THE AMERICAN PLAN

A NOVEL

DAVID WEISBERG

HABITUS BOOKS

The American Plan

978-0-9983840-0-9 (Hardcover)
978-0-9983840-1-6 (Paperback)
978-0-9983840-2-3 (eBook)

Publishing Services, AuthorImprints.com; Cover design, Michael LaBash

Published by Habitus Books, Berkeley, California

info@HabitusBooks.com

for
Natalie

PART I:
CUBA

An American like that, with money
and connections, could get away
with anything in Cuba.

1

FOR THE THIRD AFTERNOON RUNNING Philip Narby hung about the crummy little sidewalk café, watching for Sylvio. Two hours now, long enough to go through a pack of Chesterfields, four bottles of Hatuey beer, last week's *Time* magazine and just about every word of the *International Herald Tribune*. He was sick of it, waiting like a leashed dog for a lowlife like Sylvio. And if Sylvio didn't show? That meant skulking around the stairwell of some decrepit apartment house, seeking out one of Narby's other acquaintances who might have what he wanted, and with a good chance of getting swindled.

Narby ordered another beer and picked up the *Tribune*. He read the story again, with its glimmer of hope: the North Koreans had finally accepted the U.N. terms for a preliminary exchange of prisoners. Narby knew very well the kind of horseshit the military and the State Department fed the press. Still, it made sense. Ending the war now had advantages for all concerned. Mao could boast that his peasant army had fought the nuclear-armed Americans to a draw. Stalin could stop hemorrhaging tanks and fighter jets. And Eisenhower could make good on his promise to bring our boys back home, get his ticker-tape parade down Broadway. The only losers—once again—were the no-account Koreans themselves. The Poland of East Asia.

There were other factors: the prison camp riots, the pointless slaughter back and forth, fighting over a few square miles of barren ground, the mounting political cost. Even the Reds had to appease their own masses once in a while. Two, three more months and his purgatory would be over. Once they started demobilizing, with thousands of young men just like him coming home everyday, Narby could slip back into the country, hiding in plain sight.

At the moment, however, Narby had more pressing concerns. The tremor in his leg was acting up, though probably it was only nerves. And his side was starting to throb. By the weekend he'd be in considerable trouble. If it came to that he'd have no choice but take whatever he could get. But he drew the line at injecting himself. That had been a dangerous mistake. The girl he was with—even a worse mistake—had panicked, pulled a knife. Afterwards, he'd been sick for a week, scared out of his wits.

That was another item on his list for Sylvio. He'd been a month without. The girls Narby met through Sylvio were of an entirely different class, and he always took adequate precaution. He wanted that La China again, the mixed-blood girl with the dark skin and the green oriental eyes. It wasn't very nice, very gentlemanly, paying for it. But he had his animal needs. Besides, he hadn't asked to come to Havana, having to live like this, like an animal. The whole country was a goddamn cesspit. The mere fact that Narby didn't mistreat them, didn't beat them or demand unnatural acts, made him something of a moral paragon.

Narby scanned the narrow street, the opposite corner and down the block of dingy three-story houses, their iron balustrades draped with laundry. You could recognize him right off, that raffia hat with the red band, Sylvio's sign that he was open for business.

Who the hell was that? Straightening from his slouch Narby picked up the newspaper and then, casually, turned the page, lowering and then raising the paper. A well-dressed American—possibly a European, but definitely not Cuban—walking towards the café. There was nothing around here for tourists, no hotels or casinos or high-class brothels. It was far from the Malecón and the Vedado. Maybe he was lost, though the man's gait and posture—steady, calm—suggested otherwise.

The man was taking a seat about ten tables down the sidewalk. He asked for a cortadito and a bottle of water. Good Spanish, but the broad American vowels gave him away. Even more disconcerting—because it was unlikely that a well-heeled American would have any business in this obscure pocket of Havana—was the sense, the near certainty, that Narby had seen him before: a tall, trim, elegant-looking man in his forties with light brown hair, wearing a beautifully cut pearl-gray suit, with that relaxed, loose-limbed attitude. Except for those first weeks in Havana, when Narby hardly knew where he was or what had happened to him, he scrupulously avoided the bars and beaches and the fashionable streets around the Prado, or any place where Americans congregated. And he made a point of rotating among a half dozen newsstands, at odd hours, making no pattern.

Turning the page again Narby chanced another look. God damn it, the smooth son-of-a-bitch was watching him. The bank. Now he remembered. Only last Monday Narby had made a withdrawal at the Banco de la República. Passing in the entranceway. Their eyes had met. Or was Narby imagining things? He was always a bit keyed up on those bank runs, signing the slip at the international counter, feigning impatience when the clerk insisted on matching the signatures.

He'd been so obsessed with finding Sylvio that Narby had forgotten all about it. That greasy little scum. It was all Sylvio's fault. Screwing with him, never letting Narby know when or where, jacking up the price because he thought he had Narby on a string. And now Narby had left himself exposed, trapped.

Or maybe not. The Philip Narby at the bank was clean-shaven and coiffed, in a silk sports shirt and linen trousers and oxfords. The Philip Narby hanging about, drinking beer, was rather unkempt: a week's growth of beard, wearing cheap canvas trousers and an old sun-bleached polo shirt and tennis shoes—a young man on a lark, bumming around the Caribbean, trying to make up his mind whether to finish college or put on the harness and take that job in his old man's office. But what if the American had been tracking him since Monday? Had Narby been so blind, so careless, as to let that happen?

Folding the paper he leaned back and sipped his beer, absently gazing down the street, channeling his nerves into the pantomime while keeping the man in his peripheral vision. The American got up, was walking toward him. The man had come to kill him. If he pulled out a gun, shot Narby right here and now, who was going to stop him or chase after him? The toothless old men playing dominoes, the barefoot kids running along the street, the halfwit hawking tickets for the bolita? An American like that, with money and connections, could get away with any-thing in Cuba.

His suit jacket, hooked with one finger, was slung over his shoulder. In his other hand he carried a coffee cup. He was nei-ther armed nor dangerous. On his face he wore a solicitous, genteel smile.

Maybe the man was only a queer, interpreting their little peek-a-boo at the bank and again, just now, as an invitation. He certainly looked more like a queer than a killer.

"Hello. Again." The man nodded, looking down at Narby. "Mind if I join you?"

"Sorry," Narby said, catching his breath. "Must be a mis-take. No, thanks."

The man continued, smiling. "No. No mistake. I'm quite sure. We met in Tokyo. Though briefly, I admit. May I?"

Without waiting for assent he put down the coffee, pulled out a chair, and draped his jacket over the back. "Believe me, I'm as surprised to see you here as you seem to be, seeing me."

"Why should I be surprised, since I don't know you?" Narby said flatly, averting his face. "Besides, I'm not that way, if that's what you're looking for. Each to his own, friend. But you've got the wrong guy."

The man raised an eyebrow, momentarily flustered, and then he laughed. "No, no. Nothing like that. Don't you remember? We were introduced, but for the life of me I can't recall your name." He offered his hand across the table. "I'm Bill Knowles."

The name startled him. Yes, Narby knew it. Very well, in fact. But the face, the voice, held no particular meaning. He shrugged, declining to shake the man's outstretched hand and feeling a vague satisfaction as Knowles, looking a bit foolish, withdrew it. "All right," Knowles said, his tone confidant despite the rebuke. "Presumptuous of me, I suppose. Barging in on you like this."

A crumpled pack of Chesterfields lay on the table. Noticing it, Knowles reached back and from his jacket pocket took out his own. "Funny, how trivial things stick in the mind," he said, pulling a cigarette and lighting it and then dropping the pack between them. "You smoked Chesterfields. So did I. They didn't carry them at the PX in Tokyo. You had to get them on the black market. You told me so yourself."

Narby remembered that, about the Chesterfields, buying them on the street, the cartons piled in the trunk of a car. But that was earlier. His memory about certain things that happened later was still confused. Knowles was trying to unnerve him, with his cool gray eyes. Narby met them for a second then looked away.

"Help yourself."

Narby took a cigarette. Knowles had his lighter out but he ignored him and struck a match. Leaning back, he sprawled his legs under the table. "So what?" Narby said, deciding on a tack.

"Lots of people smoke Chesterfields. You're mistaking me for someone else. But, thanks for the smoke."

"All right. No harm then if you indulge me for a moment. If I'm wrong then I'll go away." He smiled again, his complexion warm but not suntanned, the earthen shade of a pale potato. "It was at the Kansas City. A month or so before Korea, summer, pouring rain. The monsoons. You came with Ted McCoy. He brought you along. You worked for him, as I recall. Something of a protégé, it seemed. Tokyo. Summer of 1950. Come now, you can't deny you were in Tokyo."

"Why should I deny it?"

Knowles laughed, gently, easily. "No reason at all. Just as there's no reason you shouldn't remind me of your name."

"You followed me from the bank, didn't you?" he said, too quickly, reacting instead of thinking. His leg under the table was trembling. "You've been watching me for days."

"What bank? Look, I sat down for a coffee and I saw you, recognized you. Don't be fantastic. Why in the world would I follow you?"

"Then what the hell are you doing around here, in this neighborhood? Aren't you afraid of getting rolled? Look around, friend. You'll ruin your expensive suit, sitting on that filthy straw chair."

"You're in some kind of trouble, aren't you? Maybe I can help."

"How do I know you're really Bill Knowles? I've got some pals around here. All I have to do is whistle and you're in for it. Whatever you are."

"Of course I'm Bill Knowles. Here. May I?" The threat had no effect. He reached into his suit jacket, cautiously, and took out a business card. "I'm with the Allbright Paper Company. We have a warehouse not far from here. It was a pleasant afternoon, not too hot, so I decided to walk. I've cut through this neighborhood before. Never had any trouble."

It was happening again: information without memory, as if someone were using Narby's mind as a filing cabinet. He ought to keep his mouth shut. But he didn't like that superior smile, that smirk. "It's phony. There is no Allbright Paper Company. All the paper in Japan under the Occupation came from a company called Putnam. You lied then, and you're lying now."

"I was right," Knowles said. He leaned forward to tap his cigarette against the ashtray. The smirk was gone. "That's what made such an impression, frankly. What you said to me that night at dinner, at the Kansas City. That you didn't buy into all that 'losing China' hysteria. And something else, about natural resources in Indo-china. A little naïve, I thought. But I said to myself, McCoy's young friend, he's quite an original."

"MacArthur wanted you out of Asia." He was reacting again, but he couldn't hold back. "Willoughby hated you even more, hated everyone connected with State, with Frank Wisner, despised anyone with the taint of Acheson or Roosevelt. But they couldn't touch you. Not like me. One phone call from MacArthur's people to Washington and I'm sent straight to Pusan. To the Naktong."

"Calm down. It's all right. You served at Pusan? With Task Force Smith? That was bad. Brutal. But… well, here you are, all in piece and far from the fray, taking the afternoon sun with a beer, relaxing with the *Herald Tribune* and the war still grinding on. Now," he said, smiling again, "how's that?"

"You tell me."

"Well, maybe I could, if only you'd remind me of your name. Whatever's happened, we're on the same side, right? You obviously know enough about me to realize that, yes?"

"The enemy-of-my-enemy kind of thing? That what you mean?"

"Well, yes, if you must take it that way. Still. Isn't that good enough?"

"Depends. Maybe there are more than two sides. More than one enemy."

Knowles shook his head slightly and picked up his coffee, crossing his legs, his smile fading, leaving his face neutral. His fine sky-blue shirt was splotched with perspiration and he loosened his tie.

"Unfortunately, for some men, everyone is an enemy. I could find out, you know. Besides," Knowles went on, the slate-gray eyes assessing Narby, the wharf-rat clothes, the beard and the sprawl and the jiggling leg, "you don't exactly project the picture of peace and prosperity. Not that it's any of my business. Frankly, it's nothing to me. It's just my innate curiosity. I don't like hanging threads."

So, Knowles obviously didn't know about the bank account, about Sid Black, because if he did, then he would know that the ratty clothes were just a ploy. And up to now the ploy had worked. With the exception of Sid Black, no one knew Narby was in Havana. In fact, Knowles had failed to recognize him at the bank, had failed to make the connection. It was Narby who was the more acute observer. Knowles had simply stumbled upon him somehow. Probably they staked out the international newsstands, keeping tabs on foreigners and stray Americans. If only Narby had a little more to go on. He couldn't survive like this much longer, hiding out in his hole of a room, clinging to dope pushers like Sylvio, siphoning off more and more of Sid Black's money.

Narby shifted in the uncomfortable straw-bottomed chair and flicked the butt end of his cigarette into the gutter. The tables were turned a bit. He had more on Knowles than Knowles had on him. He ought to take a chance.

"Wouldn't want to leave you hanging. My name is Narby. Philip Narby. Mind if I bum another smoke?"

Knowles blinked, his lips parting slightly as if to speak, closing, parting again. "Philip Narby?" he said. "But. I would never forget a name like that. No. It was more all-American. Some monosyllable out of Twain. Jim or Tom. It suited you, I remember. Still does, even here, so far from the Mississippi."

"You calling me a liar?"

"Goodness no, not at all. It's more like… a discrepancy. Help yourself," Knowles said, smiling again, nodding at the pack of cigarettes. "Philip Narby," he repeated. "I won't forget this time. My apologies."

The bastard was playing some kind of mental game. "Who's this man you mentioned, McCoy?"

"Ted McCoy. He was at Harvard, two years ahead of me, so I didn't know him well. But it was nice to get reacquainted, when I saw him in Tokyo. He was working for one of the Civilian Sections of the Occupation. Bad luck, that. One of the first reservists to get sent to Korea. Very sad. He was dead within the week. They found him by the side of the road, with three or four others. His hands were tied behind his back with wire, a bullet hole in his temple. No taking prisoners back then. But. If you were at Pusan, you know all that. Don't you, Philip?"

What the hell did that mean? Was he calling Narby a coward, a traitor? "You think I was going to give them another chance to kill me? MacArthur and Willoughby and the rest of them. They're the traitors. They had this machine, this torture. Electro-shock. Because when I came to, I couldn't remember anything. As if it were my fault!"

"Slow down, Philip. You were captured? Where? When?"

God damn it! There was Sylvio, strolling by on the other side of the street with his hands in his pocket, whistling, the straw hat with the red band cocked to one side. He had what Narby needed, all right. Only Sylvio wasn't about to stop and do business with some unknown American sitting next to Narby. If Narby got up now he could catch him at the plaza, where Sylvio would usually linger for a few minutes, chatting with his pals or using the urinal.

"I have to go. Don't get up. Don't follow me."

"But… Wait. Here." The business card was on the table. Knowles slipped it into the pack of Chesterfields and handed the pack to Narby. "You can reach me at that number. Or write to that address. It's perfectly safe."

As he turned the corner Narby looked back. Knowles was watching him but he kept his seat, a well-dressed American sitting quietly amongst the dirt and disorder of the rundown neighborhood. Ten minutes later, after leaving Sylvio, Narby circled back, coming from the opposite direction and careful not to show himself. Knowles was gone, the table cleared, the old men playing dominos, just as before. Perfectly safe, he muttered to himself. They'd be watching him from now on, could pick him up whenever they wanted. Or maybe they were looking for someone else and wanted to use Philip Narby as the bait, out front, exposed. Just like Korea, stringing them out along the hillsides like clay pigeons at a shooting gallery.

He'd made it out of Korea alive, against all the odds. He could beat the odds again.

2

FROM THE BOTTOM OF THE WARDROBE Narby pulled out the manila envelope, soiled and creased from wear, and tossed it on the table. He'd been carrying it with him for a long time, since January of 1950. He must have addressed the envelope shortly after being introduced to Knowles at the Kansas City in Tokyo, perhaps that same week:

> Bill Knowles, VP of International Sales
> Allbright Paper Co.
> c/o Business Interests Division
> Unites States Embassy, Hong Kong.

But for some reason he had never sent it. Well, it wasn't too late. The enemy of my enemy—maybe that was good enough.

What had Knowles called him? Ted McCoy's protégé. Jim or Tom. Who the hell did Knowles think he was dealing with, some pansy office boy? Granted, the name Philip Narby was a fake. But it had kept him alive, supplied him with money, bought him time. Protected him.

Son las once de la noche en la Havana hermosa, con la música de la Orquesta Aragón.

Eleven o'clock. Narby turned down the radio, poured another Bacardi and shook two pills from the brown bottle— large, white, ovoid, stamped "Lilly U 53." Calmantes, Sylvio called them, certainly a more soothing innocent word than narcotic or dope. It was the same stuff they had given Narby in the hospital in Kobe after taking him off the morphine. Dolophine. The GIs in Japan called them "dollies." They would combine it with amphetamines, Benzedrine, splash. Basically, a dolly-splash was a milder form of speedball, another splendid innovation of the U.S. Military Occupation Forces under the command of General Douglas MacArthur, Supreme Commander for the Allied Powers.

It was an expedient, a stopgap measure. Once he was home he'd quit, get proper medical care. In Tokyo, before Korea, before things started going wrong, he hadn't even been a drinker. Not like the rest of them. Despite the chronic pain, the occasional tremor, his physical condition was excellent: an hour of ocean swimming every morning, and in the evenings a hundred pushups. There were no signs of the addict's moral or spiritual decay.

With one swallow he took the pills with the Bacardi and then lay on the bed, waiting for the dope to kick in.

The run-in with Bill Knowles had shaken him pretty badly. He had waited this long, two months, to risk another withdrawal at the Banco del Repúblico. That afternoon, after the bank, he had taken two taxis, sprinted across a plaza and then hopped a bus. Narby was quite certain no one had followed him.

Even if Knowles hadn't been looking for him their meeting was no accident. Two months now and Knowles had trusted him, given him leeway. It was some kind of game or test. He was waiting for Narby to make the next move. There was no other explanation.

Besides, how much longer could he go on like this, operating in the dark, cut off from the world? With every passing week the end of the war lurched a bit closer, back and forth across the 38th parallel. Thank god it was Eisenhower in office, a General and a Republican. If it were Truman, the McCarthy gang would have him crucified for giving away the North to the Reds, crying "defeatism, appeasement." But Eisenhower could pull it off, even with the red-baiters nipping at his heels. By mid-summer at the latest Narby would be home.

He was going to need help clearing his name, proving he wasn't a deserter, a coward. Who else was there to turn to but Bill Knowles?

For two years now Narby had been holed up in this room. Those first weeks in Havana were still something of a blur. Straight from the harbor—arriving from Santo Domingo, by way of Manila and Singapore, following the Great Crescent across the Indian Ocean—he had checked into a tourist hotel near the Nacional carrying nothing but a rucksack, wearing the outfit they had given him at the hospital, the suntan trousers and flower-print aloha shirt, cheap PX stuff, the very picture of the blowhard off-duty American serviceman, right down to the penny loafers.

That was shortly after the Inchon invasion. The newspapers were full of it, how MacArthur's daring gambit had turned the tide against the Reds, a swift and total American victory just around the corner. And yet there he was—a twenty-five year-old man, single, able-bodied, prime meat for the draft board—wandering around Havana in a daze, surrounded by the hordes of American tourists.

It had taken him a few days to work up the nerve, but then he had done what Sid Black had asked—deposited the money. And that same day two MPs, probably on leave from Guantanamo, probably drunk, had walked right past him, nearly bumped into him. If they found him they would arrest him for desertion, send him back to Korea to finish off the job they'd bungled in Pusan. Just as they had done to Ted McCoy. Found dead by the side of the road, his hands bound behind his back with wire and a hole in his temple. Someone from K.M.A.G. had made it look like a typical N.K.P.A. execution. And, of course, the Korean Military Advisory Group took orders directly from Supreme Command, from Willoughby and MacArthur.

At least he'd had the presence of mind to realize the danger and get the hell out of that part of Havana. After moving from hotel to hotel, each one a rung lower on the ladder of comfort and luxury, he had found this place, this room, in a rundown working-class neighborhood of foreigners and immigrants.

Every Monday he deposited the rent through the dueña's slot on the ground floor and the next day she changed out the sheets and towels. Shower and toilet down the hall, a payphone inside the entryway to the building. Africans, Chinese, Greeks. Narby was the only American. Everyone kept to himself. Despite the disreputable character of the neighborhood, he'd never had any trouble. The only occasions he felt uneasy were when he dressed to go to the bank. But that was only once a month, and he could usually hail a cab on the nearby plaza, keeping his exposure on the street to a minimum. If someone ever broke in to his room, the thief would be more than satisfied with the wad of small bills Narby always kept in the dresser drawer.

The real money, about three thousand dollars now, was wrapped in an Army-issue rubber poncho, stashed beneath the bottom drawers of the wardrobe.

At least Narby didn't have to worry about Sid Black anymore. If Black were still alive he would have long ago put a stop to the bank withdrawals. The U.S. Army had taken care of that, sent him right back into the slaughter. Narby supposed he should feel sorry for Black—a short, barrel-chested, dark-haired Master Supply Sergeant. Black, too, had been with Task Force Smith, had given Narby the salt tablets at the port of Pusan, had helped him get the hell out of Asia—not out of the goodness of his heart, but because Black had an urgent need to get his money out of the country. Well, it hadn't quite worked out the way either of them had expected. Narby had escaped and Black was dead.

Sergeant Black had run quite an operation in Japan until Korea screwed it up for him. Everything from scrap metal and surplus war materiel to pornography, everything run out of that supply depot ...

Click click click. Now he understood: Ted McCoy had become acquainted with Sid Black because the paper supply, the shipments from the Putnam Company of Macon, Georgia, went through Black's depot. Ted McCoy liked the best cigars, the finest Scotch whisky, contraband Russian caviar, all those good things like the Chesterfields that you couldn't get at the PX. He was one of Black's regular customers. "My enterprising little Jewish friend," McCoy liked to say. McCoy had a lot of those snobbish country-club attitudes. Narby had never really trusted McCoy. All in all—though it made Narby squirm to be so damned cynical—he supposed it was better this way, with McCoy out of the picture.

The dope did that sometimes, at least on the way up. Cleared his mind, brought things into focus. The relief came now in warm waves and pulses, up from his feet and legs and washing him in a clean white weightless clarity.

He sat up on the bed and had a smoke. Some day he'd have to write a letter to the Eli Lilly Company commending them on the purity of their product.

He was all right. He was going to make it.

In the beginning Narby had let the room depress him. The walls were tinted a rancid shade of peppermint green and splotched with scab-like patches where the damp had gotten under the plaster. The window gave on to an alley filled with trash and rotting fruit thrown out from the vendors' carts. All his life he'd been used to a certain level of comfort, of coddling. In Tokyo he'd even had his own house, a handsome little wooden bungalow with a garden and a housekeeper. But all that had been a delusion, a mistake. He'd been on the wrong side of things, working for the wrong people.

It was beautiful, really, his little rancid scabrous cell. An American like him, a good boy from a solid background, couldn't buy his way into a shithole like this.

In his better moods the situation rather amused him. Because without his tags they hadn't been able to identify him at the military hospital in Kobe. For all anyone knew, Tom or Jim—or whatever the hell his name had been back then—might very well be one of those unreported POW's they were bickering over in Panmunjon, held in a prison camp deep behind the 38th parallel. Given the way Philip Narby had been forced to live these last two years, holed up in a room like this, you could hardly say he was a free man.

A mirror was affixed to the flimsy door of the wardrobe. Narby stood and with his shirt off gently ran the tips of his fingers along the scars, inspecting the skein of puffed ridges and welts that ran along his left side, up from his hipbone and zigzagging to just under his armpit. The pain came from inside, as if some hideous parasite had burrowed in his flank and was gnawing its way out. But after two calmantes and the Bacardi he felt almost nothing.

He was an inch, maybe two, over six feet, rather lean, reddish-blonde hair, powdery-blue eyes. With a fresh shave and haircut, because he'd made the bank run that afternoon, he looked pretty damned good. Except for the scars. He'd seen it plenty of times—the kids at the beach where he swam, the women he paid to have sex, turning away, gawking, careful not to touch.

That was another thing he'd quit once he was home. It was what men did in wartime. Just like they married their hometown sweethearts once things returned to normal. Only Korea wasn't a legitimate war. It was a botch up, a lie, from the very beginning. Maybe this time around the girls back home wouldn't be so willing.

It was strange. Some things he remembered as though it were yesterday. Like Martha, Ted McCoy's secretary. Around forty, a divorcée, a bit of a smart aleck, a little thick in the waist but shapely, a brunette with dark eyes. It was maybe a week after the North Koreans had crossed the parallel. McCoy and the other reservists in the office, the former OSS men, took it as some kind of joke. Show 'em a little Yankee firepower and the Reds will turn tail, just like that... the airlift made Stalin look weak and now he's worried about Berlin... it's a feint, a diversion. A paper tiger.

Coming into the office that morning he had found Martha in tears, nearly wailing. When she saw him she threw her arms around him, crying into his shoulder, her body shaking with sobs. "It's Dick. Oh god. He's dead. Dick's gone. No no no."

It was her fiancé, Captain Richard Loerber, part of KMAG, the Korean Military Advisory Group stationed in Seoul. It wasn't even a war yet and Loerber was dead, just like that. Mauled by the paper tiger, cut down by a feint.

What fixed the memory, Narby supposed, was the sex feeling. Because he and Martha had flirted, had come close to having an affair, his first, the older divorced woman and the younger single man from the office. After work, after too many drinks, she had let him kiss her, open mouthed, let him unbutton her blouse and get a good feel. But that was before Martha went for Loerber. For a woman in her situation, a man like Loerber would have meant a last chance at a normal married life, maybe even a kid, if she wasn't too old.

When he had comforted her that morning, her body pressed against him, quaking, it had crossed Narby's mind. He could have her now. It excited him, even if he didn't really want her. At least, not while he was sober.

Three weeks later Ted McCoy was dead. No one was joking anymore. The fun, the bragging, was over. And he realized that his turn was next. It was just a matter of time.

Or music—sometimes that would shake him up, make him remember. Like the Beny Moré they were playing on the radio, the Latin Bing Crosby. As a kid he had played trumpet in the high school band. He would listen to the radio for hours at a stretch, a station out of Chicago with all the big band and swing music programs, Harry James, Bunny Berigan playing "I Can't Get Started with You," things like that. Brought to you by Chesterfield Cigarettes. But it wasn't like an ordinary memory. Nothing attached to it, no affection, no longing, no intimacy. It was information, cold and lifeless. It might as well belong to someone else. Whatever had happened to him, to his mind, it was for keeps. He was Philip Narby now. The name meant a hell of a lot more to him than Jim or Tom.

He poured another Bacardi, half a glass, and sat at the table. After meeting him at the Kansas City, Narby had intended to send the envelope to Knowles by diplomatic courier. Something had changed his mind, or interfered. A twenty-three-page document with detailed references to classified military files. Unsigned. By now Narby could recite by heart the salient points: U.S. Brigadier General Charles Willoughby willfully, illegally, aided and abetted a known wanted Japanese war criminal, Colonel Tsuji Masanobu, to evade capture... winter of 1946... providing money and intelligence to hide Tsuji, procure weapons, with the intent to organize a neo-fascist militia... concerted and organized efforts within the highest ranks of the Supreme Command for the Allied Powers... Tsuji's responsibility for massacres of American troops in Singapore… the Bataan Death March… torture of Chinese and Philippine and American prisoners… inhuman acts of cannibalism.

It was certainly information worth killing for. Not that anyone could touch MacArthur himself now, not after he spit in Truman's face and stage-managed his triumphant return to civilian life, *Time* magazine's "Man of the Year" and still perhaps in the running for the Republican ticket if Eisenhower's heart gave out before the next election. But what about Willoughby, head of Military Intelligence for MacArthur? They might be able to go after Willoughby.

He undid the clasp, slid the document out, put it in the new envelope and addressed it to Bill Knowles at the Allbright Paper Company's Havana office—writing from memory because he had destroyed the business card the very same day Knowles had given it to him. There was nothing wrong with Narby's mind. If he had lost his mother's face, his father's voice, it was only because such things were useless to him now.

3

THAT NIGHT—JULY 29TH, 1953, three days after the signing of the Armistice at Panmunjon—Narby put on the PX clothes he had worn the day he stepped off the boat in Havana: aloha shirt, khaki slacks, white socks, brown loafers. Back then he had worn a crew cut, shaved every morning. Now he looked like a castaway from a shipwrecked cruise liner, or a tourist after a two-week bender. Or perhaps a solider letting loose after three years of hell.

He gave the room a final regard: the green walls with the cancerous splotches, the collapsing bed, the attar of mildew and rot. A prisoner of war. That was his fallback, a last resort if he were found out. They had held him at a camp near the Yalu, tortured him with electrical shocks, crammed their filthy Red propaganda down his throat. How'd you make your way back to the States, son? Couldn't remember, not a damn thing except that awful rancid color of his cell walls, the stink.

That was another thing Knowles had missed. It wasn't the Reds who had threatened Narby with electro-shock. If the U.S. Army ever got their hands on him, figured out who he really was, they'd probably put him right back on the gurney, pick at his brain for information. Scrub him clean him of any residual pink.

He threw the rucksack over his shoulder and went downstairs. In the entryway he stopped at the payphone. None of the other tenants spoke English; most of them hardly spoke Spanish. He could talk freely.

After five rings someone picked up. "Hello... Buenas noches... Quién habla?" A relaxed self-assured American voice with broad New England vowels.

"It's Philip Narby. I'm leaving. Tonight."

"Philip. I was hoping to hear from you. I'm very glad you called."

"Did you receive the package? I sent it around the end of May?"

"Yes. Yes I did. But there was no return address, so naturally I couldn't confirm ..."

"I risked my goddamn life carrying that thing around. You understand that?"

"Of course I do. And I commend you for it. But, Philip... you're leaving? How? When?"

"What are you going to do about it?"

"Sorry?"

"What are you going to do with the information I sent? Don't you understand? That's why they killed McCoy. Because he knew."

There was a pause. "Philip. Listen to me. It's not wise to discuss details like this over the telephone. We need to talk. Face to face. It's absolutely necessary. Tonight, if at all possible. I can meet you wherever you wish."

"Not possible. There's a boat waiting for me. Not the ferry, obviously. I can't travel in the open."

"Yes. I see that now." There was a pause. "You're going back, aren't you? Because the war is over. Because they're demobilizing."

"That's right. A face in the crowd. What other choice do I have?"

"What will you do then, Philip? Have you thought it out?"

There was almost four thousand dollars in the rucksack, wrapped in the rubber poncho. "Something will come to me. I've made it this far."

"I told you once before that I could help you. I'm telling you again. Where are you landing? I'll arrange a contact."

There was a clicking on the line. He understood that, given time, a telephone call could be traced to its origin. "Better I contact you. When it's safe."

"Yes, but ..."

He hung up, pushed open the door, and walked quickly in the direction of the old city until he found a taxi near Bolivar Plaza. It was another calm night, muggy and overcast with a gentle breeze. Good conditions for the crossing. By morning he would be in Florida.

The dock was outside the city limits, about ten miles south of the Port of Havana. The harbor patrol was conducting random searches of private boats coming into Cuban waters, probably searching for weapons. Only a few days ago, in fact, there was something on the radio about a rebel attack on the barracks at Moncada. But it was unlikely the patrols would bother with a charter boat going out for a little night fishing.

The breeze on his face through the taxi window felt good. He was perspiring from nerves. The bulge in his pocket, the little brown bottle, reassured him. Along with a supply of Dolophine he had picked up about two dozen splash—unmarked yellow capsules, something like bennies—to help keep alert during the crossing and when he landed in the morning. He had to be careful with the splash, though. It could burn you out fast.

The ocean came into view, the seafront promenade. A chorus line of streetwalkers leaned over the balustrade, displaying their backsides—a stretch of the Malecón favored by American Navy personnel on leave from Guantanamo. Beyond the seawall the ocean rose in dark roiling swells. Not many whiteheads. Usually the waves here came spraying over the rocks, but tonight the wall and sidewalk were dry. He was in luck. He lit a cigarette and leaned back and closed his eyes, waiting for the calmantes to ease him down.

Twenty minutes later the taxi stopped at the edge of a steep hillside sloping down toward the sea. From there the road, winding down to a cove, was unpaved. The driver refused to go any further. Narby could see a light down near the water's edge and he could make out the dock and maybe half a dozen boats. He paid the driver and got out and began to walk, the rucksack slung over his shoulder. There was nothing around, just a few fishermen's shacks. The darkness had a pale milky texture from the moonlight diffusing through the thick cover of cloud. He could hear the lapping of the tide against rocks and pilings. At the bottom of the slope, near the foot of the dock, he turned and looked up at the road and the jungled hillside above. The taxi was gone. Nothing, no lights, no cars coming or going.

The pilot, or captain, or whatever he was—some kind of Englishman, with a pitted red face and a rather impressive overhanging gut—had told Narby to go to the boat at the end of the dock. He lit a cigarette and walked out on the planks. The other boats were dark; the one at the end had a single light at the bow. From what he could see of it, the craft didn't exactly inspire confidence—a rust bucket, the strip of hull exposed above the waterline slime-green and crusted with barnacles, and the deck cluttered with junk.

"That you, Smith?" someone called out.

"Yeah. It's me. Sylvio's friend."

The man on board came forward. "Put out that bloody cigarette, god damn you! You're going to blow us all to hell. You're standing by the petrol tank, you fool."

"Sorry." Narby flicked the cigarette into the water. "Take it easy."

"Let's have the money."

"All right." He had already separated out the amount. He pulled the bills from his pocket and counted. "A hundred now, a hundred when we land."

"Two hundred now. A hundred when we land."

The pilot's shirt hung open. Narby took in the slouch, the ugly temper, the foul smell. The pilot was half-cocked—a beer swiller, judging from the gut.

"Sylvio said two hundred."

"I don't care what that greaseball told you. It's three hundred. You want to get across, don't you? Take it or leave it."

So, there was going to be trouble. He ought to have anticipated something like this. But there was no time to argue. "All right. But only half now. Half when we get there."

"Forget it. Get lost. Sod off."

Narby shrugged, turned around, and started down the dock.

"Smith! You want the harbor cops down here. All right. Fuck all. Hand it over. And no more bullshit."

Standing halfway down the dock, out of the pilot's sight, Narby counted out the money from the bills in his pocket. He had only twenties. He walked back to the boat and handed it over the rail. "A hundred and sixty. Ten-dollar tip, for the excellent service."

The pilot grunted. "Over here." He lowered a portion of the rail and Narby stepped on board. "Get down in the cabin, with the other one. Down those steps. No lights. No smoking. And keep your voices down. Don't come up until I tell you it's clear."

"The other one? There's someone else?"

"Yeah. So what? Stop dithering. We're wasting time."

"That wasn't part of the deal. Look here, damn it, the last thing I need—."

"Shut up. Hear that?" There was the sound of a car on the road at the top of the slope. "The cops come around every few hours, fishing for bribes. Now get the hell below or get off my boat. And no refunds, mate."

It was impossible. There was no way Knowles could have followed him. "Who's down there? What does he look like?"

"What does he look like? Like a spic. Dark and greasy."

"A Cuban?"

"He ain't no fucking Irishman. Go on. Get out of sight."

Would Knowles have sent a Cuban? He tried to push away the thought. What about Sylvio? There'd been plenty of opportunities for Sylvio to jump him, rob him, if that's what it was about. It made no sense. He stepped over the clutter—tangles of rope, rusted traps, boxes of screws and machine parts. There was a raised bridge and on the other side two mounted swivel chairs. The boat had once been a fishing charter, big enough to venture out as far as the Gulf Stream or even to the Keys. The passage to the cabin was low and ducking his head he noticed, buried among the junk, the hook-end of a gaff, its long wooden haft wedged under the base of the mounted chairs. From the lower step of the passage, if he had to, Narby could lean over and grab the handle and wrench it free.

The other man was sitting in the cramped dark airless space, his hands folded on his lap. Narby hesitated on the third step. The man didn't move. Watching him, Narby nodded and put down the rucksack. The ceiling was low and he had to bend his neck. After a moment, deciding it was safe, he sat on the opposite bench, his knees nearly touching the Cuban's. The man was tense, on guard. The pilot might have lied to the Cuban as well, about the money, about someone else coming on board.

The boat began to rock, the deck overhead creaking with the weight of the pilot as he climbed to the bridge. The starter clicked, the engine firing and sputtering and quitting and clicking again until the engine sputtered into a sustained gurgle. Then they were moving, slowly, a breath of air flowing into the cabin, carrying sickening fumes of gasoline and burning oil. And something else, sweet, vaporous. Like Sylvio. An affectation of the Cuban male. The man across from Narby was doused in cheap cologne.

For some minutes Narby remained still, concentrating, fighting off the nausea that sometimes came when the Dolophine kicked in. And on top of the calmantes he had taken two splash. As soon as they got out of Cuban waters he'd go up on deck, get some air, no matter what the pilot had said. Only how long would that take? Maybe this perfumed joker knew something about it. With his hands folded like that, sitting up straight, he looked like a nervous schoolboy.

"The pilot, the captain," Narby said, "you know him? You trust him?"

"Sorry," he answered. "Little English."

"El Capitán. El gordo. Es bueno? Me too. Poco Español."

His eyes adjusting to the gloom, Narby could make him out now: a compact torso in a white cotton-drill suit and dark tie, an elongated neck and face, flared nose, a pencil-line of moustache, shellacked hair. Dark-skinned but not a Negro. Mulatto.

"El Capitán? Un cerdo. A pig. Pero necesario? No?"

Narby smiled. The little man was ok. Looked about the same age as Narby. They made an effort to converse. He gave his name as Ernesto Campos. "Está como un baño esta noche, la mar." Calm as bathwater. They were bouncing now at a fair clip, the engine roaring at full throttle.

"Hell, you could almost swim across if not for all the sharks. Tiburones."

"Yo. No puedo nadar. I no swim."

"No? Too bad."

An embezzler, a bank clerk, possibly, or an accountant absconding with the firm's cash drawer. The valise at the Cuban's feet was probably stuffed with someone else's money.

Narby stood, his head grazing the ceiling of the cabin. Maybe the pilot didn't want them to come up because he was headed back toward Havana, planning to keep their money and give them up to the police. If something went wrong, boxed up together like this, he and the Cuban would naturally pull together. Could they navigate the boat if the pilot had to be subdued? Maybe Campos was thinking the same thing. Maybe he was wondering what the hell this unshaven Yankee clown in the flower shirt had done to warrant such a desperate departure.

His mind was turning in circles. He needed air, a cigarette, needed to see for himself. "I'm going up. Should be all right by now."

"No. Por favor. Please. Better here. Debajo. Escondidos. Hidings."

"Think so?"

"Please. Siéntese. Seat down. For to wait."

The man was nearly pleading. Narby crouched in the low narrow space and pulled the flask out of the rucksack. "This might help. Ron. You like?"

"Claro que sí."

"Salud."

Narby hadn't counted on sharing. He passed it to Campos, watching him in the gloom. The man had a good thirst. Not too much, damn it. Narby took another drink and somewhat reluctantly passed it again to Campos. If he liked it that much, why didn't he bring his own? Every man for himself. If something happened and they were in the water, well, it was just too bad. Narby screwed the flask closed and put it in the rucksack.

He realized now it had been a mistake to take the splash so soon. Yellow capsules. Weren't they usually blue? Maybe Sylvio was in on it. Maybe it was some kind of poison.

Campos was too quiet, too composed. The Cuban was getting on his nerves. The man clearly had nothing on his conscience. Whatever his crime, his hands were clean. All Cuban money was filthy. Stealing, embezzling, bribing—it was built into the system. Same with Narby. Sid Black's money was dirty. It was no crime stealing a dead man's money, putting it to some better purpose. Bill Knowles would understand. Knowles was certain to help, now that Narby had handed over the evidence against Willoughby. Only what would Knowles want in return?

He sat down again, fidgeting and sprawling on the stinking cushions. Drinking might help. Or make it worse. He needed a goddamn cigarette. His fists were clenched. Why the hell was the Cuban looking at him like that?

"So, where you going? A dondé? Someone meeting you on the other side?"

Campos blinked his eyes. "No understand."

Playing dumb. A wise ass. "A dondé con esto?" Narby kicked at the valise. "Dinero. Sí?"

"No. Mis cosas. La ropa. Clothes-ing."

"Yeah. Let me see. Abre." Narby tensed, ready to jump the dapper little son-of-a-bitch if he pulled a knife or gun. "Open it."

Campos shrugged and hoisted the valise onto his knees. It wasn't locked, and he clicked it and turned it toward Narby. Clothes, neatly folded. A leather shaving kit. Couple of books in Spanish. Probably the money, the bonds or certificates, were sewn into the lining. What had he paid the fat man with? Why should Narby pay, and not Campos? "Porqué? Why are you here? What have you done?"

Campos set the valise down, brushing the dust off his drill trousers. "No puedo decir. I can no say."

"You're some kind of thief, yeah? Ladrón. Criminal."

Campos shook his head. "Estudiante. Medicina. I am student for to be doctor."

"Sure you are. And I'm Florence Nightingale. Porqué? Porqué usted aqui, conmigo? En la barca. En la noche."

Campos stroked his delicate moustache with two fingers. It was the most vigorous gesture he'd made all night. "La politicá," he said, after a moment. "La lucha politicá. Me entiendes?"

What did that mean? Cubans had no politics. It was just one golpe after another, changing nothing. The Americans ran the country. The utilities, telephone and electricity, the copper mines, the big sugar mills, all in American hands. Maybe Campos had stiffed some upper echelon thug in Batista's administration and was running scared. "Yeah. I get it. Me too, amigo. Politics. Conscience. I'm going to make a surprise landing. Like Normandy. Like Inchon."

"I no understand."

"Forget it." Narby stood, filling the space, and picked up his rucksack. "You can stay down here, for all I care. I'm going up."

Coming from the dark of the cabin the cloud-dimmed moonlight against the deck was almost bright. He held on to the side rail, the warm wind flapping his shirt and pulling at his hair, the boat bouncing with reassuring regularity. Now he could breathe. He had to calm down. Behind the boat the churning twists of phosphorescent wake foamed milky green. In front there was only the parting of the water and the night, the bow plunging into a vapory black vacuum. He looked up at the bridge. The pilot's chair was empty.

The fat man had nestled himself on the deck, propped on a couch of life preservers and canvas tarps, a wooden crate rattling with beer bottles just within his reach. "Hey," Narby shouted against the wind and the engine noise. "Aren't you supposed to be up there? Steering a course."

"Automatic rudder," he shouted back. "Mind your own fucking business. I told you not to come on deck. Get below. "

"I need some air. And a cigarette. That all right?"

"Make it quick."

He crouched, shielding the match, then stepped toward the stern out of the pilot's sight and pulled out the flask, smoking, staring into the blankness. He had made a mistake. Nothing good could come out of returning like this, like some low skulking pervert. He should have taken his chances on the ferry. Or given himself up to Knowles.

Thank god the water was calm and the motion of the boat steady. In the open air he began to subdue the panic. The cheap tin flask had leached a metallic taste into the rum. Narby swirled it, drank the last swallow and flung the flask into the sea.

After a while he went down into the cabin. Campos was reclining against the cabin wall, his short legs dangling from the edge of the bench, his eyes closed. Narby watched him until he was satisfied the Cuban was asleep. He sprawled out as much as the space allowed, using the rucksack for a pillow. But when he closed his eyes the dread would tighten behind his temples. He sat up, waited a minute, tried again, restless, coiling and uncoiling on the filthy cushions.

At some point he must have drifted off, despite the splash. When he came to—thinking he had only just closed his eyes, with no sense of having slept, no relief—Campos was gone. A gray tint of light showed through the passageway. He checked his watch: 5:30. His mouth and throat were dry. It took him a moment to straighten and stand, concentrating on the pain, drawing it back and containing it to his left side. He went up. Campos was crouched behind the outer bulwark of the cabin, protected from the wind, his knees drawn up and the valise wedged against his side.

"Amigo. You got some water? Agua."

The Cuban pointed to a plastic jug at his feet. Narby turned away, shook two calmantes from the bottle, and washed them down with the water.

The sea had a dull leaden cast, melting without distinct horizon into the gray haze of sky, the rising sun occluded behind the thick cover of clouds. The pilot was back on the bridge. Narby stepped three rungs up the ladder and shouted: "How much longer?"

"An hour, give or take. Stay out of sight, for chris'sake."

"Where are we putting in? What town?"

"Nowhere. In the mangrove channels. There's a landing no one uses. Hidden. That's what you wanted, ain't it?"

"Is there a road? A bus station, or somewhere I can get a lift?"

"How the bloody fuck should I know? Mangrove. Mosquitoes. Some old niggers hanging about. Now get out of sight. Unless you want to explain yourself to the Coast Guard."

Within half an hour the sun grew discernible, a fierce concentrate of heat raging behind the clouded horizon. The Cuban, still huddled, was chewing on a sandwich. Campos had made provisions, thought ahead. A little food might do Narby good, settle his stomach until the dope-sickness passed. But he wasn't about to ask for a handout.

Instead he concentrated on the horizon, the narrow band of yellow beginning to show between the water and the wall of cloud. The boat slowed, turning. In the distance the coastline suddenly rose up, a low dark green ridge rimming the haze. The pilot was standing, looking for something, then turning again and steering a course parallel to the coast. "Both of you," he shouted. "Get below until I tell you it's clear." Narby went down first, followed by Campos. The Cuban wasn't quite so dapper after spending the night on deck.

"Someone waiting for you? A friend. Un amigo, para ayudar?" The Cuban seemed not to understand. Narby tried to summon the words. "Dónde estamos? Cual... lugar de Florida? Sabes?"

"Un lugar. Sin nombre. I not know name."

"Probably one of the Keys, yeah? There's a highway up to Miami. We can probably hitch a ride."

Campos shrugged in incomprehension.

"You wouldn't… Conoces un hombre se llama Bill Knowles? Un Americano. Un hombre elegante, bien vestido. Bill Knowles?"

"Quién?"

"Forget it."

They were slowing. The engine quieted to a gurgle. Narby felt the boat maneuvering. Suddenly, they jolted to a stop. The engine spluttered a few times, then died. The pilot was shouting for them to come up. Narby grabbed the rucksack. Campos came behind him with the valise.

But they hadn't landed. The boat was rocking amid masses of towering mangrove. Narby could see the shoreline some two hundred yards in the distance, a low wall of dark-green brush. The pilot was leaning his enormous bulk over the rail, peering down into the water.

"We're hung up on a fucking bloody sandbar. This channel's no good. We need to push off and try the next one. You're going to have to get in the water. Both of you."

Narby leaned out over the side. The hull had run up against a hump of ridged white sand that rose just under the surface. "What do you mean, get in the water?"

"What the bloody Christ do you think I mean, you clod? Climb down and heave us off. I'd do it myself if I weren't so god-fucking fat. The longer we sit here the more chance someone will see us. What the hell are you waiting for? You too, amigo. En el agua. Push. Em-poo-hay." He made a pushing gesture then pointed down to the water. "Hurry it up."

"Where's the ladder?"

"No ladder. Just jump. You can step there and grab the rail to get back up. It's only knee deep. Don't tell me you're afraid?"

Narby stripped off his shirt, kicked off the loafers, and rolled up his trouser legs. Campos's face had gone blank with apprehension. The little clerk didn't want to dirty his nice new suit, Narby supposed. But then he remembered: the Cuban can't swim. Though it was shallow around the mangrove there was a long stretch of deeper open water between the boat and the shoreline.

"You stay here," Narby told him. "I'll try to push us off myself. Understand? You. Stay here."

Grabbing the rail he stepped over and turned around to face the boat and leapt backwards, his knees bent and his feet sinking easily into the cool sand. Twice, his bare back pressed against the filthy crusted hull and his legs planted in the sand, Narby pushed until he was winded, his face running with sweat.

"Can't you start the engine while I push?" Narby yelled.

"I know what I'm doing," the pilot shouted back. "It's going to take both of you. I can't start the engine till we're free. Get down there," he said to Campos. "Hurry, for chris'sake."

Tentatively, the Cuban removed his jacket and imitating Narby rolled his white drill trousers to the knee and climbed over the rail. Narby helped him down. "Like this," he said, putting his back against the hull again. But Campos was too short to get much leverage. Together, they heaved once or twice. Suddenly the boat rocked. Narby looked up quickly. The pilot had climbed onto the bridge. The engine gurgled to life. There was a short burst and the boat jerked into motion, the hull grinding easily over the hump of sand and the bow pivoting away from them, toward the open sea. The rucksack, the money, the little brown bottle, were on board. There was no time to think.

As the bow pivoted Narby leapt and grabbed at a piece of rope dangling off the stern, his legs swinging dangerously close to the propeller. For a second he felt his feet dragging in the water as the boat accelerated. If he swung too far he might get caught in the blades. Gripping the rope with one hand, his palm and shoulder burning, he reached frantically with the other and found the rail and heaved himself up, crawling over and falling onto the deck, the forward momentum pitching him against the junk and the empty beer bottles.

He had to be quick, before the pilot could react. The haft of the gaff was in front of him. On his side, sprawled on the deck, Narby wrenched it free and struggled to his feet. The pilot had seen him and was coming down. As if it were a drum major's baton Narby raised the gaff and rotated it, swirling the hook away and planting his feet. He arched forward and swung and he could feel the impact vibrating down the haft, the blunt end of the gaff thudding into the pilot's enormous gut, pitching the fat man forward as he doubled over and then crumpled face down onto the deck.

With no one at the wheel the boat began to bank chaotically, like a wild horse suddenly set loose. The pilot, moaning and wallowing, tried to raise himself. Straddling the man's mass Narby raised the gaff and brought it down at the base of the thick fat-folded neck. The pilot went limp, his face flat and inert against the deck. Narby raised the haft again. But the careening motion put him off balance and it came down without force, the blunt end of the gaff grazing the pilot's neck, jostling him as one might poke at a snake or rat to test if it were dead. The empty beer bottles were rolling crazily about the deck, piling up against the body then rolling away.

Narby stood, averting his face. In his moment of terror the fat man had shat his britches.

Steadying himself with the gaff Narby grabbed onto the ladder, climbed to the bridge and took the wheel, pulling back the throttle until the boat slowed, the bow swinging around gently. From the bridge he could see Campos now, a bedraggled childlike figure in his rolled trousers, aghast and abandoned in the knee-deep water. Narby let the boat come closer and then cut the engine, and the boat drifted silently until it nestled into the thicket of mangrove. Quickly, he hopped down from the bridge and extended himself over the rail to help Campos climb up.

The little Cuban was staring at the pilot, prone and splayed and befouled amidst the junk.

"Suspira. No es muerto. Yo puedo hacerlo." Campos picked up a length of pipe that had spilled onto the deck. "I kill him. Yes?"

"No. Stop. We might need him."

Campos backed off.

Narby picked up a tangle of sea-blackened rope. Holding his breath against the stench he placed his foot on the fat man's back, lifted the pilot's arms until the wrists crossed, and wrapped the rope three times around one wrist and then the other, yanking the rope with violence until it cut into the soft fatty flesh.

"Let him alone. We've got to find somewhere to land. Before someone sees us."

The sky had gone white, a shimmering shadow-less haze. For a maddening half hour they wandered the billowing islets of mangrove, testing a channel and then backing away when the hull scraped bottom.

"Mira," Campos called out. Slathered in sweat, his white drill suit ruined, the little man had nevertheless preserved a measure of composure, his pomaded hair oiled flat, the cinnamon-skin of his elongated face virtually unblemished. "Tierra firme."

It was a small cove with a muddy sand beach. Narby could see pine trees rising behind the mangrove. The ruins of an old dock, rotted pilings and planks, jutted out into the turbid brown-green water. Narby brought them in as close as the boat's draw allowed, about twenty yards from the shore. Wading through the warm shallow water he and Campos ferried their things—the rucksack and valise, their shoes and clothes, the jug of water—onto the mud beach.

"Qué hacemos? Con el barco, el gordo? What we do?"

"I don't know. He's got my money somewhere. El dinero. We ought to get a refund, don't you think?"

"No understand."

"Money. How much did you give him?"

"I give the money ayer. Before. Yesterday."

"Well, he's got mine somewhere on board. Wait here. I'll take care of it."

Narby waded back to the boat. The pilot was breathing in gasps, wheezing, his befouled body pitched on its side. He'd probably come to before long. The thought of going through the fat man's trouser pockets, touching him, made Narby sick. He kicked at him a few times in the gut, but with little force. "My money. Where's my money, you fucking bastard?"

The man could hardly breathe, let alone answer. Narby climbed to the bridge and searched the shelves beneath the throttle. Finding nothing, growing anxious with each passing minute, he rummaged the midsection of the boat where the pilot had wallowed most of the night. Nothing. The gaff had rolled back under the swivel chairs. Narby picked it up and held the rusted hook at the pilot's throat. "You hear me. I'll rip this right through your windpipe. Where's my money?"

It was pointless. He was wasting time. Like a man diving into a cesspit he held his breath and crouched and forced his hand into the pilot's pocket. The man's panic-loosened bowels and bladder had oozed everywhere. Gagging, Narby pulled his hand away. It wasn't worth it.

Campos was watching from the mud beach, batting away the flies and mosquitoes. "I'm going to take the boat out, point it out to sea and let it go," Narby called out, making a pantomime of steering. "OK?"

Whether he understood or not Campos nodded. As Narby climbed to the bridge Campos yelled, "How you return? No go far."

"Nadir. Muy fuerte en el agua, yo. No problema."

There wouldn't be reef sharks so close to land, not danger-ous ones, anyway. Just bottom feeders, he figured. It was ugly water, malodorous and stagnant though it flowed through the mangrove into the open Gulf. But for the moment there was no fear in him. Only the desperation to be free of the boat and the pilot.

Within a few minutes he had taken the boat beyond the labyrinth of mangrove. Using rope and some long machine screws—he didn't have time to figure out the automated rudder—he tried to lock the wheel in position. He put the throttle about mid-way. Satisfied, the boat chugging straight into the open sea, he climbed down from the bridge. The pilot was on his stomach again, lolling with the rocking of the boat with his cheek flat against the deck. His hands, bound behind his back, had turned beet-purple. Narby considered weighting him with the anchor and dumping the still-breathing mound of flesh overboard. When they found the boat out at sea there would be no trace. Wasn't that the way of self-preservation? Hadn't he earned the right, after what they had done to him in Korea? The pilot had brought it on himself.

He could let the pilot die, but he couldn't kill him. Not like that, in cold blood. It wasn't mercy. He simply didn't want to have to think about it later. So far, he'd acted spontaneously or with necessity. That was enough.

Hurrying, he straddled the rail near the aft where he could jump clear of the propellers. He looked back one last time and leapt.

As he surfaced and turned around Narby saw his mistake. The force of his jump had been enough to swing the hull eastward. The boat might eventually angle back toward the coast. Or with luck the currents might still take it out to sea. There was nothing he could do about it now.

He swam with strong well-formed strokes, his legs kicking straight and churning the water. The coiled aimless violence that had assaulted him in the cabin, the dread, had been purged away. He had always been a strong swimmer. In the water he never hesitated, never lost control. It was a good omen, after all, coming ashore like this on nothing but his own power. Perhaps he was more in command of the situation than he realized.

4

THE COVE, OR WHATEVER IT WAS, was little more than a narrow crescent of mud and sand hemmed in by thickets of mangrove and coastal scrub, the dock a skeleton of rotting timbers. Chunks of worm-eaten lumber, posts and planks, lay scattered about the beach. Narby drank from the jug, letting himself dry off before getting dressed. To ease his concern he kneeled, rooted around in the knapsack for the Chesterfields, found the little brown bottle and opened it to confirm the contents and then put it back and lit a cigarette.

"Care for a smoke?"

Campos had spread out his jacket and shirt on a piece of lumber. Stripped to his undershirt he looked rather pathetic, the cotton clinging to his thin torso, his ribs protruding, his dark face beaded with sweat. "Si, gracias."

Narby lit one off his own and passed it to the Cuban. Campos took a drag, and then, with some effort, he said, "At the boat. You help me. My life. Many thanks you. Contra el gordo. Muchas gracias." He put out his hand. "Camarades, sí? Usted y yo. We make friends."

"Why not?" Narby had abraded his hand grabbing the rope, and perhaps pulled something in his shoulder or upper back. His left side was throbbing. He shook the Cuban's hand. "Comrades."

"Por favor. I am Ernesto."

"Ernesto. Good. I'm Philip."

"Felipé."

"Close enough. So, got any idea where the hell we are? Dondé estamos? Conoces?"

"Creo que si. I thing so. Mira." Using a stick he outlined the bottom half of the Florida peninsula in the mud. "Here Miami. Here Key Waste. Here Tampa." He traced a line running south from Tampa toward the Keys and stopping halfway made an X. "Aquí. Mas o menos." Then, from Tampa he traced another line, south and then curving east. "Hay un camino de Tampa a Miami. Se llama Tamiama Trail. We go this way."

"How do you know? You've been here before?"

"No me. Los otros. They say me, the others."

"Where's the nearest town? How do we get to the road?"

Campos turned, looking helplessly at the wall of scrub and mangrove.

"I not know. Es peligroso. La jungla. Necesitamos una machete."

"Yeah? Well, we don't have a machete. Someone brought in all this lumber, took the trouble to build a dock. There's got to be a way out of here, a town or settlement nearby."

It was a foul spot, swarming with mud flies and mosquitoes, the brown shallow water giving off a putrid odor, the breezes from the Gulf choked off by thousands of billowing mangrove islets. The heat was gaining intensity, the sky a flat grayish-white haze. Narby paced along the wall of underbrush. "We're going to have to push through. Bushwhack. I'll carry the water jug. You ready?"

He watched as Campos methodically unrolled his trouser legs and then folded the shirt and the white drill suit jacket neatly into the valise. What next, a squirt of cologne? The man was ridiculous, a preening sissy. On the other hand, not more than half an hour ago he'd been ready, eager even, to crush the pilot's skull with a pipe. Despite everything the Cuban still gave the impression of meticulous self-possession, his hair combed back and the pencil-line of moustache only slightly malformed. The little clerk had guts, stamina. Whatever his cause, embezzled money or political backstabbing, it was seeing him through, protecting him.

Narby led the way, thrashing through the underbrush, Campos behind him holding the valise at chest level, like a shield. He thought he had found an old footpath, then lost it, then found it again, or maybe it was just his imagination, an optical illusion of the tangled thickets. But then, suddenly, they stumbled onto a dirt road wide enough for a vehicle, heavily overgrown but with a set of shallow wheel ruts still palpable under Narby's feet.

He took a drink and handed the jug to Campos. In the heat, with the effort of pushing through the thickets and keeping off the mosquitoes, Narby estimated an hour until they were out of water.

"Any idea which way? Cual direccíon?"

They were out of the mangrove, in the midst of some kind of jungle. Campos set the valise down and walked several yards in either direction, playing the boy scout. Between the rather sickly looking pine trees, their scaly blackened bark slathered with coagulated yellow sap, rose a dense underbrush of vine-twisted palmetto bushes, the blades of the fan-shaped fronds knife sharp to the touch. If the road petered out they'd have no choice but go back toward the cove and start over.

"Ningun idea. What you think?"

"This way. Let's go."

"Pero porqué? Why to go that way?"

Narby looked at him and shrugged. "All right. The other way, then. If it makes you feel better."

Campos laughed. "No. La primera. Por allí. Es mejor. Tienes buen instito, Felipé."

"Think so? Let's hope you're right, comrade."

They walked in silence, numbed by heat and exhaustion and the monotony of the jungle, halting every ten minutes to sip from the jug. The road held, though it was obvious no vehicle had passed this way in many months, maybe years. After an hour, stopping again, Narby could bear it no longer. He turned away from Campos, saying nothing, and found the little brown bottle. Might as well go out with a positive attitude. There was barely enough water left for a good swig. He took a few drops to wet his mouth, and then swallowing repeatedly with the thick tacky spit coating his tongue and lips—three dollies and two yellows—forced them down his gullet.

"Medicina," he said to Campos, catching his breath. The pills had nearly choked him. He held out the jug. "Here."

But the Cuban was staring at the dust. "Felipé. Mira."

A boot print. And another and another. Someone had walked that way recently, perhaps that very morning.

"All right," Narby said, hoisting the rucksack back on his shoulder. "Maybe we can catch up to him. If they speak English, I'll handle it. If it's Spanish, it's up to you." He still wasn't convinced they had landed in Florida. "Me entiendes? De acuerdo?"

"Yes. I am agree."

It wasn't long before Narby saw someone ahead in the distance, a tall dark figure coming toward them on the path. "Let's stop here. Better to let him approach us." His throat was cracked and sore. He took a last swallow from the weightless jug, so that he might speak clearly.

Ernesto had opened his valise. Amid the waste of the fetid jungle the Cuban felt compelled to put on a crisp white short-sleeved shirt. Dressed, he snapped the valise closed and held it at his side. If not for his mulatto skin and the pencil moustache you might mistake him for a travelling bible salesman.

Catching sight of them the figure stopped for a moment, then resumed his slow pace. Narby could see him now: a tall Negro man with grayish-white hair, wearing a set of overalls over his bare torso. Some kind of farm worker, Narby supposed. His broad chest, the powerful exposed arms and shoulders, suggested a younger man, despite the tufts of white hair.

Narby put up his hand in greeting. The man stopped, still some twenty feet distant. "Hello. Good morning."

The man nodded. "Mo'nin.'"

"You speak English?"

He stood, looking in their direction, but indirectly, cautiously. "I suppose."

"We're lost. Is there a town around here? A place with a telephone? Can you give us directions?"

"What you want?"

"Just looking to find our way to the nearest town. Our boat. Well, we got stuck on a sandbar. Had to wade ashore. Back there a ways. In the mangrove. Damn easy to get hung up in all those sandbars, yeah?"

"Ain't none of my business. You best talk to the Cap'm."

Narby strained to understand the man's thick accent. "I'm sorry. Talk to who?"

"Cap'm. He in the sto'. Up'ta road."

"A store? Is it far?"

"Nope. Round the bend."

"Thanks much, friend. I appreciate it." He turned to Campos. "Let's go."

Deferentially, the man waited for Narby and Campos before he continued on, stepping into the brush to let them pass, his eyes lowered.

After a moment, Narby glanced back. The man had disappeared into the jungle.

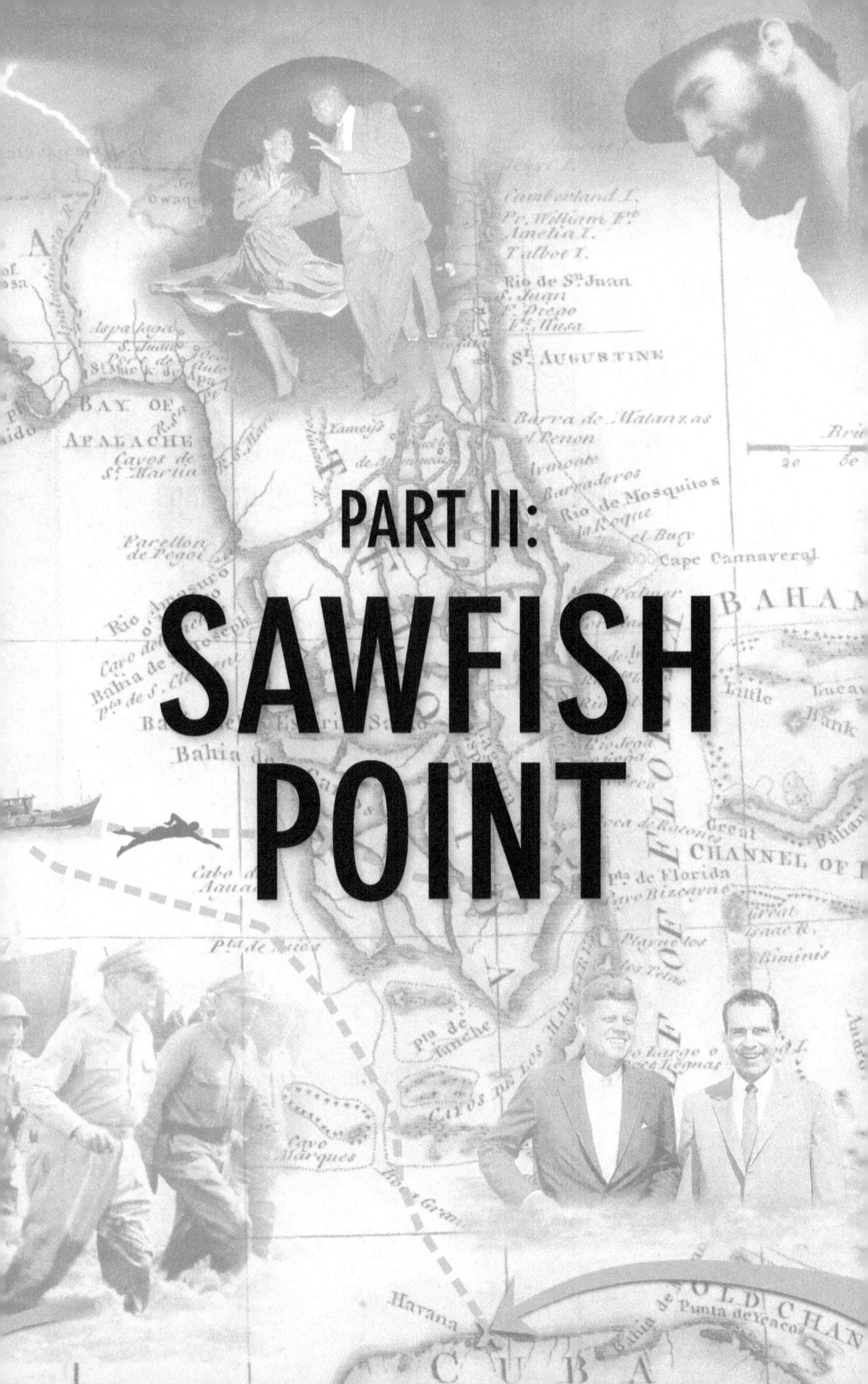
PART II:
SAWFISH
POINT

Their puny movement was in tatters.
Poor dapper Ernesto. He'd wind up getting
himself tortured and killed, for nothing.

1

NARBY HAD NOTICED HER YESTERDAY, at the library when he came to look through the telephone directories for banks in Miami. A blonde with a sweet smile, a decent figure, especially when she turned in her chair and the outline of her bra showed against the thin white cotton blouse. She had noticed him, too, though they hadn't spoken. The fan by her desk was blowing the loose curls of piled hair across her forehead and she had brushed them back in a way that seemed coquettish, provocative—a deliberate gesture, perhaps, to show him that she had no wedding ring. Only, yesterday he hadn't had the presence of mind to confirm it. It could have been her right hand.

He stood a few yards back, browsing the shelves near the circulation desk. As soon as he saw that she was alone, he made his move.

"Hello. I'd like to apply for a library card."

"OK. You just have to fill out this form." She handed him a piece of paper. "Have a seat."

He could smell her perfume. "Thanks. Mind if I borrow your pen?"

"Here you are." As she handed it to him he saw the ring, the small rather cheap-looking stone.

He began writing. Ignore the ring. Keep going. "Just got into town," he said. "Thought I'd get a library card, first thing. Kind of makes a person feel at home."

"That's so nice. What brings you to Myerton?"

"Not sure really." He laughed, looking up now. "Just got out of the Army. Kicking around a bit, looking for somewhere to settle down. Here, where it says permanent address. Well, to be honest, I don't have one yet. All right if I just put down where I'm staying."

"I don't see why not."

"Great. Thanks. I'm a big reader." He looked down again, writing. "Novels. History. Current events. Even a little poetry." He signed the card—after two years the Philip Narby signature had become second nature—and slid it across the desk, smiling, careful to catch her eyes in a causal, passing way. Brown, rather plain. "Everything filled out correctly?"

"Yes. Mr. Narby," she said, reading it off the card. "Looks just fine." She took a little breath. "If you don't mind my asking, were you over there in Korea?"

"For a while. Yes."

"Welcome home, then. Frank, that's my husband, well, they haven't sent him home yet. I know it's ridiculous, but, well, maybe by chance you know him? Frank Swanson? He's a second lieutenant. With the, well, I can never remember which Division he's with."

"Frank Swanson? No, doesn't ring a bell. Well, it's a big Army. Don't you worry. He'll be home soon enough."

"Oh, I'm not worried."

He looked directly at her now. "No. I don't think you are."

"Excuse me?"

He smiled. "So, when do I get my library card?"

"Oh. We mail it to you." There was a slight warble in her voice. "Only takes a day or two."

"Great." He softened his gaze, cocking his head. "I've been away a long time. It's good to be back. A bit lonely, though."

"Your family must be thrilled that you're home."

"Yeah, well, like I said, I'm not from around here. No family to speak of. But that's a long story, best told over a drink. A cocktail. Mrs. Swanson."

He had to hurry. A mother with a couple of kids were bearing down on the circulation desk. "You will have a drink with me, won't you?" She would neither speak nor look at him. But she didn't seem too offended. "Maybe I do know your husband. See, we have something to chat about. Maybe I have some news." He stood up, a child at his side, the mother yanking it away by the hand. "Thanks, Mrs. Swanson. I'll drop by tomorrow. See if that book I'm looking for is back on the shelf. So long."

He went out and walked down the street, past the McCrory's Five-and-Dime and the Rexall Drugs and cut across the courthouse square. The town was called Myerton, the seat of Lacoosa County, Florida. Except for half-a-dozen substantial buildings clustered around the town square—the courthouse and jail and sheriff's office, the First Federal Bank and the Arcade Movie Theater—the place was a backwater. There was a train station, but the passenger trains didn't even bother stopping until October when the winter tourist season began, and even then only twice a week. Across the tracks was the Negro section. There were as many Negroes as Whites, Narby had noticed, maybe more, but the Whites kept them pretty well corralled.

The heat was wretched, far worse than Havana. The town sat ten miles inland from the Gulf, on a wide brackish-water river, surrounded by mile after mile of thick pine and palmetto jungle. No blue Caribbean sky here: just a pasty grayish-white glare from dawn until mid-afternoon. It was a little after three. Like clockwork the thunderheads were piling up in the east, over the cypress swamps and grasslands. In half an hour the sky would turn black and it would rain in torrents for maybe twenty minutes, just as it had every afternoon since he'd landed, ten days ago. Ten days and already he was sick of it.

Narby gave it a fifty-percent chance that he would take the librarian to bed. He only needed to get a little liquor into her, make her feel as if he really did care about Second Lieutenant Swanson getting home safe and sound. He only wanted to comfort her. Or maybe not. Maybe he ought to play the 'let's run away together' card. There was no doubt she was attracted to him. Very attracted. Same feeling he'd had about Martha, McCoy's secretary. Only Martha hadn't been afraid. The only hitch was if the Lieutenant showed up all of a sudden. There was still a lot of chaos in Asia. The GIs they could send home, but they'd want the officers around for a while, to keep order.

On a side street off the courthouse square there was a little place called the Smoker's Den, a tobacco shop and newsstand. Narby had found it on his second day in town, looking for Chesterfields and the *Herald Tribune*. The entrance was five steps below the sidewalk, in a kind of half-basement. On the bottom step Narby hesitated. Through the window he saw someone at the counter. But a second later the glass door swung open and the customer brushed past him, grunting "scuse me," his head down, a flat brown-paper package under his arm.

The shop was empty now and Narby went in, setting off the little brass bells that were tied with a piece of yarn to the inside handle. Below street level, with the tinted plate glass window, the ferocious glare was subdued. The air inside was cool and dry, with the sweet aroma of cherry pipe tobacco. The shock, passing from the swelter and glare to the cool softly illuminated shop, his shirt damp with sweat, was spine tingling, like diving into cold dark water.

The proprietor had disappeared momentarily into the back. It was a tight cluttered space, packed from floor to ceiling with cigarette cartons, jars of tobacco, boxes of cigars, displays of pipes and lighters, a spinning magazine rack, an odd assortment of masculine items—models of old ships, folding knives, wallets, money clips, chess sets—crammed into every nook. At the alarm of the bells the shopkeeper reappeared, pushing through the beaded curtain hanging behind the glass cases.

"Hello, sir. Ah. Welcome back."

Two days ago Narby had stopped in, and along with the newspapers and magazines he had bought ten more cartons of Chesterfields, a leather wallet, and one of the more expensive Zippo windproof lighters. This was his third time in the shop.

He nodded across the counter, giving the magazine rack a slow spin. "Afternoon."

"Is there something I can help you find?"

"Yeah. I'm looking for the *New Yorker* magazine. You carry that one?"

"*New Yorker*? No. sir, I am afraid not." He smiled. Narby had liked the looks of him from the very first: a thickly built square-faced olive-skinned man, with coarse dark hair and a black moustache threaded with gray, his high prominent nose sloping down from his forehead between dark, wet, oblong eyes. Some kind of Arab, Narby guessed. Lebanese, maybe, or Egyptian. An immigrant. Someone who didn't belong, not in a town like this. "If you wish, I can try to order it from my distributor."

"Yeah? Good. And while you're at it, how about the *Atlantic Monthly*. Can you get that one, too?"

The man tore off a piece of brown wrap from a roll under the counter and wrote down the titles. "Frankly, if you do not mind my saying, you are the first customer who has ever asked for these publications. I cannot guarantee I can get them straight away. Or at all. But," he said, looking up, smiling with his square white teeth, "I will do my best."

"Thanks. I appreciate it."

He let his eye wander for a moment and squatted down to look at the lower shelf of the glass case. "Can I see one of theses flasks? The middle one."

"Of course, sir."

The merchant spread a square of velvet on the countertop and set the flask down, as if displaying a piece of jewelry. "Fine quality leather. All glass inside. Notice the hinged screw top. Usually four dollars. Today, three-fifty."

Narby had flung the cheap tin flask into the Gulf the night of the crossing. He could use another. "Fine. I'll take it. And I need some more cigarettes."

"Chesterfields, yes?"

"That's right. Give me a couple of cartons."

The shopkeeper reached behind to take them down from a shelf behind his head. Narby had already trashed the cornball PX outfit, the aloha shirt and penny loafers, and the wharf-rat rags, too; had bought new clothes, had a haircut, was shaving every morning. Maybe he ought to drop the Chesterfields, as a precaution. "You've got some interesting brands, here. What are these? Imports?"

"Yes, sir. These are English. And these from Canada. A little more expensive, but well worth it."

"All right. I'll give them both a try. What about this?" He pointed to a dark blue pouch. A lot of the locals, he had noticed, rolled their own cigarettes. "Danish shag. That any good?"

"Yes, indeed." He took the pouch from the humidified section of the case and unsealed it, offering Narby a sniff. "Aromatic, is it not?"

"Nice. I'll take that, too."

The more Narby spent, the more the Arab would trust him. From the rack he picked out the latest *Time*, the *New York Herald Tribune* and a *Miami Herald*. The *Tribune* was three days old, the *Herald* current. He put them on the counter.

"That should do it, for now."

"Please, sir. If you like these tobacco brands you must tell me as soon as possible. I do not keep back stock but I can order more, as soon as you wish. Most of my customers, sir, they stick to the tried and true."

"I'll do that. Name's Philip Narby by the way." He held his hand out over the counter.

"Very pleased to meet you, sir." The Arab had quite a grip. "Please, Mr. Norby, is it? Mr. Norby, everyone here calls me Hank."

"All right. Good to meet you, Hank."

As Hank tallied the bill on a scrap of paper, Narby told him that he was new in town, wasn't sure how long he'd be staying, how glad he was to have found a shop like this, a friendly face. Narby peeled off a twenty. The shopkeeper went into the back, behind the beaded curtain, to make change. When he returned, the tiny shop still empty, Narby decided to risk it.

"Hank. I'd like to ask you a favor."

The proprietor leaned forward, needlessly lowering his voice. "Of course, Mr. Norby. There are other magazines available, which I cannot openly display."

"No. It's nothing like that. Look. I was wondering if I could have some mail sent here? I'm living a ways out of town at the moment and, well, there's no delivery. Since I'll be coming in here regularly, well, it's convenient. It's nothing much, a letter now and then. You think you could do that for me?"

The Arab nodded. "Of course, Mr. Norby. That way, we shall see each other more often. Please, use this address." He wrote it on the scrap of paper. "I will keep your letter safe and sound until you come fetch it."

"Thanks. I appreciate it." No doubt the shopkeeper thought it was some love intrigue. Good. Narby took his package, said goodbye, and swung open the door. Only five minutes in the cool subterranean atmosphere and stepping out into the glare and heat was like slamming into a wall.

2

NARBY HAD A ROOM at the Glo-Bel Motor Court, a roadside motel on Highway 40 a few miles north of town: eight plywood and concrete-block tourist cabins arranged in a semi-circle, with a larger, more homey structure at the end where the manager lived. There was nothing else around, just the pine wastes and the two-lane highway. At the edge of the motel's gravel parking lot sat a ten-foot-high neon contraption in the shape of a church bell—hence, the name of the motel—ridiculously grandiose considering the gimcrack accommodations. At twilight, when the manager switched it on, the thing glowed a ghastly pink and green, emitting a loud obnoxious buzz. If the idea was to lure in the motorists speeding down the lonely highway at night, it wasn't working. Except for the manager and his wife, Narby had the place to himself.

Narby pulled in just as it started to pour. His second day in town he had bought a '49 Chevy pickup. It was cheap enough, banged about and eaten with rust but in decent running order, and inconspicuous. The locals' vehicle of choice, apparently. The tags were good for three years and the salesman, pleasantly surprised that Narby was such an easy sell, signed the title transfer and told Narby to fill it in at his leisure. When Narby mentioned that he'd misplaced his New York driver's license, the salesman had said, "the huh what? Driver's license? Ain't no such animal down here in Flo'da. Just drive on the right, stop on the red, and don't run no one over, and you be just fine."

Holding the package from the Smoker's Den over his head, against the rain, he dashed across the lot. Cabin 101. Eight dollars a week, the off-season rate. All in all it was a step up from the rancid green room: a closet-sized kitchenette, a Formica table with four chairs, a tiny sitting room with a rocker and a lamp, the bedroom just big enough for the dresser and double bed, a bathroom with a metal shower stall. With screens on all the windows and a screen door and the electric fan at least he wouldn't suffocate in his sleep. About the only time it cooled off, just a little, was during the storms when the wind kicked up.

He tossed the package on the table, unbuttoned his shirt, washed the sweat from his face at the sink, opened the cabinet and poured half a jelly-jar of bourbon. Jim Beam, instead of Bacardi. When in Rome. Forget Havana. He'd never been in Havana. He was a soldier boy from New York, or maybe Chicago, set free after three years of hell, looking to start over. Isn't that what you did in places like this? Start over.

The only thing about Cabin 101 that set Narby on edge were the roaches, enormous winged monstrosities that the manager, an old man named Dindridge, called palmetto bugs. Dindridge had given him a spray-can of insecticide, but you had to coat the little shits until they dripped before it had any effect. So he took to squashing them with a shoe, their fat carapacial corpses oozing a thick white malodorous paste. After a good slaughter, though, they seemed to keep away for a few days. Must give off the smell of death.

He took a few sips and lit a cigarette. The sky was blue-black, the rain pounding the tarpaper roof. He stood by the screen door, in the breeze, watching the gravel in the parking lot splatter with mud. Cutting back on the dollies—conserving them rather pointlessly since he'd be out soon, no matter what—meant he was drinking more. So what? It kept him steady, restored him to his natural equilibrium. He could handle it, as long as he kept fit.

Back in Tokyo, McCoy and his ilk could certainly bolt it down. Just about anyone who mattered in the Occupation started quaffing at lunchtime. Section Heads like McCoy went for the high-class stuff, the Chivas. He'd go through a bottle every couple of days, it seemed. If they had ferreted out the lushes the way they had the lefties and the queers, there wouldn't have been anyone left. The stenographers and janitors, maybe.

In the shoebox bedroom he peeled off his shirt—drab cotton work clothes purchased at the five-and-dime—and threw it on the bed. He was going to have Mrs. Swanson, right here. Give the bed springs something to sing about. She might not find his scars very seductive, but hell, how could she refuse a war hero? Tomorrow, or the next day. Once he had her clothes off, how different could it be than with a whore? Maybe they could talk a little, afterwards. He could use something like that right now, a little tenderness from a real woman. Or maybe not.

From the dresser drawer he took paper and pen and sat at the table. The cabin had no phone and Narby wasn't fool enough to place an international call from the Myerton post office, in public. Besides, he had to handle Knowles with care. It was easier in writing. Tell him just enough. Keep him interested, guessing. Narby knew more about Knowles than Knowles knew about him. He planned to keep it that way.

Have landed undetected.—Not quite true, because of that man Carl Vetch. But it was preferable that Knowles think so.—*Need information on Ernesto Campos. Cuban. Mulatto. About twenty-five, short, slender, cinnamon skin, dark eyes, black hair, mustache. Finicky dresser. Claims to be a medical student. At present in hiding in Miami. Very likely involved in anti-Batista violence. Also, Carl Vetch. American. Southerner. About forty-five. Medium height, flabby, glasses, light-brown thinning hair. Slovenly. Bad teeth.*—That was a nice touch.—*Connected to Putnam Paper Company. PPC contracted with Civilian Censorship Division in Tokyo re control of paper supply.*—That should prick up Knowles' ears.—*Vetch's role with Putnam unknown. Will investigate from this end. Reply to safe address: PN c/o Smoker's Den, 47 Fifth St., Myerton, Florida.*

He sealed the letter in an envelope and addressed it from memory. In the morning he'd drop it at the post office, before meeting with Vetch. Then he would have to wait.

The rain was letting up. He considered returning to the library, waiting outside in the truck until she finished for the day. And do what? Follow her home? Proposition her? Drag her into the jungle and rape her?

He poured another glass of Jim Beam—jelly jars, only the finest crystal stemware for guests of the Glo-Bel Motor Court—and began to peruse the newspapers he had bought, his eyes flitting from Seoul to Iran to Berlin, his concentration wavering. He had buried the money, wrapped in the rubber poncho, in the dense brush behind the cabins, under the roots of a palmetto bush. It wouldn't do to lug the rucksack around like some kind of hobo, and the cabin wasn't safe. You could break in with a toothpick. He kept five hundred in his pocket, at all times.

If Narby needed to get out of town suddenly, without time to return to the motel, he'd have something to tide him over.

Narby had a bad feeling about Carl Vetch.

Carl Vetch was the man who the Negroes living in the pinewoods called "captain." That morning ten days ago, while the Cuban Campos had waited outside, Narby had gone into the store, or whatever it was, an elongated broken-back shack standing in a clearing littered with junk, dark and airless inside, the shelves bare. He had asked for water and directions and, if possible, a ride into the nearest town, giving Vetch the story he and Campos had agreed on: two visitors down from New York City, out fishing. Their boat got hung up on a sandbar. The outboard motor had burned out; they'd been forced to wade ashore, and eventually they had found the dirt road.

Vetch gazed at Narby through the thick dusty glasses, one lens cracked, the steel rims eaten with rust.

"That so?"

Narby asked again for water.

"Don't sell no water. I got sodee pop. You want a sodee pop, cost you ten cent."

Narby reached in his pocket. Stupidly, he hadn't thought to make change in Havana. That had been a mistake. Vetch got one look at the twenty and just like that changed his tune. "Sho. I can give you a lift in my truck. Only. Don't like to leave the store unattended during the busy morning hours. No telling how much business I might lose. Un'nustan what I mean? Now what you want? I got Nehi grape, I got on'ge, got Cola-nip peach. Ain't none too cold, I'm afraid. Juice went out again, cause of the storms knocking out the line. They's two of you, is they? I spect we can squeeze in. Ain't no New Yoke taxi cabs round here. Hah."

They settled on a price: the twenty, with the cost of the sodas thrown in. Narby brought two bottles out to Campos and told him that he'd found a ride to the bus station in town. But right away there was trouble. Vetch came out from behind the store—rotting grey planks, the broken-backed roof littered with pine needles and moss, the porch collapsed on one side, rubbish spread everywhere. The busy hours—the man was a joker, some kind of white trash, slobbering at the sight of a twenty-dollar note. Yet the moment Vetch saw Campos and took in the Cuban's dark skin, showing even darker against the crisp white shirt, his face went sour. "Who that? That your fishing partner? No Nigras or dogs up front. Your boy can ride in back, in the bed."

With his limited English, Campos hadn't understood Vetch's slurred drawl. But apparently he understood where he was, the rules of deference to be obeyed if they wanted to get out of that jungle in one piece. Silently, Campos climbed over the filthy tailgate. Narby handed him his valise and got in the cab beside Vetch, the rucksack on his lap.

The drive out of the jungle took an hour, most of it slow going over rough ruts and washboard, the low pine branches and palmetto fronds scraping against the hump of the hood. Vetch asked a lot of questions, made a lot of noise as if he were entitled to an explanation.

"I been living out here for over fifteen years, son. In all that time ain't no stranger ever come round Sawfish Point, like you just done. Not with no roll of twenty dollar bills in his pocket. Hah! What you doing round here with that dolled up Nigra? What you got in that sack? I know what you up to, son, sneaking round that mangrove in a boat. You was looking at that land, wasn't you? Like that one they sent down here last winter, with his surveying tube. Only he was from Putnam. You ain't from Putnam. Air you?"

The dope—the dollies and yellows Narby had forced down, just when Campos had seen the boot prints in the road—was kicking in. Click click click. Putnam. Left for dead in a ditch along the Naktong, running half way around the world, two years of cowering in Havana, and now he was picking up the thread. He'd seen the invoices with his own eyes, in Martha's desk. There was no Allbright Paper Company. The CCD bought paper from Putnam, shipped from Georgia to Yokohama and then passing through Master Supply Sergeant Sid Black's warehouse.

"You mean the Putnam Paper Company?"

"Sho. Only down here it's all gum. They got they pulp mills up north in Macon. Sawmills all round Georgia and the Panhandle. Big operation, them Putnam boys. Only these pines way down here ain't good for nothing but turp'tine. Ain't hardly good for that neither. They done shut down all the stills bout five years ago. Them trees all tapped out. But I spect you know all about that, now don't you, son?"

They hit a stretch of gravel road and turned south on the U.S. highway, picking up speed. Five miles later they crossed a drawbridge over the Lacoosa River and drove into Myerton. Vetch pulled the truck over a block from the Greyhound station. A small crowd, men in fatigues and garrison uniforms, was milling around on the sidewalk in front, probably waiting for connections to Tampa or Miami. And probably more inside the station—the first of the exodus from Korea. Narby was wearing the aloha shirt, the suntan trousers and penny loafers. An off-duty non-com, decked out in classic Tokyo PX style. Splattered with mud, stinking with sweat. He would no doubt be an object of great curiosity.

"Ain't no one round here knows Sawfish Point like I do. Ain't no one knows what Putnam did down there but me." Vetch kept the motor running, as if waiting for Narby to make up his mind. "You interested in buying up that land, you best be careful, watch yourself. Things ain't what they seem like. Never is."

He didn't exactly relish the prospect of chumming it up with those homesick soldier boys. He ought to follow up the Putnam thread, wait a few weeks until the demobilization had spread thin.

"In that case, maybe we should talk, before I head back to New York."

"Ha. I knew you was looking at that land. I got plenty to tell you, son. If you ain't with Putnam, then I bet you against em. Just like me."

"Maybe so." He could see Campos in the rearview, climbing out over the tailgate. "Just a minute. I'll have a word with… with my boy. I don't suppose I need him anymore. He can catch a bus for Miami from here, yeah?"

"Sho. Only he got to wait round back with the rest of the Coloreds. This ain't New Yoke, son. A Nigra all dolled up like that, he best keep his head down."

Narby got out and pulled Campos back beside the truck. "You can get a bus to Miami. I'm staying here for a while. Quedarme aqui un poco. Watch yourself, amigo. Cuidado. There's a separate Colored waiting room in the back. Detrás. Just stick with the Negroes. Vaya con los Negros. Me entiendes?"

"Entiendo muy bien. Racismo Americano. I go with the Blacks, yes?"

"That's right." Narby felt a pang for the dapper little embezzling medical student, or whatever the hell he was. The rough ride in the bed of the truck had nearly done him in. Still, Campos had managed to keep his white shirt relatively clean. "You have money? Dollars? For the bus?"

"Yes. Gracias. Mira." He took a pad from his jacket pocket and scribbled something down and tore out the page. "For to find me in Miami. Comrade."

As Campos walked toward the station Narby looked at the paper. *LI-berty 2-2422.* A phone number. Below that, a date: *Viente-seis de Julio.* Why the twenty-sixth, when today was the thirtieth? Some kind of code, maybe. In a week or two, Narby would catch the bus to Miami and ask the Cuban face-to-face.

He got back in the truck. "I need someplace to stay. Somewhere quiet where I can get some rest." A couple of soldiers were wandering down the street from the station, carrying duffel bags. "Maybe someplace a ways out of town."

"Sho. I know just the place."

3

NARBY PARKED THE TRUCK a block from the Rexall's Drugstore, took a swallow from the flask, and with the letter to Bill Knowles in his hand walked toward the post office.

Rexall's carried legit splash—diet pills, Benzedrine inhalers for asthma and bronchitis—though none of it had the kick of Sylvio's yellow capsules. But without the Dolophine to smooth it out, to dull the pain and lull him to sleep, the splash was a bad idea. For Dolophine or Codeine he would need a prescription. In a small town like Myerton, a stranger with no identification, no Army discharge papers, with nothing but a web of scars to give him credibility—he could hardly stroll into a doctor's office and ask for narcotics.

A few days ago he'd sat at the Rexall's soda fountain and drank a malted while he read the paper. No locks or gate protecting the pharmacist's counter, as far as Narby could see. An old geezer in a white lab coat sifting pills into bottles. You could come in with a gun, a stocking over your face, demand that he hand over all the narcotics. The only cops he'd seen around town were a pair of overstuffed deputy sheriffs, driving in their bubble-gum machine or having coffee and donuts at the Gladiola Café, bullshitting with the locals, cowboy hats cocked back. Real sons of Dixie. It would take a hell of a lot of nerve, but it might be done with minimal risk.

At the post office he slipped the letter into the box. A week, maybe ten days, before he heard back. As long as Narby kept up the best-customer routine, he supposed he could trust Hank not to open the letter. Should have instructed Knowles to seal his letter with a kiss, keep the Arab thinking it was an affair of the heart.

This was Narby's third meeting with Vetch. It was obvious now that the man had no awareness of Putnam's international business, hadn't a clue about Ted McCoy or Bill Knowles. Yet it was in Narby's interest that Vetch continue to believe that he had come from New York with the intention of buying land. Vetch was the sole witness to Narby's unorthodox homecoming. He might seem like a nothing, a countrified clown, living out in the jungle in that pile of rotting planks he called his store. But there was something cunning about the man, something driving him, an outrage or injustice. Better to make him think Narby was on his side than dismiss him as someone who didn't count, someone harmless.

A block from the Gladiola diner Narby caught sight of him, waiting in his truck. Vetch got out and they went in together. In front was a counter with stools, and beyond it a dining room with booths and tables. There was the usual handful of red-necked working men slouched over their food. And a couple of tables of local gentry, beefy sun-tanned men in short sleeves and neckties, yucking it up. An old couple sat in silence by the window.

Vetch said he'd been living in Lacoosa County for fifteen years. Yet no one in the diner nodded or said hello. If anything, people seemed to look away.

They took a booth in the back. Vetch wore the same dingy yellowed shirt with the red stripes, armpits traced with sweat stains, his broad pasty face nicked from the morning's shave. Behind the glasses his eyes were small and dark, like buttons pressed into dough. The crack in the lens gave him the air of an abused weakling, the schoolboy who'd been knocked around for being a wise ass.

"Breakfast is on me, Carl. Get whatever you like."

"Mighty kind of you. One of them New Yoke spense accounts, is it?"

Narby smiled. "You got me all wrong, Carl. I'm low man on the totem pole."

"That right? Any man can just up and leave a motorboat like that, he cain't be hurting too bad. Hah."

"I told you, Carl. The motor was burnt out. A cheap little skiff, not worth the trouble to salvage."

"Could've had them Nigras haul it out for you, no trouble at all. Hah. Probably done drifted off with the tide by now. Pity. I could use me a skiff."

"Well, if it turns up, consider it yours."

"I believe I will."

The waitress took their order and poured coffee. Narby took out the pouch of shag tobacco. "Cigarette?"

Vetch picked it up, sniffed at it. "Kind of sweet and wet. No, thanks. I been smoking Top since I was ten year old. Spect I'll be coughing on it in my grave. Hah."

"Suit yourself." Narby lit his cigarette.

"Well? You been talking to them Putnam men? What they tell you? They set you a price?"

"No. Not yet. Besides, I'm waiting to hear your side of it. You said you had a proposition."

"Sho. Only it ain't so simple. Fore I let you in on it, you got to un'nustan how things is out there in Sawfish Point. How they was, when Putnam had they camp going. Had em forty, sometime fifty Nigras out there. Six stills burning night and day. Cause they had they quotas, see? Only them pines ain't giving enough gum. Only way the Cap'm reach his quota is to push them Nigras harder and harder. But Nigras just men, like you and me. Push em too far, they just quit."

"I don't get it, Carl. I thought you were the Captain. That's what they call you out there, isn't it?"

"They call me Cap'm cause they respect me. Sho. Only I ain't never been no Cap'm of no camp. You seen my store. I was more important than any Cap'm. Camp Commissionaire, that's what I was. Any fool mean enough with a whip and a Winchester can be a Cap'm. That last we had, Higginbotham, meanest son-of-a-bitch you ever laid eyes on. He done shot three Nigras, he did, fore they sent him away and closed up the camp. Commissionaire, now he the one with the smarts. See, I used to feed and clothe and liquor up all them Putnam Nigras and such. Kept the account books, made sure them boys never paid off they debt to society. Lynchpin of the whole system. Without that bookkeeping they got no right to hold them prisoners more than six month. It's the Commissionaire and the store and them account books that make it all legal. Even them Judges over to the coat-house tell you the same. Sho."

The waitress came with their order. Vetch arched back, as if he feared she would spill it in his lap. As soon at his plate hit the table he began to shovel it in—eggs, bacon, grits, biscuits swimming in pale viscid gravy—washing it down with quick slurps of coffee. Narby watched, more amused than disgusted.

That word Vetch liked so much, was it Negro or Nigger? Must be hell for the Colored people around here. In the kitchen behind the counter, Narby could see a Negro man in a stained white apron, bent over a griddle. It might be over a hundred degrees in the kitchen. Not that Narby felt particularly sorry for them. But if he ever saw a Negro pick up a knife, stick it to one of these smug southern bigots, Narby sure as hell wouldn't lift a finger to stop him.

"Mind if I have that there biscuit, since you ain't eating it?"

"Be my guest." He slid the plate to Vetch.

"What's wrong, son? Y'all don't favor grits and gravy up there in New Yoke?"

"Let's get to the point. What's your proposition?"

"All right, since you in such a rush." He nodded, a bland smile on his face. "Sho do appreciate the breakfast, son. Only, when you pay the ticket, don't be hauling out that wad of twenties, like you done in my store. You best be careful. These boys round here don't much like that Yankee superior attitude, all haughty and high. Just telling you for your own good. Mr. Nawby. Truth is," he said, lighting a cigarette, "I ain't like these dumbass crackers round here. They got they heads in the sand. And that's putting it politely."

"Thanks for the advice. I'll remember that."

"Here's some more advice. That land round my store don't belong to Putnam no more. That road you and your dolled-up Nigra came walking on, out of the mangrove like a couple of skunk apes, stinking like mud. That road don't belong to Putnam neither. I had me a contract with Putnam and they done broke it. That land belongs to me now. They owe me. I got me possession. Sho. Only I cain't prove nothing. But I saw what old Higginbotham done, shooting them Nigras in cold blood. Tapping trees on land that don't belong to Putnam. Poaching on other folks' property. I'm the only White man round here that seen what they done. Them Putnam boys up in Macon figure that don't matter. Figure they can just find some Yankee buy up that land without asking no questions. Only hitch is old Carl Vetch. Old Carl Vetch ain't going nowheres. And I got them Nigras with me, too. Them that still living out in the camp. Sho. They got they women and children out there now, they pigs and chickens. Cause I let em. Un'nustan?"

Vetch had worked himself up. Narby didn't like the attention they were drawing. "We should discuss this in private, Carl."

"Maybe so." He shook his head, tapping his ash into the pool of grease on his plate. "Dumb-ass crackers."

"You go on outside. I'll pay and meet you by your truck."

"Sho. Only. Watch them twenties. Hah."

4

AN HOUR LATER, AFTER MAKING a number of calls from the phone booth in the Rexall's, Narby walked back to his truck. His inquiries had been successful. The Bank of Coral Gables had an affiliation with the Banco de la República in Havana. International wire transfers, withdrawals and deposits—it could all be done from their main branch on Aragon Avenue. Yesterday, he'd picked up a couple of tourist maps at the Sinclair service station. Coral Gables was adjacent to Miami, a four-hour drive, more or less, cutting across the Everglades down the Tamiami Trail.

He had tried to call Campos. A woman with accented English had answered. She didn't think anyone by the name Ernesto Campos lived in the building, but she would take a message, just in case. "His friend from the boat," Narby had told her. "El camarada del barco. I'll call again. Telefonearé otra vez."

Campos wasn't taking any chances. Narby had a pretty good idea why. There'd been a story in the *Miami Herald* three days ago, buried on page eight, about a botched rebel attack on a Cuban Army barracks in the town of Moncada. The Cuban government called them criminals, claimed that all involved had been killed or arrested, the attack little more than a minor annoyance, an act of desperation carried out by fanatics. But there it was—the attack had occurred on July 26th, the date Campos had written down along with the phone number. July 26—one day before the signing of the Armistice ending the Korean War, three days before Narby and Campos had met on the boat. That's what Campos had meant by "politicos." No doubt, Batista had thugs all across the Caribbean hunting for collaborators, enemies of the State. If they ever found Campos, they'd drag him back to Cuba, torture him good and long before standing him up against the wall. The dapper little medical student was running for his life.

Only one thing didn't add up. Campos was dark-skinned, a mulatto, like Batista. The mixed race and Colored Cubans were Batista's biggest supporters. Narby knew that much just from reading the Cuban papers and the *International Tribune*. On the other hand, if Campos really was a medical student, that might put him on the side of the intellectuals, the liberals and socialists. Narby would find out soon enough. In any case, no matter how deftly Batista coddled his American handlers, there would come a time when they'd tire of the blatant corruption. The rebels would be wise to play both cards—nationalist and Western-bloc—while keeping the communists away from the table.

He'd like to help Ernesto. With luck, their interests might coincide, as they had on the boat. If not, then it was every man for himself.

He got in the truck, but instead of heading to the Glo-Bel he went south this time. After a few blocks the downtown area petered out into streets of drab stucco bungalows and trailer parks, and then the open two-lane highway. Cattle land, gladiola farms, a stand of swamp cypress in the distance. The turn off to Punta Rasca came up suddenly after a curve and he made the turn rather fast, squealing the tires. A narrow potholed road ran for about two miles through pine thickets, and then past mangrove and coconut palms and coastal grasses, dead-ending at a small marina: a gas pump, a shack, a couple of floating slips, and a landing dock. Narby pulled over and got out to take a look. The water was a milky translucent green. Maybe a half mile offshore he could see the largest of the barrier islands, Sanmora. He'd noticed it on the map. There was no bridge, but there was a ferry. He crossed the road to the shack-like office. It was unattended, but a schedule was posted on a piece of cardboard. The ferry made a morning run at 7:30 and an evening run at 6:00. He would come back tomorrow, to catch the early ferry.

The other side of Sanmora, on the Gulf, would have sand beaches, clear open water. He longed to swim, exercise his body, feel himself in the water again. Only not in that viscous brown tepid soup off Sawfish Point.

He sat on the dock, drinking from the flask, smoking, watching the pelicans' effortless glide inches above the surface of the water. Without the Dolophine the pain came at odd intervals, no longer a throb but quick stabs as if there were hooks with wires embedded deep in his flesh on which some sadist took occasional pleasure yanking. So far there had only been two mornings when the agony had kept him in the cabin, doubled over, or trembling under a tepid shower. He was better now. All in all, it seemed propitious, substituting the drink for the dollies. Dope fiends were pariahs, but boozers and alcoholics, as Narby very well knew, might be destined for great things.

On the dock was a spigot and hose. He took off his shirt and washed away the sweat and the stink, and let his hair dry in the wind as he drove back to Myerton.

She was shelving books from a rolling cart. When she reached for the upper shelves the fullness of her breasts pressed against the sleeveless cotton blouse, dark blue with little white polka dots. He waited, looking at a newspaper, until she was hidden between the rows.

"Hello, Mrs. Swanson."

"Oh. Hello." She continued shelving, showing no surprise, not looking at him.

"Philip. Remember?"

"Yes."

"You must have one, too?"

She looked at him, quizzically. "Pardon? Have one what?"

"A first name. Like Helen. Or Cindy Lou."

"Janet."

"Janet. Now there's a piece of intelligence worth knowing."

She looked at him again, backing off, holding the book she was shelving in front of her chest, as if protecting herself. "Pardon?"

"I was in Army Intelligence. In Korea." She looked away, quickly, because their eyes had met, and pushed the cart down the row. He followed behind. "Any word from Lieutenant Swanson?"

"Since yesterday? No."

Just a shade of annoyance, as if she were enjoying it despite herself.

"I could find out, if you'd like. It might take a week or so. I know the right people to ask."

That stopped her. "Could you? That would be very good of you."

"I'll need some more information. Nothing technical. Whatever you know about where he's been stationed, how long, that kind of thing."

"He didn't really say much about that. Not that I can recall. I'd have to go through his letters."

"That's a good idea, Janet. Go through his letters when you get home. And then we can talk about it tonight."

She moved away, turning her back as she pushed the cart. He heard the swish of her skirt. Her perfume hung in the air. Walking behind her he saw now that she was wide in the hips. On the threshold between voluptuous and heavy. Not thick yet, like Martha. But nothing left of girlhood. He went around the other way, and met her on the other side of the shelves, facing her. Nothing of girlhood in the eyes, either: brown, dull, tired, but excited, afraid. That seemed to be what was driving him: her fear of succumbing, of betraying Frank.

"How about a drink? Tonight. Just to talk."

"I'm a married woman." Her whisper had a forced harshness. "I'm sorry. No. I can't."

"Yes you can. It's easy. Nobody will know."

"Are you crazy? I don't know you from Adam. Leave me alone. Please."

"I'm at that motel on the highway, a couple of miles north of town. The one with the big neon bell. Cabin 101. I'll wait for you. You can park around the back, out of sight, if that's what's worrying you. Janet. I can help you find your husband. Only, when he gets home, don't expect him to be the same. Not after Korea. Let me tell you about it. Let me prepare you."

She turned and walked away, leaving the cart. In reality, she was quite plain. That didn't matter. Something had started. He would see it through.

★

The rains were heavy that afternoon, the wind fierce, almost a gale. Dindridge, the manager, had mentioned something about a tropical storm down in the Keys.

At sea, on the way to Yokohama, they had just managed to skirt a typhoon. December 1949. On the U.S.A.T. Caprice, an Army transport ship requisitioned to ferry Occupation personnel from Seattle to Japan. He had huddled in his room below deck, sick to his stomach. And last fall, in Cuba, a hurricane had ripped across the middle of the island, tearing the heads off the palm trees, washing out whole towns. It wouldn't take much of a blow to turn Cabin 101 into a pile of sticks. But by sunset everything had quieted, the air dead and thick with the sweet sodden odor of vegetal rot, the usual burst of insect noise and then, as darkness fell, the electrical buzz of the neon bell. Narby lit one of the pic-wic coil mosquito repellants. After a storm the little bastards would rise up in clouds, squeezing through the chinks in the screens, avid for blood.

It was the first time since arriving—eleven days ago—that he felt calm. For the moment the pain had abated. He would take only one Dolophine tonight. In a week he'd be done with it, for good. He was up to a quarter bottle of Jim Beam a day. He would do his best to hold it at that, find somewhere to swim and exercise, to stave off the negative physical effects, the torpor and the gut.

He poured another inch in the jelly jar, listening to the cars passing on the highway, the tires hissing on wet pavement, distracting himself with the papers.

The wire story on the front page of the *Miami Herald* described the prisoner-of-war exchange. "Operation Big Switch." From the Americans came accusations of torture, forced confessions, brainwashing: *they put a towel on my face and poured water on the towel. When I passed out, they brought me to by stabbing me with burning cigarettes. They wanted us to sign confessions denouncing the American system, to go along with the communist line. Some of the guys couldn't take it. It wasn't their fault. After that, they weren't the same.*

He clipped the article and put it in the drawer. After an hour, tired of reading, he took another shower and put on clean clothes, a pair of dungarees and a white tee shirt. As he ran the towel over his hair he heard the car, first the hiss and then the tires crunching the gravel and then, as he had suggested, pulling behind the last cabin.

She cut the motor, and then nothing, only the electrical buzz—sitting alone in the car in the dark, struggling, afraid, or maybe hoping Narby would come out and cajole her, force her. Then the car door opened, and the percussive slam, and footsteps on the gravel. He swung open the screen door and she stepped inside, stood by the table, clutching her purse against her chest. "Hello, Philip. Well. I'm here. I shouldn't be. But I am. I don't know why." And then, finally, she looked at him. "Maybe you can tell me."

"Would you like a drink? All I've got is bourbon, I'm afraid." He held up his glass. "On the rocks, in a Welch's jelly jar?"

She laughed. "OK. A small one. Thanks."

They sat at the table, as far apart as the diminutive space allowed. "You're not from the South, are you?" he asked, because her accent was flat rather than twanged.

"No. I. Frank and I. We moved down here after we were married. From Muncie." She sipped at the drink. He hadn't noticed before—up close, her eyes appeared slightly crossed. She had redone her makeup, her red lipstick glistening. He switched off the harsh overhead bulb, leaving only the light from the shaded lamp by the rocking chair, falling softly on her blonde hair. She wore it more naturally now, like a girl, letting it fall to her shoulders. "How about you?"

"I guess I've been kicking around all my life, even before my stint in the Army. From Chicago, though, if you had to pin me down. And Tokyo, before the Korean mess."

"Japan? Frank was over there, too. I guess it's silly to worry. I mean, the fighting is over." She was doing a good job of avoiding his eyes. "Only I thought I would have heard something right away. That he was coming home right away." She let herself glance at him now, a fleeting visual caress. "I'm sure I'll hear something tomorrow, or the next day. Don't you think?"

He shrugged. "Cigarette?" She took a Chesterfield and he lit it with the lighter. "Do you have children?"

She got up, the cigarette in her hand. "I shouldn't be here. This is wrong. I should go."

"Maybe the reason you're here, Janet, is because your husband isn't so eager to get home. Maybe you know that. If that's the case, then it doesn't really matter. That it's wrong."

She stood there, rigid with nerves, smoking in quick, jagged pecks. "We don't have children. We tried. And then... he was gone." She stubbed out the half-smoked cigarette in the ashtray. "All right. Let's talk." She sat down again, smiling a bit falsely. "What line of work are you in? I mean, now that you're out of the Army."

"I'm looking to buy some land." That would do, for now. "I inherited a little money from my family. Not much, but enough. Some place warm. Where the natives are friendly."

She wasn't really listening. He reached across the table and took her hand. She let him. "It's all right, Janet." He stood up and led her by the hand into the little box of a bedroom. It was dark. They kissed, Narby pressing and Janet yielding. He knew right away that if it was going to happen, it would be all his doing. He reached into her blouse and caressed her breast over her brassiere. It excited him, but only as long as he kept his hand there, touching her. Not only do it all himself, but keep himself interested, too. He unbuttoned the blouse, unhooked the skirt, as if disrobing a department store mannequin. When she was on the bed, on her back with her eyes closed, not moving, not talking, he thought, I don't have to. If I stop here, it will better later. Tomorrow. No. She'll never come back.

It was quick, silent but for the groan of the gimcrack bed-springs. She had barely shuddered, barely touched him, just his shoulders and upper arms. About the only thing alive in her was the warmth of her soft padded flesh and her thudding heart.

They were both filmed with perspiration, tacky and adherent as he pulled away and stood by the bed. "Want a shower?"

She opened her eyes now. She wasn't unhappy. Didn't appear bitter or angry. She shook her head no.

"I'll be right back." When he got out of the bathroom she was already dressed, cradling her purse. He held the towel in front of him. She avoided looking at him.

"I'm going to go."

"You all right?"

"I don't know."

"I'll drop by the library. Tomorrow. OK?"

"If you want."

He stood by the screen door, the stiff motel towel wrapped around his waist, watching her car pass through the penumbra of ghastly pink-green neon light.

She hadn't touched him there—in the dark, she hadn't even seen them. The scars.

5

IT WAS ONE THING, to do it at the bank in Havana. But here, under American eyes? Did he have the nerve to pull if off?

With over three thousand in cash buried behind the cabin, there was no need to rush things. More reason, then, to make a test run soon, while the pressure was off. Get a feel for the bank, the tellers. When and if the need arose, he ought to be prepared.

He left at dawn, stopping at the Sinclair station to gas up. South of Myerton, past the turn off to Punta Rasca, the highway skirted the Big Cypress Swamp and then curved eastward, crossing the Everglades. For the first hour, except for a couple of flatbed trucks packed with Negro farmhands, he had the road to himself. Then there was nothing, just the black ribbon of tar cleaving the grasslands, the illusory puddle of silver wavering at the horizon under the hot blanched hazy sky.

He drove with his elbow crooked out the window, the air blasting his face, wearing dark glasses against the glare. To break the monotony he swerved at a bunch of fat turkey buzzards that had alighted on the shoulder to feast on a dead possum, watching them rise up lazily and then, in the rearview mirror, drift back down without the least sense of alarm. Then he played a game with the flask: he would take a swallow only when he saw another human. A car passed, he drank. On the side of the road, a thatched hut under which a half-naked brown man sat selling bags of oranges. He drank. A highway patrolman on a motorcycle behind a lone tree, looking for speeders. Of questionable humanity, so he didn't drink. A fisherman standing on a sluice pipe over a drainage ditch, dangling a long bamboo-stick pole. He drank.

At the Dade County line—billboards for airboat rides, a stand of melaleuca trees, a motor court, a bar-b-q barn—he quit the game and tried the radio again, twisting the dial until music came through the static. A swing band. He recognized it right away, those piano chords that went splank... splank splank. Count Basie.

Big deal. He had liked music as a kid, played the trumpet in the school band. So what? It meant nothing. It was for other people. He pulled over, under the shade of the tall willowy pines planted along the ditch. Count Basie, Benny Goodman, Artie Shaw. But no father, no mother. A house, an attic window looking out through the tops of the elms. He must have listened to the radio up there. Better reception. From Chicago, if you had to pin him down.

He unfolded the map. Greater Miami and Miami Beach. Ten more miles, down Eighth Street and then south on Le Jeune. He unscrewed the flask, thought better of it, and closed it. He felt all right, or at least good enough. He pulled out on the highway. There was more traffic as he got closer. The music stopped, then the jingle for WQAM and then the news, the urgent assertive rapid-fire voice: *give us a minute and we'll give you the world. American leaders are still struggling to assess the Soviet Union's claim, announced last week, that the communists had successfully tested a hydrogen bomb, the most powerful weapon in existence. In South Korea, some 3,000 American soldiers are still unaccounted for after the first prisoner exchanges with the communist-controlled North. American authorities voiced grave concerns about ever learning their whereabouts. And how about those Yankees! After pitcher Whitey Ford's decisive 5 to 1 win against Cleveland this weekend, they are poised yet again to win the American league pennant and just perhaps become the first team in history to win five World Series in a row. Now how about that?*

Three thousand unaccounted for. Tom or Jim or whoever the hell he was, never to be heard from again. A lucky break for Philip Narby.

After the turn onto Le Jeune, the side-of-the-highway lowlife disappeared. He passed gardens and courtyards, red tile roofs and wrought iron railings, arched passageways draped with bougainvillea, dappled sunlight filtering through the banyan trees. He circled the small downtown area once or twice, past the rows of fancy shops, the storefront offices and the bank, noted the coffee shop on the corner, and parked the truck several blocks away on a quiet residential street. It wouldn't do for Mr. Philip Narby, a man of some means, to be seen climbing out of a banged-up 49 Chevy pickup. He clicked open the leather brief case—another overpriced item from the Smoker's Den—stowed the flask, and climbed out.

It was a quarter past eleven. The sidewalks were quiet, a trickle of women shoppers, mothers with kids, a couple of business types. The off-season. No one paid him any notice. He went into the coffee shop and sat at a booth by the window and ordered a ham sandwich and a coffee. In the five-and-dime work clothes—gray short-sleeved shirt opened at the neck, damp with sweat, plain dark trousers, black shoes—he might be a repairman, a mechanic. He rolled a cigarette, aware of the tremor in the fingers of his right hand. Why be nervous? It was only a test run, without risk.

After paying the bill he went into the washroom and locked the door. Stripping to the waist he washed at the sink, hands and face and armpits, and slicked his hair and then changed into the freshly laundered linen and silk—the Havana bank clothes he had packed in the brief case that morning—and then pausing to assess himself in the mirror: a young man of leisure, a sport, with a sailing yacht docked at the Dinner Key Marina. He had concocted a plausible tale, the details—if he needed them—drawn from the *Yellow Pages* and the Sinclair tourist map and the advertisements in the *Miami Herald*. Back and forth from Cuba, a little business, a little pleasure. Staying at the Hotel Atlantique out on Miami Beach, fully air-conditioned and open throughout the summer. Damned careless of him to lose his checkbook. He had called his bank in Havana. They informed him he could make a withdrawal from their affiliate in Coral Gables.

The bank occupied the ground floor of an office building on the next block, a bluff-white Miami-limestone façade with gray-tinted plate glass windows. Narby pushed through the revolving door into an open spacious lobby. Cool and dry, muted light. Like the Smoker's Den. Swish of perfume, leather upholstery, polished wood, residual cigar smoke. The sea-green carpeting lent the room an aquarium-like glow. Lighting a cigarette he went to the desk where the withdrawal slips were arranged in slots and began to write. There were four tellers, all women. Young, rather pretty, at least from where he stood, wearing identical yellow cardigan sweaters. Quiet at this time of day, this time of year. No uniformed guards that he could see. From across the room one of the tellers, the brunette, caught his eye. He smiled, looked away, continuing to write. Very pretty, indeed.

Why not just do it? Forget the trial run. Ask for two hundred. Nobody would risk defrauding a bank for such a measly sum. If they refused, he'd shrug it off good-naturedly.

He crumpled the slip and took another, made it out for two hundred and approached the teller, the brunette.

"Good morning, sir," she said brightly. "What can I help you with today?"

"Good morning." He returned her smile, the passing flirtatious glance. "I'd like to make a withdrawal." He pushed the slip across the counter.

"Very good." She looked at it. On the branch location line he had written Banco de la República, Havana. Obviously, she wasn't simply going to hand him the money without a question or two. "Just a minute, Mr. Narby," she said, getting off her stool. "I'll be right back."

She took the slip into one of the offices behind the teller windows, leaving the office door open as she consulted with a gray suit planted behind a desk. Tight fitting skirt, superbly flattering. He would see Janet tonight, their third tryst. His heart dipped at the thought. The brunette was more his style. He fidgeted, looking around casually, tapping his finger on the counter. No guards, no cops. A woman like that would have a dozen men sniffing after her. Same with the other tellers, like fashion models or high-class call girls. That made the bank officer in the gray suit the pimp. The Sylvio. The observation seemed to quell Narby's nerves.

"Thank you for waiting, Mr. Narby," she said, smiling, solicitous. "I see that your account is with our international affiliate in—"

"That's right. In Havana. I'm back and forth quite a bit." Slow down. It's just a mild annoyance. "The folks over at the bank in Havana told me I could use this branch. Is there some problem?"

"Well, Mr. Narby. I'm afraid we don't have the signature cards on file here."

"I understand. Well, here's the thing. I'm only in town for a few days and it seems I left my checkbook at the hotel in Havana. And I've run short of cash. Simple as that." If she undid one more button, the view from where Narby stood would be much improved. Nice touch, that, the sweaters in the sweltering August heat. Like a striptease. The more layers, the more delayed and heightened the gratification. "You do provide international banking services, don't you"—he leaned back to read her nameplate—"Miss Prentice?"

"Yes, we do, Mr. Narby. In that case, I'll get Mr. Wilson. I'm sure he can help. Just a moment."

Despite the frigid air-conditioning he was breaking a sweat. Wilson got up from his desk, a pale flaccid man with thinning hair and loose jowls, his white shirt bunched at the belly. "Pleasure to meet you, Mr. Narby." They shook hands across the counter. "How are you today?"

"Fine, thanks. Well, a bit frustrated. As I explained to Miss Prentice, I left my checkbook at the hotel in Havana."

"Yes. She explained that to me. Let's see what we can do. Might I please see some identification, Mr. Narby?"

"Well, you see, that's the problem. My passport, and all the rest of it, is in Havana." He held up the brief case. "In my other brief case. I took the wrong one. But the bank in Havana told me I could drop in here. That if I had the account number, it shouldn't be a problem."

"Hmm." Wilson was giving him that once-over look. As if they were rivals, perhaps. Maybe Wilson had something going with Miss Prentice, took her into the vault after closing. Wilson's only advantage, as far as Narby could see, was that he was on her side of the counter. The boss. If she refused, maybe she'd lose her job.

"Why don't you call the Marina, over at Dinner Key? All the fellows down there know me."

"Where are you staying while you're in town, Mr. Narby?"

"On the Beach. At the Atlantique. In fact, I used the last of my cash taking a cab over here. I've got an appointment down-town in half-an-hour. Someone's showing me some property for sale. I thought this would be the easiest way, since you're an affiliate."

"Sorry about that. Once we get your identification, we'd be happy to start an account for you. I could get the ball rolling right now and …"

"If it's that much trouble, forget it. I'll see if I can get my bank in Chicago to wire me cash at the Western Union. Damned nuisance." He turned to go.

"Just a moment, Mr. Narby. Let me try to get through to Havana on the phone. Give me two minutes." Wilson gave him a man-to-man nod. "Sorry for the inconvenience."

"All right." Narby nodded back, glancing at this watch. "See what you can do. I appreciate it."

Wilson disappeared into his office, closing the door behind him. Maybe he was calling the police. Narby ought to get the hell out now, while there was still time. Miss Prentice took her seat behind the window. It was now or never, he supposed. Might as well stick around for the view. "Have you been to Havana, Miss Prentice?"

"No. I'd love to, though."

"It's great fun. A big party, really. Everyone lets their guard down. Do you like to gamble?"

"I don't know. Never tried it."

"The casinos are a real kick. Even if it's all rigged in their favor. And the shows. The Tropicana, now that's something to see. A bit risqué, though. For us buttoned-down Yankees."

She laughed. "Oh. I wouldn't mind that."

"Do they let you out in the evening?"

"I'm sorry. Do they what?"

"The bank. What time do they let you out of that cage?"

She looked away, the creamy white skin of her neck showing a flush of pink. Wilson bustled out from his office. "Good news, Mr. Narby. They confirmed your account number. Here's what we'll do. If you'll just complete these signature cards. That way, next time you visit, there won't be any delay. Donna, please put Mr. Narby's transaction through. You know, Mr. Narby, the Bank of Coral Gables offers an array of financial services. Might I suggest ..."

There must be a pile of money still sitting in the Philip Narby account. Wilson had certainly changed his tune. "Maybe next time, Mr. Wilson." He signed the cards and slid them to Miss Prentice.

"Please. Call me Bob."

"Next time, Bob. Matter of fact, I'm thinking of relocating to Miami. I'm sure we'll have another chance to talk." Miss Prentice would understand. The remark was entirely for her benefit. "In a bit of a rush, at the moment."

As she handed over the bills the teller gave him a warm, more than professional smile. He was bank approved. He was in the game.

"Of course. I look forward to it. Have a good day, Mr. Narby."

As he walked down Aragon Avenue Narby fought the urge to look back over his shoulder. He ducked into a men's clothing shop, browsed the racks idly for a few minutes, went out again and circled the block. Nobody. In the truck he clicked opened the brief case, had a drink from the flask as he cranked the engine, heading out Le Jeune and then north on the Tamiami. It was too easy. Someone was helping him, someone in Havana.

Bill Knowles must have taken control of the account. Because Sid Black was dead. It made sense. Narby needed money to operate. Next time he'd withdraw more, the monthly maximum. Maybe Knowles had fixed that, too, making Narby's access unlimited.

Somewhere in the middle of the Everglades, the fat drops of rain beginning to splatter one-by-one against the bug-smeared windshield, he pulled over to change into the workingman clothes. Seven hundred in his pocket—the five hundred emergency money and the freshly plucked two. About thirty-five hundred buried behind the cabin. What more proof could he want? They were planning something big for him, for Philip Narby. As long as he remained Philip Narby, he was safe.

6

THE THIRD TIME HE CALLED the woman said, un momento. Narby could hear a child crying, garbled Spanish in the background.

"Digamé."

"Ernesto? Soy Felipé. Tu camarada." Silence. "Con los instintos buenos. With the good instincts."

"Felipé. Dondé está?"

Narby explained. He was in Myerton, the town where Campos had boarded the bus for Miami. The only witness to their unofficial entry into the country had been the storekeeper out in the jungle— un tonto, a fool of no consequence. They had gotten out of Cuba and into the U.S. undetected, invisible. "Like ghosts. Como fantasmas."

"Si. Fantasmas," Campos laughed. "Like goats. Por el momento vivo aqui como un Negro, en el barrio segregado.

Estudio Ingles. I study English. You come to Miami. Make practice. OK?"

"Yeah. Sure. Look, Ernesto." Narby was in the phone booth at the back of the Rexall's drugstore, the glass door pulled closed. "Mira. El viente-seis de Julio. Yo entiendo muy bien. Entiendo a Moncada. Yo peudo ayudar. Somos en el mismo lado. I can help you. We're on the same side."

"Como? Por qué? How you help? For what?"

"Porque no me gusta nada a Batista. He's no good for your people, and he's no good for my country, either. Puedo obetener dinero. I can find money. For your cause."

"No dije mas. No good talk teléfono."

"Agreed. Puedo venir a Miami."

They made an arrangement. Narby would call back in a week, at this same hour. Campos would tell him where and when they could meet safely. Narby hung up. He bought some toiletries, aspirin, rubbing alcohol, and five packs of Benzedrine inhalers. He'd been in here enough times, spent enough money around town, that the store clerks nodded now when they saw him. Good looking young fellow. Just out of the Army. Quiet, staying out there at the Glo-Bel. Seen him over at the Gladiola with Carl Vetch. Vetch's nephew or something.

After Rexall's he stopped at the Smoker's Den. Under the sweat-damp shirt the refrigerated air sent a shiver up his spine.

"Mr. Norby. I have your *Atlantic Monthly*. But the *New Yorker*, I am sorry to say, has not arrived. I will contact my distributor today and get to the bottom." The Arab had stopped apologizing about the special-order surcharge. A man like Mr. Narby didn't quibble over a few extra pennies. By now Narby had sampled all the imported cigarettes, English, Turkish, even the Egyptian Ovals. "If you are ever in the mood for a fine Cuban cigar, I have special reserve. Partagas Oro. Shade grown. Hand rolled. The Rolls Royce of cigars."

"Thanks, Hank, but I'm not a cigar man." Another customer came down the steps, setting off the brass bells. Narby moved aside, his back to the man, pretending to look at the pipes displayed in the case on the wall.

"Give me two boxes of them Dutch Masters. And one of them picture magazines."

Hank handed over the goods in a brown paper bag and tendered the change. The bells rang, the shop empty again. "Mr. Norby. A letter for you. It arrived yesterday." Suppressing a smile the tobacconist handed it to Narby over the counter. The envelope reeked of perfume.

"Here, Hank. For your trouble."

"Please. Complimentary service. It is my pleasure."

Narby sat on a bench in the courthouse square under one of the moss-heavy oaks and inspected the envelope. The gummed edge had not been disturbed. He opened it carefully. The strand of hair he had placed under the flap was still there. Good. Hank had passed the test. And at the same time Narby had no doubt confirmed the Arab's suspicions about a secret love affair. He tore the envelope in half and dropped it in a trashcan. He'd stop in again before meeting with Campos. By then, there would surely be something from Knowles.

As he turned the corner he saw Vetch leaning against the truck— dingy red striped shirt, the harsh hazy light glaring off the cracked glasses—gnawing at his fingernails. The man had been dogging him around town, pressing Narby for a definitive answer to his inane propositions. Vetch seemed to carry the fetid jungle around with him like a contagion. His teeth were worn down to brownish nubs, like stumps rotting in stagnant water. And he stank. But what disgusted Narby more was Vetch's air of superiority, his condescending attitude. His insistence that he and Narby were somehow partners, co-conspirators against the Putnam Lumber Company. The mere sight of him—the plump sausage-like figure wrapped in the sweat-stained balloon-seller's shirt—was beginning to turn Narby's stomach.

Vetch straightened up, running his hands down his belly-mounded shirtfront.

"Where you been, son? I came round the Glo-Bel couple times, but you ain't there much. Leastwise your truck ain't. You all right?"

"What do you want, Carl? I'm busy."

"I got it all figured out. Made some drawings, to show you what I mean."

"Drawings of what?"

"The Fish Camp. Like I told you. You had your dinner yet? Y'all fancy bar-b-q up in New Yoke? They's ribs over at old Grunsten's place, up the highway."

"Looking for another free meal, Carl? Well, you're out of luck." "No matter. Let's go on over to your place, so I can show you."

Narby didn't like standing on the street where people could see them. "Get in the truck, Carl."

Narby drove out of town, crossing the drawbridge over the Lacoosa River and past the shacks crowded side-by-side on the other side of the wide cattail-choked ditch. Before reaching the Glo-Bel he turned off the highway onto Burnt Farm Road where the barbed-wire cattle pastures began, drove until the pavement gave out, and cut the motor. Without the breeze the cab of the truck was sweltering. He kicked open the door to let in some air.

"All right. We can talk safely here. What do you want, Carl?"

Vetch flicked his sodden cigarette butt out the window and unfolded a piece of limp soiled paper. "Here's the way I see it. This here's the store. This here's the gas pump. I already got the lectric and the well. These here are the tourist cabins, out the end of Sawfish Point, at that cove where I got the boat ramp and such. Going to get me one of them ice machines too, so I can keep bait and sodee pop and beer. Problem is getting them County boys to do what they's obliged. After they put in that lectric wire the County supposed to improve the road out to my land. Only when Putnam done pulled out, they reneged. More or less cut my throat. Now, I figure once we get the deed to that land, make it legal and such, the County going come round, too. Hah. Maybe I'll even join up with that Cham'er of Commerce."

"That's all very interesting, Carl. Very impressive. But I'm sorry to tell you, the Company in New York said no go."

"I ain't talking bout that New Yoke Company you say you working for. I'm talking bout me and you. I done told you. I know what them Putnam boys did out there, poaching them pines on other folk's land. Breaking the law. Breaking my contract. You and me, we could get that land cheap if we go about it the right way. Cause you got the money. You can get one of them New Yoke lawyers to write em a letter. That'll scare em. Sho. Besides, I got me possession. We sitting on something big. You cain't see it now. But wait until Thanksgiving and Christmas, all the way through Easter. All them folk driving down to the Keys and such on the highway. They got to pass right by that road. Ain't no other way. We put the sign out on the highway, we get my road fixed, ain't no one going to drive another eight hour when they can get the best fishing in the whole damn state right here. Tarpon, snook, snapper, bonefish. Crab, too. Whatever kind of fishing them tourist folk want. They buy they bait and tackle and provisions at my store, and the gas for they cars and boat motors. They stay in my cabins, put in the water at my ramp, tie up at my dock. See what I mean? I done thought it all through.

"You and me, Nawby. Fifty-fifty. Once them Putnam people un'nustan what's what, they going sell for less than fifty dollar an acre. You cain't walk away from that, son. Don't be a fool."

"What makes you think I have money, Carl? You think I'd be staying at that dump on the side of the highway, or driving this busted up truck, if I was as important as you seem to think?"

"I seen the way you and that fancy Colored come up my road. And then you buying a dime bottle of Cola-Nip peach sodee pop with a twenty dollar bill. And that sack you was toting. Wouldn't let it out of your hands for nothing. I don't know where you really from or what you really is. But I know you got money. I know you like it out there on the highway, away from folks. Even this here truck, kind of like you want folks to think you some country boy running away from his Daddy's farm.

"I ain't no dumb-ass Florida cracker. They's something between us, son. We alike, you and me. They something breathing down your neck, like a hound. I know that feeling, too, son. All too well."

It wouldn't take much: one swing of a machete, an ax handle, a gaff. Vetch was soft, half rotten already, felled with ease. Drag it a hundred feet into the thickets and no one would ever find the body, no one suspect that the buzzards were circling for anything more unusual than a dead possum. He doubted anyone would even notice Vetch's disappearance, or at least not until long after Narby had moved on. If it ever came to that.

"Sorry, Carl. I can't help you." He lit a cigarette, slammed closed the door, started the engine and turned the truck around. "I'm sure you'll find a more suitable business partner."

The moving air gave Narby a chill. He was drenched with sweat.

"Ain't no need to decide today. Think on it, son. Fifty-fifty. Why, you get your investment back in no time. Sho. You a good boy, son. Anyone can see that. Come from a good family, educated and such. You lucky that way. Some of us ain't so fortunate. You can drop me over to the coat-house. I got me some business at the County Clerk. You know where that's at, don't you? Right next to the Shurf's office. Sho."

7

YESTERDAY, AGAIN, HE HAD MISSED the morning ferry to Sanmora. So the next day Narby rose at dawn and took the long drive, past the ditch-side shacks, over the drawbridge and through downtown Myerton, past the trailer parks on the south end of town and then more barbed-wire cattle enclosures, passing two flatbed trucks packed tight with Colored farm hands, then more pine and palmetto scrub until the turn off for Punta Rasca.

The ferry was pulling up to the landing dock. He got out, paid his twenty-five cents, and waited in the truck. The early morning air was clear, the placid water of the estuary glinting in the low harsh sun. There was the smell of gasoline, the salty rot of the shallow mangrove-stained water, a burnt tar odor rising from the creosote-coated planks of the dock. The ferry was a flat barge, big enough to carry half a dozen cars. That morning only a single car was coming from the island, and Narby the only one waiting to cross. The ferryman waved him on board, told him to put on the brake, kicked a couple wooden wedges under the tires and hooked a rusted chain across the end of the open deck. Narby got out and watched as they chugged toward the island, a long curving strip of mangrove behind which rose the low vine-tangled coastal jungle. A huge blue heron stalked near the shore, thrusting its long neck as it pecked and hunted in the mud. There were seagulls and pelicans and other birds Narby didn't know, wading or skimming or circling above the mangrove.

"Ferry out at six o'clock," the ferryman informed him. "Miss it, you spend the night."

A dirt road from the ferry landing connected to a paved road running along the spine of the narrow island, deeply shaded at that hour of morning by the tall shaggy pines planted along the shoulder. After a mile he came to the Village, a cluster of simple wooden structures arrayed around the inlet that opened onto the estuary: schoolhouse, post office, fire station, general store, little whitewashed pine-plank houses set up on pilings. The Village marina—a warren of docks crowded with fishing boats and motorized dinghies—sat at the center of the town, where a bridge crossed the inlet. He pulled over and went into the general store, an orderly well-stocked space with groceries, hardware, and nautical and fishing supplies. A group of men with weathered faces stood by the front counter, talking and drinking coffee. They watched him come in. Narby nodded, said hello, asked if they sold a map of the island.

They looked at each other and laughed. "No sir. No map. Don't need one. Ain't but one road and you just came on it. What you looking for?"

They weren't southerners, or at least, not southerners like Vetch and the people in Myerton. "Nothing, really. Just thought I'd explore. Maybe take a swim. Is there a public beach?"

"Down by the lighthouse. Just drive south. Past the ferry. Can't miss it."

"Thanks." Before leaving he bought some bread and cheese and a can of deviled ham. No friendly chatter, no further information exchanged. That sat fine with Narby.

Aside from the Village there seemed to be no other towns or settlements. Some of the scrub along the road had been cleared for cattle pasture and there were small groves, grapefruit and lime, and a field of watermelon. The lighthouse was a gaunt, iron, utilitarian structure, with a cottage for the keeper at its foot. There were no cars parked in the dirt lot. Narby grabbed his rucksack and headed out past a couple of picnic tables toward the water. The beach was empty, an unbroken stretch of white sand backed by low dunes and coastal jungle that appeared to run the length of the island. Except for the lighthouse Narby could see no other building, no sign of habitation. The sea was more green than blue, the waves gently rolling in and foaming on the hard-packed sand.

He walked for half an hour, his feet in the warm water. Masses of shells had washed up during high tide and lay exposed, bleaching in the sun. The dunes were dotted with feathery grasses and sea-grape, a low-branching tree with round rubbery leaves and clusters of hard nut-like fruit. Behind the dunes grew a thick tangled forest: coconut and silver palms,

cabbage palmetto, tiny-flowered bushes, marlberry, privet, aca-
cia, laurel, all twisted together with vines and tendrils. Looking
for shade he put his sack down at the foot of a sea-grape growing
between two dunes. With the sea breeze, even in the harsh sun,
it was idyllic compared to the sweltering inland pine wastes. He
sat for a moment, eating a little, taking his first drink of the day
from the flask, having another cigarette, staring out at the sparkling green water. He had his swimsuit with him but it hardly
seemed necessary, so after his cigarette he stripped naked and
ran like a savage into the surf, scattering a flock of sandpipers. The slope was gentle, with no discernible undertow. When
it was deep enough he took a long leaping dive and swam, up
and down, out and back, careful to judge where the gentle current was taking him by keeping his eye on the rucksack, feeling
the different layers of water ripple across his skin, warm at his
chest and cool at his stomach and waist, and almost cold when
he let his feet dangle straight down. The water was clear, showing the white sand bottom and the schools of minnows darting
frantically as he kicked and stroked. But after a while he saw
nothing, felt nothing but the propulsion of his body through
the gentle swells, his heart working in a hard steady throb, his
lungs pumping, his muscles in fluid co-ordination.

It was the first time he'd been in the water since leaping
from the boat, inadvertently nudging the bow landward. Three
weeks ago. After running out of fuel the boat surely would have
drifted out to sea. Whether or not the pilot had survived was
none of Narby's concern.

He swam until he was tired and then let himself float on
his back, the cool salty water rocking him in a lazy undulating
rhythm. But the sun was beginning to burn his face. He waded
out. The beach was empty. There was no need to hurry, hide
his nakedness. He laid out the stiff Glo-Bel towel, put on his
swimming suit, and sat cross-legged in the meager shade of the
sea-grape, eating a little more, drinking water and sipping from
the flask. For a moment the beauty of the island obliterated

everything that had ever happened to him. Even his scars seemed to disappear, the saltwater as it evaporated in the breeze tightening his sun-warmed skin in a tingling embrace. Like Robinson Crusoe, Narby thought, at first bemoaning his miserable fate, shipwrecked on a deserted island, but then thankful, humbled, because he alone of all his shipmates had survived the storm, because Providence had thrown him not on some barren craggy shore but a green virgin land with fresh water and fruit, with the food and drink and tools that Crusoe had salvaged before the wreck sank out of sight.

A psychological trick—Crusoe had played it to the hilt, even twisting his blasphemy into a blessing-in-disguise. Playing both sides, pitting the devil against an unforgiving God while Crusoe himself, the self-effacing mortal, watched from the wings, bucking himself up with his mind games and getting filthy rich into the bargain, if Narby was remembering the story correctly. Ended up buying the whole goddamn island, cashing in on those plantations in Brazil, racking up millions.

It was one of Tom or Jim's favorite books. Narby ought to check it out from the library, read it again. He was going to see Janet tonight. At her house, this time. Park the truck around the corner, she told him, come around to the back door, after ten. She didn't like meeting him at the motel. It made her feel dirty. Still no word as to when Second Lieutenant Swanson was expected home. Or so she claimed.

As he stood, pulling on his T-shirt, he heard something in the distance, a buzzing that seemed to be coming closer. He grabbed the sack and moved away from the dunes, out in the open to get a better view. It was a plane, flying low, coming straight up the mangrove coast from the south. After a minute or so he could make it out better: a small plane with pontoons for landing in the water. Realizing he was exposed, a lone figure against the white sand, he moved back behind the dunes, and as the plane was about to pass overhead he ducked into the jungle, enduring the swarm of mosquitoes.

The buzz persisted as if the plane were circling, then it faded and then, suddenly, stopped. He wondered if they had seen him, and where it had landed. He waded knee-deep into the surf to get a better sightline down the long gently curving beach, but there was no sign of the plane. There was still plenty of time before the ferry left. He decided to continue walking north, ankle deep in the surf to avoid cutting his feet on the piles of washed up shells. It was hotter now, the sky beginning to haze, the horizon growing indistinct. After a while he noticed the dunes were lower, the jungle behind them growing closer to the shoreline. He came to an inlet, a black-water creek that wound through the jungle and emptied into the sea. Probably fed by a spring somewhere in the interior of the island, the source of fresh water for the Village. Though here, at its mouth where it met the salt water, the creek looked rather forbidding, a brackish malarial soup. The tide was coming in now, the inlet perhaps twenty yards wide, maybe five feet deep. He could easily swim across and continue walking, but he didn't want to leave his sack or get it soaked. He took off his shirt and holding the rucksack high above his head waded across, the water flowing in from the Gulf swift and cool. At the mid-point it was deeper than he had guessed, the water coming up to his mouth, but the mud bank rose quickly again and he climbed out on the other side.

When the tide was at its highest the inlet might be too deep to wade. The current might very well take a weaker swimmer by surprise.

He stopped to drink the last of his water. Next time, he'd bring two canteens. It was a rather fantastic spot, the confluence of creek, jungle, dunes and sea, like something out of *Treasure Island*. Another favorite of the missing soldier, Tom or Jim.

Past the inlet the beach widened again, the dunes high enough to block the view of the jungle, with sea-grape bushes growing in the gaps. Something caught his eye: a wooden walkway, built about a foot off the ground, coming from between two dunes and marked with a private property, no trespassing sign. He stepped up. The walkway led to a manicured lawn and garden, entirely hidden by the dunes. And behind the gardens, a large house, a mansion of some sort with a swimming pool and tennis court. There was no sign of anyone about. This had nothing to do with the Village, which lay on the opposite, estuary side of the island. In fact, it looked like something you'd expect to find in New England: the weathered gray wood, the ocean-view terraces, like the estate of some well-to-do maritime merchant.

Having as close a look as he deemed prudent—there might be guard dogs, or trip wires—he walked back to the dunes. After a short stretch of beach there was another, identical walkway, with the same private property sign. Again, he followed it as it passed between the dunes. Another well-to-do property, this one in a modern style, sleek concrete and metal and glass, with a cantilevered terrace jutting from the second floor. Deserted, but well maintained: the swimming pool, the grass lawn, the masses of bamboo and flowering bushes.

The mansions—eight in all, each with its own walkway threading the dunes—were practically invisible from the beach. They had been spaced far enough apart to ensure privacy, the jungle intervening like a natural barrier. The seaplane might very well have something to do with whoever lived here.

Past the row of mansions there was nothing, only the dunes and jungle and the white sand beach. It was getting late. He had a two-hour walk back to the lighthouse. If he didn't turn around now he risked missing the ferry. The seaplane must have put down on the other side, on the estuary where the water was calm. Or perhaps it had landed in some spot hidden in the mangrove. He'd seen planes like that in Japan, with pontoons, flying low up and down the coast. Army intelligence working for SCAP, for MacArthur. It was a good thing he'd had the presence of mind to duck into the jungle. Apparently, someone was keeping an eye on the island.

On the return ferry to Punta Rasca he was again the sole passenger. The storms were coming late that afternoon, the wind just now picking up, the eastern sky clotting with blue-black thunderheads. From the vantage on deck, half way across, he could see the entire estuary. There was no sign of the plane.

The swimming had been excellent. He would come back every few days, perhaps with some surf-fishing gear in the bed of the truck, for appearances sake. After a while he and the ferryman might get to know each other. Narby could begin to ask questions without drawing attention.

No one was waiting as they pulled up to the slip. Whoever had crossed over from the island that morning wasn't returning today. He climbed back into the truck. The ferryman kicked away the blocks under the wheels.

"Not much traffic today," Narby said through the window.

"Nope. Never is in August."

"That right?"

The ferryman nodded. A tight-mouthed sullen old man. One of the Villagers, Narby supposed. A different kind of Southerner.

Around eleven that night Narby tapped on the screen door at the back, by the kitchen. Janet let him in. It was a one-story ranch style house with a yellow stucco finish. She was wearing a sleeveless floral print dress, her hair freshly piled, lips glossy red. With her wide hips the dress was less than flattering. She looked better in a skirt and blouse. There was a *Ladies Home Journal* spread open on the kitchen table, next to an ashtray full of lipstick-stained butts and an empty glass, the rim smeared with red. From somewhere inside the house a radio was playing quietly, cornball country music. She'd been sitting there since ten, waiting for him.

"Hello, Janet." She wanted him to greet her with a kiss, he supposed. But he held back. "You sure this is all right? Me being here?"

She smiled, her mouth a little twitchy. "What would you like to drink, Philip?" She opened one of the cabinets. "There's rye whiskey, bourbon, gin. I could fix you a martini."

"Thanks. Just bourbon. No ice."

"All right." She poured a rather stingy amount into a tumbler. "There you go." She picked up the lipsticked glass from the table. "Salud." They toasted, quite mirthlessly.

"You're sunburned," she said. She reached out and put her palm against his face. "Hot."

"Went to the beach. Took the ferry to Sanmora Island. Have you been out there?"

"Once. It's not very convenient, with only that one ferry. Frank says—well, let's not stand here."

She led him to the living room, the curtains drawn, dark but for one lamp in the far corner and the glow of the radio dial. Despite a push of air from a ceiling fan it felt closed and musty. The music has stopped and there was talking and she switched it off and they sat on the sofa. She set her empty glass on the coffee table. Narby kept the tumbler in his hand. He'd been drinking all night, more than usual.

"You were saying. About Frank?"

"About Frank? Oh, only that Frank says that the people out there don't like outsiders. That's why they don't want a bridge. Or better ferry service."

"Can't say I blame them. So, any news about Frank?"

"No."

It was better at the Glo-Bel. A married woman coming to a man's motel room meant only one thing. Being here, in their home, their bed, would cloud things. It was a mistake. "Maybe I should go, Janet. You look beat."

"Philip. I don't know what's happening to me. I've never felt this way, not even with Frank. Don't go. Be with me."

"All right. Only, don't take it so damned seriously. It's only because you haven't seen Frank in so long. When he's back you'll feel different. Beside, I'll be long gone by then."

"What do you mean? Where are you going?"

"I don't know. I told you. I don't know where I'll settle down, finally."

"I'm going to leave Frank. I've decided. I'm going to ask for a divorce. Look." She held out her hand. There was a band of paler skin where the ring had been.

"Is that really what you want?"

"Yes. I decided that even before I met you, Philip. It has nothing to do with you. Don't flatter yourself."

"Well, then. Good for you." He stood up, holding the empty glass. "Mind if I help myself? Can I get you another?"

In the kitchen, pouring a drink, he tried to argue himself out of it. But the animal inside needed feeding. He went back to the living room. "Come on." He held out his hand and she reached up from the sofa and he pulled her up. "In here?" He nodded to the hallway.

"Yes."

She must have put away the photographs, his clothes, anything suggesting that someone else had lived there, shared her bed. Just as well, because Frank wouldn't be the same. One by one, the girlfriends and wives and children were going to have their eyes opened, their hearts wrung out to dry. In cozy little bedrooms just like this, with flowery curtains and frilled pillowcases. Thank God Narby had been spared that, having to squirm through the homecoming, pretending. Thank God he wasn't like other men.

Silently, in the dark, they undressed. On the bed, on her back as usual, she wrapped her arms around his neck and shoulders, kissing him on the mouth again and again until he had to pull away. "Turn over," he said, rather matter-of-factly. "Get on your knees."

"What?"

"Turn over."

"But why?"

"Because I like it that way." He was thinking again of La China, the mixed-blood girl in Havana.

"But. I don't understand."

Half a dozen times now and each time she had lain inert on her back, her big hips splayed flat on the sheets, her pelvis pinned to the mattress. That wouldn't do anymore. "Just turn on your stomach. Put your arms to your side."

"But. I can't."

"Come on, now. I can show you." He started to tug at her shoulder.

"What are you doing? You're scaring me, Philip."

"I need you this way. Don't be scared."

"Is it because of your injury? Those terrible scars?" She had never mentioned it before. Now she began to whimper. "I don't understand, Philip. Talk to me. Hold me. For God's sake, Philip, what's the matter with you?"

Probably he had drunk too much, been out in the sun too long, the hours of walking and hard swimming. And he had used two Benzedrine inhalers, in the truck, about half an hour ago. A bad idea, especially with nothing in his stomach. He let go of her shoulder and stood up and steadied himself with one hand on the dresser.

"I'm sorry. I'll go. It's not your fault."

"You're goddamn right it's not my fault. What do you think I am?" She pulled the sheets up to cover herself. "Don't go. Please. Can't we just talk? About you. About what happened to you, over there. In the war."

"Not such a bright idea. Look. I'll swing by the library in a couple of days. I've got a lot on my mind." He dressed as he spoke. "Just stay there. I'll leave by the kitchen door."

"I love you, Philip."

"Don't say that. It's not possible. It's something else. Only you don't know what it is yet."

He closed the screen door behind him, slowly, making no sound. Even so, as he passed between the houses and across the lawn a dog started barking and he sprinted to the truck, his head down and his shoulders hunched, the way a man runs under fire.

8

HE WAS BACK ON THE SPLASH, the less-than-satisfactory Benzedrine inhalers, buying five packs at a time at Rexall's—for his chronic bronchitis, if anyone asked. If only he could get his hands on Dolophine or some narcotic equivalent, for the pain, he'd quit the splash for good. Cut back on the drinking before it got out of control. He'd played it over in his mind a dozen times: walking into Rexall's before the lunch hour when it was always quiet, pulling the stocking over his face, taking the gun from under his shirt, telling the old man behind the counter to cooperate, or else. There had to be another way. He hadn't come this far to debase himself like that.

He had to stick it out a little longer, wait for instructions from Knowles, find out what Campos knew. A week, maybe two, and he'd be out of Cabin 101 for good. The place was grating on his nerves, the roaches springing at him out of the darkness, the rain beating on the tin roof, the buzz of the inane neon bell, the boiling heat. Having Janet here had only made it worse. Made him crave everything she couldn't give him. Well, he wasn't done with her yet. Not until Frank was back. And maybe not even then.

He'd been to Sanmora again. The beach deserted, as before. He had another good swim, far out in the gentle green swells. And he had another look at the mansions. Winter homes, obviously, for people with plenty of money. People with yachts and seaplanes at their disposal.

It was over an hour's drive from the Glo-Bel to the ferry landing at Punta Rasca, but as the crow flies Sanmora was maybe two miles from the mangrove cove where he and Campos had waded ashore. Sawfish Point, Vetch called it: thousands of acres of sweltering pine waste where the Putnam Lumber Company had operated the turpentine camp. Maybe Knowles had intended for him to come ashore on the island. Not Sawfish Point. The son-of-a-bitch pilot had fouled everything up. Perhaps the seaplane had been sent not to hunt Narby down but to rescue him.

Tomorrow he would drive to Miami, call Campos, as arranged. Make a second visit to the bank in Coral Gables. The money was there, ripe for the gleaning. He needed to avail himself of it while he could, not waste time.

It was raining again, the afternoon deluge. He'd already inhaled four bennies. There were still six left, because he had stopped at Rexall's again. No doubt, the hick-town pharmacist was catching on. It might not be long before they refused to sell to him. Goddamn cheap jittery dope. His nerves were bad enough. Shirtless, sweating, the little electric fan Dindridge had given him trained on his face, he dropped to the floor and did another fifty pushups, and then took another cold shower. After that, an inch of bourbon. The counting, keeping a schedule, gave order to the empty time. The waiting. When the clock struck six, he indulged in another inhalation. After the initial kick he sat at the table to continue his work, combing the batch of newspapers and magazines he had picked up at Hank's, clipping whatever seemed relevant: *twenty-three American war prisoners refuse repatriation, will stay with their Communist captors; troops loyal to the Shah of Iran besiege Mohammed Mossadegh in Tehran; new communist Prime Minister of Hungary Imre Nagy promises a "people's democracy."*

Just as the rain was easing he heard Vetch's truck, sloshing across the sodden gravel lot. He put away the clippings, cleared the table, and stood at the screen door, blocking the entrance.

"What do you want?"

"Mind if I come in, son? We got to talk."

"Why? We concluded our business some days ago."

"This is more of a social call. Hah. Come on, now. I'm getting soaked to the bone out here."

"I'm not feeling social, Carl."

"That so? Well, in that case I got no choice but to take it to the Shurf. They's a mess out there and hell if I'm going to be left all on my own to clean it up."

Narby stepped back and opened the screen door. Vetch came in, dripping on the linoleum. His glasses were fogged. He pried them off, blotting them with the hem of the dingy red striped shirt, his little black button eyes receding deeper within the pale sockets and the round, pasty, sweat-beaded face.

"Whew. That's better. A man stand out in that rain long enough, he start to slime up like some old cypress knee. Hah."

"Let's make it quick, Carl."

"Scuse my appearance. Didn't have no chance to freshen up. Mind if I use your conveniences?"

The man's stink was filling the cabin. "Go ahead."

Narby rolled a cigarette with the shag tobacco, poured an inch of bourbon and swallowed it and feeling nothing poured another. Vetch came out, smoothing his palms down his shirtfront. "Something to drink, Carl?"

"Jim Beam? Drinking the good stuff, eh? Kind of early for the cocktail hour, ain't it? Well, considering the matter at hand, don't mind if I do."

Narby passed him a jelly jar. "A farewell toast. I'm leaving in a day or two. Sorry things didn't work out. If this Fish Camp idea is such a sure thing, as you claim, you shouldn't have any trouble finding another investor. Salud."

Vetch sat across the kitchenette table, gazing at Narby through the cracked lens, his mouth hanging open in a bland half smile, exposing the brown nubs of teeth. "Longer I be round you, son, more curious I get." He paused to taste the bourbon, smacking his lips in appreciation. "You like one of them trick pictures in a magazine. Is it two faces, or is it a flower vase? Longer you look on it, the harder to figure out."

"Get to the point, Carl."

"Why you so jumpy? You ought to relax, son. Settle in. You ain't going to New Yoke anytime soon. You ain't going nowhere."

"Yeah? Why is that?"

"Them Nigras living down in the old turp'tine camp—my camp. They found your boat. Sho enough. Tangled up in that mangrove."

Narby felt his legs tense. "It's just a dingy. Keep it, if you want."

"Now don't you fret, son. See, whenever our Colored folk down here find someone else's mess, they run. That's cause they smart, see? They know that if that mess gets found out, them Coloreds going to take the blame, no matter what. See what I'm saying? They find some mess of trouble they ain't going to run to the Shurf. Only White Man they tell is me. That's cause they trust me, cause I let em stay in the camp with they women and they animals. That's why they call me Cap'm. Out of respect. We got us an arrangement, them Black boys and me. Un'ustan what I'm saying?"

"I don't know what the hell you're talking about. Whatever it is, it's got nothing to do with me."

"It ain't no dingy you come on. They's a mess on that boat, son. Big old fat stinking white mess. Burned up by the sun and half gnawed to the bone by them buzzards and maggots. Hands all tied up, too. What's left of them. Dead White man about the worse mess a Nigra can find, cepting a White Woman. Hah. And that stink. Jesus almighty. I figure, that there poor soul been putrefying bout three weeks now. Bout the same as when you and your fancy Colored man come dragging yourselves up my road. Now, ain't that curious?"

Strange, but after the initial jolt the news brought relief, almost calm. The thing had become definite. Narby had believed that he was showing a little mercy. Now he saw it had only been weakness. It could have been done efficiently, without this new complication. He wouldn't make the same mistake twice.

"As I said, it's got nothing to do with me. Just a coincidence."

Vetch took another sip, smacking his lips, shifting his weight in the chair. The thunder came again, faintly, the storm rolling out toward the Gulf. "We done been playing make believe all along, ain't we? I knew it the minute you came into my store. I knew it when you seen them soldier boys over at the Greyhound. Them coming back from Korea."

Even now in the midst of blackmail the man was pathetic. Narby felt nothing, no hate or anger, his fear ebbing out into that unremitting low-frequency dread that had shadowed him since Tokyo. Vetch was pleading for help, the sorry shrunken eyes behind the broken glasses, his swollen hands on the table open and supplicant, his fingers bitten and torn. It wasn't only money. Vetch wanted someone to take his side, to console him. With a few carefully chosen gestures Narby might very well turn the dead pilot into Vetch's enemy as well, Vetch's crime.

"You're too clever for me, Carl. I ought to have known I couldn't fool you. Not for long, anyway."

The former camp commissionaire leaned back, his face mutating, showing a mild surprise. "You damn right. I ain't like these crackers round here. Small-minded nits, they is. Mean, too. Don't even know how to treat they own Colored. That's what I'm saying. You and me is different. But now, that don't change the fact that they's a dead White Man out there on Sawfish Point, and I got to figure out what to do with it. I reckon I ought to go to the Shurf. Ain't that right?"

"I don't see any need to bother the Sheriff, Carl. As long as the men who found it keep quiet."

"They do what I tell em," Vetch said quickly. "They as eager as you is to be rid of it. Erase all that co-incidence. Matter of fact, them boys going to help us. Way out in Sawfish Point ain't no one going to see or hear or even smell that stink. Get em to haul that boat out in deep water and sink it once and for all. Them sawfish and hammerheads and crabs take care of the rest."

Apparently, the buffoon was eager to make himself an accessory.

"Course, instead of sinking her, we could salvage that old boat. Got some kind of foreign registration number on it. From over yonder in Cuba, is it? Like your Colored Man? Hah. I could use me a boat like that."

"Don't be stupid. Get rid of it. Sink it."

"If that's what you want. Only. It's going to cost you. Them Colored boys done paid off they debt to society. These days got to pay em wages for they sweat. Come to think on it, that boat belongs to me now, cause it wershed up on my property. Seaworthy boat like that, coming all the way from Cuba. That's worth plenty."

"All right. Fair enough. How much do you want?"

Without hesitation, as if ever since walking through the screen door he had been itching to unveil the predetermined sum, Vetch said, "thousand dollar."

Narby laughed, sloughing off a bit of tension. "You're joking. I don't have that kind of money."

"You want it sunk? You want that mess cleaned up, with no one the wiser? You got to pay. Otherwise, I'll leave it to the County Shurf to tidy up. Let the taxpayer foot the bill. Hah."

Narby had to push back. How hard could it be to beat down a man who slobbered over a twenty-dollar bill? Besides, a little back-and-forth would bind Vetch even tighter. Offer him enough to feed his delusion, keep him distracted until Narby was finished with him. "Three hundred. Take it, or get the hell out."

"Come now. No call to get unfriendly. It's just a calculation, that's all. Beside, we together on this. We going to build us that Fish Camp, ain't we? It's like paying yourself. Making yourself an investment."

"If we're together, a thousand dollars would mean half for you and half for me. So, I'm offering six hundred total, half for you and half for me. That's three hundred. Take it or leave it."

Vetch took out the paper pouch of Top and rolled a cigarette, scattering flakes of dry tobacco. "You got a point there, son. But I'll take five hundred, cause my share's bigger. I got me possession. You can give yourself one hundred out of the six, and that way you and me both get what we want."

"Four hundred, Carl. That's as much as I can afford. You want me in on this, don't you? Four hundred and you take care of that mess."

"Four hundred, huh? And you and me gunna partner up for the Fish Camp? You gunna put that in writing?"

"Four hundred."

He raised the jelly jar to drink, little webs of white crud showing at the corners of his mouth. "Ah, that's the good stuff, all right. Well, let's just call it a deposit. How's that? A four hundred dollar deposit. And I ain't doing nothing on credit. I need it now. Upfront. I know you got the cash, Nawby. It's in that old sack you was toting when you come dragging yourself up my road. Now ain't it?"

"Tomorrow. Come back in the morning. I'll have it by then."

"Hid it somewheres, did you? That's what I would've done myself. Only a fool leave a sack of money in a little old cardboard matchbox like this. All right. Tomorrow morning," he said, putting out his hand. "Shake on it."

Narby did it quickly, blanking his mind.

"Them boys'll take care of it. Don't you worry." Vetch pushed back the chair, grunting as he stood. "I be on my way. Now that the rain's over. You stick with Carl Vetch, son, and we'll beat em both. Beat whatever's hounding you and beat all these dumb-ass Florida crackers. I be back in the morning, all right. Sure as the sun rise."

Holding open the screen door Vetch turned, nodding toward the bottle on the table. "Take it easy with that stuff, you hear? Good-looking young fellow like you don't want to go to that ugly place. Not yet."

9

ALL THE TELLERS WORE THIN yellow cardigans, top buttons unfastened, showing a creamy inch of vortex-like cleft. Miss Prentice—Donna—had window three. Slim hipped, well-provisioned, with soft brunette hair and polished smile and bright eyes. Narby nodded pleasantly at her from across the cool lofty room, the air laced with perfume and leather and a faint tang of cigar smoke. Not that she would remember him. There would have been many men, many transactions, in the intervening weeks. But it was her job to make the client feel special, the only man in the world whose money mattered.

He had intended only to fill the four-hundred-dollar hole inflicted by Vetch's blackmail. But instead, impulsively, he made the slip out for a thousand. After all, there was no way to be certain that Sid Black was dead, that Knowles had taken over the account, that the money would remain so readily accessible. He had to consider as well the cost of his own well-being, his physical and psychological equilibrium. Combat bonus, his own personal GI bill.

"Good morning. I'd like to make a withdrawal, please."

"Good morning." She glanced at the slip. "Mr. Narby. Nice to see you again. How are you today?"

"Nice to see you, Miss Prentice. I'm all right. Well, actually, a little behind in the gaming department." He laughed. "I swear, every one of those damned casinos in Havana is rigged."

"I'm sure your luck will change."

"You know, Miss Prentice. I think you're right." He let his eyes bear down on her, unbridled. "I think today might be my lucky day."

"Just a moment, Mr. Narby." He watched as she turned and walked into the office, the seductive tandem shifting underneath the taut, dark blue crepe skirt. Wilson—pale, flaccid, gray—followed her back to the window.

"Mr. Narby," he said, thrusting his hand over the counter. "Bob Wilson. Welcome back. Everything is perfectly in order now. I just wanted to let you know. Personally."

"Hello, Bob. That's good to hear."

Prentice sat at her window and under Wilson's watchful gaze opened her cash drawer. "How would you like that, Mr. Narby?"

"Twenties, please."

She counted out the bills.

"As you might know, Mr. Narby, the Bank of Coral Gables offers a wide array of banking and financial services, domestic and international, some of which might have distinct advantages for someone like yourself. Tax advantages, for example. If you have just a moment, I'd be happy to discuss some of the changes to your account you might want to consider."

"Thanks Bob, but I've got a lunch date. Some other time."

"You bet. Here's my card. Let me know if you need anything at all while you're in the Miami area."

I need Miss Prentice. In your office. With the door locked and the blinds down. And you out of it. "Sure thing, Bob."

She counted out the bills a second time, laying them on the counter for Narby's verification. Lightly suntanned hands, slender tapering fingers, nails pared and buffed. Wilson hung about, just behind her, doglike. Narby supposed he'd have to wait until his next visit to get her alone, proposition her. So much money, such a desirable woman, their fingers nearly brushing as he lifted the bills off the counter.

He walked out this time free of the urge to look back down Aragon Avenue, unburdened of the fear of a hand coming from behind, clamping down on his shoulder.

As before, he had parked truck on a shady residential street several blocks from the bank. He opened the door, brief case swinging at his side, cigarette between his lips, the sporty bank clothes beginning to wilt and splotch in the heat. It wouldn't do to show up again in the same silk and linen, he realized. He ought to refurbish the disguise. For Miss Prentice's sake.

The Cuban had instructed him to call at two o'clock. It was just noon. He pulled the flask from the glove compartment. Might as well find someplace to stay, get cleaned up, before meeting Campos. Tomorrow, early, he would drive back up the Tamiami, beat the worst of the heat. From Le Jeune he made a left on Eighth Street, toward the roadside motels he had passed on the way into town. The vision lingered: the stack of bills, her slender hand, his gaze drawn down into the creamy white cleft.

Fifteen hundred dollars in his brief case. His lucky day. Why in hell would a man like Philip Narby spend a day like this in some roadside dump, drinking by himself? Philip Narby, who docked his yacht, the Kansas City, at Dinner Key Marina. Philip Narby, who, if asked, had an ocean view suite at the, what was it called, that fabulous new hotel on Miami Beach? The Atlantique.

He pulled into the parking lot of a marine supply store and unfolded the Sinclair service-station map, flipping it to the blow-up of Miami Beach on the other side: Eighth Street to Biscayne Boulevard and then crossing Biscayne Bay on the 13th Street Bridge, Florida A1A. *The General Douglas MacArthur Causeway.*

Now wasn't that heart warming? Streets and bridges and school auditoriums all across America honoring the great hero, *Time* magazine's Man of the Year. The butcher, the traitor, the egomaniac. Even at Bataan, Old Dugout Doug had been a coward, a fake. But the masses needed its heroes, just as it needed its arsenal of atomic bombs. Heroes who were traitors, bombs that could never again be dropped. It wouldn't do to fling about nuclear-armed warheads if the other side could simply fling them right back. Hydrogens now, the latest thing in mushroom molten death. *Destroyer of worlds*. Wasn't it just a tad late for your touching retrospective pacifism, Professor Oppenheimer?

There would be no bridges or schools named after Bill Knowles. Not even Eisenhower knew. Didn't want to know, so he could play hero-dumb with complete conviction, good soldier that he was. And the Dulles brothers? They knew just enough, gave orders at the uppermost layers. But beyond that they had no control, or even awareness.

He rolled a cigarette and swung the truck around, heading the opposite direction. On the causeway the wind picked up, the choppy water of Biscayne Bay sparkling like shards of bright green glass, dotted with thousands of effervescent whitecaps. He could see the verdant Bay islands, the Mediterranean villas with the lawns sweeping down to yachts moored at private docks. At the hump of the bridge the serried skyline of hotels rose into view, and beyond that the cold cobalt blue of the Atlantic.

Collins Avenue, the main drag, was lined with night clubs and restaurants and hotels—white stucco, glass brick, brushed steel, everything glaring in the harsh sun, landscaped with palms and hibiscus and bursts of bougainvillea. At night the street would probably light up like fireworks. At midday, though, in late summer, it all looked rather bleached out, fossilized. Through the gaps between the hotels he could glimpse the white sand beach, the dark sea rising up slightly as it met the horizon. If nothing else, he'd have a good long swim.

The Hotel Atlantique sat at the corner of Collins and 22nd Street. He pulled into the semi-circular up-sloping driveway. The liveried doorman shot him a look that gave Narby second thoughts. It was the rust-eaten redneck truck. Averting his face he drove past the canopied entrance and out the other side, as if he had pulled in by mistake, and found a parking garage on Michigan Avenue about ten blocks away. His clothes were a sopping mess, his sweated hair tangled from the wind. But what did that matter if he had money? He broke open a Benzedrine inhaler, took a snort, and a drink from the flask. He waited a few minutes and took another, longer drink. That was it: the kicker, the tip into clarification after the long morning's priming.

From the garage he walked across Michigan and then up Lincoln Road—the Fifth Avenue of Miami Beach—past boutiques and jewelers, half the shops closed until the winter season, passing under the gaudy spectacular marquee of the Carib Theater. Taking in the scenery, the women, the well-built ones who took advantage of the heat to show some bronzed flesh, legs and midriff and shoulders, swinging their big bags, faces a bit mask-like, the bright lipstick and deep eyeliner against toasted skin. A hard and brittle sex appeal. For looking only. No flirting, no touching. Wives out shopping, he supposed, the hubbies, the Wilsons, ogling creamy young secretaries in cool tinted offices.

At the corner he hailed a cab. "The Atlantique."

"The hotel? Buddy, it's right there, half a block away."

"I know. Drive up Collins a ways, maybe double back on Ocean. Give me a little tour. It's my first time in town."

"A tour? What do you mean —"

"Ten bucks." He leaned forward and handed the driver the bill. "Show me some of the sights, five minutes, then drop me at the hotel." "You got it, pal."

The breeze would cool him off a bit. He didn't want to show up at the Hotel on foot.

They drove by the Roney Plaza and north on Collins until the Firestone Estate and then turned back on Indian Creek. Past the hotels Miami Beach was nothing but a long wide sandbar with a creek running through it. Like Sanmora, only bulldozed, scraped clean of jungle and mangrove.

"Hear they're going to tear it down," the driver was saying. "Used to be a lot of those big private spreads right on the ocean. Oil men, rubber men, railroad men. Not any more. How many more hotel rooms do they think they need?"

The cab pulled into the circular drive. A white-haired Negro doorman in gold buttons and epaulettes, the one who had scared him away in the truck, opened the cab door. "Any bags, sir?"

"No. Just this." The Smoker's Den attaché.

The air in the lobby was bracing, colder even than in the bank, with an odd chemical smell. Miami Beach's first all-air-conditioned year-round luxury resort! Why wait for winter? Get in front of the crowd. He had his pick of rooms and took a one-bedroom ocean-view suite on the ninth floor. The bellhop—another aging Negro—took him up the elevator and unlocked the room door and Narby tipped him a dollar. It was like a damned meat locker, with that same chemical smell. He threw open the drapes. Through the sliding glass doors the heat and light came flooding in, with a rather operatic drama. He slid the door open and stepped out on the terrace into the stiff breeze, the roar of the surf muffled by the height and the wind. The ocean stretched to infinity. At the horizon, sharp as a razor's edge, towering masses of cloud rose up into the powder-blue sky.

The swells looked to be about two to three feet. There would be strong currents, and a good deal more turbulence when the storms rolled in. Already the sides of the striped canvas cabanas set up on the beach were buckling in the wind. The hotel-builders had erected a series of rock jetties that extended some thirty yards out into the water, apparently to delineate one hotel's beachfront from the next. To clear those jetties he'd have to swim straight out into the bigger swells. Damned stupid, Narby thought. You could already see what was happening:

some of the strips of beach between the jetties were wide, but others had eroded to half the width. One day there'd be no beach left at all and the sea would come crashing right up to the hotel seawalls.

It was 12:40. The Benzedrine had keyed him up, his muscles twitching. There was time for a swim before calling Campos. He gathered the stack of bills from the brief case and found a hiding place in the bathroom, under the sink in a gap between the wall and the cabinet. In the dresser he left his wallet with about fifty in cash—a habit from Havana. Downstairs, in a shop in the lobby, he bought a pair of Lastex trunks and changed in one of the cabanas. Except for the cabana boys the beach was fairly empty. No one around to gawk at the scars.

Beyond the breakers and the rock jetties the swells tossed him up and down, intent on flipping him over and forcing the sea down his lungs. He managed about half an hour, using all his strength to simply keep from drowning. At the first crack of thunder, with the rain pelting his head, he caught a wave and came tumbling back to the beach. The exertion was exhilarating.

Back in his room he showered, called room service, had a sandwich and a beer as he sat on the loveseat watching the storm, the glass doors slid open, the warm ocean air counteracting the frigid chemical flow that poured down from the vent. The place might be a big leap up from the Glo-Bel, but there was something cheap about it, jerrybuilt—the ugly rock-jetties, the stale too-cold air, the rust forming in the metal tracks of the sliding doors—an indelible quality of gimcrack and corrosion seeping through the veneers of glitz.

It was two o'clock. He made the call. This time Campos himself answered.

"I'm here. In Miami."

"Felipé. From where you call?"

"A hotel. On the Beach. Why don't we meet here, in my room?"

"Miami Beach?" The Cuban laughed. "Here I am Negro. Un Colorado. Me comprendes?"

"Yeah, I get it. So what?"

"The Negro no permitted in Miami Beach. Only for labor. For to clean, make garden. Yankee racismo. Very strong."

There was a restaurant called El Castillo in Overtown, the Negro quarter just east of downtown Miami. They arranged to meet in an hour.

The storm had swept through rapidly. By the time Narby went out the sun was bearing down again, raising steam from the wet pavement. He drove back over Biscayne Bay and though downtown Miami, like a chunk of Chicago broken off and transplanted in a hothouse, and bumped across the railroad tracks and then turned north on NW 2nd Avenue, into Overtown. The sidewalks were busy with Black people, a rather well-heeled crowd, Narby observed, far better off than their ragged country cousins on the Gulf coast. He parked on a side street fronted with narrow, wooden single-story shotgun houses, some well-maintained, others badly weathered and sagging. The restaurant was across the avenue. At the intersection, noticing the cop on the corner—the only other White face, as far Narby could see—he hesitated, stepping back until the cop strolled off in the opposite direction, tapping his nightstick against his leg. Calmly, quickly, Narby crossed the street and passed through the propped-open double doors.

El Castillo was a big, noisy, high-ceilinged cafeteria-like room, fans whirring overhead, the walls lined with red-upholstered booths. Campos sat at the back. Seeing Narby come in, vigilant, the Cuban stood halfway, nodded across the room, and sat again, not wanting to attract attention, Narby supposed— though a White man traversing the restaurant would no doubt raise a few heads. On the back wall an artist had painted a colorful mural: an edenic seaside Caribbean jungle done in a naïve style, the trees drooping with mangoes and papaya and bananas. The place rattled with rapid fire Spanish and southern

Negro patois and banging cutlery. There was music from a jukebox—the same stuff Narby had heard all over Havana, the blaring horns and criss-crossing drums and the tensely-pitched male voice. Beny Moré, or one of his imitators. They could talk here without being overhead.

"Good to see you, Ernesto."

"Todavia vivamos, sí? We are still alive."

"Well. We're not dead."

Campos wore a crisp white short-sleeved shirt, a cigarette pack bulging the pocket. His hair was slicked back, his moustache freshly trimmed. From the looks of it—two empty ceramic demitasses, blackened by the thick Cuban coffee, the ashtray full of butts—Campos had been sitting there for a while, a bit anxiously, probably, because Narby was late. As he sat Narby got a good whiff of cologne—like an animal giving off its scent.

"You are staying now in Miami Beach?" Campos asked, lighting another cigarette.

"Just for a day or two." The waitress was at their table, a young Negro woman. Narby ordered a beer. Campos declined another café Cubano.

"You are good, Felipé?"

"Sure. And you? Everything all right?"

"Puede ser. Can be. I practice correct English. OK?"

"You're doing fine."

"We can to know each other, yes? For to trust. Like on sea. We talk like comrades. Brothers. No of sangre. No brothers from blood. Brothers de la mente."

"Brothers of the mind? De acuerdo. I accept." The waitress came with his beer. As she turned and moved away Narby's eyes lingered for a moment, her form shifting under the thin waitress's uniform, her legs. Darker than La China. More woman than girl. More woman than Negro.

Campos was eager to talk, explain himself. "I study for to be doctor. Medicina. Havana Universidad and also two years at University in Francia. Specialize. For psicología. Sigh-kolo-gee.

But then I must stop to study." He paused, lit a cigarette. His hands were steady, but the Cuban was on edge, his eyes darting about, his syntax deteriorating as he went on, though his English had indeed improved. He told Narby about his older brother Ramón, a union organizer murdered by Batista's police, about his own involvement with Juventud Ortodoxía and el Movimiento. They were organizing to oppose the corruption of the new regime, to overthrow tyranny and restore the Constitution of 1940. "You read in newspaper the Moncada attack, at Santiago? This is what I escape. Like I tell you. The army broke it. Murder. Prison. Tortura. Now, for this day, se llaman el Movimiento Viente-Seis de Julio. Movement of twenty-six July."

"But there's something that doesn't fit. You're dark-skinned. I thought Batista had the support of people like you. The Negroes and mulattos. Your leader, this lawyer Castro who they captured. He's White. Anglo European."

"Yes. But for this I am." He struggled for the words. "Is the problem of concienca, Felipé. The consciousness. Here, I am Negro. Here, I hide in Negro skin. Disfrazado. In Cuba I am… como dice Aristóteles. Political Man. Because I come over the colonial consciousness. No. Over come. I overcome what they poison to my mind, la mentalidad de los imperialistas. La mente colonizada."

It was like a thought uttered years ago but still hanging in the air, half-finished—*it's Indo-china we ought to be worried about, getting the French off their backs. The Chinese will find their own way, without the Soviets. Not even Mao can change that. It's in their history, oldest damned civilization on earth.*

There was the sensation of being in two places, two moments, blurred into one. Suddenly, Narby knew what to say. "You're not communist, are you? With all this business about imperialism? That kind of talk will get you nowhere. This man, Castro. He's not in with the Soviets, is he?"

"Not communista. Nunca. The Communists in Cuba, they take from Batista with one hand, and give to Batista with the other." Campos took a breath, paused to light a cigarette, leaned forward. "Somos Nacionalistas. Patriotas. Como los patriotas de la revolución Americana. We are nationalists, like American Revolution. We fight solamente for our country. La Patria. For Cuba. Me entiendes? Is possible to be anti-imperialist and not communist. Yes?"

The natty little man had broken a sweat. One after another the tiny beads forming beneath the tight slicked-back hairline began to slither down his face. He blotted himself, gingerly, dignified, with the waxed-paper napkin, the name of the restaurant, El Castillo, printed beneath a line drawing of El Moro Castle, the fortress guarding the old port of Havana.

"We will revolver, el Movimiento. Batista will go down. Criminal. Asesino. We have in Cuba idioma. Paredón." Campos thought for a moment, stroking his moustache with the tip of his finger. "It is meaning like: on the wall, the wall where you make execution."

"Up against the wall."

"Eso es. Yes. Up against the wall." He stubbed out his cigarette. "Y que piensas tu, Felipé? What you think now?"

"What do I think? As long as you don't call yourselves communists, then I'm with you. Viva la revolución. That son-of-a-bitch Batista deserves whatever's coming to him." He raised his glass and drank. "By all means. Paredón."

The sensation had passed, the same blurring uplifting exhilaration he had felt that night, years ago, at the Kansas City in Tokyo. The night he had met Bill Knowles. Like now, they had sat at a table at the back. The place had been packed, too, only with diplomatic staff, Division heads, top Army brass having dinner with their bare-shouldered diamond-studded wives. The American proconsuls of the Asian Pacific, gorging on Omaha steaks flown in that very same day. And here, in El Castillo: a crowd of Negroes, laughing and carousing as if without a care in the world, powerless downcast people. Yet somehow, it was the same.

He felt the Cuban's hand gripping his forearm. "For what I tell you, Felipé, I can die. Because you prove me your fidelidad in the sea, I tell you. And you, hermano? What are you? What you run? Why you on boat?"

Already, he was composing the next letter to Knowles: *Evidence of communist influence in Cuban rebel movement, despite nationalist rhetoric. Campos hiding in Negro section of Miami. Infiltrate 26 July group? Advise.*

"My situation is not so different from yours, Ernesto. I am a patriot, just like you. And a traitor, an enemy of the state. Just like you. Do you understand what I am saying?"

"I understand more better than speak. Yes. Tell me."

Narby envied them in a way, these people all around him who cared nothing about losing China or the Russians swallowing Eastern Europe or Uncle Joe juggling the bomb. At least the Soviets paid the Negro lip service, if only for propaganda. Narby had clipped the article just yesterday: *Two non-commissioned POW Negro officers have reportedly refused repatriation to the US, choosing to live under the grim thumb of communism rather than return to their home and families. Brainwashing? Or are these men sending a message, confused and delusional perhaps, about conditions here in the homeland?*

"I can't explain it. You'll have to trust me. I was running for my life. Like you. From people in my own government, in the military. Corrupt people, as bad as Batista. Now I have to hide, like you. And like you, I'm not alone. I work with a group of men, good men, very smart men. They've sent me here. To help correct the corruption before it spreads."

"Is conspiracy? These men that you work?"

"More of a counter-conspiracy, a push back. The important thing is, we can help you. Only stay clear of the Soviets. Keep the communists out of it and I promise, we'll help you get rid of Batista."

"Why you want to help?"

He gave it a moment's thought. "Because you're going to win." The formulation satisfied him, so he continued. "It's inevitable. Don't get me wrong. The Americans won't give up on Batista so easily. Same mistake we made in China, backing the Kuomintang. My people, the people I work for—we don't want that mistake to happen again."

"And what you want for return? What you want from Cuba?"

He shrugged "Nothing that we won't get anyway."

"You are cínico. Nihilisto."

"Maybe so. I am also your friend. Brothers of the mind, right? In the end, that's all that really matters. That's why I'll help you. Because I like you. And I don't like Batista. Men like Batista make me sick."

Campos's eyes had softened. He held his cigarette to his lips for a moment, as if in a kiss. "We must wait. To see what Batista do with Castro and the others. We have people in Mexico City, Caracas, New York. Only now we must stay tranquilo, quiet. I must continue my study for medicina. Psychology. This is revolutionary science, Felipé. The mind of the Cuban people. To make them understand. That is the big struggle of all. Now, we need money to eat, to live somewhere. Later, it is necessary to buy weapons."

"All right. Money. It won't be much, not right away. Later, when I get approval, they'll be more. A lot more. Money and weapons. I guarantee it."

If Campos was surprised he did a good job hiding it, flicking the ash of his cigarette, his eyes darting around the noisy crowded room. "When? Tomorrow?"

No wonder things at the bank had gone so smoothly. Narby would need plenty, to gain the revolutionary's trust. Knowles had anticipated each and every move. "All right. Tomorrow. Here?"

"No. Too much people. Telephone to me, por la mañana. I tell you where, and you come. Solo. Alone. Only you."

10

NARBY WATCHED FROM THE TERRACE as the sun went down, the cloud-streaked sky turning coral pink and russet, darkening into violet, an enormous moon pendulant over the choppy leaden water. He went inside, broke open a Benzedrine inhaler and sat for a few moments on the love seat, drinking from the flask, smoking a cigarette, making up his mind. It had been a good day's work. He deserved a reward.

He descended into the lobby. A stubby sun-browned man in a wilted seersucker suit, hat titled back over his shiny forehead, approached him. He was taking bets on the Yankee game. "You look like a gambling man," he said, his voice low and winking and shabby. "I'm here everyday. Ask the concierge. That's my office." He pointed to an armchair in the opposite corner of the lobby. "I put in more hours than the mayor. What'll I put you down for, pal?" He pulled a notepad from his pocket.

"Five bucks. On Detroit. " It was a long shot. The Yanks seemed invincible that season. Not that Narby paid much attention. But he read the papers. The headlines were full of it. As the man tore off his receipt, Narby inquired in a tone of indifference if he happened to know a bar or nightclub in the vicinity where one might meet an attractive young lady. "Alton Road," the man offered cheerfully. "Just the other side of Lincoln. Plenty of little joints over there. It's pick and choose. Get my drift?"

Despite the heat Narby decided to walk, his mind blanking, his nerves tight. When he reached Alton Road he went into the first place he came to, the window flashing with neon, and sat at the bar and ordered bourbon. It was dark and warm, the smoky air churned but hardly cooled by a pair of oscillating floor fans. For a moment he had the sensation, utterly impossible, that he had been here before. It was the music—a swing band, coming from a radio or phonograph. Like the Count Basie he had heard on the truck radio. He let it pass through him, not wanting to listen. Maybe it meant something, maybe not. Like the false intelligence they send out during a war, to sucker the enemy.

It didn't take long. She came out of nowhere and sat two stools down, pulling a pack of cigarettes from her purse and then taking her sweet time lighting it and snapping closed the purse and blowing out a plume of smoke in one long lip-pursing exhalation. Piles of hair and burgeoning flesh, gleaming nails and mouth. He asked if he could buy her a drink. He moved closer, sat next to her, watched her lips close over the rim of the glass and then dehisce, leaving a viscera of lipstick and saliva. After a few minutes they left together and he hailed a cab. He tipped the White cabbie, tipped the Negro doorman and the Negro elevator operator, letting her witness his generous nature. She called him honey and big fella. When he told her what he wanted she said, I don't do that, sweetie, and he said, but you can, if you try. How much to motivate you, inspire you? And she said, but that's not on the menu, my sugarplum. And he said, it may not be on the menu but you've got all the ingredients. I've got the recipe. Pulling off his damp silk shirt, she said, you certainly are one well-constructed piece of man. And he said, run your hand up and down, here. Don't be afraid. It won't hurt you. And she said, Christ, what did they do to you? And he said, nothing you can't make better. Nothing I can't make you make better.

The next afternoon, on his way out of town, Narby pulled the truck over at a roadside vegetable stand on the Tamiami Trail about three miles east of the Miami city limit, an open shack with a palm-thatched roof and hand-lettered signs for tomatoes and corn and squash. He got out and waited at a picnic table under a row of tall shaggy pines that grew along the ditch—Australian Pines, like the ones that shaded the road on Sanmora Island—watching the people under the thatched roof picking produce from the wooden bins: poor Whites, migrants and hill-billies, Negroes in farmhand clothes, Indian women in long dirty brightly-colored dresses, with brown leathery skin, Seminole or Miccosukee.

After a while a car pulled up, an old model Buick. Ernesto climbed out of the passenger side, the murky figure seated behind the wheel waiting for him, the motor idling.

Narby took the envelope from his pocket and walking back toward the truck handed it to Campos. The Cuban nodded, walked on, and Narby sat in the truck, watching Campos buy a few items from the bins and then return to the car. It backed up, turned, and headed toward the city. Viva la revolución.

There had been another story in the *New York Times* yesterday, and a piece in *Newsweek*. Their puny movement was in tatters. Poor dapper Ernesto. He'd wind up getting himself tortured and killed, for nothing. Philip Narby would help usher him along to his martyrdom. And even if against all the odds they managed to topple Batista, would it really matter? It had been the same with the Jacobins, the Bolsheviks, and probably the Chinese next. Revolutions ran on blood. When they ran out of Batistiano blood they'd have no choice but to bleed their own.

11

SIX STEPS BELOW STREET LEVEL the Arab's tiny cluttered shop was a well of cool air and muted light. Every few days Narby stopped by, usually in the late afternoon after the closed sign appeared on the inside of the glass door. Narby had a special tap and after a moment, standing on the steps looking down through the tinted glass, he would see Hank parting the beaded curtains, coming to let him in. The aroma of mint tea steeping in the back room mixed with the smells of pipe tobacco and cigars and newsprint. Like the air of the souk in the old country, Narby supposed.

Danish tobacco, imported cigarettes, another windproof lighter, the leather attaché, the special-order magazines including the pricey *Foreign Affairs*: it added up. Narby's money was keeping the Arab afloat—Narby and the trickle of cowboy-hatted pot-bellied burghers of Myerton who stopped in for Dutch Masters and the exorbitantly priced illustrated publications, wrapped in brown paper, that Hank kept under the counter.

For three months now Narby had been sending weekly communiqués to Knowles. So far, there was only one letter from Havana in response, and that had come almost six weeks ago. Possibly, their mail was being intercepted. But Narby doubted it. Bill Knowles was smarter than that, and too well connected.

Good to hear from you, Knowles had written. *Your situation interests me, very much so. At the moment I'm afraid I can't do much for you from this end. Obviously, you know how to survive quite well on your own. I admire that. As for the paper business, it's in both our interests to keep that confidential. As for everything else you mention, by all means, stir up the pot and see what settles.*

But there were letters from Campos now, updates on the exile's existence in Overtown, news of fellow revolutionaries arriving in Miami, fleeing Batista's secret police. Unfortunately, Campos never revealed actual names, only noms de guerre: Pombo, Sierra, Panchita, Moya, and the intriguing El Coriano, the Korean. Though never acknowledged, it was apparently a quid quo pro: every time Narby handed off the money at the tumbledown roadside vegetable stand, a letter from Campos would arrive a few days later. Narby would then forward the information to Knowles, always withholding a few details, against some future need. It worried Narby that after that first, rather vague letter—had he missed something? a code he was supposed to know?—Knowles had grown so damned negligent in responding. But the money from the Coral Gables bank continued to flow. He was in the game, his backers behind him. At least for now.

Despite the money, Narby couldn't let himself forget that there were powerful men who wished him dead. He was guilty of desertion during wartime, bank fraud, and perhaps even murder. Nor had he fully recovered from his wounds, though the nightmares haunted him now with decreasing frequency: the Lieutenant pounding on the radio, crying like a kid and cursing the dead battery, pleading for a runner, and then Tom or Jim zigzagging down the hill, the paper with the coordinates crumpled in his fist. In the dream he's almost flying, like an Olympic hurdler floating over boulders and trenches and barbed wire, his feet barely touching the burning smoking ground. And then the needles, the hooks, being yanked out of his side, his guts leaking through the jagged slits, pitching forward onto his face into the ditch, the hot shit-flecked water pooling in his open mouth.

It wouldn't be long before the Jim Beam and the Benzedrine turned on him, the medicine worse than the infliction. The pharmacist at Rexall's had started asking questions. So now Narby was buying his inhalers and keep-alert pills now from a dozen different pharmacies around Miami—stocking up ever since reading the story in the *Tribune*. Seems there had been an epidemic of bronchial asthma ever since our boys came home from Korea. Brave young men, bugging out on splash from sea to shining sea. There was a do-gooder campaign gaining momentum to take amphetamines off the shelf, require a prescription. About the only thing more ugly than coming off splash was being on it too long, too much, a raving hollow-eyed skin-crawling oblivion. Either way—letting them have it or cutting them off—there would come a day when some of those boys, three years of slaughter and privation festering in their hearts, would go berserk in the streets.

No doubt, if he skulked around, there was dope to be found in the dive bars along Alton Road on Miami Beach: cocaine, heroin, possibly codeine if not Dolophine. But he had sworn to himself: no more Sylvios, no more sweating it out in rundown cafés. As for buying sex, no intermediate was necessary. There was something excruciatingly desperate about the loneliness of an over air-conditioned Miami Beach hotel suite with an ocean view. Narby could certainly afford more conventionally attractive companions than the Alton Road regulars. But it seemed less shameful, almost an act of pity or altruism, with the cheap blondes, the last-time-around cocktail girls. As a matter of course he paid generously, even when they refused his more intimate requests.

Janet Swanson, so unsatisfactory from the start, was out of the running. The Lieutenant had returned. Narby saw them around town, the stocky sullen man with a heavy square jaw and a Marine Corps crew cut, walking with a slight limp, yanking Janet alongside him by the hand. One day, on his way from Hank's, Narby had almost bumped against them in front of the Arcade Theater. Janet had looked away, but the husband glared at Narby. In a fit of guilt, she had probably confessed to Frank that some man had preyed on her while Frank was away, that in her loneliness she had foolishly allowed him to speak to her, hold her hand, even kiss her. Apparently, Janet's honor wasn't worth a public confrontation, and they had kept walking. You ruined her, Narby would have liked to tell him. No wonder she's terrified of sex. You made her, Frank. She's all yours.

Still, there was something there. He felt it every time he saw her at the library, keeping his distance, the space between them alive, heavy with charge. With the blouse stretched across her breasts, her eyes and lips and hair done up, in the daylight world of ordinary existence, she represented something forbidden him—the love of a wife, a mate. But because it was Janet, it felt not like a loss but an advantage.

The first cool spell of the season came at mid-October, the morning fresh and the sky, clear at last of the glaring haze, an ethereal blue.

He pulled out of the Glo-Bel on to the highway and then, after a mile, turned west on Burnt Farm Road. The pavement ended with the last barbed wire fence, the road crumbling to loose rock and dust as it met the jungle. From there, the ruts leading to Vetch's store plunged into the underbrush. To the left ran another, newly cleared path, wide enough for a truck. Vetch's sign marked the fork—a rectangle of hand-sawed plywood nailed to a scrub pine, the letters painted with a stencil: VETCH'S FISH CAMP. WORMS BEER GAS. CABINS FOR RENT. BEST FISHIN' IN FLORIDA! GUARANTEED!!

The Southerner had apparently taken his cue from Madison Avenue, creating demand ahead of supply. Because there was still nothing there: no road but the ruts, no gas pump, no boat launch, no habitable cabin. True, Vetch had used some of the blackmail money to make a few improvements to his hovel. His electric bill paid he had lights now, a radio, a pump for the well, a new icebox. The man still believed that he and Narby were partners. Give it another six months and the pilot's remains, the wreckage of the boat, would have rotted long past recognition. By then it wouldn't matter what Vetch believed, or who he told. No one would pay the least attention.

Narby veered left onto the freshly cut path. It hadn't rained in weeks and the mud, mixed with the pulverized debris of the underbrush, had hardened. The jungle was sparser here, mostly saw-palmetto and Spanish bayonet and clumps of coarse grass. He drove a quarter of a mile until he came to Vetch's truck, parked in the middle of the dirt roadway.

Twenty yards beyond, the men were working with shovels and pick-axes and machetes, clearing the next section of road. Vetch sat in the truck, the door swung open and his legs dangling out, a shotgun cradled between his legs with the stock resting on the running board.

Narby got out and watched. At Narby's request Vetch had put together a work crew. There were eight that morning, Negro men who lived in the old turpentine camp, the men Vetch called "my nigras"—a couple of them still in their prime, the rest of some indeterminate advanced age. The years working for Putnam, virtually enslaved, had marked them: the stooped postures, the missing fingers, an earlobe torn off, dark skin scored with pale pink scars.

Narby lit a cigarette and walked over. Cap'm Vetch, the overlord. Soft and smug and lazy. New rifle, new boots, crisp straw hat, a new brightly striped shirt from the McCrory's Five-and-Dime. Though he still wore the rusted steel eyeglasses, tightly stretched across his face, the cracked lens glinting in the morning sun.

"How's the work progressing, Carl?"

"All right, I spect. Only they's two kind of progress. White Man progress and Colored Man progress. What we got here is splitting the difference. Hah."

"What's with the shotgun? Afraid of a workers' rebellion?"

Vetch spat out a fleck of tobacco and ran his tongue over the nubs of teeth. "Rattlesnakes. I seen my share of men go down by snake bite back in them Putnam days. I'm here to protect em."

"Then why aren't you standing out there next to them, where you might actually do some good? Besides, we could use an extra hand, another shovel."

"All right. Tomorrow I'll see if I can find us a couple more boys. They's work out the veg'ble fields now, and the gladiolas. We going have to pay em a few pennies more, but they'll come if I fetch em in the truck."

"As long as you're sitting there, doing nothing, why don't you pitch in? A little exercise might do you good."

"That's Nigra work, son. Colored don't want White folk messing with they work, just like White folk don't want Colored messing in they business. You leave this to me, Nawby. White man start working neck-a-neck with Coloreds, they lose all respect. Sho. That's a natural fact."

"You're just goddamn lazy, Vetch."

Narby flicked away his cigarette, picked up a shovel from the bed of Vetch's truck, and walked to where the men were working. It was stupid brutal work, chopping at the brush, digging out enough of the stumps and roots so a vehicle could pass. The men were stripped to the waist, streaked with sweat. Narby stood apart and started to dig. After a few moments he stopped, pulled off his sopping undershirt, heedless of showing the scars, and moved to the front where a tall powerfully-built older man, his head covered in grayish-white hair, was swinging a machete. Narby recognized him—the man he and Campos had encountered in the jungle that morning, wearing the same overalls against his bare chest.

"Good morning."

"Mo'nin," he said, not looking up from his work.

From where they stood Narby could see the white string stretched between short wooden stakes, sticking up in the brush ahead, marking the intended width and direction of the next section of road. He stepped to the side to get a better view and looked back at the length already cleared. Straight and uniform.

"That's a damned good job. You've done this kind of work before? Building a road?"

The man let the machete rest and straightened up. He was two or three inches taller than Narby. "Yes, sir."

"What else do you know how to build?"

"I done stone work. Brick. Carp'try. Gardening." He looked over Narby's shoulder, toward Vetch's truck, and turned away, swinging the machete.

It wasn't a typical Southern Negro accent, clearer, with a vaguely British lilt. "Mind if I ask your name?"

Without stopping he said, "Sam."

"Good to meet you, Sam. I'm Philip. Philip Narby."

The man nodded. Narby decided to work alongside him. The other men stayed a few yards behind. Vetch had raised himself, standing on the running board, watching.

"Goddamn hard work," he said, catching his breath. "You used to work for Putnam, did you? In the turpentine camp?"

"For a spell."

"You live out at the old camp, now? Out in Sawfish Point?"

"No, sir. Used to. No more." He straightened up, wiped the sweat from his face with his hand, and started chopping again at the brush.

He wondered if Sam had been one of the Negroes who found the boat. Still, he wasn't about to ask. Because it had never happened. "Where do you live now?"

"Over to the highway."

Narby's hands were already beginning to blister. Next time, he'd bring work gloves. After a few minutes he stopped. "Look, Sam. I might have some more work for you, after the road's cleared. Better work than this. You interested?"

The man let the machete rest. His eyes, filmed as if with dust, were set wide above high flat cheekbones, the dark skin of his face scored with tiny pits and abrasions. "Yes, sir. I could use me some decent work."

"Good. I'll let you know."

Narby walked back to the truck and threw the shovel in the bed. There was a tall filthy rusted tank of water with a spigot sitting on the tailgate. Narby leaned over and opened the spigot and let the cool water dribble down and fill his mouth.

"That Nigra water," Vetch said, coming up to him, holding out a canteen. "This here for the bosses. What the hell wrong with you, making a damn ass out of yourself? They laughing at you, Nawby."

Ignoring him Narby pulled his shirt on. Vetch had no doubt noticed the scars.

"What that Sambo say to you? Listen to me, son. That's a bad one. He done stole from me, took from the store. Only I let him go after I made him pay up, cause he just a dumb old Nigra like the rest of them. So dumb he think he smart. Hah."

"Try to find two or three more men for tomorrow. I want to have the road cleared by the end of the month."

"That's good with me. Only like I say, you got to pay em more. If they's work out in the fields, they going to take that first."

Narby figured Vetch was cheating him, skimming from the top before paying out the men. That would end soon enough. "All right. Whatever you think it takes. I'll be back in a few days."

"You leave it to me. You just getting in the way here, mucking up the flow. You ain't got no Nigra sense. That's for sho."

Narby stepped back into his truck and unscrewed the flask, looking out over the low scrub. It was harsh ugly land, waste. But with the cooler weather, the nascent road bed imposing a bit of order and purpose, he began to see it differently. He owned two hundred acres, with an option for more at the same price per hundred. Land no one wanted. Not even the County Clerk's office had an accurate plat. Secluded, without public roads, land like this might come in very useful. At the least, it was a way to park some of the money, establish a cover. People in town were getting to know him by sight, by reputation. Philip Narby was a landowner now, a man invested in the future of Lacoosa County.

Still, he always carried at least five hundred in his pocket.

12

THAT FALL NARBY WAS MAKING the trip across the estuary to Sanmora Island two or three times a week. Except for the tight-mouthed ferryman, there was rarely anyone else on board. The few cars or trucks that seemed to cross regularly were on the inverse schedule—Villagers who went into Myerton in the morning, for work or shopping, and who Narby would see waiting at the marina in the late afternoon as he rode the ferry back to Punta Rasca. If the ferryman had any curiosity about the anomalous young stranger he never expressed it, never asked Narby a question, never answered Narby's occasional inquiry with more than a nope or a yep or a shrug of indifference.

The island was about ten miles long and a half-mile wide at its broadest point. A single paved road, shaded by the tall shaggy Australian Pines, ran most of the island's length, more or less down the center, with the gaunt iron lighthouse at the southern end. The Village, a hamlet of fishermen and farmers, lay on the protected, swampy bay side. No more than five hundred inhabitants, Narby guessed. As far as he could tell, except for the row of mansions nestled in the jungle behind the dunes, the rest of Sanmora was undeveloped, and for good reason. The low narrow barrier island would be exceptionally vulnerable to tropical storms. A tidal surge from a strong hurricane might very well breach the lowest dunes, and the heavy rains flood the freshwater creek. The Village, facing inland, with many of its houses built on stilts, had no doubt withstood any number of maelstroms. But the mansions, of recent and expensive construction, were entirely exposed. Whoever had built them was a gambler, willing to exploit the pristine beauty of the dunes and the warm bright clear turquoise water, the thalassic breezes and exotic coastal jungle, despite the high chance of disaster.

Narby came to swim and wander the miles of deserted beach. He brought food, water, tobacco, bourbon and Benzedrine. Three times now, ducking into the scrub, he had watched the seaplane pass overhead, though where it landed, or its relation to the opulent unoccupied mansions, remained a mystery.

In late November things began to change. He was waiting in the truck at Punta Rasca as the ferry approached, the water of the bay slivery smooth, the billowing masses of red mangrove stark and glowing against the oblique morning light, thousands of birds—pelicans, herons, scarlet and white ibis, the comical roseate spoonbills—stalking and floating, dotting the placid surface. Three vehicles crossed from the island that morning: a truck and an old Chevy Bel-Air, typical ferry traffic, and to his surprise, a black Mark II Lincoln Continental. Over the next few weeks there were others: a Thunderbird convertible, a Mercedes-Benz sports car, and service vehicles coming over from Myerton—Mike's Landscaping, Ace Pool and Plumbing, Bullock's Plaster and Drywall.

Normally, Narby didn't go through the Village, turning south on the main road from the ferry landing toward the beach access at the lighthouse. But one morning he decided to follow one of the trucks that had crossed on the ferry with him. Passing through the Village, he noticed two rather luxurious yachts docked among the fishing boats and dinghies at the marina, the polished teak and chrome catching the morning sun. About a mile beyond the Village the truck turned into a hidden driveway of some sort, through a breach in the thickets. A chain hung with a PRIVATE PROPERTY sign blocked the way.

Narby pulled over and watched: the driver drove his truck up to the chain, unhooked it, pulled through, and then got out again to hook it in place. Narby could easily do the same, but he was quite certain that the private road led to the mansions. The only other way to reach them, short of bushwhacking the jungle or landing a boat or seaplane at the beach, was from the lighthouse, a two-and-a-half mile trek along the dunes and then crossing the mouth of the creek.

By mid-December he began to encounter them on the beach. The first, long part of the walk—from the lighthouse to the creek—was deserted as usual, a Robinson Crusoe realm of jungle and sea with never a footprint but his own impressed in the wet sand. Still, he was careful, and no longer dared to go naked. At the creek, when the tide was low, he would wade. At higher tides he would fling his rucksack across and swim, the rapidly moving water of braided cool and warm pushing him seaward. Once on the other side he put on a shirt, covering the scars.

The first one he saw was a woman of some years, maybe fifty, dressed in a flowing blouse and a billowing skirt that reached her shins, her face shaded under a wide-brim sunhat. She was walking barefoot along the surf, collecting shells with great concentration, bending and picking up, inspecting, putting a few specimens in the basket slung over her shoulder and discarding the rest. They passed within twenty yards, saying nothing, though of course she had noticed him. The next time, a week later, it was a middle-aged couple, cocktails in hand, their red Irish setter bounding along the sand beside them; and then, two children playing in the waves, supervised by an older sister or more likely a nanny, sitting on a canvas chair under a beach umbrella. People from New York, Boston, Chicago, he supposed, arrived for the winter season. People who were wealthy enough, influential enough, to command their own yachts and seaplanes and build opulent houses that stood empty nine months of the year. People who obviously didn't care to mix with the ordinary run of tourists in Miami Beach or Havana.

When the opportunity showed itself, Narby decided, he would initiate contact. But he had to be careful. No matter how unlikely, there was always the chance someone might recognize him. Of course, he would deny it, just as he had with Bill Knowles. Merely to think about all that made him queasy. If only he could get rid of him forever, this person that Knowles had burdened with the name Tom or Jim, this thing that dogged him, always threatening to come out of the shadows. Hadn't it died already, bleeding and gasping in that shit-water ditch near the Naktong River? It was best not to think about it, expunge it from his mind.

One day in January he walked nearly the entire length of the island, miles up the beach past the creek and the hidden mansions, almost to the northern tip of the island. On his way back—late afternoon, the sky streaked and blustery, a cool wind coming off the Gulf—past the wooden walkways but before the reaching the inlet, he noticed someone up ahead, standing ankle deep in the foam, gazing out over the water. A young woman. Alone. He had never seen her before. He would have remembered.

When he had first caught sight of her, from a distance, she had been looking in his direction. But as he approached she had turned her head. In a minute he would pass within five feet of her. Close enough to exchange hellos, or be snubbed.

She was shading her eyes with her hand, her hair—tawny blonde, the color of wheat, cut shoulder length—flying in the wind, her blouse and loose white trousers rippling, wrapping about her torso and legs.

He was in bathing trunks, an old T-shirt, his hair matted from swimming, the battered rucksack slung over his shoulder. He hadn't bothered to shave that morning. Like some kind of beach bum. On the other hand, he was in excellent physical condition. None of the mansion men—at least the ones Narby had passed on the beach over the last two months—could say the same.

Coming closer, realizing how attractive she was, striking even, his determination wavered. Whatever she was staring at seemed to absorb her, though to his eyes there was nothing there, just the bright undulant surface of the blue-green water, livelier than usual with the wind. Maybe he wouldn't speak, but neither would he veer away.

He was about to pass. Quite naturally, as though they already knew each other, she turned his way and said, "Look," and then gazed back toward the water, shading her eyes and pointing with her other hand. "Do you see them? Dolphins. You can just make out their fins breaching the surface. Over there. Look."

So he stopped and stood beside her.

After a moment, she said, "Oh, damn. They're gone."

But because he hadn't known precisely where to look, hadn't fixed his eyes on one spot, Narby's vision was more mobile and he saw them come up. "There they are. Over there."

Her hair whipped about her face. She was almost his height, with broad shoulders. Her face, lightly freckled, complimented the complexion of her hair, blonde and tawny and fresh.

"Yes. I see them. How magnificent. Such freedom and grace."

They said nothing more, watching until the fins disappeared again.

"I don't think we've met, " she said, giving up on the dolphins, somewhat abruptly turning and facing him. "I'm Willa Branton." She put out her hand, shaking like a man, a strong quick grip.

"Philip Narby. Pleased to meet you."

"Hello, Philip Narby. Odd, I thought by now I knew just about everyone on the island. At least by sight. I certainly haven't seen you at Tara's. Haven't seen you at the Mucky Duck. Post office? Turner's store? No." She cocked her head, like a curious dog. "Explain yourself, stranger." It was a joke. She was smiling.

"Just taking a walk. I live on the mainland. Out in the county."

"Oh. I see." She paused. He felt as though she were sizing him up. She wore no make up. Her eyes were green, striated with flecks of dark brown, her lips full and pale. "You must be one of those interlopers everyone talks about at our meetings. Did you know that?" She laughed softly. The wind had a damp bite. She wrapped her arms about her torso, either because she was chilled or perhaps because he had been looking at her a bit too intently.

"An interloper?"

"Let me show you." Taking a few steps toward the dunes she picked up a stick of driftwood and etched a line in the wet hard-packed sand. "We, the owners of Island Property, own the rights to the beachfront right up to here. You, the stranger, must stay on this side. The tidal zone. Unfortunately, as much as certain people around here would wish, the ocean itself is not up for sale. Not yet, anyway."

She was smiling, kidding around, prolonging what otherwise would have been a passing, forgettable encounter.

"All right." He leapt over the line, his feet sinking into the muddier sand. "That better?"

She laughed. "My well-intentioned neighbors," she said, waving the stick in the general direction of the mansions. "What they'd really like is to draw the line there." She hurled the driftwood out into the waves. "But it's illegal. It's damned un-American. This land is your land, this land is my land. From sea to shining sea."

He might have thought she was drunk or high, but her voice was steady and her eyes focused and intelligent, in full control. It was something else.

"You live here. On the island?"

"Just down the strand. When I'm not in New York." She reached in the pocket of the loose white rippling trousers. "Would you like a cigarette?"

"Yeah. Thanks." His took his windproof Zippo from the rucksack. Huddling next to her he cupped his hand to shield the flame as he lit her cigarette. She was very close, then she backed away, and he turned, hunching against the wind to light the cigarette she had given him.

"Must be a front blowing in. Brrr. Aren't you cold? Going this way?" She indicated north, back toward the mansions.

She had seen him coming down the beach, walking in the opposite direction. It was an invitation. "Sure. Why not?"

As they walked she deflected her attention out toward the water. "God, I love it here." She looked at him again, more deliberately now—his trunks, the damp T-shirt, his matted hair. "You're a swimmer?"

"Yes. Keeps me fit. How about you?"

She shook her head. "Not a chance. I love to look at it, smell it in my hair, feel it on my skin. I don't think I could ever live away from the ocean for very long. But going in deeper than my knees. Frankly, it gives me the shivers. In fact, it terrifies me."

What kind of woman would talk like this, to a man she didn't know? She was at least thirty, he guessed. But he couldn't figure her as a wife or a mother. "That's too bad. Even if you don't swim, there's no reason to be afraid."

"A reason? Since when does fear require a reason? Besides, I find it interesting. Inspiring, actually. To love something that arouses fear. We have our pact, the oceans and I." She paused, as though reconsidering. "How far out do you go?"

"I don't know. Maybe thirty yards. It drops off pretty quick."

"As far as where those dolphins were swimming?"

"Sometimes."

She walked with her feet in the sheets of rolling foam, looking at him and then away at the water and then down at where her feet sank into the fine-grained mud. They were close enough to touch.

"I find the most amazing things on this beach. Enormous conch shells, strange black leathery seedpods, rusted old trinkets, turtle eggs, a dead baby octopus. I even found the proverbial bottle with a note in it. No kidding. The ink had bled and blurred, so I couldn't make it out. Some poor shipwreck is still out there on his desert island, hoping to get rescued. That's part of our pact. I don't go in, don't disturb, and in return the sea offers up its mysteries." Again, she cocked her head. "Like you, for instance."

He tried to find something to say, but decided only to smile. A half-step behind her he noted the outline of her thighs, her buttocks and breasts as the wind wrapped her tightly in the diaphanous clothing. He couldn't very well reach out and paw this kind of a woman, couldn't talk to her or leer at her the way he did a whore, the way he had with Janet. Or Martha. Or Miss Prentice as the bank.

They had passed the first of the walkways that jutted out between the dunes. She led him away from the surf. At the foot of the third walkway with its private property sign, she stopped.

"Here's my place," she said. She took a last drag from the cigarette and flicked it, sparking, into the sand. "I'd ask you in. Poor thing, you're all goose bumped. Don't you have a jacket or something? But, well, it's not a good time. At the moment."

She had stepped up onto the walkway. Over her shoulder he could see the house, the modern one: three boxy rectilinear structures of smooth silken-gray concrete set at angles to one other, the facades broken with geometrical precision by picture windows of various sizes. On the second floor a cantilevered slab of concrete, a terrace of some sort, thrust itself forward, hovering over the edge of the swimming pool.

Her hair was flying. She pushed it out of her eyes.

"Another time, then."

"It's a big mess at the moment. I have to clear out some old junk first, you see. And then. Well, the fact is, I leave for New York on Wednesday and I'm not sure when I'll manage to get back. But. Well, you aren't going anywhere, are you?"

"No plans to."

"You'll be here next fall. October. Yes?"

"Chances are good."

They were standing only a few feet apart. The wind was at his back now, gusting, like a hand nudging him toward her. "Tell me your name again."

"Philip. Philip Narby." He hesitated, then said, "and you're Willa Branton."

She laughed. "Good memory. So, you won't forget, will you?" "Forget?"

"To find me. In October. On the beach, just like today. In fact, I dare you."

"Dare accepted."

"Good. I'll have everything cleared out by then." As if it were nothing, she stepped closer and leaned forward and kissed him on the mouth, quickly, lightly, without embrace. "That was foolish," she said, bringing her head straight, shrugging. "I don't give a damn. There are things you either know right away, or never."

She glanced back over her shoulder, at the house. Now he understood. There was someone inside, waiting for her. "So long, Philip. Until October."

He watched her stride the length of the walkway, her arms wrapped about her. The garden was bordered by a low hedge and a gate. She unwound her arms, unlatched the gate, disappearing at it swung closed behind her, not once looking back.

13

HE WOKE UP LATE, FEELING SICK. In a few hours he would meet with Campos. He had to get up, put a little food into his stomach, maybe take a swim. Clear away the nightmares.

This time it was Ted McCoy who had strapped him to the gurney. And Sid Black whose body lay crumpled on the side of the road—the road Tom or Jim had traveled, in the back of convoy, from the port in Pusan into the hills behind the Naktong River—his hands bound behind his back with wire, a black oozing hole perforating his temple. And then Narby was running down the steep hillside, ducking from invisible fire. Only how he could run and be strapped in the gurney at the same time? Because it was only a goddamn dream.

He got out of bed and went into the sitting room, pushed aside the heavy curtains and squinting against the sun slid open the glass door to let in the ocean breeze, clear the room of the chemical air-conditioning smell, the stale smoke and perfume. The night had been a waste, a humiliation. He had paid fifty dollars, for nothing. She wasn't bad looking, at least not by Alton Road standards. But after the initial stimulation he had lost interest, hadn't been able to finish. It had put him in an ugly mood. In a rather ungentlemanly tone of voice, as he recalled, he had told her to leave.

Standing under the shower he tried to remember, twist the blur of the evening into focus, retrace his steps. He couldn't afford to make a mistake, to do something stupid and then, even worse, let it slip his mind.

Yesterday afternoon, as before, everything had gone smoothly at the bank, no questions asked even though he had increased the amount of the withdrawal to fifteen hundred. Still, it was goddamn nerve wracking, worse than Havana because Wilson was always hanging around with that dullard's solicitous smile, looking over the teller's shoulder as she counted out the bills. Looking down her blouse, too, into the creamy vortex. And as before, stepping out of the bank into the glare and the heat, that surging current of thrill and relief, like a shot of dope. That was dangerous, because it made him careless. Stupid, too. Because the money wasn't really his. He ought never to forget that. He was working for Bill Knowles.

After the bank, the drive from Coral Gables to Miami Beach, crossing Biscayne Bay over the General Douglas MacArthur Causeway, parking the truck in the Michigan Avenue garage and then hailing a cab to take him to the Atlantique—the diversionary maneuver with the garage was perhaps no longer necessary, but it was part of an established sequence. He ought not risk forgoing it, simply for the sake of convenience. Oh his way to the room he might have stopped first at the hotel cocktail lounge for a drink. Playing the little staring-game with the bored wives or the single girls who came down to Miami Beach in groups, to see who would look away first; a game he would always win. Or was that later, on his way to Giovanni's for dinner? But he remembered a swim, the ocean rather placid in May. In either case, before leaving the room he would have taken what money he needed for the evening's entertainment and hidden the rest, seeding the dresser drawer with a couple of twenties. He'd had plenty to drink by then, and because he knew he'd be stopping at Stennart's on the way out town, to replenish, he had been rather liberal with the dope, too. The fifteen-hundred had given him ideas, Knowles or no Knowles.

He had dined at Giovanni's, on Espanola Way. The raven-haired hat-check girl liked to flirt with him, but when he had tried to follow up, she had laughed, taken aback, informing him that she had a steady boyfriend. He was too avid, too direct. All the usual preliminaries—the getting-to-know-you chit chat, holding hands at midnight beneath a starry sky—to him it was like a chant in some dead language, the rituals of an extinct civilization. The whores, Martha, Janet. That was all he knew. And the woman on Sanmora, Willa Branton. The way she had kissed him. He got all worked up, just thinking about that kiss. About what might happen, next October.

After Giovanni's it was more a blur. He had picked her up at one of the Alton Road dives, brought her back to the hotel. But at what point had he paid her? Suddenly, trying to remember, he suffered a slight panic. He got out of the shower and dried off and went into the sitting room. The attaché was on the coffee table. He lit a cigarette and sat on the love seat and opened it. Papers, magazines, clippings, his black notebook, a few articles of clothing, tobacco, but no money. Because of course he had hidden it. He went into the bathroom and kneeling opened the cabinet under the sink, looking inside and then reaching in, around the drainpipe, and running his hand against the back. But he had been given a different suite this time, on the ninth floor. There was nothing there. He checked the dresser drawers, under the mattress and the cushions of the love seat. Nothing.

No matter how far gone he had been, would he have been so stupid, so desperate, as to let her see it, tease her with it? After his rather humiliating failure, after telling her to leave, he perhaps had taken another white pill, to help him sleep. Sometimes, after a night of heavy drinking, the dollies—or whatever the hell it was that Stennart was selling him—made him black out and there would be a gap in his memory, a blank hiss like an erasure on a tape recording. He checked the door: bolted from inside. After she had left, no one had disturbed him. The money was somewhere in the room.

It would have excited her, excited both of them, fanning out the fifteen-hundred, touching it, whipping up her entrepreneurial imagination. They had gotten into it rather deep. But all the while it had been an effort to keep himself interested, at attention. He had a picture now: on her back, her legs up in the air, and him bearing down, and then there was a knocking, someone banging. An obnoxious distracting noise.

Narby put out the cigarette and went into the bedroom. Kneeling on the bed he reached behind the headboard and yanked out the fat white envelope, stuffed with twenties. Just the right thickness. He had wedged it there last night, to stop the headboard from smacking against the wall.

He unclenched, counting the bills. It was all there, minus last night's expenses. Christ, he had to be more careful with the dope. More than that, he needed a real woman. The pay-as-you-go approach had lost its appeal. It was making him sick.

He called room service and got dressed. An aging Negro in a white coat with gold buttons delivered coffee and a mess of ham and eggs. It was just as Campos said. The only Negroes on Miami Beach were bellboys, dishwashers, maids, garbage men, laborers. The Miami Beach City Hall ran the town as if it were a private country club. He turned on the television and watched as he ate. The McCarthy hearings. Again. That petty nonsense with Schine and Cohn and the Army. The baggy-faced lush from Wisconsin was on the defensive. *Mr. Welch, you are not the first individual that tried to get me to betray the confidence and give out the names of my informants. You can go right ahead and try until doomsday. You will not get the names… I don't remember… I don't recall… I wouldn't know.*

Playing dumb. Still breasting his hand of commies and queers and traitors, the same bluff over and over and over. Apparently, McCarthy's usefulness was finally coming to an end. His handlers were turning on him. Same China Lobby crowd that had backed MacArthur and Willoughby. Like a rabid dog that finally had to be chained, put down.

Two weeks of this inane disgraceful mewling. Biggest show on earth. Kept the masses distracted from what was really happening, like the French falling to pieces in Indo-china, the debacle in Dien Bien Phu. The old European bullies had lost their nerve and the Americans would have to take up the slack. With Korea finished the rest of it was starting to boil up. North Africa, Indonesia, the banana republics, Arabia. The proxy civil rebellions, the tribal wars. Under the new conditions the blunt-headed bomb-drunk generals were worse than useless. With all their lip service to liberty and democracy and self-determination, the Americans were going to have to find a smarter way to go about it. Keep the White faces behind the scenes. Have Yellow men kill Yellow men instead. Pit Black and Brown against Black and Brown. The Soviets would no doubt follow suit.

He pushed aside the breakfast dishes and administered his morning dose of bourbon. *I will not name them… I will not betray… the love of my country… no conception of the insidious communist infiltration that my ceaseless investigations… my duty… my country… my God.* You had to hand it to him. Played it to the hilt. Method acting, like Brando in the role of that motorcycle tough. Narby lifted his glass. "Here's to you, tail-gunner Joe."

After a moment he switched it off, took the bills from the envelope, separated out the five hundred for Campos and began copying the serial numbers into the black notebook. The Cuban was getting stingy with the information. The 26 July Movement was reorganizing in Miami, as well as in Caracas and Mexico City. The leader Castro was still imprisoned on the Isle of Pines. Batista was probably keeping him alive as some kind of bargaining chip, a concession to public sentiment. That much Narby had gleaned from the newspapers. What he wanted from Campos was names, where they were buying weapons, their ties to other nationalist movements, their contacts in the Soviet Union. Maybe Campos was playing him a bit. That was entirely understandable. But Ernesto was sentimental, a romantic, his mind clouded by all that hocus-pocus about colonial consciousness and the will of the people. That gave Nary the advantage. The more Campos believed in Truth, the more susceptible he was to delusion and manipulation.

Besides, their friendship was genuine. Narby wished the Cuban no harm. Batista was scum, human garbage momentarily lifted by the accidental tides of history. Their affection, their mutual hatreds, would serve Narby well. Sooner or later, Campos would let his guard down.

In the meantime, Narby was recording everything: the serial number of every note he handed over, every scrap of conversation he could remember, every detail of their meetings. There was a chance, of course, that Knowles might not want that money too readily traced. The circulation of those bills might tell a rather embarrassing story. From Master Sergeant Sid Black's illegal operations in Occupied Tokyo, through Seoul, Manila, Havana, Coral Gables, Miami's Colored Overtown, and then perhaps to Mexico City or Caracas and exchanged for weapons. If the arms dealer had a yen for gambling or a taste for those peculiar sexual entertainments that only Havana could provide, one of the twenties in Narby's hand right now might very well wind up in the pocket of Batista himself, taking his cut from the casinos and brothels and casas de exhibiciónes.

Narby had no means of interpreting Knowles's silence. Aside from that one vague letter months ago, not a word. Like the silence of God, Narby supposed, the old Robinson Crusoe gambit. If things went well, despite the misfortunes of ship-wreck and desertion, He was behind you. Watching your back. In return, you kept the account books, tallied them up and deliv-ered them to Him in your prayers.

Unfortunately, there was no time for a swim. Narby closed the flask, finished dressing, availed himself of a Benzedrine inhaler and packed the attaché. The heat was bearable that afternoon, so he decided to walk from the hotel to the parking garage on Michigan Avenue. In the truck he changed out of his sports clothes—the silk and linen refurbished that winter at a Lincoln Road haberdasher—into a T-shirt and a pair of khaki trousers and sandals.

The new drop-off spot was a truck stop on US 1 in North Miami. He got there early and found a good vantage, parking on the shoulder about thirty yards down the highway, partially hidden behind a stand of melaleuca. Narby figured they'd be coming from the south. Campos seemed to have three or four drivers at his disposal, each with his own car. And they were usually late. Another Cuban trait, like the fog of cologne, the crisply laundered shirts and the finicky moustache.

At ten after two he spotted them, an olive-green Ford Victoria, a 49 or 50. He jotted down the tag number and put the truck in gear. The driver never got out of the car, but Narby got a good look at him as they turned off the highway, a hulking swarthy oval-faced man in dark glasses, with thick black curly hair. There was a potholed asphalt parking area on the far side of the gas pumps. The Victoria pulled over and waited. Narby stopped at the first pump and told the attendant to fill it and check the oil. He got out of the truck, the envelope tucked into his waist, and walked over to the soda machine. Campos followed a few seconds later, digging in his for pocket for a coin.

"Hello, Ernesto."

"Felipé. Como está?"

"What's your pleasure? Grape? Bubble Up?" Narby pushed the dime through the slot, mashed the button, and after the thump took the cold wet bottle from under the flap. "R.C. Cola? I didn't press that one. It's a goddamn monopoly." He snapped off the cap and handed the bottle to Ernesto and put in another dime. With his other hand he pulled out the envelope and turning, his back to the machine, passed it to Ernesto.

"Gracias, amigo."

They moved to the side, drinking the sodas, two travelers striking up a casual conversation: a compact nattily dressed businessman of suspect complexion and a working man, tall, well-built, fair skinned and blue eyed. "Ernesto. I can't keep doing this blindly. I've got my own people to report to. Mis jefes. My bosses. They want something more for their money."

"No pasa nada. We only for to organize now. Keep from Batista's police. We lose two friends, la semana pasada, en Mexico. We are afraid for Castro, en la cárcel."

"That's not good enough. You can't just sit around, waiting. Hiding. Tiene que golpear. You have to hit Batista again. Show the people that you're still strong. Let me help you."

"Puede ser. Only is very dangerous."

"You don't get it, do you? You think you'd be standing here right now, alive and breathing, if my friends and I weren't already in on it? Who the hell do you think is keeping Batista from putting your precious Fidel in front of the firing squad? Me entiendes? We have people on the inside. Ready to go. There's no other way."

"I can no decide only myself. I am only small part."

"Mierda. Take charge, damn it. While you still can."

Campos smiled. "You are American individualist. Cowboy. You have no understand for the collective action. Without the people, we are nothing. I am nothing." "Sometimes you need a cowboy to round them up, these people of yours. Lead them to greener pastures. A la tierra de promisión."

"Like you Americans do for los Indios? For los Negroes? Very nice. Muy agradable."

The hulk in the green Victoria was getting impatient, nodding his head at Ernesto from across the lot.

"One month. I give you answer." He tossed the empty bottle in a trashcan and returned to the waiting car. The Victoria turned around and pulled out onto the highway.

Narby walked back to his truck. The station attendant was wiping the dipstick. "You're almost a quart low, pal. Looks like you got a leak somewheres. Want me to add some oil?"

Narby's hands were sticky from the soda. Sugar. Oil. Copper. Magnesium. Rum. Gambling. Dope. Beach resorts, country clubs, cigars, marlin fishing, the sex trade. The gateway to the Caribbean and the oil fields off the coast of Mexico and Venezuela. It was quite a shopping list. But what about the Cuban people? They were indeed an untapped resource. Only what were they worth? Perhaps Campos had a point.

"Sure. Might as well toss half a dozen more quart cans in the back, while you're at it. Wouldn't want to run out of oil, now would I?"

Thirty minutes later Narby pulled into a seedy little strip of shops just off Eighth Street, near the Miami city limits. At the far end of the parking lot was a glass and metal door, *Stennart's Drugs and Medical Supply* stenciled on the top pane. He pushed it open. It was a narrow chaotic space, more storage closet than shop, the high metal shelves crammed haphazardly with bottles and cartons and boxes, the air sour, a hospital stink of ammonia and ether. At the back, behind a rusted mesh grate, was the pharmacist's window. Narby pushed the bell and the window slid open.

"Yeah?"

"Good afternoon."

The face—gaunt, putty gray, thick horn-rimmed glasses— squinted. "Oh. It's you."

"Three boxes. More, if you have them."

It was illegal now to sell Benzedrine in any form without a doctor's prescription. But Stennart was a private business- man. He had every right to unload his back stock, accumulated before the regulatory changes. With supply low and demand high, prices were at a premium. And Stennart didn't like to sell more than three boxes at a time. Narby had inquired about Dolophine. Nothing doing. But Stennart had unmarked bottles of pills—sleeping aids, analgesics, muscle relaxants—that he was willing to throw in for twenty a piece. Use at your own risk.

In the parking lot Narby broke open two inhaler capsules, and then swallowed a couple of pills, a blue and a white. Fifteen minutes out of Miami, past the last gimcrack motels, the radio signal decayed into static and he turned it off. It was a long hot tedious drive, four hours across the glaring expanse of mud and tall grass, with only the little islands of hardwood trees and outcroppings of royal palms scattered in the distance to break the monotony.

Green eyes, pale wind-chapped lips, long seductive legs. Kissing him on the mouth, as if they were already lovers. Willa Branton. He hadn't stopped thinking about her for a single day.

True to her word, she had disappeared. They had all disap- peared: the shell collector, the dog walkers, the drink-in-hand beach strollers, the children and their nanny. Since the middle of March, the dunes behind the mansions again deserted, the two yachts docked all winter at the Village marina gone, or perhaps put into dry dock. No more flashy luxury cars on the ferry. No buzz of the seaplane.

The Villagers called it the "Colony." Narby had looked up the records at the County Clerk's office in Myerton. The land—about five hundred acres of coastal jungle—was registered to a single entity, Isadora Land and Trust, P.O. Box 49, Wilmington, Delaware. Dalton Pembaker, General Partner. If the owners of the individual mansions held deeds to their properties, they had not been recorded at the Clerk's Office. The name Willa Branton appeared nowhere in the documents.

What would he do until October, until he saw her again, made good on the promise of that kiss? If it weren't for Frank he'd pick up with Janet, just to tide him over. Hang around at the library, provoke her until she broke down, take advantage of her desperation, even rape her if he had to, just to get her to feel something, to crave it. It was Frank's fault. What the hell had he done to her? Maybe Frank's balls had been blown off in Korea. Maybe that was why Frank limped and scowled, boiling alive in his own impotent flesh. Maybe it was Frank who needed to be batted around. Maybe that would thrill her, shock her out of her paralysis—watching Narby, her lover, beat the living crap out of the gimpy lieutenant and then, together, both of them driving out to the cypress swamps and dumping the body, fresh meat for the alligators.

Narby began to laugh. It was a Benzedrine jag. He was going to burn out if he wasn't careful. And he was going to need something more than a fantasy to appease him. Until October.

It was six o'clock by the time Narby reached the fork where the pavement ended, Vetch's idiotic Fish Camp sign nailed into the trunk of a scrub pine. Narby's road veered left, an unpaved swath cut through the shoulder-high palmetto scrub. He drove at a crawl for another quarter of a mile, the truck lurching from side to side, until he came to Sam Water's flatbed parked in the clearing.

He was late. The men, having quit for the day, were resting in the bed of Water's truck, waiting—a crew of six that week, men from the turpentine camp or from Henderson Avenue, the Negro section of Myerton. They had made good progress. There had been no rain for weeks and everything was dry, the mosquitoes down. Waters was still at it, working by himself, measuring and marking a stack of two-by-four planks, wearing his usual overalls over a bare chest, tufted with whitish-gray hair. The man never wasted a moment, never fooled around. Narby no longer went through Vetch. Sam Waters worked directly for him now.

"Hello, Sam. Sorry I'm late. Looks like you had a busy week."

Waters stopped his work, looked up.

"Mind showing me what you've done."

It was a simple island-style house, like the ones Waters knew from the Bahamas, where he had grown up. They had cleared a good-sized patch of land with shovels and axes and machetes, pulling out the larger stumps with chains hooked to the bumper of Waters' flatbed. The foundation, the four corner-posts built of limestone blocks, was nearly finished. The house would rest two feet off the ground. There would be a wide porch, windows with louvered shutters that hinged from above, everything designed to maximize air flow and shade. Every few weeks Waters told Narby what materials they needed and Narby bought them and had Waters pick everything up in his truck: native limestone cut from the Florida rim, bags of mortar and cement, lumber— Waters had recommended the durable, more expensive Dade County pine rather than the inferior pine from the sawmills up north in Perrine.

"What's all this?"

The entire space of the building's footprint was covered with a layer of chalky-white crumbled rock.

"That kill off all the weeds and them. We spread that this morning. Don't want nothing coming up under the floor."

His voice was deep, easier to understand than the others. Waters had migrated to the Florida Keys from the island of Eleuthra some forty years ago, a teenager looking for work with Flagler's railroad, clearing mangrove. There was still something vaguely British beneath the Southern Negro talk he had picked up since then.

"I don't remember buying any of that."

"No, sir. We dig it up. They's patches all round here. Wherever they ground is bald." Waters reached down and picked up a fistful and crumbled it in his hand. "They's sea shells and such. Cain't nothing grow root in that. Dry hard, if you wets it. Spread it on the road, too, if you want. Makes a fair hard surface."

"Good. Let's do that."

"Only we need more water. Cain't tote that much in the truck."

"All right. Let's get the well drilled. You know anyone who does that?" Narby preferred to hire Negroes, to let Waters arrange things himself as much as possible. The fewer White people in Myerton who knew, the better. Over the last six months Narby had purchased three tracts in Sawfish Point, a total of three hundred acres now from the Putnam Lumber Company and another hundred from a rancher in Ocala who had given up on the idea of clearing it for cattle pasture. The name Philip Narby was on record at the County Clerk's office, but he doubted that anyone other than Vetch and the tax collector had taken much notice.

"I know a man in Tampa with a rig. Maybe get him down to drill it. "

"Good. Let's go over the payroll."

Waters went to his truck and came back holding a few sheets of soiled paper. Narby made a pretense of checking the figures. He wanted Waters to like him, trust him; wanted the men in the crew on his side. He handed the paper back to Sam—noticing, again, the grayish film over the man's eyes, the skin of his face textured with thousands of tiny scars and pits and scalds, as if he had been splashed with burning liquid or acid—pulled a roll of twenties from his pocket, and peeled off the week's wages.

"There's a little extra. For the good work."

Waters merely nodded. That was fine with Narby. They understood each other, man to man.

14

IN ALL THE TIME NARBY had been staying in Cabin 101, the manager Dindridge had never kept the neon bell burning past ten. But last night the thing had been left on, throwing its lurid pinkish-green glow across the gravel, the electrical buzz rattling until dawn. What was more, Narby had noticed a light in the rooms behind the motel office, where the withered old man lived with his wife. Narby had waited and waited. He didn't like leaving that much money in the cabin, even for a single day.

Around midnight, growing impatient, he had stepped out. A moonless overcast night. The tint of neon coated his skin like a glaze. A car passing on the highway, anyone watching from the motel office, might see him, their eyes drawn as if toward a lone freakish figure creeping across a stage. He had walked to the truck, opened the door pretending to look for something in the glove compartment—a pointless charade, perhaps—and then returned to the cabin.

He couldn't risk being seen—passing in front of the cabin and then inexplicably disappearing into the underbrush behind the motel. Couldn't risk Dindridge hearing the low but unmistakable sound of feet scraping gravel, the rustle and crackle as he pushed through the thickets.

It was the same tonight: ten-thirty already and the neon bell still burning and the lights on in the office window. And now there was a car parked in front of cabin 108, a Pontiac sedan with Ohio plates. Earlier, he he'd heard children's voices, squealing. It was safer to wait until just before dawn, the underbrush dripping with dew, swarming with mosquitoes. How loathsome it was, this skulking and creeping in the filth.

Narby stood by the screen door, shirtless, smoking, looking out into the lot and the absurd bell and the darkness of the highway. It wouldn't be long, two more months perhaps, until the house was finished. With his own private road, his own well for water and a gas-powered generator for electricity, surrounded by miles of jungle, he would be protected, coming and going as he pleased, answerable to no one. He could keep out whomever he wished, hide whatever needed to be kept hidden.

Unconsciously, he realized, he'd been running his fingers up and down the rough fleshy ridge of scars. Caught in the weird neon light diffusing through the screen door the scars appeared even more hideous. How would she react? Would it disgust her, arouse her pity? Or draw her in, fascinate her? He guessed the latter. She had dared to kiss him in a blatantly sexual manner, a complete stranger, something found washed up on the dunes. His disfigurement, his distance from other men, would attract her.

As he turned to pour another drink, something caught his attention—coming down the dark empty highway, flickering through the underbrush, an intimation of head beams. Then the sound of a truck. Vetch's truck. He put down the bottle and opened the kitchenette drawer and took out the knife, a six-inch serrated blade. There wasn't much of an edge to it. But a swift jab, the point plunging into Vetch's throat or gut, would suffice. He set it on the Formica counter, within easy reach from the table, and covered it with a dishtowel.

The beams grew brighter. The truck slowed and turned, the rusted roof of the Ford showing purple under the pinkish-green neon as it pulled into the lot, the engine spluttering and the tires crushing the gravel.

By now, Vetch might have figured things out. Though perhaps he was only coming to demand his cut of the men's wages, to bitch about Narby paying Sam Waters directly. He went into the bedroom and pulled on a T-shirt. The attaché with the money from yesterday's withdrawal sat on the dresser. Narby had managed to avoid Vetch for almost a month. Or had he? All the while, Vetch might have been following him at a safe remove, perhaps all the way to the bank in Coral Gables. Some instinct for survival had given Vetch the hope that there might be money, here, in the cabin. The same instinct that had led Vetch to the boat and the dead pilot.

It had been quite simple, everything paid in cash, the documents signed in a realtor's office in Tampa. Unincorporated county land, without zoning or regulation. He had divided up the Putnam tract and to placate Vetch, to keep the Southerner's mouth from running, had deeded the land surrounding the store to Vetch—twenty-five acres of pine waste. But the strip of land between Vetch's store and the mangrove estuary now belonged solely to Philip Narby. Vetch was setting up his pathetic fish camp, the plywood cabins and the dock and boat launch, on Narby's property. The ruts connecting Vetch's store to Burnt Farm Road and from there to the highway now passed across Narby's land. If Vetch ever again tried to blackmail or threaten him, Narby would put up a gate, block access, have the dock torn out, the cabins burned to the ground.

Narby stood out of the light, watching through the screen. Vetch cut the motor and got out of the truck, slamming the door, his bulbous form silhouetted against the carnival neon of the bell. The ex-commissionaire stepped up to the cabin door and tapped rather genteelly.

"Nawby? You in there? It's me. Carl Vetch."

Narby stepped forward.

"What do you want?"

"Hah. It's Sad'day night, Mr. New Yoke. This ain't business, Nawby. It's a pus'nal call. Mind if I come inside?"

His voice was oddly relaxed, almost wobbly. Decked out in newly laundered clothes, the red-striped shirt and brown trousers unstained and pressed. His thinning brown hair was slicked back, the round flat face freshly shaved and nicked. And he reeked of talcum powder, like an old lady in church.

Narby unlatched the screen door. "Christ, Carl. You getting married?"

"Hah. Come to think on it, maybe I am." He nodded at the bottle of Jim Beam on the table. "Ain't you going to offer me a drink? It's Sad'day night, after all." He was half crocked. In the lit-up buoyant phase. That was always an unknown, which way a man would go, toward gushiness or belligerence, with the next drink.

"Have a seat, Carl." Narby pushed the bottle toward his guest and took down a jelly-jar glass. "Help yourself."

Vetch lowered himself into the chair, blowing out a breath. "Thank you. That fan feels right refreshing. Hot night like this, a man needs to cool down. Release his heat." He reached for the bottle, then uncorked it and carefully, almost gingerly, poured himself an inch. "It's the good stuff, is it?"

"Only the best around here."

Narby leaned back, his hand on the counter. He'd never seen Vetch so defenseless. One swift motion, a few seconds of existence wrenched out of eternity, and it would be finished, the knife handle protruding from Vetch's windpipe and then Vetch gurgling a bit, tipping and falling backward in the chair. Only there would be a great spurt of blood and perhaps prolonged writhing.

Narby watched as Vetch poured and took a drink, setting the glass down with the inebriate's deliberation, as if afraid it might shatter. "What's on your mind, Carl?"

Bending forward the Southerner pulled from his trouser pocket the paper pouch of Top and a white handkerchief. He put the tobacco on the table, pried the cracked steel-rim glasses from his face and dabbed at his forehead. Without the eyeglasses, exposed to the air, his small dark button eyes receded further into the pale sockets—the eyes of something that lived under rocks, or in a cave. "You going to sit and have a drink with me, or ain't you?"

After a few drinks Narby could easily cajole him back to truck. Far better to do it there, in Vetch's own truck. Then he would drive the body back to the store, haul it inside, and walk the three miles through the jungle, in the darkness, back to the Glo-Bel. None of the Negroes who stopped by for a nickel of chewing tobacco or a soda pop would dare report it. It might be months, years even, before any White person found him, putrefied beyond recognition.

"All right." Narby sat at the table. "To your health."

"Hah." Vetch didn't bother to clink glasses. "Smooth. Maybe I ought to switch to Jim Beam from that old swill I be drinking all these years. Now that I got the resources." He set down the glass and ran his palms down the front of his shirt. "Nawby. There's something I want to clear the air about. Between you and me."

"Yeah? What's that?"

Vetch began to roll a cigarette, scattering the flakes of tobacco. He'd even taken care to clean the dirt from under his thick, yellowed bitten-down fingernails. "It's about them Coloreds."

"They don't owe you anything, Vetch. They're free to work for me. It's none of your business."

"Hah. They ain't working for you. They working gainst you. That's what I come to say. You don't know nothing bout the Colored Race. I come to shows you."

"What is it with you people down here? Still can't comprehend that you lost the Civil War? All the Negro man wants is to be left alone. Earn a decent living, like anyone else. Why the hell do you hate them so much?"

"Hate em? Hah! I don't hate em. I love em."

Narby laughed. "You love Negroes? Is that the Negro people you're referring to, Carl, or some specific Negro? Go ahead. I'm listening."

"Sho. You folk up North don't know nothing. How many Nigra boys you play with when you was a chile, Nawby? How many drunk Nigras you haul out a ditch fore the snakes eat em? Damn it all, you ain't never touched a Nigra in your life. You Yankees got your Colored towns just like ours. Worse than ours. Cause you make believe Colored and White the same. That's cruel, you ask me. No sense in it, down right mean. Treat a Colored like he a White man and that's his doom, sho as if you shot him in the head. White folk and Colored folk like male and female, un'nustan? They needs each other different so White can be White and Colored can be Colored."

"You're a regular Gunnar Myrdal, aren't you? Can't say I follow your logic. Have another drink, Carl. Explain it again."

"I ain't going to splain it. I going to show you." He paused to light his cigarette, letting it hang on his lower lip, his mouth agape, exposing the rancid nubs of teeth. "Where's that little ole flask you like to tote everywheres? Fill it on up. You coming with me."

"Where?"

"Over to the White House. Hah. We going to visit ole Eisenhowa. Sho."

Narby shifted in the chair. "What's that? The White House?"

"Only you cain't go like that. Get wershed up. Put on a proper shirt." Vetch laid his hands flat on the table and pushed himself up. "Bring some of that money you got hid away. I be in the truck, so you can get it. Go on, now."

Vetch went out. Narby heard the door of the truck open. Vetch was waiting for him. He poured another drink, his mind blanking for a moment. Not deciding, but simply reacting, letting the pound of his pulse direct him.

Then he got up and took a shower and shaved, neither hurrying nor taking his time, dressing in a short-sleeved sport shirt and a pair of clean khaki trousers. There was fifty dollars in the pocket. More than enough, Narby decided. From the dresser drawer he took a folding knife, rather small but with a very sharp steel blade, of Swiss manufacture, one of Hank's more expensive trinkets. In the kitchenette he filled the flask with Jim Beam. At every step—in the shower, buttoning his shirt, putting the knife in his pocket—he attempted to argue himself out of it. Only there was nothing there, no proposition or counter proposal.

He went back into the bathroom and cracked open a Benzedrine inhaler, the drug taking effect immediately, like the flash of a camera and then the long-fading afterimage, the blot of brilliance gradually converging into darkness. Outside, turning the key to lock the cabin door, he stopped. The attaché was on the dresser. There was a light on in the motel office. By the glow of the bell, if he were watching, Dindridge could clearly see him getting in to Vetch's truck, see them driving away. After so much care, so much vigilance, ten months now in the gimcrack cabin, with all the effort of burying the money in the jungle, how could he be so cavalier? But again, he had no answer. Only the sensation that he was still in control, that his will superseded any other consideration.

Vetch started the truck. Narby got in. He could smell Vetch's talcum powder, mixing with the truck's endemic stink, the sweat and grease-blackened upholstery, the burning oil and cheap tobacco.

"Vetch looked him over. "That's better. You got money?"

"Yeah. Let's go. If we're going."

"Hah! I knew you was a Nigra lover, too."

They pulled onto the deserted highway. Narby drank from the flask and handed it to Vetch. Vetch took a drink and gave it back, his hands wrapped tightly around the wheel. A few of the shacks along the ditch showed dim light in the windows or kerosene lamps hanging on the front porches. Over the bridge the highway continued into town, toward the courthouse square. But Vetch turned left instead, and then right again, bumping over the railroad tracks.

Narby had never come this way. The street was riddled with potholes, the pavement half crumbled. On either side, low sagging wood-slat buildings alternated with overgrown vacant lots. The pine-pole street lamps were spaced far apart, somewhat randomly, throwing cones of dirty light. At certain corners people were gathered in front of illuminated doorways, angular men in wide brim hats and women in tight dresses. Bars and juke joints, Narby supposed, the fronts decorated with painted metal signboards: *Jax Beer Ale Stout, the drinks of friendship. Nehi Soda. Call for Phillip Morris!* Some of the buildings were houses, where people sat on the porches and front steps. As they drove past Narby could hear the muffled stomping music, laughter, the voices calling to one another.

"This here's Hend'son Avenue. Colored Town. They sho know how to joy themselves. Hah. It's a barrel of monkeys round here on Sad'day night."

After three or four blocks the streets grew quiet and dark, the groups of houses separated by longer stretches of waste and weeds. Vetch turned, and turned again. They passed two low barracks-like buildings, housing for the migrant farm workers. Then nothing, just dark vacant lots, then a burned down house, the ruins surrounded by a riot of weeds and vines. They crossed the tracks again.

It was a large three-story country house, painted white, with a wide wrap-around porch, standing alone at the end of a pitch-black street. About half a dozen cars and trucks were parked in front in the dirt, haphazardly. There was a light, on the porch over the front door. The upper windows showed a dull glow behind closed curtains.

Vetch pulled over, parking the truck away from the others, and cut the motor. "Let's have that whiskey."

Narby took a drink and passed it to Vetch. Vetch took a long pull and wiped his mouth with his foreman. "All right. Come on. And don't say nothing until we get inside. Stranger cain't just walk in there. Un'nustan?"

That he was dependent on Vetch to get inside made Narby uneasy. But what did it matter? He would be rid of Vetch soon enough.

They got out of the truck and Narby followed Vetch up the porch steps. There was a dog barking somewhere close by, perhaps just behind the house, an angry snarling vicious bay. The dog was chained, Narby supposed. If anyone gave the house trouble, they would let it loose.

Vetch rapped on the door a few times, looking straight at the peephole. "It's Cap'm Vetch. I got a friend with me this time." He stepped aside. "Stand here under the bulb. Let em see you."

Narby stood in front of the door, letting Vetch parade him like a fool.

The lock clicked and the door swung open. Vetch went in first. They entered a darkened paneled vestibule with an oily smell: candle wax, smoke, heavy perfume. Vetch closed the front door behind them. Another door, to the side, opened. A Negro woman in a plain housedress, holding a cigarette, greeted them. "Evening Cap'm. Who you got there? Another Cap'm? Or is he just private first class?"

"This is my associate. All the way down from New Yoke." Vetch turned to him. "You got a name you want to give em?"

"Philip."

The woman looked him up and down. She might have been attractive once, when she was young. He could discern her loose breasts sagging under the dress. It was probably her house. "That's a nice name. Philip. Kinda royal-like." Her voice was deep, raspy, but easy to understand. She put the cigarette she was holding to her mouth, standing in the inner doorway, gazing at both of them as she took her time, theatrically blowing out the smoke. "All right. Come on in. Make yo'self at home. Gals be down sho'tly."

They entered a large parlor, dimly lit by two shaded floor lamps. A ceiling fan turned overhead, stirring the oily air. The Madame, or whatever she was, went up the wide staircase. There were three sofas and a couple of armchairs, the floor covered with an oriental rug. Two men—despite the gloom Narby saw they were White, middle-aged, like the men who ate breakfast at the back tables at the Gladiola Cafe—sat on a sofa, talking quietly with a Negro woman who sat between them, very close. She appeared to be draped in a negligee. The man on her left had his hand on her knee. The men took no notice of him or Vetch.

Narby sat in an armchair on the other side of the room. From upstairs, through the ceiling, he heard movement. Vetch came over and said quietly, "You on your own now, Yankee Doodle. Here." He pressed something into Narby's hand, a small square foil packet. Two women, one behind the other, were coming down the stairs. "When we's done, I meet you outside, in the truck."

As she stepped from the stairs Vetch went up to the first woman, full-figured and draped in a loose, un-girdled robe. She laughed quietly. Narby heard her say "cap'm." Vetch called her by name, something like Florence. The one behind her was petite. She wore a short flouncy negligee, showing her thighs. Narby stood and she came up to him.

"Good evening," she said. "How you feeling tonight? You good?"

"Fine, thanks. And yourself."

"Hot." She gave a little laugh. "Can I get you sump'm? Glass of wadda? Some ice tea?"

She had the same dense accent as the workers. Narby had to repeat the syllables in his mind until they formed words. "A glass of water. Yes, thank you."

"My name Becca." She paused, as if she sensed the incomprehension. "You know. Like Ree-becca."

"Hello, Becca." She was very young, with short hair and thick lips painted red. "I'm Philip."

"Pleasure to meet you, F'lip." A foot shorter than Narby, she looked up at him, but indirectly, as if gazing at some spot on the wall over his shoulder. She was smiling for him, posing, letting him assess her, decide if she was to his taste. After a moment, she said, "Everything awl right?"

"Yeah. Sure."

"Then why don't you go on up. Room five. I bring your wadda for you, hon."

"Fine. Room five."

Vetch and his companion had already ascended. The stairs led up to a darkened hallway of closed doors, four on each side. Two light bulbs, painted over with opaque blue, dangled overhead. The walls were scuffed and shiny. Tacked on each door was a rusted tin number. Narby found room five and went in, closing the door behind him: a narrow bed with sheet and pillow, a folded towel, a sink against the wall, a dirty white curtain over the window, open to the hot airless night, a table with an ashtray and a lamp, a chair, a waste basket, a hook on the back of the door.

Narby sat next to the window and lit a cigarette. He felt nothing. No excitement, no repulsion. The squalid room, the particular traits of the girl, her talent and disposition, would determine whether or not he would see it through. He thought again, uncomfortably, about the girl from Alton Road he had had to send away. The desire, which he craved the way a man wasting away from disease craved an appetite, would have to come to him now from outside, almost as if against his wishes.

There was a perfunctory knock. She came in.

"Here's your wada." She put the glass down on the table, sat on the bed, shook off her bedroom slippers and crossed her leg, inspected the sole of her foot. "'Scuse me. Got a splinta' or sump'in." Her negligee had ridden high up her thigh. Her skin was smooth, taut and lustrous. "You a friend of that Cap'm?"

"No, not really."

"Oh. I thought you was."

Smoking, he leaned back in the chair, watching her pick at the sole of her foot. She reminded him of a painting, probably one Tom or Jim had seen as a boy at the art museum in Chicago, depicting a dancer, a ballerina, holding one foot, her leg bent in the same way, with the same attitude of concentration. Only the painting was colorful, gay, a scene drawn from the backstage glamour of the Paris ballet. Not a Negro girl scraping at a splinter in a dank squalid room. Yet there was a similarity of posture, even of purpose, if Narby wished.

She let her foot go and looked up at him and smiled.

"Would you like a cigarette?"

"Sho."

He gave her one that he had rolled from the shag tobacco and standing by the bed lit it for her. Her eyes were big, soft, the whites yellowed and mildly bloodshot. She was very young, a teenage girl.

"Thank you." She scooted back on the bed, her legs dangling. Her breasts, small but full and round, showed through the negligee. "That's sweet tabacca. Nice. Why don't you make yourself more comfortable, hon. Don't be shy."

He finished the cigarette and began to undress, turning so that the scars were facing away from the lamp.

"So, what you want, hunna'pot? Honey F'lip. What you like Becca to do?"

"I'm sorry. What did you say?"

"Sugar, you got to tell me what you want fore you get all involved. So's I can tell you how much. Unna'stan?"

"How much do you want?"

She laughed. "How much you got, hon?" She stood now and with a single motion lifted the negligee over her head and tossed it on the chair. "You like me? Have it all for ten dollar, hon. Just put it on the table, fore we got all involved."

He had hung his trousers on the hook. He reached into the pocket and took two bills, a ten and five, and put then on the table. "I like you more than ten dollars."

"Well ain't you sweet. Awl right. Come over here."

Standing over the sink she washed him and then dried him with the towel. "You got a johnny, hon? You don't got your own, that be fifty cent extra."

"Yes." He took the square of foil from the trouser pocket.

After a few moments, caressing each other on the bed, he was ready. He pressed on top of her, cradling the back of her head. Her short hair was stiff, with a chemical smell, and her hipbones dug into him. He let go of her head and put his hands under her buttocks, cupping and lifting. The floorboards creaked with the weight and movement, the metal leg of the bed scraping the floor. He could look into her eyes now, but when he tried to kiss her on the mouth she turned away. So he went at it harder, struggling a bit too strenuously, not wanting to risk any loss of sensation, so that it finished sooner than he would have liked, more out of exigency than a release of pleasure.

Sitting on the bed as he pulled his clothes on, she said, "You a good looking man. Them fat ones pret near crush a gal."

Standing to button his trousers he could feet the folding knife in his pocket, pressing against his thigh. "You mean the Captain? A fat one like him?"

"Nah. Cap'm always take Flo'nce. She his regular Sad'day night."

"Captain been coming here a long time?"

She shrugged. "I don't know. Since last summer, I reckon."

So, the blackmail money he had paid Vetch wasn't just for the fish camp. It was a good thing for Vetch that he had his own girl. Because looking at her now—she had slipped on the negligee, the sheer fabric rippling down her smooth, taut body—Narby understood that it would happen again and again until he got what he wanted from her.

"Sump'm a matter? Ain't that how you like it, hunna'pot?"

"It was all right."

"Just awl right?" She reached out and with the back of her hand caressed his cheek, her eyes focused just over his shoulder, and ran her fingers through his damp hair. "Mebbe we do better next time. I get to know you, mebbe I lets you kiss me. For real. You ask for me next time, won't ya? Becca. Say it for me, hunna'pot."

"Becca."

"That's right. Becca be here, every Sad'day night. You a nice good looking man. You'll see. Becca treat you right."

He finished dressing and went down the stairs and through the door into the vestibule. At the sound of the outer door closing and then his shoes clicking down the porch steps, the dog started up again, whining and snarling against the chain. There were only two cars now, parked in the dirt. Vetch was waiting in the truck. He got in and Vetch cranked the motor. They passed the burnt-down hulk, bumping over the first set of tracks, and turned on to Henderson Avenue. "Well," Vetch said, "you get your dollar's worth, did you?"

"You could say that."

Narby noted the landmarks. The dark clumps of houses scattered amongst the overgrown lots, the corners where the men gathered, the pools of light falling from the crooked poles, over the railroad tracks, the sharp turn and then crossing the river, back on the highway. He could find his way without Vetch. The Madame would remember him. Because he had paid more than she had asked, and the Madam would get her share.

"Those men. Sitting downstairs. You recognize them?"

"Sho. That big fat one, that Harlan Bodell. He sell in-surance. The other, that Wally Mason. Used to be county commissioner while back. He the boss of that Winn Dixie supermarket. Manager. Hah. Ain't nothing but a butcher with the blood wershed off his apron. Fambly men. The upstanding gent'men of the community."

Narby thought for a moment. "Haven't you ever had a wife, Carl? A girlfriend?"

"Nope."

"Ever have a White woman?"

"Nope. First gal I did it on was a Nigra. All us boys did it with Colored gals, up in the woods behind the paper mill. My old man, whoever the hell he was, did the same. Sho. And his pappy done the same before him. That's the way people like us do down here. A Dixie tradition."

"Maybe that's because no White woman could stand to touch you."

Vetch kept his eyes on the road. His voice was neutral. He took no offense. "I spect you right. Besides. Ain't no call to dirty up some nice White girl. I know that. Best to keep filth where it belongs."

"Don't you have anyone around here? Any friends? Any family?"

"Everyone got to have a fambly somewhere. That's a fact of nature. My mama, now, she was a Georgia fact. My pappy, well, seems he crossed so many state lines ain't no one knows what kind of fact he was. Up Georgia, they put me in the jailhouse once. I ain't never going back there. I'm my own fambly now. My own fact. Un'nustan?"

"That's god damned poetic, Vetch. Jolly for you."

Vetch smiled. "Now that I done tell you my true confessions, it's your turn, Nawby. I seen them scars, running down your side like barb wire. What happened that make you like that?"

"Car accident. Long time ago."

"That so? I ain't never seen nothing like that from no car crash. Seen it on boys come back from war. That what it look like to me."

"You must have seen some action, Carl. In Germany or Italy or the Pacific."

"Nope. With all that turp'tine and resin and such that we be shipping up to Jacksonville and Tampa, Putnam got us a special dispensation from the fed'ral gum'ment. Never went to war. Never had a mind to. I ain't never had no argument with no German, no Jap. Got enough folks right here close to home ought to be shot at. Hah."

"What about Pearl Harbor? Didn't that make you want to fight?"

"Weren't my quarrel. Same thing with that Ko-rea mess. They couldn't get me for that one. Too old. But I figure, young man like you, you just the right age. That where you get them wounds, ain't it? In Ko-rea."

"Car accident, like I told you."

"Ain't nothing to be shamed of. Whatever it is you done. Whatever it is made you run. Every man for himself. That's the way it is, war or peace or in between. Sho."

It was dark up ahead. Dindridge had finally shut down the bell for the night. Now he could hide the money. Vetch pulled into the lot.

"Stay away from me, Carl. Don't come by here anymore. Leave Sam Waters and those men alone. You got what you wanted. You got your land. We don't need each other anymore. It's finished."

"Ain't nothing finished, Nawby. But—so long as they's no trouble. Maybe it's best we go our own ways. For now."

He watched through the screen door until Vetch's truck disappeared into the darkness. The money, the attaché, was on the dresser, just as he had left it. He'd wait an hour, to be safe, and then he'd have to crawl into the brush behind the cabin and grub around in the filth for the rubber poncho.

15

August, 1954

NARBY STOOD BY THE PROPPED-OPEN DOORS, a copy of the *New York Times* tucked under his arm, scanning the big noisy room and the row of booths along the back wall, under the colorful Henri Rousseau-style mural of a prelapsarian Biscayne Bay. It was 2:15. He figured Campos would be here by now.

Not wanting to linger at the entrance he lowered his gaze and made his way toward an empty booth. A bit conspicuous, a White Man sitting by himself, but now that he was here, he wasn't about to turn around and leave. He lit a cigarette and unfolded the newspaper, looking up when the waitress came to take his order. When she brought his beer, he laid the paper aside and gave the room another glance. Apparently, Campos was going to make him wait.

The place was crowded. There was a top layer of racket— the whirring of the overhead fans, loud talk and laughter, the clatter of cutlery—and under that, if you listened, a pulse of music issuing from the jukebox, a jump blues and then Billie Holiday singing *Mean to Me* and now a Beny Moré number. Some of the Negro patrons were rather light-skinned. Against another background, in less flamboyant clothing, they might pass as European. No one seemed to pay Narby any mind. Probably, they thought he was a cop. Or maybe they were having too good a time to give a damn.

Was Campos trying to unnerve him, making him hang around like this? Or maybe the Cuban was in trouble. He'd give him until three and then, after one more beer, he'd leave, just as casually as he had strolled in. That was the difference between now and Havana. Between waiting here at El Castillo for Campos and that day, well over a year ago, when Knowles had cornered him at the sidewalk café. It wasn't a pleasant memory. He still remembered that damned smirk on Knowles's face, the Buddha-like calm in his limbs and voice. Not that Narby could claim he was entirely in control of the situation. But he had been operating for a year now, on his own. The Philip Narby account had held—it was all his, to do with as he wished. He was going to press Campos, force the Cuban's hand.

Louis Armstrong. *I've Got the World on a String*. No doubt, there were men in this very room who had been stationed in Tokyo, or fought in Korea. Yet there was zero chance anyone here would know him, recognize him. Zero chance that a man like Sam Waters, for example, had any interest whatsoever in Narby's past or his scars or where he got his money. The race prejudice against Negroes, Narby had come to realize, might be used to his own advantage. It was more effective, after all, than "hiding in plain sight," trying to blend in with all the other blue-eyed sandy-haired hometown heroes. The U.S. Army, the southern bigots, the state constitution of Florida, the esteemed burghers of Myerton and Miami, had divided the world in two, Black and White. Narby need only cross the color line to disappear.

Imagine someone like Ted McCoy, like Bill Knowles, with his bespoke suit and Brahmin accent, blundering into a place like El Castillo! Or Tom or Jim—that eager Midwestern boy who had gone all limp in the knees listening to McCoy brag about Harvard and the O.S.S. and London during the blitz and the McCoys' summer place on Martha's Vineyard—Tom or Jim, consorting with Negroes? What a laugh.

Lighting another cigarette, looking up, he saw Campos at the entrance, a small tightly wound figure in a bright crisp white shirt. Narby wasn't about to spring up like a jack-in-the-box. Let the Cuban gawk, expose himself. He slipped the lighter in his pocket and leaned back in the booth, perusing the newspaper.

"Felipé. Excuse me. I am too late."

"You mean *very* late. Not too late. If you were *too* late, I wouldn't be here, now would I?"

Campos sat across from him. "Yes. I remember now. American phrase for to learn 'very' and 'too.' You can never be *too* rich or *too* thin."

"That's right. It's in the Constitution, tucked into some amendment."

The Cuban took out a pack of Lucky Strikes. Narby watched, looking for signs of distress. The immaculate moustache, hair slicked back, not a strand out of place, the freshly laundered shirt, his nails buffed and polished—but as Campos lighted the match Narby noted the tremor in his fingers.

They hadn't seen each other in two months. Campos had finally broken the silence, writing to Narby at the Smoker's Den. Just as Narby had wished.

The Cuban sat straight, almost rigid, cigarette in one hand, the other resting on the table. Campos had acquired a handsome new wristwatch, with a genuine alligator-skin band. Perhaps Ernesto was skimming off the Movement's funds. The embezzling clerk—Narby still couldn't shake that first impression.

The Cuban was waiting for Narby to start. "Everything all right? Your big man is still alive and well, on the Isle of Pines. Yeah?"

"They hold him for el juicio. The trying. Batista—." He stopped, the waitress at their table, and ordered a café Cubano. "All the judge, they are of Batista. For to do what Batista want. Prison or execute."

"Maybe so. But don't you see what Batista's doing? As long as he holds Castro, the Movement"—he lowered his voice, though with all the noise it was hardly necessary—"the Movement is paralyzed. He's found your weakness."

"How you mean?"

"You're supposed to a people's revolution, right? But without this single individual, this Fidel Castro, you'll fall apart. Batista's holding him as a hostage. It's quite simple, really. You won't move, for fear of getting Castro killed. It's better for Batista to keep the Movement from acting, keep you paralyzed, rather than risk the Movement's re-organization once Castro is eliminated. You understand? Twenty-Six July is playing Batista's game. You've put too much importance in one person."

"Maybe I agree. Maybe I can no say to the others what you say. Because is very dangerous. *Too* dangerous."

Narby shrugged. "You could call Batista's bluff. Stage an attack. Assassinate one of Batista's judges or a general."

Campos stared at him. The waitress set down the thick ceramic cup. Narby ordered another beer.

"You think is easy? To make assassination. After Moncada, Batista kill many innocents. Many torture. For one assassination, many good people has to die."

"How about smuggling someone onto the Isle of Pines, into the prison."

"To escape Castro?"

"No. To kill him. Given the circumstances, Castro might be worth more to the Movement as a martyr. Un santo. With Castro out of the way the Movement could settle its internal squabbles and begin to act."

Campos gave out a short nervous laugh. "Who will be new Castro, Felipé? You? Gringo cowboy. Like William Walker. Like what you do in Guatemala?"

So, that's what it was all about. Narby figured it would come up, sooner rather than later. Jacobo Arbenz, the duly elected president of Guatemala, had been ousted a week ago. The American newspapers had dubbed it an anti-communist, populist-nationalist coup.

"Arbenz overthrew himself. Too communist, even for his own downtrodden people."

"Mierda. Arbenz was no communista. He was patriot. This I know. Is not possible, that he is communist."

"Appropriating land owned by American corporations? Buying weapons from the Soviets? Come on, Ernesto. Arbenz was toeing the Stalinist line. Don't be naïve."

"No tienes razon, Felipé. You have error in thinking. Is historical fact that imperialism can no exist at same moment with indigenous nationalist movimientos. Imperialismo de la Frutera. The Junited Fruit Company. In Cuba we know much about these thieves. Arbenz want to stop them, only for to follow Guatemala law, Guatemala constitution. For this action of patriotism, Arbenz receive the golpe. Entiendes bien, Felipé. When the Americans no sell more weapons for Guatemala Army, Arbenz is necessary to buy weapons from los Rusos. Arbenz have no choice. Is conspiracy in United States government, Eisenhower y Dulles y Wall Street, for to make international rationale for golpe."

"Who told you that, Ernesto? You sure as hell didn't read it in the *Saturday Evening Post*."

"Mis informadores." Campos put out his cigarette and leaned forward, his voice just above a whisper. "In Opa-Locka. One hundred o mas Guatemaltecos. Secret U.S. Army training camp."

Opa-Locka. Ten miles north of Miami. One of those Gold Coast boomtowns that had been abandoned after the big 1926 hurricane. During the Second World War the army had built an airstrip out there, at the edge of the swamp. It was common knowledge that the Americans had been backing their own handpicked man in Guatemala. Colonel Castillo Armas. Every podunk banana republic seemed to have a bunker full of Colonels, ready to throw each other over at a moment's notice. But the papers reported that the anti-Arbenz forces had been organizing in Nicaragua, not in southern Florida. And right in Narby's own backyard. Why the hell hadn't Knowles given him warning? Now, Narby looked like a fool.

"Not the Army," Narby said, carefully sifting his words. The waitress set down the beer. He took a moment, drinking half the glass. "The U.S. Army is a very blunt instrument, Ernesto. Big artillery, tanks, missiles, that's more their style. This wasn't an Army operation."

The Cuban stared at him, his face tense, blank—just as Narby had seen him on the boat, the lead pipe in his hand.

"It's Central Intelligence, not the Army. C.I.A."

"Is the same. C.I.A. or Army. No?"

"As a matter of fact, no. Not at all."

Campos didn't budge. He wasn't buying it. He wanted more.

"It's like I told you. Some very powerful men in the U.S. Army want to see me disappear. Permanently. Someone from C.I.A. helped me get out of Cuba. Is helping me now. And therefore, indirectly, helping you, as well. Helping the Movement."

"Como Grecia, during civil war? Como Turquía?"

"That's got nothing to do with what's happening now. Greece and Turkey were just a bit of tidying up after the war, cleaning house before Stalin came to visit. Guatemala—well, that's more like Iran." He was only now making the connection himself. "Yes. More like Mossadegh and Iran."

"You are C.I.A. man?"

Narby shifted his legs under the table. "No. Not Army and not C.I.A. I don't belong to anyone. Look, Ernesto. You have to understand. There's no way around American interests, American domination. Not anymore. Not after what the Soviets pulled in Eastern Europe, not after Berlin, not after Uncle Joe cobbled together his own H-bomb. Not after China. Half of Washington was wailing that we lost China, like a mother watching her baby being eaten alive by sharks. They had the atom bombs ready to fly. They were this close to turning Peking into a heap of fried rice. MacArthur's finger was twitching on the goddamn trigger. Fortunately, Truman cut off his hand just in time."

The filing cabinet. Somehow, he knew. Truman had signed the order on Guatemala years ago, all the way back in 1951.

"From now on, Ernesto, every measly five-cent chip on the table, every lousy scrap of earth, is going to be fought over like it was Pennsylvania Avenue. Forget about keeping America out of it. It's a waste of time. Concentrate instead on which Americans you want on your side. Play one against the others.

The Army, the Air Force, the State Department, the diplomatic corps, the Mutual Security people, the Foreign Aid bankers. The McCarthyites and the striped-pants Alger Hiss crowd. The rabid anti-communists and the Adlai Stevenson anti-anti-communists. Sugar people, copper people, oil people, uranium people. Gamblers and alcoholics and gangsters and sex maniacs and any number of homosexuals. Men who would sell out an entire country like Cuba just to keep their yacht-club privileges at the Miramar. Or to keep their mistresses. There's even a few people still kicking around who put their money on democracy and freedom-for-all—well, up to a point.

"Let me help you choose your friends, Ernesto. Help you get on their good side."

"Go on. Dígame, Felipé. How I get on good side?"

"This man Castro. If Batista decides to execute him, who's next in line?"

Campos looked away, lighting another cigarette. After a moment, tapping the ash, he said, "el hermano. Raúl."

"Yeah? He cut from the same cloth as brother Fidel?"

"Fidel Castro no is communist. Never. Pero, el hermano. He is de la Juventud Socialista. Socialist Youth. Es mas izquierdista."

"In that case, you better pray for Fidel. Better yet, I'll pray for him. I'll let my contacts in Havana know how vital it is that Fidel remain our anti-Batistiano of choice. You understand, Ernesto? Batista can be bargained with. And if he can be bargained with, he can be fooled. We'll come up with something. Some kind of truce or amnesty. Maybe get Castro out of the country for a while."

"De verdad?" With the tip of his pinkie Campos gingerly removed a speck of tobacco from his upper lip, looking away with indifference, or contempt. "How you say? Talk is cheap, Felipé."

"Talk is about all the Movement has right now, amigo. Better make it smart. Get rid of all the anti-imperialist commie-sounding catchphrases: no nationalizing, no land reform, no appropriating natural resources. What you want is: democracy, freedom, liberty, over and over and over. Castro's got to ring that bell until he's sick of it. Quote George Washington and Jefferson, that kind of thing. And maybe, just maybe, he might get someone in the American Press to back him up."

"Como un loro. How you say? Bird who repeat words for master."

"Parrot. Maybe so. Look, tell your own people—your campesinos and trade unionists and socialist boy scouts—tell them anything you like. But to the outside world, what you have to do is make Batista look like the enemy of American business interests, make everyone think that Batista is the opposite of the American way of life. Convince everyone that it's Batista and his corrupt pals, and not Castro, who will drive the Cuban people right into the arms of the commies. Let me tell you, it doesn't hurt that Batista has Negro blood, either. Negro features. And that Castro is White. No offence, amigo. And maybe pick up a motto while you're at it. Something like, *the 26 July Movement—America's Best Friend!*"

"You know these people? C.I.A. Who give Arbenz the golpe?"

"Christ, Ernesto. Don't get stuck on that. Arbenz gambled and lost. There are men in the CIA who support your cause. Very smart, very open-minded men. You'll need them on your side. Arbenz tried to have it both ways. Learn from his mistake. Don't repeat it."

"Why, Felipé? Good friend of CIA. Why you on boat same night as me? Who tell you I am at Moncada?"

"No one. I told you, I'm not CIA. Not Army."

"I no believe. I am sorry." Campos put out his cigarette and swung his legs from under the table. "Adios."

"Wait." Narby took a pen from his pocket and wrote the name and address on a waxy El Castillo paper napkin. "Here. He's the CIA chief in Havana. El jefe. He's using the Allbright Paper Company as a cover, una trampa. Go ahead. Check it out.

See if I'm lying. It's treason, you understand. If they ever find out I gave this to you."

Campos let his eyes pass over the napkin, folded it into a square and slipped it in his shirt pocket. Half out of the booth he hesitated, then stood, saying nothing, and walked away.

The jukebox started another song. Nat Cole. *It's Only a Paper Moon.* He motioned for the check, putting his money down but then waiting, listening, as if the words were meant for him alone: *but it wouldn't be make believe, if you believed in me.*

16

MAYBE KNOWLES WASN'T C.I.A., AFTER ALL. But who, what, was the C.I.A.?

Narby had a good idea: former O.S.S. men mostly, a lot of McCoy types from Harvard and Yale, well-scrubbed scions who had been young and eager working for Roosevelt and Stimson during the run-up to the war, New Dealers and do-gooders. They'd had an open playing field under Truman and Marshall. But the new H-bomb crowd—the there-will-never-be-another-war warriors like MacArthur and LeMay, the rabid China-lobby set like Knowland and Luce—hated them. And so did Brigadier General Willoughby, MacArthur's G-2, head of Intelligence.

MacArthur and Willoughby had despised the O.S.S., because the O.S.S. was too close to the Alger-Hiss contaminated State Department. Pampered Ivy League Commies and Queers. Indeed, the O.S.S. had threatened to expose the phony intelligence MacArthur's lackeys were bringing out of Korea. MacArthur needed to convince Truman and the Joint Chiefs that Red China would under no circumstances enter the war, assure them that he could take the entire Chosin Peninsula smack up to the Yalu with minimal force, minimal cost. A cake-walk. But the O.S.S. had aerial photographs. Their men on the ground, dropped behind enemy lines, had observed massive Chinese troop movements along the border, the silent nimble padded-jacket hordes swarming like ants over the mountain passes, their bugle-call clarions ringing through the iron-hard air of winter. Hardened veterans of Mao's Revolution. It was all in the filing cabinet. Misinformation, lies, treason.

The enemy of my enemy. Knowles had the document now, proof of Willoughby's collusion with Tsuji Masanobu, the Japanese war criminal. Maybe Willoughby had hunted down Knowles, a clean kill, his corpse fed to the sharks that raked the Florida Straits. If Knowles were dead, there might be no one left who knew enough to turn off the tap, and the money would keep flowing. The last withdrawal, a rather astonishing twen-ty-five hundred. He'd been so damned keyed up not even Miss Prentice's creamy vortex had quelled him. Sid Black was dead, that much was fairly certain. But Narby preferred to believe that Knowles was alive and well; that Knowles had neglected to answer Narby's letters simply because there was no reason to risk doing so, as long as Narby kept sending him information about M267. As long as Knowles, in turn, kept Narby's operation funded.

But if Knowles were C.I.A., or some offshoot? Maybe strug-gling to keep his position, now that the Dulles brothers, estab-lished anti-Hissites, had taken the agency under wing. So what? Narby was in business for himself, just as he had told Campos. The fact that someone high up wanted Narby dead merely con-firmed his worth, the intrinsic value of his services. If some-one didn't want you dead, you weren't in the game. If someone didn't want you dead, you didn't matter.

He gave it a day, twenty-four hours, time enough for Campos to share the revelation of the El Castillo napkin with his co-con-spirators in Havana. The following afternoon, around three, on his way out of town, Narby stopped at the Western Union on Flagler and NE Second Avenue. Standing at the counter, unshaven, in his workman's canvas pants and T-shirt, a cigarette hanging from his mouth, Narby filled out the canary-yellow form. *EC et co. has stumbled upon Allbright's position. Suggest you close shop or take other precautions to protect your business interests—.*

Hadn't Knowles himself instructed Narby to stir up the pot and see what settles? Maybe he'd been a bit impulsive yesterday, a bit imprudent. In any case, it was his duty to warn Knowles. Or, if not Knowles, then whoever it was who was now fielding Narby's communiqués in Havana. With luck, Campos's people would find out just enough to glean that the information on the napkin was correct, and thus he would win back Campos's trust. With luck, Knowles, though put out, would be forewarned with sufficient time to minimize the damage, and Knowles would realize that Narby had taken the risk in order to keep close to Campos.

But was it really treason? Knowles himself had refused to reveal his true allegiance, had insulted Narby's intelligence by clinging to the Allbright Paper cover. Besides, if Knowles was in fact C.I.A. and now turned against Narby to protect himself, Narby knew exactly who to alert concerning the incriminating document now in Knowles's possession. Unless, of course ...

He backed away from the counter, blanking his mind. It was the splash, Stennart's yellow pills, whirlpooling the endless ouroboros-like possibilities, addling his thoughts. Just send the goddamn telegram. Nothing was fixed. He had to be flexible, improvise. Narby still knew more about Knowles than Knowles knew about him. He took a breath and continued: *Why does the cobra continue to spare the caged mongoose?* Narby had contrived the code words months ago. Cobra was the son-of-a-bitch Batista. The snake-eating mongoose was the young bearded lawyer, Castro. *Who the hell is running the zoo? As ever—*He thought for a moment. The clerk behind the counter was watching from under his visor. He decided against his normal sign-off, PN. Tom? Jim? But then, smiling at the inspiration, he wrote: *El Coreano.*

Fifteen minutes later, on his way out of town, he pulled into the potholed parking lot fronting the dismal row of shop fronts. The spectral gray-skinned pharmacist had hinted last month of an anticipated 'overstock' of Phenaphen. Narby had said he wasn't interested. But now, perhaps, he was. Just a bottle or two, to tide him over.

Odd. The door was locked, in the middle of the day, the glass pane papered-over from the inside. He banged, gently, trying to peek through a rip. It was dark. He could make out a row of shelves, collapsed, boxes spilled into the aisle. He stepped back, letting go of the handle. Someone had trashed the place. The cops. Or competing dope peddlers. Next door to Stennart's was a bric-a-brac shop, the Jolly Roger. Junk with a vaguely nautical theme that the old woman who ran the place called antiques. Narby had been in a few times, pretending to browse. He didn't like to go into Stennart's if there were other customers. So he would wait, browsing, until he saw them leave.

Maybe she knew something. He strolled in, making noise. The proprietress came out from the back, a blowsy heavy woman with disordered gray hair, a pair of glasses on a chain dangling from her neck.

"Howdy. Welcome," she said, settling on the stool behind the cluttered desk.

"Afternoon."

"Looking for anything special?"

"No, not really."

"We got some nice costume jewelry, just in from an estate sale last weekend. Nice gift for your gal. Or your mother. Priced to sell."

Becca deserved a little gift. The woman brought out a felt-lined tray and he picked a necklace of real-enough looking pearls, set in gold-leaf floral clusters. Three dollars. The woman's voice grew warm. "How about a ring or earrings to go with?" She smiled at him. "Sure is a lucky gal."

"No, thanks."

"Need any furniture or garden items? We got furniture in the back. Building materials, too. Window frames, columns, doors."

Waters had begun to frame the walls last week and they needed a front door. He strolled though the rows of junk. Along the wall were a number of bulky items, webbed with dust. Something caught his eye: a heavy, black, thick, wooden slab with two vertical rows of rusted iron studs. It looked very old, more portal or gate than door. The woman was at his heels.

"Now ain't that something? Story behind that piece, there is. All the way from Grenada, Spain."

He clamped his cigarette in his mouth and with both hands pulled it forward. As a front door it would certainly dissuade the casual intruder. The rusted misshapen ironwork had acquired the tint of dried blood. "From Spain?"

"Yes, sir. Imported back around 1915, so I understand. You know those Moorish style buildings they put up around Opa Locka? That was the craze back then, in the teens and twenties, all that Spanish-Araby style and such."

"Where?"

"Opa Locka. Wait a minute. I'll show you."

She moved off, rummaging through one shoebox after another, and came back holding a postcard. "Here. See that? That's a copy of one of the buildings in the Alhambra, over there in Grenada, Spain. Built dozens just like that. Half of them been torn down by now. We get the salvage from time to time."

He flipped over the old hand-colored postcard and read the legend. *Post office and City Hall. In the enchanting City of Opa Locka, Florida.*

"Genuine Spanish. Yep. Maybe two, three hundred years old."

Narby laughed. It would keep out the barbarians, the Huns, the Crusaders, the Guatemalans, the M.P.s, the C.I.A. Keep out Vetch. "It looks like it."

"Been sitting in the shop for two years. I'll give it to you cheap. Just to make space. You don't see a piece like that every day. Just give me a minute. I'll call Willie and he can help you load into your pick-up."

"How much?"

"Thirty dollars."

"I'll give you fifteen."

"Well. Seeing how we need space. And since you bought the pearl necklace. How about twenty?"

"Seventeen-fifty."

"You got yourself a deal."

As she was writing up the ticket Narby asked if she knew whether the pharmacy next door was still open for business.

"Now that's a shame. That was maybe two weeks ago. Came for him in an ambulance, they did. Mr. Stennart, that's his name. Don't know more than that. Shop's been closed up, ever since."

He counted out the money. "He have family around here? Mr. Stennart?"

"Don't know. Can't say I knew him very well. Strange bird. Not exactly the neighborly type. Why? You one of his customers? Come to think on it, you've been in here before, haven't you?"

"No." He smiled. "Never."

She handed him the receipt. "Willie'll be here in a flash to help you load it. Go on and pull your truck around back."

He pulled the Chevy around. The squat concrete building couldn't have been more than a few years old, yet already it was crumbling under the tropical climate, the damp working its way into the stucco, everything flaking and corroded and streaked, weeds and vines growing through the gouges and cracks. A malarial stink rose from the puddles pooled about the trash bins in the alley behind. The back door of Stennarts—wood, but reinforced with a metal grating—sat partly off its hinges, secured by a heavy padlock. He could come back after dark, perhaps, with a crowbar. If he had the nerve.

The woman stood with her hands on her hips, watching Narby and Willie, a young Negro workman, lift the massive door and slide it into the bed of Narby's truck. Narby climbed into the cab and started the motor, waving Willie over to the window. "Here you go." He handed Willie two dollars. The man looked at it, rather dumfounded.

"Thank you. Mighty kind."

"Say. You don't happen to know what happened to Mr. Stennart. The fellow who owns the pharmacy?"

"Who?"

"Stennart. The druggist next door. They took him away in an ambulance two weeks ago."

"Don't know nothing about that."

Vetch was right. A Black man had to be out of his mind to admit anything to a White, no matter what. "OK. Take it easy, friend."

SHE NO LONGER CAME DOWN the wide staircase into the parlor in her loosely girded satin robe, no longer teased or offered him a glass of water, acting cool, playing as though he were heating her up.

If she wasn't ready, the Madame, or whatever she was, greeting him in the vestibule, would tell him how long. Ten minutes, half an hour. He didn't care to wait inside and went back to the truck, parked in the darkness some distance from the house, smoking, drinking from the flask, the invisible dog snarling against its chain. When he saw the porch light blink a few times he would return, slipping the Madame a few dollars, sometimes a five, an extraordinary gratuity that guaranteed his request for privacy, to avoid brushing shoulders with Vetch or any of the others as they stumped down the stairway or sat in the dimly lit parlor waiting or making their choice—heavy sluggish men pawing the thighs of their consorts like farmers at the state fair, showing off their prize cows.

Every Thursday and Saturday at the same hour. Most nights the Madame admitted him without delay. He climbed the staircase unaccompanied, his head down, eyes averted against the dank of the hallway with its blue-tined bulbs and the row of narrow doors with their rusted tacked-on numbers. Rapping lightly, he would wait until she told him to come in—the room was unlocked—not moving from where she sat on the bed, smoking a cigarette, naked under the negligee, her legs crossed, her skin glistening lightly from the heat, a pale coating on her dusky face and neck and breastbone where she had dusted powder. Her voice was tired, high and cracked, perpetually hoarse as if she spent her days shouting. On the table a fan rattled, weakly swirling the plumes from her cigarette.

She had told him she was twenty-two. He guessed eighteen. He sat on the chair, trying not to look at her quite yet, slipping off his shoes and then unbuttoning his shirt.

"You doing all right, Becca? Damned hot tonight. That fan keep you cool enough? You could use a new one. Maybe I'll pick one up for you. If you'd like."

So many Thursday and Saturday nights and he had never dared ask about her life outside. Only the banal inquiry into exigencies, confined to the narrow room: cigarettes, lingerie, lipstick, skin, hair, mouth, whatever he could see or touch or smell.

"I doing all right, now that you here, honna'pot." She leaned back: slight, sharp hipbones, the flat smooth breastbone that shone in the dull light, the small hard conical breasts that pointed outward. "You all sunburn. Look at your hand. What you do, get like that, sugar?"

His thumbnail was black, his hand swollen. He had mashed it an hour ago, unloading the heavy door from the truck. "Just a little accident. Damn near broke my thumb." He stood, disrobing. He always arrived showered and shaved, immaculate. The ritual of standing over the sink, Becca washing him, had been dispensed with. They had established other rules.

Sitting on the bed she reached out and took his hand as if to inspect the hurt but then lifted it to her face, pressing the palm against her surprisingly cool cheek and then with the tip of her tongue licking at the base of his injured thumb until his entire thumb was in her mouth and she sucked it, as a child would its own, her eyes rolled upward, melting into his, until she released him, a sly childish smile passing over her lips.

"You the best looking fella in the whole county, honna'pot. Don't go spole it by banging yourself up."

On the edge of the narrow bed she rose to her knees, so that as he stood in front and embraced her, her face and the stiff mass of her tightly curled hair, showing black and bronze in the lamplight, nestled under his neck. After a moment he pushed her back by the shoulders and lifted her negligee over her head. At first, months ago, she had spurned his kisses, turning her mouth away. But now, as he bent over her, she parted her lips, letting him devour her, a wolf feeding in a hot red carcass. She uttered no moan or sigh, only a low gurgle up from her throat, dry and inexpressive, Narby standing and bending and feeding, she on her knees on the bed, her head tilted back, her tired yellowed eyes open and impassive, her cool dry hand running up and down the skein of scars and welts twisting upward from his hip.

She was his now. He handled her in a way that she would allow with no other man. Or so she led him to believe. He had quit the Alton Road call girls, had finished with the remnants of Janet. He was hers, too, in a way he sought with no other woman. She understood him. She explained, with the cool dry palms of her hands and her thick cracked lips and her narrow hips, that love could be found in oblivion with a Negro girl of no more than eighteen, in a sordid second-story room on a pitch black street of weeds and rubble and vacant lots with the burned down house at the corner and the pools of dirty light in front of the juke joints and the storefront churches on Henderson Avenue. A crack in the universe, wheeling in space, opened solely for him, for them.

When he lay her on her back she stopped him to unroll the johnny over his stiffened sex with her pixie fingers, his heart thudding in a measured self-willed mania, gripping the back of her head, his hands grappling her hair, her eyes rolling back as he bore down, slowly at first, gradually increasing the speed and intensity, the legs of the bed scraping the floor, until her arms went limp at her side and a thread of drool ran from the corner of her mouth. There was a point, a node of nearly unbearable sensation, and he paused and withdrew very slowly, arching his back like a cat, and rather roughly turning her on her belly and beginning again, his mouth open and his teeth against the nape of her neck, the metal legs scraping, yawing, catching against the pine planks like the blade of a warped saw.

"Go on," she muttered. "That the way you like it, ain't it hon? I ain't got nothing you can't have, hon. Plenty more of that for you, sugar. You my special Sad'day night thunderstorm. You gwine to wash me away."

After some moments, as the ritual demanded, she would cajole him to turn over, on his back, and she would sit astride him, making her puny weight felt with the pressure of her sharp hipbones, leaning forward with her palms flat against his chest, pressing down with all her strength as if to squeeze out his heart. She was various and mobile, at one moment her torso tense as steel and then going limp and liquid, slithering on top of him like an eel.

He held back, flipping her over again, and then on her side. When she intuited his willingness, or perhaps deciding it herself, she slid away and took off the johnny. "Come on, now. Let it rain, hon. Let it pour down. Give me that lightning."

Afterward, for a few moments, Narby held her in his arms, cupped side by side on the sweated sheet. It was like holding a crippled sparrow, rescued from the sidewalk after falling from its nest, her tiny quick bird's pulse and her weightless limbs fluttering to be released from the hands that had saved her, captured her. Contrary to custom he paid afterward now, as if the money were unimportant, a formality. Had she asked, he would have set her up in an apartment, in Overtown or Coconut Grove in Miami, made her his mistress, his concubine. But she didn't ask. He knew she wouldn't. Because that would spell the end of it, the end of whatever life was her own beyond the narrow room, miserable as it might be, and she would resent him for it and he would neglect her, and grow tired of it. Like man and wife, he supposed.

She never thanked him. She would take the money, count it, showing neither surprise nor gratitude. "You best pay me good. You done spole me for everyone else, hon. I cain't hardly move. You done put me on my back for the entire evening."

He pulled the faux-pearl necklace from his pocket. "I thought you might like this."

She sat up on the bed, hardly glancing at it. "That's pretty. Sweet of you, hon. I wear it next time, if you like. Sad'day night."

The oblivion, the animal animus, had drained out of him. He was restless now to get away, out of the room and down the stairs and outside to his truck, thirsting for the flask. On occasion he might give her a parting caress. But it was false and a bit stupid, so he simply said goodbye and opened the door, leaving her as he had found her, sitting on the bed, naked under the negligee. At the top of the stairs he heard heavy footsteps from below, scraping across the parlor. If it were Vetch, if Vetch uttered a single word to him, Narby swore he would strike him.

But at the bottom of the stairs, his head down, he encountered no one and let himself out through the vestibule and down the porch steps into the darkness.

It was quiet, almost silent. He could hear the links of the chain frantically uncoiling, and then the catch in the dog's furious bark as the collar bit sharply into its throat, the whimpering and snarling as it struggled against its own inane fury. Poor goddamn brute, left alone night after night in the dirt yard behind the house, in the pestilential heat, no doubt mangy with ticks and worms. Someone ought to put it out of its misery.

18

THERE WAS NOTHING TO DO NOW but wait. Wait for Campos to re-establish contact. Wait for instructions or rebuke from Havana. Wait until October, when she returned to the island. Week after week, aside from the handful of hours with Becca, or a passing word with the Arab tobacconist, Narby spoke to no one but Sam Waters, hardly saw a White face save that of the sullen tight-lipped Sanmora ferryman.

He was anxious to leave the Glo-Bel Motor Court, rescue his money, wrapped in the rubber poncho, from the filthy hole in the jungle behind the cabins. The walls of his house were up now. He could ascend the porch steps, walk through the roofless rooms. Simple, box-like island-style architecture—a central passageway with a bedroom on one side, the kitchen and bathroom on the other, and at the back a large open room enclosed by screened panels. The wide-eave tin roof and hinged wooden shutters would deflect the sun and protect against the violent storms. A well-ventilated house of limestone and coral rock and

Dade County pine, with the ancient oak-and-iron front door from Grenada Spain via the ruined folly of Opa Locka. Sam did all the wiring—the electricity supplied by a gasoline-powered generator—and the elemental plumbing that would pipe in fresh water from the well and drain the waste out into the jungle.

Narby had a good rapport with Sam Waters. The strapping white-haired man was intelligent, skilled, an honest and indefatigable worker. And clever enough to dissemble his contempt for 'Cap'm' Vetch, to play the humbled deferential Negro employee. The debt-peonage system that had supplied the Putnam Lumber Company with free Negro labor had been outlawed since 1947, but the county still boasted a thriving KKK, a thicket of Jim Crow prohibitions and curfews, with Sherriff Bullock making the rounds of Henderson Avenue in his bubble-gum machine to remind the Colored folk, lest it slip their minds, that they were a mere one slip-up away from prison, or worse. Lynching might have fallen from favor, but up at the State Pen in Raiford *Old Sparky*—the local newspaper's pet name for Florida's short-circuit prone electric chair—had taken up the slack. The Sunshine State was averaging one Negro male execution a month, sometimes two, if the hunting was good.

Working side by side, they would talk—or rather, Narby would ask Waters about his life and Sam would answer in his laconic manner. Born in Eleuthra, in the Bahamas. Came over as a teenager during the brown wilt that destroyed the island's pineapple crop. Cleared mangrove for Flagler's ill-fated Key West Railroad. Worst work a man could do, killing work, clearing mangrove, standing in knee-deep water and pulling out the roots by a chain tied around your waist. But after that, Waters got lucky, finding employment for the Tractor Prince, James Deering, building Vizcaya, Deering's castle on Biscayne Bay. That's where Waters honed his masonry skills with limestone and coquina, fashioning the courtyards and fountains and formal gardens. When that work dried up, during the Great War, he lived for a while in Coconut Grove, close to the big Christ

Episcopal Church. But with the railway finished and Vizcaya built, the City of Miami didn't want a lot of idle Colored laborers hanging around. That was a bad time. Waters got out, traveled all the way up to Perrine to work in the sawmills. But after a year or two they didn't want Negroes in the mills anymore, neither. The only work to be had was in the fields, cutting cane. It was better than clearing mangrove, but not by much. Then, after all the bank runs, the panics, there wasn't even work in the cane fields. That's when Putnam got him, over in Glades County.

"I was setting on a bench, minding my own business. Deputy come up to me and say, you got a job? And I say, no, sir. Ain't no one got a job nowadays."

They were resting in the shade, on a block of limestone, smoking Narby's hand rolled shag tobacco. The other men were eating their lunch in the bed of Sam's truck, washing it down with the cold Cola Nip Peach sodas Narby kept in the ice chest.

"The cop didn't like that, did he?"

"No, sir."

"Well? What did he say? What was the charge?"

Sam's broad flat face was stiff, his complexion etched with thousands of tiny abrasions and scars, and his eyes clouded, the whites tinted gray. Narby supposed it was the result of some accident, an exposure to lye or acid. A kind of mask-like face that hid the attitude, the superiority, perhaps, of the man behind it. "Don't recall exactly. Something like, 'Shut your mouth, nigra. You under arrest for vagrancy and resisting an officer. They gwine to give you five to ten, boy.' "

"Son of a bitch. So, they brought you up in front of the judge, right? Same kind of a son-of-a-bitch as the cop, maybe his uncle or cousin. And they told you it was either five years up in Raiford or pay a fine."

"That right."

"And lo and behold, there appeared a representative of the Putnam Lumber Company, another S.O.B., who so generously offered to pay your fine, which in turn you would repay by working at the camp. Way out in the jungle. And buying all your provisions from the Company store, the Commissary. On credit against your wages. Vetch's store."

"Weren't Cap'm Vetch up there. They send me up to Alachua. Up in the long leafs. Swinging the hack and collecting the gum." He stopped, apparently taking some pleasure in the rich sweet Danish tobacco. "Weren't long for I wished I was back in the mangrove. Ain't no whipping with that. And at least the railroad pay us. Up in Alachua never saw no money, not a cent. Everything ate up by the store, them books they keep."

"Our own little homegrown Nazi Germany. But, well, you got out of it somehow, didn't you? When you were down here, in the Sawfish Point camp. With that Captain Higginbothom, and Vetch running the store."

Waters flicked away the ragged butt and stood. He was taller than Narby, stronger, despite the white hair. "Best be getting back to it fore the storms come on."

"You're not afraid of Vetch anymore, are you? Granted, he's White. But just barely. If you know what I mean."

"No, sir."

"You tricked him somehow, didn't you? You got something over on Vetch and made him fix the books. That's how you got out. That's why he hates you. The rest of these men, the ones that still live in the old camp, Vetch talks about them like they're spoiled children. Pets. But not you, Sam."

"Don't know nothing about that."

"Yeah. I figured you'd say that." Narby stood, his legs trembling slightly. He was sweating heavily, and it was only ten. "All right. I've had it for the day. I'll see you Friday."

"Yes, sir." He bent to pick up his tools.

"Sam."

"Yes, sir."

"If Vetch ever tries anything, ever bothers you or threatens you. Well, you come to me. He's nothing around here. He's finished. Understand?"

Waters merely nodded and stepped on to the unfinished porch, motioning for the crew to get started. Narby went back to his truck, wiping the sweat from his face, and sitting in the cab took a long drink from the flask—the drink he'd been anticipating, holding off on, all morning. Closing his eyes, the sting of the bourbon in his mouth and filling his throat as the ease of relief seeped into his limbs, unlocking his jaw and loosening the clench of his shoulders. He took another, and after a moment opened his eyes. Standing on the porch Waters had been looking at him, watching Narby drink.

Apparently, the church-going Colored Man disapproved. A couple of weeks earlier, Narby had offered him the flask, taking a drink first and holding it out. Waters had refused, shaking his head, lowering his gaze, with perhaps a glint of pity behind the opaque clouded eyes. It wasn't the mixing of races that had made Waters defer. They had shared a canteen plenty of times.

Narby started the truck and turned it around, lurching over the churned-up dirt and mud. How dare that nigger look at him like that? With that smug scowl of disapproval, worthy of a pompous father. He wondered if Waters knew about Becca. All the Blacks around here knew each other, picked at each other's sores like a horde of apes. Maybe he was just a big joke to them, paying Waters twice, maybe three times, the going rate for Negro labor, throwing away fists full of cash on the little black whore, young enough to be Waters' granddaughter. Laughing behind his back at the profligate White fool.

With Stennart out of business Narby was rationing, compensating with more booze. He recognized the violent mood coming over him, the craw of the Benzedrine-need raking his brain, his spine. It was too late now to catch the morning ferry to Sanmora, swim it off. Besides, she wasn't there. Not until October. The woman who had kissed him, wantonly, tasting of lust.

So what if they laughed behind his back? They were niggers and he was a White Man. The last laugh would belong to him.

19

THE LAST WEEK OF SEPTEMBER. Still no letter from Campos. Nothing from Knowles. Perhaps Narby's indiscretion on the El Castillo napkin had set off a fatal chain reaction—Knowles exposed, the C.I.A. in turn alerting Batista's police to Campos's whereabouts in Miami. Narby had seen something last week in the Negro newspaper, the *Miami Times* (the *Miami Herald* reported only black-on-white crime) about a Mr. Charles Bonn, *unemployed Negro male, mid-twenties, of no fixed address*, shot dead in front of the Harlem Square Theater in Overtown, three blocks from El Castillo. A delinquent gambling debt was the presumed motive. Campos no doubt had more than one alias. Well, it was too late now for Narby to pay a visit to the Negro morgue—Jim Crow prevailed, even in the afterlife—and ask to see the body.

Narby had no other contacts in the Movement. Without Campos he had nothing for Knowles. Unless, of course, he invented—something new about Putnam, perhaps, or rumors of rebels training in the remote wastes of Sawfish Point. That might work in a pinch, but sooner or later he'd have to feed Knowles something with meat, with blood. Like the Guatemala business.

He had no choice, then, but to operate on the assumption that Campos was not in fact Mr. Charles Bonn. That he was alive, and that Bill Knowles, silent and cunning, possibly operating under a new cover, was still counting on him. On Philip Narby.

Campos was a romantic. They had faced death together, had lifted each other up. The bond of affection would overcome any doubts. He would come back to Narby, take him deeper into his confidence. Once the charismatic Castro was out of the picture—Batista might drag things out for a few more months, but sooner or later Castro would be stood against the wall—Narby would convince Campos to split with hard-liner brother Raúl and form a splinter faction. After all, Campos was a Moncadista. He had been with Castro, had risked his life, from the very beginning. His opinion would carry weight with the others.

Frankly, though, Narby wondered if Campos really had what it took be a leader, weighed down with all that useless intellectual ballast about the revolutionary science of psychology, winning over the minds of the ordinary folk, evolving their consciousness. He might beguile the ox-cart campesinos with some siren song about la tierra and the immemorial rights of the yeoman farmer. But what about the urban classes, the clerks and bureaucrats and layers of middlemen tightly intertwined with the criminal element, with gambling and the sex trade and dope, the bribery and patronage that was as endemic to the island as the Royal Palm or the mojito? You couldn't root out corruption like that with educational collectives and folkloric festivals. It had to be cut from the body politic with a knife, the offenders branded as counter-revolutionary, rounded up en masse and herded into stadiums. Revolution was not a science, not a philosophy. It was a lead pipe.

Campos certainly had nerve. He was willing to kill, strike with the pipe, in a moment of crisis. But for revolution, one needed a more sustaining ruthlessness. A mind that could willfully blank itself—the antithesis of consciousness.

On his way out of town Narby stopped in at Hanks. Nothing from Miami, nothing from Havana. But the Arab was in a rather exuberant mood. "Mr. Norby. Please. A gift for you on this important occasion."

He handed Narby a box of imported Egyptian Ovals. They were very strong, harsh cigarettes, packed with twice as much tobacco as the phony Hollywood-American version, the Camel. "So," Narby said, smiling, guessing the source of the tobacconist's happiness. "You're a Nasser supporter, are you?"

"He is a great man, indeed. He will be for Egypt like Ataturk for the Turks. The Suez is now Egyptian. Forever. Nasser will be a good friend of America, Mr. Norby, because Egypt is a free country. Independent of the British. Like America after the revolution. He is good for America. Good for all the Arab peoples."

Of all the strongmen rising out of the colonial rubble, Nasser seemed the most competent, the most cunning. The Suez might very well be his trump card, or his noose. "So, you're Egyptian, Hank?"

"American citizen," he said quickly.

"Right. Well, now that the Suez business is arranged maybe Eisenhower will cough up all that foreign aid. You folks, I mean the Egyptians, could certainly use it. Better to get it from Washington than Moscow. In any case, congratulations."

The tobacconist leaned forward, his thick-fingered nut-brown hands flat on the glass-topped counter. "Thank you, Mr. Norby. May I add, sir. It is only the Jews now who are the problem. The Jews' control of the English banks is a well-known fact. Without these Rothchilds and Cohens making mischief, there would be no Jewish State on Arabic soil."

The Israeli Air Force had just purchased a squadron of American P-51 Mustangs. The French, too, would soon be delivering a big basket of weapons to Ben Gurion, especially if Nasser pushed them on Algeria. The Egyptians had good reason to worry about their Hebraic neighbors. "I'll see you in a few days, Hank." Narby swung open the door, the brass bells ringing him out. Perhaps he ought to drop another perfumed letter addressed to PN in the mail, just to keep Hank on his toes.

He drove south, toward the cypress swamps and the grasslands. Two more weeks and he was out of the Glo-Bel for good. A Negro contractor from Tampa had dug the well. Waters and Narby had installed the generator in a shed away from the house, to reduce the noise. It was a crude set up, but it worked. The light fixtures and ceiling fans were in, the tin roof sealed and the leaks staunched after the last downpour. If they got through the rest of the hurricane season without a big blow, the roof would hold up fine. As soon as moved in, he would contrive a place to hide the money, perhaps install a safe under the floorboards. No more skulking in the jungle behind the cabins in the middle of the night, digging in the filth.

For the last two months Narby had been buying plants from a nursery in Dade County, on the Ingraham Highway, south of Coconut Grove. Melaleuca, Australian pine, bougainvillea, strangler fig, bamboo, gardenia, honeysuckle. And fruit trees for the orchards: coconut, key lime, mango and papaya, avocado, plantains, carambola from Malaya. Waters, who had worked at the gardens at Vizcaya, told Narby what to buy. Sooner or later, the Whites of Lacoosa County would want to know what the hell Narby was doing with all that jungle. Now, he had a cover—one of them eccentric Northerners, with some kind of experimental farm, growing things no one wants to eat but the monkeys in the zoo. No wife, no family, rugged fellow, some kind of free spirit. Heard he was kin to that old dog Vetch, but he sure don't look it. Got a bunch of Coloreds out there working for him, too. Ain't no White men going to work all the way out there in Sawfish Point, that's for sure. Coloreds'll take any work they can get. That's what they for.

To make the ride tolerable he allowed himself one-and-half Benzedrine tablets, and unlimited Jim Beam. Stennart's was still boarded up. Every time Narby passed he thought about the Phenaphen. The only thing stronger than his wish to get off the dope was his yearning to be back on it. He was still sick. He would be sick the rest of his life. There was no cure, no redemption. Only an endless grubbing for palliatives and stimulants and depressants, the endless chase for dollies and bennies. All desire, he had concluded, tended toward the speedball.

He checked in to his usual suite. It no longer mattered if he showed up a bit disheveled, climbing out of the taxi reeking of the Tamiami Trail and Jim Beam. All the Negro bellhops knew him by now, Mr. Narby, a generous tipper. The White cabana boys, too. That crazy swimmer with those hideous scars, some kind of Johnny Weissmuller, goes way out even when it's storming. There'll be a day he won't come back. Storms don't get him, the sharks will.

Around eight he swallowed two more bennies from his dwindling stock and dressed: midnight-blue Italian silk sports shirt open at the neck, chocolate-brown linen trousers with a soft crease, excellent Swiss leather shoes, a jaunty narrow-brimmed panama-weave hat, his cigarettes in a Smoker's Den silver case, the flask in his hip pocket. A sport-fisherman's deep tan, his reddish hair a bit frazzled and bleached from the sun. Philip Narby, the very picture of a South Florida bon vivant. All that was missing was the thirty-six foot cabin cruiser docked at the Dinner Key Marina.

There was a new item on the menu at Giovanni's: snapper ala putanesca. It gave Narby a laugh. Excellent code name for an action. Operation Whore's Snapper. He flipped opened his pocket notebook and recorded it. But by the end of the meal he wasn't feeling so clever. With enough Jim Beam he might stretch it out, but after the initial lift the splash would flatten and his nerves begin to shred. He paid the bill and retrieved his hat, the frank suggestive once-over at the slim-hipped raven-haired hat-check girl more habit now than an expression of any lingering interest. Even if she responded, what would he do? Ask her out on a date, chat about the sultry weather or the Yankees? What Becca gave him would only disgust her. Frankly, when it came to women, that was all he really wanted now—to establish that need, that satisfaction, immediately. Once it was out of the way, the wolf fed for the night, a woman might perhaps mean something more to him. Or not.

He strolled down Espanola and then across on Euclid and up Lincoln, toward Alton Road. Mid-week in the off-season, a dead steam-laced night. The streets were empty. He had to find it. Tonight. Now. He considered taking a cab up to Normandy Shores or Surfside, try his luck in one of the honky-tonks along the northern end of Collins. He'd been before, twice. There was gambling, organized prostitution, all the cops on the take, the stupid shit-eating grins of the hired thugs who kept things from getting out of hand. The same loud pushy crowd he'd avoided in Havana, vulgar in that red-faced triumphant way that only Americans could exude. He wasn't in the mood for that. He didn't have the stomach for it.

When he reached Alton Road he turned south. All the dives looked more or less the same: the dull brick facades, the neon flashing in the window, the placards advertising beer and cigarettes, the solid gunmetal doors about as inviting as a prison gate. The queers and transvestites hung out at Roberto's, along with a certain type of man who pretended not to notice that the girls were really boys. The Tiki Lounge had B-girls, teases, cajoling you to buy them one champagne-cocktail after another, at best letting you get a quick feel under the table or during a close dance. The Roost and Bradford's were more dependable, if you liked the kind of Blondes and Redheads who despite their precipitous cleavage had never stood a chance of making it in pictures, or as magazine models, or who had given up their careers in burlesque for a more lucrative, if dangerous, trade.

A few no-name joints seemed strictly for drinking, dank wells where in the silent company of your fellow lushes you could drown yourself on the cheap, from dawn to staggering dawn.

There was a place further down Alton, around the corner on Fourteenth. The Ship Ahoy. Darker inside than the others. A couple of mildewed lifesaver rings and a ship's wheel hung on the wall to give it the nautical touch. He sat at the bar, resting his hat on the empty stool beside him, and ordered a double Jim Beam, looking around casually as he lit a cigarette. Maybe ten other people, in singles or couples. Not much in the way of chatter. No laughing. Same music as last time, faintly audible above the blowing fan. The new Negro jazz. No blaring horn sections, no tinkling pianos, the harmonies almost bitter. Nothing like what Tom or Jim would have heard on the radio station from Chicago, the big bands, the Basie-style swing. Narby could listen here without resentment.

He sat for a few moments, drinking, growing impatient. How had he managed it with Sylvio? He couldn't bear to think about it. The jukebox was along the back wall. Narby took his drink and walked over to look at the selections. A couple was sitting two booths down. He'd seen them twice before. Phantom people, in perpetual gloom. This time he would approach. What did he have to lose?

The music stopped. He consulted the cards, flipping back and forth, and then dropped his coin, pushed the buttons and watched the disc drop. The Miles Davis Quintet. Looking up, the music flaring in rapid rhythmic jolts, he saw that the woman in the booth was gazing at him, over the shoulder of the man sitting across from her. Nodding her head, as if in approval of his play, his taste. A gaunt woman with straight, rather stringy hair. She looked damned high. And not, he guessed, from booze.

He smiled at her in acknowledgement, took a breath, and stepped over. "Good evening," he said, looking her in the eyes and then, quickly, looking at the man slouched on the bench across from her, his back propped against the wall. "I'm not intruding, I hope."

The man began to straighten. There was something next to him, a stick or club. He was reaching for it. Narby took a step back, almost flinching. But it was only a cane. The man had gripped it to help him straighten. He was crippled.

"No," she said. "Not at all." She was assessing his appearance, the bon vivant clothes and sportsman's tan. "Pull up a chair. Why don't you?" Her voice had a lag, as if it took a little push to get the words from her brain to her lips. She was floating.

The man, too, was sizing him up, rather more aggressively. But he wasn't objecting. Narby reached behind and slid a chair to the end of their table. "Thanks." He took the silver case from his shirt pocket. "Cigarette?"

He held it open for her, and then offered it to the man. He shrugged, as if coming out of deep thought. "Thanks."

"I'm Philip." He didn't offer his hand. "Nice to meet you."

"I'm Audrey. This is Derek. My husband. Likewise. Nice to meet you, Philip."

They looked alike. Gaunt, stringy. Older than Narby, in their late thirties, perhaps. The husband wore a crumpled long sleeved shirt and a narrow tie, the knot loosened and the shirt open at the top. He hadn't shaved, looked like someone who hadn't cared to wash or change clothes for a day or two. The kind of shaggy wharf-rat neglect Narby himself had fallen into in Havana, the same jittery distraction.

Narby flicked his lighter for Audrey. She considered him as if from some great distance or through a fog, squinting and then opening her eyes wide. Thin, flat-chested, her blue dress hanging limp from her shoulders, like a surplice with loose flared sleeves. Derek scooted back against the wall, gripping the handle of the cane. "Seen you before," he said. He spoke with more assurance than his wife. "What ill wind blows you this way, friend?"

"Just seeing the sights. Looking to relax." He picked up his glass and drank it off. "They water these drinks down any more, I might give up drinking all together. I thought perhaps I could find something a little stronger. Something, you know. Different."

"Everyone's scratching around for something different. The new thing. New car, new shoes. New chick."

Audrey laughed. "Derek! So," she said, turning, "what do you, Philip? What's your line?"

"I'm a businessman. A broker. Real estate. Not very interesting, but it's a living."

"Could have fooled me, " Derek said. "I would have guessed something more civic-minded. Like, say. Law enforcement."

"Oh, Derek. He's not a cop. He's too good-looking."

"Don't be fooled, baby. Can't you see the Irish in them there eyes? He's under cover. One of Hoover's Federales."

"Look. I don't want to bother you." He addressed them both, looking back and forth. "If you could help me find what I'm looking for, I'd be most appreciative." He kept his voice low, steady. "Pills. Dolophine. Codeine. Benzedrine. Phenaphen. I'll pay you for any helpful information."

"What's wrong, man? Don't you want to meet Mr. Jones? Not that Audrey or I have any idea what you're talking about. Do we, love?"

"You see, Derek," Audrey said, drifting back. "He's not a cop. Cops always looking for junk. Or weed."

"Women." Derek shook his head deprecatingly, flicking the cigarette in the ashtray. "You married? Because let me tell you, man. It ain't worth it."

Narby put a twenty on the table. "That's just for talking to me. For letting me sit here."

"It's marked. Don't touch it, Audrey."

"But. Derek. What about Morocco? Isn't this what we talked about?"

"Christ. Button it, would you."

Her face crumpled, as if she were about to cry. But then she drifted off, swaying in the booth, her eyes losing focus.

"Is there a pharmacy that might help me? I was using Stennart's, out on the Eighth Street. But he's closed down. Or maybe a Doctor who writes prescriptions."

Derek was looking at the money now, slouching, tapping the cane against the floor, under the table. The music had stopped. "You like that sound?" Narby said. "I'll put on another record." He stood. "I'm not what you think, Derek. Not even close." He chose another Miles Davis Quintet, taking his time, and sat down again. The twenty was gone. "All right. What do you say?"

Derek shrugged. "Don't know what you're talking about, man. But you're dead on the mark about the music. Sound of our times, man. The Negro knows what's going on, the sinister undercurrents. He can hear it down in his soul. You dig?"

Audrey had stopped swaying. Her eyes were closed, her arm resting on the table. The loose sleeve had ridden up to her elbow, showing a few scabs and black-and-blue marks. Like that girl in Havana, the mistake.

"We're on the same wavelength, Derek. Can't you see that?"

"But you're clean, man. Trackless virgin territory. Didn't they teach you the basics in vice? Give it up, pal. We're just a nice married couple, out for a quiet evening. Isn't that right, baby?"

Audrey opened her eyes. "Derek. We need that money. I told you, I'm not going back to Mexico. Morocco, baby. That's where it's at. Like we talked about."

Derek smiled, nodding toward his wife. "She gets like that, man. An episode. Epileptic schizophrenic hysteria. She's a live wire, man. Touch at your own risk."

"What do you do, Derek? I mean, aside from squatting in this hole, sucking down booze?"

"The old provocation trick. Won't work, man. Spit all over me, man. I ain't budging."

"He's a teacher." Audrey said. "High school English. He's a poet. Aw come on, Derek. Look at the guy. He's scared. He's bugging." Audrey reached out and put her hand on Narby's arm. It was cold against his skin. "I know what it's like. Christ, Derek. Have some compassion."

"*In Xanadu did Kubla Kahn a stately pleasure dome decree.* Tell me who wrote that. You tell me, I'll help you out. Your typical Fed is not well-versed in the English Romantic tradition."

Narby placed his hand over Audrey's, looking at her. "I'll give you a hundred, if you can help me."

"Lay off her, man." Derek gripped the cane, struggling to lean forward. "Don't trip her wire, man. Identify the poet and win a trip to Xanadu. The contest ends at midnight."

"Maybe we should get out of here, Audrey." He could feel her fingers wriggling under his hand, yearning to intertwine.

"I've got money. I know people. If Derek doesn't want to go to Morocco, we'll go without him."

"It's not his fault," she moaned. "He's a beautiful man. Even without all that."

Derek squirmed on the bench. "Shut up, bitch," he said, rather quietly.

"You were in Korea. Weren't you, Derek? So was I. I'll show you. I was wounded, pretty badly. We could help each other."

"You mean, so you can fuck my wife? Because they let you out of Korea with your balls still between your legs? Lucky for you, man. Hey Baby, this is one hell of a cop."

"Derek. Don't talk like that."

"Who's the poet, Jack? One guess."

Narby shrugged. "Robert Frost?"

Derek started to laugh. "You're a riot, man. That's hilarious. You ought to be on Ted Mack. Wrong, man. You lose. The contest is closed."

Narby stood. "Sorry to have bothered you."

"Derek," Audrey whined. "Don't be such a goddamn ass."

"It's only fair, love. He's got the balls. I got the knowledge. Never the twain shall meet."

He might still get something out of Audrey. But he couldn't stomach it. He smiled at her and turned away. Behind him, he heard Derek, raising his voice for the first time. "It's Coleridge, man. Samuel Taylor. Remember that. Might come in handy one day, piece of intelligence like that."

20

HE REMEMBERED LEAVING THE SHIP Ahoy around ten and wandering into Bradford's and after that Roberto's, sitting at the bar watching one of the queers in a long tight dress, draped in a Spanish mantilla, dance the flamenco. He kept moving, three or four watered downed drinks at each stop. All the high-class clubs along Dade Boulevard, like Ciro's and the Copa, were closed for the season, but the dives and striptease joints were open year-round, every night until five in the morning. No rest for the low life.

It was still dark when he made his way back to the Atlantique. He had walked straight through the lobby and out to the terrace bar, nodding at the night clerk who knew Narby by sight, past the swimming pool and down the concrete steps of the seawall. The cabanas were folded down for the night, the beach chairs stacked. The moon had set, the sky overcast and starless, the sea calm and ink-black, the waves foaming milky green as they broke and rolled up the sand. Wide awake and yet mortally exhausted, his head lolling and then snapping upward as if something kept calling him to attention, intoxicated to the point of an illusory sobriety, he had considered going in, figuring that if he swam hard enough, long enough, he would then be able to sleep. Straight into the briny void with strong confident strokes.

Unbuttoning his shirt he came closer to the surf, drawn forward by the soporific murmur of the waves sloshing against the jetties, the twinkle of tiny lights miles far off shore, cargo or cruise ships riding the invisible black horizon, beckoning him. Suddenly, as if stepping into a puddle of warm blood, he jerked back. His handsome Swiss shoes were soaked, caked in grainy mud. He plopped down on the sand and fumbled at the laces. The shoes would drag him under, impede his quest to swim out to the ships. So that was it, not a mere idle plunge but a mission. Dope smugglers, no doubt. Enormous crates brimming with Dollies and Bennies. That poor son-of-a-bitch junkie Derek, castrated by Korea. Derek was right about the poem though. Derek's intelligence had been correct. It was in the filing cabinet, only too far back, in the section marked Tom or Jim, English Class, Teacher's College, 1947. Derek was perhaps someone worth cultivating. In exchange for such valuable information Narby would keep Derek's wife content, supply Audrey with the missing parts. Only they were enemies, he and Derek. Just as he and Frank Swanson were enemies. That was how it went down, with Korea. A phony war, a United Nations publicity stunt that went sour, posing no threat to God or Country, with no women or children or homeland to defend, allies and enemies alike an undifferentiated horde of laundrymen and gooks toward whose fate one was at best indifferent, at worst contemptuous. Enraged and terrified and confused you directed your hated, your outrage, toward your own instead—hated the man next to you, the soldier below you who sucked the last drop of water from the canteen or took the last blanket or grabbed the only working rifle. Hated the General who ordered you to stand or die, hated the officer, who also hated the General, who ordered you to run down the exposed hillside to deliver the paper with the artillery co-ordinates, because the radio was dead, because some little Jew Sergeant had sold off all the replacement batteries on the black market in Shinbashi. So much hatred, so many enemies close at hand.

Some time passed as he sat on the sand, absorbed in these remembrances—time enough for the sun to pink if not yet breach the horizon. His shoes off, the sand between his toes, he understood that he was ready now for his voyage outward. Only perhaps he ought to rest for a moment longer, gather his resolve. Besides, he still had his trousers to contend with. He lay back on the damp sand and closed his eyes.

The two cabana boys found him, curled up against the glaring morning sun, rousing him a bit roughly until they realized he was a guest of the hotel, the crazy swimmer, the big tipper, and then helping him brush off, making like it was a joke. He left the wet gritty clothes in a heap outside the door to his suite and called down for laundry service, telling them to have everything ready by two. After a shower he managed a few hours of fitful rest, then got out of bed and ordered breakfast and the newspapers. The first drink of the day was always unpleasant, but by the third his throat relaxed. It was a matter of chemistry, attaining the right admixture of alcohol and then monitoring it, adjusting throughout the day. And the night. Every day. Every night. For the rest of his life.

Calmer now, he opened the attaché: exactly two of Stennart's white pills left. The last of the batch. His will had been good. He had conserved. Two would be sufficient to calm him for the afternoon's work, at the bank. Because this time he was going to withdraw three thousand, despite having withdrawn half that much less than three weeks ago. The success of Guatemala was only a first step, he had realized. The base at Opa-locka was too exposed now. For whatever came next—Venezuela, perhaps, or the Dominican Republic—a more secure location was required. Sawfish Point. Two thousand acres of remote jungle. The funds to purchase ought to be in place well beforehand, and untraceable. He had to act now. Today. This very afternoon. No wonder Knowles had gone silent. At this critical juncture an intercepted message might put the entire operation at risk. Just as Narby had anticipated, he was now in the forward position, running things on his own initiative. They would follow his lead. They were waiting for his next move.

When his clothes came, clean and pressed, he took two yellows—the bennies, too, would soon be gone—dressed, packed the attaché, and went downstairs to check out. The white-haired gold-buttoned epauletted Negro doorman hailed him a cab that took him five blocks to the garage on Michigan Avenue.

Keep your mind on Miss Prentice. Or her avatar. Any teller would do, as long as the blouse underneath the yellow cardigan sweater was unbuttoned to bank-regulation standards, the creamy vortex exposed. He crossed the bottle-green sparkle of Biscayne Bay, climbing and descending the hump of the General Douglas MacArthur Causeway and then wending his way, this time down the scenic route on Biscayne Boulevard and Brickell and up through Coconut Grove until he hit the Miracle Mile and found parking on a quiet shaded street of banyans and strangler figs, the coral-rock garden walls and arches of the faux-Spanish villas festooned with masses of bright bougainvillea.

He sat for a moment, gazing at the two white pills cradled in the palm of his surprisingly steady hand. The last of it. Something else would come along, another Stennart's, a sympathetic physician, a more compliant Derek. There was always the Rexall's in Myerton, the slow-moving pharmacist behind his window like a sitting target and the fat deputy sheriff shooting the bull at the Gladiola Café or cruising down Henderson Avenue in his bubble gum machine, keeping vigilance over the darker race. Along the Tamiami stood any number of gun shops and shabby side-of-the-road establishments, their signboards screaming ICE BAIT AMMO BEER. It was perhaps time to acquire a sidearm. Though Narby understood that a man like Bill Knowles would never carry a weapon. For a man like that, a gun was a concession to fear and desperation, was it not?

Closing his eyes he waited until the first waves of narcotic quietude rippled and mixed with the jagged agitation of the yellows, just now attaining their plateau. Reassured, he climbed out, smoothing his freshly laundered blue silk, adjusting the jaunty narrow-brimmed hat, and with attaché in hand strolled toward Aragon Avenue. The South Florida sportsman bon vivant. Wilson would no doubt assail him again—investment opportunities, savings schemes, tax dodges. By instinct, Narby supposed, any banker might grow frantic at the sight of so much money fleeing his vaults, month after month. Sooner or later, he would have to do something about Wilson. Perhaps engage Miss Prentice to divert the banker in his office, the door closed and her skirt hiked, while Narby went about his affairs.

The enormous afternoon glare bouncing off the white lime-stone façades penetrated his dark glasses, provoking a mild squint. Inside, as always, a cool bath of dry air, the sunlight muted through the tinted glass, the aquamarine glow of the carpet, the smell of leather and perfume and a trace of cigar smoke. He stood at the counter, slipping the dark glasses into his pocket, and filled out the form, blanking his mind. As he lay down the pen one of the tellers smiled at him from across the lofty room, looking away just as their gazes meshed. He was without doubt the most appealing man in the vicinity. If only his good looks, his sportsman's appeal, were as fungible as cash. If only he could walk up to her and, in the same way he would exchange the withdrawal slip for the money, say, I'd like you, please. Naked. In my hotel room, or the truck, or on some deserted beach. Or right here, right now, behind that partition. In exchange for me.

He'd had her before, maybe twice. She would do. He strolled over, his nerves jangling despite the muffle of the calmantes. At the window his eyes searched out the vortex, a ship in the storm seeking safe anchor.

"Good afternoon. Nice to see you. How can I help you today?"

"Good afternoon. Miss Bryant, is it?"

She smiled. "Yes."

"Here you are, Miss Bryant." He slid the withdrawal slip across the marble sill. She took it, examined it. From his vantage, the slip was perfectly aligned with her cleavage. He thought he detected a slight excitement in her breathing, a bead of dew-like perspiration twinkling in the exposed cleft.

"Just a moment, please." She rose. She had stopped smil-ing. The slip in her hand she stepped into one of the small offices behind the tellers' windows and closed the door. He watched through the panel of rippled frosted-glass—an upright and rather well-endowed female blotch, handing the slip to the male blotch seated behind a desk. The male blotch rose. Narby could see that it was clutching the telephone receiver. There were agitated movements: the blotch waving at, or waving away, the female. She opened the door. He could see it on her face, the strained smile, the warmth of attraction wiped clear from her eyes. She was scared.

Narby took a breath, turning slightly. A tall heavy-set man in a blue blazer was coming out from behind a desk in the far corner of the bank lobby, near the entrance to the safe deposit boxes. At the same time, the blotch behind the frosted glass was coming through the door, following the teller. Its face came into view: red, the eyes nearly popping. The teller in the next window pivoted in her chair, as if alerted to some danger. They had been waiting for him. It was some kind of ambush.

Turning, he saw a clear path across the plush aquamarine carpet to the revolving doors. The hulking man in the blazer, coming straight at him now with rapid steps, apparently unarmed, would try to intercept him. He would have to run. Now. No. Wait until he's closer, so he couldn't angle across, like a football player evading the tackler. He heard someone say, "Excuse me. Mr. Narby." The blotch had its arm extended. One more second. He had to hold himself back, as if bound by a chain, tightening beyond endurance. His breath hissed through his teeth. Let them come closer, let them see that he had nothing to hide, nothing to fear.

"Yes," Narby said, turning his head, smiling, raising the attaché slightly as if to defend against a blow or swing it in attack.

"If you'd be so kind—"

The blazer was within arm's reach. Narby lurched forward, as if to butt him, and the man stepped back.

"Mr. Narby!"

Now. He ran for the door, a demeaning yet prudent bolt, the attaché slowing him only slightly, and thrown by its swift revolution plunging into the heat, the blinding glare. No police. Not yet. The sidewalks, the rather precious Coral Gables shops and boutiques, deserted in the midday swelter. Executing a few diversionary turns, he sprinted down Galiano, past the last shops, then slowing as he entered the neighborhood of lushly landscaped villas and garden apartments. For a moment he panicked, thinking he had forgotten where the truck was parked. But there it was, in front of him. Feeling the wet of his back against the seat he understood that it was only sweat—that his life, his blood, was still contained within him and under his command. He was trembling, goddamn it, but not so bad as to impede him from inserting the key at the first try, starting the truck, driving slowly down the street until he hit Le Jeune and then left onto Eighth Street, and then after two lights turning on a side street, zig-zagging down the blocks of shabby little Florida bungalows and then, turning back along the rank overgrown alleys that ran behind the commercial buildings along the Tamiami. He recognized the back of the junk shop where he had loaded the old Moorish door and next to it the padlocked back entrance to Stennart's. His breathing was returning to normal. He craved a drink and pulled into the alley, taking the flask from the glove box.

No one was following him. No one had seen him get into the truck. The bank knew Philip Narby only as an account number, a signature, a disguise. Besides, it wasn't their money. They were acting on behalf of another. Not Knowles. Narby was certain of that. Knowles wouldn't have been so clumsy, so obvious. Knowles wouldn't have failed. He leaned forward to peel off the sweat-soaked silk and he pulled on a T-shirt and then lit a cigarette and drove the truck out of the alley and back onto the Tamiami.

It was Sid Black. He was alive. Back in business. It had taken him this long—whatever was left of him—but he had finally straightened out his affairs and staunched the weeping wound of the Narby account. Obviously, Black had alerted the bank, perhaps that very week. It was the name Philip Narby, and not the exorbitant amount on the slip, that had sent the teller into a spin. She, and all the other tellers, had been warned. The thought comforted Narby somewhat. A man like Sid Black cared about nothing but money. Fanatics, romantics, egomaniacs, men like Willoughby or Campos, might be manipulated or seduced but never reasoned with. But a clever Jew like Black would understand that if he wanted his money back, he would have to bargain. Because the money was filthy. The crates of contraband booze and cigarettes, the scrap metal stolen from the Japanese bases, batteries and gasoline and electric wire and machine parts, whatever Master Supply Sergeant Black could siphon off and sell at one of the sprawling outdoor markets at Shinbashi or around Ueno Station. Or the Russian caviar, the expensive cigars and champagne, stuff the PX couldn't carry that he sold personally to men like Ted McCoy, coming around the office like the goddamn Fuller Brush man. Pornography, too, the magazines wrapped in cellophane that Narby had found in the bottom of Black's desk drawer that day in the warehouse when he had been searching for invoices from the so-called Allbright Paper Company.

It was highly unlikely that Sid Black would be reporting his losses, the theft of his money, to the police or the MPs or the Internal Revenue Service. Highly unlikely that he would encourage the Bank of Coral Gables to pursue the matter any further. Black had had his chance to get his hands on Narby, and he had failed.

He was beyond the city limits now, speeding past the billboards for airboat rides and alligator wrestling, entering the Glades, vast and empty and hostile. It would be a relief, after all—to never again have to go through that song and dance at the bank. Even with all the land he had purchased he still had about twenty thousand dollars, wrapped in the US Army-issue rubber poncho, buried in the fetid swarming thickets behind the Glo-Bel motel. No mortgage, no car payments, no wife, no kids, the house in the jungle virtually finished, and thirteen hundred acres, more or less, of trackless pine and palmetto wastes, protecting him like a heaving sea of barbed wire. For a hunted-down wharf rat, a deserter, he had done rather well for himself. A regular Robinson Crusoe. Hell, he felt like celebrating. He reached over, his eyes on the road, one hand on the wheel, clicked open the attaché, and popped two yellows in his mouth.

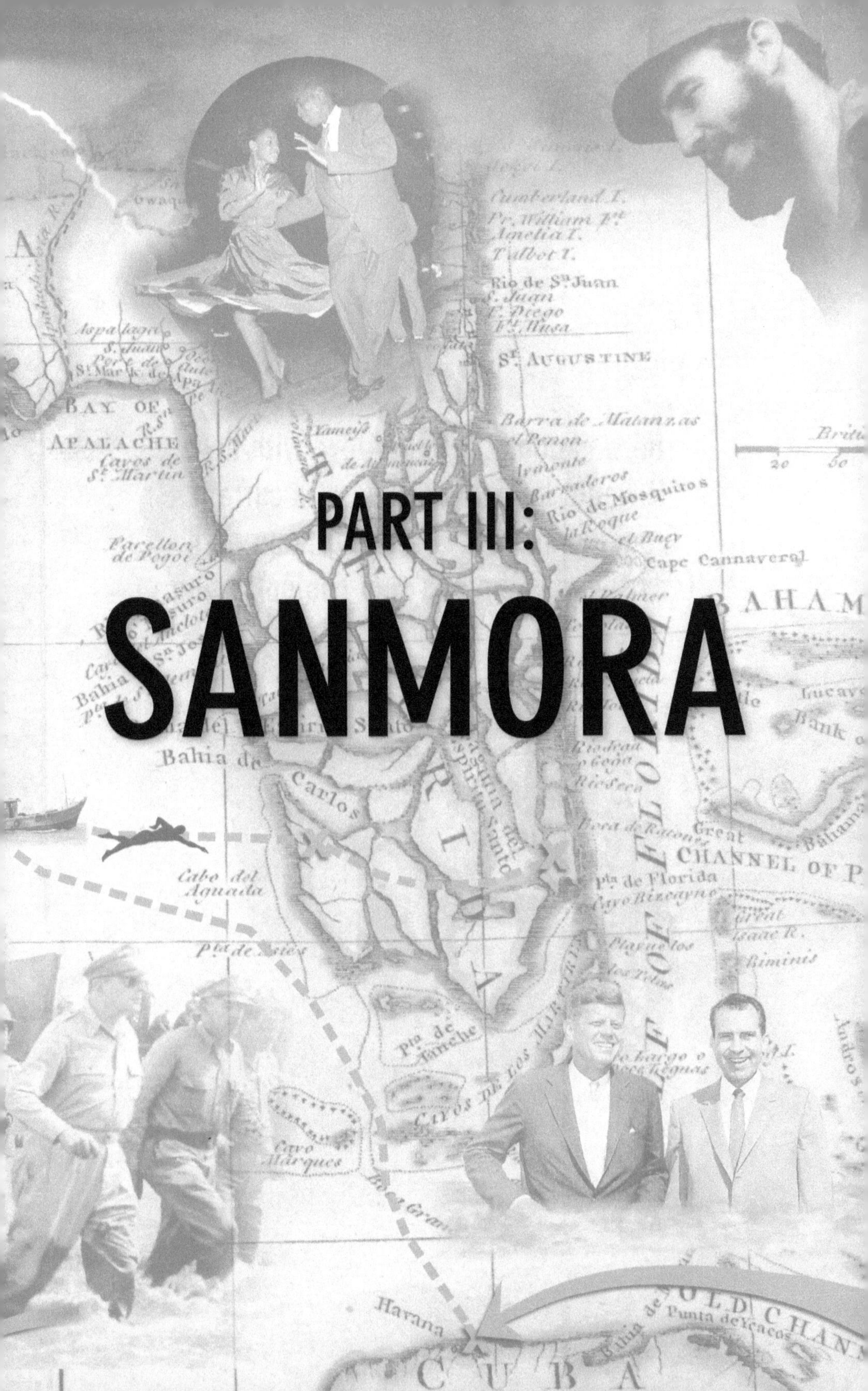

PART III:
SANMORA

He was going to fall in love with her.
It would be like a sickness, a current
dragging him out. Dragging them both.
Only she was the one who couldn't swim.

1

NARBY STOOD ON THE PORCH looking out at the jungle beyond the clearing. The morning sky was crystalline blue, the air dry and cool and free of swarms. To the banal caw of crows and blackbirds were added the polyphonic twitterings of a dozen migrant species. Yesterday, along the estuary and the mangrove coast, he had watched thousands of exotic shorebirds—spoonbills, black skimmers, arctic terns, yellow crowned night herons—crowding out the commonplace pelicans and gulls. Eight months out of the year a pestilent low-lying mosquito-infested tract of pine and palmetto scrub, but now, the hurricane season over, with the first cold snap, Sawfish Point approached paradise. It was a stunning if transitory respite from the feverish tedium—like a shot of dope for an addict in the throes of abject craving, the jungle unclenching, flooding the land with sweetness and light. No wonder they called it the high season.

He went inside, leaving open the antique Moorish slab that Waters had rigged up into a front door. The kitchen was crude: a second-hand icebox, propane stove, a cold-water tap over a rust-streaked porcelain sink. Sufficient to boil coffee, fry an egg or cook a steak. He poured another cup, laced it with bourbon, and sat at the table in the back, the largest room in the house, the walls fitted with screen panels. Behind the house Waters had planted stands of bamboo and fruit trees: mango, key lime, avocado, papaya. One day the room would be deeply shaded, embraced, by the gardens and groves, a tropical bower.

The furnishings, like the front door, had come from the second-hand junk and estate-sale shops along the Tamiami Trail:

a pair of high-backed throne-like wicker chairs, an overstuffed claw-footed sofa, a threadbare Persian rug, lamps with water-stained silk shades, bookcases pocked with insect holes, a cracked marble coffee table. After the narrow rancid room in Havana, after the Glo-Bel plywood cabin, it was all rather quaint and commodious.

Beneath the rug, under where the table now stood, Waters had installed a small fireproof safe, accessible through a hinged opening in the floorboards. He trusted Sam Waters. What choice did he have, really? He had to trust someone. The Bahamian had become indispensible, as had Narby to Waters, or so Narby hoped. He had doubled Waters' weekly salary, praising the man's skill and diligence and integrity. With the road still in need of improvement, constructing the gardens and the pond, putting up fences, preparing the wiring to connect sooner or later to the Lacoosa County power lines, expanding the rudimentary plumbing, perhaps adding some outbuildings—there was plenty to keep Waters busy. In concession to the man's private religious or moral scruples, or whatever the hell it was, Narby kept the booze out of sight.

For the present, Narby was steering clear of Miami Beach and Coral Gables and the rest of White Miami. It was possible, though unlikely, that Sid Black was still looking for him. Black might have hired a private detective. Best to lay low for a while, until Black reconciled himself to his losses. Black had used Narby, and in turned Narby had used Black. As far as Narby was concerned, they were square.

He opened his black book and looked over the notes from his last meeting with Ernesto Campos. Twice now since the Cuban had re-established contact after their argument over Guatemala, they had arranged to meet at El Castillo. Charles Bonn—of no fixed address or occupation, the man shot dead in front of the Harlem Square Club that summer—was obviously not Ernesto Campos. But Narby suspected that the unsolved murder held a warning. Perhaps Campos felt the same. Campos had said nothing about Bill Knowles, or whether his comrades in Havana had attempted to verify the information written on the napkin. As if by tacit agreement, both men had simply picked up the game where they had left it: money, weapons, building the Movement, making allies, propaganda, the need for more action, more violence.

Castro was still in prison, awaiting trial. The Movement was stalled. In the Cuban press there was talk of reform, reconciliation, though no one really believed it. It was politics, Batista giving his torture machine a rest before cranking it up again once the outside world looked away. Campos merely said, "We must wait." After Guatemala and Iran, with the Huk rebellion in the Philippines steadily losing ground, Campos had little choice but to entertain seriously Narby's prediction: without the CIA on their side, or at the least taking a neutral stand, the Movement would fail.

In the meantime, to appease his revolutionary fervor, Campos was continuing his studies in the mass psychology of decolonization. Through his academic connections in Havana the Cuban had managed to matriculate as an exchange student at the University of Miami School of Medicine. "There I am not Negro," he explained to Narby. "I am Spanish. Un poco de Gitano, dark like Andalusian. Like I tell to you, Felipé, race is psychological, not physiological. It is an error of bad consciousness."

Through the bird racket Narby heard Waters pull up in the flatbed. He closed the notebook, kneeled under the table to put it in the safe, and then finished packing the rucksack. On his way out, he informed Waters that he would be gone all day. "Good morning to start digging," Waters said, the pick-ax slung over his shoulder. "Might as well start on that pond. That all right?"

"Fine. You got some help?"

"Mebbe. I go see if I can fetch a couple of them lazybones from the camp. A good day to work is a better day to loaf. So they say." He might have even cracked a smile. Narby wasn't sure. Waters wasn't much for kidding around, but the pleasant weather was infectious.

Starting in mid-November, the Sanmora ferry ran twice a day, two trips out and two trips back. Along with the exotic shorebirds the high-season luxury-class cars had returned, the Lincoln, the Mercedes Benz. Two beautiful yachts, a sailing vessel and a sleek cabin cruiser, had docked at the Village Marina. The seaplane came and went, perhaps once a week, buzzing the coast, never touching down within sight. Over the last few weeks Narby had passed most of them on the beach: the smartly dressed shell collector, the cocktail-in-hand dog walkers, the children with their nanny. Of the eight villas hidden in the jungle behind the dunes, he noted that six of them were at present re-occupied.

October. They were to meet on the beach, by chance, as before. December now, and still no sign of her. Twice, when no one was around to see, he had mounted the raised walkway and peered over the gate in the hedge, trying the handle and finding it locked. The swimming pool was still covered by the tarp. No lights inside, no movement. The house—the sleek concrete boxes with the steel-framed windows and the cantilevered terrace—appeared deserted. Perhaps, having regretted her indiscretion, her rather sluttish behavior, she was avoiding him, hiding. Maybe she'd been drunk or high, though at the time he hadn't thought so. Or maybe she was only a liar, a tease? Or perhaps something had happened to her. How the hell should he know? It was getting on his nerves. Because for the last three weeks he found himself lingering along that stretch of dunes, hanging about, like a lost dog. The others were beginning to notice, he thought. He was getting careless.

A few days ago, on the beach, he had nodded in passing to a rather sturdy looking man, mid-fifties, iron gray hair and moustache, dressed in crisp plaids and khaki, smoking a pipe. Narby had a hunch it was Dalton Pembaker—the name he had seen on record at the County Clerk, Executive Director of the

Isadora Land and Trust Corporation. The man had nodded back, as if perhaps sending a signal of recognition. Why not risk it, next time they passed? Say hello, start a little conversation. Drop the name Bill Knowles. Stir the pot and see what happens.

He parked the truck in the dirt lot next to the utilitarian metal lighthouse—built during the Spanish-American War, Narby had learned. The island made a strategic vantage for keeping vigilance over Cuba and the Caribbean, less obvious and exposed than Key West.

A few wintering visitors—even in the high season tourists rarely bothered with Sanmora, with no hotels, no restaurants, and the inconvenience of the ferry—were picnicking under the tall shaggy pines. Narby avoided them, making his way down a side path, the rucksack slung over his shoulder, the pines giving way to native coastal shrub, the flowering vines and clumps of tall tufted grass, prickly pear cactus, and sea-grape bushes—so called because the Villagers made jam out of the hard, clustered berries—that grew at the foot of the dunes. In the bright winter air the island attained perfection, the cool ocean breeze playing against the warm brilliant sun, the surface of the turquoise water sparkling, the gentle breakers sending the sandpipers scurrying across the foam.

Fifty yards or so shy of where the black-water creek breached the dunes to empty into the Gulf, he went for a long swim. Afterward, he drank from the canteen and the flask and ate a bit of whatever he brought in the rucksack. The drink was all he had now. The drink and the craving and the intermittent pain.

After his swim he spread a towel on the sand and sat crossed-leg, shirtless in his swimming trunks, smoking and drinking and gazing out at the ocean. Letting his mind drift. He wondered what he would be now, Tom or Jim, if he had refused the congressman's offer, had never boarded the *U.S.A.T. Caprice*, Seattle to Yokohama. If he had simply ignored the unsigned document someone had laid on his desk that morning, fed it to the incinerator instead of showing it to Ted McCoy, who had laughed at him, dressed him down, and then, outraged, sending it to Bill Knowles at the embassy in Hong Kong. But it would have already been too late. Someone had chosen him, obviously, picked him out of the crowd.

Suddenly, he felt a prickling and stinging against his back, something striking him. He jumped up, twisting around, flinging his arms out.

"Hello, pirate. Watching for the Jolly Roger?"

She was standing a few feet behind him, smiling. His shirt was on the towel. The scars were on full display. His fists were balled; he lowered his arms. "Damn it. I almost slugged you."

"Sorry. It was a dirty trick. But. I couldn't resist."

It had only been a handful of sand and pebbles. He had overreacted. His pulse was pounding. He took a breath. "Sneak attack," he said, trying to joke, whisking up his shirt. "It's not fair."

"That's the general state of the world, isn't it? Not fair." She was wrapped in an opal-green shawl, over a swimsuit, apparently, her bare legs showing.

"I was beginning to think so. But now, maybe I'll change my mind."

She laughed, cocking her head to one side, looking him up and down and pulling the shawl tighter against the breeze. "Been for a swim?"

"Yes. How about you? No. I remember. You don't swim."

"Very good. What else do you remember?"

"Your name. Willa Branton. Your house." He pointed in the direction of the creek. "That you'd be back. In November."

"That was the idea," she said. "Well. Only a few weeks late." She made a little pout with her mouth. Her lips were full, pale, because she wore no make up. "Forgive me?"

He could pretend that he hadn't been searching for her, waiting. But it was perhaps more to his advantage to flatter her. "I suppose so. This one time."

She was looking down at his things: the beaten-up ruck-sack, the flask on the towel, the pouch of tobacco. He'd gone without shaving for a couple of days. The shirt draped over his shoulders, hiding the scars—the original bank shirt, in fact, purchased years ago from a shop along the Prado in Havana—old now, frayed, faded by the sun. His hair tangled from the swim, his breath no doubt stinking of cigarettes and bourbon. And it wasn't even noon. Apparently, she didn't care.

"Feel like a stroll?" The winter sun brought out the red in her short brown hair, ignited the dark flecks in her green eyes, showed the symmetrical smattering of freckles across her cheekbones. A face without flaw or distraction, fresh and warm and inviting. "I've been out all morning. Walk me home, and I'll make you a cup of coffee. Or something stronger, if you prefer."

"All right." He gathered his things and slung the sack over his shoulder. "Lead the way."

They walked barefoot just at the waterline. He discerned the outline of her body in the swimsuit, shifting under the shawl: her high round breasts, the flat stomach, her well-shaped der-riere and long legs. "With this weather, well, I wish I had made it back earlier," she was saying. "My god, it's sublime. And the birds. Have you seen them, on the other side of the island? The flamingoes and the spoonbills? Sometimes I think I should give up New York entirely. You live here round year, don't you—oh, shoot. I'm sorry." She stopped and faced him. "I'm at a disad-vantage, I'm afraid. I can't recall your name. You told me and I wanted to remember. I thought I had. Really."

"Philip Narby."

"Philip Narby." She looked him in the eyes. "I won't forget this time."

She turned and began to walk again, looking out at the water, quite aware, he supposed, of his intent gaze, assessing and admiring. When they reached the inlet she stopped, sud-denly glancing behind her, as if she had lost her way.

"Oh, Christ. What the hell is this?"

"The creek. You must have crossed it earlier."

"Yes, of course, how else, only. This river wasn't here. It was just a little stream. I can't walk across that."

"How long ago?"

"What?" She sounded annoyed.

"How long ago did you cross it?"

"Hours. It was very early. I walked all the way to the lighthouse. On the way back, that's when I saw you get out of the water. But how the hell are we going to get across?"

She was actually frightened. Narby laughed. "You must have crossed just after low tide."

"It's not funny." She frowned, looking behind and then over the dunes, hoping for some other way around.

"It's all right. We can swim. It's only twenty yards or so. I've done it plenty of times."

"I told you. I'm not a swimmer. I can't manage it." From the mud bank she gazed down at the dark rippling channel, her brow creased. "God. It's deep. I can't see the goddamn bottom."

"Hold a minute." He put the rucksack down and waded up to his chest, his shirt unbuttoned, letting his shirttails float. "You can make it up to here, yes?"

"I don't know. I suppose."

"All right," he called. "Just a minute." As he reached the midpoint of the inlet, the water up to his chin, he let himself be dragged a few feet by the undercurrent and then planted his feet in the muck, gauging how difficult it would be to ferry her across. Raising his arms overhead he pushed across, his feet sinking to the ankles in the muck, the water at his chin, until he felt the bottom sloping up. He could walk across without his mouth going under, but just barely. The tide was still coming in. Ten minutes more and it would be too deep. He yanked his feet from the mud and swam back.

"It's OK. I can walk and you can hold on to me. You won't go under. I promise."

"What are my options?"

"Well. We could wait for the tide to go out, but that would take hours. Or we could walk back to the lighthouse. My truck is parked there. I could drive you home. If you prefer."

"If only I could see the bottom. But I can't. Oh, shut up, Willa." She gave a nervous laugh. She was terrified. "All right, Tarzan. Sweep me off my feet."

"Easier without that," he said, indicating the shawl.

In her anxiety she had wrapped herself tightly. Sighing, she let the shawl drop on the sand.

Gripping her hand Narby led her into the channel. As the water rose toward her chest she draped hers arm over his shoulders and, quite naturally, he lifted her, gently, as if she were an invalid. But the weight made his feet sink deeper in the mud. It took all his strength and balance just to move a few yards. "Maybe you should try to wade a little further," he suggested. "Until it's up to your neck."

"No chance, Tarzan."

"All right. Let's try piggyback. Hike yourself up, as high as you can."

The mud underfoot was too soft. His mouth went under, the incoming current pushing him off balance. He was going to tip. The important thing was to keep her head above the water. Suddenly he lost his footing and his legs gave way. She screamed, wrapping her arms around his neck, nearly choking him. But as he fell he had also pushed hard against the bottom and by luck there was a ridge of firmer sand and his head came up right away, and he was back on his feet. From there it was only a matter of trudging. A few yards from the bank she climbed off and waded alongside him, still gripping his hand.

The bank was steep. He stepped out and then helped her up. They disengaged. She ran her hand through her wet hair, then shook it out. "Wasn't so bad. You make a damn good seahorse. Oh hell. We left our things, your bag."

He shrugged. "No problem." Showing off, he took a running start, dived into the channel and with a few strokes reached the other side. His shirt was sopping. He took it off, not caring at the moment, and stuffed the shirt and her shawl into the rucksack. "Heads up," he shouted.

"OK," she cried out, her anxiety released, playful again now that she was safe. "Let her rip."

Like a discus-thrower he uncoiled and launched the rucksack across the inlet. She tried to catch it, but it fell at her ankles. "Whoops." She picked it up and brushed off the wet sand. "Does that mean I don't make varsity?"

He swam back and climbed up the bank, the water running off his body. She was watching, admiring. Despite the scars. She held out the rucksack, as if to hand it to him, but as he reached for it she dropped it and embraced him, kissing him on the mouth, pressing her body, covered only by the swimsuit, against him. But then, as he was lowering his hands around her waist, she pulled away.

"Thanks for the lift," she said. "Would you mind giving me my shawl?"

He picked up the sack and withdrew the shawl. She wrapped herself, like a mermaid, he thought, and they began to walk again, saying nothing more until they reached the wood-plank walkway. A pair of rubber thongs had been left there and she slipped them on. "Be careful of the splinters." He drew up his arches as he stepped. The planks were warm from the sun. The gate through the hedge was unlocked. In the garden, the dunes cutting off the breeze, it was suddenly warmer, the air smelling of gardenia and honeysuckle, almost cloying, like a hothouse. The tarp covering the oval swimming pool had been removed. The water, crystal clear and the surface skimmed of detritus, made a tiny gurgling sound.

Now, for the first time, he saw the house clearly. He had perhaps seen the same kind of architecture in Chicago, or in the parts of Tokyo that had escaped the bombs and fires. Silken-textured concrete walls, plate-glass windows of various sizes framed in burnished steel. It was all rectangles and squares, the various parts of the house—the first floor and the smaller second floor and another adjacent building—set at odd angles to one another. A concrete slab, a terrace fitted with a steel-cable railing, jutted out from the second story, dramatically cantilevered so as to command a panoramic view of the dunes and the jungle and the sea.

Next to the pool was a curved, blue-tiled wall with a showerhead. "Rinse off, if you'd like. It's cold water, though. Would you prefer a hot shower?"

"No. It's fine."

"I'll just be a minute, then."

She went in through a wide glass door, apparently unlocked. The row of mansions was like a private domain, hers and Pembaker's and the rest of them. Maybe she wanted him to follow her inside, to take her as she undressed for the shower. Maybe she was like Martha, divorced, only younger and still beautiful and therefore without desperation. He had worked up a bit of lust for Martha, as he remembered it, but at same time he had pitied her. He had never really wanted to see Martha naked. He had only wanted to imagine it, to shape her in his mind. That single glimpse of Martha's breasts, which had lost their appealing firmness and shape once her blouse was undone, had been rather off-putting. Even drunk, he doubted he would have had the stomach to go through with it.

He rinsed and found a towel, took off his suit and put on the dry clothes he had brought in the rucksack, loose canvas trousers and a T-shirt, clothes fit for a day scraping barnacles, bumming around the dock, beachcombing. Sitting in one of the pool chairs, sprawling his legs, he took a few swallows from the flask and ran his palm over his cheek. He was pretty damn rough looking. She'd seen the scars, of that he was certain, had probably felt them, too—the gnarled flesh against her bare legs when she was slipping around on his back. He rolled a cigarette. The ultra modern design, everything sleek and perfectly maintained, with the gardens and the pool, at least two acres of beachfront property—even in Lacoosa County that would cost plenty. Part of the divorce settlement, he guessed. Or perhaps the house wasn't hers. Perhaps it belonged to some man who let her live here in exchange for romantic favors. The idea excited him, because the man wasn't here now, clearly. Only, how could he be sure?

He got up and walked across the deck of the pool and peered through the glass door. He could see no one inside. He pushed down on the handle. She had left it unlocked. He went in. To the left was a hall and a closed door, behind which he heard a shower running. Turning right led to what looked like the main room, spacious and lofty. The western wall was dominated by a soaring single-paned window looking out on the gardens. At the other end were stairs, polished blonde-wood steps set into a floating metal-frame staircase, the railing echoing the railing on the terrace, contrived of slender steel cables. The other walls, colorless like putty, were smooth and bare. The floor was some kind of dark charcoal-speckled stone or marble. A set of low dark wooden cabinets and shelves ran opposite the window, filled with books and record albums and a phonograph. Oddly, the furniture, and there wasn't much of it, had been grouped in the center of the room: a low black-leather sofa, two chairs made of leather straps and chrome, a chrome-and-glass coffee table, all of it arranged on top of a rug with a black and blood-red geometric design, providing the only splotch of color against the grayish neutrality of the walls and floor.

He found an ashtray on the coffee table and put out his cigarette, turning when he heard the door in the hallway open. Willa came out, her hair wet, wearing a sleeveless summer dress that fell just above her knees. Her legs were bare, and she was barefoot. Not realizing he was inside, she stepped out to look for him by the pool. He watched through the picture window. In the sunlight the dress was somewhat translucent, giving the impression that she had nothing on underneath. "Philip?" she called out.

"I'm in here."

She turned her head and came back inside.

"There you are. Nice and dry?" She smiled. She wore no make up, no ring or jewelry.

"I hope you don't mind my coming inside."

"Of course not." She came closer. Indoors, in the muted light, her eyes were more gray than green. "Make yourself comfortable."

"Thanks." He sat in one of the chairs. It was low and sharply angled, like sitting in a leather sling. From this lower vantage, through the window, he could see the top of the dunes and the branches of a sea grape, framed like a composition, a nature study. The rest was sky, the morning's pure winter blue beginning to blanche and haze as the sun rose higher.

"I suppose I should make good on my promise."

She was standing, looking down at him. All he need do was extend his arms and he could draw her forward from the waist, lifting the hem of her dress and pressing her sex into him, against his face, his mouth. As he did with Becca. Don't mix things up. If he tried something like that she would slap him, throw him out. Or maybe she would go along with it, encourage him. "I'm sorry," he said. "Your promise?"

She laughed. "A coffee. Or something stronger."

He should leave, before he lost control. She would end up slapping him, or worse, laughing in his face. Wasn't she laughing at him now?

"You must be hungry, after all that exercise," she went on. "Rescuing the damsel in distress. Let me see what I have in the kitchen. OK?"

"Sure. Thanks."

She gave him a curious look. "It's quite all right," she said. "There's no one else here. I live alone."

The door to the kitchen was across from the stairs. Behind the stairs was a dining table, set in a niche. He got up, took the flask from the rucksack, had two good swallows, put it back, put the tobacco pouch in his pocket and sat again. From above he could feel a gentle flow of air, and he could hear a slight hum from some kind of air-conditioning system. He looked up at the high ceiling, a smooth plane crisscrossed like a tic-tac-toe board with four steel beams, the entire room based on a machine-like interlocking of steel and concrete and glass. He knew about Frank Lloyd Wright, Louis Sullivan, the Bauhaus. Because he was from Chicago, if she asked. The house had something of all that, only more severe, more advanced. There might be electronic listening devices built into the walls, or surveillance cameras.

"Here we are."

As she entered Narby stood up, like a gentleman.

Willa carried a tray —a platter of sliced fruit and cheese and crackers, an open bottle of chilled white wine, wet with condensation, and two glasses—and set in on the low table. "I thought a glass of wine was more apropos. To celebrate your feat of heroism."

She meant the creek. "*Our* feat of heroism. You held on like a real trooper."

"Like a frightened school girl. But thank you. Cheers."

They toasted and sat, Willa taking the sofa and Narby the chair, facing each other. She drew up her legs, curling on the leather cushions like a cat. The dress rode up her thighs, showing her legs. "I don't usually walk in that direction, toward the lighthouse," she explained. "We—I usually walk north, towards the point. Have you been up that far?"

"Many times. What made you walk that way this morning?"

"What do you think?"

He shrugged. "Mind if I have another glass?"

"Help yourself." She was watching him. "Are you a wine aficionado? I brought back quite a few good Sauvignons from France this summer."

"I'm more of a bourbon drinker, actually."

"Sorry. Not a drop of bourbon in the house."

"No problem. I'll make do." He took another drink, to show her he liked the wine well enough.

She uncurled and walked to the cabinet that ran the length of the wall and took a cigarette from a mother-of-pearl box. "Cigarette?"

"Sure. Thanks."

She lit her own and came over to him and held the box open. He took one. She put the box down and leaned forward, snapping the lighter. As he touched the cigarette to the flame he could see down the front of her dress, her nipples pressed against the white cotton. She wasn't wearing a brassiere. Then she curled again on the sofa, smoking, half smiling. After a few seconds, tapping the ash, she said, "let's get to know one another, shall we?"

"Why not? Ladies first."

"All right. Willa Branton. Age thirty-four. Never married. No children, needless to say. Born Davenport, Iowa, 1920. Holyoke College, class of 1942. Currently residing at 257 Bedford Street, Apt. 3, New York City. Winter residence, 4 Isadora Way, Sanmora, Florida. Represented by the Sidney Janis Gallery, something East 57th Street. What else? Ah. Religion. Undecided." She raised an eyebrow. "Any questions so far?"

"Sidney Janis Gallery?"

"Yes. There's no reason you should know it. It's one of the more interesting galleries in town these days and, well, considering the town, one of the more interesting just about anywhere, I would think. An art gallery."

"You're a painter? An artist?"

"You say it as if you don't believe it."

"No. Only, I've never met a painter before." She was waiting, so he added. "Are you famous?"

She laughed. "Depends on what you mean by famous. I've exhibited in Paris and Berlin and Rome, as well as New York and Chicago. Some of the critics like me, some not as much. Even the severe Greenberg seems to favor me. Sales are up.

Somewhat. But if you mean, do I make tons of dough? Have I had my photo on the cover of *Life*? Well, in that case, I'm still languishing in obscurity."

Was she making fun of him? He shifted in the chair. "I've been out of the country, actually. It's been years since I've visited a museum or art gallery."

"Oh. Where have you been? Maybe you're the famous one, not me."

"Asia and the Pacific. The Philippines. Indonesia. Hong Kong. A long way from Paris and Rome."

"Aha. Entirely beyond my sphere of influence. That explains your not knowing all about me."

She was smiling, being clever again. Quickly, before she could ask more, he said, "What do you paint?"

"What do I paint? You mean, landscapes or portraits or things like that?"

"Yeah. I guess so."

She thought for a moment, smiling at him, holding the cigarette. "My work falls more into the category of the non-representational or non-figurative. Some people would call it abstract art. But I don't."

"It was a stupid question. Sorry."

"Not a stupid question at all. It's just the old conundrum. Picture worth a thousand words, that kind of thing."

It struck him, just then, that the walls, the neutral-putty expanses of smooth concrete, were unadorned. "Guess I'll have to go to New York. Or Paris or Rome. See for myself."

"Maybe not so far."

"No?"

"I have a studio here. I'm working on some new paintings. When they're ready, I'll show you. If you like."

"Good. Save me a trip." He wanted to get up, touch her, lift her dress. She was teasing him, maybe. Or telling him it was all right, that she wanted him. He took a breath, leaning back. "So, you come down here from New York, to paint?"

"Yes. To get away from the New York circuit. It's becoming something like a hall of mirrors. From the Cedar Tavern all the way out to Springs. But here. The dunes and the jungle, the shifting colors of the sea, the isolation. It's nothing so ordinary, so direct, as inspiration. It's more like, I don't know. Access. It gives me access to a certain... " She stopped. "I'm talking nonsense." She uncurled, leaning forward to put out her cigarette. "Have you seen the sea turtles, the loggerheads? You have to come at night, in a bright moon. During the first weeks of April. Up they come, out of the hissing void, clawing their way toward the dunes, searching for a spot to bury their eggs. It's the most extraordinary thing I've ever witnessed. Prehistoric. Out of this world."

"No. I've never seen them."

"I can show you. There's a place they favor, just past the Pembakers. In April. I'll take you."

She would stay, at least until April. Four months. Pembaker was here, too, on the Island. He'd been correct. "I'd like that. Very much."

She ate a slice of apple from the platter and poured another glass of wine. He followed her lead, taking some apple and cheese. Tell her anything, keep things moving. Don't mix things up.

"Your turn," she said. "Mr. Philip Narby. So, what sent you all the way to Asia and the Pacific?"

He reached for the box and took another cigarette. "Government work. But I quit that, some time ago."

"What kind of government work?"

He shrugged. "Nothing interesting." He tried to shift, move his legs, but the low angled chair was constricting. He could only lean forward, or else lurch completely out. "State department work. Business-interests section. Paper pushing. Bureaucracy." He hadn't thought it out. It didn't matter. She wouldn't know what he was talking about. Like him, with the art.

"Really? You hardly seem like the paper-pushing type."

"I'm not. Like I said, I quit."

"And now?"

"Not much to tell. I came down here about two years ago, bought some land out in the county. In Sawfish Point, if you know where that is. About fifteen miles north of Myerton."

"No, I don't. It's not much, is it? The town. Myerton?"

"Crackers and rednecks. A few country lawyers, the usual big-bellied deputy sheriffs. Train station. Gladiolas, winter vegetables, truck farming. Not much in the way of modern art, as far as I know."

"How appealing," she said, clearly amused. "And your land? What do you do with it?"

"It's scrub, mostly. Pines and palmetto. No paved road, no electric, no telephone line. Pretty damn worthless, really. I built a little house, out in the sticks. We're putting in some groves, tropical fruit and hardwoods. Not that I have any intention of farming. It's something in the way of an experiment," he added, "to see what the climate can support."

"We?"

"Me and Sam Waters. He works for me." Then, realizing what she was asking, he added, "Single. No children."

Her eyes were glistening, intent on him. "What else?" She took another cigarette, leaning forward, showing him again, allowing him to look. "Are you often on Sanmora? Do you own land here as well?"

"No. I come to swim. That's all. Three times a week, usually. It's the only open coastline in the county. The rest is all muck and mangrove."

"It does you good, the swimming. I can see that. You mentioned a truck, didn't you? You come by the ferry? Or do you have a boat?"

What the hell was he waiting for? He pushed out of the chair and sat beside her on the sofa. She said nothing, her eyes widening as he kissed her and then gently pushed her down onto her back, her dress riding up her thighs. Her lips and skin were cool to the touch. A mild perfume of violets rose from behind her ear, noticeable only as he pulled away. "I like that," she said, her voice surprisingly calm, and he kissed her again, sliding his hand up her thigh and finding her naked underneath, understanding now that it was not a game or a test. She began to moan, running her hands under his shirt while he fed on her mouth, her tongue.

She was underneath him. He felt her palm flat against his chest, pushing. He angled upward, thinking she would stop him now, tell him that he had gone far enough, to get off. But she only raised herself sufficiently to pull the dress over her head, dropping it on the floor, and he took off his trousers and T-shirt, the soft leather of the couch adhering and then dehiscing from her cool rather flawless skin as he shifted her about, raising her slender hips to put her into position, her eyes shining like some wet grey mineral, clear and hard. He was rigid now, ready, and he entered her and he felt her go limp, taking him in without resistance, as if her system had been anticipating him all the while, avid to be filled.

My god, she was moaning, my god, please, please, twisting underneath him, spasming right away, three or four times. After a while, sensing her willingness, he withdrew, pulled her up by the shoulders and put her on her knees, so that she was draped face-forward over the back of the sofa while he stood behind her. Beads of sweat had formed in the channel of her spine, little drops of dew that seemed to hypnotize him as he flexed, her arms spread out and resting atop the back of the sofa, her face averted and her hands gripping and squeezing the leather, her hips squirming, the taut flesh of her ass pressing into him even as she seemed to buckle and collapse from the effort, one spasm after another in rapid succession.

They finished on the rug, on their sides, Narby behind her. The stark lofty room glowed with the winter sun filtering in through the soaring pane of glass. Their breathing quieted, leaving only the slight mechanical hum. He moved away, propped on one elbow, and she turned and lay on her back, looking up at him, her face drained of color. The narrow tuft of damp reddish hair swelled from between her thighs, her round breasts puckering upward toward the light, pink heliotropic buds. He leaned down and kissed her again and then stood and began to dress. As he pulled on his shirt he became aware of a slight stinging against his back, scratches where she must have clawed at him with her nails.

What now? He looked around for the rucksack and not caring what she thought he took out the flask and drank, three greedy swallows. Maybe, in fact, she would want money. She was very good, very experienced. He had taken her from behind the way he did Becca and like Becca she had known how to move, how to make it last. Money would certainly make everything simpler. He always had plenty on him, in case he had to leave town suddenly. He looked around the room again, the luxurious extravagant emptiness. Didn't real artists live in attics or run-down farmhouses, warming their hands on an old stove? What the hell was she, really?

She got up and slipped the dress over her head and lit a cigarette. After a moment—she seemed to have lost her cleverness, her shamelessness—she said, flatly, "if you're worried, don't be. It's not the right time in my cycle. Not a chance."

"I'm not worried."

"Good."

"Look. Maybe I should leave."

She picked up the empty wine glass from where it had tumbled onto the rug and poured out what remained of the bottle. "Would you care for some more?" she said, drinking it off. "I've got Scotch, if you'd prefer."

He unclenched a bit, watching her drink. "No, thanks."

"Well, I would." She walked away and came back with another bottle and filled the glass again. He stood by the window, looking out, smoking. He would finish the cigarette and leave. She came up behind him. "It's the best time of day. The light."

"That so?" He moved away and put the cigarette out in the ashtray. Why should he hang around? So she could laugh at him again? Maybe she'd been instructed to keep him here, find out whatever she could and then signal for help.

"Look. Philip. If you don't mind. I'm going into the studio. I can't miss an afternoon like this. I have to work. Until I lose the light."

"Good for you." He bent down to pick up the rucksack. "See you later."

"When?"

He shrugged. "Like I said, I come around here to swim, every few days."

"Tomorrow. For dinner. Just after sundown. I'll make some steaks. You bring the bourbon. All right? Say, six o'clock?"

"Six? But I'll miss the return ferry."

"Stay the night then."

It was impossible. They would come for him, kill him. "You're kidding? I mean, you're not afraid? After all, you don't even know me. Even if —."

"As a matter fact, yes, maybe I am a little afraid. Still. I'm willing to risk it. How about you?"

Already, now that she was dressed, he was imagining her naked again, as if, too excited, too determined, despite the intensity of his ejaculation, he had missed the very thing he was craving. He wanted her again. He wasn't going to be able to rest until he knew it would happen again. And again.

"Yes," he said. "Why not?"

"Good." She paused. "It's all right, Philip. It's natural, to be awkward like this. I don't mind. I don't care about that. It'll work itself out, one way or the other. Tomorrow, then."

She was gone, through the doorway that led to the kitchen. He slung the sack over his shoulder and walked out, past the pool. Standing at the gate in the hedge, turning around, he noticed what must be the studio, on the far side of the garden, a separate building like a garage, a single-story box of concrete and glass. He waited until he saw her come out a side door and walk across a flagstone path, unlocking the studio door and then closing it behind her, not noticing or perhaps not caring that he was still in the garden, watching. After a few minutes, satisfied that she had told the truth, that she was in fact working, painting, he opened the gate and walked between the dunes and down the beach toward the lighthouse.

By the time he reached the fork that led to his property, his road, it was night. It occurred to him that Becca would be waiting for him. He had come at this hour every Thursday, for months now. To make up for it, next time he would give her double.

The house, the jungle, was dark. He sat shirtless in one of the throne-like wicker chairs in the room at the back, lighting a kerosene lamp because he didn't want to bother with the generator, didn't want the noise. The silence seemed to spread about him like a series of ever-expanding concentric waves of which he, Philip Narby, was the center, the still point. The sense of satisfaction that had come over him—he couldn't remember ever having felt like this—called for yet another swallow of Jim Beam, another cigarette. A satisfaction that was greedier than fear or failure, that clamored to be fed, appeased. She had let him do to her the same things he did to a scrawny little Negro whore. She had liked it, wanted more. Again and again. The not-quite-famous Willa Branton. Things he hadn't even known how to do with a woman until Becca had shown him. *You done good honey, you my Sad'day night special.*

2

DARKNESS FELL QUICKLY. Waiting by the creek he watched the sun sink into the ocean and then, with only a smear of residual light to guide him, waded across. He stood at the foot of the walkway, gazing up at the house. There was a light in the window upstairs—her bedroom, he supposed. A rippling aquamarine glow from the pool reflected up the smooth concrete walls. He was certain no one had seen him approach. Just after sunset, she had said. Six o'clock. What was he waiting for?

He flicked his cigarette into the sand and tried the gate. It was unlocked. The gardenias were stronger at night, sweeter, the sharp smell of chlorine cutting through the perfume as he passed the pool. The French doors were ajar. He entered without knocking and stood in the entryway. There was a room to his left, the door pulled to, but not shut. He took a breath and swung it open. But it was just an unoccupied room, with a bed and a dresser and a closet. And the bathroom where she had showered yesterday. The bed was unmade, without sheets or a spread. He looked in one of the dresser drawers. Empty. A guest room, probably, with no sign that anyone had stayed here recently, or that she was expecting anyone. Maybe she entertained all her overnight guests upstairs, in her own bed.

He considered stepping back outside, knock, announce himself. But instead he went into the living room and put down the knapsack and took a cigarette from the box on the cabinet. A Gauloises, a strong French brand. Hank didn't carry them. But Sid Black had, because there were a lot of Francophiles and poseurs working for the State Department in Tokyo—men who feeling deprived by the banal PX offerings would have bought them by the carton. Why would she smoke French cigarettes? But maybe the cigarettes weren't hers.

The house was quiet, only the faint mechanical hum. He could hear her moving about in the kitchen. He could sneak up the stairs. But he'd have a good look at her bedroom soon enough, he supposed. He flicked the lighter. The table was set for two, with candles and wine glasses, the romantic touch. He ran his hand over the back of the leather couch, lightly, as he would touch a woman's skin, because he was remembering how they had made use of it. He didn't want to startle her. But now that he was here, inside the house, he rather liked the feeling, as if he had earned some special proprietorial right. Out the big picture window he could see the blue glow of the pool and the corners of the garden, illuminated by two outdoor lamps. The lights in the living room were dimmed. Still, with no shade or drape over the window anyone lurking in the garden or peering over the hedge would have a decent view of the proceedings. Apparently, she didn't care.

Cocktail glasses and an ice bucket were set out on the low teak cabinet. He took the bottle of Jim Beam from the rucksack, dropped a cube into a glass and poured a drink and sat on the sofa, sprawling a bit. He was clean-shaven, in a silken shirt and good linen trousers. Making use of the sporty Lincoln Road clothes, now that the bank business was finished.

After a moment she came out, gripping a bottle by the neck and ferrying two glasses in the other hand. Betraying only the mildest surprise she halted in midstride, smiling, apparently not bothered that he had let himself in, perhaps even liking it. She wore a short black cocktail dress with narrow shoulder straps, cut low to show the tops of her breasts. Her legs and feet were bare. No makeup, no jewelry.

She came forward and set the bottle and glasses on the coffee table.

"You've made yourself at home, I see. Good."

He rose, holding the tumbler of bourbon, and rather stupidly said, "Can I pour you a drink?"

She looked skeptically at the Jim Beam. "I was thinking more along the lines of champagne, to kick things off."

"Right." But he simply stood there, staring at her. She didn't look away, but after a few seconds, smiling again, said, "I've got something on the burner. Mind popping it? I'll be right back."

He sat down, turning the bottle, cold and wet with condensation, in his hands. In fact, he had never in his life opened a bottle of champagne, had seen it done only in the movies. The foil around the neck was loose and he peeled it off. There was a wire with a loop at the end and he untwisted it, but the cork didn't budge. It was very good, expensive stuff, he supposed. Dom Pérignon. Like the champagne Sid Black delivered to McCoy and Black's other well-heeled customers. He pulled at the cork. Nothing. So, what the hell was he supposed to do now? In the movies it always exploded open effortlessly, foaming, to the great merriment of Fred Astaire or Cary Grant or whoever the hell it was. He drank off the rest of the bourbon and refilled the tumbler with Jim Beam. She was trying to make a fool of him, he supposed. He didn't mind, as long as he got what he came for. On the sofa and rug first, and then, later, upstairs, in her bed, he decided. Twice, three times. All night long.

He took another Gauloises and kneeled down, wanting to have a look at the shelf of record albums that sat below the phonograph. When she came back into the living room, he said. "Sorry. I'm not a champagne drinker."

She gazed at the peeled unopened bottle. "Well, never too late to start. Here. Let me get it."

"No. Just tell me how."

She was smiling, having a good time at his expense. "Push under the cork with your thumbs and work it loose. Hold on a minute." She came back with a dishtowel. "Here. Wrap it around the neck. So we don't spoil the rug."

He did as she said and held the cork in the towel as it came off, absorbing the gush, and he filled the two crystal flutes just to the brim until the foam settled.

"Well done," she said. "Shall we drink a toast?"

She wanted him to say something. "To the island. And it's beautiful—wildlife."

"Yes. On land and sea."

It tasted like nothing, thin and effervescent. Without waiting he poured another glass, trying it again, like someone sampling the goods before deciding to buy.

"You don't like it," she said, watching him, amused.

"It's all right, I suppose."

"Here." She got up and fetched the Jim Beam and filled his tumbler half with bourbon and then topped it off with champagne. "A champagne cocktail, of sorts. How's that?"

He tried it. "Not bad." He took another sip. "A definite improvement."

She laughed. "To the Jim Beam, or the Dom?"

"Both. A higher class of boilermaker, you could say."

He was sitting in the leather-sling chair and she was on sofa, as before. He couldn't take his eyes off her. "Smells good. What's on the menu?"

"Steak. Roasted potatoes. Salad. I wasn't sure what you liked, so I stuck to the basics. Shall I put on the steaks? Or we could wait."

"Let's wait."

She looked at him, returning his stare with her cold, mineral gray eyes. "Yes. Let's wait."

She wanted it as much as he did. He pushed out of the chair and sat next to her and they kissed, pausing to drink, and then kissing again and again, her head back, her mouth wide open and hot. He slid his hand under her dress, up her thigh. She was naked underneath and she spread her legs. Understanding, or guessing, he gently probed with his finger and she slunk down, encouraging him, already wet, his finger all the way inside her now as he stared down into her eyes, kneading the nape of her neck with his other hand and then kissing her.

She was like a man, not bothering with a lot of prelude or small talk, not concerned with protecting herself, obeying only the heedless animal desire. They did it as before, using the sofa and the chair and finally on the rug, with him behind her. She had spasmed at least half a dozen times, rather violently, before he finished. He lay with his arms around her, physically overwhelmed, trying not to think, not to care what it meant or what she might expect of him. Blanking his mind.

Willa disengaged first, pulling her hips away and turning on her side to face him, kissing him lightly as she got to her knees, with no sign of shame, and then standing and slipping the dress over her head, leaving him sprawled naked on the rug, admiring him the way a man admires a woman.

She was looking at the scars. He sat up and reached for his shirt.

"I'll put on the steaks, now. Yeah?"

"Great. I'm starving."

"Me too."

She went first into the empty guest room, the bathroom. To wash, or whatever women do afterwards. He dressed, his limbs and lips tingling, the power of the sexual release echoing, soft little shudders down his shoulders and spine. It exceeded anything he had experienced with Becca. The way she turned rigid, her complexion darkening, almost purple, the violence of her pleasure or climax or whatever it was that the woman felt. Maybe Martha would have had the same reaction, if he'd had the stomach to see it through. Or poor Janet, if it weren't for her gelded ball-and-chain, Lieutenant Frank Swanson. He pictured her again, quite vividly, standing slump shouldered by the dinette table in the gimcrack little Glo-Bel cabin, trembling with fear at the very idea of it. Terrified of her own nakedness.

Why the hell was he thinking of that?

He made himself another champagne cocktail, going easier on the Jim Beam. There was a line he shouldn't cross, because he still didn't know why he was here. If he hadn't already crossed it. The goddamn bottle was half empty. He needed something in his stomach, that was all.

Squatting, one hand on the top of the low cabinet to steady himself, a cigarette clamped in his mouth, he flipped through the shelf of record albums. Edith Piaf, Jacques Brel, The Weavers, Woody Guthrie, Edgar Varese, Charles Ives, Claude Debussy. The names were familiar. From Tom's or Jim's days as a student at that pathetic teacher's college, Narby supposed. Hadn't one of the Weavers run afoul of H.U.A.C.? At the end of the shelf, as if set apart, the complexion of the album covers, so to speak, changed. Miles Davis, Bud Powell, Sarah Vaughn, Charlie Parker, Thelonious Monk, Chet Baker—the only white face in the crowd—Clifford Brown. He chose one, slipped the disc out of the cover and put it on the turntable. Not a scratch or mote of dust, as if it had never been played. The volume was set low. He sat on the sofa, smoking and waiting and listening. Feeling damned good. Who said he'd had too much to drink? It was going to be a night like no other. Philip Narby, finally getting his just rewards. Crawling out of that shit-water ditch for the last time. The sound of the trumpet was pliant and beautiful, but it wasn't joyful. Not like Count Basie, not like swing and jump blues. It wasn't mournful. It was neutral, suspended. Like the sex feeling once it was used up and fading, in that lag before it built up again, rising in the blood.

"Philip." Willa was at the table. "We're ready."

It was a rectangular table, a thin slab of charcoal-dark wood with the smooth lustrous finish and rounded edges of a river stone, resting on trestles made from aluminum tubes. They sat across from one another. There were steaks, done rare, roasted potatoes, salad, French bread, and a small plate of olives. An uncorked bottle of wine flanked by two candlesticks stood between them. She had filled his glass. Red, this time. To go with the meat—he remembered that now.

She began to eat. The steak and potatoes first, not the salad, reversing the normal order. She wasn't fussy about manners, one elbow resting on the table, eating for the sheer pleasure of it. He waited a moment, and then, overcome with appetite, lowered his head and unselfconsciously lashed into the meal.

"You like it?"

"I don't think I've ever tasted anything so damned good in my life."

"There's another steak in the fridge."

"No. This is plenty. Thanks."

She was watching him now, maybe expecting him to say something. She helped herself to the salad and passed the big wooden bowl. He put some on his plate, following her lead. Or was she looking over his shoulder, across the room and out the window, into the garden?

"So, you like the new jazz," he said, shrugging off the impulse to turn his head and look over his shoulder, deciding on a tack.

"Sorry. The what?"

"The record album I put on. The new jazz."

"To be honest, I haven't been listening." She paused. "I don't know. I don't think I've ever heard it before. What is it?"

"Miles Davis. You've got a couple of his records in your collection."

"Oh. Those. The jazz records. They aren't mine. Someone left them here. You're welcome to have them, if you'd like."

"You want me to turn it off?"

"No, of course not. I only said they're not mine."

"Well, if you're so eager to give them away, you must not like this kind of music."

She thought about that for a moment. "Not necessarily. Perhaps it's because I associate the records with something unpleasant. Someone unpleasant."

"You mean the person who left them here?"

"Yes. But. Things are exceedingly pleasant at the moment, don't you agree? Music can always acquire a new association."

"True."

"I like new things. The newer the better. Besides, it's not fair of me. One shouldn't judge a work of art by the company it keeps."

He had the feeling, again, the she was mocking him, but at the same time admiring. "What do you mean by that?" he said, blandly.

She smiled. "Nothing. Are you finished? Let's move to the sofa, then. I'll bring the wine."

She sat with her legs tucked underneath her, her arm resting on the back of the sofa. Not as close as before. For a few minutes she remained quiet, smiling at him or letting her head hang back with her eyes closed as the music played, as if she were listening intently, losing herself in the sound. He would have her again, very soon. He got up and turned the record over.

"How do you like it now?"

"I'm already hearing new possibilities." She pulled herself up, straightening to light a cigarette. "Look," she said, "I don't know what you're thinking. What just happened. Yesterday afternoon. An hour ago. Well, there's no shortage of spontaneous acts in my past. But I have to tell you. I want to tell you, Philip. There's never been anything like this. I don't go around picking up men on the beach and bringing them home and— quite the contrary. I'm rather guarded about my privacy. Very selective about who I reveal myself to. I don't expect you to make much sense out of what I'm saying. Not now, anyway." She paused, taking a long drag on the Gauloises. "When I met you on the beach a year ago and then again yesterday, I knew that just possibly—I can't put it into words. But yesterday afternoon. It was something like the proof of a first axiom. Yes. The theory, the intuition, being that you're something very different. Rare. A renegade from the white-collar herd. That somehow, our contingencies notwithstanding, we found each other. At the right time, under the right circumstances."

"What about the man who left those records here? Was he one of the herd?"

She laughed. "Yes, since you ask. It seems he was."

"He was here, wasn't he? That day when we met and you said you couldn't ask me to come inside?"

Rather than act insulted or put upon, she seemed to welcome the interrogation. "Yes. But it was over and finished by then. Physically, he was present. The way a crate in the middle of the living room, waiting to be shipped out, is present."

"You find him on the beach, too? Does he live around here?"

"Christ, no. He's a Long Island scion, some secondary character wandering the lawn at a Gatsby party. It was foolish of me to ever get involved with someone like that. He's far away now, gone for good. I assure you."

"What's his name?" he asked, easily, not thinking he would get anywhere.

She looked at him oddly. "Richard. Richard Lansdale. Why? Does it matter?"

"No. Just a habit of mine. I like to know people's names. Even if I never meet them."

"Is that how you remembered my name? Because you thought you'd never see me again?"

"Maybe."

"What about you, Philip? A man with your looks. There has to be a girl somewhere. The one you left behind, the one that got away. The one chasing you. Come clean."

"Not really. Nothing serious. When I was posted abroad I was always on the move. Three months here, six weeks there."

"A girl in every port. That kind of thing?"

She meant whores, probably. "If you want to put it like that."

"Is there anyone now?"

"Not since I came down here." She wanted more. "Not since I met you."

"Very propitious, then. Ideal conditions." She raised her wine glass. "To us." They drank a toast, moving closer. "What do you think of the house?" she said, hoping to veer from what was coming, to give it a little more time, he supposed. "It was the third or fourth house in the Colony, after the Pembakers' next door, and the Atlees'. It's a Beckworth. The architect. Commissioned by a very dear friend of mine. Endicott Ward, the writer and art critic. I had met Cott years ago, when I first came to New York. Anyway, it was just after my first group show at the Janis, and Cott was traveling to Europe that winter and he asked if I wanted to stay in his beach house for a few months—a remote unspoiled Florida atoll, he called it. Rent free, because he knew I was pretty broke. He thought it would be a good place for me to paint. With the studio and the solitude, the dunes and the sublime February weather. To *produce*, as he likes to put it. I was looking for a new tack, getting fed up with the Tenth-Street gang. So, though I had no idea what it would be like, I took him up on the offer.

"Everyone's gone mad about old farmhouses these days. Knock on the door of any barn within fifty miles of Manhattan and instead of a farmer you'll find a stockbroker or the vice president of an insurance company or, even worse, an illustrator for one of the slicks. The bohemian-managerial class, with a few genuine craftsmen sprinkled in, to keep things honest. But here! It was as if I'd found my very own rabbit hole, my magic looking glass. I couldn't believe it when Cott told me he was planning to sell. Not that I had the money. Not back then. But he didn't want to sell to just anyone. Anyway, he got the rest of the Colony behind it, especially the Pembakers, and we worked out an arrangement. Extremely generous of him. As it happened, my next show sold surprisingly well. We're all squared up now."

"Sounds as though he's more than just a friend. This man Endicott." When she left the room, or later when she was asleep, he would write them down: Richard Lansdale. Endicott Ward.

"Cott? He's old enough to be my father." She laughed, hardly offended by the implication.

They started to touch, kiss, keeping their clothes on as though they could imagine themselves still innocent, discovering unimagined thrills.

"Mind if I put on another record?"

"Please do. I'm beginning to get an entirely new appreciation for this music. Whatever it is."

It was more deliberate this time, slower, less varied and almost mechanical, as if they were trying to grind each other down, purge themselves for the evening of the burden of lust. Later, he remembered being surprised, excited, by the rigidity of her nipples, nearly as hard as a man's erection. Over and over she cried out, short bursts like an animal yelping in pain. When he came, though, the intensity of his pleasure was diminished—the second time in less than two hours, with too much drink—and something else took its place, some hollowness or coldness that he hadn't realized was there, and he clung to her on the rug, blanking his mind of all but the faintest pulse of suspicion, the record finished and the phonograph hissing as the needle scraped against the blank at the center of the disc.

"I'm going to take a quick shower," she said after a while, gently decoupling and getting up. "You can take one down here, in the guestroom, if you'd like."

On his back on the rug he watched her climb the stairs, gripping her dress in one hand, like a rag—stark and beautiful with her square shoulders and short tawny hair, her long legs and the curve of her back as it dipped to meet her small round behind, her breasts soft and upright and gently shifting as though kneaded by invisible hands. As she reached the landing, he saw the damp reddish tuft, the glistening smears on the inside of her thighs.

He was going to fall in love with her. It would be like a sickness, a current dragging him out.

Dragging them both. Only she was the one who couldn't swim.

3

HALF THE TIME THEY WENT NAKED, in the house and by the pool. No one saw them, no one knew he was there. If the seaplane had flown by, he hadn't heard it. The residents of the Colony respected her privacy, because it was understood that she came to Sanmora to work, to immerse herself in painting. She was a serious artist, her fame starting to spread. She didn't want to show him the paintings in the studio, not yet. It was some kind of game, he supposed. For the next two days, despite the quality of light, the studio remained locked, her work put aside for his benefit. As if the sight of her paintings might somehow interfere with her astonishing unbridled pleasure.

They were on the terrace, the cantilevered slab that hung over the garden, watching the spectacle of the winter sunset over the Gulf. They'd been in and out of bed all day, with a stroll along the beach, drinking steadily since lunch. She'd probably had an entire bottle of wine by now, was holding it pretty well. The air was still balmy from the afternoon heat, the sky remarkably clear, a single bank of wispy streaks above the horizon glowing coral-pink and red, the sun enormous and molten as it descended into the darkening sea. Willa wore a short kimono-like robe, loosely tied. Narby was in bathing trunks, shirtless and barefoot. Standing at the cable railing, he could see miles down the dunes in either direction. The other seven houses of the Colony, tucked back into their jungle clearings, were virtually invisible, unless you knew they were there. It was as if they had the island to themselves.

"Philip. Would you mind making me one of your cigarettes? I really prefer them to the Gauloises."

He rolled two and gave her one. The attraction, the thrill, came in pulses and waves, rising and breaking. It would build again as night came on. During the troughs she told him about the New York art scene, the personalities, the critics and cura-tors and galleries. What came through mostly was her confi-dence, her arrogance. That she was on to something that these other painters—Kline, Rivers, Johns, Kelly; all men, he gath-ered—couldn't see. She had distinguished herself from the pack, sprinted ahead. The remote island retreat was a sign of her independence. Nobody but this man Endicott Ward and the Janises knew where she disappeared for the winter months, as if the secret location held the key to her ascending status.

He told her about the jungle around Sawfish Point, the two-rut road through the thickets, the rustic house and the newly planted groves, mentioning some vague financial dealings in Havana and Miami, things he had started up after quitting the government. She didn't press him with a lot of questions. It gave her a kick, he realized, to see him as some kind of exalted beach bum, a drifter with means. "The way you are with me, the way you've been since I first saw you on the beach," she had told him, "a beautiful stranger, a gift of the sea. The way you fuck me, Philip. Like a god."

She liked to sprinkle in filthy talk, as if she would do or say anything to make him hang around, get him back in bed. Was that how it had been with Richard Lansdale, until he had disap-pointed her?

She stood next to him at the railing, smoking, talking now about the sunset, how she saw it. Artist jabber. "There's this moment when it begins to sink very quickly, as if the sea is suck-ing down the sun, drowning it. Leaving this dull dark orange glowering, as if the horizon is burning out. I find it interesting. As if light and dark were masses rather than values or quali-ties, physical bodies in time and space." She gazed at him, going quiet for a moment. "I can never quite tell what you're looking at, Philip."

"Sorry," he said. "It's just that I'm not used to it. Being with a woman. Someone like you."

"I can understand that. Perhaps, tomorrow morning, Philip, as wonderful as these last two days have been, well, maybe you ought to go. I really have to get back to my painting. I'm sure there are things that you need to attend to, as well. Yes?"

"I was planning to. On the morning ferry."

"I see. And then?"

He shrugged. "You tell me."

She thought for a moment, wrapping the kimono tighter, covering herself. "Here's the thing. The whole relationship syndrome. I don't want that, Philip. I've had that, more than once. It drags me down."

"Yeah. So, what's your point?"

"Let's go inside," she said. "I'm getting a chill. Downstairs. We'll have a bite and talk."

Sitting at the table, another bottle of wine opened, he felt the tension easing. They would be back in bed soon. Tomorrow morning was still a long way off. Her beauty, her desire, overwhelmed him. He would do anything to have her, again and again. They agreed that he would return in a week or so. He would stay as long as it felt right. They would act spontaneously, by intuition. He would always find her here, after sundown, the studio locked up for the day. Alone. The only rule was that nothing should interfere with her painting. "Without my painting, Philip, I'm nothing. You wouldn't want to see me, be around me, if I wasn't happy in my work. I assure you."

Their agreement, the food she had prepared—a simple stew made with fresh fish she had bought at the Village market—restored him. The arrangement would allow him to keep an eye on the island, and have a damned good time doing it. Eventually, he would make contact with Pembaker, the head of Isadora Land and Trust. Or the other one she had mentioned, the co-founder of the Colony. Dan Atlee.

After the meal he put on a jazz record and led her to the sofa. Each time he made it a little rougher, pulling her hair, pinning her down. She convulsed for what seemed like minutes, her body roiling in rapid jolts, her nails digging into his back and shoulders, her complexion turning almost purple. He hadn't thought he could come again, but the absoluteness of her pleasure, her utter abandon, brought him to it. Every time it was different. Every time it was more.

After a while she got up to shower. Wash him out of her. Maybe she had some other means of protecting herself. Whatever she had used with Lansdale.

She came back, her hair wet, wearing a light clinging dress. He had put on a pair of loose fitting short pants, leaving his shirt unbuttoned. They sat close on the sofa, holding each other, the music playing quietly, a tenor saxophone darting over jagged piano chords and a walking bass. If he were an ordinary man, he supposed, he would tell her he loved her, eventually ask her to marry him. Because the idea of losing her, of her being with another man, was intolerable.

"Philip. Those scars. Do you mind if I ask?" She sat up and facing him held his hand.

Why lie, feed her that bull about a car accident, as he had told Vetch and Sam Waters. "A run-in with a mortar round. Or maybe a grenade. Didn't really see it coming. From behind, possibly. What they amusingly call friendly-fire."

"I'm sorry. I don't understand."

"Korea. I was wounded." With Knowles he had blurted it out, in a panic. All that was over. Philip Narby could make of it what he wanted now. Use it to his advantage. "Fifty-thousand dead or crippled. I got out all right, I suppose."

"How horrible. You were in the Army?"

"Not exactly. I was living in Tokyo, working with a government Information Agency, part of the Occupation Forces. As a civilian. Anyway, with all that hysteria about the Reds, about Berlin and losing China, and the Army in a shambles, well, once the fighting broke out, after the Communists overran Seoul, just about every able-bodied American male was given a uniform and a rifle. There was no time for training, no time to learn how to clear a jammed M-1. Seeing as I was already in the neighborhood, and able-bodied, I was hardly in a position to refuse." He paused. Go slow. Not too much. "You must have known someone who got sucked up in the draft, summer of 53. A brother or cousin. An old flame."

"Actually, no. I was in Paris that summer. And the following year as well."

"What were you doing in Paris?"

"Studying art. More like worshipping. At the Church of the Deux Magot, the cult of post-impressionism. Well, two years of French male chauvinism cured me of that." She paused to light a cigarette. "Do you want to talk about it, Philip? About what happened."

"Why?"

"Why?" She gave a short amused laugh. "Because it must have left a very deep impression. Must have changed you, somehow."

"It changed everybody. Even if they don't know it."

"And how is that?"

"The consequences. The politics behind it."

She shrugged. "Frankly, I don't pay attention to politics. My mind doesn't work that way. I'm asking about *you*. What *you* felt, what you saw. How you endured it."

"You read the papers, didn't you? Even living in Paris, you must have formed some opinion. About the U.N. resolutions? Truman firing MacArthur, right in the middle of it? The bickering over the exchange of prisoners?"

She looked a bit put off. "I'm sorry. I can understand you not wanting to talk about it. I'm just glad you're all right. That you are who you are. That you made it here. To me."

"But I am talking about it. Here." He pulled her hand and ran it up and down his left side, under his open shirt. On the thickest scars he felt nothing, the flesh cauterized of sensation. Instead of recoiling she caressed him, her eyes closed.

"It must have come from an angle, from above. I was running down a hillside. Some lieutenant had volunteered me. He was screaming, pounding the radio with his fists. He needed a runner. Someone to run the co-ordinates down to command, to artillery. Because the radio was dead. I had it in my hand, this little scrap of paper. It was very very hot. Not like here. Scorching, like a furnace. There must have been a lot of noise, gunfire, artillery rounds, air cover. But all I can remember is running fast over the rough ground, everything burnt up, leaping over boulders and fallen trees and heaps of rubble. With only this quiet whooshing in my ears. Like being underwater. And I felt weightless, too. Because of the fear, I guess. It empties you, hollows you out. So that you're afraid but you don't feel it anymore."

It was good to tell it like this, calmly, precisely, with her hand cool against his side and his lust appeased. What was the harm? It could have been any poor son-of-a-bitch, pitching down that hillside.

"That's when I got hit. A mortar round, or a grenade, something spewing shrapnel. We were in retreat, you understand? Despite Walker's stand-or-die orders. Behind the Naktong River, about a month before Inchon. Worst fighting of the whole goddamn war. They had to blow the bridges that very night, even though there were people crossing, women, kids, running from the North Korean Army. So, like I said, it could have come from anywhere. Our fire, their fire. Doesn't matter. There were plenty of others. Dead bodies, I mean. Some of them pretty damn mutilated, armless, headless, half rotted away. Anyway, I must have landed in a ditch. It was farmland, rice fields. So there were irrigation ditches. That water maybe kept me alive just long enough. Even though it wasn't exactly, well, clean. They're very poor people. Peasants. They used whatever they had to fertilize their crops. You understand what I'm saying? Face down in the ditch for hours, my guts leaking out. Right here, where your beautiful hand is right now. Or at least that's what they told me at the hospital back in Japan when I came to a few days later. Bandaged like a mummy. Blacking out from the pain, or the morphine. Both, probably. Fortunately, I still had all my parts. In good working order. Only problem with that was, if you were still whole, they'd send you right back."

"My god. What a nightmare. But look at you now. You're magnificent."

"Yeah, well, as you might imagine, I wasn't too keen on another deployment. Not that I didn't want to serve my country, and all that. Make the world safe for freedom and democracy. Show Stalin who's boss."

"It's revolting. All the red baiting and rabid patriotism. It's play-acting. A form of mass psychosis. Just as Freud claimed. The unleashing of the death instinct, the triumph of Thanatos over Eros. A symptom of the sickness of our way of life, our repressed degraded culture. Just look at the men who claim to run things. Brutal sexless polyps. Like that eunuch Richard Nixon."

Narby laughed. "You must be a democrat, then. A Stevenson supporter, I'd guess."

She stood up, letting his go hand. "No. I'm not anything. One herd is the same as another."

"Where are you going?"

She gazed down at him. "The biggest mistake an artist can make is to get involved in all that. If anything, art is the antithesis of the yapping newspaper-newsreel-textbook version of existence. History, politics, law. It's all noise. If you really want to create something new, something authentic, you have to believe in it without reservation. Let it consume you. As if nothing else mattered." She turned, as if to walk away.

"Willa. Where are you going?"

"To get another bottle of wine. We're running on empty, darling."

4

ON HIS WAY OUT, STEPPING from the elevator into the lobby, Narby bumped shoulders with him. A man with a woman on his arm. They were laughing, probably a bit juiced. Going up to the man's hotel room, no doubt, to continue the fun in private. Brushing past Narby, absorbed with his companion, he hadn't bothered to look up. Maybe Narby wouldn't have noticed either, except that the man was a good six inches shorter than his well-proportioned friend. A short barrel-chested man in a shiny snug-fitting suit with a tense triangular-shaped face, the wide forehead tapering down to a dimpled chin, dark complexion, dark thinning hair.

Narby climbed into one of the idling cabs waiting beneath the covered portico. A fairly common Jewish type, he told himself. They tended to congregate at this end of the Beach, Ocean Drive and lower Collins. It was eight months since the trouble at the bank. Black wouldn't have hung around this long, without the slightest clue, wasting his time. Push it out of your mind.

"Where to, pal?"

Narby pulled the handbill from his blazer and read off the address.

The driver pulled onto Collins and headed toward the causeway. "Hey pal. That's in Colored town. You know that, right?"

"There a problem?"

"No. Only."

"Only what?"

"I'm just saying. If you're headed over to Railroad Front. Well, it's not the choicest spot. In my opinion. I been driving in this town since forty-seven. What I mean to say, if what you're looking for is some female companionship. I know just the place. Nice, safe, clean. Nice looking classy girls."

"Not interested."

"OK. You're the boss."

He lit a cigarette, looking out the window as they climbed the causeway, the ocean air soft and warm against his face. Out on the moonlit bay the lights on the sailboats and yachts swayed in the gentle chop, like happy drunks. So what if it was Sid Black? He wouldn't dare go to the police, civilian or military. That business with the radio batteries, the aluminum and scrap metal. They could hang Black for less than that. Early the next morning, or even tonight when he got back, Narby would check out of the hotel. Just in case. Black was the only person aside from Bill Knowles who could trace him back to Havana, back to the hospital in Kobe and McCoy and the C.C.D. That was reason enough to be cautious, to stay out of his way.

He glanced at the handbill. *The fabulous Billie Holiday and Her Orchestra. One Night Only. At the world renowned Harlem Square Club.*

He was done grubbing around Alton Road, trolling the Ship Ahoy and the degenerate fringes of the Beach. Overtown would be more conducive to his mood, his needs. He had to be careful, that's all. Not look like he was looking for it.

Another thing. Coming out of the elevator, Black hadn't noticed him. If indeed it was Sid Black. That gave Narby the advantage. Instead of checking out of the hotel, maybe he ought to stick around, find out why the hell Sid Black was still in Miami. It was possible, though very unlikely, that Black was in on the whole thing. McCoy, Knowles, Angleton, the Harvard-Princeton-Yale-O.S.S. cabal with their country-club attitudes—a swarthy little Jew like Black didn't fit the mold. It wasn't good form, Narby supposed, to procure pornographic magazines, contraband booze and cigars, from someone you considered your equal. They had used Black just as they had tried to use Narby. If you looked at things from a certain angle, he and Black were on the same side. Or maybe not. Everyone was on the same side, from a certain angle. Just as everyone was an enemy.

"Here we are, pal. Watch yourself."

The Avenue was crowded, brightly illuminated from the street lamps and storefronts and the flashing marquees. Inside the theatre lobby a small mob pressed against the ticket window. Everyone dressed to the hilt, flashy suits and wide-brimmed hats, the women in flouncy dresses and gowns. Narby was hatless, with his collar open because he didn't like to wear a tie. His shoes could stand a shine. Maybe that amused them, the Negro besting the White man in matters of style. But no one seemed to notice, no one looked his way. He bought his ticket and after a short wait held it out to the usher.

"Excuse me, sir," the usher said, not touching the ticket. "Over there, sir. If you please." He gestured toward the stairs across the lobby. "Up the mezzanine."

"I prefer it down here," Narby said, smiling. "It's general seating, right?"

"Please, sir. Take the stairs, please."

"Is there some problem?"

"No, sir. No problem at all. Only, if you would please take the stairs. Thank you, sir."

They were pressing behind him, eager to get in. He shrugged and stepped aside and ticket in hand climbed the stairs up to a narrow curving balcony, with about thirty small round tables covered in white clothes. At the front was a balustrade and he could hear the noise of the crowd rising from below. Half the tables were occupied, couples or foursomes. Now he got it. Negroes downstairs and Whites up here. A few of the patrons casually looked up at him from their drinks and chatter. He spotted a waiter and pointed to an unoccupied table next to the railing, and the waiter motioned for him to sit. No one bothered to take his ticket, so he put it in his shirt pocket.

Down below, they were having a good time. Hundreds of Black people squeezed into the cavernous room, sitting at tables or standing on the dance floor in front of the stage. It was quite an uproar. Narby sat down and lit a cigarette. It was a good view of the stage and the crowd. Warm, though, the air hung with smoke and the odor of the crowd, their perfume and cologne. When the waiter swung by Narby ordered a double bourbon and a cold beer, nodding in a friendly way at the couple sitting several tables away when they happened to glance in his direction.

He couldn't quite figure it. The Whites kept out of Overtown. All the big Negro stars—Holiday, Nat Cole, Billy Eckstein, Count Basie—played the grand nightclubs on the Beach, along Dade Boulevard. Why would they bother coming here, crossing the color line? He kept his gaze lowered, watching the stage. When his drinks came he looked up again. The people around him—well dressed, more sporty and restrained than the crowd below—seemed quite at ease, waving and talking across the tables as if it were some kind of private party. He was the odd one out. Maybe he ought to finish his drink and leave, before he drew too much attention.

The lights overhead were dimming. An announcer took the stage, the musicians filing out from the wings. The band was going to warm up the crowd before Lady Day made her grand entrance. They began to play a swing tune. A cry of approval went up and the crowd on the dance floor below, already packed, began to pair off and move to the beat. No one on the mezzanine seemed to be listening, continuing their convivial chatter. It was a very good, very tight orchestra. He recognized the modern touches in the arrangement. As the waiter passed, Narby motioned for another bourbon. If he was going to stick around he might as well settle in. Forget about the ghost of Sid Black.

During the second number Narby noticed someone on the far side of the mezzanine, a tall heavy-set man in a glossy dark suit with a red necktie, his ostentatious gold cufflinks catching the light as he raised his arms, a smoldering cigar deftly scissored in one hand. He was moving from table to table, greeting each and every couple in a large, husky voice, some of the patrons standing to embrace or kiss him on his rather flabby, suntanned cheek. Some kind of big shot, Narby assumed. Maybe it was his party. Narby averted his eyes for a moment, watching the orchestra and the dancers below. No doubt about it. He was making his way across the mezzanine, like a politician working a room.

Narby touched his shirt pocket. He had the ticket. He hadn't asked to be seated in the mezzanine. He looked up again. The man was in his fifties, his head shiny under the thinning hair, a broad fleshy face, shining brown eyes and an elastic smile, his bulk like some powerful but deceptively harmless animal. Expensive, well-tailored clothes, if a bit showy. Despite Narby's aversion to anyone approaching him like that, and with nowhere to hide, he sat up, smoking, watching the man with a certain fascination, rather openly now, as if more or less encouraging him. Daring him. If the man asked Narby to leave he would protest, showing his ticket.

As he came closer, table by table, Narby lowered his gaze. The saxophone player was taking his solo. He appeared to be one of the youngest musicians on the stage and his playing reflected it, an angular style with unexpected breaks in the rhythm, though he never entirely deviated from the solid swing of the players behind him. He wasn't playing for the dancers, Narby thought, sensing the big man's presence at his side. Playing for himself, inside the music.

"Good evening." He was standing at the table, holding the cigar, smiling, though not quite so broadly. "Glad to see you're enjoying the show."

"Enjoying it very much."

"Don't tell me," he said. "We met last winter." He snapped his fingers, as if trying to conjure something out of the air. "You're with American Airlines. Am I right?"

Narby smiled politely. "Sorry. No." He stood up, easily, having anticipated the need to do so. "In fact, I don't think we've met. I'm Philip Narby."

"No? My mistake. Pardon me. Art. Art Goldfarb. Pleasure to make your acquaintance, Mr. Narby. Philip. Please. Sit. I didn't mean to interrupt."

"Quite all right."

"You're here with your wife?" Goldfarb asked, though the other chair was empty.

"No. On my own, tonight."

"Nothing wrong with that." Goldfarb glanced down at Narby's table, the empty glasses. "In that case. Mind if I sit for a minute. I've been on my feet all evening. Warm in here, too. Sometimes I say to myself, Art, you should put in air-conditioning. But the expense! A theater this size. Besides," he said, sitting with a slight grunt, tapping his cigar against the ashtray, "the music is so hot no one really complains. Not the folks downstairs, anyway." He laughed. "Packed house tonight. For Billie, it always is."

"I'm certainly looking forward to hearing her sing."

"Fifteen minutes and she'll be out. So. You caught her at Ciro's last weekend, did you?"

"No. I'm only in town for a few days."

"That right?" For a moment Goldfarb's attention was diverted. Another couple had come up the stairs and Goldfarb waved to them. "That's Charlie and Maxine Eberhard. Known them for years. Charlie's a big jazz aficionado, a real swinger from way back. Lives in the Gables. You know the Gables? All those red roof tiles? That's Charlie. He owns the factory. Hell of a nice man, Charlie. Maxine's a gem, too."

Up close Goldfarb's demeanor acquired a different aspect. When the smile on his broad loose face relaxed, his lips lapsed into something like indifference, or perhaps disgust. Under the bright eyes sagging half-moons showed yellowish against the warm, tan, lightly mottled complexion. "Only in town for a few days? Where you visiting from, Mr. Narby?"

"Not far. Across the state. Near Myerton, if you know where that is."

Goldfarb looked a bit surprised. "Myerton? The Gulf Coast? That's cattle country over there, right? Winter vegetables, flowers."

"That's right."

"Well," he laughed. "If you're not with American Airlines— you're in cattle? You do have that rugged silent rancher look. Like Montgomery Clift, come to think of it. In *Red River*."

Narby shook his head. "Real estate," he said.

"That right? How's the housing market in that neck of the Florida woods?"

"Fair. But I'm more on the investment side. Large private holdings. Land trusts. That kind of thing."

Goldfarb seemed rather absorbed in Narby's story. "Very interesting. A lot of virgin territory out there, I imagine. So, where do you work out of?" He squinted, leaning back in the chair, taking a puff from the cigar. "You're not from New York. Takes one to know one. Detroit maybe. No. Chicago?"

"Used to be. But, I'm down here, full time now. I guess I like to be close to the action. Besides, who needs those Chicago winters?"

"I'm with you on that. I've been down here for twenty-five years. Out on Miami Beach. It's been one hell of a ride, too. Myerton? Very interesting. Well, welcome to the Harlem Square Club." He nodded toward the stage, the orchestra still playing, the dance floor packed. "You're in for a real treat tonight, Mr. Narby. Something very special. But, excuse my curiosity. The fact is ..." he paused, tapping the cigar. "As you obviously have noticed, this is a Negro theater. In the Negro section of Miami. I don't recall ever meeting a White patron such as yourself, who simply bought a ticket at the window and walked in, as you seem to have done."

"What about all these people?" Narby said, indicating the mezzanine. He smiled. "What about you, Mr. Goldfarb?"

The big man laughed. "Oy. Stupid of me. I assumed. Here." He leaned forward and took a card out of his jacket pocket.

"I should have introduced myself properly. I own the Harlem Square Club. And a few other, lesser venues in the neighborhood. And the Continental on Dade Boulevard. You know the Continental? On the Beach."

Narby glanced at the card. *Arthur B. Goldfarb, president, Gold-Art Management and Productions, 1700 Michigan Avenue, Miami Beach, Florida. The gold standard of entertainment in South Florida.*

"Pease. Don't get me wrong. You're very welcome here, Mr. Narby. But, let me explain. When one of the big acts, someone like Billie, comes to town, well, she always does a show or two over here. For her own people. You understand how it is. I like to get a group of my old friends together. Music lovers. Jazz fans, like Charlie. Or Jack over there. Cultured, sophisticated people. Because sometimes the shows over here are quite spectacular. There's a different feel, a kind of buzz. Because of the connection to the audience. You follow? Naturally, when I noticed you sitting here, my first thought was. Do I know this man? Did I invite him? It's a surprise, that's all."

"I hope I'm not intruding."

"Of course not. Because, now, we're friends." He opened his arms, slightly. "Welcome."

"Thanks. The funny thing is, I wanted to sit down there. Closer to the stage."

"And they stopped you, did they? Sent you up here. Good to know they're on their toes. Because. Well, it crossed my mind, when I noticed you sitting here. By yourself. That you weren't here solely for the music."

"Oh? How's that?"

"We have an ordinance in Miami. Prohibiting mixed-race audiences. Not that the authorities really give a damn about what happens around here, in Overtown. But. Well, it's politics. A peculiar complication of the entertainment industry, you might say. But. You're not a policeman. I see that now. Very definitely."

"I'll take that as a compliment." It was rather amusing. Philip Narby, mistaken for a cop.

Goldfarb laughed. "As you wish. Still. I find it hard to fathom exactly how you wandered in here, into an all-Negro theater in a Negro neighborhood. All the way from Chicago. Or Myerton. Or wherever it is you're staying."

"The Atlantique."

"Nice hotel. Under new management. In fact, I just met the new owner a few weeks ago. A real hot shot. Down from Baltimore. The hotel business, the entertainment industry, real estate—it all goes hand in hand on the Beach. Who knows? Maybe we'll have occasion to do business one day. But my curiosity still has the better of me."

Goldfarb was someone worth knowing. He would have connections in Havana and Washington. If there was trouble with Sid Black, perhaps he could help. "No mystery," Narby said. "I'm keen on jazz, like your friends. Swing, big band, the modern sound. All of it. Anyway, I passed by here the other day." He stopped, pulled the handbill out of his pocket, and showed it to Goldfarb. "I've got a friend who lives around here. There's no ordinance against that, is there? Whites and Negroes being friends?"

"Not yet," said Goldfarb. "But there would be, if the crackers had their way."

"Anyway, I was passing by two days ago and they were handing these out. That's the whole story. Frankly, I don't go for all this race prejudice. If I want to have a drink with a Black Man. Or a Black Woman, for that matter. If I want to sit in a Black theater. Well, it's no one's business but my own. I've been a lot of places, Mr. Goldfarb."

"Please. Call me Art."

"I've been a lot of places, Art. I've been in some tough spots. But even in Korea—well, let me put it this way. I've got no gripe against the Black Man. The Yellow Man. The Jewish Man. So, why not drop in to see Billie Holiday? I was lucky they had a ticket left. I'd be sitting down there, right now, if that usher of yours hadn't blocked my way."

"Let me shake your hand, Mr. Narby."

"Philip. Call me Philip."

"Philip. I share your sentiments. Point for point. It's the same with my friends, here. We're all very liberal, very forward-looking people. Unfortunately, we have to work within the constraints of the system. I feel terrible for the artists, performers the caliber of Billie, or Nat Cole, or Eckstein. It's an outrage, frankly. But, change comes slowly. People like you. Like us. We're making a difference. Am I right?" Goldfarb raised his arm to the waiter making the rounds. "Jimmy. Bring Mr. Narby here—what would you like? Whiskey? Scotch?—Bring Mr. Narby a bottle of Chivas. On the house."

"That's not necessary."

"My pleasure," Goldfarb said, rising from the chair. "Please. Don't get up. Very nice to meet you, Phil. Next time you're in town, drop by the office. A lot of moving and shaking in Miami these days. The Beach, the Gables. Broward. South Dade. We'll talk. Enjoy."

5

THE STAIRS, THE CORRIDOR, THE DOORS, like a carnival funhouse of crazy corners and tipped planes. But he held fast to the general direction, the current of his intent. In the vestibule past the ticket window he set his sights on the leather-padded double doors. He pushed through, the doors pushed back, he tried again. But it wasn't the weight of the doors. It was a man, a very large very black man in an usher's uniform.

"Sir. Pardon me. Upstairs sir, please. The stairs are this way, sir."

Almost whining, like a child. A man big enough to crush Narby with one fist, yet his eyes were glazed with fright.

"It's all right. I'm a personal friend of Mr. Art Goldfarb. Sure I am. He's right up there. Go ask him yourself. He told me, he said, 'Philip, enjoy yourself.' Now, if you don't mind, please, my good man. Clear the gangway."

Against the name of his employer, wielded by a white patron, without precedent to guide him, the usher was helpless.

Drifting through the disorder of tables and chairs, halting to steady himself, taking a few breaths before pushing onward, toward the snazzy ever-shifting crowd on the dance floor. Maybe he was too goddamn drunk to know what the hell he was doing. But he was not too goddamn drunk to know that he was doing exactly what he wanted. Maybe they were staring at him, or staying out of his way, or ignoring him. With the boat lurching to and fro, tipping side to side, it's a free for all, every man for himself.

At the threshold of the dance floor he came to a rest, flummoxed by the thicket of jutting elbows and hips and backsides, an impenetrable wall of flailing Negro flesh. He was dancing, too, only on the inside, whirling like a gyroscope to prevent himself from toppling over. The concentration required merely to remain upright, to resist reaching out to ballast himself upon the backside of some voluptuous maiden, was so fierce that it excused him from all other mental responsibility. He wasn't even laughing. It was the music. He was a jazz man. In the know. All the latest sounds, the newest records.

Unable to penetrate, feeling suddenly exposed as he came to a rest, he moved again, snaking along the periphery toward a spot near the wall. The house orchestra was blowing a big finale. Finding the spot empty, leaning against a pillar, he went through the complicated manual operation whose sequential actions, if carried out correctly, resulted in a cigarette between his lips.

"You fall from the sky?"

Someone speaking to him. From behind the pillar. Narby turned. "Did I what?"

"Ain't you supposed to be up yonder?"

The speaker was quite close, almost shouting in his ear. Narby leaned away to get a focus. A smiling slender young fellow with a long funny face, topped by a porkpie hat. "Am I?"

The man laughed. Pointed nose, white teeth, red mouth, shiny green necktie, his Adam's apple protruding sharply through the black-yellow skin of his up-tilted throat. "They done tossed you out of heaven above? Or did you jump?"

"I jumped," Narby shouted. "Better down here."

"That a fact? Then you all right and air tight."

"The tighter the better. Don't you agree?"

"Sure. Only you got to be loose with the juice to get the right kind of tight. You dig this sound, man?"

"Deeply. Very deeply." Narby turned toward the stage, listening with his eyes. "I know it. I know I know it."

"What you know, man? Hey, Jack, the man here says he knows *it*."

Narby looked at him again: the elongated face, the porkpie hat, the Adam's apple. "It's a Dizzy number. Sure it is."

The man had triplicated. There were three now, disputing. "Naw, man, that ain't no Dizzy tune." "That's Fat Girl, not Dizzy." "Bird played it first, you fools." "No he didn't." "Yeah he did."

The orchestra went into a stop-time cadenza. During the crack of silence, Narby licked his lips, tasting the word as it came up. "*Manteca*. It's called *Manteca*."

"Nah, man. You wrong. It's called *Tanga*."

"Ask Chick, man. Chick'll know."

The orchestra blew a tremulous wailing fermata chord, the conga beating out a dying flurry. The crowd broke into whistles and cheers. On the stage, wiping away his sweat with a handkerchief, the bandleader said, "That's a hot one all right. Whew. A hot one for this hell of a hot town. A tune by the great John Birks otherwise known as Dizzy Gillespie. *Man—teca.*"

Someone clamped Narby on the shoulder. But he was among Negroes. There was nothing to fear.

"My man!" The porkpie hat said. "I knew he was right. *Tanga!* Fat Girl! Shit, you coons go crawling back to the swamp. Me and my man here are in the pocket. Didn't I tell ya' it was Dizzy."

"Tango?" Narby said, laughing. "That wasn't a tango."

"Naw man. Tang-a."

"Where's everyone going?" Narby asked.

"Shows over, man."

"Night's young," Narby said. "I'll wait here for the next set." He patted the pillar as though it were an old friend.

"Ain't another set. It's bagged for the night. But you all right, man. Sneaking down here with da darkies to get up close. Ha."

"I'm Philip Narby." He held out his hand. "You're all right yourself."

The porkpie hat slid his palm across Narby's open hand. Some kind of secret Negro handshake. "I go by Bobby. Wherever I go, Bobby goes. He never gets ahead, never falls behind. You something else, man. Phil-lip whatever-you-said. We ain't too formal down here on the floor. One name is one too many when they looking for you. Dig?"

"Bobby." He remembered now having left half the bottle of Chivas upstairs. That was a shame. "Come on. I'll buy you a drink. Some place with jazz. Bring your friends, too. All three of you."

Again, they disputed, leaving Narby against the pillar, the crowd ebbing away. "Come on, man. Let's meet those cats out back." "We ain't bringing that cracker, Bobby." "Don't you call my man a cracker." "Don't be messing with any of that." "Man's cool. Knows his shit from shinola. Jumped down from way up high and landed square on his feet. He's a cat, not a rat."

Apparently, Bobbie prevailed. He was ushered down a flight of stairs, out a metal door, and into a narrow space between high walls, a dimly lit alleyway slick from the rain. If only they would speak more slowly he might understand, get a word in edge-wise. The air was a thick warm mist. At the end of the alley, as through a slot, he could see the glow of Second Avenue. There was the stink of grease blowing from a big rattling exhaust tube, and the jungle funk, lush and green and sweetly rotten. They were huddled on the metal landing, under an awning. The door swung open and three or four more came out, wearing shiny black suits and narrow ties, musicians, Narby supposed, everyone laughing and slapping hands while he merely nod-ded, standing apart from the huddle, flicking away his cigarette butt. He was there and he wasn't there. He felt the drizzle on his head, against his face. It felt good, but then he would be wet, and it would feel bad. He took a breath, clawing his way up from the trough of a wave, the drink dragging him down and then tossing him up. Like the lights of the boats, swaying on the chop of the Bay.

"You fellows can really swing," he said, breaking in. "You played the hell out of that Dizzy tune. I knew it was *Manteca*. I used to live in Havana. I have all your records."

"That's a good one," one of the musicians said, turning, smiling at him. "Cause they ain't never put me on a record. I'd sure like to hear me one day."

Everyone laughed. "I mean Dizzy. And Parker. You fellows are fantastic. You're out in front. Like Miles Davis and Monk. How do you do that? Play fast and slow at the same time? Stretching it out and then bringing it back."

Bobbie introduced him, made his case. The cat that fell from the sky. He got his slaps. One of them, the tenor man, was called "Cannibal" because of his habit of eating everything in sight. Don't worry, Phil, he won't eat you cause you ain't no cracker. Narby told them he was from New York. No shit? Cannibal was headed up there next week. For keeps this time. Only town in

America a man could make some bread making real jazz. Black or White.

Narby reached in his pocket for a cigarette.

"Here," Bobby said, "try one of mine."

It was already lit. Hand rolled, as Narby preferred. The end was wet. Negro spit, mixing with his own. It wasn't as though he hadn't tasted it before, swallowed it, lapped it up between Becca's legs. Honey for the honna'pot. He took it from Bobby's hand and put it to his lips, wondering at the unusual sharp aroma. Not even Hank carried this brand. Seek and ye shall find. His lungs full he held it for a few seconds and then let the blue smoke stream smoothly from his nostrils into the warm misted air, his eyes closed. Click click click.

"What did I tell you," Bobby was crowing. "Phil from New York. Landed on his feet, like a real true cat."

6

THE NEXT MORNING HE AWOKE around noon and after breakfast in his suite went for a swim to clear his head, paralleling the shore for a mile against the current and then doubling back. The water warm and milky green, the swells gentle under a brilliant sky. In a swimsuit and dark glass, unshaven, the towel draped over his left shoulder to cover the scars, Narby doubted Sid Black, or anyone for that matter, would recognize him. Nevertheless, he had exercised caution, taking the stairs rather than the elevator and by-passing the lobby by cutting through the poolside bar.

Willa was in New York. Some business with the Janis gallery, she had explained. They'd been at it now for six weeks. Narby would show up, spend a few days, swimming, walking the long deserted stretches of dunes, reading, listening to jazz records while Willa spent the daylight hours in the studio. In the evening she would prepare a simple dinner. They drank wine and Narby's boilermaker champagne cocktails. The sleek machine-like house became their playground: in the pool, draped over the low-slung chrome and leather furniture, sprawling on the thick rug, gripping the cable railing on the cantilevered terrace. He marveled at his good fortune in finding a woman like that, who didn't give a damn about marriage or children or propriety, whose need seemed as great as his own. Finding her in the middle of nowhere, the wastes of Lacoosa County. But was it really chance? He thought not.

She would be back in a week. But come April, with the return of the miserable Gulf Coast weather, the swarming mosquitoes and black flies, she would pack up for New York until next November. He preferred not to think about it. When the time came, he'd figure something out. Convince her to stay. Make her need him, crave him, even more.

After his swim he took a shower and sat on the loveseat, looking out over the placid ocean nine stories below, the glass doors slid open to counteract the frigid air-conditioning, and poured out two inches of Jim Beam. He was managing well enough now on the State Department Diplomatic Corps regimen: Irish coffee for breakfast, a pick-me-up around eleven, two or three stiff ones at lunch, then steady-as-she-goes nips, maybe a couple of beers as well, until the cocktail hour. After dinner it was from each according to his liquor cabinet, to each according to his capacity. He rarely got blind drunk anymore. Just enough to pacify the parasite, feed the Naktong Worm.

The Harlem Square Club had proven very interesting, very fruitful. He lit a cigarette and picked up Goldfarb's business card. The entertainment industry might provide a viable cover, with conduits to both the Black and White worlds, operating half in the shadows. Goldfarb, the loud heavy-set ostentatious

Jew, and the elegant silent patrician Bill Knowles—it amused Narby to think of them working together, unawares.

Things were heating up in Cuba, it seemed. The newly appointed U.S. Ambassador, Arthur Gardner, was a pal of Batista's. To cozy up closer to the Eisenhower Administration, Batista had finally cut his ties to the leftist labor unions, outlawed the Cuban Communist Party and closed down their newspapers, *Hoy* and *Ultima Hora*, and banned the Young Socialist Movement. That meant a lot of young hotheads and petty political gangsters out on the street, looking for retribution. Narby guessed that the 26 July group would absorb any number of the disaffected, regardless of Castro's anti-Red rhetoric. It was a three-way contest now: Eisenhower and the Republicans, the C.I.A. and the liberal wing of State, and the Soviets. If Castro were smart, if he ever managed to get out of prison, he would steer smack in the middle: a good-humored, clean-handed populist with no other goal than to restore Cuba to a constitutional democracy. But chances were Fidel Castro was finished.

He put aside Goldfarb's card and opened the crumpled brown-paper lunch sack. He'd been too damned drunk last night to gauge its strength or effects. Mary Jane, reefer, hemp. From Mexico, Narby supposed. He dumped it on the table— twenty dollar's worth—separated the dried leaf from the sticks and seeds, rolled a cigarette and stepped out on the balcony. Maybe if he smoked enough of it he'd work up the guts to go downstairs, pick up the house phone in the lobby and ask for Mr. Sid Black's room. If they patched him through, he'd simply hang up and pack his bags. If the operator informed him that no one by that name was registered at the hotel, then he could stop all the backstairs skulking.

At first there was only a slight warmth up his spine, a quickening of his heart. When the butt burned too close he flicked it over the balcony railing and stood for a moment, rather enjoying the view, the shifting blue-green colors of the sea and sky, the soft ocean air against his face, the hypnotic wash and crash of the waves, wave after wave. There was something to it, after all. They ought to pipe the stuff through the vents, mixed with the polar air-conditioning. Make it the high season, all year round.

He went inside and rolled the remainder, a dozen or so cigarettes, and put them in the pouch of shag tobacco. Bobby, with the long crescent-moon face and the porkpie hat and the sharply protruding Adam's apple. And the jive talk. Told Narby he could usually be found around the Harlem Square or one of the bars off Second Avenue. He'd be easy enough to recognize.

Maybe he ought to smoke another. Better to wait, he decided, see how long it lasted, how it blended with the Jim Beam. He pulled on a dark polo shirt, a pale yellow hat with the brim pulled down, and dark glasses, and took the stairwell to the lobby. The place was bustling, people passing back and forth from the front desk and the sitting areas to the lounge and the poolside bar, everyone stimulated by the arrival of the cocktail hour. Someone was using the lobby phone. But there was another, next to the concierge's desk. He waited a moment, took a breath and walked over, nodding familiarly to one of the senior bellhops. He was put on hold. His pulse was up. Good. He was ready for anything, he supposed.

"Hotel Atlantique. Front desk. How may I assist you?"

"Yeah. I'd like to speak to one of your guests. A Mister Sid Black."

"Just a moment, sir…. Mr. Sid Black… I'm sorry sir, no one by that name is registered."

"What about Sidney Black. Or S. Black?"

"No, sir. No Blacks. I do have a Green," the voice joked.

Narby hung up. That was that. He could relax, unclench. Enjoy Bobby's cigarettes.

"Excuse me. Mr. Narby."

He swung around. It was the bellhop, a white-haired Negro. Narby was a regular guest, a good tipper. They all knew his name. "Yeah. What's up?"

"You looking for Mr. Black?"

"Who told you that?"

"Sorry, sir. Sorry. Didn't mean to eavesdrop. Only I'm standing right here. None of my business, sir. Excuse me."

"No. That's all right. Go on. What is it?"

"Mr. Sid Black?"

"Yeah."

"He's here, sure enough. Only he ain't no guest."

What was it? Some kind of riddle. "OK. I give up. If he's not a guest, what is he?"

"He the new owner. Bought the hotel, back in December."

"New owner? You sure? Maybe it's a different Black. About this tall, dark eyes, bald on top. Maybe forty years old."

"That's Mr. Black, all right. Down from Baltimore."

"And you say he's here? At the hotel? Right now?"

"No, sir. I ain't seen him so far today. But he comes round most days, toward evening. You want me to tell him you looking for him, Mr. Narby?"

"He usually comes around in the evening? About what time?"

"After sundown. Most days. I'll be sure to give him your name, Mr. Narby."

"That won't be necessary." He had to think. His heart was pounding, the dope momentarily looping his thoughts. "Look. I don't want to get you into any trouble with your boss. The thing is. Don't mention it to Mr. Black. He might get upset. He's a very private man. He might not like it, if he thought someone was interfering in his business. His personal life."

"I don't know nothing about it, Mr. Narby. Never heard a word."

Vetch's dictum held. The worst thing for a Black man was getting caught in a White man's mess. "Thanks. Here. For your trouble."

"Thank you, sir. Enjoy your afternoon, sir."

He went up to his room, called down to the front desk to have his bill ready, and packed his valise. Take it easy. He wasn't running anymore. From anybody. He sat on the love seat and poured a drink and lit a cigarette. The important thing was to keep two steps ahead of Black. He remembered what Goldfarb had said, that it was all the same, the hotel business and the entertainment industry and Miami real estate. It was probably as corrupt here as Havana, only in a more polite and democratic fashion, the hotels and the nightclubs and drugs and prostitution and illegal gambling and money laundering and tax dodges. Politics, Goldfarb had called it. He'd bought dope right in Goldfarb's nightclub, hadn't he? Maybe it was just business as usual for Black, with a veneer of legitimacy now that he was out of the Army-surplus business, so to speak. Black obviously had better reasons for being in South Florida than merely tracking down Philip Narby. For all he knew, Black had given up on him by now, written it off as a business loss. He ought not jump to negative conclusions, ought to look on the Robinson Crusoe side of things.

The stuff seemed to be wearing off. There was something too it, though. It amped him up, but not in a nervous jittery way, like the bennies. He'd handled himself well just now, downstairs. No one was going to chase Philip Narby out of Miami Beach. He took one of the dope cigarettes out of the tobacco pouch, went to the balcony, smoking only half because it kicked in more quickly than the first.

In the lobby, settling his bill, he noticed that it wasn't only the ocean scenery that had improved with the help of Bobby's dope. Legs, breasts, behinds. They all seemed to clamor for his attention, his appreciation. It was all rather funny. He nodded to the bellhop on his way out. Narby supposed he had given the old man a bit of a fright. No doubt, he'd be relieved never to see Philip Narby again, despite the exorbitant tips. Outside, the doorman hailed him a cab.

The newer, more fashionable hotels were further up Collins Avenue. That was the trend. The older places, south of Lincoln and along Ocean Drive, were going to seed. Further north, where Collins ran along Indian Creek, they were tearing down all the big private beachfront estates, with plans to put up bigger gaudier hotels. He told the driver to head up Collins. When they had gone ten or so blocks Narby told him to pull in to the next hotel. The Calvado. Glass brick and neon, winding stairs and curved ornamental walls. But behind the newer façade and the tacked-on glitz, more or less the same set- up as the Atlantique: two wings around the swimming pool and a tower in the middle, the lobby cocktail lounge and poolside bar, just about every square foot dedicated to the consumption of booze and the art of procuring. Men looking for warm bodies. Single girls scheming to meet eligible bachelors.

He hesitated for a moment, scanning the lobby, and approached the front desk.

"I'm very sorry, sir. We're all booked up. High season, you know. We do on occasion get cancellations. But I'd have to check with the manager. I don't know if he's available at the moment. Perhaps, if you came back later."

Narby passed him a five. "Maybe you could check on that right now. Yeah?"

"Of course, sir. Just a moment." He disappeared into the office and returned seconds later. "You're in luck. We do have one cancellation. A deluxe suite, in the main tower. One of our nicest rooms. Full ocean view, balcony …."

"What's the rate?"

The clerk wrote a sum on a piece of notepaper. It was twice what Narby paid at the Atlantique. They were going to milk him, it seemed. Still, the women were perhaps better looking here, the air not quite so frigid and metallic. He gave the lobby another glance. "Fine. I'll take it."

At the newsstand off the lobby he bought the *Miami Herald* and the *New York Times* and *The Atlantic*. The Negro bellhops were younger here. The one showing him to his room looked to be Bobby's age. Leonard, according to the name tag. Maybe he wouldn't have to go back to Overtown to get what he was looking for. When they got to the room Narby tipped him. "Thanks, Leonard."

"Thank you, sir. Very much. If there's anything else I can get you, sir. Anything you need. Just ask for Leonard."

"I'll do that."

He spent an hour reading the papers, clipping articles, jotting notes, taking puffs from the half-cigarette, the glass doors opened to the ocean air. The United Nations Security Council had condemned Israel for the raid into Gaza. Forty Egyptian soldiers dead, scores wounded. In response, Ben Gurion laid out the evidence that Nasser was covertly supplying arms and intelligence to the Palestinian fedayeen. The British had just ratified the Baghdad Pact, hoping to wean Iraq away from their fellow Arabs. The Shah of Iran safely in the C.I.A.'s pocket, Nasser whipping up his pan-Arabic supporters, Iraq's King Faisal practically a member of the British House of Lords, the French selling weapons to the Israelis while shoring up Algeria, the non-aligned Nasser playing everyone against everyone: the Americans against the Soviets against the British against the Israelis against the Palestinians against the weaker Arabic states—things were barreling toward a blow up. Probably ignite over Suez. Oil fields, shipping lanes, vast stretches of strategic real estate—it made Cuba seem very small potatoes. Except for one factor. Havana was ninety miles from hometown U.S.A. Our own Monroe-Doctrine backyard playground.

The sun was setting, the streaks of cloud over the Atlantic burning pink and vermillion, the ocean dark, like molten lead. Pity to enjoy the view all alone, in his beautiful tenth-floor suite. The stuff, he noticed, whetted his appetite. He was starving. And not just for food.

He had a drink in the cocktail lounge downstairs. To look rather than touch, he supposed. Since taking up with Willa

Branton he hadn't had another woman. Not even Becca. He let his eyes roam: average girls, secretaries down for a weeklong holiday with a couple of girlfriends, taking the Orange Blossom Special from New York or Philadelphia or Baltimore. Giggling virgins. Janets-in-the-making. A wife, mature and experienced and wanting more, giving him the eye surreptitiously while her pot-bellied hubbie yakked it up about some prizefight. He was wasting his time. He paid, took a walk along the beach and then went out for a decent meal. A few hours later he took a cab up Collins. He had stopped in a few times at the more established burlesque houses and stripper joints around Lincoln Road, the Place Pigalle, Chez Paree—places where, if you were willing to shell out for the overpriced liquor, you could sit amongst tables of married couples and red-faced men in high-waist pants and fat ties smoking cigars, and watch women with names like Honey Harlow or Tempest Storm strip down in some phony dance to a G-string and pasties. And that was it. Show over. Buy another bottle or get the hell out.

But further uptown, past the Normandy Shores Golf Club, there were little places that, if diligent with the bribes, escaped the scrutiny of the Vice squad. The Paddock, the Shack, the Vault. The jokes were filthy. No one was spared: Kikes, Niggers, Wops, Micks, Eisenhower's schlong, Marilyn Monroe's toilet habits, Hemingway's fish fetish. The girls didn't dance, they jerked. In the end, everything came off and the lights would dim. After a moment they'd come out from backstage in negligees and sit on your lap and you bought them champagne. The private rooms were down a hallway, cordoned off by a curtain. No married couples here, only men, alone or with their consorts.

Narby sat toward the back. It was hot and crowded and dark. The black walls appeared to glisten and swell, oozing with the collective sweat of the onlookers. One of the girls on stage Narby thought very pretty, a slender red head, a bit on the frail side. He watched her through the filth and the din, trying to catch her eye. Only something was wrong with her. Unhooking her brassiere she nearly tripped, the heel of her shoe catching on a gouge in the scuffed wooden platform, then righting herself, laughing with a kind of terrorized giggle. The crowd howled back, booing her. Someone yelled out, "She's weak, she needs to feed the pussy." She answered the heckler with her middle finger. There was a scuffle in the front, shouting, chairs pushed over.

Narby stood, his fists clenched. He lurched forward, only to be repulsed backward by an enormous hairy paw against his chest. "Keep out of it, pal."

"Says who?"

The paw attached to a massive downy arm. Two-hundred fifty pounds, crew cut, sunburned jowls, small insipid eyes bored into the lumpish head, aloha shirt big enough to sail a ship, khaki pants. Right down to the penny loafers, lightly splattered with vomit. "Says me, pal. They're just having a little fun. Sit down. Or take a walk."

Marine or M.P. Time of his life in Japan during the Occupation, the cheap pan-pan girls and cauldrons of booze, then the Korean shit storm, and then back home after years of slaughter and waste, a burn out, a nothing. The hometown girls turning away as he came down the sidewalk, leering, maybe a little jail time for drunk and disorderly, the jobs that never worked out, and then this. Same work, really, as the M.P.s. Keeping the rape and whoring and drunkenness within acceptable parameters, always managing a little fuckee-fuckee for himself on the side.

"Hands off. I hear you."

The bouncer nodded, lowered his arm. Narby felt the small rodent eyes crawling over his face.

"You in Korea?"

"Maybe I was. You?"

"PFC Narby. Eighth Army. Artillery. Company D. Went in with Task Force Smith. Second month of the war. The Pusan perimeter. A real good time."

The bouncer gave a thick laugh. "Marines. X Corps. Inchon. We saved your ass, pal. Looks like that's my task in life. Cause I just saved it again. You want a fight, take it to the fucking Chinks."

It was like throwing acid in your face, invoking Korea, thinking he might solicit a shred of camaraderie. He looked around, his guts sinking. What was he doing here? The men were pigs, the women more abject than the most desperate Havana whores. The redhead was down on her hands and knees, licking something off the stage to their jeers and hoots. He had to get out of there before something happened, a fight, a police raid. He had the dope cigarettes in the pouch in his pocket. That would be the end of Philip Narby. They'd find out who he really was, strap him back on the gurney, scald his brain with electro-shock until he told them what he knew about Willoughby and Knowles and McCoy.

He was outside. He wandered along Collins. Up here, north of the hotels, he could see the ocean from the street, the waves foaming white in the moonlight as they rolled up the sand, the salt wind in his face, his hair. He wanted only Willa. They had met for a reason.

A pair of headlights came cutting through the thick damp air. Narby jerked, looking for somewhere to hide, ready to throw himself in the ditch. But as it passed under a streetlamp he saw it was only a cab. He raised his arm and it pulled over.

"The Atlantique. No. Forget that. The Calvado."

Sid Black was in Miami Beach. Buying hotels, going legit. A man like that couldn't afford trouble. Wouldn't want people digging in to his past. They could hang Sid Black for what he had done. Black might be alive, but as far as Narby could see, he was nothing but a ghost.

7

AS HE DROVE PAST HENDERSON AVENUE, crossing the bridge, he felt a pang of remorse. He hadn't settled things with Becca, hadn't paid her for the lost nights. It made him uneasy to think about it, the parlor downstairs with its suffocating air of candle wax and dime-store perfume, how he had first gone there with Vetch, the panting toad-like men sunk in the sofa—men who, by now, would have taken his place on Thursday and Saturday nights.

He stopped at the fork. Vetch's ruts veered to the right, plunging into the brush, paralleled by the sagging power line. In cramped handwritten letters, squeezed onto the bottom of the childlike signboard, Vetch had added yet another induce-ment to the promise of cozy cabins and spectacular fishing and beer and bait and ice: *off-season rates all year round!!!* Narby had to laugh. The greater the man's delusion, the more violent, perhaps, his reaction when he discovered how completely he'd been fooled. Even the Negroes living out in the defunct camp, men who once feared Vetch, were laughing behind his back. The Great White Cracker Clown.

The windows had shutters now, painted sea-green, the porch under the wide eaves painted coral-white. Island colors. He blew the horn, got out and lowered the tailgate. Crowded in the bed were more fruit trees and saplings, melaleuca and Australian pines from the nursery on Old Cutler Road, along with pots of bamboo and other exotics, plants that grew at a prodigious rate in the hothouse climate of Sawfish Point. Waters understood how to plant and fertilize. There was furniture, too, from the bric-a-brac shops along Flagler and the Tamiami: a brass floor lamp, another water-stained Persian rug, and a couple of junked oil paintings in cracked, faux-gilded frames. Narby had a taste for seascapes, harbor scenes, ships tossed in storms—Robinson Crusoe stuff. The more darkened by dust and neglect, the better.

Waters was there six days a week. He and his crew were working behind the grove that morning, digging the pond. They came around from the back of the house and started to unload. To Narby's surprise, the ancient Moorish door now pushed open with ease, and clicked closed. There was a sliding bolt lock, too. Since he'd been gone Waters had re-hung it and installed new hardware. Waters no longer waited for Narby to tell him what to do. He simply came every day and did what was needed, making improvements and repairs, handing over receipts if he had bought supplies, and Narby paid him, usually without question.

Waters had lived alone ever since his wife died years ago. His two children were grown and had moved away. It would be good to have someone on the property at all times. Someone Narby could trust. Someone who depended on him. He was waiting for the right moment to make Waters an offer: the Bahamian could build himself a small house, a cottage, close to Narby's, live rent free in exchange for keeping an eye on the place, plus of course his regular wages for construction and maintenance and gardening work. He would draw up some kind of agreement, if Waters wanted it in writing.

He went into the kitchen and washed the grime off his face, took a beer and a hunk of cheese and a box of crackers from the icebox—the cupboards were useless against the ants and roaches—and sat in the room in the back. Through the screens and the fledgling grove he could make out Waters and the men, digging holes for the new saplings. Somehow, without Narby's consciously willing it, the house had formed a personality, tangent to if not reflective of his own. It was full of junk, but junk that had once been priceless. A detached and castoff place, like rooms from an old estate that had broken away and been washed out by the storms and the sea and then tossed up in the middle of nothing, a wasteland where once a garden might have blossomed. He even had a library now, an entire wall of roach and mildew spotted volumes—leather and cloth-bound and paperbacks from the used book stores around the University of Miami—along with the stacks of newspapers and magazines and the notebooks and folders in which he organized the clippings. An old library table served as his desk. The high-backed throne-like wicker chairs, where he sat and read and drank into the night, and the scroll-footed caved-in sofa, upholstered in brocade, where it amused him to think he might one day entertain guests—have Bill Knowles to tea. Or perhaps cocktails with Brigadier General Charles Willoughby, swapping stories of the Occupation, how Lord Charles, as they called him behind his back, had fixed the war tribunals and jerry-rigged intelligence for the glorification of the Supreme Commander. Entertain the famous Willa Branton, on her back and her belly and her knees.

From the pouch he took one of Bobby's cigarettes. He was down to six, half his supply. There were probably stronger strains. Bobby might have sold him the dregs, because Narby was White. A cracker. An ofay. Narby's enlightened attitudes didn't enter into it. The Whites had all the power. If a Black man had a chance to put one over on a White, he'd be stupid not to take it.

Refreshed, buoyant, he went out the back door and through the grove, the young trees already bearing winter mango and avocado. The pond was Sam's idea. At the moment it was nothing but a big hole. Beneath the layer of rich topsoil, the ground was white and chalky, a mélange of sand and shell and marl—the same stuff Waters had spread under the house to prevent anything from growing below the raised floor. Now there was a huge mound of it, dumped at the foot of the pines about twenty yards behind the pond. The material would come in useful later, to surface the rough dirt lane that ran from the fork to Narby's house.

Only three feet deep, the ground water had already begun to seep in, the bottom of the pit turning to slurry. Once it was finished, the sides shored up with cement, they would fill it and replenish regularly with clear well water, Waters had explained—like Vizcaya, where they had grown giant lily pads and lotus flowers, with willows weeping along the banks.

"Everything good, Sam?"

"I spose. That's some good spec'mens you brung home. We get to the rest tomorrow or next day. They be fine in them pots for now."

"Nice job on the front door."

Waters nodded. Narby could read nothing from the man's face, the stiff scarified complexion and filmed-over eyes. The dope cigarettes gave off a rather acrid lingering odor. He wondered if Waters recognized it. Too bad Waters was such a tee-totaler, a prig. Narby wouldn't mind having someone to share a drink with now and then, a kindred spirit amidst the wastes of Sawfish Point.

"I'll give you a hand tomorrow. I could use the exercise."

Waters stopped digging, blotting his face with a red cloth. "Cap'm Vetch came round. Yesterday."

"What did he want?"

"Nothing. Just to look round, I spect. He seen your truck weren't here. Didn't say much."

"I told that son-of-a-bitch to keep away from here. You didn't let him go in the house, did you?"

"No, sir. He didn't ask." He paused, measuring his words. "You don't want him coming by, you best be around, Mr. Nawby. I can't stop him." "Remember that gate we talked about putting up? Where the road crosses the property line. That should keep anyone from driving in, unannounced. Let's start that tomorrow. The pond can wait."

"O.K."

"You boys want some cold soda pop?"

"Wouldn't refuse."

Narby came back cradling five bottles. They sat on the unearthed chunks of limestone that Waters was using to build the low garden walls. Narby passed around a pack of

Chesterfields—left over from the cartons he had bought long ago from Hank. The workers looked old enough to have been around in the days of Captain Higginbotham, tapping the trees for Putnam, forced to spend all their wages in Vetch's store. A notch up from slavery. They said nothing, just nodded. They belonged to another world.

The next day, after putting in a few hours of early morning labor, Narby drove into Myerton and parked in front of Rexall's. Janet would be at the library by now. He wondered how he would feel, after half a dope cigarette, looking at her, talking to her. Even if she had wanted, Janet wouldn't have known how to reach him, not since he'd left the Glo-bel. He crossed the court-house square and went down the half flight of steps, setting off the brass bells. There were magazines waiting for him, and spe-cial-order Danish shag. The cool subterranean shop was empty. Hank came out from behind the beaded curtain.

"What do you make of that raid on Gaza?" The proprietor and his most loyal customer were in the habit of discussing the news from Hank's native land. "Looks like things are heating up for Nasser."

Hank nodded. "It is the British. The Jewish bankers. They are prodding the Israelis to embarrass us." He shrugged. "No matter. Nasser is too smart for them. Even the United Nations is on his side. Egypt has been a great civilization since the time of the Pharaohs, Mr. Norby. The rest of the world understands. Even President Eisenhower. Soon, so too will the Jews and the British. I have no worries. Well," he said, a bit slyly, "no worries except for the natural worries of a father."

"A father?"

"Yes. To you, Mr. Norby, I can announce. My wife is now six months with child. Expecting."

"Hell, I didn't even know you were married, Hank."

"Excuse me. It is something very personal. For people of my faith. But you I can tell, Mr. Norby. Because you are a true friend."

"Congratulations." Narby tried to sound sincere. "That's wonderful news. Keep me posted, all right?"

"I will indeed, sir."

"And best to your wife."

At that, Hank merely nodded.

It was four blocks from the Smoker's Den to the library. Janet turned away, keeping her distance, refusing to acknowledge him. Despite having a shed a few pounds, she looked worse. Bedraggled, worn down. He couldn't be sure, but it looked like a bruise on her arm, and a splotch under her eye, covered over with make-up. If only she would let him help her. He would talk to Frank. One Korean veteran to another. Like throwing acid on his face. He shrugged and walked out.

The girl working at the Piggly Wiggly Supermarket gave him a suggestive smile. She wasn't much to look it. A plump homegrown White Myerton maiden, freshly dropped out of high school. Flat broad face, like a pig. But her ass wiggled provocatively enough under the uniform. A wiggly piggly. The dope cigarettes, he noticed, gave things a poetic sheen.

He piled the groceries in the truck and drove along the strip of shops on the highway just south of downtown. There were three package stores in Lacoosa County. He rotated among them, buying Jim Beam by the case. And two gun shops. It was foolish to live out on Sawfish Point unarmed. Narby hadn't touched a gun since Korea. Even then, he hadn't fired it. Had flung it away in terror, running down the hill—a jam-prone M-1, surplus junk from the Second World War. A pistol, he was thinking, something he could carry in the attaché or keep hidden in the truck. And perhaps one of those automated Browning shotguns he'd seen advertised in the papers, for the house.

In fact, there was a gun shop just down the highway from the package store. He pulled into the dirt lot, between two equally battered pick-up trucks. But then he thought, smarter to buy the guns and ammunition in Miami, where there was no chance of being recognized. At one of the redneck gun shops along the Tamiami, or in the sporting goods department at the Sears Roebuck.

Or maybe he was just a coward. It still haunted him. He should have let Campos swing the pipe. Should have thrown the pilot overboard, the anchor wrapped around the fat stinking still-breathing corpse. Why buy a gun if he didn't have the nerve to use it? Better to kill Vetch with Vetch's own rifle, if that's what Narby needed to do to protect himself. Or poison. Make it look like suicide. Out there, all alone in that wretched store, bankrupt and diseased, without a woman or even a dog to ease his desperation. Because if they suspected foul play, started poking around the records at the County Clerk's office, they might piece something together.

He was daydreaming. A reefer jag. He pulled the truck out of the lot and puffed on the stub of dope cigarette as he drove through town, flicking it away when it burned his fingertips. He was bringing lunch for Waters and the men. Thick slices of roast beef and cheese, a fresh loaf of bread, corn, pickles, potato salad, and key lime pie for dessert. Make Waters feel at home. Give it another month and he'd plant the idea about Waters building a place for himself on Narby's property. Living there as a groundskeeper, of sorts. Rent free, with a decent salary. Treated with respect.

Crossing the bridge Narby passed the deputy sheriff driving his bubble gum machine in the opposite direction. He rather doubted the local constabulary could identify the smell, or even knew what the hell it was. Still, he ought to be more careful. Maybe mix it with the fragrant shag tobacco, to mask the peculiar odor. That way, he could smoke it whenever he wished.

But then, after crossing the bridge, he pulled onto the shoulder and swung the truck around. He had forgotten to pick up the lumber and corrugated metal for the gate, and the chain and padlock. To keep Vetch out. To avoid violence, if at all possible.

8

WITH AN HOUR OF DAYLIGHT LEFT, he assumed Willa would be in the studio. As usual, he let himself in, surprised to find her in the living room, on the leather sofa with a glass of wine. Waiting for him, apparently.

"Hello, Philip." She rose, and standing, they embraced and kissed. She leaned back and looked at him, scanning his face. "I'd half convinced myself you weren't real. That I had imagined you. In my lonely hours."

"Well, here I am. In the flesh. "

"I missed you, Philip."

"Yeah?" He had missed her, too, terribly. But why admit it, now that she had said it for him? It gave him the advantage. "Show me."

She laughed a little, withdrawing, teasing. "Would you like a drink?"

He helped himself from the bottles on the cabinet. The wine was in an ice bucket and he refilled her glass and sat close to her on the couch, his hand gently caressing her leg, short sensual strokes up to her thigh. But instead of yielding, reclining, she scooted up, placing her hand over his. "Could you make me one of your shaggy cigarettes? I missed those, too."

"Of course." She wanted to talk a bit, he supposed. Before getting into it. "How was New York?"

"Good. Very good."

She was excited. Something had happened. "Yeah? Tell me."

"Sidney wants to mount another solo show. The entire gallery, this time. And they've chosen me again for the Biennale. Next year, in Venice. It seems as though I've been noticed. Well. More than noticed."

"Who's Sidney?"

"Sorry. Sidney Janis. He and Harriet own the Janis Gallery. Sidney wanted to tell me in person. So he waited until I was in the city. It's quite a story. About a month ago three men sauntered in to the gallery. An odd trio. Two of them were dressed like stock brokers. Not Brooks Brothers, either. More Savile Row and Bond Street. Sidney said it was as if they had just stepped out of a vault, reeking of cash. But the other one, the one clearly in charge—he was draped head to foot in a flowing white robe and a headdress. With a beard and dark glasses. Like something out of central casting. Turns out he's a Saudi Arabian sheik. Floating on a sea of oil five times the size of Texas. He told Sidney he was looking to augment his collection of contemporary American art, which he hangs in his London town house, in Mayfair. He was there for hours. Looking at everything, stroking his beard. And damn if he didn't walk out with six paintings. Had one of the stockbrokers write the check while the other hailed a couple of cabs. Three Willa Brantons. Sidney wouldn't tell me what the other three were. Said the Sheik wanted to keep it mum, for the moment." She paused, arching her eyebrows, tapping the cigarette against the ashtray. "I suppose I won't have to sweat paying the bills this month. For once."

"That's great, Willa. Congratulations."

"It's what I needed, Philip. Things have been very precarious for me these last few years. Thank God for Endicott. And Sidney and Harriet. It's a rung on the ladder. There's still a long way to climb. Because I'm rather ambitious. About everything I do."

"I see that."

"And because I'm a woman, it's going to be twice as hard. One thing I hated about Paris, Philip. If you're an old cow, they accept you. But an attractive woman who is a serious artist, an intellectual? They treat you like a freak, a curiosity of nature. Or else you're consigned to the shadows of some more powerful man. Like de Beauvoir, dogging that little dwarf Sartre. It's goddamn demeaning. But in New York, it's different. Sure, it's still a boy's world. The Tenth Street crowd, the Cedar Tavern gang. But in New York, if you're a woman and a serious contender, they merely hate you. I don't mean they're queers or anything like that. Not that I give a damn if they were. But once a woman bores her way in, proves herself somehow, then they treat you like one of the fellows, slap you on the back and stick a cigar in your mouth, while cutting you to pieces behind your back. I'd rather be hated than pitied. Wouldn't you? Could you pour me another glass, darling?

"The thing is. Yes, there's Notre Dame and the Louvre and the little bookstalls along the Seine, the Place de Vosges, Montparnasse. All the charming cafés. But the age of Monet and Matisse and Cezanne is finished. Even Picasso has succumbed. It's like a disease that you have to catch, the Parisian virus, in order to become immune. Don't get me wrong, Philip. I'm not extolling the good old American Way, either. I mean, for Chris'sake, look at the Flying Dutchman de Kooning, or even worse, Pollock. We have this cowboy mentality. It's like a brawl in the saloon and what's left over, the mess the next morning, is what passes for the new painting. So-called abstract expressionism. A clumsy redundant term. Why not call it expressive abstraction? Or finger painting?

"They're frontier romantics, you see. What I'm after is something entirely different. How can I explain it? The brawlers, they let accidents happen. I *make* accidents happen. They pick and choose among their mistakes. I create productive mistakes. Pregnant abortions—to use a metaphor from a more female perspective."

The trip to New York had put her on some kind of high horse. The bottle of wine was empty. She'd probably been drinking all afternoon.

"You know what I love about you, Philip? I can see it on your face. You don't give a damn about any of that." She leaned over and kissed him, cradling his head for a moment and then letting go. Something was wrong. She was holding back.

"That's not true. You're in with the Arab oil sheiks. That's damned impressive."

She laughed. "O.K. I deserve that. Sidney told me that my sheik didn't even bother to take off the dark glasses. He hardly saw what he was buying. I don't know. Maybe he saw things better than most. Maybe he was looking for something so—so alive that one could sense it, even in the dark."

"Come here." He kissed her, running his hand up her leg under her dress, feeling her breasts. She was wearing a brassiere and panties. He felt her go a bit rigid, and he backed off. Maybe she was waiting for him to say he had missed her, too. Grovel a little. Maybe she had someone else, in New York. How the hell should he know?

"What about you, Philip? Tell me what you've been doing. Really. I want to know."

He shrugged. "Working on the house with Sam Waters. I told you about him. Remember? Putting in the grove and the garden. Spent some time in Miami. On the Beach."

"Oh. What were you doing there?"

"Visiting friends. Business contacts. I've got a little project going. With some people in Miami. And Havana."

She looked at him quizzically. "Something to do with the property you own?"

"Indirectly." He had to think. He'd smoked half a stick earlier that afternoon, before his swim, but it had worn off. "Mind if I put on a record? I heard some good jazz in Miami. Billie Holiday, no less. At a nightclub in the Negro section. Not the kind of place you just wander into, if you're White."

"Really? You go often? To those kinds of places?"

"I happen to know the owner of the club. He invited me." He squatted, choosing a record from the low shelf. "I'll bring you along next time, if you want."

"You know, I'm beginning to like this kind of jazz. It makes me think of you. Of us. Put on whatever you like." She stood. "If you would excuse me for a moment. I'll be right down."

She went up the floating staircase. Narby stepped outside, took a few puffs, and then, putting on the record, topped it off with a bourbon, and then poured another glass, for sipping. Maybe she would come down in a more receptive state.

He waited on the couch, sprawling, his eyes closed and his head back, the frenetic saxophone rather calming, as if in its extremity and confidence it purged him of doubt. He didn't hear her come down the stairs, but suddenly he felt her—standing behind him, running her fingers through his hair, pulling and kneading his scalp. She leaned over and kissed his neck and he could feel her naked breasts against his shoulder and chest. "Darling," she murmured. "I'm in the throes of a rather heavy menstrual period. Bleeding like a stuck pig. Not very sexy. But I missed you so, darling."

She came around from the back of the couch, naked but for a pair of dark red panties, and kneeled between his legs. "I've been thinking about this all day. Since I can't have you just now, in the way I'd really like, I'll have you this way. Just relax, darling. Let me show you how much I missed you."

It seemed to be over in a minute—she hadn't pulled away, hadn't flinched, savoring him, and now he could hardly move—yet the record had finished and in the wake of an almost unbearable pleasure he could hear the slight hum of the house, the wash of the waves coming across the dunes. The sofa faced the wide picture window. It was night. Anyone in the garden or bothering to peer over the hedge could have seen, watched. That was part of it, he realized, whatever it was she wanted from him.

"Look at you," she said, her hands still gripping his thighs. "In ancient Rome they would have rendered you in marble, darling. The Swimmer."

She got up and slipped on the short silken robe and he put on his shorts and his shirt, letting it hang unbuttoned. She liked him like that, liked to run her hand over his belly and chest under the shirt, as though the scars were some kind of tease.

He put on a record and she brought out another bottle of wine. "I'm afraid the cupboards are rather bare. Didn't get a chance to run over to Turner's today. Sorry. You're probably hungry."

He picked up the rucksack. "Surprise." He had stopped at the Village store that afternoon, before parking at the lighthouse. During the high season, with the residents of the Colony back on the island, they stocked fancier items. He had cheese, bread, grapes, cured ham, things for a salad. He put the sack on the table and arrayed his catch.

"That's wonderful, Philip. Very thoughtful."

As they ate she began to talk again about New York. "They all want to know about the island. Where it is, who else lives here. Endicott and I decided some time ago to keep it a mystery, as far as possible. Not even Sidney knows where we are, exactly. It's very gratifying, to not have to play the game all the time. To be able to step out of it, be somewhere where my work and my time are all my own. To be with someone like you."

"Why not chuck New York altogether? Live here year round." He loved her. Only he couldn't say it. Not until she said it first. "I'd like that."

She smiled at him, brushing her hair away from her face. "So, I ought to tell you. Sanmora might still be a well-kept secret, but you've been found out, my darling."

"What do you mean?"

"You've been noticed. We've been noticed."

"Yeah? How so?"

"I went for a walk on the beach earlier this afternoon. Taking a break. It's always more difficult to get back into it, after a hiatus. Anyway, I was taking a break from the studio and I ran into Tara on the beach."

"Tara? Who's that?"

"Tara Pembaker. She and her husband Dalton have the next house down. I told you about them. Dalton was the first one to buy land here. More or less started the Colony. Anyway, I ran into Tara and as always she wanted to chat. Gossip. She's a very nice, very charming intelligent woman. You've seen her, I'm sure. Collecting her shells. An attractive middle-aged woman. Likes to wear those oriental kaftans and bamboo bracelets and such. She's very good about never bothering me, never barging in. But if she catches me on the beach, that's a different story. Or at one of the Colony get-togethers. And she's old friends with Endicott. So, naturally, I'm fond of her. Anyway, she asked me about you. She'd noticed us out walking a few times."

"What did she ask?"

"One thing I like about Tara. She's unflinchingly direct. She asked if you were my new boyfriend. That's all. She and Dalton like to dote on me. The age difference, probably. Tara's old enough to my mother. And because of Endicott, I suppose. Anyway, Tara has a bit of the matchmaker in her. She knows Richard, actually. Quite well."

She stopped to light a cigarette. "Richard was the man I was seeing last year. I believe I told you. In reference to the jazz records. He left them here. Well, they're yours now, darling. Aren't they?"

Richard Lansdale. He'd written the name down. "What did you tell her?"

"I said we were friends, still getting to know each other. Of course, she'll think what she wants. But for the time being, she seemed satisfied with that."

"What else? My name? Where I live?"

"Does it bother you? That I spoke to her."

"No. It's only… I don't like people interfering."

"It's hardly interfering. Anyway, I told her the bare minimum. You're Philip. You live on the mainland. You do something with land, real estate. That's all."

Her tone had changed. Or was he imagining it? "What about Richard Lansdale. What does he do?"

"Well. If you really want to know. He loafs. By loafing I mean he works in his father's white-shoe law firm. Richard is a spoiled son-of-a-bitch. It took a while for me to grasp his appalling essence. For Christ's sake, Philip, don't tell me you're jealous."

"Depends. Did he fuck you like a god?"

She stared at him, unflinching. "As a matter of fact, no."

"Sorry. I shouldn't have said that. " He loved her. He wasn't going to let anyone interfere.

"Apology accepted. Only now that you've broached it, don't push it away. Richard was more like, I don't know. A bullish dog. Always asserting his dominance. A quick utilitarian discharge. To be absolutely blunt. You and Richard are virtually different species." She paused, tapping her cigarette. "Please, Philip. Say whatever is on your mind. Only once you've said it, don't take it back afterward." Her voice softened. "And I'll do the same. Not say things and then take them back. That's the coward's way."

"Fair enough. So, did you fill Tara in on that side of things? The dog and the god."

That made her laugh. She poured another glass of wine. "Somehow, I omitted that piece of intelligence. Though Tara would no doubt relish the information. Look, Philip. I told you from the beginning. I don't want to turn this into a *relationship*. Whatever it is between us, whatever we have. Let's keep it that way. Easy, free, moment to moment. Night to night."

"Sure. I'm all for it."

"Are you certain?"

"This woman, Tara. She wanted you to stick it out with Lansdale, didn't she? Marry you off to him, or something?"

"Possibly. But she knew it wasn't right. Probably Richard complained about me to her. Things went sour with Richard rather quickly. But because it had become an established relationship, with all the expectations, the pressure." She took another drink of wine. "Stupidly, I had agreed to be engaged. Consequently, we stayed together far longer than was natural. Or pleasurable."

"No worries on that score this time around. Marriage isn't in the cards. Not for me."

"Nor for me. Of course, you realize it's harder this way. Being natural. Without the banalities of convention, most people fall apart. Either from their own insecurities, or the wrath of public opinion. At least we have the Island to insulate us."

"What about the rest of them? Your neighbors?"

"The Colony? Harmless, rather tepid people. Family people. Button-downed New Englanders. They wouldn't dream of butting in. It's only the Pembakers and the Atlees who, how should I say? Keep watch."

Like the seaplane? He remembered how it had borne down on him on the dunes, scouring the coastline. "Dalton Pembaker. Tara's husband. He's the head of the Trust, isn't he?"

"The Trust?"

"Isadora Land and Trust. That's who you bought the house from, isn't it?"

"No. I bought it from Endicott. He took care of all the paperwork. I just signed."

"He didn't tell you about Isadora?"

She shrugged. "Perhaps he did. Why? Does it matter?"

"Probably not. I'm just curious. As someone in the real estate game."

"Frankly, all that kind of thing is lost on me. Trusts. Corporations. Institutes. They're phantoms, smoke screens. There's the individual, and there's the world filtered through one's senses, one's perception. The rest is noise, illusion, a paper reality. Even the Rockefeller Foundation. I'm more than happy to receive their largesse. But it means nothing to me. And it shouldn't. Only the individual creates. As an artist, attach yourself to a group, a claque, a movement, and you're finished. Like 'abstract expressionism,' darling. It's propaganda. An advertising slogan. Even Sidney and Harriet admit that. No real artist would take it seriously. It's just a way of selling, making money. So I can continue to create, without the wolf breathing down my neck."

"Sounds radical to me," he joked. "You're not some kind of subversive, are you?"

"Maybe I am. You should ask Dan Atlee. It's his favorite topic of cocktail-party conversation. The Red Tide. Communist Infiltration. God and the Free Market. It's quite amusing."

"Dan Atlee. The other one who started the Colony, with Pembaker?"

"Yes. Dan and Sheila own the Cape Cod, with the gray shingles. On the other side of Dalton and Tara. If you meet him, he'll no doubt invite you to go out marlin fishing, or tarpon, or whatever species it is he's hoping to exterminate. On the Miranda, his thirty-odd foot pride and joy. He's quite the he-man sporting type."

One of the yachts docked in the Village Marina, Narby supposed. "Have you gone out on his boat?"

"No. Not my style. No swimming. No boats. I let the ocean alone, and it brings me gifts. Remember?"

"I do." He thought for a moment. "I suppose I should meet these neighbors of yours. Since they're keeping watch."

"There's always the Pembakers' parties. They throw two every year, one at the start of the season, which we've missed, and one at the close, before everyone packs up. Around the ides of March, typically. Dalton could tell you all about the Colony, the Trust thing or whatever it is, since you're so interested."

"What is Pembaker? A lawyer?"

"No. A publisher. He owns newspapers."

"Which ones?"

"I don't recall the names. They're published abroad. Venezuela and Chile or Mexico, I believe. He's really quite interesting, compared to the rest of them. Rather influential, so I understand. You'd probably like him. And Tara, too."

"And the one with the yacht? Atlee?"

"Dan. He's something with shipping. Tankers. It goes with the boat fetish. Dan's the one who first spotted the Island. Or so the legend goes. I believe he was in the Navy. Or was it the

Marines? Dalton and he are a bit like father and son. Dan's somewhat the junior partner in running the Colony. I can't say I much care for Dan, one way or the other. Sheila, the wife, well, she's something of a milquetoast. Dan's the kind of man who requires a wife like that, I suppose. The mouse wife. Nothing at all like Tara."

"Dan's the all-American patriot, yeah? The anti-communist crusader?"

"He certainly goes on about it at the Colony parties. Of course, he's usually drunk at that stage. I think Dalton likes to tease him. Bait him. The thing is, Philip. Now that the cat's out of the bag they're going to gossip about us. It might be better to stage a pre-emptive strike. Let me introduce you in the flesh. Give you corporeal confirmation, so that when they see you swimming, or on the ferry, they'll at least know what you are. Beyond that, they can think what they like."

"If you want." Perhaps Pembaker was waiting for Narby to make the first move. They had recognized each other right away, hadn't they, the day they had nodded in passing on the beach. It might have been Pembaker in the seaplane, searching for someone who fit Knowles' description of Philip Narby.

"What are you thinking about? You look as if you're a million miles away."

"I'm just wondering. When are you going to show me?"

"Sorry?"

"Your paintings. You must have finished some of them by now. I mean, how do I know that you're really the famous Willa Branton. You might be an imposter. I want proof."

She laughed. "All right. Tomorrow. Afternoon, when the light is best. I promise."

9

THE STUDIO STOOD NESTLED in the garden, between the house and the jungle. Endicott Ward was not himself a painter. He had added the studio building—a single-story concrete cube, set an angle to the stacked cubes of the house—for the benefit of his artist colleagues and friends. But Willa liked to think that the studio had been destined for her alone, for the great work on which she was now embarked.

Narby followed her along the flagstone path. It was another sublime subtropical winter afternoon, bright and cool and carrying the salt tang of the Gulf. After a light lunch and a few glasses of wine, Willa—still inconvenienced—had done to him again what she had done the night before, as if the intensity of the pleasure might predispose him toward a finer appreciation of her work. Or perhaps it was only to insure that, gratified, drained of desire, he would be less distracted, less tempted to confuse Willa's personal beauty with that of her creations.

The studio door was bolted She unlocked it and let him in. It was bigger inside than it appeared, a soaring white light-flooded space smelling of oil paint, a dullish glare reflecting off the polished concrete floor mottled with drippings. She cranked open the bank of louvered windows and then, with a long pole, the skylight window above. "I close it up at night, because of the humidity and the salt."

Unlike in the house, there was no hum, no mechanical ventilation or cooling. The sound of the surf drifted in, softly, filtered through the dunes.

He had expected a clutter of canvases, squeezed tubes of paint and old coffee cans full of brushes. Instead, there was a monastic asceticism. In one corner stood a large easel and a simple wooden chair. Against the back wall, opposite the windows, was a narrow daybed covered with an old chintz spread, a stepladder, and a built-in cabinet with drawers, containing her supplies. Above the cabinet was what appeared to be a series of vertical metal racks, maybe twenty in all, each as wide as a door, that opened on hinges like the leaves of a book. "I'm working with large canvases now," she explained. "I don't want to be confined. I need the field of possibility to be virtually limitless." Standing in front of the racks she raised her arms and began to swing them open, one after another, each rack holding a single canvas. Most appeared blank; others showed only a few smears or splotches. When she came to the second to last rack she pulled the ladder over and standing on the third rung removed the canvas and ferried it across the space, lifting it over her head like a piece of plywood, and placed it on the easel. Then, back on the ladder, she removed the canvas from the last rack and leaned it against the wall, next to the easel, the light from the windows falling on its surface without glare.

"These two I consider finished. As much as anything can be finished. Stand back a little, Philip." From a cabinet drawer she took a pack of Gauloises. The smoke mixed pleasantly with the paint vapors and the ocean air. He stepped back further, understanding better now the considerable appeal of the studio, the smell and the air and the light, the serenity. Even the sounds—the cry of the gulls, the faint wave-wash from across the dunes—were like a caress. The studio was a world unto itself, a chamber of sensual self-absorption.

The way Willa talked about herself and her reputation, with that boundless self-confidence—he had expected, hoped, to be duly impressed. For a few minutes they stood some feet apart without speaking, their gazes meeting on the painting set on the easel, its ravaged blistered surface. Lucky for him she didn't want a first reaction, that she demanded instead this sustained wordless attention, as if rapt in prayer.

A week ago, in Miami, he had dropped by the library to consult any art books they had on contemporary American painting. Willa's success was apparently too recent to be recorded in books, but he had seen reproductions of others like Pollock—one of the 'Cedar Tavern gang' who seemed to be the favored object of Willa's contempt. Narby didn't get it, frankly, but at least the Pollock pictures presented a frenzied surface, the paint covering the canvas and replacing its emptiness with an idea. He could see nothing of that in the work now in front of him. Half the canvas was blank, raw, as if she couldn't be bothered to fill it all up with colors or shapes. No solid forms, no striking colors, no bold strokes. Only a bland faded-out sporadic splotching, yellowed and grayish, spread so thin you could see right through it. But he had stopped looking. There was nothing to see. Instead, he was raking his imagination for something to say.

What the hell did he know about it? If the critics and gallery owners and oil-sheik collectors all agreed that her painting was the hottest item going, who was he to argue? What did it matter, anyway? He was down to the butt of the cigarette. Willa had finished hers and stamped it out on the splattered concrete floor. He did the same and took another from the pack and sat on the daybed, keeping his gaze fixed but concentrating on the studio instead of the easel, the smell and the quality of light and the flow of air falling from the skylights, the serenity. Like a chapel. It wasn't a job for her, or a profession. It was a religion.

He waited it out, until, after her second Gauloises, she came over and sat next to him. "What are you thinking, Philip? Don't worry. You won't offend me. You can't."

He ran his hand over his mouth and the morning's growth of beard. Then, because he had just thought of it and had no time to reconsider, he said, "I believe it."

"You believe it?"

"Yes. Isn't that the only thing that really matters?"

She looked at him, her eyes agate-green in the studio light. "What a waste. Art history and the critics and the journal articles." With her cool palm she caressed his cheek. He sat still, not touching her, because he didn't get it, was still waiting.

"How did I ever find you, Philip Narby? Three little words, and you've said everything. Everything."

After a moment she stood. "Philip, darling. I've just seen something. In my mind. I need to work. Right now, as a matter of fact, before it fades." She turned to face him. "You'll be here when I'm finished. Won't you? I'd like that. Very much."

"So would I."

Apparently, he'd hit just the right note.

10

NOT A WORD HAD BEEN SAID, but they understood. Their love affair, its careless intensity, ought not be transported. She had not invited him to visit her in Manhattan, and if she had, he would have refused.

From mid-March until November—like all the Colony mansions tucked behind the dunes—the sleek machine-like house would stand empty, the pool covered and the windows shuttered against the tropical storms, silent but for the hum of the air-conditioning system that was kept running, even with the house vacant, against the corrosive heat. But Narby's presence had altered things. Apparently, Willa couldn't bear to be apart from her lover for too long. Twice now since leaving for New York— despite the miserable off-season weather—she had returned. Narby picked her at up Ratliff Field, the regional airport in Myerton. The fact that her lover had no telephone, that arrangements had to be made through letters sent care-of a Myerton tobacco shop, only seemed to increase Willa's fascination. As did the battered pickup truck and Narby's negligent appearance, unshaven, in ragged work pants or cut-off shorts, a T-shirt draping his broad-shouldered swimmer's body, his shaggy russet hair. His fearlessness of the ocean. His haphazard means of procuring a living from the pine wastes of Sawfish Point—the antithesis of her former fiancé's nepotistic corporate sponging. His blunt unpretentious manner of speech, suggesting the rejection, rather than absence, of good breeding and other social refinements. His capacity for drink. His stamina in the techniques of love. The skein of death-defying scars running from his hipbone to his armpit, as if he had been granted a second life, another chance.

From the airport they drove to Punta Rasca where they waited in the miasmic heat for the six-o'clock ferry. She told him about New York, the gatherings at the galleries and the Modern and the Guggenheim, her Greenwich Village studio, the guesthouse at Endicott Ward's summer compound on Cape Cod. In return, he offered a few phrases, scant of detail: work on the property with Sam, meetings in Miami and Havana concerning his various investments, the nights listening to jazz at the Negro clubs in Overtown.

Twice now, she had stayed for five days. The blink of an eye. Between the heat of the day and the mosquitoes at night they hardly went outdoors, lulled by the cool dry mechanical sterility of the air-conditioned house, an artificial erotic oasis in the midst of jungle and sea and scorching dunes. When their time ran out, he drove her back to the airport and sat with her in the hangar-like waiting area for the twice-a-week connecting flight to Miami, both lovers rather exhausted by the hothouse concentration of sex and drinking, already on edge, already starting to crave each other again, knowing that it might be months before the craving would be appeased.

The next day he drove to Miami Beach, parking the truck in the garage on Michigan Avenue. Filthy from the hot drive, he wiped his face, put on a fresh shirt, and went into the street to hail a cab. The Beach was seeing more summer tourists now, but it was midweek and the Calvado was half empty. Narby had his pick of the upper-floor suites. He unpacked, showered and dressed and went down to the bar for a drink and a look around. If some firm hot little brunette flung herself at him, he probably wouldn't refuse, but he wasn't particularly looking for it. Not looking, not paying, not groveling. Willa had changed all that. He supposed he trusted her. The way they had gone at it, a five-day orgy, both of them rubbed raw by the end of it. If he wasn't looking for it, he figured, then she wouldn't either.

He had left the money in the attaché up in his room. Five hundred for Campos and a hundred for Bobby. And five hundred in Narby's pocket, the emergency funds he always carried in case something prevented him from getting back to Sawfish Point, to the strongbox underneath the floorboards. He could never let himself forget. There were powerful people looking for him, men who would like to pick his brains apart, see him dead.

From the stool at the end of the bar Narby could keep his eye on the lobby. He rolled a cigarette and ordered a gin rickey. Under Narby's influence Willa had graduated from her steady diet of wine and bubbly. They had settled on the gin rickey as their summer refreshment. A booze soda pop. It was pleasant now, sitting by himself, to be reminded of her taste, her mouth cold with ice and gin.

Before going out that evening he would put the money for Campos in the hotel safe. Five hundred—a sizeable outlay, considering that the Narby account was finished. Batista had granted an amnesty for all political prisoners. Castro had been released from prison and things were moving again. He had to keep Campos close.

The Calvado was certainly a step up from the Atlantique. Newer, better maintained, snappier, more expensive. Ever since Narby had learned that Sid Black was in the hotel business he'd taken an interest in the shifting economic landscape of the Beach. The further north on Collins Avenue, away from Lincoln Road and the relics on Ocean Drive, the shinier the glitz and flabbergast. At Collins and Forty-fourth Street, where the oceanfront Firestone Estate had once stood, rose an enormous new hotel with a vast curving façade—the Fontainebleau, though on the radio ads they called it the 'Fountain Blue.' Coral Gables and South Miami still wrung out the Spanish theme, the red roof tiles and wrought iron, the Grenada this and Seville that. But on the Beach it was all phony Gallic-chic.

Narby knew more about Sid Black than Black knew about him. Knew more about all of them: Brigadier General Charles Willoughby. Bill Knowles. Carl Vetch. Ernesto Campos. Dalton Pembaker. Willa Branton. In addition to the Atlantique, Black owned two other hotels. Only instead of going up—north on Collins, toward the spectacular new Fontainebleau—Black had been buying down: the Ebb Tide and the Sand Dollar, three-story concrete-and-terrazzo hovels on Drexel, blocks from the ocean, and both in disrepair. In fact, the Atlantique, hardly five years old, the first fully air-conditioned hotel in Miami Beach, wasn't looking very good, either—the maimed coconut palms and wilting bougainvillea, the streaks of shit-colored rust dribbling down the blistered stucco, the wafts of mildew mixing with Freon in the icebox lobby. Narby made sure to have a look every time he came to the Beach, strolling past Black's hotels in his tourist get up, the dark glasses and sporty short-brimmed hat pulled down over his brow—occasionally even daring to pop in for a drink at the Atlantique cocktail lounge. Narby guessed that Black had no clue that he was still here, in South Florida. Nevertheless, he was careful.

Black was letting his hotels run down, even though he had only acquired them within the last few months. Now why would he do that?

He had another gin rickey, went back to his room and changed into his bathing suit. After a swim and a nap he went out to buy the papers and spent the afternoon in his suite reading. Later that evening, after dinner at Giovanni's, he caught a cab to Overtown. A young Negro singer named Selma James was appearing at the Harlem Square. Narby guessed that Goldfarb and his private party would not be in attendance on the balcony that night. Goldfarb's Miami Beach nightclubs on Dade Avenue were closed for the season. Selma James wasn't an attraction for Whites, not like Billie Holiday. Narby had never heard of her. But frankly, he wasn't going for the music.

He had the cab drop him by El Castillo. Even in the summer heat the sidewalks along Second Avenue were crowded. There were no seasons here, high or low. No tourists. Narby had dressed for the occasion, his neck chafing under the bright blue tie. He undid the collar button, loosened the tie, and walked with the brim of his hat pulled over his brow, his eyes averted. As if that could disguise the fact that he was White.

About half a block from the theater he saw them: a pair of his race brethren in blue uniforms had positioned themselves under the marquee. Broad backs, buckled necks, legs spread apart, a sidearm at one hip and nightstick at the other. He stopped, standing under the awning of a shoe repair store, and lit a cigarette. He could wait for them to move on, but they appeared fixed, twin pillars through which every Negro patron was compelled deferentially to pass. Technically, Narby's presence at the club would violate the law, the mixed-race ordinance. Without Goldfarb there, maybe they would let him in, maybe not. But he couldn't risk having some cracker cop ask him questions, draw attention, right in front of the theater.

He turned around and walked back toward El Castillo and then turned left on the next block and then left again, circling around the back of the theater toward the other side where the alley came out to the avenue. The narrow side streets had none of the avenues' life or glamour—low, sagging, wood-slat buildings, the darkened shotgun houses and bars without names and storefronts with no merchandise in the windows. Between the wooden street lamps, spaced far apart, lay wide trenches of darkness. His shoulders were hunched, his hands rolled into fists. Someone coming out of the shadows with a knife wouldn't give a damn if he were White or Black. Beneath his clothes he could feel the slithering layer of sweat.

Reaching the avenue he turned left and then ducked into the alley, his shoes clicking against the pavement, echoing up the narrow space. At the end of the alley two men stood on the raised metal landing by the backstage door, talking quietly and smoking, their hats and shoulders sheened by the red bulb overhead. At his approach their voices dropped. One of them bent over for a moment, as if tying his shoe.

Narby took a breath. "Good evening, gentlemen."

"Evening to you." A tight, deep voice. Not exactly friendly.

They were blocking the way to the door. From the bottom of the steps, looking up at them, Narby said. "Maybe you could help me out. I'm supposed to meet a friend inside. He told me to come around this way. Through this door."

They looked at each other. They were wearing dark suits, collars open under their ties. "You took the wrong turn off the highway, Mister," one of them said. "Ticket window out on the Avenue."

"Yes. I'm aware of that. Only. My friend said he'd meet me back here."

They looked at each other again. "Don't know nothing about that. You better inquire at the ticket window."

"How about I just buy my ticket here. From you gentlemen. Just tell me how much. Ten dollars? Twenty?" Cautiously, he opened his jacket and reached inside for his wallet.

"Who's this friend you looking for, Mister? Maybe I know him."

They didn't look like bouncers, or toughs. He could just step up, push past them. The one who spoke was taller than Narby. Big enough to push back.

"Bobby."

"You looking for Bobby?"

"Yeah. Know him?"

"Shorty. Go inside and find Bobby. Who should we say is asking?"

"Mr. Ofay," said the other. Shorty. The wiseass.

"Name's Phil," Narby said, ignoring the slur, addressing the tall one. "Tell him it's Phil, from the Billie Holiday show. He'll know."

Shorty muttered something and went through the door.

Narby could smell it now, lingering in the air. The tall one had hidden it under his shoe. Instead of the wallet Narby took a pack of cigarettes from his jacket pocket and shook one out. "Cigarette?" He stepped up onto the landing. "What's those?"

"Gauloises. French."

The man took it and tapped one out and handed it back. Narby flicked his lighter and extended his arm. The man leaned back a little. Narby supposed he'd never had a White man light a cigarette for him.

"Tasty," he said, exhaling. "You from France or something, Mister?"

"No. New York."

"Ha. I knew you wasn't from round here."

He put out his hand. "Philip Narby."

The other one shook, a quick tight pump. "Red."

"Nice to meet you, Red. You a musician?"

He laughed, a quick snort. "I better be. Cause I'm going in there to blow, soon as they ready."

"What do you play?"

"Horn. Alto."

"Like Bird."

"Ha. You could say it like that." He took another drag, direct his glance an inch or two over Narby's shoulder. Checking him out, keeping aloof. "You dig Bird's sound?"

"Sure. All the new players, they're trying to catch up to Bird now, aren't they? Not just alto, either. Sonny Rollins. John Coltrane."

Red shrugged, leaning back on the railing, smoking. "Bird's boss. But he ain't no Prez. Ain't no one can touch Prez. Ain't no Hawk, neither."

Narby could see now that Red was forty, maybe older. "I get you. Still, up in New York, everyone's a Bird-watcher these days."

"I'm going up there, myself. Got some gigs in the works. Used to be tight with Fat Girl. He introduced me, before he bought it. Man, I sure wish Fat Girl was still round."

"Good for you. Tough town, though." Narby thought for a moment. He remembered something he'd read about, in *Metronome*. "Got your cabaret card, do you?"

"Say what?"

"Your cabaret card? You got to have one in New York. If you want to get paid."

"Oh yeah. That. I get me one, by and by."

"Yeah? It's not so easy, if you're from out of town. Let me know if you need any help. I know the right people. In city hall. I could help you with that. Seeing how you're helping me out."

"No shit?"

"Sure."

"What's your bag, man? You blow, too?"

"Not anymore. I'm more like—a promoter. Matter of fact, I'm looking to put some shows together down here. In Miami. If I can find the right talent."

"What kind of shows? Dance shows?"

"No. Something different. Small combos, forward-looking sounds. Hard swinging stuff, but cool. Maybe do some recording, too."

"I'm your man," said Red. "You ready to produce, you come talk to me."

"You dig Miles?"

"Sure, man. I dig all those new sounds. Progress, man."

"Black Man's progress."

"Amen."

Narby flicked away the butt. With his right foot he rather gently tapped Red's shoe. "Don't you need to get ready? Get into the right mind set, to go in there and blow?"

Red smiled. "I knew you was a viper," he said, bending down, laughing, bringing up a stout half-burnt hand rolled cigarette, flattened but not crushed. "It's Shorty gets all hincty. Thinks every ofay is a narco. Ha. I could see you was a viper from a mile off."

"Here." Narby handed him the lighter.

They passed it back and forth. The door swung open. A red porkpie hat. The high-cheekbones and pointy chin, long face sloped inward like a crescent moon.

"Well. If it ain't the man who fell from the sky. What's this? Tea for two."

Narby passed him the cigarette. "Hello, Bobby."

"You know this cat, Bobby?"

"Sure I know him. He's a jazz freak, true and blue. What you doing sneaking round here, man?"

"Those two Irishmen in blue suits, standing by the ticket window. I didn't want any trouble."

"Good thing you stopped, man. You can't go in there tonight. Selma, man, she's strictly race music. Chitlin and soul. You dig? No blancos in the arena. Not even up in the sky." He paused, took a final drag and flicked away the tiny stub. "You got balls, Phil. You young enough to use em, so you too young to lose em."

Shorty stuck his head out. "Come on," he said to Red, "before they can your ass."

"You keep me in mind about that show you producing," he said to Narby, going through the door. "You just tell Bobby. He knows where to find me."

After the door shut, Bobby said, "Not here, man. Over on Ninth Street. Jack's. Just go on in and be cool and have a drink. Anyone asks, tell em you waiting on Bobby. You got the bread?"

"Sure."

"Cool. Give me half an hour. Ain't no one going to goof on you over at Jack's. No Clydes admitted."

"Jack's. On Ninth Street."

"Just off the avenue. Blue electric sign. Kind of spluttering."

The dope had kicked in, a searchlight sweeping across the back of his eyes. "You got what Red's smoking?"

"Where you think he cop, man? From the Jolly Green Giant?"

"Half an hour," said Narby. "I don't like to be kept waiting."

"That's cool. Busy man like you." Bobby eyed him, up and down, his tapered suit, the Lincoln Road Italian silk tie. "That's some deluxe vine, cat. You looking bad. Wrapped up and boxed. Up in the clouds with your shoes on the ground. What's that show that Red's talking about?"

"Something I'm thinking of putting together. Bringing the New York sound down to Miami."

"That's cool." Bobby thought for a second. "You in business with that Hymie Goldfarb? One that owns this place?"

"No. I'm looking for my own place."

"Over to the Beach? Ha. You going to bring those bad New York motherfucker cats down there, to No-Black-Man's Land? That's a joke."

"No. Not the Beach. Maybe here, in Overtown. Negro music belongs here, right?"

"Look, man. I got to go." He opened the door. "I see you at Jack's."

"Half an hour, Bobby. Don't keep me waiting." He bounded down the steps, through the alley. It must be laced, judging from the take off. Heroin or cocaine. A few minutes later he was sitting in a booth at Jack's, a dingy juke joint on a side street, quiet at this early hour of the evening, no one looking at him, no one bothering him. Protected by his shield of Whiteness. He dropped a few nickels in the box and waited. Tomorrow, after meeting with Campos, he'd make a visit to Goldfarb's office. Goldfarb might be able to advise him. Yeah. His own place, here in Overtown. Where no one would ever look for him. No more hanging around, no more grubbing for dope. It was a pleasant jag: Philip Narby in control of things, for once.

11

THEY ARRANGED TO MEET at a diner on Poinciana, an inconspicuous greasy spoon bordering the Negro section of Coconut Grove. The cinnamon-skinned revolutionary was living in South Miami now, not far from the University. His suave manner and natty dress and his status as a medical student had gotten Campos out of Overtown and he had applied for permanent resident status. But he was still a hunted man, still a Negro outside his small circle of medical colleagues and anti-Batista sympathizers.

Narby sat in the parking lot, smoking a cigarette. Hank's Danish shag blended well with Bobby's reefer, masked the acrid smell and sweetened the ashen aftertaste. Contrary to the Dolophine, the marijuana, mildly analgesic and pulse-quickening, not only buoyed him up but seemed to reroute all his nervous energy into his muscles and loins. Medicine for the sex drive. When they yanked the amphetamines off the shelves last year they ought to have put marijuana in its place. For Korean Veterans' Use Only.

He was in a T-shirt and work pants and hadn't bothered to shave. When dealing with the Miami Negroes, Narby preferred to look sharp, show some style. But in the White world he was more comfortable as the wharf rat, the drifter. He swung open the diner door. Campos was in a booth, drinking coffee, an open book and papers spread on the table.

"Amigo," Narby said, setting down the sack.

Campos stood and embraced him, reeking of cologne.

"Studying for exams?"

"No. I am translating."

"May I?" Narby picked up the book. *Peau noir, masques blancs,* by Frantz Fanon. "You read French?"

"Yes. I was in Paris. One year. I am translating into Spanish. Can you understand?"

"Black skin, white masks?"

"Eso es."

He had two years of French at the Teacher's College. German, too. He had dreamed of going to Paris or Berlin. But the Harvard boys had kept him out. Shunted him off to the sewer of Asia, MacArthur's fiefdom. "Not really. What is it? A novel?"

"No. It is analysis of the psychological effect of European colonialism on the native, the Arab and the African. The phenomenon of the black bourgeoisie. How the slave, the colonial, becomes an accomplice in his own degradation. Muy feo. Pero verdad. The situation in Latin America is in fact more complicated. But it is necessary analysis for Cuba. For this I translate. To create political consciousness for my people."

The Cuban was in a crisp white shirt, his hair slicked back, moustache trimmed, clean as a whistle. "Sounds like a lot of unnecessary work. I mean, if the people don't oppose you, does it really matter what the hell they think? People like a winner. It's only natural. After the coup, once they see that you and your group are on top, and that scum Batista is gone, they'll want to be part of it. The grass is bound to be greener, yeah? As long as you improve conditions a little, ease off the police corruption and oppression, get some food into their bellies, medicine for the sick kids, things like that, their consciousness will follow. Acuerdo? For that, you'll need money. Foreign investment. Lots of it." He nodded to the sack. "You spoke to Fidel? You saw him?"

"Yes. He was in Nueva York, and here in Miami. Brevemente. For five days only."

"Did you deliver my message? When can I meet him?"

"I am sorry. Now he is in Mexico City."

"Damn it, Ernesto. I gave you that money right after Batista announced the amnesty, to set up a meeting. What happened?"

"We have re-organization. The situation is different, now that Castro is in exile."

"You're setting up with the faction in Mexico? Is that it? I thought the Miami group was in charge?" Narby wanted to offer Castro the land in Sawfish Point. The old turpentine camp could be turned into a training facility. This time, unlike the Guatemalans in Opa-locka, the Press would never get wind of it. No leaks, no unwanted attention. He would explain to Castro that Eisenhower and Dulles could be brought on board, just as long as the rebels soft-shoed any talk about land reform or nationalizing the utility monopolies or the mining concessions. Trimming those Rasputin beards might not be a bad idea, either. Sooner or later, Castro was going to need backing by a major power. The alternative, the Soviets, would be a terrible mistake. It would be a damned shame if after all the blood and sacrifice Cuba wound up as the Poland of the Caribbean.

"It is not decided. There are disagreements." He was drumming his fingers on the table. His nails, usually immaculate, were bitten ragged. A splash of coffee had stained the margins of Fanon.

Narby lit a cigarette and offered one to Campos.

"No, gracias. I am given up on tobacco. The medical evidence is conclusive. The smoking will kill you, Felipé. Cancer. Sugar, tobacco, rum, gambling—my country is a factory of insalubrious vices."

The Cuban laughed, lightening the mood. They had crossed the dark ocean together, saved each other's life.

"Ever since Moncada you've been waiting for Castro's release. Now that's he free, you don't exactly seem on top of the world. What's going on?"

"I can no say."

Narby hoisted the rucksack on the table, pushing the papers aside, and rather carelessly pulled out the packet of twenties. "Use it for whatever you want. Weapons, assassinations, a new suit of fatigues for El Barbaro and his merry men. Hell, you can use it to pay your tuition for medical school, for all I care. A cash-for-consciousness program. But I have to know. The people I work for have to know. And it has to check out. Or else, amigo, we're both in trouble."

"Por favor. Quiete."

He dropped the bills on the table. "Talk to me."

Campos sighed, sliding the packet off the table. "When they increased the international sugar quotas, this is when Batista made the amnesty for all political prisoner. Because he have money for to make mas sobornos. More brides."

"Not brides. Bribes."

The waitress came to their table. Narby ordered a beer and a ham and egg sandwich. "Over easy. Not too runny." He gave her a flirtatious wink, though she was pushing fifty, and stringy.

"How about you, hon? More coffee?"

"Yes. Thank you."

"You got it, fellas."

"The liberals say Batista try to be more moderate. But is joke. Same time as amnesty, many killings in Havana. Batista's police make look like terrorism. Fidel is in Ciudad Mexico two days only and one car for him explode. But he escape. Me comprendes? Batista not want to execute political enemies inside Cuba, because it look very bad. Better to free and make exile and kill them outside Cuba. Better to make them fight each other. I cannot decide what is more. The brutalidad of Batista or his stupidity."

"What about Prío? Is he still behind you?"

"Yes. And no. They will make meeting at Mérida, with Justo Carillo. Only Carillo says golpe, ahorita. Now. From inside army. Without support of labor or the other parties. He say he will make Fidel mayor of Havana. Prío give money to all anti-Batistiano groups. So that he can—como se dice?—have seat at the table. Mira, Felipé. These groups—the communists, the old Ortodoxos, the Auténticos, Prío's people, the Directorate Estudiante, the Socialist Youth—they do not want to come together."

He took a sip of coffee, dabbing nervously at his moustache and brushing away a fly. "There are fifteen men who were with us at Moncada, who escape to Guatemala and were with Arbenz. Hombres muy peligrosos. They hate everything American, Felipé, because of what C.I.A. do against Arbenz. Now, we are in arguing. Todos. Over which one will be first to attack Batista. Over who get money for weapon, for make militia."

Narby had taken out his black notebook. Making notes now. Because, unfortunately, the dope's electrifying effect on the nervous system seemed to play tricks with his memory. "Don't worry, Ernesto. It's in code."

"Is necessary to unify with a single leader. One man. I am sorry you no meet Fidel Castro. Then you will understand why we have total faith. He has no doubts, no hesitations. If the reasons for his decisions are not always evident, it is no for me to question. I was to go with Castro to Mexico, with the central group. The Moncadistas. But, instead he take Manuel Marquez and El Coreano."

"El Coreano?"

"Miguel Sanchez. He is Cubano, but he fight with American Army in Korea. He has military experience, for to make campo de entrenamineto. Trainings camp. I am for to be health officer. But Fidel tell to me they already have. Is an Argentine doctor who come to Mexico after C.I.A. golpe in Guatemala. Castro say I must stay here, in Miami. For to organize all groups to support Veinte-Seis de Julio. Make propaganda."

Campos sounded disappointed, almost bitter. The medical student was perhaps being pushed aside. "All the more reason for you and I to work together, Ernesto. You have to get Castro to push out the radicals and fanatics. It's in both our interests. Acuerdo? Once the fanatic element is neutralized, it will be easier to get the money flowing in Fidel's direction. Real money, not these little gifts of mine. And weapons. Aircraft. Artillery. Me entiendes?"

"Puede ser. Only no C.I.A."

"Didn't I already prove that to you?"

"Yes. That one you tell me, in El Castillo. He is no more in Cuba."

"What do you mean, no more?"

Campos shrugged. "I can no say."

"Let me talk to Castro, directly. Can you arrange that?"

"No now. Impossible." Campos sifted through the papers on the table and handed Narby a booklet. "Here. You must read. His elocuencia is very powerful. An illiterate animal like Batista cannot understand. But the people, they will understand. Is Castro's speech, when they make his trial."

"*La Historia Me Absolverá*. History… will absolve me." Narby laughed. "That's a good one."

He flipped through, catching a phrase here and there, most of it too high blown for his street-and-newspaper Spanish. Forty-five pages of lawyer's prose, sprinkled with national-ist fervor. *Dictadura. Tierra. Trabajdores. La Patria. Sangre. Capitalistas.* Clearly, a pitch to the home crowd, preaching to the choir. Maybe that's why they let him go. So they could shut him up at home while letting him play the fool in exile. It was bullshit, maybe, but damned impressive, the incredible hubris of this virtually powerless man, this people's Svengali. They had sentenced Castro to twenty-five years for treason and yet miraculously he was already out of prison. Still, the chances of Castro making it out of Mexico alive were nil. He had too many enemies. Even among the 26 July Movement—the men who had made Castro into some kind of prophet—there was danger. There was no hatred greater than that of the spurned disciple.

The waitress brought their food. "You fellas need anything else, just whistle." She gave Narby a smile. "I told em not too runny, hon. O.K.?"

Narby slipped the booklet into his rucksack and brushing away the flies began to eat, washing the sandwich down with the cold beer. "What else did Castro tell you? He assign you any other jobs?"

"We speak of the future of Cuba. I make program for to eradicate racismo y los religiosos atrasados. Clinicas colectivas para la sauld mental. For to liberate los pobres de los misticismos de los Católicos y los cultos Africanos. Psychological problems muy profundas, impedimentos for to develop a just society. For the people to make their historical destiny."

"You're the only one in Castro's circle with dark skin, yeah?"

"It is not matter."

Narby shrugged. "Maybe that's why Castro didn't want you in Mexico, with the inner circle."

"Siempre el cínico. You look always for the worst, Felipé."

"And you, for the best. An optimist. Between the two of us, maybe we'll get it right. Besides, what about my good instincts?"

Campos smiled. "Como en el barco. En la jungla."

"So, what's his name? This Argentine doctor who was with Arbenz?"

"I can no say."

The egg was overdone, dry and flaky. He took a couple of bites and pushed the plate aside, bait for the flies. "You can't say? Or you don't know?"

"Se llama Ché. This is all I hear."

"Tell Castro I have a location. Very hidden, a couple of thousand acres, with easy access to the Gulf. I could clear away enough jungle for an airstrip, to get weapons in and out. Much closer to Cuba than Mexico, too. Just let him know."

Campos nodded, collecting his things. "Mira, Felipé. Next time, you come to my house, yes? I make you comida Cubana. Cerdo asado con moros y cristianos, platanos, una salada de aguacate."

"Sounds delicious. What's your address?"

"No here," Campos said, rising, embracing his friend. "In Havana. When she is free. Muchas gracias for the gift. We won't forget."

He watched as Campos walked toward Poinciana Avenue, his white shirt brilliant against the storm-darkened sky, rippling in the rising wind. A green Plymouth pulled up from around the corner and Campos got in.

Of all Batista's adversaries, Castro was the most visible, the most public and charismatic. The man was nothing if not an original. Narby could certainly appreciate that. But it was a long way from Mexico City to Havana. Without ships, without air cover, an invasion from abroad would be suicidal. In the meantime, the Movement was doing its best to sow dissent and chaos within Cuba: sabotage, work stoppages, assassinations, defections from the army. Only, if there were too much chaos, one of the other groups might get the upper hand before Castro had a chance. An interesting situation. Even if Campos were being pushed out, he'd be valuable. He knew plenty. He was pretty jazzed up on those mental health clinics. If Castro didn't promise to appoint him minister of health, or whatever, maybe Campos would turn elsewhere.

Narby closed his notebook and picked up the pamphlet. "*History Will Absolve Me.*" It was the language of a dictator, not a man of the people. A cowboy-hero. Castro and History, walking alone, hand-in-hand into the sunset.

12

GOLDFARB'S MIAMI BEACH OFFICE was in a new high-rise on Jefferson, a few blocks from Lincoln Road. Narby rested for a moment on a shaded bench, finishing the cigarette and then standing to brush off his suit. Saks Fifth Avenue. Powder-blue, like his eyes, a tropical weight silk-and-cotton blend, freshly laundered and delivered to his hotel suite that morning. He knew what he was after. The how, the why, would come to him. It was no good trying to think too far in advance, rehearse. Better to be flexible, because you never knew how people might react.

Nevertheless, to ease his mind, he ducked into the gloomy air-conditioned bar across the street. Arthur Goldfarb and Sid Black, two Jewish Miami Beach businessmen. Entertainment and hotels. There was a good chance they knew each other. So what? Better to dive right in then skulk around the edges, leave things to chance. That's what had landed him in Korea, face down in the shit-water ditch, his guts leaching out—letting circumstances, other people, get the jump on him.

Never forget where you come from, son, some sincere sap had once advised Jim or Tom. A night-soil ditch along the Naktong River, September 1950. Tom or Jim had disappeared, and Philip Narby had been born. Then and there. Before he had ever heard the name Philip Narby. Before Sid Black had given him the forged papers and the account number. In the ditch, and then in the hospital at Kobe, hovering between life and death, not knowing who he was or what had happened to him. Before running into Black in the hospital garden, Black hobbling around on crutches, hailing him, recognizing him because he worked in McCoy's office. Before they threatened him with electro-shock.

It was supposed to make you proud, keep you on the straight and narrow—remembering where you came from, the little town, the ma-and-pa humble origins. Pure homespun American bullshit. Still, in his case, it was rather amusing to apply the adage.

He paid for his drink and passed from the icy gloom into the ferocious glare, the heat. Like penetrating a wall of fire. In the lobby he consulted the directory for Gold-Art Management and Productions and rode the elevator to the sixth floor.

A secretary or receptionist sat behind a high desk. "Hello. I'm Philip Narby. I spoke to Mr. Goldfarb earlier today. He asked me to drop by."

"Hello, Mr. Narby. Please, have a seat. I'll let him know you're here. "

That was a surprise. Stout, efficient, matronly. Dark sensitive eyes, though. He had expected more of a Wilson-Prentice type arrangement, a creamy vortex. He waited on the couch, hat in hand, looking around at the promotional posters for Goldfarb's nightclubs hanging on the wall. No doubt Goldfarb had plenty of hot showgirls to handle, whenever it struck his mood. No need to grope the office help.

"You can go in now, Mr. Narby."

"Thanks." He smiled as he passed, looking her in the eyes. It never hurt to make a little overture.

"Hello, Art."

"Come in. Have a seat. Good to see you again, Phil. What can I do for you?"

Goldfarb was in shirtsleeves and vest. On the wide mahogany desk the remains of lunch, served on fancy china, had been pushed to one side. At Goldfarb's elbow a cigar smoldered in an ashtray. Otherwise, except for the telephone-intercom and a few framed photos and a neat sheaf of papers, the desk was clear.

"Thanks for making time. I appreciate it. That was a hell of a show, by the way."

"Which was that?"

"Billie Holiday. Where we met. At the Harlem Square Club."

"Back in April. Right. Glad you enjoyed it." He picked up the cigar. "So, remind me, again, Phil. Who are you with? American Airlines, right?"

"No. I'm not with anybody, Art. I manage a large tract of land, over in Lacoosa County. On the Gulf Coast. Among other holdings."

"Lacoosa County. Myerton. Right. Now I remember." Goldfarb was looking him over. "So, what's on your mind?"

"227 Ninth St. North West." Narby shifted in the chair. "A little juke-joint bar. A place called Jack's."

That got his attention. Goldfarb leaned back in the capacious swivel chair, the cigar clamped in his mouth. He was a big man—mottled sun-browned balding head, full nose and lips, softly bagged eyes, hanging jowls and pendulant earlobes. Even in his shirtsleeves he liked to show off—a bejeweled tie clasp, gold cufflinks and wristwatch, the ring with an emerald stone. A luxurious office, too, cool but not iced, the daylight filtering through the sixth-floor view of Biscayne Bay, the bottle-green water in the distance sparkling in the sun. The wall behind the desk was plastered with photographs of Goldfarb, smiling and relaxed, posing with his celebrity pals: Goldfarb and Bob Hope, Goldfarb and Ava Gardner. Martin and Lewis, Milton Berle, Julie London. On the other wall, opposite the window, there was Billy Eckstein, Lena Horne, sprightly Nat Cole with one arm draped over Goldfarb's bulky shoulders. The wall for Coloreds only, apparently.

"Jack's?" he said, releasing a plume of smoke. "Should that mean something to me?"

"It ought to. You own it."

"You mean the property? Northwest Ninth?" He leaned forward and pressed a button on the intercom. "Sylvia. Could you bring me the book on the Overtown properties. Thank you." He looked up again at Narby. "Presuming you're correct, that Gold-Art Management holds that piece of property, what is it in particular that interests you?"

"I was there a few nights ago. It's just what I'm looking for. The narrow bar in front, the room in back with enough space for a bandstand. It would have to be renovated, though. I don't mean to be out of line, Art. But the place doesn't appear to be in good repair."

"Hold it a minute, Phil." Sylvia came in with the books and put them on Goldfarb's desk. "Thank you, dear. All right. Let me see." He flipped through. "Ninth Street. Here it is. 227. Same tenant now for three years. No complaints, rent usually on time." He closed the book. "The thing is, Phil. I don't bother myself much with that end of the business. The accountant keeps track. I believe we acquired that property in a larger purchase, with several others. Maybe it's not in pristine condition, but it's certainly no worse than how we found it. In any case, what's it to you?"

"I'd like to take it over. Lease it."

Goldfarb emitted a short laugh. "What on earth for?"

"I want to open up a business. I'd like your help, Art. Your expertise."

"What kind of business?"

"A jazz club."

"You're talking about a night club?"

"No. Just drinks and music. No dinner service, no comedians, no floorshow, no dancing. No torch singers. Just music. Modern serious jazz."

Goldfarb seemed amused. "Serious jazz? Like who? Give me some names."

"Miles Davis. Charles Mingus. Thelonious Monk. Sony Rollins."

Goldfarb puffed on the cigar, shaking his head and frowning. "Never heard of them."

Narby opened the attaché case and dropped the magazines on the desk. *Downbeat. Metronome.* "These guys are attracting a lot of attention. Winning all the polls."

Goldfarb gazed blankly at the covers. "That's New York. Fifty-Second Street. Greenwich Village. Let me save you some pain, Phil. There's no audience for that kind of music here, White, Colored or otherwise. I can fill the Harlem Square with

Billie Holiday. I can fill it with Selma James or Ray Charles. Because they're entertainers. But you're not going to get colored folks to pay money to sit with their hands folded on their laps listening to some stoned guy in dark glasses and a beret honking on his horn for five minutes at a stretch. What the hell gave you such a meshuggah idea?"

"I've been talking with people, Art. In Overtown, in the Grove. There's no place to hear this kind of music in Miami. With the right publicity, the right ambience... "

"Hold on. Back up. First of all, what were you doing over there? On that block in Overtown?"

Narby dug into his suit pocket for a cigarette, his mind skittering a bit. "It's a free country. I went for a drink. Scouting, I suppose you could call it."

"You're looking for trouble, my friend. If you're determined to lose your money opening a jazz club, as you call it, I advise you to consider more practical venues. Why not fix up one of those honky-tonks north of the Beach? It's fairly relaxed up there. Relatively inexpensive."

"The gangsters run those places. You know that, Art."

Goldfarb shrugged. "So? You pay a little for protection. It's like a tax. A business expense."

"It's Negro jazz, Art. It's got to be in Overtown. But not just for Colored."

"You can't have a mixed audience in Miami. It's the law. Not unless you have permission, separate seating. Even at the Harlem Square, there are no Whites at most of the shows. Only when I invite my friends, for something special. The only White people who'd be willing to go down that street at night wouldn't be worth having in your club. I assure you."

"I'll take that chance. What is the tenant paying now? Whatever it is, I'll top it. If I make improvements, I'll pay for them out of my own pocket."

Goldfarb laughed. "They have a lease, my friend. Even down here on the Sewanee River, Negroes have contractual rights."

"When does it expire?"

"Like I said, I don't bother with that side of the business. I'd have to ask Morty. But, they're reliable tenants. No complaints. Why should I futz with a sure thing?"

Narby lit a cigarette. "They're pushing dope in there, Art. The bar's a front. Dope and prostitutes."

"Am I my brother's keeper? Like I said, they're good tenants. That's a problem for the vice squad, not me."

"But it's your property. You might be held responsible. For aiding and abetting."

"Am I hearing things, or did you just threaten me?"

"Of course not. It's only..." Narby leaned forward, changing tack. "Look, why not help out the community, Art? A place like Jack's, it's not good for anyone, not for you or the Colored people. Why be associated with something like that? Christ, I'm no do-gooder, Art. But if you can help yourself and help others at the same time, why not? A jazz club with serious musicians, with a more elevated clientele. Even if it's all Colored. That's a hell of a lot healthier than what's going on there now."

Goldfarb was looking at him now with a bit more attention, trying to figure him.

"I'll run the place myself. Take all the risk. Only, I'd like your help. It could really fly, you know. Catch on. If it loses money, it's my money, not yours."

Goldfarb seemed to be mulling something. After a moment, chewing the cigar, he said, "If I sold you the property, instead of leasing. That would be a different matter."

"All right," Narby said quickly. "I'd consider buying."

"That way, there's no question of liability. And, of course, when ownership changes hands, the current lease can be terminated. Legally."

"Good. If that's what it takes."

"But. You'll never get a loan. Not for that property. Not without a solid business plan."

He took a moment to finish the cigarette, leaning across the desktop and stubbing it in the ashtray. "Why pay interest to a bank? Maybe you and I can work something out. What's the selling price?"

"You're determined to lose your money, aren't you?"

"Maybe so. But at least I'll have an interesting time doing it."

"I'll talk to my accountant. Give me a few days. Where can I reach you?"

"I'm staying at the Calvado. Better if I call you."

"Do me a favor, Phil. Think it over. Take you're time. You're asking for trouble, and when the trouble comes, don't look to me to bail you out. Fair warning, O.K.?"

"Yeah. Fair warning. It's my show. Still, I thought, maybe you could help me out, with the bookings."

"We'll see. First things first."

Narby nodded at the photo on the desk: a plain-looking heavy-set woman and two fat kids, standing before a sprawling Spanish-colonial, lush with palms and hibiscus. "That your family?"

"Yes," Goldfarb said, indifferently. "My wife and the boys."

Going home to that every night. The showgirls would compensate, Narby supposed. "Lovely. You must be very happy."

"That's my business. Making people happy. Because most of the time, people are miserable. If everybody were born happy and stayed that way, I'd be out of a job. Now, if you'll excuse me."

Narby stood. "I'll give you a call."

"Make it Wednesday. And watch yourself. Think it over, all right?"

13

IT WAS A FAIR MORNING, the sky cleared of its perpetual haze after last night's thunderstorms, the first harbinger of the pleasant winter weather to come. Narby sat at the table in the back room, copying the serial numbers for the next round of payments and making the packets: one for Campos, one for Red, one for Bobby, and the last for Goldfarb. Out the screens, through the grove, he could see Waters and a couple of men working near the pond, planting melaleuca and screw-pine saplings. He stopped for a moment, watching, smoking. The first stick of the day. A fifty-fifty blend. Half now, and then a puff every so often, to keep things at a pleasant pitch. He sat again and finished his work and then kneeled under the table and lifted the boards, putting the packets in the strongbox, and then showered and dressed. There would be a letter from Willa soon, any day now. He would check at Hanks, fill up the truck, grab a few things at the store, maybe have a bite at the Gladiola Cafe.

He got in the truck and lurched slowly down the rutted lane. The cooler weather changed everything, played its tricks. Through the scrim of dope the jungle appeared benign, almost beautiful—a sea of dense underbrush and above that the palmettos, thousands upon thousands, thrusting their knife-sharp bladed fans upward towards the sun, and above the palmettos the spectral latticework of the black-barked pines. His road, his jungle. He came to the gate, climbed out, unlocked the padlock and unwound the chain and drove through and got out again, locking it behind him. As far as Narby knew, Vetch hadn't come around in months. No one had come around. Only Narby and Sam and the workers.

Where the jungle thinned the truck bounced up onto the washboard road that skirted the barbed-wire cattle enclosures. With all the insect-borne diseases and the rank grasses that grew wherever they had cleared away the jungle, there wasn't much profit in ranching this far south on the peninsula. That land could be he had, too. More expensive than the Putnam acreage, but still at wasteland rates. Land prices were beginning to rise, even in Lacoosa County. If only he had some money coming in he'd buy it all, right up to the highway.

When he reached the courthouse square he spotted the mailman working his way across downtown. He parked and decided to eat first, at the Gladiola. They nodded to him now, said howdy. White T-shirt, work pants, leather sandals. Hardly ever see him in town. Philip Narby. Used to live over to the Glo-Bel till he moved out into the pines. Got a crew of Nigras working for him, out Sawfish Point. Growing some kind of experimental farm. Came down here right after Korea. Something happened to him over there. Made him into a loner. So they say. A good looking young man, too. Shame.

He sat by the window and ordered a plate of ham and eggs and grits. Looking at the *New Yorker* and then out the window, watching the sidewalk and the main street. Out of habit, he supposed. He'd seen Sid Black again, twice. Once, about a month ago, getting out of a taxi on Collins Avenue, and then, a few days later, sitting in the lobby of the Calvado. But instead of drawing back, hiding, Narby had behaved as though Black were nothing. A ghost. Walked right past him. And Black—shiny neon-blue suit, big cigar, talking a mile a minute—hadn't noticed him. Because Black wasn't looking for him, had given up. Maybe the last thing Sid Black wanted was to deal with Philip Narby. Now that he was a Miami Beach businessman, Black would want a clean slate, with nothing to remind him of all that—the stolen Army surplus, the scrap metal and radio batteries, selling Chesterfields out of the trunk of his car, delivering pornographic magazines and other contraband goodies to men like Ted McCoy. Only why would a legitimate businessman acquire three hotels and then let them run down like that, as if he didn't give a damn about his own property, his own business interests?

As he finished his coffee he saw Janet drive past in her Buick. Frank was beside her, in the front seat. They parked down the block. Frank got out first. He was hunched over, holding his hand against his face, cradling his jaw. Looking like hell. Janet got out and together they walked down the block, two feet of poisonous air between them, and entered the building next to the movie theater. Frank yanked the door open and, rather ungentlemanly, went in first, the door almost closing in Janet's face. About five minutes later—Narby was in no hurry now, sipping a second cup—Janet came out. By herself. Walking down the other side of the street. He was watching her, staring, and she must have felt it, because as she passed she suddenly looked up. This time she didn't avert her face. On the contrary, from across the street, stopping dead in her tracks, she locked her eyes onto his. Froze. And then, giving herself a little shake, looking down at her feet, she crossed the street and came into the diner.

What the hell was she doing? He rose, hoping to intercept her, but it was too late. She was through the door. Half a dozen customers were sitting at the counter, the quiet hour before the lunch crowd. Bullshitting, killing time. They all noticed her, of course. If she wanted everyone in town to start gossiping, that was her business, he supposed. He leaned back, took a breath.

"Can I sit down?"

"Of course."

She laid her handbag on the table. Her face was drawn, her makeup rather carelessly applied. She had on a skirt and blouse, the blouse buttoned to the neck. Suddenly, the temerity that had inspired her to march across the street seemed to drain away. She went limp, her head hanging.

"What is it, Janet? What's the matter?"

"I can't stand it—"

"Not so loud. Maybe we should talk somewhere else."

She raised her head. "You have to help me, Philip. I can't stand it anymore." She was whispering now, almost panting. "Please. Help me."

"Take it easy. Here. Drink some water."

"I went by the motel. Two, three times. Looking for you. They said you had moved out into the country somewhere. I couldn't find you. Oh god, if Frank finds out I'm here, talking to you."

"Where is he now? I saw you and Frank get out of the car."

"He's at the dentist. All his teeth are falling out. It's horrible. He'll be there for an hour, at least." She let her mouth hang open, her eyes unfocused, as if she could bear neither to look at him nor look away. "I never want to see him again. God, I don't know what to do." Her hands were writhing in her lap. "Oh, God. I'm so scared. Help me. Please."

"Calm down. It'll be all right. What is it exactly that you want me to do, Janet?"

"You'll help me?"

"Of course. If I can."

"You still care for me, don't you, Philip? Even a little?"

"Look, let's get out of here. Just get up, pretend you came in for a friendly hello, and leave. Get inside your car—"

"I can't. Frank took the keys."

"Christ. All right. My truck's parked around the corner. You know what it looks like?"

"Yes."

"It's not locked. Just make sure no one sees you. Get in and, well, just stay low, lie down on the seat. I'll be there in a minute."

"Get in to your truck. Lie down on the seat. Stay low," she repeated, as if receiving instructions for some difficult maneuver. "I'm sorry. Where is it?"

"Around the corner. To the left. You'll see it. If someone's there, take a walk around the block and come back."

She stood. "Nice to see you again." Her voice was stiff. Ridiculous. "So long."

"Janet. Your bag."

He handed it to her. She was close to tears, trembling. "So long," he said. "Take care."

After smoking a cigarette he paid the bill and walked out. He had to admit, she looked better now, had lost weight, and with her face drawn like that, her emotions brimming, he felt the urge to kiss her, touch her. See what it was like. From behind, through the back window, the truck appeared empty. In fact, he was almost surprised to see her there, supine on the seat, her bag resting on the grimy passenger-side floor. He got in. Her head was pressing against his thigh. He started the motor. A few minutes later, past the Glo-Bel, he turned onto one of the unpaved country roads and pulled over, the truck nestled against the brush.

"You can sit up now."

She pulled herself up and using the rearview mirror made a feeble attempt to put her hair back in place. "Like cops and robbers," she said, trying to make a joke.

He ought to keep his hands off her. Because if he touched her now, he'd be stuck with her. "What's going on, Janet? What did he do to you?"

"I have to move out. I hate him. I can't stand to be in the same room with him. It makes me sick. The way he shouts at me. Pushes me around." She paused, biting her lower lip. "Do you have a cigarette?"

He gave her one from the pouch, already rolled, and lit it for her, and then lit one for himself. "I thought you said you were going to get a divorce. Did you bring that up with him?"

She laughed, an hysterical outburst. "Are you kidding? He'd rather see me dead. It's like living in a nightmare. I'm going out of my mind, Philip. Do you understand?"

"He hits you?"

"No. Just pushing. Calls me names. When he's drunk. His goddamn beer cans all over the house. His filth. I wish he'd never come back. I wish he had died over there. Oh, God."

He held her while she sobbed, her head pressed against his shoulder, his hands flat on her back. He could feel the bra strap under her blouse, her chest heaving gently but then quieting. She sighed and leaned back, wiping her eyes with the back of her hand. "Do you still care for me, Philip? Do you still like me?"

"How can I help you, Janet? What do you want from me?"

"I'm sorry I was like that with you. I was so confused. Waiting for Frank to come back. Not knowing what it would be like. I felt so guilty. So ashamed. Well, I don't feel that way anymore. I don't care. I want to live. That's all there is to it. I can't go back. Oh, Christ," she said, her voice breaking again into a sob. "What am I going to do? I want to live, Philip. Just a normal life. Like everyone else."

He could do with her whatever he wanted, right now, in the truck. He felt himself stiffening, his thighs tense, his heart thudding. It was a tremendous effort simply to keep his hands from unbuttoning her blouse, reaching down under her skirt. He thought about Martha—that day when she found out that Loerber was dead, her life in ruins. Sobbing into his shirt, pressing herself against him, looking for someone to take away her pain. "You ought to move out. Is there anywhere you can go? Any family?"

"Only my mother. But she's all the way in Muncie. I thought about that already. A thousand times. Only, how? Frank has the car. He took all the money out of the bank, all our savings, hid it somewhere. He doesn't even have a job. Besides, why should it be me? Why can't he get out and leave me in peace? I don't want to go back to my mother. It's not fair. Oh, god. Why can't he just disappear?"

"What time is he getting out of the dentist?"

"Around noon. I'm supposed to meet him there. Drive him home. They're pulling out three teeth. He said they'd give him something for the pain, that he wouldn't be able to drive."

"It's just eleven. I can drive you home. I'll wait while you pack a bag and then I'll take you to the bus station. You can take the next bus out. Just get on it, it doesn't matter where it's going. Just as long as he can't find you."

"On what?" she snapped. "I've got about a dollar in change in my purse."

He reached into his pocket. "Here. A hundred dollars. You can live on that for a while, until you make it back to your mother's. Then you can find a divorce lawyer. I can give you more. If you need it."

She was staring at the money. "Philip. I… I can't take that. Thank you, but. It's not right."

"Well, what the hell do you want, then?"

"Please. Don't speak to me like that. Can't you see what's happening to me?"

"You want me to talk to Frank? Convince him to leave you alone."

"Could you do that? Make him stay away from me?"

"Sure. Easy. You pick him up after the dentist, while he's groggy from the pain medicine. I'll be waiting for you, at your house. You help him inside and then clear out. I'll talk to him. Get him to take a vacation, think things over."

A wild look came over her face. "Really? I mean. But, how could you do that?"

"How? What difference does it make? You want him gone, don't you? Chances are, he won't be coming home from his vacation either, not where I'm going to send him. You'll find where he hid the money, sooner or later. In one of his suit pockets, probably."

"But …" She backed a way. He could see all of her, with her skirt pushed up above the knees from squirming about on the seat. "You mean, you would threaten him?"

"Get rid of him. Isn't that what you want? Then you and I can, you know, get back together. Because you won't be confused anymore. Because Frank wouldn't be coming home this time around."

"Stop. Let me think." She looked at the money again. "Are you sure you can spare that much?"

"Sure."

She took it and put in her bag, silently, the cigarette between her fingers trembling as she opened and closed the clasp. "It's very kind of you, Philip." She wouldn't look at him now, staring down at the bag, the clasp. "I'll pay you back. I promise. Do you—you live somewhere out in the county? Maybe. When things change. After the divorce. Maybe I could come see you."

"Sure. Only I don't have a permanent address right now. Just look me up in the phone book, next time you're down from Muncie."

"You don't like me anymore, do you? I thought, well, when you came around the library, even after Frank had come home… But I guess I was wrong."

"Sure. I like you. That's why I'm helping you." He cranked the engine. "Let's go, before it's too late. I'll take you home. Run in and pack a bag as fast as you can. Then I'll take you to the Greyhound. I'll wait in front of the station, until you catch your bus. Just in case Frank snaps out of his stupor and catches on."

He turned around and a minute later they were back on the highway, heading into town. She looked out the window, her hair blowing. The top button of her blouse had come open. She hadn't bothered to pull down the skirt. He'd given her the money. Why not treat like her a whore, a very expensive one, at that. Take what she was offering and then forget about her.

"Sorry. Don't remember the street."

She told him where to turn. A drab little stucco house in a yard of browning sod, a pile of junk rotting under the carport. He'd never seen it in the daylight.

"I'll wait here. Hurry up."

Saying nothing, she got out. He watched her open the door, go in, her hips swinging, her ass. Things might be bad with Frank, but at least she wasn't numb anymore. He waited, fingering the half stick in his pocket. What the hell was she doing? It was already 11:20. He got out of the truck and went to the front door. It was unlocked. He went in and closed it behind him. The air inside stank, like a cage that hadn't been cleaned.

"Janet? Where are you?"

He heard her in the bedroom. The suitcase was open on the bed, a few articles of her clothing carelessly tossed in. She was sitting on the mattress, limp, her face blank. "Come on, Janet, for Christ's sake. Hurry it up."

"I can't. I want to, Philip. So very very much. But I can't. Where will I go? Tell me, Philip, where will I go?"

"To your goddamn mother. Get up."

She reached over to unclasp the handbag bag. "Here. Take back your money."

"You better keep it. In case you change your mind."

"Where can I find you? Please, Philip. Don't leave me alone."

"You still work at the library?"

"Yes. Mondays and Wednesdays."

"I'll come by. In a week or two. We can talk."

"You promise?"

"Hide the money where Frank can't find it. You're going to need it, sooner or later. Understand?"

She nodded. He looked at her one last time, sitting on the bed. Don't touch her. Leave her be.

He walked out quickly and took a spin in the truck, finishing the stick, and then drove downtown. Frank's car was still in front of the dentist's office. He parked and walked across the courthouse square, stepping down and peering in the window before pushing open the door, setting off the brass bells.

The shop was empty. At the sound of the alarm the Egyptian came out from behind the beaded curtain, a rather exaggerated smile plastered across his wide face, showing his big front teeth under the thick mustache. "Good day, Mr. Norby. How are you today, sir?"

"Good enough. How are you, Hank?"

"I was hoping you would come today, sir. I have some very great news."

Narby didn't feel like chatting. There was time to go back and get her before Frank got home, take her to Sawfish Point. Waters would be there, but so what? "Yeah? What's that? Win the Reader's Digest Sweepstakes or something?"

"No, Mr. Norby. Much better. Wait please." He ducked behind the beads and came back with an enormous black cigar clamped in his mouth, and another in his hand. "I save this for you, Mr. Norby," he said, holding it over the counter.

"I'm not a cigar smoker, Hank. You know that."

"Please, sir." From his sweater pocket—he wore an open cardigan against the air-conditioned chill of the cluttered little subterranean shop—he took a pair of tiny scissors, a cigar cutter, snipped the end and handed it to Narby. "To celebrate. Yesterday, I became a father. A boy, may God be praised. A boy is a blessing. A girl, too, is a delight. But a burden."

"That's wonderful, Hank. Congratulations." He reached over the counter and shook Hank's square, blunt-fingered hand. He was genuinely fond of the Arab. He ought to show some enthusiasm. "All right. Let's stink the place up."

He passed Narby the cigar.

"Hell, Hank. This is a good one, isn't it?"

"The best in the shop, sir. Top of the line Partagas." He held up a lighter and Narby drew, bringing it to life, the thick sour smoke coiling in his mouth.

Having absolutely nothing to contribute on the subject of babies, the shop owner beaming and nodding, Narby said, "So, how's your wife? She recovering all right?"

"She is well, thank you. Very kind of you to ask. Very considerate, Mr. Norby."

Maybe he ought to follow Frank home, make sure things didn't get out of hand. He wouldn't mind divesting Frank of those painkillers, either. He had tried to help her, hadn't he? There was nothing between them anymore, never had been.

Once Willa was back, she'd disappear from his thoughts. Only the idea of Frank touching her, pushing her around, made him feel like a coward, a weakling.

"I'm sure you'll make a wonderful father, Hank." Whatever the hell that meant.

"George," he said, exulting in the celebratory cigar, burning up his most expensive inventory. "George Gamal. This is the boy's name. What do you think of that, Mr. Norby?"

Gamal, as in Gamal Abdel Nasser. He was making a fool of the British over the Suez standoff. Eisenhower wanted nothing do with it. And now the Soviets were paying lip service to Egyptian independence. The only winners would be the Israelis, who would no doubt take advantage of the crisis to grab more territory, in the Sinai or Gaza. Still, Hank had reason to be proud. "Gamal. Very good, Hank. But why George?"

The shopkeeper raised his thick eyebrows. "Because of George Washington. Father of America."

Smart. If Hank knew what was good for his family, they'd keep the Gamal for home use only. "Damn good cigar," he said. "Maybe you'll change my mind about these things."

"You have very good taste, Mr. Norby. I noticed this, ever since you first entered my store. Please," he said, his smile fading, lowering his voice, "may I take a moment of your time to show you something, Mr. Norby?"

He fidgeted, trying to blank Janet from his mind. "Sure. What is it?"

The tobacconist came out from behind the counter and after peering through the plate glass window and up the steps he flipped over the *Will Return in Five Minutes* sign and pulled down the shade. What the hell was going on? Narby tensed, letting the cigar burn in his hand, watching the Arab as he bent over behind the counter and from below the cash register pulled out a wooden cigar box.

"Mr. Norby. For two years now you have been coming to my shop. Always you have spoken to me with kindness. With intelligence and respect. To me comes your mail, and for this we trust each other. I show you this now because of your kindness, because you are a true friend."

With his thick fingers he opened the lid and extracted a small black and white photograph with scalloped edges. "Her name is Nawal," he said, placing it on the counter as if displaying a precious gem.

The face of a plain-looking young woman stared up at him, of middle-eastern cast, the beads of her dark eyes slightly crossed, a scarf hiding her hair, her expression blank and mildly startled.

"My wife. The mother of my son," he said gravely.

Back in the old country they kept the women hidden behind a curtain. Hank was bestowing a great honor on him, Narby realized. Like a blood brother, or something. "She's lovely, Hank. Nawal. A beautiful name."

He let Narby gaze for a few seconds and then, delicately, lifted the photo with his fingertips and returned it to the box, nestling it flat among the meager collection of keepsakes: a few photos, exotic coins, odd pieces of silver and ivory, a gold chain, a tiny blue bottle.

"When Nawal is feeling stronger, you shall come visit us at our house, Mr. Norby. Then you will meet George Gamal."

"I'd be delighted, Hank."

The tobacconist returned the box to its shelf under the cash register. What care, what tenderness. Narby had nothing to show in return, nothing with which to answer the Arab's invitation. For a moment it pained him, that some small-time immigrant shopkeeper might experience a depth of feeling, a wealth of emotions, that he would never know, never understand.

Hank unlocked the door, turned the sign. "Any mail for me?" Narby said, rather flatly. The passing pain had left him cold.

"Yes, sir. A package. And a letter." He went behind the counter and brought it out—a box of jazz albums that he had ordered from New York. And a letter from Willa.

"You should really let me pay you something for your trouble, Hank."

"I will not. You cannot make me," he said, laughing. The man was in raptures.

Narby had the cigar in his hand. "O.K. In that case, I'll take a box of these. The Partagas Oros."

"Aha. I have made of you a believer."

"Maybe so, Hank."

"They are fifteen dollars for twenty, Mr. Norby. You are sure?"

"Yep."

"Perfectly fresh. I can guarantee. Stored at the correct humidity. Just a moment. I will get them."

Minutes later he walked back to the truck, the goods under his arm. Frank's car was gone. Too bad for Janet. He got in, tossing the costly half-smoked cigar into the gutter, and opened the letter. It was a card, with a reproduction of a painting by Paul Klee. *Dear Philip, how I long for you. Your touch, your taste, my beautiful man. But it won't be long now. I plan to arrive on the 23rd. Only this time, no need to meet me at the airport. I'll be driving. It's a surprise. A gift I gave myself. Come to me as you always have, out of the sea, something rare, a treasure. I'll be waiting. Ready for anything. Your very own, W.*

14

SHE RETURNED THAT NOVEMBER at the wheel of an Italian sports car, a two-seat cream-colored Alfa Romeo Guilieta Spider with a convertible top—the spoils of her latest sale from the Janis gallery, following her triumph at the Venice Biennale. There would be another solo show that spring, and a touring exhibition of America art sponsored by the Rockefeller Foundation, traveling from West Berlin to Rio de Janeiro. A Willa Branton now hung in the Ambassador's library at the U.S. Embassy in Mexico City—*Sporadicism # 7*. Narby had seen it in the studio last March. Washed-out amorphous smears of thinly applied paint, showing nothing, suggesting nothing, lacking even the elemental charm of a child's daub. Apparently, the line separating fraud from genius was difficult to discern—not only with Willa's work, but that of her peers, as well. Like that joker Pollock who had died in a drunken car crash that summer. "Jack the dripper. The overrated son-of-a-bitch," as Willa put it. "The Pollock meat has finally met its grinder. Still, it's good for Sidney and Harriet. Pollocks are going to double, triple in price. He hadn't done shit in years. Couldn't even drip anymore. Christ, though, I feel sorry for Ruth. His mistress. Lee knew all about it. Everyone knew. Ruth was flung out of the car, you know. In one piece, thank God. Maybe now she'll crawl out from under his cloud."

The only New Yorker she seemed to admire, when she wasn't defaming him, was an older painter named de Kooning, a transplant from Europe. "His brushstrokes, Philip. What magic."

He wondered if Willa could draw a human face or a woman's torso, outline a tree with any degree of accuracy?

They had no trouble picking up where they had left off, Narby back and forth, spending three or four nights at a time, swimming, walking the dunes, exulting in the spell of extraordinary weather and the beauty of the island, listening to jazz in the evenings while drinking gin rickeys and bourbon and white wine. Willa took it easier now, spent less time in the studio, more time playing. She had seen her gynecologist in New York, been fitted with a new diaphragm. Just to be on the safe side, she explained. Apparently, the Dr. had given her a clean bill of health, and by association, Narby, too—lucky, considering his former habits. Pleasure for the sake of pleasure, with him and only him, Willa had reassured. With a powerful sexual attraction like theirs fidelity was something natural and animalistic, a physical compulsion from within rather than a repressive social law or an acting-out of insecurity and fear. And though she hadn't asked—not directly, at any rate—he volunteered that it was the same with him, that he hadn't been with another woman, hadn't wanted it. True enough, in a way. Despite Willa's delight in filthy sex talk, the determination with which she sought and attained one climax after another, he understood that she didn't want him to think she was overly-permissive, an easy target, a loose woman. Frankly, he didn't know what to believe. All he knew was that he would do anything to keep her, that he would let no one interfere.

It was a month after she returned, just after dawn, when he heard the plane, faint and then closer and then faint again. Not fully awake, he was uncertain if the sound were real or imaginary, some half dream in which Willa's somnolent breathing and the sound of the waves had confounded him. The bedroom was dark, the early morning glow seeping around the edges of the curtain. He got up, splashed cold water on his face, threw on a pair of trousers and a flannel shirt, grabbed the tobacco pouch and, leaving the curtains drawn, slid open the glass door and stepped onto the terrace.

The sun had not yet cleared the jungle, the air tremulous and pellucid with the first light of day. He stood at the rail, scanning the sea and the dunes and the sky. Maybe it was only the gulls, though the sound was quite distinct. The seaplane might be circling the island, or raking the coast, back and forth, as he had witnessed on more than one occasion. He waited, sitting in the canvas chair, smoking. He had a constant supply now and rarely took his tobacco straight.

He was about to go inside when he heard it again, faint but steady. He looked out over the water. A low-flying speck, growing larger as the sound became clearer, glinting in the low sun. It seemed to be hugging the mangroves south of the island, sweeping back and forth within a limited range. And there was someone out on the dunes. He hadn't noticed him before. Whoever it was had come out, as had Narby, to watch for the plane. It was Pembaker. He was certain.

Quietly, he stepped back inside, put on his swimming trunks and grabbed a towel and went down stairs and out the back, past the pool and the garden, fragrant with gardenias and honeysuckle, through the gate in the hedge and down the plank walkway that passed between the dunes to the beach.

He had met Pembaker twice now, but only in passing, in the presence of Willa, who had introduced them. Willa had been back and forth to New York so often, a consequence of her new notoriety, that they had missed the Pembakers' parties. Besides, Willa didn't like the idea of being thought of as a 'couple,' so she hardly went out of her way to socialize with Narby around. He draped the towel over his shoulders and strolled in Pembaker's direction, south, toward the creek. A sturdy good-looking man, mid-fifties, with iron-gray hair. A publisher, Willa had told him. He owned English-language newspapers in South America. Venezuela, was it? And Chile and Mexico. The Allbright Paper Corporation had offices in Venezuela and Brazil, if in fact Allbright existed as anything more than a name and a handful of international addresses, printed on glossy business cards. Narby had known it was phony, a cover, even before leaving Tokyo. Maybe Pembaker's newspapers were phony, too.

He had to be careful, not say too much. Let Pembaker show his cards first. Pembaker—Narby could see now that he was correct—had turned and was headed back, away from the creek and toward the Colony. What a coward Narby had been in Havana, scared witless by the suave mild-mannered Knowles. No one would ever make Philip Narby cower like that again.

Recognizing him, Pembaker raised his hand in greeting. Willa's boyfriend, the one from last year—who had obviously spent the night and was here on the beach in the early morning, fresh from her bed. A worldly man like Pembaker, no matter how loyal a husband, might naturally feel a bit of envy.

"Hello." Pembaker spoke first. He was in khaki trousers, rippling in the breeze, a short tan windbreaker jacket and tennis shoes. Despite a few superfluous pounds, he was in decent shape.

"Good morning."

"Out for a swim? Glorious day, isn't it?"

"That it is."

"I'm surprised to see anyone out this early. I usually have the beach all to myself at this hour. Willa's here, I take it. When did she arrive?"

"A few weeks ago. She was quite eager to get back to her studio."

Pembaker laughed. "Among other things, I'm sure. We only got back two weeks ago ourselves. On the Miranda, with Dan and Sheila."

"The Miranda?"

"The Atlees' boat. Thirty-four foot Wheeler cabin cruiser. Dan picked us up in Norfolk. Came down the inter-coastal and then across the Keys and Florida Bay."

"I noticed it last spring, docked in the Village marina."

"That's the one. You much of a boater?"

"Not really." Pembaker was curious, all right. "More of a swimmer," he said, smiling.

"Yes. I watched you one day. You're fast. Swim in college, did you?"

"A little." What else had Pembaker seen? "It's a habit now. Keeps me out of trouble."

"Maybe I'll join you one afternoon. I ought to get in the water more often when I'm down here. " Pembaker looked out at the sea for a moment. "I believe Willa told Tara that you're a year-round resident, in the County. Near Myerton."

"Sawfish Point, actually. About fifteen miles north of town."

"That's cattle and lumber country out there, isn't it?"

"Used to be. The lumber people pulled out years ago. As I understand, it was a big turpentine operation. Pine resin. The

Putnam Lumber Company. That's all gone now. Still some cattle ranches around, though."

"Interesting. How long have you been down here, in this part of Florida?"

"Couple of years." He considered for a moment. "After coming home from Korea."

Pembaker put out his hand. "It's always an honor to meet a fellow veteran." They shook, Pembaker's grip rather exaggerated, Narby thought.

"You in Korea?"

"No. Missed out on that one, thank heaven. Second World War. European theater. So, were you Navy? Marines?"

"No. Eighth Army. Field artillery unit. Nothing special."

"Nonsense. That's the meat and bones of it. The infantry. Good to see you came out of it so well. Have you met Dan yet?"

"No."

"You two could swap some stories, I bet. He rode in with the Marines, part of the Inchon invasion. Got caught up in that nightmare by the Chosin Reservoir. But. I don't want to hold you back from your swim."

At the sound Narby turned his head, looking over his shoulder. There it was again, a speck against the yellow morning sky, the buzz rising above the wash of the surf. "Another resident of the Colony," Narby said, "coming in by seaplane?"

Pembaker looked up, following Narby's gaze, as if he hadn't noticed the plane until now. "Coast Guard," he said, after a moment. "Or maybe one of those crop dusters the County was planning to fit out, to spray for mosquitoes. Have you heard anything about that? Something needs to be done, considering how bad they can get."

"No, I haven't." The speck was circling back again, miles south of the island. Pembaker was lying, Narby guessed. "I could have sworn I've seen that plane before, though. A seaplane with pontoons. It touched down on the other side on the island. In the bay."

"Recently?" Pembaker sounded incredulous.

"May or June. Sometime last summer."

"Hm. Must have been an emergency in the Village. I'd know if any of our people were coming in and out by seaplane. We're a pretty tight-knit group." He laughed. "Maybe Dan's got a new toy he hasn't let me play with."

"Willa tells me that you and Dan Atlee started the Colony, built the first houses. She calls you the 'founding fathers'."

He laughed. "Well. Something like that."

"You certainly found an idyllic piece of earth."

"Yes. It's a special place." He smiled. He was standing with his hands thrust into the pockets of his jacket, his legs spread apart. "We want to keep it that way. Private. Unspoiled."

"I don't blame you," Narby said. It sounded like a warning.

"As long as we can dissuade the County from building the causeway, we stand a pretty good chance." He looked at Narby. "Being a year-round resident, you probably know some of the county commissioners, yes? George Dankworth? Bob Sunderland?"

"A little," he lied. "As a rule, though, I steer clear of local politics."

"Too bad. We could use some inside influence. Get someone more rooted in the county on our side."

"Well. I do own quite a bit of land, almost two thousand acres. Unimproved, though. No roads, no power lines or water. The County leaves me alone and I return the favor. At least, for now."

"Ranch land, is it?"

"Pine scrub, mostly, and some mangrove flats along the estuary. I've got a small experimental farm going. Testing out some tropical species, fruit, ornamentals. With a partner from the Bahamas. A botanist. But mostly, I'm just sitting on the land, for now. Waiting to see what happens. I'm in no rush."

"Interesting. You'll have to tell us more. Frankly, we're in something of a tug-of-war right now. With the County, the State, even the Department of the Interior. My wife Tara is on a wildlife conservationist campaign. She's in with the Marjory Douglas crowd. Let me tell you, Tara is a very determined individual. And it's not just the Colony that's involved. It's the entire island. Well. I'll let you get on with your swim. Good talking to you—Philip, yes?"

"That's right. And you're Dalton."

"Call me Dalt."

"O.K. Dalt. A newspaper man, correct? A publisher."

"Correct. Nothing you'd be perusing with your bacon and eggs, though. We run a consortium of newspapers for the American business community abroad. A mix of local and international news, working with the wire services, A.P. and U.P.I. Mostly in South America."

" You don't have a paper in Brazil, do you?"

"As a matter of fact, yes. *The Rio Reporter*. A weekly."

"Maybe you know a friend of mine. Bill Knowles. V.P. at the Allbright Paper Company. They've got paper mills down in Brazil. Name ring a bell?"

Pembaker considered for a moment. "Bill Knowles. Sounds familiar, but no, I can't say I know anyone by that name. An American?"

"Yes. Well. Just thought I'd ask."

"I'll have Tara get in touch with Willa. We'll have you two over for cocktails, once we're settled. How's that?"

"Great. I look forward to it."

He watched Pembaker trudge across the sand, up toward the dunes. The man knew something, was holding back if not outright lying. They were feeling each other out, speaking at oblique angles. He had a positive feeling about Pembaker, though. The man had something fatherly about him, but in a good way, not patronizing or overbearing.

It was the other one, Dan Atlee, he ought to be worried about. It was lucky that Narby had been drawn out by the sound of the plane, that he'd had a chance to talk to Pembaker like that, privately, before meeting Atlee—almost as if Pembaker had come out to warn him. Altee was at the Inchon invasion—that had been MacArthur's show, a piece of supreme luck that could just have easily been a disaster, like MacArthur's cowardly fuck-up at Bataan. Inchon had been MacArthur's last hurrah before Truman finally worked up the nerve to fire him. Atlee did something with shipping, Willa had said. Oil tankers. An ex-Marine, a war hero, the sportsman with the ostentatious yacht, a blustering red-baiter—Atlee obviously considered himself a big man. So what? If there was going to be a fight, if Atlee was on MacArthur's side, it was Narby who would throw the acid first.

He continued down the beach toward the creek. The plane had disappeared. Well past the last of the mansions, he went for a long swim, his mind blanking. But he couldn't clear Atlee out of his thoughts, that nimbus of dread that now hovered over the man's name. It was only a matter of time—weeks, perhaps days—before they met, face to face. He had to be prepared.

After his swim he lay on the sand staring into the depthless winter-blue morning sky. Why so damned skittish? He wasn't in Havana anymore. The cowering wharf-rat was dead and buried. No more whores, no more skulking. Look how far he'd come. He had money, he had land, had the place in Overtown now, in control of his own needs. He had Willa Branton. He'd even killed a man, the pilot. Indirectly, perhaps, but the result was the same. If he had to, Philip Narby could do it again, only this time deliberately, without weakness or hesitation.

He walked back, staying close to the dunes, not wanting to run in to any of the other Colony people. They would no doubt have been informed by the Pembakers of his presence, Willa's 'friend,' an outsider in their midst who had to be tolerated. Harmless people, Willa had called them. He passed through the gate in the hedge, showered by the pool and went up the stairs, expecting to find Willa still in bed. But the bed was empty. He'd been out for two hours, he realized. He put on a pair of cut-off shorts—it was warm, the morning chill burning off with the ris-ing sun—and went downstairs. She wasn't in the living room or the kitchen. He walked around to the studio and tried the door, but it was locked. The Guilieta was parked in front, so she hadn't gone into the Village. He went back, around the studio building and through the garden and out the gate. Whenever Willa went for a walk on the beach she left her sandals at the end of the walkway. But there were no sandals. He went inside and called out. And then a second time, louder. Foolishly. The house, so stark and angular, was not amenable to hiding. Where the hell was she?

In the kitchen he found warm coffee in the pot. The kitchen was rather filthy, the living room and dining table too, dirty dishes, wine and liquor bottles, ashtrays spilling over. Housekeeping hadn't been on their minds, obviously. His knap-sack was in a corner, over turned. He picked it up and checked the contents: two more tobacco pouches—one pure, in case Willa wanted a cigarette, the other his medicinal blend—another lighter, cigarette papers, magazines, a notebook, the flask, the money. All there. What did he think, that she had stolen from him?

He sat on the couch and rolled a cigarette. Then he put on one of the jazz records he had ordered through the mail. Thelonious Monk. It was striking music, primitive and sophisti-cated all at once. But what attracted him most was that it wiped out the Count Basie, the Benny Goodman, all that confusion from the days of Tom and Jim. Wiped it out and at the same time confirmed it, contained it. He wondered if he could get this Monk character to play at Sir Jack's—the name was Red's idea, retain-ing the name of the old juke joint but imbuing it with a little class. To go with the refurbished name, the hot-cool mood, there was a new ice-blue neon sign, hung right above the entrance. The repairs were costing more than Narby had anticipated. Bobbie and Red were perhaps taking advantage of him, his trust. Still, as long as they kept it within bounds, he'd look the other way.

Ultimately, following the advice of his accountant, Goldfarb had decided not to sell outright, but instead had made out a 'contract-for-deed.' A kind of installment-plan. It might cost Narby a little more that way, but it was preferable. He wanted as little notice as possible from White Miami. The arrangement kept the name Philip Narby off the property records at the Dade County Clerk's Office. And as far as anyone in Overtown was concerned, the place belonged to Red and Bobby. Colored Men working for Colored Men. The White Man, the money man, stayed out of sight—except when he came around to deliver the pay packets, enjoy himself a little, stock up on Bobby's produce.

Sprawling on the couch, lost in the music, tired from his swim, he must have dozed off. When he came to, he was craving a drink, hadn't had one all day and it was almost noon. He was about to get up for the bottle when Willa came from the kitchen. "There you are," he said. "I've been looking for you."

She stood over him, her face neutral. She was in her work clothes, the paint-splattered T-shirt and shapeless cotton trousers. "When I woke up you weren't in bed. You were gone for hours. I thought you —"

"Thought what?"

"That you'd left, gone home, without a word. Or—drowned."

He laughed.

"It's not funny. People drown all the time. Even the strongest swimmers."

"Sorry. I forgot that you get the creeps, about the water."

"The creeps?" It was her turn to laugh, at him, he supposed. She was taking in the state of the room, the mess. "Philip, I have to ask you something."

"Go ahead."

"You might have noticed. I'm not spending as much time in the studio, these last few weeks."

"Yeah, well, all work and no play. So?"

She ignored his levity. "It's not good for me. I'm losing concentration. Over the last three years I've been doing my best work here. I need to keep that going. The continuity. The intensity."

"I get that. Sure."

She took a deep breath and sat down next to him. "The island—well, it's not a vacation for me, as it might be for you. It's the opposite, in fact. My work is really what brings me here, what makes me stay. I can't lose that dynamic. I can't afford to toy with it."

She wore no brassiere under the T- shirt. Her hair was in her eyes, and her face, pink from the sun, gilded by the light from the window, beguiled him with its mask of innocence, the flawless skin and the dusting of reddish freckles and the full pale lips. He must have been dreaming about her, because he was feeling aroused. "How about we go by the pool?" That excited her, doing it outside, in the daylight.

"Philip. Please." She stood, deflecting his touch, and took a cigarette from the box on the cabinet. "I need to be in the studio. For the rest of the day. Alone."

He recognized the cutting indignant tone. Only it had never before been directed at him. That was new. "You're annoyed about this morning, aren't you?" He considered telling her about the plane, but then he'd have to explain. "I couldn't sleep, so I thought—"

"It's got nothing to do with that, Philip. Don't be absurd." She lit the cigarette, turning away. "I told you, I have to get back to work. Seriously. I can't do things in half measures."

"Where were you? I got back over an hour ago. I was looking all over. Didn't you hear me calling?"

"No. I was in the studio. Where I should be, right now."

"No you weren't. The door was locked. I tried it."

"I didn't want to be disturbed."

"With the lights out? You told me that winter mornings were rather dark in there. That the afternoon light is what you're after. You were painting in the dark?"

"I wasn't painting. I was looking. Sometimes, I can see better, feel it more strongly, when it's dark."

"Feel what?"

"Whatever it is that compels me to paint. It's not mine. I have to find it, chase it. Hunt it down. Don't give me that stupid smile, Philip. You haven't a clue what it's about."

"Then maybe you can explain it." But he knew she couldn't. Just as she couldn't explain her paintings or why anyone would think so damn highly of them.

"Philip. I need your help." She was pacing the room, smoking. "The way things are between us, it's rather overwhelming. That's the reason I haven't been able to engage fully, to lock myself up in the studio. Until this morning. It seems as though I can only be overwhelmed by one thing at a time. I need it back. That kind of intensity. Look at this place, the disorder, the neglect. I don't like disorder. It unbalances me. But I didn't even see it, didn't care, until this morning. When I woke up and you were gone, and I waited and waited and you didn't come back."

"O.K. I understand. Look, go back in the studio. I'll tidy up, drive into the Village and pick up some groceries. You can paint all day, and tomorrow, and the next day. Whatever you need to get back on track."

She shook her head. "Philip. You have to leave. For a couple of weeks, at the minimum. Leave, and then for Christ's sake, come back."

He got up. It was some kind of game. "No problem. I've got plenty to do. More than you can imagine."

"Please. Don't take it like that. I love you, Philip. I don't want you to go. I'd like nothing more than to fuck you all day long, rub my cunt all over you, put you in my mouth, to feel you inside me, filling me up. I can't get it out my mind. I've never had a man like you. But I simply don't know of any other way, but to ask you to leave. To make you promise that you'll come back."

She had said it. But it was rather expedient at the moment, was it not, her proclamation of love? He wasn't about to hand it back so soon. "Whatever you want, Willa." He went upstairs, gathered his clothes, brought them down and stuffed everything in the sack. "I'll spend the rest of the day on the beach. I can catch the afternoon ferry." He didn't want to touch or kiss her goodbye. It was some kind of game. She had her rules, and he had his, he supposed.

"You're upset. I'm sorry. You have to understand. It's as if I have to become a machine, without identity, without personality. That's why the whole relationship idea is so useless. But we can still have this, this thing. Whatever it is, between us."

"It's fine. I've got plenty of business to take care of."

She stopped her pacing, looking at him, her face drained. "When will you come back?"

"Couple of weeks. I'll show up. No fanfare, no bells and whistles. Like before."

"Of course. Yes."

He went out through the garden. The truck was parked at the lighthouse and he walked down the beach, just as he had the day they met. When he got to the creek he stopped, remembering how he had ferried her across like a frightened little girl, her wet legs slipping against his back and sides, and how she had kissed him. The tide was out now, the creek not much more than a runnel.

He'd spoken to Pembaker on the beach, very early. Then he came back and Willa was gone. Not in the studio. He didn't believe her story. And now, suddenly, she needs to be alone? Maybe she'd been watching, had run over to Pembaker's to compare notes with Dalton after their little seaside tête-à-tête. It made no sense. Nothing about Willa made much sense. At least he could console himself with the fact that he still knew more about Willa, about Pembaker, than they knew about Philip Narby.

15

THE NEWS FROM ORIENTE PROVINCE was bleak. Batista's Information Ministry was hardly a trustworthy source, but there had been confirmation in the American press, a UPI wire story and an independent report in *Diario las Americas*, the Spanish language paper published in Miami. Fidel Castro was dead. His luck had run out.

Narby knew more than the brief dispatches in the newspapers. For the past six months Campos had been feeding him quality information: the training operations at the farm in Santa Rosa outside Mexcio City, under the direction of Miguel "el Coreano" Sanchez and the medico they called Ché and Alberto Bayo, who had fought against Franco during the Spanish Civil War; a second botched attempt on Castro's life; the raid by the Mexican Federales, no doubt in concert with Batista's secret police, on a cache of weapons concealed at the safe house in Lomas de Chapultepec.

It was nearly impossible to fathom Castro's thinking—cramming eighty armed men aboard the *Granma*, a small private yacht designed to carry at best twenty passengers. There would have been scant room for weapons or extra ammunition, for food and water and medical supplies. Such a pathetic force, already strained from the trip from Mexico across the Gulf, would require immediate and widespread support on land. That's where Frank País had come in, operating out of Santiago, where Batista's grip over the local population was the weakest. País had been charged with organizing a widespread uprising to coincide with Castro's clandestine landing: strikes, marches, work stoppages, small-scale attacks on the symbols of state corruption, the factories and sugar mills run by Batista's wealthy cronies. The insurrection—theoretically, at least—would tie down the police and the army while the band of armed revolutionaries came ashore and organized in the wilds of the Sierra Maestra. Unfortunately, on the appointed day, only a handful of actions materialized—instead of insurrection, only petty sabotage and a few placards. To make matters worse, the amateur mariners aboard the *Granma* had landed in a desolate swamp. Struggling to get their weapons and supplies on solid ground, the rebels had been spotted by an air force patrol. Panicking, the group floundered, split up. A company of Batista's army pursued them into the mountain jungles of the Sierra. Castro himself and half his force were killed that very day. A thousand soldiers were now hunting down the forty or so stragglers, the last of El Barbado's men.

The entire fiasco might have been prevented if only Campos had convinced Castro to meet with Narby, to consider his offer. Narby had been ready to clear a landing strip and a staging area, hidden in the jungle and the thickets of mangrove. Hell, the Negro men working for Narby might have thrown in their lot with the rebels, when the time came. With Narby's help, with more men and a larger boat and a secure base in south Florida, with the right tone in their anti-communist pro-constitutional-democratic Cuba propaganda, M267—as the Movement now called itself—might have succeeded where Castro had failed. Well, it was too late now.

The other anti-Batista groups—the radical workers' movement, the socialist PSP, the Student Revolutionary Directorate— were certain to take advantage of M267's demise. Some were hardliner communists, men who from the very beginning had been critical of Castro's reluctance to invoke the global struggle against neo-colonial American capitalist hegemony. Men who would eagerly seek assistance from the Soviets. Castro might be gone, but the problem of what to do with Batista, or who would fill the vacuum when the dictator's time ran out, remained.

He hadn't seen or heard from Campos since the news broke, two weeks ago. Narby would console Campos, commiserate, assess the damage. The point was, with his position weakened and his ideals crushed, the dapper little medical student might be more willing now to provide Narby with access to Prio's people in Miami. Even more, Narby was eager to make contact with Frank País, who only a year ago had merged his more radical group, the A.R.O., with Castro's organization. Chief of Action and Sabotage. That was kind of man whose trust, even friendship, Narby wished to cultivate. Even if Knowles were out of the picture, information about País and Prio and the others would prove most valuable—to the C.I.A., the intelligence section at the embassy in Havana, the Latin America desk at State. It wasn't money Narby wanted in return. It was protection. Assurance that if the Army ever tracked him down he would be granted a pardon against charges of desertion during wartime and disseminating classified information. Protection against MacArthur and Willoughby.

There was one additional copy of the document Narby had relinquished to Knowles before leaving Havana. Tom or Jim had typed it out word-for-word and mailed it from Tokyo, maybe two weeks before they had sent him to Korea to die. In a sealed envelope, to his mother, with instructions to store it unopened in a safe place until her son's return. A small town, a hundred miles outside Chicago. He could picture the house, the leafy street, the room in the attic where the radio reception was good, the fields of corn at the edge of town shimmering in the late summer sun, the local teacher's college where he had taken classes in French and German after losing the Pepsi-Cola scholarship contest, his only chance to get into Harvard or Princeton. Hoping, praying, to be sent to Europe, to be part of it.

The serial numbers duly recorded, he put the packets in the attaché, took a shower, packed his rucksack, and sat for a few moments in the high-backed wicker chair, watching the smoke from his cigarette waft out of the screens into the grove, the mild winter-morning sun threading shafts of light through the branches of the mango and avocado and carambola. He was meeting Willa at ten, at the Sinclair station on the Tamiami south of town, where he could leave the truck for a few days. It was bound to be an altogether more pleasant crossing than his previous trips—speeding across the Everglades in the Guilieta with the top down, one hand on the wheel and the other caressing Willa's thigh beneath her dress.

He heard Waters flatbed coming down the rutted lane. But when he went out on the porch to greet him, he saw that it wasn't Waters. It was Vetch. Waters was careless, would sometimes leave the padlock open. There was someone next to Vetch in the cab. Someone small, a child perhaps. Vetch nestled the truck into the shade of the Australian pines and got out. Unarmed, in a checkered shirt today instead of his usual dingy balloon-seller red stripes.

"Morning," he said, stopping ten yards from the porch steps, gazing up at Narby, his glasses glaring in the sunlight. "Mind if I come up?"

"Who's that in the truck?"

"This here sho turned out to be a nice house. That high and mighty Nigra did you a damned good job. Charged you five times what you should have paid, though. That ain't right. You be giving that boy all kind of foolish ideas. But then, you never had no Nigra sense."

"What do you want, Vetch? Who's that in the truck?"

"Someone that want to talk to you. Sho. Only she kinda shy. Out here in the open, in the daylight. Hah."

Sitting quietly in the cab, half hidden in the shade. He couldn't make out the face, but he knew. She was looking at him, watching. He should have killed Vetch when he'd had the chance, that day when Vetch showed Narby the drawing of the fish camp, sitting in the truck out on Burnt Farm Road. He could it do it now. With a garden shovel or an axe. Sink it into his gut, just as he had plunged the handle of the gaff into the pilot.

"What's a matter, Nawby? Done lose the power of speech? Or maybe you quit on poor little Becca cause you done lost the power of sump'm else. Maybe it's them Ko-rean War injuries, flaring up. Giving you a malfunction. Hah."

Seething, silent, he went inside and out the back door and into the grove and found the axe and came back through the house and stood in the doorway. "Get off my property. And stay off."

"You fixing to cut some firewood? Hah. You done broke her heart, Nawby. Worse than that, you done left her high and dry. Without a Daddy to take care of her. Didn't say goodbye or nothing. All them Sad'day nights she was waiting on you. Waiting on her Yankee benefactor. You sho liked to pay her plenty. Too much. Same as you done with that son-of-a-bitch Sam Waters. I told you. Give a Nigra money you ruin 'em. Spend it all on drink and useless finery and they wind up worse off then they was before. You done ruined her, you did. You gotta pay, Nawby. It's only fair. You owe her."

Holding the axe across his chest Narby stepped down from the porch.

"I'm only trying to do good. For the Nigra people. Ain't that what you Yanks want, for us southerners to treat em fair and square? Well, here I am. My heart's a-bleeding."

Vetch backed away. But he didn't seem afraid, his mouth fixed in a slack bland smile, showing the ragged stumps of teeth.

"If I ever see you with her again. If I ever hear that you're bothering her. Touching her."

"You ain't man enough to do it. Hah. Why don't you call on the Shurf? Report me for trespassing? You wouldn't care for that, now would you? Having the Shurf come round, poking his nose in your business."

At the sound of Waters' flatbed Narby lowered the axe. Vetch turned, seeing the truck approach, and began to retreat toward his pickup. "She living with me now, out in the store. Sho. We shacking up, cause she ain't got no one to take care of her no more. No one to buy her liquor or pay for her doctor. You ought to come round one day. Have tea with me and the Missus.

Hah. You think we done finished our business, do you? Well, think again, Nawby."

Vetch climbed into the truck and began to turn around, just as Waters pulled past. Waters parked and got out and watched the truck disappear down the lane. "What he want?"

"Nothing."

"Who that Negro gal with him?"

"Nobody. Forget about it."

"What you want with that axe?"

"Don't leave the chain unlocked, Sam. Even if you're only gone for an hour."

"Yes, sir."

Narby was bathed in sweat. He dropped the axe in the dirt and went inside to shower again, change clothes. Waters was unloading the flatbed when he came out with his rucksack and the attaché. "I'll be gone for a few days, maybe a week. Keep an eye on everything. You can stay here. I'll pay you extra."

"I do that, if you want."

"Good."

Against a White, a Colored man was powerless to protect his own property. But Vetch would most likely keep away, as long as Waters was around.

The Sinclair Station was ten miles south of town, where the highway skirted the cypress swamps. He parked the truck around the back, among the other heaps, and had a word with the attendant. Willa was waiting for him in the Guilieta, parked in the shade away from the gas pumps, the top down, her head wrapped in a colorful silk scarf, her eyes hidden behind a pair of dark glasses.

"You drive, darling. I'll take in the scenery."

He tossed his things in the narrow space behind the seat and put the car in gear. The smoothness of the mechanism, the sudden pounce of speed, elated him. Within minutes they passed into the vast shimmering plains of soughing grasses, the clumped hummocks of hardwoods and royal palms rising in the distance like lonely outposts. In the whipping wind, with the roar of the engine, there was no point in trying to talk. She wore a short sleeveless dress, the silky material like a second skin slithering against the form of her body and her bare legs.

There had been two months of her moods, two months of his erratic coming and going, never quite knowing what to expect. But then, by mid-February, with two more paintings finished to her exacting if incomprehensible standards and shipped to Sidney Janis, her mood had lifted, the abrasive edge rubbed smooth. She began to show a renewed curiosity about her lover, to take an interest in his affairs, his life beyond their island romance. So, he had invited her to come with him to Miami. She was looking for some new angle, he supposed, some new vantage from which to figure him, to enjoy him. The same for Narby. The last two months had been a trial of sorts, he concluded. But on her terms alone. The island was her world, her domain. Now, for a few days, he would be the one in control.

Frankly—after New York and Paris and Venice, after Provincetown and East Hampton—Miami Beach had never entered her imagination. It was a tourist destination, part of the degraded mass culture, as blandly unappealing as a Norman Rockwell illustration or an inane television advertisement. But he promised her something different, far from the normal run of site seeing.

They crossed the General Douglas MacArthur causeway, the water choppy that afternoon, an agitated deep green speckled with thousands of whitecaps. "Biscayne Bay," he said. "On the other side, that's Miami Beach."

"It's an island?"

"More like a sandbar, reinforced with about a million tons of concrete."

"By the way, where are we staying, darling? Glamorous or quaint? Bungalow or penthouse?"

He'd considered, then rejected, the Fontainebleau and the Eden Roc, the enormous glitzy new hotels on the northern end of Collins, all that phony Francophilia, the corporation ad-man atmosphere. "Neither. Guess again."

She laughed. "All right. How about—sleazy?"

"Not quite. It's a special category."

"Is it where you stay, when you come on business?"

"Usually."

"Good. I want to observe you in your native habitat."

Instead of diverting to the Michigan Avenue garage he drove up Ocean Drive and lower Collins. It might amuse her, he thought—the old Jews hogging the benches in Lummus Park, the hotels designed to look like cruise ships, the pink hulk of the Roney Plaza with its absurd Andalusian bell tower, the neon-rimmed stucco facades with the art nouveau flourishes and plaster-of-Paris rococo reliefs moldering in the tropical climate. Parading slowly with the top down, in the chic two-seater, the handsome young couple was noticed, admired, envied.

The new class of super hotels on upper Collins had hastened the erosion of chic into shabby, a process on the Beach, Narby had noted, as inexorable as the erosion of the sand beaches behind the hotels. Like the Atlantique before it, the Calvado had begun its decline into irrelevance. Cigar smoke and ash and spilt whiskey had settled in the folds of the drapes and the nap of the carpet. Cigarette burns dotted the chintz bedspreads. Rust rimmed the bathroom fixtures and the vents, the air never quite clear of the funk of mildew and Freon. The Calvado's lyre-shaped swimming pool, once the talk of the town, had become a tank, lined with sand and vegetal sediment. Half the palms in the courtyard were headless. The lobby cocktail bar had the air of a neglected aquarium, the patrons suspended like eels in a smoke-swirled algal gloom. Still, the regular clients came back season after season, attached to some romantic memory of their first visit. And there were the oddballs, touts and lonely traveling salesmen, bleary eyed couples who moved with a dope-fiend slowness, call girls who couldn't cut it at the high-rolling hotels uptown.

They had a tenth-story ocean-view suite. Narby called down for gin rickeys. Willa stepped out on the narrow terrace, gazing at the muted variations of turquoise and blue, the dark swaths of seaweed and zones of glistening sparkle, the rollers churning in, rougher than the Gulf. A single ocean liner, in silhouette, floated on the distant horizon.

He came from behind and embraced her. She hadn't said a word since he had handed the keys to the Guilieta to the white-haired Colored doorman in epaulettes and gold buttons. "Nice view, isn't it?"

She turned to face him, kissed him on the mouth. "Spectacular."

"And the hotel?"

She laughed. "It's rather on the edge, isn't it? Like us? Excuse me for a moment. After that hot ride, I need a nice cool shower."

She came out of the bathroom drying herself with the stiff over-starched towel, not bothering to close the bedroom door when the bellboy knocked with their drinks. Narby took the tray at the threshold and tipped with his usual generosity. He went to terrace with his drink, smoking, and Willa came out to join him, naked, her hair damp. Someone in the next suite, stepping out on the adjoining terrace, would certainly get his money's worth. She began to kiss him, tugging at his trouser waist. He undressed. Facing the sea—ten floors below, the pool deck and poolside bar and the strip of beach below dotted with tourists—she gripped the balustrade and he pressed against her, from behind. Her small round breasts hung over the rail. She leaned further, raising her hips.

For a moment they must have lost their bearings. Her feet were off the ground, his arm tight around her waist, holding in her position, his hips slamming against her as she loosened and then tightened in response. Before they realized what was happening she was half over the railing. Narby heard the creak and before it was too late he leaned back hard, pulling her with him, and they tumbled into the room.

Narby landed on his back, on the carpeted floor. They might have fallen to their death. Willa didn't seem to care, to understand. She had managed to keep her balance, stay on her feet. Standing over him now she lowered herself, straddling him, grinding into him. She rode him until she was worn out, wave after wave of climax and release, and then gently he helped her off and draped her over the love seat and finished, slowly and deliberately until he lost control.

After a while he said, "They should fix that rail. It's a damned hazard."

She looked at him, finally understanding, laughing. "My god. That would have shaken them up down by the pool. I believe we would have landed on the diving board."

"You all right?"

"Just my knees, darling. They're rubbed raw."

He inspected her wounds, kissing each kneecap tenderly while she lay back on the love seat.

He went for a swim while Willa took a nap. In the water, he began to have second thoughts about taking her to Overtown, to Sir Jack's. Well, it was too late now. He couldn't very well leave her at the hotel. When he got back to the room she was in her robe on the love seat, reading a Mary McCarthy novel and sipping white wine. He took her for dinner at Giuseppe's on Espanola Way—*snapper alla putanesca* and a bottle of Chianti— and then, passing by the palatial Carib Theater on Lincoln Road, they decided to go in, to see *Bridge on the River Kwai*. After that they stopped for drinks at the Five O'Clock, a piano bar. They sat in a cozy little booth, topping up with more gin rickeys, the music quiet and rather anodyne, Narby thought. Willa was pretty far gone, leaning against his shoulder, her hand on his leg under the table, gently kneading.

He'd had a look at that rail, before they'd gone out. The bolts were coming out of the concrete. A couple more good thrusts and it would have collapsed.

"It was all very impressive, Alec Guinness, the scenery. But why the same infantile drivel, over and over? Boys and their guns. Men being men. Honor. Courage. Stiff upper lips. Have you seen *The Seventh Seal*, Philip? It's one of the very film fews, the very view films …" She laughed, a sloppy giggle. "The very few films I think important."

"It's bullshit. Propaganda. Supposed to show the horror of war. What a joke. That was more like summer camp. The real horror can't be shown. They'd hunt you down, kill you, if you tried to show what really goes on, back at Headquarters, back in Washington. Korea should have put an end to movies like that. Did for me."

"Talk about it, darling. It will do you good."

She was drunk. He could say whatever the hell he wanted. "I wasn't even a soldier. They tried to kill me, because I knew too much. MacArthur's people. Just like they killed McCoy. Just like they killed fifty-thousand boys and men. So MacArthur could run for president. There was another million dead, too. But they don't count, cause they're Yellow. Better dead than red, eh? They tried to kill me, and I fooled them. I'm not really Philip Narby. It's a fake, a name from a bank account. I'm a deserter. I work for Bill Knowles, or whoever replaced him. Bill Knowles. That name mean anything to you?"

She was slumping, her hand running up and down his thigh, coddling him under the table. "Who? Doesn't he write for *Partisan Review*? Oh darling, you're not a fake. You're the most real. I know a fake man when I meet one. Believe me. You're as real as they make them."

He got her outside and they took a cab back to the Calvado. Her arm slung over his shoulder, he led her through the lobby, steadying her. It was around midnight. They were waiting for the elevator, Willa nestled into him, nibbling at his ear. That's when Narby saw him. In the lobby. Talking to the desk clerk. Dark shiny suit, smoking a cigar. A man escorting a drunken young woman up to his room at midnight might not warrant notice in a hotel like the Calvado. But Willa's giggling, her flimsy dress, drew the clerk's prurient attention. And Sid Black, his back to the elevator, turned his head, looking over his shoulder, just in time to see them before the doors closed.

In the suite he put Willa to bed and stayed up, smoking and drinking, sitting on the love seat, waiting for the knock on the door. But it never came.

16

THE NEXT MORNING, WHILE WILLA SLEPT, Narby drove the Guilieta over the Bay to see Campos. There was going to be a struggle among the factions to fill the void, accusations about what went wrong and who was to blame. This time, hoping to catch Campos off guard, Narby was coming unannounced. Ernesto was no doubt in the thick of it, and eager for allies. Narby would renew his offer of help—not only to the remnants of M267, but to all interested parties.

History Will Absolve Me. For all of Castro's hubris, his insane optimism, the manifesto had impressed Narby: Castro's calm, erudite courtroom plea for liberty and democracy and the rule of law, the man's astonishing bravado even as he faced a life sentence. Not that Narby had ever harbored any illusions about Castro actually practicing what he preached. Under cover of all the lip service to Thomas Paine and the American Revolution, the tract was larded with promises of egalitarianism, radical land reform, loosening the grip of United Fruit. Eisenhower and

Dulles would never allow an island-nation ninety miles from mainland U.S.A. to drift leftward. When the time came, the C.I.A. would no doubt aid and abet the overthrow of Batista, but only with the proviso, tacit or explicit, that they reserved the right to oust whoever took the reins, if they misbehaved.

Still, for Castro to end like that—floundering in a swamp, shot down like a dog, his followers and sympathizers rounded up for another orgy of murder and torture. At first, the news of Castro's death had seemed a vindication, proof that Narby had been correct—behind Campos's iron-willed Saint Castro stood the doomed naïveté of a fool. But now, on his way to see his friend, Narby felt only pity. And opportunity.

Ernesto's apartment was just off the highway, south of the University, on the ground floor of a drab two-story cinder-block building. The Guilieta might provoke questions. Narby parked down the block, out of sight, and walked. Coming around the side he could see Campos through the window, sitting at the kitchen table, drinking coffee, studying his medical texts, apparently. Strange, he seemed calm, almost content. Narby moved closer, peering in through the screen. As he did so, Campos's phone rang. The Cuban rose to answer. Narby listened through the open window. The rapid fire consonant-stripped Habanero Spanish was difficult to follow, except for the familiar noms de guerre: Crescencio, Nico, El Cazador. Alejandro—that was Castro's latest codename. What the hell was going on?

Campos hung up and sat again, working at the kitchen table. Narby drew a breath, walked around to the front, and knocked. "It's me," he said, "Felipé."

Campos threw open the door. "Felipé," he gushed. "You have come for to celebrate. Please. Come inside."

Had the little man lost his mind with grief?

"Por supuesto, we knew it was another of Batista's pathetic lies. But this! This is more than we could ever hope. For this kind of gift we cannot pay someone." Narby shook his head. "Ernesto. What in hell are you talking about?"

"Ah. You have no seen."

"Seen what?"

From a pile of newspapers stacked on a kitchen chair Campos picked up a copy of the *New York Times* and recited in his best English: *Fidel Castro, the rebel leader of Cuba's youth, is alive and fighting hard and successfully in the rugged, almost impenetrable fastnesses of the Sierra Maestra, at the southern tip of the Island. President Fulgencia Batista has the cream of his army around the area, but the Army men are fighting a thus-far losing battle ...*

"Let me see that."

Campos handed it over. That morning's paper. A front-page story, with a photo: a rebel in army fatigues, a powerful yet sensitive young man, lightly bearded, holding his rifle aslant his chest, gazing up soulfully into the jungle canopy. Beneath the photo, to prove his identity, was a facsimile of Castro's signature, dated only three days ago. He was alive. The man was a goddamn miracle, back from oblivion a second time. How could it be?

"This man, Hair-bert Mateus"—the Cuban couldn't quite get his tongue around the reporter's name, Herbert Matthews— "he will be American hero of our revolution, a journalist poet, a patriot."

Narby perused it, unbelieving. *Thousands of men and women are heart and soul with Fidel Castro... a new deal for Cuba, radical, democratic, and therefore anti-Communist... the Army might yet get him, but in present circumstances he seems almost invulnerable.*

"I make you a café Cubano. Please. Sit to read. It is more better than Hemingway, yes?"

Overnight, so it seemed, Castro had gone from an intermittent sideshow in the blood-soaked carnival of Cuban politics to an unstoppable force of history. Just as Castro himself had prophesied. That Batista had put out false information about Castro's death was predictable enough. But the article went far beyond reporting the fact of Castro's survival after the botched landing of the *Granma*, holed up with a handful of his men in the Sierra. Someone very high up, with influence over America's largest newspaper, had decided that Fidel Castro was worth boosting. Campos was right. You couldn't bribe someone to write this blather. Matthews was positively singing, playing Homer to Castro's Odysseus—the exile's return, thirsty for righteous revenge.

He turned back to the front page, unable to take his eyes off the beatifying photo. "Is there independent confirmation of this?"

"Yes. I learn tambien there will be change in American policy. Stop to sell weapons to Batista. Change of diplomacy. The C.I.A. change too, yes?"

"Maybe so. I'll see what I can find out."

They talked for an hour, Campos offering Narby little sugar-powdered cakes to go along with the sweet oily black coffee. Having disciplined himself against the indigenous vices of rum and tobacco, the Cuban's weakness for dulces apparently remained a point of honor. It was Frank País, rebounding from his failure with the general insurrection, who had arranged the meeting in the Sierra between the *Times* reporter Matthews and Castro. Now that Castro's return had rekindled the armed struggle, the next step was to coordinate the 'llano' and the 'sierra,' the middle and civil servant-class dissidents in the towns and cities and the rebels fighting in the dirt-poor mountains of Oriente. The young heroes of M267, whose spectacular survival had a Hollywood appeal, were far too few and ill-armed to go it alone. Public opinion, domestic and foreign, might tip the struggle in Castro's favor. Already, only two weeks after Castro's return, the Movement had operatives in Havana working to put together a post-revolution alliance with political moderates and the professional classes, with men like Raúl Chibás and Roberto Agramonte. Such a proposed alliance, Campos explained, would prove that Castro was anything but a radical, that fears about wholesale land seizures or restrictions on private enterprise were unfounded.

The wolf, out if its cage, was going to don sheep's clothing.

"Dulles is going to let his Caribbean chief make the call on what to do about Castro," Narby told Campos in return. "Don't put the cart before the horse, my friend. There's too much tension right now between State and the Joint Chiefs and Congress to get a clear picture of any real policy change, no matter what the *New York Times* says. The *Chicago Tribune* won't be so amenable, I assure you. Still, Castro would do well to stroke the American press like a pussycat. Even the beard might work in his favor, now that he's hiding out in the jungle. You know, the backwoods look, more Abe Lincoln than Karl Marx."

As they parted Campos embraced him. "Soon, Felipé, they will call for me to come home. You come with me, yes? Help us for to build the new society. A new America, but with no racismo, y sin la pobreza. Is possible. Is no just a dream."

"I think I'll stay put for now. But thanks for the invitation."

He had come to pity, but the tables had been turned.

"This dress? Or something more demure?"

"The short one. With the scoop in front."

"It's a bit revealing. When I bend over. Don't you think?"

She was naked, having just stepped out of the shower. "Maybe a little. Nothing wrong with a little revelation, now and then."

She laughed. "You won't mind then? If other men look."

"Let them look. So long as they don't touch."

She slipped on her panties and sat in front of the mirror, combing out the tangles. "Aren't you going to tell me where we're going?"

He smiled. "No. Trust me. It's something different."

As she looked in the mirror, combing, she said, in a rather off-hand manner, "Philip. Do you love me?"

He was standing behind her, taking a shirt from the closet. She was looking at his reflection, at the scars. "I think so. I mean, I don't care for anyone else, don't want any other woman. Sorry. I can't say it any other way."

"Don't be sorry. Don't apologize for how you feel." She stopped, turning to face him. "You came quite close to death, didn't you? It must have changed you somehow. Like, I don't know, like an animal that's badly wounded and then recovers and becomes stronger. But wary, cautious. Always hanging back a little, always on the periphery." She turned to the mirror, her comb. "I can't stomach the sort of men who always have to push themselves into the center of things. They're boors. They believe in all the social nonsense, the status grubbing. You're ten times the man they are. Because you let me be myself. You're not afraid of it, are you?"

"Afraid of what?"

"The fact that I don't want babies. I don't want a husband. I don't want a mate. I only want love." She put down the comb and stood and slipped the dress over her head. "Zip me, would you?"

They ate dinner at a dark little place with dripping candles and gypsy music and Romanian steaks smothered in onions. In the car he lowered the top.

"We're leaving the Beach?"

"That's right. Can't find this kind of thing on Miami Beach."

"Animal, mineral, or vegetable?"

"Animal," he laughed. "And vegetable."

He took a cigarette from the pouch, steering with one hand. "Here. Try this."

"What is it?"

"Medicine. Take a couple of puffs. It won't hurt you. I promise."

She ducked down against the wind to light it and took small cautious puffs, coughing. "It's rather harsh. You're trying to drug me, darling, aren't you? How romantic."

He laughed. After a moment, he offered it again.

"No, thank you. Maybe later. That explains the aroma. I thought it was some new brand of tobacco."

"Watch out," he said. "It might make you go mad. With the giggles."

She started to giggle. "That's funny. How funny the word giggle sounds. When you're giggling."

He reached over and slid his hand under her dress and squeezed her thigh. She squealed, gripping his wrist, laughing rather wildly. "Don't! You'll make me wet my dress. Stop! See what you've done. You've made me silly."

"Don't worry. I'll make sure you get home, safe and sound."

"Where are we going, Philip? Can't you tell me now?"

"Nope."

"Not some kind of burlesque show?"

"Of course not."

"Good. You're so good, Philip. Too good, too original, for that. Besides, all those women are frigid. That's why they can strip in front of fat ugly strangers. They don't feel the slightest pang. All right. I know. The jai alai. Is that it?"

They drove past the cluster of tall office buildings and crossed the railroad tracks. The sidewalks became lively again, the avenue illuminated with flashing signs. He drove down Second Avenue, past the Harlem Square and the Lyric Theater and the Rockland Palace.

People were looking at them, a White couple in an exotic sports car, on display with the top down. "Philip? Are you sure you know where you're going?"

"Of course."

"Philip," she said, a sudden sobriety tightening her voice. "Is it safe here?"

"You're safe with me."

"Really. Philip."

"Trust me. Relax."

She leaned her head back and closed her eyes. "I'm being silly. You've rendered me silly. Of course I trust you."

"Good."

They passed the fortress-like Saint John the Baptist Church. The side streets were dark. He turned. Sir Jack's was midway down the block. The ice-blue neon sign glowed against the dark shabby storefronts and sagging porches: a neon arrow, angled at the middle and pointing toward the entrance, with the words SIR JACK'S spelled out in gothic-type letters. The sign might draw you in, if you happened to peer down the street. At the moment, the sidewalk in front was empty.

He parked a few doors away, the neon reflecting off the metal skin of the Guilieta, raised the top, and reached behind the seat for the attaché.

"It's perfectly all right. Everybody knows me here."

"They do? What's that for, love?" She meant the attaché.

"Come on." He took her by the hand and they crossed the street. The new metal door was to dissuade break-ins. He swung it open and they stepped inside.

Red sat at the first barstool—tall, with a graying moustache, his eyes a bit bloodshot, his fedora tipped back on his head, smoking a thin crooked cigar. Music, a jazz combo, came from the back room.

"Phil. How's my man?" Red shook his hand.

"I'm good. How's everything tonight?"

"So so. For a Friday."

Red was the manager. He booked the musicians, too. Depending on the night, who was playing, Red would sit in once in a while. His playing hadn't kept pace with the newer sounds, his dexterity impaired by arthritis. Or so he claimed.

"Red. I'd like to meet you a friend of mine. Willa."

Red looked at her now. "A pleasure."

"Hello, Red."

Narby leaned over the bar and greeted the bartender, a woman named Denise, someone Bobby had recommended.

Pleasant looking. But a motherly type. So they didn't bother her too much. "Two gin rickeys, Denise. We'll be in back. Red. I'll catch you in a few minutes."

He took Willa's hand and led her through the bar into the back room. Half the tables were occupied, about twenty-five people. They sat on the banquette. The lamps and sconces were dimmed by red shades, the air hazed with blue smoke. A quintet was on the bandstand, the bass player—a tall young man in a tight charcoal-gray suit, white shirt, blue tie, his face glistening with sweat from the exertion and the spotlights—was finishing his solo. The drummer kicked in, then the piano. A wave of applause rose as the trumpet took up the melody. The band was good, very tight. A cool relaxed swing.

Willa pressed against him, holding his hand.

The band went into the next tune without stopping, a ballad, the trumpet player—short and stocky, in an open-necked blue shirt, his cheeks bulging, his eyes closed—breaking up the phrases, reinventing the standard flow of notes.

Denise brought their drinks. Another night without a single White face, despite the advertisement Narby placed every Friday in the back pages of the *Miami Herald. Sir Jack's. Jazz every night. The only place in town for modern hot cool bop swing. Never a cover. Air-conditioned for your listening comfort. All welcome!*

The people in the back room were mostly friends of the musicians, he guessed. Sir Jack's did most of its business in the front, with the barflies. He put his lips to Willa's ear. "You like the music?"

"Yes," she said, almost murmuring. "It's melting into my ears." She turned to look at him, close enough to kiss. She was high, her eyes bright and a bit glazed. Nervous, too. Clinging to him. "How did you ever discover this place?"

"It's mine. I own it."

"You're joking."

"No joke. We opened last fall. While you were in New York."

"This is your—your business venture?"

"One of them. More a hobby, really." He lifted the highball. "Wish me success."

She drank, just a sip, wary of losing what little was left of her equilibrium, he supposed. Letting her eyes dart about the room. Was there a single Negro among Willa's art crowd in New York, or Paris, or Venice? Her prejudice was that of omission, he figured. She wanted nothing to do with the sterile corporate drudges, the white-collar puritanical dross of American life, the Dick Nixon types, the sexless-polyps, as she called them, who ran the world. Well, this should be more to her taste. If she could swallow it.

He lit a cigarette and gave it to her and lit one for himself. "Just tobacco," he reassured her.

The trumpet veered into a solo, flurried notes bursting forth and then dispersing, leaving space, and then clusters, making the ballad bristle against its own lush slowness. For Florida musicians they were top shelf. But if you were young and Black and talented, sooner or later you went to New York, and never looked back. Like Fats Navarro from Key West, who had played with Bird and was dead at twenty-six. Or the Adderly brothers from Tampa, Nat and Julian "Cannonball"—when Narby had met him, they called him "Cannibal"—making waves now on 52nd Street and in Greenwich Village.

After the patter of claps, the tall bass player leaned down over the microphone. "Thank you. That was something we call"—he paused, looking quizzically at the drummer—"*You Never Knew*. Or something like that." They all laughed, as if in secret communication. "Ain't that what you call it? No? That's cool, cause that's what I was playing. Y'all stick around. We're just taking a short pause. To refresh."

Out of nowhere Bobby appeared at their table. Same elongated crescent-moon face, sharp nose, protruding Adam's apple. But the moustache had evolved into a neat little goatee. In place of the sharkskin suit and vermillion vine there was now a tunic-like collarless shirt with yellow and green stitching, and a braided-leather necklace; in place of the red felt pork-pie hat, a black beret.

"Hello, Bobby."

"What's shaking, Phil? Long time no see, man. Where you been hiding?"

"This is my friend, Willa."

He made a little bow. "Pleased to meet you, mam'selle."

"Good evening."

"Hah. No wonder you been hiding, man."

Willa smiled at the compliment.

Bobby was a semaphore, a beacon, an advance warning. He knew the streets, the beat police, the dealers and junkies and pimps, could separate the inveterate drunks from those who merely liked a good time, had acquaintance with all the best players in town, knew all the places in Overtown and Allapattah and the Grove that sold jazz records and second-hand instruments. Narby paid Bobbie a hundred a month, to help Red. And Bobbie sold marijuana. Reefer. Tanga. But never junk. The gangsters from out of town had commandeered the heroin trade. "Mixing it up with another Black man is one thing," he had told Narby, "but man them Jew and Guinea motherfuckers is evil, like them sharks cruising between here and Havana, smelling for blood." Besides, Bobby considered junk bad for the community, bad for the Race. Not like tanga. That was soul stuff. Bobby even sold to the preacher down the street.

"You heard these cats before?"

"No. I don't think so."

"You dig it?"

"Yeah. They from around here?"

"Trumpet man down from Tampa. Ass-ugly, but he can blow. Bass player from Augustine. Pretty boy, ain't he?"

"Maybe we should offer them a regular gig. Make them the house band."

"Yeah, that's cool. Only when we going to bring down some of them mean New York motherfuckers, like you said? Listen man, I got a letter from a friend last week. Living up in Harlem. He's shedding with Charlie Mingus. Can you dig that? Man, that's the baddest shit I ever heard. Big serious heavy deep cat. Got the consciousness, too."

"The problem is, Bobby, we can't get anyone like that down here for just one gig. We'd have to line up other gigs, more dates. Otherwise, with all the travel expense, it's not worth their while."

He had tried to convince Goldfarb to share bookings. But the clubs on the Beach were going the opposite direction, the White crooners like Sinatra and Pat Boone, or sticking with the older generation, Nat Cole, Sarah Vaughn. Rock n' roll, too, now, that it was hitting the charts. But jazz? Music without lyrics that you can't dance to, can't sing along with? A losing proposition. Goldfarb wasn't interested. Besides, Narby doubted if the younger Negro players could stomach playing in Miami Beach anymore, no matter how good the pay.

"You'll work it out, man. I got faith in you, brother." Bobby jerked his head. "Couple cats out back waiting for us. Come on."

He didn't want to drag Willa out into the alley. She was slumped against him, smoking, her hand on his leg under the table. "After the next set."

"Sure, man." Bobby got up. "Catch you later."

"Everything all right?"

"Mmm. Very all right. Who was that?"

"Bobby. One of my business partners."

She was moving her head, her hair swaying from side to side. "What other business ventures you hiding up your sleeve?" She laughed.

"How about another drink."

"I don't think I should." She paused. "Well. All right. One more. Yes."

He went to the bar and came back.

"Your house, out in the woods, Philip. What's it like?"

"Rustic. I'd say. Rustic to primitive."

She kissed him, their faces close. "Will you take me there? Show me."

"Yes. Anywhere you want."

"Philip. When I asked you." She shrugged, kissing him again. "Philip. Do you have other women?"

"Sure. A harem. A different girl for every night."

"No, darling. I'm serious."

"Really? You seem more drunk than serious."

"You doped me up!" She laughed. "Remember?"

She had spoken a little too loud. He stroked her under the table, lowering his voice. "No one who really matters. Only you. Like I told you. It's love."

"When I'm in New York? Or when I make you go away, so I can work? There must be any number of women itching to take their clothes off for you, darling. For all I know you might have a little wife somewhere, stashed away for rainy days. Don't laugh. I've seen it, I've met them. These men who have little wives, stashed away. And children, too."

"So?"

She leaned away, as if to get him in focus. "No. On second thought, no. You're too original. Even for that."

After the next set, the music very good, enthralling to those who had an ear for it, Narby turned to her. "Willa. I've got to do a little business." She was fading in and out. "I'll be right back."

He started to get up. She latched on his arm. "Don't leave me alone, Philip. Please."

"Just give me ten minutes."

"I'll go with you." She said it rather too loudly.

"All right. Take your purse."

He took her by the hand. There was a storage room behind the bar, piled with liquor boxes, mops and brooms, extra chairs. He pulled one out. "Just sit there."

"What happens in here, Philip?"

Bobby and Red came in, shutting the door after them. Narby could see that they didn't much like Willa's presence. He lifted the attaché on top of a pile of boxes and clicked it open. Red handed him the account book and showed him what money had gone out, what had come in. Narby gave it a cursory glance and handed two of the packets to Red.

"Your lady friend all right?" Bobby said.

"Sure. Just a little too much too drink."

"I'm fine, thank you," she said. "It's like when I was a little girl. Ducking into the closet to hide from the grown-ups." She laughed.

"That's right," Bobby said, laughing with her. "No grown-ups allowed." He turned and took a brown paper grocery bag out from behind the boxes. "This is the soulful shit, Phil. Even better than the last. Grown to order from south of the border." Narby took a moment, feeling the heft of the bag then reaching in and taking out a handful, smelling it and examining it in his palm. "Here," Bobby said, "have a taste." He handed Narby a stick and flicked his lighter. Narby took a deep drag, held it in his lungs, then slowly let it stream from his nostrils, filling the closet with blue smoke.

"Yeah. O.K. So what's this, two pounds?"

"Kilo, man. We do it scientific. Two point two avoirdupois."

He rolled the bag closed and stuffed it in the attaché and gave Bobby his packet.

"That your Italian job outside, man? That some slung chariot."

"It's Willa's," he said.

"No shit? Mam'selle got style."

"The cops come by yesterday," Red said. "Same old garbage. Nothing to worry about."

"I'll be back in a couple of weeks. Book these guys for the month, if they can stick around. O.K.?" Sooner or later, he was going to break down and ask Bobby. But not tonight, not with Willa there.

"They be around. Only look at the house tonight. It ain't enough. You know that. We need that big name, man. Like you always said."

"Miles Davis. That big enough? I'm working on it. Trust me."

17

THE WEEK OF THE PEMBAKERS' end-of-the-season party Narby had seen Willa's name in the *Wall Street Journal*, in an article about George Blanero, a Republican congressman from Indiana who had been awarded a Gold Medal of Honor from the American Artists Professional League "for his congressional exposure of Communism in art."

The fourth-term legislator, perhaps the most outspoken of his peers, has identified all modern art movements—surrealism, Dadaism, futurism, cubism, and abstract expressionism—as "a glorification of the insane and the indecent, a public outrage perpetrated on the good sense of the American people by a cabal of Ivy Leaguers and the fashionable Alger Hiss crowd who control the museums and organize the big exhibitions." Disputing fellow Republican Nelson Rockefeller's more generous characterization of contemporary American abstract art as "free enterprise painting," Blanero condemned such artists as "tools of the Kremlin."

"If you knew how to read them," Congressman Blanero asserted, the ostensibly meaningless globs and splatters and zigzags of abstract art contained "secret codes and maps revealing strategic NATO and U.S. weapons sites to our enemies behind the Iron Curtain." Asked to provide names, Blanero produced a roster of many of today's most prominent painters, including the recently deceased Jackson Pollock, Franz Kline... and Willa Branton. The

Congressman declined, however, to identify which artists in particular might be guilty of treason.

The man was a rabid dog in the McCarthy mold. Still, it made Narby think. The touring exhibitions had skirted the apron of the Eastern Bloc: Helsinki, Stockholm, West Berlin, Munich, Vienna, Trieste, Istanbul. Would the tours not provide excellent cover for espionage and propaganda operations? Blanero was a crackpot, but perhaps the rabid dog, barking up the wrong tree, had picked up the right scent.

Willa had no politics. She called herself a radical individualist, an existential sensualist. She hated systems, corporations, mass-produced culture, the herd mentality, the whining traditionalists, the Brahmin champions of good taste. A self-style renegade—and yet, she enjoyed the largess of the wealthiest cultural institutions on earth, the Museum of Modern Art and the Rockefeller Foundation. It wasn't a contradiction. It was a plan, an idea. Not her idea, certainly. If Willa and her ilk were in fact anyone's tools, they were hanging in Dulles' CIA shop, not the Kremlin's.

Since their escapade in Miami, Narby and Willa had grown closer. He no longer disguised the dope, no longer played at being some mysterious man whose means of existence were shrouded in secrecy. His money, he told her, came from a dead man, a buddy from the Army killed in Korea. Something like an inheritance. He bought up land to park the money, because he hated banks, trusted no one. He lived in the jungle, surrounded by a thousand acres of pine waste, because he didn't want to be bothered by a lot of nosey neighbors and niggling regulations. He bought a rundown Negro bar and turned it into a jazz club, on a whim, because he dug the music, liked hanging around the players, the scene. He followed his own rules, flaunted his own eccentric tastes and desires, associated with anyone he damned well pleased without regard to status or propriety. Yes, he liked the dope, too. It cooled the fire of his war injuries and inflamed his passion. Made him see color where the rest of the world saw black and white.

"You have a problem with that?"

"Not at all, Philip. I wish it did the same for me. But a puff or two only makes me tired and unfocused. Or worse, it makes want to crawl away somewhere and hide. I believe the clinical term is 'induced paranoia.' I'll stick to wine and cocktails. And fucking. You got a problem with *that*?"

He laughed.

"I'm so glad you're coming to the party. Tara's looking forward to meeting you."

"What else did you tell her about me? Give me a head's-up."

"Very little, actually. I've hardly seen her this year, or any of the others. All the wives, they're dying to lay their eyes on you, up close. I just hope it's not too boring. There'll be a lot of island talk, Colony business. As usual."

While Willa dressed he stepped out onto the terrace. He would finally meet Dan Atlee, face to face. Veteran of the Inchon invasion, of the retreat from the Chosin Reservoir. Narby's story might sound plausible to an outsider, but to someone like Atlee who had served under MacArthur? He ought to stick as close to the truth as possible: Eighth Army, twenty-forth Infantry, Task Force Smith. Defending the Pusan Perimeter. Blowing the bridges over the Naktong during the height of the N.K.P.A. onslaught, hundreds of civilians—old men, women and children—tossed in the blasts like confetti, bodies flung into the darkness of the river below. The killing heat. The thirst. The loss of radio contact, the misdirected mortar fire. Trying to hold the hills behind the Naktong. The order to "stand or die." Hit by enemy fire. A month at the hospital in Kobe. A little R 'n R in Tokyo, a little I 'n I—intercourse and intoxication. Sent back, of course. Like everyone else whose arms and legs and balls were intact. But then what? He hadn't thought it through.

The worst POW camps were up by the Yalu. Half the prisoners dying from infections and disease and starvation, or freezing to death. And the torture, holes burned in the skin, castration, tongues ripped out. Electro-shock. Brainwashing. Wasn't that what Knowles had assumed, that Narby had been held prisoner? If Altee wanted to play the hero, the what-did-you-do-in-the-war-Daddy game, Narby might be cornered into playing that card. No matter what Atlee had been through, nothing could come close to that. Where he was captured, what they had done to him, how he had managed to escape—it was locked inside, inaccessible, a fortress of unbearable shame and suffering. Swaths of his memory burnt away, like green pastures scorched to a blanket of ash.

He took a few drags off a stick and went inside. "Want a drink?"

"No thanks, darling. I—well, yes, why not?"

He went downstairs for a bourbon, to settle his nerves, and came back up with a glass of wine for Willa.

"They all consider themselves patrons of the arts," Willa was telling him, "but it's never about the art itself. It's the galas that excite them, or the Opera, the board meetings where they rub shoulders with the high and mighty. Remove one of my paintings out of that world of Rockefellers and Van Dorens, out of that social frame, and they'd just as soon wipe their feet on it. Frankly, that's the way it should be. If you think about it. I put gas in my car, but do I give a damn about Dan Atlee's oil tankers, his pipelines? Do I understand all that? Of course not. They understand me as a professional. They're impressed with my rising stock, my rank in the standings. It's the wives, actually. They have to get their thrills by sucking it off the culture sphere. A sublimation of the sex drive. After the good catch, after the honeymoon, after two or three children, with the important man-of-the-world husband working late, away on business for weeks on end. The cocks fly the roost and the hens are left at home, restless. Frantic."

"But you like Tara, right? Isn't she friends with Endicott Ward?" Ward was the famous art critic, Willa's champion, the man who had sold her the Sanmora house on such favorable terms.

"Yes. Tara's above the cut. I do like her. Very much. That's why I'm wearing this long skirt. Like a Sicilian peasant. She expects me to be different, to play my part. She would be terribly disappointed if I came dressed like the rest of them, in some casual cocktail smock from Bergdorf's or Saks."

Narby wore a silk sports shirt, open at the neck, and linen trousers. The Miami Beach bon-vivant clothes. "This all right?"

"You're too damned handsome for your own good. Christ, they'll be drooling all over you. Yes. Just the right touch of the bourgeois, darling. But you don't fool me. I know what's underneath."

It was dark when they left, walking down the dunes hand in hand.

The walkway leading from the dunes to the Pembakers' garden had been festooned with flaming torches atop bamboo poles. Willa led him through the gate. There was a wide lawn flanked on one side by a tennis court and on the other by a swimming pool twice the size of Willa's, glowing blue from the underwater lights. More torches were scattered about the yard, oozing an oily black scented smoke that kept off the mosquitoes. There was a flower garden, a vine-twisted pergola, and beyond that, gathered on the large flagstone patio, thirty or so people—the Colony—their faces softly flickered by the torches, bathed in the soft nimbus of the blue and green electric flood lamps hidden in the bushes. Behind them rose the terraced bulk of the house, a three-story seaside castle of dark weathered wood and rough hewn stone, the kind of stolid suburban estate against which Willa's steel and concrete bunker asserted its cold sleek defiance.

Narby recognized most of them: the dog walker, a couple of shell collectors, the surf fisher, the novel reader, the bearded stroller. Two Negro women in maids' uniforms circulated among the guests bearing trays of pinkish champagne cocktails and canapés. Pembaker was holding forth to the gathering. He and Willa stood at the edge of the group and listened.

"So, I'm afraid the causeway is going to happen, whether we like it or not. The Village is behind it, pretty much a hundred percent. Frankly, they outnumber us. Still, we can delay it, maybe for another two or three years. And in that time, if we're smart, we should be able to put in place sufficient roadblocks to hinder any further haphazard development. At least on our side of the island."

"But doesn't the Village understand what havoc the causeway will bring?" It was the bearded stroller. "They've never liked outsiders, Dalt. Why the hell are they changing course? The ferry's good enough. If a little inconvenient."

"It's economics, Jerry. They can't survive on fishing anymore. And they certainly can't survive only on what we spend every season. There's the irony. We broke open the isolation. They've had a taste of the modern world. They've heard the boom."

"What about the toll? If it's high enough, that might dissuade the hoi polloi. Was there talk about the toll?"

Narby glanced around, trying to figure which one was Atlee.

"It's too early for that. But certainly that's something we'll pursue when the time comes. Anyway, what I wanted to tell you about was the sanctuary issue. It was all quite amusing," Pembaker went on. For a man in his fifties he was in good shape, exercised and vigorous. A good three inches shorter than Narby. In a blue blazer and sharply pressed trousers and Oxford shirt open at the neck, his thinning brown hair combed back, his sun-reddened complexion a bit purple, from the web of capillaries pushing under the skin.

"Let me see if I can get him right. Commissioner Sunderland." Pembaker cleared his throat, puffed out his chest a bit. "Well, Mister Pembayka, I don't see why the pay-pul of Lacoosa Counta need to give away good drainage to some passel of buds. We got 'nuff buds to go all round Lacoosa County twenta times. We got us crows and egret and redwing blackbud and pigeons and yella bella sapsuckers in ev'ra tree and yard from heya to yonda and back again. Way I see it, them buds ought to be setting aside some land fo' us human folk."

Narby laughed with rest of them. He'd heard about it from Willa, Tara's crusade to establish a bird sanctuary in the marshes on the bay side of the island. Tara was a nature lover, a preservationist, a follower of John Muir and Marjorie Douglas, champion of the Everglades. For the others, probably, the sanctuary was just one of the roadblocks, as Pembaker had put it, a way to limit the Villagers' rights over parts of the island.

One of the wives, a woman in her forties, wearing an emerald-green satin Chinese smock with oblong ivory buttons, interrupted. "Well, " she said, addressing the group as though Pembaker weren't there. "I don't see why Dalton doesn't just pick up the phone and call Fred Seaton. Why don't we go over their heads, with the National Refuge Act?" Narby recognized her. It was Tara. "Surely the man who's going to make Alaska a state could bring some pressure to bear." She looked at her husband, a pleasant wry smile on her face. "Is it really necessary, Dalton, to dicker with these local suzerains?"

The group turned toward Pembaker, waiting for his answer. He reached into his blazer pocket and took out a cigarette and a lighter. After a meditative exhalation, he shook his head thoughtfully. "Tara plays hardball." Everyone laughed. It was a charming quirk in their relationship, referring to each other like that, in the third person. "Look, here's the thing," he continued, striking a less jocular tone. "We don't want to alienate these local fellows. We've got the causeway initiative to worry about, the easements for the marina, the dispute with the Village over beach access. Do we really want them to think of us that way, as a bunch of "—he twirled his hand in the air, conjuring the right phrase—"a bunch of Federal agents? Yankee carpetbaggers?"

"Next thing you know, hell, they'll be bitching because we ordered them to let their Negroes go to school," the bearded man said, provoking a few laughs.

Pembaker frowned. The maid with the tray was standing a few feet away. "Look. There's going to be development. Ultimately, that's a good thing. For Florida, for the South. We all know that. At present, we've got the very best of it, right here. That gives us a huge advantage, a forward position. We play our hands right, play carefully and graciously, we'll get most of what we want. I assure you. Not everything, but the essentials. And we'll no doubt increase the value of the Trust. Five, maybe ten fold. Besides," he said, arching his eyebrows, his face tightening, looking at his wife: "I called Fred Seaton. About two hours ago. We're discussing an executive order."

The group let out a laugh, a few claps. Tara looked at him, only mildly thankful. "That's our boy," she said, coolly.

"But not until we've gone the other route, as far as possible. I want a couple of the commissioners in on it. To make it look like it was their idea all along. Bob Sunderland and maybe Andy Crawford. They know we can still give the County a lot of grief about that causeway, if we put our minds and wallets to it. Crawford likes to horse swap. He's telling me that with all this Negro integration trouble"—the maid's presence didn't seem to matter now—"he's lost all faith in the Democratic Party. A bred-in-the-bone son of Dixie contemplating a move to the Republicans! Now how do you like that?"

There was a lull. Narby heard himself addressed.

"What do you think, Mr. Narby?" It was Tara, looking his way through the group. They parted a bit, everyone turning. "I understand you live out in the county, north of Myerton. Have you had much dealing with the commission or the zoning board, or whatever they call themselves? We could use another opinion here, one a bit less, well, less vested in our particular interests."

He slipped his hand from Willa's. He didn't appreciate being called out like that. But Tara was smiling at him. A not unattractive woman, despite her age. "I doubt I can be of any help," he said, getting his bearings. "I'm pretty much on my own out there." They were waiting for him to explain. "I supply my own electricity, my own water, maintain my own private road. It's all a bit primitive, at the moment. I doubt that the County even knows I'm out there. Well, except for the property taxes. Which frankly don't amount to very much." He stHHh He stopped. It was a dead end.

A man in a polo shirt and a crew cut, younger than Pembaker, someone Narby didn't recognize, said: "That's ranch country out there. That mixed Brahman breed. Do you have cattle, Mr. Narby?"

"No." They were waiting for more. "No cattle where I am. I bought up acreage from the Putnam Lumber Company. They had pretty much finished their operations out there, and... "

"Turpentine, wasn't it? Rosin? A damned good business, especially during the war. If you could keep the labor costs down."

"That's right," Narby said, looking at his inquisitor. A tightly wound man with a stolid oval face. "But eventually the trees gave out."

"Prices fell like a stone when the Asian market opened up again. Same thing that happened with the price of rubber, after we defeated the Japs." The polo shirt cocked his head, as though he was correcting Narby in front of the group.

Narby turned to Tara. "There's really nothing out there. Scrub pine, palmetto brush, possums and rattlesnakes. I don't get in anyone's way. And I don't go to the county for anything, really." She was smiling at him, admiring him. "Hm. Maybe I should call Fred Seaton, too. Apply for statehood."

They laughed. Willa had moved away, the better to watch him perform, he supposed. He was the outsider, someone of interest. They would have an idea of who he was, from Tara. Willa's friend, possibly a new fiancé.

"The bigger point I'm trying to make," Pembaker said, taking up the thread, "we're on the threshold of a big change. These old boys down here might play dumb, but they see what's coming down the pike. That's why we have to act now, and act with prudence. We can't think of it as us versus them anymore. We need to form a wedge, so to speak. Jerry, Dan, you know what I mean. The more money that moves down here, money from the north, the more pressure there's going to be from Washington. Especially with labor issues, and integration, of course. That's to our advantage. If they can help us with these strictly local matters—the causeway, zoning restrictions, easements, beach access—well, we can offer them leverage with Washington, offer to use our influence."

Tara began to laugh. "Goodness sake, Dalton. We're not negotiating with the Soviets. We're talking about a bird sanctuary and beach access and a bridge or two. Not a missile treaty."

Dalton took it in stride, laughing alongside her. A few of the woman in dresses and bare legs had started fidgeting, rubbing their ankles. "I'm getting bitten alive," someone finally said.

"How about we move inside," Dalton suggested. "We're mixing martinis. And the ever-popular daiquiris."

"The food's on the buffet. Please, everyone, help yourselves." Tara stood by the French doors, rather striking in her shimmering green Chinese outfit, making certain everyone obeyed. Narby kept his spot on the patio, smoking, hanging back until Willa came up to him and took his hand. She waited until the last of them had passed inside.

"Tara. This is Philip. Philip Narby."

She held out her hand. She was petite, a pretty face only lightly etched with middle age, a bit impish, her chestnut hair cut shorter than Willa's, hanging in a fringe across her forehead and ears. Nice soft mouth. "So very nice to meet you, Philip. Thank you for coming. I hope I didn't put you on the spot?"

"Good to meet you, Tara. No. Not at all."

"Good. Besides." She paused, looking as his face. "I can't imagine Willa Branton taking up with anyone faint of heart."

Willa laughed.

Tara laid her hand on Narby's arm. "I'm terrible, aren't I? But you'll get used to me. Willa, has Philip seen the loggerheads yet? They're late this year. I hope we don't miss them."

She meant the sea turtles that made the moonlight pilgrimage up the dunes every spring to lay their eggs in the sand. Tara spoke for a moment about a few other not-to-be-missed species that dwelled on their island paradise, the yellow-crowned night heron, the roseate spoonbill, the magnificent frigate bird. "Sanmora is blessed, really. I so hope Dalton can get things moving on the refuge. God knows I've sprained my wrist writing letter after letter."

Narby's gaze drifted inside, through the doors. The polo shirt. That had to be Dan Atlee. They hadn't even been introduced and already Narby felt the tension, the acid.

"Please, Philip. Go in and have something to eat. The daiquiris are made with the key limes from our garden. Wonderfully tart."

"Thanks."

"Willa, sweetheart," she said, turning away. "I have something I want to show you. Some pictures we bought in Italy. Nothing so *au courant* like your fabulous things. We're fuddy duddies, you know that. But I'd like your expert opinion. I think they aren't half bad. Endicott thinks so, too."

"Of course. Go ahead, Philip. I'll find you later."

He wasn't hungry. He went to the patio bar and took one of the martinis, freshly shaken and poured, and stepped indoors. The group was crowded around the buffet in the adjacent dining room and for the moment he was alone. It was a spacious living room with an enormous stone hearth, a ridiculous extravagance for a house in the subtropics. Dark wood walls, walnut perhaps, with built-in bookshelves, heavy wood furniture with colorful embroidered cushions in a variety of styles, Mexican looking, Narby thought, and Polynesian. On the mantel were the predictable seashells and starfish and elaborate twists of driftwood. The rugs, fairly new, had Navajo designs. Carrying his martini he glanced at the rows of books. Degas, Monet, Picasso, Arthur Dove, Thomas Hart Benton, books on natural history and cooking and gardening, tour guides of the English countryside and southern France, *Audubon's Sketch Books*, *The Arts of Pre-Columbia America*, *The Golden Bough*, leather-bound subscription editions of *Anna Karenina*, *Madame Bovary*, *Leaves of Grass*, *Portrait of a Lady*, *The House of Mirth*, *The Adventures of Tom Sawyer*. On the top shelf, the titles harder to make out, rested the more controversial volumes: *Lolita*, *Lady Chatterly's Lover*, *The Group*, *Ulysses*, *Coming of Age in Samoa*.

A few of the guests were filtering into the living room in pairs, bearing plates of food. Narby introduced himself, shook hands. Middle-aged, mild mannered, dressed in relaxed casual attire, fresh, smelling of soap and perfume. The harmless ones. He turned and saw that Atlee was still at the buffet. With his wife, Sheila, by his side. Not much to look at there. Spreading at the hips, a blowzy sunburned platinum blonde. The type that might have been a sex kitten when they'd met, in college, maybe. But then, after marriage and then the children, after Atlee came back from Korea, the loneliness and drinking would have taken its toll.

Tara and Willa appeared, coming from a hallway, and after a word with Willa—Tara seeing that he looked out of place, and without food—they separated and Willa escorted him to the buffet where dutifully, to please his hostess, he put a few things on a plate. They sat on the patio, joined by the bearded man, Jerry, a chemical engineer, retired, and his wife, Margaret.

After some desultory chitchat about the weather, the excellent local fishing, Narby said, "What did you work on at DuPont, Jerry?"

"Thermoplastic polymers, primarily. Tinkering with the variations in intrinsic viscosity for… "

"No iron-Dacron," his wife butted in. She was tipsy. "No one understands that chemistry-class lingo, Jerry. It's changing the entire garment industry. Goodbye ironing boards."

"But how does it feel next to the skin?" Willa asked, rubbing her leg against Narby's under the table. "Fine cotton and silk have such a sensual quality."

"A what?"

"You don't happen to know a fellow named Bill Knowles? He was with DuPont for a while. Maybe you ran into him."

"DuPont's a pretty big corporation. Bill Knowles? Was he at the Delaware facility?"

It was a game now. He asked everyone he met, even the musicians at Sir Jack's. He was beginning to think Knowles was a phantom, something he'd conjured up that morning in Havana, hanging about waiting for that scum Sylvio. Had the shakes pretty bad, as he recalled. A fever dream, an hallucination.

Except for that one maddeningly vague letter, delivered to PN care of the Smoker's Den. That was just like Knowles. To not even allow Narby the comfort of dismissing him as a figment.

"Yeah. Delaware. Tall good-looking guy, very relaxed, damned sure of himself. That smug Harvard smile."

Jerry looked at him as if he were raving. "No," he said. "Never heard of him."

"Well if you did, I wish you would have introduced me," Margaret chimed in with a stupid laugh.

Willa was gazing at him. It was another quirk, another layer. "That sounds just like *you*, darling," she said, stroking his hand as if they were alone. "Tall, good-looking. Sure of himself."

"More middle-aged. Maybe fifty. No? Maybe I'm wrong. Maybe he was with Dow Chemical, not DuPont. Or Allbright Paper. Never mind."

Some other guests came to join them. Narby excused himself, as if getting up to refill his plate, while Willa went to the powder room. He wandered the grounds for a few minutes, the garden and yard three times the size of Willa's, the house looming up, an enormous terrace off the second floor looking out over the dunes and the ocean. You could hide a lot in a house like this: radar and other surveillance devices, radio broadcasting equipment, crates of weapons. There was probably a fall-out shelter, too. He walked over to the hedge, in the darkness beyond the light of the torches and the flood lamps. The dunes were higher here, providing a natural defensive bulwark.

Or he could just say nothing. Yeah, I was in Korea. Don't like to talk about it. He would look Atlee in the face. "I did my duty. It wasn't very pleasant. I'd prefer to forget it. Simple as that."

He took a breath, flicked away his cigarette and strolled back toward the house, thirsty for another drink, pausing as he reached the open French doors, scanning the room for Atlee, the polo shirt and crew cut with the thick arms and thick neck. The way to the bar was clear. There were bottles out now and an ice bucket. He was about to pour a drink, the bottle in his hand, when Pembaker came toward him from the dining room. "Young man," he said, rather solicitously, gently gripping Narby's arm, "come with me. I've got something you might like. Something special."

He led Narby down a hallway, the walls hung with framed photographs, and opened a door, Pembaker closing it behind them as they entered. It was an office of some sort. There was an old-fashioned desk, shelves crammed with books and objects, three club chairs arranged around a rug, an antique-looking globe on a stand. The smell of wood and leather and pipe tobacco. "I keep the good stuff locked away." He opened the door of the cabinet against the opposite wall and took out a heavy cut-crystal decanter and two matching tumblers. "Would you care for some very fine, very old, very mellow scotch whiskey? I recommend it neat."

"I would indeed. Thank you."

Pembaker poured out an inch in each tumbler and handed one to Narby. "Cheers."

They tapped glasses. Narby made a gesture of appreciation, nodding his head after the first sip. "Excellent," he said. "Superb."

"You don't quirt soda into something like this." He waited until Narby had taken another sip, watching his reaction. "We throw these parties every year. For the Colony. It's Tara's passion. The social butterfly. I hope you don't mind me dragging you from the festivities."

"Not at all. Frankly, I'm not much for parties."

"Good. It'll give us a chance to talk. Sit down."

Narby lowered himself into one of the club chairs. "Can I offer you a little something to go with the scotch?" He opened a drawer and took out a slender silver tube and handed it to Narby. "You don't often come across these in the States. A Cohiba del Rey, in limited production. One of Churchill's favorites."

"Thanks. But. I don't usually—"

"Keep it, then. For later. One afternoon, when you're not busy, take a long walk on the beach, by yourself, and give it a try. Sometimes, in the open air, the possibilities of a perfect cigar suddenly overcome you. Then you're hooked."

Narby laughed. "All right. I'll do that." He slipped it into his pocket. "Thanks."

"This is my favorite room in the house. The inner sanctum." Pembaker began to pack his pipe with tobacco. "Every man needs a place in the house cordoned off from the domestic bustle, don't you think? But. You're young and single. So," he laughed, "you wouldn't know, would you?"

Narby smiled, taking a look around: atlases, books on Mexico, Guatemala, Peru, the bottom shelves tightly packed with the yellow spines of *National Geographic*. On the walls more landscape photographs, much like the ones in the hallway: volcanic mountains and lakes, overgrown jungle ruins, little tumbledown towns and villages, dark-skinned people in native garb, serapes and long dresses, standing placidly alongside their mules or vegetable carts. "You're a photographer?"

"An amateur. I took some of these. The others are by our newspaper staff. Have you been to Peru? To Machu Picchu? It's a once in a lifetime experience."

"No, I haven't." Narby took out the pouch and rolled a cigarette. "I'll put it on my list."

"What's that you're smoking?"

"Danish shag. I get it at the Smoker's Den. That tobacco shop in town. Around the corner from the courthouse."

"Don't know it. I'm usually pretty well-provisioned. Besides, Turner can get pretty much whatever I want these days, if I'm willing to wait a bit."

"Turner?" "The General Store. In the Village. But then, living on the mainland, you wouldn't have much use for Turner."

"I've been there, once or twice. Picking up a few things for Willa."

"Turner's an ambitious man. Not the typical Villager. He's one of the prime movers in the County's push to get the causeway built. Can't say I blame him. Considering how much he'd stand to profit." He puffed on his pipe for a moment. "Now that I've got you in here, Philip, out of earshot of the others, maybe you'd care to weigh in on this question of development. Not just Sanmora, but the County. How many acres did you say you have?"

"About two thousand."

"Riverfront?"

"No. Mostly inland, except for one section. But with all the mangrove islands, the shallow water, I'd hardly call it riverfront. More like mudflats."

"Sawfish Point, isn't that what they call it?"

"That's right."

"Would you like another splash?"

"Sorry?"

"Another splash. Of the good Scots water."

He looked at the tumbler. It was empty. Pembaker was smiling at him, as if he'd caught him out on a lie. He was fidgeting, giving himself away. "Yes. Please. If you don't mind."

"Not at all." Pembaker reached behind and took the decanter by the neck and doled out another inch. "There you are." He waited until Narby took a sip. "That's a sizeable piece. Two thousand acres. What are your plans?"

"Well, as I said, I've got the experimental farm going. But aside from that, and the house I've built. Well. No plans, really. Not now, at any rate."

"Taking a wait-and-see attitude? That your idea?"

"More or less."

"Smart. Right now, in this part of Florida, raw land is probably your best investment. The more the better, if you can get your hands on it while it's cheap. If you can afford to sit on it." He leaned back, tamping his pipe again. "That's why you were so interested in that seaplane, isn't it?"

"The seaplane?"

"You wanted to know who was poking around, surveying the lay of the land. Wanted to know the potential competition, if someone else has the same idea as you? Thought maybe it was one of us, perhaps. Am I right?"

"It crossed my mind," he said, not quite lying.

"I imagine it did. Well, in fact, you got my curiosity up. So I looked into it. Made a few inquiries with the Coast Guard, the F.A.A. It's a private plane, all right. Registered to a company in Coral Gables. Sun Vacations, or something like that. They take their more privileged clients out for airplane tours of the Everglades and Big Cypress and the Keys. Swoop over Florida Bay and up the mangrove coast a bit. They'll touch down somewhere in calm water, to give their clients a little thrill. It's a gimmick. Apparently."

"Sounds innocent enough."

"You say you've noticed that plane before?"

"Yes. Saw it the first time I was on the island, in fact. Hugging the coast, flew right over the lighthouse and up the dunes."

"And when was that?"

Narby shifted in the chair, the leather creaking underneath him, peering down into what remained of the precious whiskey in his tumbler. Sun Vacations. Why did that sound familiar? Pembaker was on his side, he could feel it. Pembaker had the advantage. He was in charge here. What choice did Narby have but to trust him? "1953. Right around the first of October. That was before I knew Willa."

"So. Before any of us had arrived that season. And how many times would you say you've seen it, flying like that, over the Colony?"

"Maybe half a dozen. Come to think of it, it's always been in the hotter months. When there's no one around. That's why I started coming out to Sanmora. To get away from the sweltering inland heat. To swim, cool off. It's the only open ocean beach in the county."

"Curious. You'd think a tourist gimmick like that would be running in the high season more often than summer."

"You think it's deliberate? That someone is watching the Colony when no one's here?"

"No, not necessarily. But I do have concerns about the Colony being vacant so many months out of the year. Sooner or later, some of us will be here year round. That was the intention from the very beginning. But so far, it hasn't worked that way. We have a man from the Village keeping an eye on things, doing maintenance, during the off months. But that's not the same as one of us being here."

Pembaker crossed his legs, caressing the bowl of the pipe. "The Colony is a unique entity. And Sanmora is a unique island, the only barrier island this far south on the Gulf with fresh water and arable land and a good harbor and stable dunes. And so far, unspoiled, if not exactly undiscovered. We tend to close ranks, when it comes to Colony business. But you and Willa seem to be quite close. Willa's already an exception, the only one of us who wasn't the original owner of her property. But Endicott vouched for her and she's become one of us now. Very much so."

He wasn't telling the whole story. The Colony, the stretch of oceanfront jungle, was owned by Isadora Trust. "Yes. Willa's told me how much the island means to her. How much she likes you and Tara."

"The point is. It seems to me that our interests might coincide in a number of ways. Your interests and the interests of the Colony. In how the County develops. The pace of development, the allotment of resources, zoning, that kind of thing. Control, really. That's what it's about. Whoever maintains a degree of control over development will be in the best position to benefit. Whether it's a good return on one's investments, or concerns of privacy, or even nature conservation. But," he said, crossing his legs again and polishing off the scotch and setting down the tumbler, "there'll be plenty of opportunity for us to discuss all that."

"I look forward to it."

"So, Tara tells me Willa is thinking of staying on this spring, maybe into the summer."

"Yes."

Pembaker gave him a rakish grin.

"She's painting up a storm these days. On a roll."

"Good for her. Well, I'm glad to hear that at least one of us will be staying on a bit longer this year. Two, actually. Willa, and you."

"I'll be sure to let you know if I catch sight of that plane again, Dalton. Or anything else that seems unusual."

"Good. Thank you, Philip I appreciate it."

There was a light tapping on the door. Without Pembaker's assent it swung open. The crew cut stuck its head in. "Not interrupting, am I?"

"Of course not, Dan. Come in. Philip. You've met Dan, haven't you? Dan Atlee. Philip Narby."

Narby stood. Atlee pumped his hand.

"Good to meet you, Philip." The moment the name was out of his mouth he turned his back, reaching for the scotch. Pembaker hadn't bothered to get out of his chair. The older man watched with a bit of trepidation, Narby thought—Atlee was pouring rather freely, half a tumbler. "I suspected you two were back here, having a little tête-à-tête." Drink in hand he faced Narby: narrow, somewhat bleared eyes, a broad flat forehead. "The old Pembaker treatment, eh?"

Had Atlee been standing behind the door, eavesdropping?

"We were just discussing Willa—she's staying for the spring, possibly through the summer."

"Yeah? First I heard of it. Good." Atlee took a drink, with no indication that Pembaker's treasured scotch was anything special. There was a wooden box on the desk. Atlee leaned over and plucked out a cigar and ran it in under his nose. He made himself at home, taking without asking. He clipped it and lit it and lowered himself into the vacant club chair, licking his lips as he took pleasure in the first draws, the coils of velvet smoke.

The better cigars—the Cohiba del Rey's in the tubes—were stashed in the desk drawer. Atlee took, but Pembaker wasn't giving away too much, apparently.

"So, what's this about Willa?"

"Philip's been telling me that she's quite hunkered down in the studio. Doesn't want to break the spell."

"I hear she's been selling like hot cakes lately. Speaking of which. Have you heard from Endicott?"

"I saw him in New York, last month. He's in Italy half the year now. San Remo." Pembaker turned to Narby. "Endicott Ward. The original owner of Willa's house. Have you met him?"

"No."

"What do you think of that crazy bunker of a house?" Altee interjected. His voice was jagged with drink. "Most people either love it. Or hate it."

"It seems to suit Willa."

Atlee turned his head. "Too German for my tastes. That bow-wow-house stuff."

"The machine in the jungle," Pembaker said, as if correcting Atlee. "That's what Endicott calls it. He's quite something, old Endicott. Knows the art world inside out, new and old. He put it very bluntly, once. 'The Europeans,' he said, 'they've got the old masters, but we've got the new ones, and pretty soon we'll buy up all the old ones, too.' Helped Willa's career immeasurably. In that game you need a champion, a tastemaker backing you. You need a Guggenheim, an Alfy Barr."

"Great guy, old Endicott. If a bit of a swisher."

Pembaker frowned. "Don't you have flight in the morning, Dan? Out of Miami." "I do. Walker's going to meet us at the ferry at five. You know, Dalt, as much as we hate the idea, sometimes I think that causeway wouldn't be such a bad thing."

"We were just talking about that. The County's plan for development. Or rather, it's lack of a plan."

"Good thing you'll be around, Phil. Philip or Phil?"

Keep away from Korea, Narby told himself. "Either way."

"Gets pretty damned lonely around here when all the snow-birds fly north."

"She'll be fine," Pembaker said. "In fact, you don't really know the island until you've spent the wet season here, watching the big storms roll in, exposed to that tremendous sun. It's part of the beauty, the romance of the place. Even with the damn mosquitoes."

"June and July. Best months for tarpon. Bonefish running like mad down in the Keys in August. Best sport fishing in the world right in our own backyard. The golden triangle. Between Havana and the Bahamas and Sanmora. You fish?"

"Not really. But I wouldn't mind trying my hand."

"Hell, Dalt. We'll be leaving the Miranda in dry dock all summer. Shame to leave a grand lady like that up on hooks half the year. Why not have Phil and Willa take her out? Tony can skipper it all right, if they're just going out for tarpon."

Pembaker thought for a moment. "I don't see why not."

"Sure." Atlee took the cigar out of his mouth and laid it in the ashtray. "Here." He jotted something down. "Just go down to the Village marina and ask for Tony. Give him this. He can skipper it for you. There's plenty of tackle on board. Tony can take care of everything, knows the best spots. Ten to one you'll land a tarpon your first time out. Start with tarpon. Now, blue marlin. That's a whole different animal."

Narby took the paper. "That's very generous, Dan. Dalton. Thanks."

"If the weather's agreeable, hell, you could take her all the way to the Keys. Tony can handle that. If the weather cooperates."

"Extraordinary, really, if you haven't been out there. The confluence of the Atlantic and the Caribbean and the Gulf. It's no wonder the Spanish and British and French fought over every scrap of island, every inch of coastline. Of all the watery earth, it's my favorite patch."

"Come to think of it, Dalt. I don't think we've ever had Willa out on the Miranda."

"No, I don't think we have."

"The thing is," Narby said, "Willa's not too keen on boats. On going out on the water."

"Why the hell not? She's a mystery, that one." Atlee's tumbler was empty. Pembaker was keeping his eye on the decanter. "A very beautiful mystery at that."

"She's a remarkable young woman," Pembaker said. "Incredible, what she's done with her painting in the years since Tara and I first met her."

"What ever happened to old what's his name? The blueblood fiancé?"

Pembaker smiled, a show of mild embarrassment at Atlee's tactlessness.

They were married men with families, past their prime. They envied him. Only in Atlee's case, it was more than envy.

"Richard Lansdale," Narby said easily.

Atlee shrugged. "Seemed like a decent sort. Sitting on a family fortune, to boot."

Atlee was trying to bait him. Narby leaned forward to roll another cigarette. Atlee watched, sitting back in the club chair, sucking on the cigar. "You know, Dalt," he said, breaking the silence, "I just can't see it. Never have. Try as I might. What do you think Willa's up to with those paintings of hers, Phil? They're some kind of landscapes, aren't they? Only foggy. Obscured by mist. Is that what it's about?"

"Well, in fact, it's not hard to grasp," Pembaker interjected. "It's all about the play of light, the play of form. Isn't that right? It's the spirit of the thing. The vitality. The Europeans don't have it anymore. We've got it now. In art, in business, in productivity. We've got the momentum. It's all of a piece."

"She sure as hell works hard at it," Narby said. "She's in that studio eight, ten hours a day."

"Nice work," Atlee remarked. "If you can get it."

"Dan's in shipping," Pembaker said, trying perhaps to deflect the sarcasm. "Oil tankers. And agricultural goods, as well."

"Banana boats," Atlee said, laughing. "Matter of fact, got a plane to catch in the morning, out of Miami International. To San Juan."

"Yes. We know. Is Sheila going with you this time?"

"Nope. Strictly business. Stopping in Havana, too, for a meeting. On the way home."

"Ah. How convenient," Pembaker said, smiling. "Have you been to Havana, Philip?"

"I spent a little time there. Some years ago."

"Most gorgeous creature I ever hooked. Of the non-human variety. Eight-foot blue marlin. Out on a charter from Havana. Two hours to play it. My arms were like rubber. It's hanging over the breakfast nook. Gives me a wink, with my orange juice. You ever meet Papa Hemingway, Phil? I have. Not impressed. You read his books? Ha. That's not the way it is. War. Women. The Spanish business." He shook his head dismissively. "The fishing lore, sure, he's good with all that. Up to a point. And booze. That he knows, like a bartender. What do you think, Dalt? Don't you think Hemingway's looking at things through pink-colored glasses?"

Pembaker shrugged. "On literary matters I defer to Tara. She's the critic in the family."

"How about you, Phil? You buy that stuff? The have and have-not theory?"

"He's all right. As a fiction writer. But I wouldn't vote for him. If that's what you're asking."

"I'll drink to that," Atlee said, stupidly raising the empty tumbler until it was almost to his lips. Twisting in the chair, he reached for the decanter. "Just a drop," he said to Pembaker. "After that, I'm in for the night."

"Philip? How about you?"

"No, thanks. I'm good."

"So, what do you think of think of this Castro character, Philip? I assume you've seen the latest. One minute he's dead, the next he's the hero of the American press."

"Can't say I know much about it. He does seem to be like the proverbial cat with nine lives. It's the second time now he's gotten out of a bad scrape. After being imprisoned and all that." He stopped. That was already too much. "What do you think, Dan?"

"Castro? You got to admire him for making a complete ass out of Batista. Yeah, they'll hunt him down sooner or later. And you can quote me on that. But damn it. The guys got balls. He's got the real Spanish blood. Batista's a dirty son of a mongrel bitch. Excuse my French. And for chris'sake, don't believe everything you read in the *New York Times*. Dalton and I know a hell of a lot more about the whole Caribbean tub than any knee jerk reporter. That right, Dalt?"

The older man in the blazer nodded. "I should think so."

"So you don't think Castro has a chance?"

"Not unless he gets outside help," Pembaker said. "A lot of it. And frankly, I don't see much coming his way. I've spent a fair amount of time in Cuba. Both Dan and I have. I know the business community, the general political climate. I've got friends in our embassy over there. If enough pressure continues to build, yes, there'll be a shift in power. But from inside. Inside the Army, or one of the established parties. That's why they brought Pazos and Chibás up to see Castro—they're from the opposition parties, established men with solid ties to industry and business. To try to temper the revolutionary rhetoric, set up some realistic notion of who would take charge after Batista falls. And when change does come, it will have to be with our support, too. But as for this romantic notion of some idealistic young lawyer with a cache of second-hand weapons, holed up in the Sierra, overthrowing the Cuban military establishment. It's pure fantasy."

Narby knew all about Chibás and Pazos. Frank País had arranged it. Dressing up Castro-the-wolf in a Brooks Brothers suit. It was a ploy, nothing more. Only he couldn't tell Pembaker that. Not in front of Atlee.

"Still," Atlee put in, "Castro's smart, steering clear of the commies, keeping himself clean from all that Arbenz anti-American crap. Only his timing is lousy. It's too soon. Yeah, he needs the politicos, though in my opinion not a single one of them can be trusted. Too cozy with the Red-infiltrated labor movement, no matter what they say now. No, what Castro needs is to get the mid-level officers behind him, the captains, the lieutenant colonels. He throws himself in too closely with the peasants, the campesinos, he'll get nowhere. Except with the commies. And that'll be it for El Comandante. The death knell."

"You've been to Cuba, Philip. What's your impression?"

"I was just there for a little fun. Not like you two."

Atlee laughed. "Oh, believe me, we've had our fun. All work and no play? Not in Havana."

"You a gambler, Philip? I'll confess. I do have a weakness for roulette. I only wish roulette had a weakness for me."

"I'd say Phil here is more a lady's man than a gambler, Dalt. Same thing, though, if you think about. It's all about taking away the spoils."

The bastard was mocking him. Splashing the first acid. But Atlee was drunk. It was Pembaker who was in charge. Pembaker who really mattered.

"We all have our weaknesses," Narby said lightly. "At least I haven't got hooked yet, like you married men."

"That eight-foot blue marlin, Phil. It's up on the wall. Understand? A trophy. Doesn't mean I don't still go fishing. Just means I can't bring home any more trophies."

"Must dampen the spirit of it, though. Knowing you have to throw them back."

"It's all good sport. Good fun. So. Is it true? What they say about artists, bohemians. The free and easy life. What about it Phil? A report from the trenches."

"Dan, that's a bit out a line."

"Just a joke." He held up his hands, as if in surrender. "Sorry. Too much liquor. No offense."

It was more than envy. "Quite all right," Narby said, forcing a laugh.

Pembaker leaned forward to tap the ash from his pipe. "In fact, it was a wayward fishing trip that led Dan to Sanmora in the first place. Isn't that right?"

Atlee leaned back, the tension in his jaw grinding the end of the cigar. "We'd heard about a flurry of sailfish strikes, even though it was early in the season. Nothing else was happening, so we cruised up from Key Largo. Put in at the Village marina and took a look around. Liked what I saw. That pristine coastline. Nothing here but the village. Looked like paradise. Back in those days."

"The winter of 1950. Dan was in the Marines then. On leave. I was living in Venezuela and I got this rather breathless airmail letter, all about an unspoiled barrier island with nothing but white sand dunes and a sleepy fishing village and an old rusting lighthouse." Pembaker laughed. "You dragged me out here all the way from Caracas. Pulled the boat right up to the beach, right here, next to these very dunes. 'It's ours,' you said. 'Let's grab it now, before we wake up and the dream's over.' Or something to that effect."

"Remember that bonfire, Dalt? Stayed up all night long, under the stars. Nothing but the dunes and the waves rolling in and the skies above. That was something. Would have been my last tour of duty, too. If it hadn't been for Korea."

"Philip was in Korea, too."

"That right? Not with the Marine Corps?"

"No. Eighth Army, Second division. Infantry." There was no avoiding it now. "You?"

Atlee shrugged, leaning back, smug, superior. "Marines. X Corps. You at Inchon?"

"No. Pusan Perimeter. Up along the Naktong. With Task Force Smith."

Atlee let out a low whistle. "That was a meat grinder, all right. Biggest fuck-up since Bull Run." He swirled the last of the scotch and swallowed, letting his head hang for a second, then looking up. "But what wasn't a fuck-up in Korea? One fuck-up after another." He raised his head, struggling against the gathering stupor. "Chosin Reservoir. Up near the Yalu. Goddamn frozen wasteland. There was this photographer, friggin' *Life* magazine. Wanted a comment, a caption for his picture. I told him: The marines don't retreat. This is not a retreat. This is an assault—in a different direction."

Atlee seemed lost for a second, staring at the empty tumbler in his hand. "Well, there aren't going to be any more fuck-ups like that. Never again. All because of Truman the chicken-hearted. You can't fight a goddamn war with one hand tied behind your back. If only they had let MacArthur have his way, we'd have the whole god damned peninsula in the palm of our hand. Could have taken back China, in the bargain. We were this close." He had leaned forward, his face going red, but then he tilted back again, like a balloon hissing air. "MacArthur was the greatest soldier ever to serve this country. To be backhanded like that, slapped down by some prissy little s.o.b. underwear salesman."

He glared at Narby. "MacArthur saved your asses, too. Without Inchon, you boys would have been paddling back to Japan without a canoe."

"I don't see it that way," Narby said, calmly. "But yes, Inchon did turn things around. For a while."

"What way *do* you see it? Don't tell me you were one of those appeasers? That you were behind Truman?"

"That's all politics," Narby said, looking at Pembaker. "I'm not much interested, one way or the other. It was a war. People made mistakes." The older man was listening with an amused look on his face. "How about you, Dalton? What did you make of the MacArthur business?"

"It was a damned tragedy, that's what I think. Dan's right. MacArthur was a great soldier, a great leader. Look at what he did in Japan, during the Occupation. It was a miracle of stamina and statesmanship that no other military man I know of could have pulled off. All right, maybe he was a bit of a show off, a grandstander. But isn't that the prerogative of genius? However. Unfortunately. No matter how much Dan disagrees. After that letter to congress, Truman had no choice but to cashier him. Chain of command. Absolutely essential. MacArthur went too far. Broke ranks. It's the lynchpin of the whole system. You don't contradict the Commander-in-Chief. Not in public. It can't be done. Not in a democracy, at any rate."

Atlee had no doubt heard it before. He hardly seemed to listen. When Pembaker finished he pushed himself out of the chair. "All right, gentleman. I have a plane to catch. Better go round up the little lady before she drinks herself silly. Hell of a time getting her up early when she's got a hangover."

Narby stood. Atlee wanted to shake his hand again. "Politics! Stinks, doesn't it? I'm with you there. War should be waged by soldiers. Not Washington. At least we made it out in one piece, didn't we? Almost. I left behind a frigging toe. Froze. Went black as a nigger's. A little memento for the Red Chinese. What about you?"

"Couple pints of blood. But I took some shrapnel home. Fair exchange."

Atlee's shake was looser this time. Damp. "Take care of Willa, O.K? Phil. What was the last name again?"

"Narby. Philip Narby."

"Good to meet you. All right, I'm gone. Carry on, you two."

They were walking back to Willa's house after the party had broken up. It was a warm moonless overcast night. The foam, flecked with phosphorescence, hissed around their feet.

"Did they get it out of you, lover? Make you confess?"

"Dalton thinks I'm some kind of a real-estate magnate. Seems a decent sort. The other one. Atlee. What the hell's eating him?"

"The he-man. He's harmless enough. Once you face him down."

"What do you mean?"

"I mean he's a bully. And like all bullies, he's terribly insecure. He'll trample you underfoot. Until you yank the rug out. Call his bluff."

"He ever try anything with you?"

She pulled him closer, instead of answering putting her mouth against his, a long devouring kiss. Then, suddenly, she was gone, running down the beach until she was lost in the darkness.

"Here," she cried out, swooping toward him again and then disappearing "Catch."

Something soft hit him in the face. He picked it up off the sand. It was her clothes, her peasant skirt bunched into a ball. "Willa? What the hell you doing?"

"What do you think?"

He ran forward, reached out into the darkness, touched her. But she slipped away. He ran after her. Suddenly she stopped and before he could avoid it he crashed into her and they fell together on the sand, rolling into the lip of the waves. She was naked, coiling around him, kissing him.

"Come on, now. Someone might walk by."

"Not here. It's too dark. No one can see." She had her hands on him, under his shirt, everywhere. Her flesh had tightened in the cool water, her breasts hard. "I want it, Philip. Now. Here. Give it to me. Like this. I don't care who sees."

"You want it like this, darling?" He rolled on top of her, pushing her down, pinning her arms over her head. A wave sloshed up all around them, in her face, and she spat out the saltwater. He pressed harder, not caring if he hurt her. "Is this what you want? Is this what you need?"

"Yes."

"You don't give a damn, do you? As long as I give it to you like this?"

"No. I don't care about anything. Just this."

And though he did as she asked, pressing his hand over her mouth to muffle her cries, he understood that it wasn't enough. She wanted more, only he didn't understand what it was, or how far he would go to keep her.

18

THE GATE CROSSED NARBY'S ROAD a quarter mile from the house: four thick upright pine posts traversed with slats of corrugated tin, cinched with a padlocked chain and hung with a *PRIVATE PROPERTY—KEEP OUT* sign. The truck idling behind him, Narby stood in the middle of the road—shirtless, batting away the mosquitoes and gnats. Someone had broken in. The gate was open. Whoever it was had pried away two of the slats, probably with a crow bar, and loosened the loop of padlocked chain sufficiently to slide it over the top of the post. It had rained last night. The mud, stiffened in the sun, showed a single set of fresh tire tracks. A truck coming in and then going out would have left two sets, slightly overlapping. He walked further down the lane to confirm his suspicion. Sam had left a few days ago to visit his son in Tampa. Narby had been in Miami Beach with Willa, had dropped her at Miami International that morning and then picked up the truck in Sanmora. So, someone had been keeping tabs, had waited until there was no one around. Whoever had broken the gate was still here, apparently—grubbing through Narby's belongings, filthying his house, tearing up the floorboards like some clawed frenzied animal, slavering for the money.

Stupid of Narby to think a gate across a dirt road could keep out vermin like Vetch. Stupid, and weak, not to have finished with Vetch a long time ago. The threats, the blackmail, taunting him with Becca—it wasn't enough for Vetch. Nothing would ever be enough for Vetch. He would gnaw away at Narby like a parasite, a flesh-eating disease. Dogging him, contaminating everything Narby touched, stealing and extorting, all the while daring Narby to go to the Sheriff, laughing in his face in front of Waters and the other Negroes.

A piece of human garbage. A nothing. And now he was here, trespassing, violating the sanctity of Narby's home, his property. It wouldn't even be a crime—a spontaneous act of lethal force in defense of one's home, coming upon a man like Vetch in the midst of thievery and desecration.

If only Narby had landed on the white beaches of Sanmora, instead of here, Sawfish Point, crawling out of the rank mangrove muck. The thought of it, the magnitude of the error, made him dizzy, an outrage beyond relief, violent and unappeasable. He had to get past Vetch, expunge him from the equation. And now, Vetch had come to him, the little piggy off to the slaughterhouse. It was out of Narby's hands. The time had come.

He closed the crippled gate and climbed into the idling truck, wiping the sweat from his face. A sweltering shadeless breezeless afternoon, the ferocity of light and heat and damp fused into a uniform indomitable pestilential haze. Bring the truck in closer, but not so close that Vetch could hear, and leave it blocking the narrow road, cutting off any chance of escape. From there Narby could walk through the brush and around the back of the house to the shed where Sam kept the pick axes and shovels and machetes. Even if Vetch had a shotgun, Narby would strike so swiftly and silently that the Southerner would hardly have time to lift the barrel, let alone aim and squeeze the trigger. One glancing hit or slash would be sufficient to disarm him, throw him into terror and shock. The rest would be easy, like pummeling a fallen piñata.

Sitting for a moment in the roughly idling truck, he opened the glove compartment and took out a small dark brown-glass bottle. Yellow pills, bennies of some sort, Bobby told him. Narby had yet to try them, their strength untested. An excess of agitation would hardly be a drawback, considering the job awaiting him. He shook out three and washed them down with the flask and then finished the half-burnt stick in his pocket. Blanking his mind. Then he drank off the rest of the water in the canteen and put the truck in gear. Bouncing, lurching, in peristaltic movement down the rutted jungle lane, judging how far he could advance without the sound of the truck reaching the house.

Then he saw it. Blocking the lane.

Get out of here, he told himself. The lane was too narrow, too walled-in by brush, to turn around. But he could put it in reverse and back up to the gate. He twisted, looking over his shoulder. The lane behind him was clear—no one waiting, no ambush, no rush of M.P.s or civilian police materializing from the jungle.

And do what? Go where? He would not run. Whatever it was, he would beat it. Destroy it.

He cut the motor, the jungle suddenly silent, and climbed out. Twenty yards in front of him, blocking the lane—a black Lincoln Continental, its hood gaping open. Abandoned, empty. Dade County plates. The stink of rancid radiator boil rising from the engine. New and shiny under the layer of grime. He circled around, his back scraping against the brush, vigilant, gazing up and down the lane. Then he saw the footprints, imprinted lightly on the still-tacky mud. One set large, one small, heading down the lane toward the house, where, he assumed, they were ransacking his things, or simply laying in wait. But who? What kind of moron would try to bring a car like this down his road? He kneeled in the dirt and peered under the carriage. A trickle of oil. Overheated, the radiator bone dry, leaking oil where the pan had cracked. Two men. They had smashed his gate, willfully trespassing, abandoned their car and walked the rest of the way. Two men in a new expensive Lincoln Continental. Idiots, madmen. Or men who perhaps hadn't known what to expect, had brought the car here not knowing where they were going, determined despite the gate and the impassable road to get to his house, to find him. Confront him. Arrest him. Kill him.

The passenger door was unlocked. Inside, oven-like, the upholstery burning to the touch, he clicked open the glove compartment. No registration, no identifying papers. Only a small square cardboard box, inordinately heavy for its size: 38 caliber 100-grain bullets, snugly arrayed little cylinders. There were five missing.

They had a gun. Loaded, ready to fire.

He found nothing else in the car. The trunk was locked. He took the box of bullets and three or four at a time flung them in every direction, as if scattering seeds into the brush. Heaving, boiling with sweat, he circled around again, to the trunk. He might be able to pry it open. There would be other weapons, perhaps. But the layer of grime on the trunk hood was undisturbed. He guessed that the trunk had not been opened. They had their weapons with them, he decided. Why bring them this far only to leave them in the trunk?

His only advantage was that he knew they were here, knew how to get into the house without being seen, through the grove and the back door. He couldn't risk walking down the road. They would be watching, waiting. He would have to push through the brush. He went to his truck and pulled on the T-shirt for protection. He knew there was a footpath running more or less parallel to the road, maybe fifty feet inside the brush, overgrown but passable. He parted the wall, crouching through the thickets, found it, could walk more or less freely, his arms and neck oozing threads of blood from where the vines and palmetto blades had scored his flesh, his skin glazed with a gray-pinkish paste of sweat and dust and blood, his breath labored but his head no longer pounding, the fear and seething and dope scouring his mind, blanking it like an electric current.

The footpath came out at the clearing near the front of the house where Sam had planted a stand of Australian pines. One of them was standing on the porch. A tall bulky lumbering man with a red meaty sweat-glistening face and black oily hair, in a checkered polo shirt, like an auto racing flag, that rode up the man's torso, exposing a ring of white belly fat. Narby stood hidden by the brush, watching him. After a moment, with great reluctance, it seemed, the man stepped down off the porch and took a look around the corner of the house, an attitude of disgust and profound torpor evident in his dull expression and the slow agonized movements and quiet moans, hiking up his black trousers every few steps with violent jerks, brushing the mosquitoes from his face, scratching his head, muttering. The gun, Narby guessed, in his trouser pocket, where it bulged.

An idiot, a thug, some low life goon. The other one, the smaller one, must be in the house, ransacking, waiting. The goon mounted the steps, hauling himself up to the porch, gripping the wooden rail. After a moment, he pushed open the heavy antique door and went inside, closing it behind him.

Narby took a breath and quickly skirted the edge of the house, through the bamboo, ducking behind the low garden walls alongside the grove until he reached the dirt-floor shed, the hot dead air inside reeking of wood rot and rodent droppings. In the corner, leaning among the shovels and rakes and various picks, their shafts dark and smooth and oiled with years of palm-sweat, his own and that of Sam and the Negro workers, he found the ax.

An ax, against a goon with a revolver? He had to think. His skin was burning from the cuts and the mosquito bites. He peeled off his shirt and wiped down his face and neck and arms and threw it to the ground and lifted the ax, weighing it in his hands, testing how rapidly he could swing or raise it and bring it down, like a batter in the deck-circle, warming up. Perhaps it was better to wait, stand his ground here in the suffocating rank darkness of the shed. Sooner or later they would come looking for him. He took his position: motionless, pressed against the shed wall, the ax cradled athwart his chest, his mind spooling out the moment of irrevocable violence, the greasy-haired goon poking his head tentatively through the shed door, raising the ax and striking, the vibration of the haft as the blade sunk into the skull—but his nerves were unraveling. He couldn't bear it. Heaving, catching his breath, he let the ax drop in the dust.

He needed water. His throat was cracking. Sam usually kept a stone jug around. Narby found it, set on a concrete block in the dark at the back of the shed. He pried out the cork and drank, the surprisingly cool water dribbling down his chin, ticking his bare chest. Waited. And again. The water seemed to settle something within him. Squatting in the dust he smoked another cigarette, gathering his nerve, blanking his mind.

The room in the back of the house had a screen door on one side. Seldom used, the bamboo there had overgrown, the door and the concrete block steps hidden, half buried in the thicket. He stood and picked up the ax and stepped out of the shed, back into the glare, crouching low, moving very slowly through the groves and the occluding shade. Keeping low, his breathing shallow, he came to the wall, solid for the first three feet and above that fitted with the screen panels. He straightened just enough to peer inside, through the bottom of the screen. Someone was sitting in the chair, the high-backed wicker throne. Not the apish idiot. The other one, the small one. He couldn't make out the face, only the form in quarter profile. Smoking a cigar. Alone, as far as Narby could see.

The goon must be outside again, on the porch. There was no time to think, to consider. He crouched, gripping the ax mid-haft in one hand, and stepped toward the door, reaching up, trying the latch, his hand trembling. It was loose, open. He straightened, putting his foot on the first of the three concrete steps. The bamboo rustled. He burst forward, the screen door flying open, the ax held approximately at the height of the sitting's man's throat.

"Don't move. Shut up."

The man let out a grunt of fright, flinching and cringing as he raised and crisscrossed his arms to shield against the blow, the cigar clamped between his jaws.

"Not a sound. Shut up. Where's the gun? Give me the gun or I'll split your head open."

"Please. I don't have a gun. I—"

"Shut up. The other one. The fatso. Where is he?"

"He's in the other room. The bedroom. Taking a rest."

The fright had loosened the man's jaw. The cigar dropped from his mouth, onto his lap. "Christ. My leg," he whined. "It's burning." Carefully, looking up into Narby's face, one arm still raised he reached with the other and lifted the cigar and put it in the ashtray, leaving a burn hole in his trouser. "He went in there to take a nap. Take it easy. I'll do whatever you say. You want me to get him?"

"Don't move."

"For Chris'ake. Take it easy. Don't be crazy."

"Call him. Tell him to come in here. Don't try anything. I swear, I'll cut your fucking head off."

"O.K. O.K. Lou. Hey, Lou." He looked up at Narby. "Maybe he's asleep."

"Try again. Louder."

"LOU. LOU. COME IN HERE FOR A MINUTE, WILL YOU?"

There was a thumping from the other side of the wall.

"Lou!" The man looked up at Narby again, nodding in acquiescence. "Come in here please, would you. Lou."

More thumping. The goon came lumbering in, his red meaty face drooping with exhaustion, his hair and clothes disordered and matted with sweat.

"What the hell."

"Put your hands up. Over your head."

"Do what he says. Goddamn it, Lou. Put your goddamn hands up."

Blinking, his mouth hanging open, stupefied, he slowly lifted his arms, the polo shirt riding up, showing the thick ring of white belly.

"Where's the gun? In your pocket?"

"Huh?"

"Empty your pockets."

"Lou. He wants the gun." The seated man spoke slowly, as if to a child. "He's going to hit me with the ax unless you give him the gun. Don't try anything. Just give him the gun. Capiche?"

"It's in there," he said, cocking his head to the side. "On the table. By the bed."

"Empty your pockets."

The goon shrugged, lowering his arms, and pulled his pockets inside out, like a clown. A few coins, a filthy handkerchief, keys, a cigarette lighter that dropped on to the floor.

"All right. Move over there. Go on." The goon shambled across the room, in front of the wall of books.

"For god's sake," the seated one pleaded, "calm down. You're going to hurt somebody."

"Shut up. You. Get on the floor. On your face, your hands behind your back."

"But it's dirty. I got —"

"Lou. Do what he says."

"O.K. O.K." He lowered himself to his knees and rolled onto his stomach, his arms at his side.

"You. Stand up."

The short one lowered his arms and pushed out of the wicker chair. Narby shifted the ax to his right hand. "Pick up the keys. Put them on the table."

He did as ordered, then stepped back. Narby took them, the keys to the Lincoln, put them in his pocket, keeping his attention split, the fat one prone on the floor and the short balding one in front of him.

"What the hell you looking at? Turn around. Go into the hall. Turn right. Keep your hands up."

"Sure. Whatever you say."

Narby followed close behind him, the ax blade hovering over the man's neck and shoulder blades. "Get over there." In one motion Narby grabbed the gun off the bedside table—a black snub-nose revolver—and raised it, point blank at the man's face, his outstretched arm locked at the elbow, trembling in outrage and fury and giddy triumph, the axe lowered now, dangling at his side, the blade unbloodied.

"Don't be crazy. I only came here to talk. Please."

"With fatso? And a gun? Breaking into my house. You're lying."

"It was open. We didn't break in. The gate on the road was open. The front door was unlocked. I swear. You got to believe me."

Short, bald on top, dark complexion, barrel chest, with the small dark eyes and triangular tapering face of a burrowing animal. "I ought to blow your fucking head off."

"Please. Put down the gun. Our car overheated. Because of that idiot, Lou. He's my driver. He carries that gun for self-defense. Look, when we saw you weren't here, we had no choice but to wait. I swear. I wanted to call for a tow truck, but I couldn't find the telephone. Please. Put down the gun."

The fear was draining away; he felt light, giddy, the tension in his limbs thrumming and tingling like plucked wires. Kill him. Be done with it. Kill them both. Drag the bodies to the car and set it on fire. Burnt beyond recognition. Yet he stood there, amazed that he was in his own bedroom, shirtless and filthy and dripping sweat, a loaded revolver in his hand, his finger curled around the trigger. And Sid Black. Cringing, at his mercy.

"It's been a long time, yeah?" Black said, slowly, gently. "Six goddamn years. You made it out okay! That's good. That's wonderful. I helped you. Don't you remember? At the hospital." Black was looking at the scars, the skein of gouges and puffed inert flesh, caked with filth. "You were pretty busted up. You had that blackout. Couldn't remember anything. We helped each other. Come on, now. We can talk, like reasonable men."

"Like what?"

Black's little eyes were remarkably clear and bright. He was scared, perhaps, but there was no terror. "Like reasonable men."

Narby laughed, the revolver—fused with his grip, gun and grip and outstretched arm locked at the elbow into a single extremity—vibrating slightly. "Reasonable men? That's a good one. You know how can you tell which man is the more reasonable?"

"What is it, a riddle? How?"

"It's the man without the gun."

"Yeah. O.K. I see your point. Look. I'm sorry we came into your home without permission."

"Don't give me any of your bullshit Jew round-around. You came here for the money."

"I came to talk. Sure, about the money. About everything. Come on, don't you remember how I helped you. With the transit papers out of Japan, the …"

"No. Other way around. I helped you. You needed to get your dirty money out of Japan. Before they sent you back to Korea. Isn't that right, Supply Sergeant First Class Black? You had no choice. You took a chance, a calculated risk. So did I. Far as I see it, Black. We're even. No. I'm ahead. I have the gun."

"Sure. You're right. We're even. Please. I'm trembling like a leaf. Can I at least sit down?"

He led Black into the back room. Lou was still on the ground, on the filthy threadbare rug. Black took the same chair, the wicker throne. "That's better. Thanks."

"Sid," the goon groaned.

"Shut up," Sid snapped back. "It's all your fault, you nitwit. He had to have the air-conditioner running. *It's a Lincoln, Sid. It's so hot outside. Lincolns don't overheat, Sid.* Whining like a baby. Do me a favor," he said to Narby. "If you're going to shoot someone, shoot that wop son-of-a-bitch."

"What do think?" Narby said, turning toward Lou. "Him or you?"

"Jesus Christ, Sid. Sid. Do something!"

"Don't Jesus Christ me, you fucking guinea."

Narby pulled the other wicker chair around and sat to face him, his arm heavy now, aching, the gun heavy, letting his arm relax against the armrest. Black leaned back, crossing his short legs, his sporty lemon-yellow shirt barely spotted with sweat, his tight tapering face—the wide forehead and sloping cheeks and knob of chin—only lightly dewed with perspiration. Nothing but jungle and waste for miles. He could kill with impunity, two shots that no one would hear, two bodies burnt to ash and scattered in the wind. Yet Black wasn't feeling it. Because Black knew him, knew he was weak, that he couldn't kill like this, face to face, in cold blood.

Black nodded at the ashtray. "Mind if I smoke? Pity to waste a good cigar like that."

Narby shrugged. Black picked up the cigar.

"Sid. I'm dying down here. I can't breathe."

"All right if he gets up?" Black said. "He's got that breathing problem. What do you call it? Asthma."

"All right."

"Get up, Lou." Sid released a coil of smoke. "Get up and stand over there. Nice and quiet."

Lou groaned, getting to his knees, pushing up, wheezing, brushing off his black pants and the ill-fitting racing-flag polo shirt.

"I just came to talk. Discuss the situation. Lou's my driver. He carries a gun, for protection. It's just a big misunderstanding."

He would have to get the Lincoln out of the road, one way or another. "You, fat man. Go fill the radiator. There's water outside, a pipe by the pump house. You have to turn on the generator first. For the electricity." He explained how to start the generator and the pump, where to find the gas can and buckets.

Lou did not look happy. "I don't feel so good, Sid. I got to lie down. This heat is killing me."

"Lou. Listen to me. Our friend here is going to help us. It's all just a big misunderstanding. Capiche? He thought we were going to rob him. Assault him. I've explained the situation. Now, we have to fix the car."

"Call the tow truck, Sid."

"I don't have a telephone," Narby said.

"Get moving. Everything's calm now. Go on, Lou."

They watched him lumber down the hall, slow, miserable, scratching his hair, hiking his trousers.

"He'll figure it out. He's not as stupid as he looks." Sid gave a short laugh. "No one could be as stupid as he looks."

"What happened to Ted McCoy?"

"What? Who?"

"Ted McCoy. I worked under Ted McCoy. In Tokyo. He was one of your—customers."

"McCoy. Yeah, sure. Look, I can't compose my thoughts with that gun pointing at my face. Please."

Narby set it on the armrest, the barrel angled away, his fingertips caressing the grip.

"Thank you. Ted McCoy was called up, as soon as the fighting started. You remember what it was like. All hell broke loose that week. McCoy was an officer in the Reserves. He was killed in action, right at the start. You were still in the office then. Still a civilian. What's wrong? After all this time, you still can't remember?"

"How did you find me? How do you know where I live? Who told you?"

"Look. I don't begrudge you. Taking some of the money for yourself. You were smart not to come back. You made the right decision, believe me. Three fucking years, a fucking waste, a nightmare. All for nothing. It kills me just to think about it. I would have done the same, in your situation."

"You went to the bank? In Coral Gables."

"As a matter fact yes. I did. That's how I met Bob Wilson. You remember Bob. He's Vice President of the bank now. We've become good friends, Bob and I. Business associates. A whole year it took me, after the end of the war, to get out of the stinking shithole U.S. Army. As if three years in Korea wasn't torture enough. No, they had to fry my nuts for another fucking year."

"I thought you were dead. The money was sitting there. Why not take it?"

Black nodded, holding the cigar, his legs crossed. "I can understand that. Only you were wrong. You made a mistake. In any case, yeah, I went to the bank. I talked to Bob Wilson. He told me that Philip Narby—excuse me, that someone passing himself off as Philip Narby—had come around that very week, to make another withdrawal. That's when I closed the account. I explained the situation, showed him the original bank documents. Bob was very understanding, very cooperative."

"You explained? Stealing? Selling off army surplus on the black market? The copper and sheet metal stripped off the Jap army bases? Selling contraband and pornography? Taking bribes from the fawning little Japs that MacArthur put in charge? Yeah, sure, I bet you explained."

Black didn't care for that. He uncrossed his legs, shifting in the chair, sucking the fat black cigar. "Who says? Where's your proof? Besides, you certainly enjoyed your Chesterfields, didn't you? Your boss McCoy enjoyed his cigars and caviar and champagne, his magazines imported from Denmark. For a married man, with that Boston pedigree, I have to say, McCoy certainly had exotic tastes. Eh, a lot of them were like that. The big shots, the goyishe officers, the brass at GHQ. In any case, that's all in the past. Over and done with. Dead and buried."

The sound of the generator, the kick and hum, drifted in through the groves. The fan overhead started to turn, stirring the molten air. Black looked up. "That's nice," he said. "The real tropical touch. Everyone's nuts about air-conditioning. In all the hotels now, like the frigging North Pole. But that's what people want. They sit and roast all day in the sun, like a piece of meat, and then they go back into the fridge. Go figure. Personally, I enjoy the heat. Even in summer. Interesting place you have here."

"But Wilson had no address for me. That was three years ago."

"Yeah. Well, after I closed the account, maybe a few weeks later, Wilson told me that the same guy came in, Philip Narby, trying to pull off another withdrawal, only he ran out before Wilson could detain him. The guy must have figured out that the game was up. That's what happened, yeah? You figured it out. That Sid Black was alive and well. Because you never went back to the bank. Did you?"

He heard the pump, the sound of the goon banging the bucket against the pipe. It would take the lumbering dolt an hour at least, back and forth down the lane with bucket, to fill the radiator. Black was regarding him as if he were some kind of startled unpredictable animal, shirtless, mutilated, streaked with filth and blood. His conniving Jew mind clicking away behind the cunning rodent eyes.

"That's right. I disappeared. And you tried to find me, didn't you?"

"For a while. But I had other things on my mind. You're a hard man to track down."

"You own hotels. On Miami Beach. The Atlantique. The Edgewater. Two others that already went bankrupt and closed down."

Black nodded, tapping the cigar. "Well well. Who's been looking for who?"

Narby stood, picking up the gun. "Care for a drink, Sid?"

"Some water would be nice. Thank you."

He wedged the pistol under his waistband and brought water from the kitchen. "Something stronger to go with it? A little bourbon?"

"No, thank you. Just the water."

"I'm going to step out for a few minutes. I want you to stay right where you are. Got that?"

"Here." Black lifted his hands in front of his chest, as if to pray. "Tie me up if you don't believe me. I came to talk. I'm not going anywhere. You got Lou's little toy. You got the car keys. He's harmless, I assure you." He lowered his hands and picked up the cigar. "There's nothing to worry about. Relax."

In the shower—the revolver on the window ledge—the cool water soothed the welts and abrasions. My name. Tom or Jim. Black must know. Only Black hadn't really known him. Just by sight, when he came around to the CCD office to dicker with McCoy. Or buying the Chesterfields out of the trunk of his car, with a crowd all around. Black had recognized him at the port in Pusan, given him the salt tablets before the convoy left for the Naktong. *It's a hundred and ten degrees out there. We can't haul enough water to the hills. It's a fucking shitstorm up in the air, a shooting gallery. We can't get low enough to drop supplies. Here. Just don't tell anyone.* And then, weeks later, maybe a month, recovering in the hospital. Sitting in the garden. Black was on crutches, a broken foot. Came up to him, to Tom or Jim. Only he still couldn't remember his name. Didn't want to remember. It was better, safer, to be dead.

He put on a good short-sleeve shirt, sky-blue cambric from a Lincoln Road haberdasher, and linen trousers, and picked up the revolver, turning it in his hand, the scored wooden grip, the fat little drum with five cylinders and the stub barrel. There was nothing to it. No mechanism but the trigger. At close range a child could kill with it. Aside from two weeks of emergency training on the beach at Yokohama—a vague impression of learning how to clear a jam, how to brace the stock against his shoulder—he had never fired a weapon. His single day of glory on the battlefield it had seemed more prudent to cast away the unreliable World War II surplus M-1, better to run and dodge the Soviet tanks, the rain of mortar shells, than shoot at an invisible enemy with pop-gun futility. He tucked the snub nose into his waistband, like a punk about to knock off a liquor store. He wasn't going to let Black intimidate him, threaten him. Narby had as much right to the money as Black. The spoils of war.

Black was standing by the screens, peering out into the shade of the grove. "What are these, fruit trees? Very pretty." Black turned, registering with a nod of his head Narby's transformation from filthy beast to bon vivant. "Live out here all by yourself, do you?"

Narby poured a bourbon from the bottle on the table, running his foot over the rug at the spot where the floorboard lifted out. It appeared undisturbed. "You said the gate was open, when you and dreamboat out there drove up?"

"That's right. Boy oh boy, that's one hell of a driveway you got."

It had to be Vetch, then. Yesterday or the day before, after Waters left for Tampa in the flatbed. "I don't get many visitors."

"I don't suppose you do. Not married? Good-looking guy like you."

"No."

"Oh. I thought maybe that was your wife. The very attractive strawberry-blonde." The cigar reduced to a jaw-pulverized butt, Sid abandoned it in the ashtray. "You're quite the couple, parading around in that little Italian sports car."

"You own the Calvado, too? Don't you?"

"No. I don't. And you're wrong about the Atlantique and the Edgewater. I sold those a year ago. I don't own any hotels. I'm in hotel management now. It's complicated, the hotel business. Not for the faint of heart. Shame," he said, inspecting the burn hole in the thigh of his trouser leg. "A good pair of slacks, ruined. Oh well. Small price to pay for the chance to finally sit down and talk."

"Is that how you found me? Spying on me at the Calvado?"

"It was you, who found me. No? Came right to me. The thing is, I must have seen you any number of times. At the Calvado, and before that at the Atlantique. I saw, but I didn't recognize, didn't connect. Like I said, I had lot of things on my mind. You thought I was dead. And I assumed, after cutting you off from the bank account, that you were long gone. So, we were both mistaken. Besides, I was doing all right, back on my feet after getting out of the Army. I have to admit, losing such a considerable sum of money, that hurt. That stung. But after I closed the account, after Wilson told me that you'd flown the coop, I said to myself, let it go. The past is past. I have a whole new life in front of me. Hell, I even met a girl and got married. Doing very well for myself, too. House on Fairway Drive, the original Carl Fischer subdivision. New car every year. Frankly, the Lincoln is a disappointment. Next year, I think I'll go with a Cadillac."

Black looked damned comfortable, sitting with his legs crossed, hardly breaking a sweat, absurdly calm, his eyes shifting about, taking in Narby and the room with its accretion of castoff junk: the moldering books and piles of papers and magazines, the trampled Persian rug and third-hand antiquities, the romantic seascape in the cracked gilded frame, everything touched with the ordure and vegetal dust of the groves and the jungle that sifted in through the screens.

"Cigarette?"

"No thanks." They heard the goon clanking the bucket. "Mind if I ask Lou to bring the cigars from the car, as long as he making the trip? I find a cigar relaxing. Conducive to conversation."

He wanted the keys. There was another gun in the trunk, perhaps. Narby got up and found the tube amidst the piles on the table. "Try this."

Black pried the tube open and slid it out and ran it under his nose, and then licked the tip and let out a whistle. "Cohiba del Rey," he said, reading the stamp on the tube. "Very generous. Thank you." He took a moment to snip the end and fire it, savoring the first velvety coils of smoke.

"Here's the thing," Black went on. "It never would have occurred to me. That you would actually take the name Philip Narby. Even when I saw you with your lady friend—and I have to admit, it was more your lady friend and the sports car that drew my attention—I still couldn't quite make you out. Back in Tokyo, you were such a clean-cut gung-ho type. White shirt and tie, sitting straight as an arrow behind the typewriter. They used to call you *the congressman's boy*. And then at Pusan, well, you were in battle fatigues. Scared shitless. Like the rest of us. I said to myself, there's the kid from McCoy's office. What the hell is he doing here? Anyway, I felt sorry for you. And then I didn't see you again until that day in the hospital. You were so busted up and confused. See what I'm saying? I was looking for the kid in McCoy's office, for that busted up young soldier, and so I didn't see you, couldn't make you out. Until you start cavorting with that strawberry-blonde, up in the tenth-floor suite. Starting driving up in that little Italian roadster. Not that I made the connection immediately. I had to go through the hotel register. You could imagine, when I saw the name. Stopped me like a brick wall. Philip Narby. And even then, I had a hard time tracking you down."

"You followed me? Spied on me?"

"I was curious, to say the least. Maybe a little angry, too. At first. You're obviously having the time of your life, living it up like nobody's business, and I'm thinking, it was my money. He had no right to keep taking and taking. We made a deal, an arrangement. I get you out of Korea, out of Asia, and you help me get the money out, deposit it in the account in Havana. Before things got worse. Which they did. For me. Because they sent me back."

"I kept the bargain. I deposited the money."

"Yes. I know. You deposited it and filled out new signature cards. I should have anticipated that. Only there was no time to ponder all the variables. You didn't seem like the type that would look for angles, break an agreement. Besides, everyone thought the war would be over in a matter of months. MacArthur kept up the bullshit, all right. The Reds showing us their asses by Thanksgiving. Our boys home for Christmas. I figured, get the money to a safe place before it's too late, and when things calm down I'll tie up the loose ends. Only it didn't turn out like that. Did it?

"So, I see the name Philip Narby on the register and my mind starts to whirl. Is this really the guy who shtupped me for fifty-five grand? He has the balls not only to stay at the hotel I manage but to register with the name Philip Narby, drink in my cocktail lounge, play around with his lady friend on my beach, in my tenth-floor ocean view suite? Pardon me, but it did get my goat. So I had Lou follow you. Couple of months ago. He said you lived on some island, that you had to take the car across on the ferry. I had the New York license-plate number traced. It was in a woman's name. Somebody Branton. Your lady friend, I take it. So, the next time you showed, I had Lou follow you again and I told him to wait around at the ferry landing. Sure enough, you came back in a different vehicle, an old truck, like a farmer. He followed you as far as he could, without you noticing. Up to the dirt road. Very curious, very interesting. So, I decided to come myself, make a visit. And here I am."

"Did you know someone in Tokyo named Bill Knowles? Someone from the embassy? Only he claimed to work for the Allbright Paper Company."

"Bill Knowles? Nope. Never heard of him."

"He told me that I ought to take out the money. As payment."

"Yeah? By what right? Payment for what?"

"Information. Information on Willoughby and MacArthur. On Tsuji, and the phony war-crimes tribunal, about bringing the Jap war criminals back to Japan to form an anti-communist militia. Information on Campos and M267. Information on the Putnam Lumber Company. You remember Putnam, don't you Sid? We're standing on Putnam land right now. Land I bought from Putnam."

"You're still all scrambled up, aren't you? Maybe you feel guilty, that you ran away. Well don't. That wasn't a war, it was a shanda. A disgrace. I spit on all of them. That Nazi MacArthur. Walker. Keiser. Ridgeway. Eisenhower and his golfing pals. I'd like to shove those golf balls down their throats. I advise you to forget about it. It was no dishonor running. It was a dishonor staying, obeying. To hell with it, yeah?"

"I didn't run. They were trying to kill me."

"They were trying to kill all of us. You're no different."

"There were invoices in Martha's file. I double-checked in your files, too, at the warehouse on Avenue D, when you weren't around. There were receipts for the paper shipments, the rolls of newsprint from Macon, Georgia, from the Putnam Lumber Company. I found some other interesting items too, at the bottom of the drawer. Magazines wrapped in yellow cellophane. And there were a couple of crates of brand new two-way radio batteries, stashed under your desk. Do you understand the difficulties of communicating coordinates under heavy mortar fire using a two-way radio with a dead battery? A battery that was supposed to have been replaced? Overwhelming, Sid. The difficulties were overwhelming."

"The past is past. Dead and buried. Whoever this Knowles character is, he's got nothing to do with me. He was selling you a bill of goods, my friend. Playing around with your unstable state of mind. No offense. But, well, you seem pretty healthy now. You and your lady friend. In the best of health."

"Why did they call me that? Call me the congressman's boy?"

Sid shrugged. "Not a clue. But boy, you were squeaky clean back then. As far as I could see, the Chesterfields were your only vice. Looks like you're all grown up now. You've got this very interesting place out here in the woods. A very nice-looking young lady. The sports car. Cavorting on Miami Beach. A taste for bourbon. Expensive cigars. Very grown-up. And grown-ups always pay their debts. Isn't that so?"

"I thought we had agreed. We're even."

"I'm willing to forgive. Up to a point. Up to July, 1953. What you took in Havana. Let's call it a wartime dispensation. Sid Black's personal G.I. Bill. But after the war, after you came home and started the funny business at the bank in Coral Gables, getting Wilson on your side? I'll consider that money a loan. How's that? A loan. And the note is due. Today. I'll waive the interest. How's that? I'm a reasonable man."

"Like I said, the reasonable man is always the one without the gun. You're hardly in a position to make demands, now are you? Stuck out here in the jungle without a car, without a phone. No one around for miles and miles. Besides, the man you should be negotiating with is Bill Knowles, not me. He authorized the withdrawals. And Wilson, too. He was more than willing to go along. It's the system, Sid. I'm only a cog."

Still, nothing of fear in Black's eyes. Not even anger. Because the Jew was lying, his mind clicking away at an entirely separate set of facts, shunting off like a train switching tracks. "Funny thing about Wilson," he said after a moment. "I never would have met Bob Wilson if you hadn't stolen from me, borrowed from me, from the bank in Coral Gables. Never would have come to Florida, either, if I hadn't been tracking you down. And without Bob Wilson I never would have started up with the hotels. Bob showed me the ropes, introduced me to the appropriate financial instruments. No, if it weren't for you, I would have gone back to Baltimore, tried to make a go of it up there. In the grocery business, where I worked before enlisting in the Army. Hard to imagine, now. Going back to Baltimore. So, in a way, I have you to thank for my success. In fact, that's why I'm here. To sustain our successful business relationship. Why break up a good thing, eh?"

"You know, don't you? You know who I am. Where I'm from."

Sid shrugged. "You're Philip Narby. I'm happy to stick with that. If that's what you want. Philip Narby. Owns quite a bit of land out here. A couple thousand acres, so I understand." He shook his head, tapping the cigar. "I made the same mistake as you, first time out. Buying property under my own name instead of a corporate entity. Still, live and learn. What's done is done. It's easy enough to remedy. Between you and me, Bob Wilson and Murray."

"Who's Murray?"

"My accountant. A highly-skilled individual. I'll introduce you. I highly recommend him."

"You want the land? Is that it?" Narby laughed. He rolled another cigarette, the blend, and poured a bourbon. Black wasn't here for the money. It was deeper. Knowles was out of it. McCoy was dead. Sid Black was the only one left from Tokyo, the only who knew what had happened to him in Korea. "What the hell for? It's worthless, it's waste. That's why it was so damned cheap. The pines around here are garbage, no good for paper or lumber or even resin anymore. You can't even raise cattle here."

"Worthless? In the Sahara desert maybe. Or the North Pole. But in America? In Florida? There's no such thing as worthless. Come on," Black said, pushing out of the chair, nearly a foot shorter than Narby, brushing away a fragment of ash that had crumbled onto his lap, scissoring the Cohiba. "Show me around, would you? I'm curious. We'll check up on Lou. See how he's doing with the car."

Narby tucked the revolver back into his waistband. "You first." They went out the front door. Black daubed lightly at his face with a handkerchief, flicking away the mosquitoes as they walked around the house—the wide porch and overhanging metal eaves, the green louvered shutters, the limestone pillars on which the box-like house rested two feet off the ground, the garden sectioned off by the low coral-rock walls, the overgrown thickets and the groves—until they got to the pond, its gleaming mirror-surface dotted with floating hearts and lilies, rimmed at the banks with a translucent yellow scum, shaded on one side by the Australian pines and soft pale-barked melaleuca and the stands of willowy bamboo.

"What's this? A lake?"

"A pond. A mosquito breeding pit."

Black stopped, looking, thinking. "Are there more lakes like this, on your land?"

"It's not a lake, Sid. It's a pond. A hole in the ground."

Originally, Waters had dug it for the fill dirt to make the pad under the house and raise the road where it dipped—muck mixed with marl, a whitish-gray slurry that dried in the sun as hard as cement and kept down the weeds and brush. The pit had started to seep groundwater and in the spring it had filled with rain and Waters had lined the sides with cement and transformed it into a pond, pumping in fresh water every season, skimming off the algae and scum.

Beyond the pond, behind the Australian pines, was a large patch of barren ground, the hard white surface cracked and sprouted with sparse weeds. A good spot to build the airstrip, when the time came. Sid strolled through the pines and stepped out from their shade into the diffused furnace of the sun, the pestilential glare. "What happened here?"

"This is where we dumped most of the muck from the bottom of the pond. Makes a passable road surface if you don't have asphalt."

Black seemed lost in thought, under some kind of momentary spell—the white ground under his feet radiating and magnifying the heat and the glare, the dead air swirled by a vortex of gnats, the stink of the household trash pile in the jungle beyond mixing with his cigar smoke. Yet for some reason Black stood there as if he were sunning himself on the Riviera. Daubing his face, his gold wristwatch catching the glare, he said to Narby, "You call this worthless? Land. Sun. Water. Thousands of acres. It's all like this? I mean, where you hit water when you dig down? And the dirt from the bottom dries out like this, clear and hard?"

"Except for the mudflats and mangrove out at the point and a few small stands of oak, on the higher ground. The rest, yeah, it's all the same. Rattlesnakes, palmettos, same scrub pine, same chalky soil."

"I can see it," Black said. "Clear as a bell. The whole thing."

"See what?"

He took the cigar from his mouth and pivoted his head slightly earthward and spit a shred of tobacco leaf. "They got an airport around here?"

"Ratliff Field. In Myerton."

"Good. We'll pick you up. We'll go in Sonny's Cessna. Get a lay of the land. Take some pictures. Then we can go over to the County Clerk's, look at the maps."

There was no point now in holding the land for the Cuban rebels. Not with Castro back in Cuba and País organizing in Santiago and the *New York Times* cheering them on, and poor Campos shoved to the margins, a bit player now, at best. Look at him, at Sid Black, standing there in the middle of the patch of barren white ground, puffing out his bull-chest under the bright yellow shirt—a target, begging to be perforated. Utterly defenseless, in the open, without even a tree to cower behind. Black first and then the goon. Narby had his hand at his waist, fingering the wooden grip of the revolver. It was one or the other. Shoot him, kill Black, right now, right here. Or else go in with him. Forget Knowles and go with Black. No one else was left, no one else who knew.

"I followed you to Miami and then I met Wilson and now I follow you here and I see it all, clear as day," Black was saying. "And just at the right time. That's what matters. That's why I know. I got the money out of Japan, and I'm thinking it's gone, I'm out fifty-five grand, but here it is, all around me, thousands of acres, safe and sound. You saved me a lot of trouble, friend. I got out of Korea in one piece and now, thank god, I'm getting out of the Beach, out of the hotel business. Just in time. That's the secret, Mr. Philip Narby. It's not about getting in. That's the easy part. Anyone can put a little money down, go to the race-track and place a bet. No no no. The secret is knowing when to get out.

"In business, in love and marriage. In a fight. In war. That's the most important thing there is. Not the getting-in. But knowing when to get out. Capiche?"

PART IV:
COCO
REEF

It was hardly likely that Bill Knowles
had sent Philip Narby to Lacoosa County
years ago for the sole purpose of
finding Dan Atlee and eliminating him.
Still, there was nothing to disprove it.

SID BLACK HAD BROKEN OPEN the filing cabinet a little wider. Narby remembered now. The humiliation, the smug hypocrisy when he had gone to Ted McCoy with the unsigned document about Brigadier General Charles Willoughby. What Willoughby had done constituted treason, collusion—not merely with the enemy but with the worst element of the enemy, the butchers and torturers. And McCoy, with his exalted American Foreign Service Civil Servant L-5 rank, had dressed Nabry down like a disobedient schoolboy. "You want me to help you? All right. Here's what you should do. Take this, this slander, or whatever the hell it is, and get rid of it. Show it to no one, tell no one about it. Tear it up, burn it. Put it out of your mind. Forget you ever saw it." And Narby—Tom, or Jim—had pleaded, almost begged. "No, Ted. I can't. You know what they're like, those people surrounding MacArthur. I dug around at the tribunal offices. This son-of-a-bitch, this Colonel Tsuji Masanobu, he's still at large. And look at what G.H.Q. is asking us to do now, damn it. They're letting the nationalist fanatics off the hook, all because of what's happening in China. For Christ's sake Ted, I know you don't go along with that losing-China hysteria."

McCoy laughed in his face. Almost threatened him. "If you're waiting for another Nuremburg, forget it. This is Asia, not Europe. I'm not talking about that Oriental-mind garbage that MacArthur hauls out at every press conference. I'm no racist. But life is cheap here. The values, the rules, are different. The world is what it is. It might rub against your sense of fairness, of how things ought to be done. But these men who you're so eager to condemn have fought in two world wars. They're heroes. What the hell have you done? What the hell have you sacrificed? What gives you the right? Who the hell are you to judge, to cry treason? Let me inform you, once and for all. If any of this gets out, the only one to suffer, the only one who's going to pay the price, my young friend, is you."

Not exactly true, as things had turned out. McCoy had paid first, his hands tied behind his back and a bullet hole in his temple. Cloaked by the fog of war they could murder at will. It was MacArthur's people who had murdered Ted McCoy, not the Red Korean Army.

He remembered how nervous, tied up in knots he had been in Havana. In Coral Gables, every time he made a trip to the bank—nervous, sick, sex starved, craving the dope, operating in the dark, never knowing who was on his side, enemies of enemies of enemies. McCoy. Knowles. The Alger-Hiss Dean-Acheson types. Humiliating him, stringing him along, calling him the congressman's boy behind his back. They had used him, and probably they had used Sid Black, too. Just as they were using Castro and M26, with the eloquent assistance of the *New York Times*. They wanted the repugnant mulatto Batista out. Afterwards, it would be easy enough to tar Castro with the communist brush. In the chaos of rebellion, the fog of war, they could slip in their own handpicked man, some obedient puppet—one of the reliable Ortodoxos, perhaps, a fair-skinned Cuban with well-established business ties, beholden to American interests.

Narby was parked across the square from the red brick courthouse. He took his time finishing his cigarette, watching as one of the deputy sheriffs came stiffly down the steps and eased himself, belly last, into the bubble gum machine. Blowing the dope-laced smoke out the truck window, within easy olfactory range of the local constabulary. Calm as could be. Not the slightest tremor, not a twitch. Just as Narby had always imagined himself—a mood of easy self-control and confidence, a sense of superiority that arose not from pedigree or privilege or pride but from sheer intelligence. Not only grasping the reality of the situation but imagining it at the same time, creating the reality in the very act of imagining it.

He waited until the deputy had driven off. City Hall, the County Court, and the Sheriff's office all shared the same building, a stolid red brick structure. Built on the site of the former United States Calvary G.H.Q.—or so the plaque in the square claimed—from where the federal soldiers had prosecuted their wars against the Seminoles. A guerilla war of raids and sabotage and retreat, the mongrel half-black Indians desperate to defend their refuge in the pine thickets and the swamps. He crossed the square, swinging his attaché, the downtown streets deserted in the ferocious heat and glare. Wearing a Stetson western-style hat now instead of the Miami Beach bon-vivant narrow-brim straw fedora, cowboy boots instead of the Lincoln Road Italian shoes, and a bolo tie.

The central corridor was empty, a space of hot air churned by a pair of oscillating fans. The county commissioners' offices were to the right, at the end of the hall. Bob Sunderland was waiting for him.

"Mr. Narby," he said, standing from behind his desk, extending his arm "Phil. Good to see you, again. Come on in, and close the door, if you don't mind. Don't want to lose any of this precious air-conditioning. Please, have a seat."

"Afternoon, Bob."

"Can I get you something to drink? A nice cold Coca Cola?"

"No, thanks." He laid his hat on the chair next to him, the attaché resting at his feet. "Hot one today. Nice in here, though."

"Ain't it? You cain't imagine what it was like in here before the County bought us poor suffering Commissioners these here window air-conditioners. I got to tell you. Used to be, my three favorite letters in the whole wide world were U, S, and A. Only now, know what they are? B, T, and U."

He held a straight face, waiting for Narby to laugh. Obligingly, Narby smiled and nodded. "I'm with you there, Bob. So. Did you get the documents I sent?"

"Sho did." He tapped at a sheaf of papers on his otherwise uncluttered desk. "I take it you got the bids from that Tampa outfit I recommended? That kind of dredging and fill you plan to do out there, that's got to be done correctly. To the code. If you go with the Snopes Company, as I recommend, well, the zoning board's going to feel quite comfortable with that choice."

Narby hoisted the attaché on his lap and clicked it open. "As a matter of fact, I have the bids right here." The Tampa outfit, Snopes Excavation and Grading, was owned by Sunderland's brother-in-law. "And the most recent aerial photographs. As you can see, Bob, I've circled the tracts I'm still concerned about." Narby laid out the papers and photo enlargements on the desk and Sunderland lowered his large loaf-like head—a man of fifty or so, with enormous ears, and two deep folds running from the sides of his nose to the corners of his mouth—moving his eyes over the figures and the marked-up black-and-white prints of jungle and mangrove.

"Hm. Uh-uh. Hm." He made a series of noises indicating what Narby took as guarded approval, repeatedly tapping the papers with the blunt tip of his index finger. "I'll need to take some time to go over all of this. Let's see here." He read down the list. "Minimum elevation requirements, easements for the road and the power poles, plat plan, drainage plans, putting up the guarantee bonds. Well, I don't foresee any obstacles. Not yet, anyway. The sooner I can impress upon my fellow Commissioners how much badly needed revenue this is going to bring to the county coffers, the sooner you can get them bull-dozers down here. You familiar with that saying—a rising tide lifts all boats? Well, that's the best argument there is for what you're proposing. That if we don't take advantage of that rising tide right here in Lacoosa County, then that tide's going to raise up someone else's boats in some other county."

"What about Commissioner Granger? His, how should I put it, moral concerns?"

Sunderland leaned back, the wooden swiveling chair creaking under his weight. A big rangy former cattleman: enormous hands, big face, long legs, and a paunch from the heavy Southern cooking. "You should have heard ole Grange at the last meeting. *We don't want no My'ama Beach going up in our backyard. That's not the kind of folks we want crowding into our County. That's not the kind of people we want buying up our precious land, using up our resources. Voting in our elections, sitting on our school board.* If there's one thing Granger don't care for, it's the Catholic religion. And if there's another thing he cares for even less, it's them slick Joosh bankers. He don't mean no harm, really. It's only that folks like him, well, they don't like change, that's all. Even when change means progress for the County. They got it in their heads that any change to the way things are is likely to rain down Nigras into their children's schools and raise their taxes and bring on who knows what other plagues from them Pharaohs up in Washington."

"Well, as you well know, Bob, I certainly don't share Commissioner Granger's point of view about change and progress. However. Like you, I do feel a responsibility to the people of Lacoosa County to respect their way of life, their traditions and such. Sure. *The Protocols of the Elders of Zion* might be going a bit far, an exaggeration. But Henry Ford was no fool. Henry Ford knew what made America the greatest nation on earth. Am I right?"

Sunderland was listening, leaning back swiveling and creaking, a look of high seriousness on his creased craggy face. "Cain't argue with that," he said.

"I take it you've been following the news. About what's happening with the stock market. Hit a two-fifty high last quarter, a record. Right? And now? It's already plunged to two-twenty. Nobody knows where it will bottom out. You realize what that's going to do to land prices? Here's the thing, Bob. We have to move fast. Because I can't compete with those Jewish developers from New York and Miami. They're going to take advantage of this financial crisis. Manipulate it for their own gain. At one end of the spectrum there's the control of the money supply and interest rates. At the other end, there's land, real estate. You follow me?"

"Sure. More or less. Go on."

Narby sifted through the papers and photographs on Sunderland's desk and separated out the relevant documents. "Without these three tracts, Bob, I can't push the project forward. I need access to the water here, and to the highway over here. These three parcels are the lynch pin that holds it all together. Putnam still owns this tract. That Ocala rancher owns this one. And this one. Well, Epstein owns that now. Same Mel Epstein who came around last month inquiring about zoning and such. And he's already made offers on these other two. Trying to squeeze me out. Obviously. They want to suck me into a bidding war, because they know I can't win. And once that Jewish-owned outfit has snagged three parcels, I'll have to bow out. The banks won't extend my credit unless I can show them a viable plan. I'll have to sell. To Epstein. I don't think that's what anyone around here wants, now is it? Not you, not the County Commissioners. And certainly not the voters of Lacoosa County."

"You been talking to anyone else about all this?"

"Absolutely not, Bob. I promised I'd keep this strictly between you and me, for as long as possible. Let you handle the Commissioners and the Chamber of Commerce as you see fit. After all, I haven't been living down here all my life, haven't raised a family here, like you. I'm more than happy to defer to your judgment. But this stock market thing changes the equation."

"I suppose it does. Tell me again. What did you pay for that land out there, back in fifty-three?"

"Thirty an acre. But that was only for this interior piece. About five hundred acres, where I built my house. We'll never see those kind of prices again, that's for sure. These other tracts were considerably more. Hundred, hundred fifty. But now, with Epstein putting on the pressure, there's talk of going as high as three hundred, three twenty-five. I can't match that. No one around here can pay that for raw undeveloped land. Epstein gets his mitts on those three tracts, right while the market is crashing, and that's it for me. Like I said, I'll be forced to sell. Cheap. Whatever I can get. And that will bring down property values, Bob. Everybody's property values, Bob, down and down and down as surely as if you had built your house, your family's home, on top of a big old gaping sinkhole."

Narby leaned back, flush with his performance. "If we let that happen, the only winner will be Epstein. And the Jewish developers."

"Not exactly the outcome we want, is it? Not the outcome the voters want."

"No, it is not. And what's more, Epstein won't be looking for his contractors up in Tampa. They'll bring in their own people. You know how clannish these Jews can be. They're liable to bring in the unions, too. Can you imagine that, Bob? Labor unions, in Lacoosa County. Don't get me wrong. For all I care, Epstein can make his millions and do whatever the hell he wants with it. Give it all to Israel. Only let him do it somewhere else. Not in Lacoosa County. Not in our own backyard."

"I got me considerable influence with the Cattle Ranchers Association. I'm going to do whatever I can to see that those tracts go to you. By the end of the week. At a price you can afford, Phil. A fair price. I'm behind you on this, one hundred percent."

"I appreciate that Bob. Damn glad to hear it. "

"Here's something else you'll be glad to hear. I had me a nice long chat with Cliff Varnell, our County Prosecutor. Had him put in a call to the State Attorney's Office up in Tallahassee.

Seems like there might be a case against Putnam after all, that turpentine poaching business you told me about. Tapping into a couple hundred acres of pine that never belonged to them. And that business with Higginbotham, about them three colored boys that died out at the camp, back in forty-two. Now you know as well as I that there ain't no chance in hell the State of Florida is going to spend a dime investigating let alone bring charges about something like that. But that don't matter, long as Putnam feels the heat. Even a little. See what I mean?"

"A couple of anonymous letters might help, don't you think? Threatening to dredge all that up again. Threatening to go to the N.A.A.C.P. and the A.C.L.U."

"Whoa. I wouldn't go that far. We don't want to taint ourselves, even hypothetically, now do we?"

"Good point, Bob."

"That man Vetch who used to run the camp commissary. He's still out there, ain't he?"

Narby shifted in the chair. Sunderland might know more than we was letting on. "Carl Vetch. Yes, he is. I know him, all right. Can't be avoided, really. After all, he's my closest neighbor. He's got maybe two, three acres. Still lives in that derelict old store. He's not a problem. Soon as he sees what's going on he'll be more than eager to sell. From the looks of it, he sure could use the money."

"You know anything about that fish camp out there? What's that about? I tried to drive out there once, take a look for myself, only that road was making me seasick. He's got no license for any kind of business. Far as I know."

"I'd hardly call it a business. A couple of jerry-built shacks out in the mangrove. Frankly, between you and me, Bob, the man's got something wrong with him, mentally. Anyway, those shacks are on property I bought years ago from Putnam. They'll be gone soon enough."

"I heard that he was co-habitating out there with some Nigra woman. Two of them living out there like a couple of animals.

If he gives you any trouble, refuses to cooperate, I could talk to the Sherriff. Have the law pay him a visit. We don't tolerate that kind of filth round here."

"I appreciate that, Bob. But I don't foresee any problem. He'll take my offer." He opened the brief case again. "You a cigar smoker, Bob?"

"On occasion."

"I think you'll appreciate this." He took out the soft metal tube and handed it across the desk.

"Co-heeba dell ray." He twisted off the cap and extracted the thick black cigar, its fragrance released into the drab little office. "Don't believe I've ever handled one of these. That's some fine-smelling cigar. Thank you much, Phil."

"My pleasure, Bob."

Sunderland leaned back, cradling the unlit cigar between his fingers. "What do you make of that hullaballoo over there in Cuba? What's wrong with them people, anyway? Can't never decide how to run their affairs, letting gangsters and corruption run rampant. No matter who's in charge. They all made from the same stamp down there, far as I can tell. Best thing for the Cuban people would be to let the U.S. Army come in and run things for a while. Give 'em a taste of law and order, a taste of decency. You been down there to Havana?"

"Once. Can't say I cared for it."

"Ha. You're all right, Phil. Only. Well, you need to let loose once in a while. Unwind, sow some oats while you're still young. Before some woman snags you for a mate. Know what I'm saying?"

Narby laughed. "Maybe you're right, Bob."

"Course I'm right. Good-looking young man like you. Served his country, did his nation proud. You deserve your fun, too."

2

THE REVOLUTION HAD CLAIMED its first martyr. Frank País was dead—chief of action and sabotage for M267, tireless and protean organizer of the hydra-headed National Directorate, the moving force behind thousands of acts of civil disobedience and militant resistance, strikes and bombings and assassinations that were beginning to loosen Batista's grip. País—the key man in the llano, the towns, while Castro nurtured his growing army of bearded long-haired rebels in the wilds of the Sierra—murdered at the age of twenty-three, betrayed by one of his own, a chivato, shoved into an idling car and taken to an alleyway in Santiago de Cuba and shot in the head. But rather than mourn, Campos had been rather ecstatic. Because the day after País was killed all of Santiago, the second largest city in Cuba, had shut down. Sixty-thousand people took to the streets to attend the funeral. There were strikes and marches and actions all over the country, a massive show of sympathy and support. Batista lashed back, tightening the noose with a suspension of the most basic constitutional rights. Now he could legally arrest whomever he wanted, shut down whatever newspaper threatened the national security. The de facto dictatorship had crossed over into de jure tyranny. His isolation hardening, huddled with his most hardcore cronies and secret police, Batista was running out of options.

"Our moment has come, Felipé. The people are no longer afraid. It is a great awakening up, a lion come from its sleep, al fin."

Two months ago Campos had begun his residency at Jackson Memorial Hospital in Miami. Between the demands of his medical training and organizing for the Revolution there was no time for diversions or small talk. They sat at the kitchenette table in the dreary little garden apartment, drinking the thick black coffee that apparently was the Cuban's only remaining vice. No tobacco, no rum, never a remark about women or sex—an ascetic with the ascetic's self-righteous discipline, as if the taming of his lusts guaranteed the purity of his dream of an egalitarian Cuba, purged of corruption and foreign domination.

Armando Hart was slated to take over operations in the llano and coordinate the next general strike—campesinos, mill and factory and transportation workers, civil servants, even the professional class. A total paralysis of the Cuban state. Weapons were flowing into the Sierra now from Miami and Galveston and up and down the Caribbean coast of Mexico. In Havana the underground groups, freshly armed, were preparing to attack, no longer afraid to answer violence with violence. Victory was within their grasp: a single tremendous overwhelming convulsion, organized from above but flowing up through the spontaneity of the masses.

"Now it comes to make choice for all people. To be with the revolution or to be with Batista. There is no middle. No place for to hide. Every Cubano must to make decision. Ahorita. Now. Today. Me entiendes?"

"Maybe so. But there's already been half a dozen attempts at a general strike, right? Not even País managed to pull it off. There's too much in-fighting. You're relying too much on the enemy-of-my-enemy logic. The closer you come to booting out Batista, the more you lose cohesion. Sure, Castro's getting most of the weapons now. The darling of the *New York Times*. But when Batista falls there's going to be a hell of a lot of chaos. A power vacuum. How many Cuban-governments-in-exile are there now? Five, six? It's going to be a big fiesta, followed by an even bigger mess."

"No. You are wrong, Felipé. Already we have plan for interim president, provisional government, new elections, the restoration of the constitution. I now work very long for making agreement. El Pacto de Miami. We are now agree to form La

Junta de Liberación Cubana. Agarmonte, Chomón, Prío, Varona. Fifteen groups here in Florida, unidos. All will put signature."

"Yeah? What about Fidel?"

"For Viente-seis de Julio I put my own signature. I am to represent Castro."

That didn't sound right. After the amnesty in May of '55, when Castro had come through Miami on his way to Mexico City, he had left Campos behind, excluded him from the core. With the crackdown following País's martyrdom, direct communication with the Sierra was impossible. Narby doubted that Campos was acting with Castro's consent. Still, Ernesto had the Moncadista prestige. He'd been in the fight, risking his neck from the very beginning. The natty little Cuban was puffing himself up, re-asserting his importance now that the wind was blowing in his direction.

"Anything in this pact of yours about protecting private property once all hell breaks loose? About the new government continuing to honor trade agreements? About the rebels laying down their weapons once Batista is gone?"

Campos shrugged. "Mas o menos. It is only paper, after all. Ultimately, the people must decide. Siempre, es la gente."

"La gente? Never met him. But whoever he is, he better be anti-communist. And you might want to suggest he get a shave and haircut and put on a suit and tie before taking office."

"I see you have new automobile, Felipé. Tres chic."

He was in the habit of driving the Guilieta whenever Willa was away. "You like it? Come on, I'll give you a ride."

"After the Revolution. You can take me in circle, how you say, after win the race?"

"A victory lap."

"Eso."

"It's a deal."

3

"HELLO, SID."

"Phil. Come in, have a seat. You remember Bob Wilson. Vice President at the Bank of Coral Gables. Bob, you remember Phil. That misunderstanding a few years ago, that's water under the bridge. Agreed? Good. This is Mel Epstein. Mel, Philip Narby. Can I get you anything before we start, Phil. Something to eat, a drink?"

"Bourbon. Scotch. Whatever you got."

"Anyone else? How about some sandwiches? Good."

Epstein rose—a tall thin mildly stooped man in glasses, with tightly curled graying hair—and went into the adjoining room and picked up the phone. Black had converted the penthouse suite at the Calvado into an office with a conference room. Fifteen stories above the Atlantic Ocean. The curtains were drawn over the sliding glass doors, the raging sunlight seeping in around the edges, the machine-chilled air swirling the smoke from Black's cigar and Epstein's Pall Malls. Several stacks of documents were laid out on the table, and a cup with pens and pencils. Narby sat, sprawling his legs under the table, and took out his tobacco pouch. They were looking at him, watching him. He was the unknown factor. The banker and Epstein wore regulation business attire, gray suit and tie. Black was decked out in a lemon-yellow crepe blazer over a dark woven polo shirt. Epstein, at least ten years older than Sid, the contrasting Jewish type to Sid's swarthy solid build—bookish, bony, pale, nervous. Wilson was pale and puffy with flushed red cheeks, chin lightly nicked from the morning's shave. Just as Narby remembered him from the bank years ago, slavering over Miss Prentice's creamy vortex.

Epstein came back into the room. "OK. Let's get started, Sid."

"First things first. Everyone relax. We're all friends here, partners. Capiche? Not a word we say goes beyond these four walls. Everyone agreed? Good. Mel. Let's get the papers of incorporation out of the way."

Epstein peeled a few sheets off the pile in front of him. "Just sign where you name is," he said, passing them to Narby.

He had driven from Campos's apartment with the top down, his hair tangled, two days without shaving, in a loose sports shirt, carelessly wrinkled. Feeling quite pleasant now, having smoked a stick crossing the MacArthur Causeway. On a high wire far above these blobs sitting around the table, watching him, envying him, waiting for him to fall. He took a pen from the cup. There were four signature lines, each with a name and title typed underneath. Men who thrived on paper, who shared nothing but a paper commonality. Paper enemies of paper enemies.

"Something wrong, Phil?"

"Maybe before I sign I should know what the hell it is I'm signing. If that's not too much too ask."

Black sucked on the cigar, regarding him. He and Black, at least, had more than paper between them. "Not at all. Mel, would you mind explaining."

"We're forming a corporation. For the purpose of purchasing and developing the property. Standard stuff, Phil. You got to have officers to form a corporation. Sid's the president, I'm the secretary, Bob is the treasurer. And, as you can see on the signature line, you're the vice president. Not that it's absolutely necessary in the state of Florida for more than one person …"

"I think he's got the gist. Sun American Land Corporation. You're the V.P, Phil. That and a dime will get you a cup of coffee. It's a formality. It means nothing. Within a year we'll dissolve it."

A phony signature on a meaningless ephemeral document—Sid Black's business model. He signed and slid it to Wilson, each man signing in turn until it reached Epstein who slipped the paper into a red folder.

"Bravo. Now, the loan agreements. Bob."

"I've got everything ready to go. Only. Let's talk about this first, Sid. Flesh it out a little. With the hotels, there was precedence. It was common practice, over the years. But this? We're flying by the seat of our pants here, Sid."

"Flesh it out?" Sid paused, swiveling in the chair, scissoring the cigar. "You're concerned about Phil, that it? Go ahead. Speak your mind. Lay your cards on the table, Bob. There's no room here for second guessing."

"Might we have a word in private, Sid? Before we go on to the loan agreements."

"Absolutely not. Like I said, we lay our cards on the table. Go on, speak your mind."

"How's Miss Prentice?" Narby interjected, lighting a cigarette. "You remember? One of your lovely tellers. The brunette."

Wilson looked at him, gauging him, weighing the off-hand remark. "It's a shame about Miss Prentice. She got married. They never stay on at the bank, once they get married. Last I heard, she was expecting."

"That is a shame, Bob. An extraordinarily charming young woman. A real asset."

Wilson smiled. "That she was."

"That's quite a harem you keep over there in Coral Gables."

Wilson laughed. "You could put it like that."

Narby glanced at Sid, sitting at the other end of the table, framed by the rim of light seeping in around the edges of the curtain. "I'm just laying my cards on the table, Sid. All you gentlemen are happily married. But I'm still single. Still looking for the right girl. Maybe Bob could introduce me."

Sid laughed. "What about your strawberry-blonde?"

"She's a lot of fun, Sid. But not the kind of girl you marry. Not the kind of girl you bring home to mother. Know what I mean?"

"Gentlemen. Can we get back to the loan agreements? I've got a hell of a lot of paperwork in front of me."

"Just fleshing it out, Mel," Narby said. "Fact is, you're getting quite a reputation over in Lacoosa County, Mel. That last tract, Sid. Eighty-five an acre, at a hundred acres a parcel. Between their Jew phobia and the stock-market crash, they're practically begging me to buy. How the hell did you manage that, Sid? Get the market to crash like that, right on cue?"

Black shrugged. "Fortune shines brightest on those who take advantage." He rapped his fist on the table. "Hear that? Opportunity, pounding on the door. It's screaming *once in a lifetime*. Let's jump on it, gentlemen. The sooner we get the loan agreements signed, the sooner they'll start to default. If we expedite things a little, we can ride this down-cycle right into the trough. There will never, never, never again be Florida land up for grabs like this. And I emphasize: NEVER. Push the loans through, Bob. You're the vice president of the bank, for Christ's sake."

"I agree, Sid. A hundred percent. Only, it's going to raise eyebrows. I need to be assured that everyone here has the legal standing ..."

"Here's how it is, Bob. Phil and I served in Korea together. He bailed me out when things were bad. I did the same for him. We trusted each other with our lives. This man is a war hero. Mortally wounded in battle. He's got scars that would make Frankenstein wince. More to the point, he's got those Lacoosa County rednecks eating out of his hand. He knows the land out there, knows the people. He's practically in bed with one of the County Commissioners. Legal standing? The man's a fucking paragon."

Epstein turned to Wilson. "There's nothing to worry about, Bob. It's no different than the hotels, if you think about it."

He was on the high wire, looking down. Black was putting on quite a show, but for whose sake? To convince Narby that Black was convincing Wilson? Setting Narby up, using him for bait?

"Explain about the hotels, Sid. I'm new to the business world. The Calvado used to be a damned nice hotel, clean, good service. What's the point of buying a hotel and letting it go down the tubes? It's like you're putting yourself out of business."

"It's Ben Novak. That's who's putting us out of business. The Fontainebleau. And now the Eden Roc and the Americana. Restaurants, night clubs, enormous swimming pools, a quarter mile of beachfront. A thousand guest rooms each, all brand new. More glitz, more flabbergast. They started this thing they call the American Plan. For one price you get room and meals and entertainment, all included. Never have to leave the air-conditioned hotel, never have to step out into the heat or the rain. You can leave your kids right in the room in front of the TV while you're downstairs swooning over Tony Bennett, laughing at Jerry Lewis, boozing it up like you're some kind of celebrity. South Miami Beach is underwater, drowning. The Edgewater, the Atlantique, all of lower Collins and Ocean Drive. The clubs and bars, the little restaurants with checkered tablecloths, that's all on the way out. Even Lincoln Road. You watch. Am I right, Bob? The American Plan is killing us."

"I didn't see it coming the way you did, Sid. But, yes, that seems to be the trend. The money is definitely moving up Collins. Though I think Lincoln Road will hold it's own."

"I wouldn't bet on it. So, here's the thing. Everybody listen. If it weren't for this man here, Philip Narby, none of us would be sitting here, about to embark on a venture of virtually unlimited financial return. I'm out of the Army and I'm looking for Phil, to clear up that little misunderstanding with the bank account. And that's how I meet Bob. And Bob tells me about the Edgewater. Explains to me how you could get in and get out. Quick."

"I only pointed out the desirability of that particular property, Sid. And because you had excellent credit, with your distinguished Army record, well, I was able to offer you favorable terms. Nothing more to it than that. I was acting in the interest of the business community. As I always have."

"Mel, that you how you remember it?"

Epstein shrugged. "It was very unusual. There were half a dozen liens on the property. Piggybacked mortgages. I've been an accountant for over thirty years and I never saw anything like it."

"So. With Bob's help I was able to purchase the Edgewater at a good price, with a small down payment. You don't mind me explaining, do you Bob? A modest little hotel, nothing fancy, fifty rooms, two blocks from the beach. Mostly a Jewish clientele, families who summer in the Catskills and come to the Beach for a week or two in the winter. Every winter the same crowd. Year after year. You'd think a hotel like that was a sure thing. Right? Wrong. Doomed. I knew it, Bob knew it, Mel knew it."

"I was still in Baltimore, Sid. What did I know? I did the books, that's all."

"So. I bought the hotel, despite the writing on the wall. And with Bob's experience to guide me, I decided to hasten the inevitable. During the high season even a modest hotel like that brings in a hell of a lot of cash. The problem is, for every dollar that comes in, ninety-five cents go out. You got the front desk staff, the housekeeping staff, maintenance on the building and the grounds, the electrical, the plumbing. With the ocean air and the salt, the blistering sun and the storms, the corrosion, people flushing their baby alligators down the toilets—it's a real headache, keeping up a hotel. But why, I asked myself. Why plow money back into a doomed enterprise? By cutting back maintenance and hotel services to the bare bones I figured I could recoup my down payment in one season. Not only that, but if I relinquished my ownership of the property while at the same retaining management, I stood to make a handsome profit. Of course, after a few years the hotel would no longer be fit for human habitation. Even the most loyal customers would get sick of complaining and go elsewhere. So, I sold the property and formed Blackburn Management. Hastening the inevitable. You following me so far, Phil?"

"Sold it? What sucker would buy a hotel that was falling apart?"

"Smart question. I told you, Mel. He's got a Yiddishe kop. The answer: I sold it to myself. To Sunshine Properties. A corporation I formed especially for the purpose of purchasing the Edgewater. While Sunshine Properties went into bankruptcy, the Blackburn Management Company did quite well. After the foreclosure Bob had no trouble finding another buyer for the Edgewater. Ain't that so, Bob? With the money from the Edgewater I formed a corporation to buy the Atlantique, and of course I hired Blackburn Management. Because of their excellent reputation. To hasten the inevitable, mind you. It's like I told you. It's not when you get in, it's when you get out. And believe me, the time to get out of South Miami Beach is now. But, of course, in order to get out, first, you have to get in. Capiche?"

Epstein got up to answer the knock at the door in the front room. 'The point Sid is trying to make," Wilson said, "is that the key to any transaction is foresight. Vision. Grasping not just one aspect of the transaction but the entire arc, from start to finish. The financial instruments available for real estate and development are remarkably elastic these days. I wouldn't want you to get the idea that anything we're doing here is any shape or form outside the boundaries of current financial norms."

"I get it. You have to get in to get out." Black was deep. Narby was beginning to appreciate Black's methods. Deeper than Knowles. "I can imagine any number of situations where that principle holds true. Foreign policy. Gambling. Politics. Relations with the opposite sex."

Epstein came in with a tray. The effort exacerbated the stoop of his paper-clip physique. A bottle of Chivas Regal. An ice bucket and carafe of water and tumblers. A platter of sandwiches cut into triangles.

"Chivas. The breakfast of champions," Narby said. "Official beverage of the U.S. State Department."

"A toast," Sid announced. "To Coco Reef."

"What the hell is Coco Reef?"

"The city we're building. The four of us. Coco Reef, a Waterway Wonderland. You think anyone is going to buy their waterfront dream-house in a place called Sawfish Point? It smells bad. Coco Reef. It rings. It smells good. It's refreshing. My wife came up with it, flipping through one of her fashion magazines. Coco Chanel. The Reef Club in Jamaica. You take a little of this, a little of that. Capiche?"

They held their tumblers: Wilson, the puffy flushed-cheek banker; Epstein, the hawk-nosed rail-thin wiry-haired accountant; and the barrel-chested Master Supply Sergeant Sid Black, resplendent in yellow crepe. "To Coco Reef, gentlemen," Sid announced. "L'chaim and salud."

"To the Pact of Miami," Narby said. "Viva la Revolución."

Epstein was thrumming his fingers on the table. He barely sipped his scotch. "Can we get to the loan agreements now, Sid?"

Wilson began to peel the sheets off his pile.

"Explain the loans to me, Sid. What's the in and the out?"

"You're taking out the loans, personal loans, to finance the purchase of the property, now that most of the owners are willing to sell at a fair price."

"The Jew-proof price. The stock-market crash price."

"The fair price, Phil. Once the elevation and easement and drainage issues are resolved in our favor—in your favor, I should say—then the property can be transferred, with the rights of development attached. You follow? So, that's the in. The out? The out is that you default on the loans. You can't pay the bank. You're broke. You're overextended. The property, the collateral, reverts to the Bank of Coral Gables. Of course, everyone knows how hard it is to unload rotten property, foreclosed properties. Especially during a down cycle in the market. Bingo. Two things happen: one, Sun American will buy the foreclosed acreage from the bank at a very handsome discount, and, two, whoever else is still holding on to a piece here or there will be more than eager to unload it. To anyone willing to buy. Jew, Gentile, White, Negro, Chinaman. What do they care? They're looking to get out. Philip Narby is free of his loan obligations, Sun American can start clearing the land and digging the canals and building the million-dollar-yacht-and-racquet-club, and we can start bringing down the buyers, showing them the progress, the fantastic once-in-a-lifetime investment. Our advertising people already have a jump. Television, magazines, Sunday supplements. I've got a deal cooking with the NBC affiliate up in Baltimore. Late night commercials, but they're made to look more like two-minutes news reports. Newsflash: Coco Reef, Florida. Anyway, once everything is in place, it's clockwork. All we got to do now is wind the clock and pull the stem."

"Buyers? What buyers?"

"The home-site buyers. Remember that word, everybody. *Home-site.* We don't sell *lots*. We sell *home-sites*. In fact, Sun American has already sold about twenty-thousand dollars worth. Ten dollars down for a waterfront homesite in Coco Reef, the sun-soaked water-world wonderland city of the future. Blackburn Oglethorpe. That's our ad agency. Nice ring, eh? We're working on the home-owner's insurance angle, too. Why let anyone from the outside profit on our dime? You build a home, you need insurance. Clockwork."

"I don't follow, Sid. How did you sell land ..."

"Tsk tsk," Sid admonished. "Not land. Not lots. *Home-sites*. Sun American does not sell land. Everyone in this room needs to understand that, inside out, backward and forward. Remember it—*home-site, contract-for-deed*—like you remember your mother's name. Sun American issues contracts-for-deeds. Period. Correct me if I'm wrong, Mel."

"I can't correct you, Sid. Because you're right."

"A contract-for-deed merely states that at such and such and date, when the monthly payments reach a certain sum, then Sun American will transfer to the buyer a deed for the

Coco Reef home-site, as stipulated on the contract. It's a promise, that's all."

"But there are no home-sites, Sid. It's all jungle. Mangrove. Waste."

"Forget that side of it, Phil. You'll be out of it by then. Free and clear of your loan obligations."

"But I keep my five hundred acres. As agreed. You can't touch it, the bank can't touch it, not even with the bankruptcy. Five hundred acres and my house and my road and the easement to the highway."

"Five hundred acres. No problem. Only, better if we swap it out. Your house happens to be smack in the middle of Coco Reef. We'll have to get the draglines in there, the bulldozers. If what you want is peace and quiet, I'll give you, say, a thousand acres—but on the other side of Burnt Farm Road, where it won't interfere. With the cash bonus from the loans, with the Sun American stock you're entitled too, I'd say you're getting a sweet deal. All things considered."

"No swap. My original five hundred that I bought from Putnam. You'll just have to work around it. After that's all settled, all the loans and bankruptcies, it's a clean slate. Right? We'll forget about all that business in Tokyo. The sheet metal, the radio batteries. We'll forget Korea, too. Hell, everyone else has. Wipe it out once and for all."

Black smiled blandly. Obviously, he'd prefer to leave the batteries and other related matters out of the negotiations. "If that's you want, Phil. OK. You understand, however, that if you ever decide to sell that land, Sun American has the right of first refusal."

"Fair enough."

"I'll have Jerry draw out a plat and Mel can draft some kind of agreement. Bob, is the bank good with that?"

"It's your call, Sid. I'll make sure that Phil's piece stays out of the loan documents."

"Who's Jerry?"

"Chief Engineer. You'll meet him soon enough."

"Let's have the papers," Narby said. "Let me in. So I can get out."

4

"WHERE ARE THE MEN, SAM? Why aren't they working on the fence?"

"They gone back to the camp to pack up. Cap'm Vetch told them they got to move out. Said them bulldozers clearing the road down by the pwant going to knock down the camp. Today or tomorrow."

"That son-of-a-bitch. You know better than to believe Vetch. The camp is on my property. You know that. The men know that."

"Cap'm told em the shurf's coming out. With them bulldozers. Those men don't want no more trouble than they already got."

"Sam. I want you to walk over to the camp and tell them that Mr. Narby says they can stay on his land. That nobody will bother them. Vetch is just trying to scare them."

"What they doing out by the pwant, with all them heavy machines? They scraping away the brush, piling it and burning it. Look like they fixing to bring out a dragline, too. I saw it sitting by the highway on a trailer, over to Burnt Farm Road."

"It's a development company. They're clearing some of the old Putnam land, along the mangrove. Building a road. Putting up a few houses. It's going to bring in a lot of money, Sam. And work, too. Decent paying jobs. Eventually, the men will benefit from what's going on. But that's got nothing to do with the camp. That's my property. Understand?"

Narby could never tell what Waters was thinking—the deep measured voice, the face etched with a thousand tiny cuts, the rigid clouded eyes, as if indignation and indifference and impotence were a single unvarying emotion. "They ain't gwine to hire no Negro man to operate machinery. Not round here. Only this." He held up the machete and let it down again. "I'll go tell em. Only you best keep the Cap'm away from them. I ain't never seen him so mad. I told em they oughtn't be laughing at him like that. Teasing and joking at him and all that, out at the sto."

"What do you mean? Teasing him about what?"

"About that woman he living with. They all know what she is. Where he found her. They go over to his sto to buy a sodee pop and they say, *Cap'm Vetch, how the missus* and commence to laugh. *Cap'm, when's the wedding?* The Cap'm chase em away with his shotgun but they come back everyday laughing and hooting him. I never seen the Cap'm so mad. Shaking mad. They lucky they ain't get shot up yet."

"The same woman that he brought around here last summer?"

"Don't know nothing about that."

Narby went inside to look again at the engineer's maps. The camp was safe for now. When the time came—after the road was paved and the first sections along the mangrove cleared—he and Sam would help them find somewhere else to live. Waters had accepted Narby's offer, had built himself a cottage on the other side of the pond, living rent free with electricity from the generator and running water from Narby's well. Narby needed him. The work, maintaining the house and the gardens, was the least of it. An old Negro man, a self-righteous prude, a person of no account, and yet for some reason Narby found it necessary for Waters to think well of him. Necessary that Waters stay with him, take his side.

What could he have done for her? Given her money, told her to leave the only place in the world she had ever known? She was like a child, her mouth dark red as if after sucking on a red lollipop, her hands cool and dry against his skin. In that dank narrow room. The things they had done together would never leave him. Even with Willa, Becca was still with him, soothing and consoling and arousing his lust. As if she had fed him something of her own life that lived inside him now.

He crawled under the table, pushed aside the corner of the rug and lifted the board. From the strongbox he counted out three-hundred dollars and took the revolver—Sid Black's five-chambered Smith and Wesson .38 caliber snub nose. Five bullets. One for Vetch—or maybe two, considering the man's thick layer of flesh, his impenetrable skull. A bullet for Lieutenant Swanson. To relieve Janet of her misery. She wouldn't make a bad-looking war widow, and as long as she remained unattached she could collect Frank's Army pension. A bullet for Dan Atlee, the enemy. Sooner or later, Atlee would see through him. He had to be ready for that. And the remaining bullet? Sid Black, perhaps. Or Bill Knowles, if they ever met again. That day in Havana Narby had been convinced that Knowles had come to kill him, to set him up, use him as bait. Perhaps Narby had been right after all. Knowles was merely waiting, drawing it out until Narby's usefulness was at end.

Or Fidel Castro. In the game of blood-splattered musical chairs that passed for Cuban politics it was Batista now who was living in exile in Miami, plotting the overthrow of the new regime. Campos had gone home to join his victorious comrades. Narby had driven him to the ferry in March and they had said goodbye, sitting on a bench in Bayfront Park. Natty as ever, meticulously groomed in a crisp white shirt, daubed with cologne, toting the same tattered yellowed valise with which he had arrived years ago—both of them, together, crossing the Florida Straits under the cloak of night.

"Felipé. Come with me. Today. Ahorita. To serve the revolution. I'll speak for you. Give the faith for you. Leave behind all this hiding, this living in la sombra."

The invitation had unnerved him. Campos had in fact represented Castro during the Pact of Miami, had apparently redeemed himself of whatever error had compelled Castro to leave him behind on his way to Mexico City, back in the spring of 1955. Through Campos, Narby might indeed get close enough to the great man to fire a single shot. From Sid Black's gun. No one, not even Knowles, could beat him at this game. Castro had been the most convenient expedient through which the more liberal cabal within the U.S. embassy had rid themselves of the embarrassment of Batista. But soon enough they would want Castro out of the picture. *La Historia Me Absolverá*. The man had a messiah complex, delivering his eight-hour rants against the octopus grip of the foreign-owned oil and sugar conglomerates. He could not be manipulated, made into a puppet dancing to *Yankee Doodle Dandy*. The more the Americans antagonized the transitional rebel government with threats of embargos and tariffs, the more they would drive Castro into the waiting arms of papa Khrushchev.

"Felipé. You can begin your life again. Only now without to be cynic. With purpose, with the living heart of an entire people beating with your own."

The sentimental gush had broken the spell. Narby laughed. "As much as I'd like to, Ernesto, I can't." He jerked his head toward the Guilieta, parked on the side of the road. "I've got to return the car. A bourgeois affectation I'm afraid, this respect for private property. Besides. It's your patria, not mine."

The mere mention of patria, Narby had learned, could bring the meanest Cuban to tears. "We'll keep in touch, Ernesto. Yeah? Once you're settled, let me know where you are. Who knows? I might come knocking on your door sooner than you think."

They embraced—not for the last time, Narby suspected—and he watched as Campos made his way across the park toward the ferry slip. As neat and prim as a traveling bible salesmen. The conquering rebels, on the other hand, had kept their beards and long hair, wearing their battle fatigues into the government offices they now controlled. The one with the beret—the Argentine poet who had stood with Arbenz in Guatemala against the C.I.A.-led coup—had just been appointed Minister of Finance. Did Campos really understand what he was walking in to?

He took the gun and the money and got in the truck. Vetch's road was still nothing more than twin ruts breaching the jungle, paralleled by the sagging power line that dipped and rose through the tops of the stunted pines. The store as pathetic as the day Narby had first seen it, the tar-papered roof sagging under the black rot of pine needs and moss, the porch collapsed at one end like a crippled drunk. The same broken gas pump and rust-eaten machine parts, the buckets and tires and vaguely nautical detritus trashed about the yard. Apparently, the so-called improvements Vetch had made with the blackmail money had reverted back into the derelict filth of his stagnant malignant existence.

He parked in the clearing under the stand of oaks, next to Vetch's Ford, and climbed out, sliding the revolver under the waist of his trousers. A thread of smoke wafted from a pipe jutting up out of the crud-layered roof. They were here. Both of them. He would march Vetch into the jungle. A classic wartime-style execution. In the distance he could make out the faint intermittent roar of Sid Black's bulldozers. Still, Becca would no doubt hear the shot, though she wouldn't see. But it was trouble between Whites. He would give her the money and she would never speak of it, not to anyone who mattered. He waded through the filth of the yard, the hammer of the yellow pills clanging in his pulse. He would get close, nuzzle the snub-nose barrel under Vetch's ribcage. He longed for some other way, the physical frenzy and release of an axe or a gaff. But he was cold inside, heavy, the violence congealed. He didn't have the nerve. It was Sid Black's gun, Sid Black's bullets. Think of it like that. Let Sid Black do it, not him.

Standing in the yard he watched as the screen door—hanging crooked, half unhinged—swung open. Vetch stood in the frame. "I thought I heard your truck. Hah. The man who came in from the swamp. You got business, Nawby, or you just come a'visiting?"

"Leave the men at the camp alone. Don't threaten them again. That's my land and you know it. Don't come near me or my house or my men. I warned you before, Carl. This is the last time."

"How about you come in for a nice cold sodee pop and we talk this over. I got me an ice box, now. Sho. So they nice and cold. I got that Cola-Nip peach you like. Hah. Never known another White man that favored peach like you do. It's the nigra's favorite."

Behind Vetch he could see nothing but the rank darkness of the store. Vetch's arm dangled down, inside the frame of the door. As if he were holding a shotgun by the barrel, the stock resting on the ground, just out of sight.

"Leave them alone, Carl. They've got nothing to do with you anymore. You got what you wanted. I'm sure you've got your hands full, now that it's the high season. Yeah? Your fish camp packed full of tourists, is it? You must be turning them away by the droves. Yeah?"

"Well, now, there's the problem," Vetch said. "Ain't no White folk tourists want to come out here with all them nigras hanging around. That's why I ain't got no business. Sho. Them raggedy nigras done scare em away. Anyways, I figure I doing them boys a favor. Setting em free. You seen all them bulldozers, scraping out a road over to the point. Some Joosh banker done take over all that land. You done lost out, Nawby. Them nigras got to get out of there soon enough, no matter what you say. Why you want to hold em down for, anyways? Ain't doing em no good living like that, like animals rutting in the dirt. Ain't you heard, Nawby? We got us a nigra-lover up there in Wershington now. Loves nigras and kisses the pope's ass. Hah! They got them nigra leaders now and all they marches and demonstrations and sit-downs. Sho. They gonna give them nigras they civil rights. Set em free! That's what I say."

Narby took a breath and stepped forward. "You're out of luck, Vetch. The cabins, the boat ramp, all the waterfront acreage, gone. To the Jew. And the store, too. Eminent domain. It's smack in the way of the new road. They'll force you out. You'll be lucky to get a dime for this pile of sticks." With each word drawing a step closer. "You wasted all that money I gave you, you fool, and now you've got nothing. Zero. You're ruined. They all hate you. The whole county despises you. Even the niggers are laughing at you." He was at the bottom of the steps now. He pulled out the pistol, his arm remarkably steady, rigid. "Drop the shotgun. Drop it and put up your hands and step down, you goddamn son of a bitch."

Vetch's arm began to move, slowly, laterally, drawing forth a shape from out of the darkness. "Wait now. I ain't armed This ain't no shotgun. You be careful, Nawby. She in a delicate way. Don't go scaring her."

He pulled her into the doorway, their hands clasped. Tiny, her arms and legs like twigs next to Vetch's thick doughy slovenly bulk, her hair grown out now, like a tangled nest sprouting from her head, her conical breasts engorged, delineated sharply beneath the thin soiled fabric of the plain cotton dress that draped her shoulders and swelled over the lump of her stomach. Her slightly bulged eyes weary and yellowed and rimmed with pink. Her lips dry, cracked. Her mouth like a little red hole against the flat cheeks, glistening with the mucus running from her tiny flaring nose.

"Becca? It's me. Philip."

She stared at him for a second, her tiny hand engulfed in Vetch's. "Where my money?"

"Let go of her Vetch. Becca. Come down here. I can help you. I'll take you away from here."

"Put away that pop gun, would you? You going to make her sick, scaring her like that. She in a delicate way. Can't you see that? What kind of man are you, Nawby?"

"Where my money?" Her voice flat, thin, a naked shameless whine. "I need money for my baby. You ain't nothing to me. Gimme my money."

Vetch had destroyed her, made her filth. Kill them both. Wipe off his prints and put the gun in Vetch's hand. A sordid murder-suicide pact, the grubbing ruined White-trash degenerate and his pregnant Negro-whore mistress, unable to bear the shame, the grotesquerie of a child born into that wallow of filth. Burn the store to the ground. If only he had the nerve. He took the bills from his pocket and dropped them on the ground. The gun still raised, his arm rigid, locked, he stepped back toward the truck. His debt was paid. The bulldozers would be here soon enough. Let Sid Black do it. Not him.

He pulled the truck around, circling the clearing and onto the ruts. He could see them in the mirror. Vetch still standing in the doorway. Becca squatting to pick up the money, her belly protruding, chasing one of the bills that had fluttered into the trash. It was incredible, insane—the human garbage was actually waving goodbye, smiling like a proud papa, his cracked lens catching the glare.

5

NARBY WAS COMING IN FROM a swim when he saw Dan Atlee, strolling down the beach. As he stepped out of the surf Atlee spotted him and waved him over. He picked up the towel, dried his face and hair, and draped it over his shoulders. He could hardly avoid saying hello.

Atlee hadn't been around much last year. This was the first Narby had seen of him all winter. That's how it was in the oil tanker business, Pembaker had explained. When things got too hectic—new wells suddenly gushing or some shipping-lanes snafu—Dan simply couldn't get away. But Narby saw if differently—Atlee had disappeared right around the time Castro took over.

"A pity you and Willa never had a chance to take out the Miranda," Altee said, after a few words of greeting.

"She's strange that way. Some kind of deep-water phobia. Anyway, thanks for the offer."

"I was watching you out there, Phil. You sure as hell aren't afraid of deep water."

Atlee's eyes were hidden behind dark glasses, his square blunt face below the crew cut raw from sunburn, his jaws tensed. No doubt he was taking a good look at the scars. Narby's credentials. He shrugged. "Not as long as the sharks stay on their side of the pool."

Atlee smiled. "Well, matter of fact, I'm on my way to the village. We just got the Miranda off her hooks and into the water. I'm keen to take her for a spin, make sure everything's in working order. Why don't you come along? We can drop a few lines and troll for tarpon on the way out, if you're so inclined. Not that exciting, Tarpon, if you've ever gone for marlin and gotten them. But for a beginner, it's good fun."

Narby shifted, turning his face away from the glare. "Nice day for it."

"Damn nice. Why don't you meet me, say, in half an hour? In front of my place. We can drive over to the marina together. I'll call Tony, make sure everything is good to go. Would do you say?"

Atlee was waiting for an answer. Why put it off? He would have the advantage. Atlee wanted him alone, on the water, unprepared. Only that's not how it would turn out. "All right."

"Good. Half an hour. See you then."

He headed up the dunes to the walkway, his mind blanking for a moment, stalling. Atlee would wait until they were out in deep water where there was no chance the body, weighted with an anchor of some sort, would wash ashore. So, there would be ample opportunity for Narby to take him off guard. Only what then? He could hardly bring the Miranda back to the marina, minus its skipper. Nor he could afford to make the same mistake twice, leave things to the drift of the currents, to chance. A yacht like the Miranda would have an autopilot. He'd get Atlee to show him. The son-of-a-bitch would no doubt want to show off his prized possession, even under such strained circumstance.

He went through the gate in the hedge. The living room was empty. He went out the kitchen door and from the flagstones, shielding his eyes from the glare, saw that Willa was in the studio. She abhorred interruptions when she was painting, or whatever the hell it was that she did in there. He'd be back by dark—she would assume he was out swimming, or hiking the beach. Well, that would be the truth, because he would have to swim back. Again.

It would save Narby a lot of trouble, a lot of worry, if people thought that Dan Atlee had taken out the Miranda that day by himself, that for some reason Atlee had wished to be alone. It would make a good story. Despite his success in the shipping industry, his beautiful winter home on the island of Sanmora, his yacht and his love of sport fishing, Dan Atlee was not a happy man. He was haunted by what had happened during the retreat from the Chosin Reservoir, the nightmare gauntlet of Funchilin Pass where he had watched his own men picked off one-by-one by Chinese snipers, blown down like ragdolls. And things were bad with Sheila. Everyone in the Colony could sense that. There had been other women, no doubt. Over the last few years Dan's drinking had gotten out of hand. No, Dan Atlee was not what he seemed. And without a word of warning, without leaving a note or saying goodbye, he had taken his beloved yacht Miranda out into the Gulf that morning, all alone, and standing at the rail for the last time shot himself in the head, the gun dropping overboard as Atlee crumpled to the deck.

Upstairs Narby took a shower and dressed, his old canvas trousers and a light V-neck pullover and tennis shoes. He wasn't going to rush. Let Atlee wait, sweat it out a bit. Every little thing, every second, every movement, had to be calculated now. He took the rucksack from the closet. He was perspiring, goddamn it, his pulse racing. A few dollies would ease him down, but he couldn't afford to go slack. He swallowed two white pills and put three yellows in his pocket. There was half a stick in the tobacco pouch. It could go either way, push him or weaken him. He stepped out on the terrace and took two deep lungfuls and then snuffed it out. If he found himself hesitating, he would take the yellows. Three at a go, when they first kicked in, would deliver the requisite jolt, a transitory but irrevocable upsurge of rage. Everything that Narby hated—everything that had stood in his way, everything that had toppled him into the ditch along the Naktong—had gathered in the form of the ex-Marine Captain Dan Atlee. A MacArthur man, a traitor-hero, the privileged scum that floated to the top. At the moment of truth, if only he could find the presence of mind, Narby would smile—*a little reward Dan, for your years of selfless service and sacrifice. From the congressman's boy.*

He took the revolver from the bottom of the rucksack. It was stupid not to have tested the gun beforehand. Too late now. It wouldn't do to alarm the Colony with the sound of a gunshot ringing in the morning air. If the first chamber didn't fire there were four more. It was hardly likely that Bill Knowles had sent Philip Narby to Lacoosa County years ago for the sole purpose of finding Dan Atlee and eliminating him. Still, there was nothing to disprove it. Once word of Atlee's apparent suicide got out, who knows? There might be a letter of congratulations waiting for him at Hank's. *Well done. You're free to go. We've taken care of everything. Wiped the record clean.*

He placed the gun at the bottom of the empty sack and over it a folded towel and a dry swimsuit and the tobacco pouch, and then, downstairs, he filled the flask and a canteen and put them on top. Provisions for a day at sea. Maybe he'd practice his dive off the stern, learn how to do it without swinging the bow off course.

It was out there, somewhere off Sawfish Point, a hulk rotting on the fetid muddy bottom, whatever remained of the pilot still lashed to the deck. If only he could erase that blunder from his mind.

He took a swallow of Jim Beam, lit a cigarette, slung the sack over his shoulder and went out the kitchen door where the flagstone path led between the studio and the garage and out to the front of the house. The Colony had its own private road, a smoothly paved black-asphalt lane that wound snakelike from one mansion to the next through the thickets of sweet-smelling island scrub, connecting to the main road about a quarter mile inland where the Colony's surplus acreage abutted the Village land. Atlee's house, a huge grey wood-shingled box, was on the other side of Pembaker's. The sweat was gathering under his shirt, his breathing shallow, his legs wobbling. He had to concentrate, hold himself tight. He was going to kill Dan Atlee, in self-defense. The son-of-a-bitch was forcing his hand. That's how men like Atlee operated, through a test of nerves. How the hell would Narby know the right moment to act? What if Atlee, understanding that the engine noise would cover the gunshot, made his move before they had even cleared the tip of the island? The ex-Marine captain, the sportsman, was no doubt well-acquainted with firearms, killing and maiming with a mere twitch of his finger. Goddamn it. Narby had never shot anyone or anything in his life. And now, all of a sudden, he was being forced to assume the demeanor, the silently seething equanimity, of a cold-blooded assassin.

Why wait? As soon as they cleared the marina. Pick up the hardest heaviest object at hand and from behind come down hard on Atlee's head as he stood at the helm. Steer the boat out into the Gulf. One clean shot to the temple, positioning the body in such a way to suggest that after shooting himself Atlee had collapsed backward and struck his head. Blood pooling everywhere, runneling across the polished teak deck. Then he would have to jump, swim. Again. The mere thought made him sick.

He rounded the bend in the road and saw Atlee backing the car out of the garage. A jet-black T-bird convertible, the top down, Atlee at the wheel, his back to Narby. He came around to the side and got in, placing the sack at his feet, and Atlee put the car in gear. Atlee liked to talk about the Miranda, the Rhode Island shipyard where she was built, the size of her twin engines and how their independent suspension allowed Atlee to pivot the Miranda around in a space no longer than her length by putting one engine in forward and the other in reverse, the ample fuel tanks for long outings to the Gulf Stream where the blue marlin ran, to Cuba and the Bahamas. He'd taken her across the Straits two dozen times. Narby ought to come along next trip. Just the men. No wives, no girlfriends. Fishing, cigars, drink, and hell, even swimming, too. Atlee had a shotgun on board for keeping the sharks at bay. There was something about the open ocean that appealed to men, called to them, he blathered on, in a way that women couldn't understand.

The words, Atlee's voice, reached Narby like the sound of gravel tossed up against a window. A warning. The man was jabbering, posturing, to cover up his murderous intent.

Atlee pulled the Thunderbird around to the dirt lot below the bridge that crossed the Village inlet. "There she is." They walked up the short slope and onto the dock. Apparently, Atlee had made sure that no one would see them—only Tony, the Villager who worked for Atlee at the marina. Tony would no doubt keep his mouth shut. Atlee would have taken the very precautions that Narby could turn to his own advantage. While they stepped over the rail Tony came down from the marina office. Narby walked toward the stern and Atlee made no attempt to introduce them. He could hear them going over details about the condition of the yacht, paying no attention to him. Tony hadn't seen Narby's face, just his back, the rucksack. The sack might have to be sacrificed, sadly. He'd been carrying it around since Havana. On the crossing with Campos. Had thrown it across the creek after ferrying Willa.

Waiting, he sat on the cushioned bench that ran along the stern, and with the sack on his lap he reached in, feeling first the cold metal of the barrel under the towel and then the scored hatching of the wooden handle, fitting his hand to its contour and then curling his finger around the trigger. Yes. He could do it. Damned easy, if you simply blanked your mind and became one with the mechanism.

"Hello, Phil."

He jerked back, startled, the gun rising as if of its own accord to the top of the sack. It was Pembaker, coming up from the cabin.

"Dalt… I didn't know you were here."

He let the gun drop to the bottom of the sack and to cover his movement took out the tobacco pouch out and began to roll a cigarette. "Didn't mean to spook you." Pembaker gave him an odd look. "Best to hold off on that. We're fueling up."

"What? Oh. Yeah." He laughed, a nervous laugh that caught in his throat. "Guess I should be more careful." He put the pouch back, pushing the gun under the towel.

"Haven't seen you or Willa in a while. How's everything down the dunes?"

"Not bad. Willa's been holed up in the studio. I hardly see her myself these days. And you and Tara?"

"Keeping busy. Tara with her letter writing and proselytizing. She'd lock up half of Florida for the birds and turtles and orchids, if she had her way. I've been back and forth a bit too much for my tastes. Still, can't complain."

Atlee came around from the aft. "Gentlemen," he said. "We're off."

The controls to the boat—the wheel and the throttles, a bank of gleaming gauges and the two-way radio—were on a raised bridge, five steps above and to the right of the luxurious teak benches lining the stern. The passage to the cabin was to the left, closed off with a pair of saloon doors. Atlee mounted the bridge and started the engines, letting them gurgle for a minute or so, the air fogging with exhaust, and then took the boat at a crawl down the wide channel that led to the estuary. Narby watched from below. It was just as he had imagined: Altee with his back to him, absorbed in playacting the role of commander. He stood and gracefully swung himself up the ladder to the bridge and stood behind Atlee, watching over his shoulder, identifying the essential controls. Pembaker remained on the deck below, standing at the side rail and looking out at the mangrove flats, the shallows dotted with white herons and egrets and blue-gray ibis stalking and poking about in the mud. The estuary, though about half a mile wide, was clotted with mangrove islands and sandbars. Atlee had to thread their way out, following the channel markers and buoys. A fire extinguisher—a two-foot-long heavy steel canister—sat bracketed to the half wall of the bridge at knee-level. All Narby need do was reach down and hoist it above his head. That would certainly give Atlee a jolt.

After about ten minutes Atlee pulled back on the throttle, the bow bouncing gently as they accelerated. Nothing was going to happen with Pembaker on board. The tension drained away, rather suddenly. He felt the wind against his face, the vibrating swaying motion of the boat beneath his feet. They were clearing the estuary and heading into the Gulf. In the distance, looking over his shoulder—because he couldn't bear the sight of Atlee's bulk, the folds at the base of his thick neck—Narby could make out three smudges of black smoke, rising from the midst of the vast inland jungle. Sid Black's pyres, the towering pyramidal mounds of bulldozed vegetation burning day and night.

Atlee spent about half an hour putting the Miranda through her paces, making notes in his log for Tony. When he was satisfied he lowered the engines to a gurgle and then shut them down, letting the Miranda drift in the choppy Gulf waters, pleasantly bobbing, Sanmora and the mainland long out of sight. He showed Narby the rest of the boat: the two sleeping quarters with oversized bunks and built-in closets, the sparkling stainless-steel galley, the dining table that folded down between two upholstered benches, the well-appointed head with a shower, sink, toilet, and medicine chest. "That's the beauty of the Miranda," he was telling Narby. "Can't beat it for fishing, or cruising for days on end. A hell of a lot more comfortable than most hotel rooms. Let me tell you, Phil, we've had some damned fun parties on board, too. The kind you don't tell your wife about." He was in the galley, taking three bottles of beer out of the small refrigerator. "Not as cold as I'd like. But they'll do."

Pembaker sat under the canopy in the shade. The rucksack was on the bench opposite. Narby sat, moving the sack to the corner against the bulwark of the cabin. Atlee opened the bottles and passed them and sat in one of the deck chairs, closer to Pembaker. "Everything in order?" Pembaker asked.

"Pretty much," Atlee said. "I've got a list for Tony. Oil pressure gauge is on the fritz. Couple of other warning lights that need checking out. And I don't like the way that left throttle sticks. Still, she's eminently seaworthy. Damn, it's good to be back on the water."

Forget it, Narby told himself. Act your part. He had to adjust his attention now, figure out what was coming next. While they talked he managed to take a yellow from his pocket and, turning his head, swallowed it with the beer.

"You feel all right, Phil?" Pembaker asked.

"Yeah. Just getting my sea legs, I guess. I'm more used to being *in* the water then on top of it. The Miranda's a beautiful boat, Dan. Really something. Thanks for the lift." He raised the bottle, feigning a bit of cheer.

"So, what's happening over in the county, Phil? Looks like they've stripped away a couple of miles of mangrove, by that stretch north of Punta Rasca. That's close to your land, isn't it?"

"Yes. Sawfish Point. It's a development company out of Miami. Sun American Land. Matter of fact," he continued, knowing how keen Pembaker was on matters that impinged on the value of his precious Colony real estate, "about a year ago I sold them a thousand acres of scrub pine. Got a nice return, too. I might sell them more, if they stay afloat. They're putting a hell of a lot of money into developing that little piece of muck that sticks out into the river. Making some kind of Potemkin village, to suck in investors. I give them a year, maybe two, before they go belly up. No one's going to buy property way the hell out there, in the middle of all that pine and palmetto waste. Still, in the meantime, I don't mind taking their money. When they go under I can probably buy it all back at half the price."

Pembaker laughed. "Sun American. I believe Bob Sunderland mentioned something about them. Jewish owned, I believe."

"Christ. Have you been over to Miami Beach lately? It's becoming the New Jerusalem," Atlee butted in. "Have to say, though, I admire how the Jews are flexing their muscles in Israel. Between the Jews and the Egyptians, I'd put my money on the Jews any day. Nasser's cagey, but he's like a momma bird hatching a nest of vipers. The things is, the Arabs have no respect for chain of command. It's a loyalty system. They're more interested in saving face than keeping discipline in the ranks. In a crisis they fall apart, like a bunch of shrieking women. Opposite with the Jews, with Ben-Gurion and Dayan. One air-raid siren and the whole damned country becomes a tightly-knit unit, a fighting machine. Look what they did to the Arabs in forty-eight and again in fifty-five, during the Gaza business. Did you hear about them nabbing that Nazi Eichmann, down in Argentina? Brilliant operation. We could learn a thing or two from them, Dalt. That's the thing about the Jews," Atlee said, standing, the bottle in his hand already empty. "In their native habitat, they're an admirable bunch. Tough, resilient. Over here, though, they never manage to fit in. Always pushing in the wrong direction. Another Black Label, gentlemen?"

Atlee went through the swinging doors and came back with another round of sweating bottles.

Pembaker wanted to know more about the development in Sawfish Point. "They've started building model homes," Narby explained. "They're using draglines to dig the canals, and then they mix the muck from the bottom with crushed shell, for fill dirt, to raise the elevation. They must have plopped down a couple dozen of these little air-conditioned stucco houses so far, with a seawall and dock in the backyard. They're calling it Coco Reef. They even have a slogan: *a waterway wonderworld*. Looks like a damned desert to me. They've scraped away everything, down to the last blade of grass. Everything done on the cheap, too, from the looks of it."

"Course they're cheap," Atlee interjected. "That's the trend, the angle, the fast-dollar track. All the more reason for us to keep things reined in tight on the island."

While they were talking Pembaker picked up a small aluminum case that had slipped between the cushions. "There's something about the bracing purity of sea air that makes me crave the stink of a good cigar." He snapped it open and handed one to Atlee and one to Narby.

"Where'd you get these, Dalt? Christ, haven't seen one of these in years."

"Bonsal sent them to me. He's having quite the time over there."

"Bonsal?" Narby said. The name was familiar.

"Our Ambassador in *liberated* Havana. For the moment, at any rate." Pembaker took a clipper, a tiny guillotine, from his shirt pocket, and snipped the end.

"I don't know Bonsal personally, but from what I gather he's been fumbling the ball," Atlee said. "Too conciliatory. We know all too well where this wait-and-see attitude leads. Now, Bob Hill, Whiting Willauer, they've got the right line. Don't you think, Dalt? So? Is State thinking of recalling him?"

"Not that I've heard." He turned to Narby. "It's our new parlor game, Phil. Predicting which way our new neighbor Mr. Castro will go, east or west. Everyone seems to be playing. Hazard any guesses?"

He knew more than Atlee. Is that what Pembaker wanted, for Narby to put Atlee in his place? Provoke an argument?

The yacht took the chop gently, a cradle's rock, the breeze pleasantly tinged by the cigars, not a sign of land anywhere, the sky spreading a pale uniform blue above the shifting lazuline waters. Anything could happen out here. No one would ever know. "Castro wants to stay neutral. That's my guess. Non-aligned. Like Nehru." He'd gone over it with Campos a dozen times. He took a moment, tasting the cigar. The yellow had ratcheted him up. "Most of Castro's people, the ones who've been with him the longest, are anti-Communist. As I understand it. Only they're dreamers. Idealists. Patriots and idealists and nationalists. That's the danger, in my opinion. They have an idea of sovereign... "

"That's all good and fine," Atlee butted in. "But we'll see what happens when they start to feel the pain of losing the sugar quota. We'll see what happens when Castro makes his move on the oil refineries and mining concessions."

"Wait a minute, Dan. I'm interested in the point Phil was making. It's a side I haven't heard much about. What's this idea they have, that's so dangerous?"

Atlee turned his head, spitting a fleck of tobacco over the side.

"They think they're different, that somehow they can stay pure, stay above politics. It's ridiculously naïve, I know. But they've got guts, real courage. There's the danger, I think. They'll say, *we won't let the Americans push us around anymore, tell us how to run things, like they've done for generations.* They've convinced themselves that they're expressing the will of the Cuban people. That's how Castro speaks, those four-hour rants. Like he's some kind of holy Cuban oracle."

"A fucking holy bore is what he is," Atlee spat out. "He'll bore his own people to death if he keeps that up."

Pembaker laughed. "Seriously, though. Finish your point, Phil."

"Wherever you throw up a roadblock for the Americans, you risk an inroad for communism, for the Soviets. Right? My sense is that Castro doesn't want that, either. But one day, sooner rather than later, he'll need something to back up the oracle, the rhetoric. One day he's going to have to come down hard on his pro-American enemies. Frankly, Dalt, I don't think Castro is a red. I don't think he's anything, really. That's his big mistake. Thinking that a tiny island country like Cuba can steer its own course. Like I said, they're dreamers."

"They're dreamers all right. Only it's a nightmare. Take my word for it, we'll have to do Guatemala all over again. I've got to admit, Castro fooled me at first, too. Well, now he's showing his real colors. There's red, but there ain't no white or blue. We ought to put the kibosh on it before the son-of-a-bitch gains any more traction."

"Perhaps," Pembaker said. "But there's more to it than that, Dan."

"Sure there is, according to the appeasers at the *New York Times.* Or that handful of beatnik loonies, what do they call themselves. Fair Play for Cuba. Christ! Come on, Dalt, look at the guy. All the classic alarms are ringing. Clamping down on the newspapers, the so-called land reform, whittling away at private property, spooking foreign investors. Castro's dreaming all right, about being the next Mao Junior, the next Stalin, tropical style. Here's the thing." Atlee leaned forward, poking the cigar in Narby's direction. "The revolution is over. Batista ran with his tail tucked between his ass cheeks. Why the hell doesn't Castro take off that guerilla camouflage and shave and put on a suit and tie? He's keeping everyone whipped up. That's why. Castro's a liar, a phony, from the brim of his cap to the toes of his combat boots."

Pembaker seemed amused. "Sounds like you've been chatting with Dick Nixon."

The ex-Marine leaned back, draping his arm over the rail. "In fact, Dalt, that was my liberal *pro*-Castro speech. Want to hear my hard line?"

"I think we can be spared that."

"Hey, Phil. Castro has a sign hanging over his desk in the presidential palace. Know what it says?"

Atlee was baiting him. "Not a clue."

"I got my job through the *New York Times*."

Narby knew more than Atlee. Knew all about how Frank País and Castro had stage-managed the reporter Herbert Matthews' trips into the Sierras. He gave Atlee a wan smile. "You don't seriously believe that almost a decade of brutal dictatorship was overthrown by a few sensational stories in a liberal New York newspaper? You grant them a hell of a lot more influence than they really have."

"You're right, Phil," Pembaker said. "Newspapers follow leads, they don't make them."

"Anyhow, it's not about Castro getting the job. In retrospect, that was the easy part," Narby said, encouraged by Pembaker's remark. "It's about how he's going to keep it."

"Not really," Atlee put in. "Not how he's going to keep it. It's how he's going to lose it. And when. And by whose hand."

"Yes, there's that." Pembaker stood. He was the last to discard the butt end of his cigar. He took a final puff and tossed it overboard. "Dan, if you don't mind, it's time to head back. I've got some calls to make this afternoon."

"Sure thing, Dalt. How about you take the helm for a bit?"

"With pleasure."

The bow was cutting through the chop, the yacht bouncing with a strong reassuring rhythm. What did they want from him? Pembaker had been watching them, like some kind of damned referee. After a few minutes Atlee came down the ladder, leaving Pembaker on the bridge. He stood beside Narby, speaking loudly against the rush of the wind.

"I noticed those scars, this morning on the beach. I had no idea it had been that bad for you, Phil. I don't blame you for being angry about it. It burned me up, too. Having to fight with one hand tied behind our backs. For a bunch of frigging laundrymen too cowardly and inept to fight their own battles. You served your country, Phil. That's all that matters in the end. My country, right or wrong. Screw the politicians and the generals. They're just the custodians. It's men like you and me who own the joint. Yeah?"

"Water under the bridge," Narby said.

"You look to be in pretty damn good shape, I've got to say. They stitched you back up with everything in the right place, far as I can see."

"No complaints."

Atlee considered that for a moment. "Man, I wish I were in your shoes. Free to play the field, without all the dodging and maneuvering. Don't get me wrong. I'd do anything for my family. But there's more to life than just the daily bread and butter. Come on, Phil. Just between you and me. Between men. Is it true, what you always hear about the bohemian types, the artists? That they play by their own rules. Play hard, too. I've known Willa long enough to get some idea. Must be pretty hot? Yeah?"

Narby turned to face him: the square sunburned face and razor-cut hairline, the flat nose and pale brutal eyes. "I don't see how it's any of your business, Dan."

"Oh. I think it is my business." His eyes fixed on Narby's for a second, and then he broke into an insipid laugh. "Just pulling your leg, pal. Forget I even mentioned it. Forget women all together. Next time out, we'll go for some big fish. How's that? You haven't really lived until you've hooked into a three-hundred-pound blue marlin. It's one hell of a thrill. Who the hell needs women, anyway? In the end, they're all a pain in the ass. The better looking the ass, the more the pain. Ain't that the truth?"

6

TWO MONTHS LATER, THE SEASON OVER, most of the Colony packed up and departed—there was a phone call. From New York, he supposed, or perhaps overseas, due to the early hour. He was already up, in the kitchen making coffee, when he heard the ring upstairs. Willa now took her calls on the bedroom extension, with the door closed. He couldn't pinpoint when exactly she had removed the downstairs phone, maybe six months ago. To prevent him from eavesdropping.

When she came down twenty minutes later, dressed for the studio in her baggy paint-daubed clothes, he asked, casually, "Who was that?"

Whatever fresh agitation the morning's call might have set off, the tension between them was always palpable now, requiring daily vigilance, like a trip wire that had to be stepped over, again and again. She wasn't in a mood to explain. "No one that concerns you, darling." She hardly paused to look at him, pouring coffee into a thermos.

"Anything wrong?"

She gave a little mocking laugh. "Anything right?"

She was locking herself in the studio for longer and longer stints, often without bothering to break for lunch, not showing herself again until dusk. She kept a cooler for her white wine and a little food, whatever she could manage to get down between the chain of Gauloises. To offset the muggy spring heat she had installed an air-conditioner. It had been two years since last she offered to show him her work in progress. It saved him—saved both of them—the strain of inventing, pretending.

When he came out of the bathroom she was gone. It was hot already, the ocean-borne morning freshness burnt off with the first rays of sun. He sat on the sofa, looking out the window. In the harsh glare the gardens and dunes took on the paralyzed artificiality of a diorama, a three-dimensional prop constructed behind a sheet of glass. An ingenious integration of machine and jungle and sea during the cool winter months, the house now sundered instead of integrated. Two worlds, incommensurate and hostile —the cool brittle interior with its sterile hum, and outside the swarming corrosive heat and damp.

He came and went as he pleased. If he felt her mood was too severe he simply disappeared, leaving a note to reassure her that he'd be back in a few days. He was convinced that the house, the studio, belonged to Willa only through some make-shift arrangement, easily overturned. She had come to the Island at the pleasure of the art critic and collector Endicott Ward, who had wanted to encourage her, nurture her talent. Only now, he guessed, something had changed. Her usefulness—or whatever it was that granted Willa the right to live in the Colony—might be coming to an end. The confidential phone calls, the desperate all-day stints in the studio, the violence of her moods—it was part of something larger.

Ever since that day on the Miranda, when he had been prepared to get rid of Dan Atlee—it was as if, at the critical moment, Pembaker had stayed his hand, whispering in Narby's ear, *not yet, not here*—he had felt mired and slow. Atlee and Pembaker were gone until next fall. Everything was on hold. Still, Pembaker had made things pretty clear, hadn't he? He wanted Narby to stick around, keep an eye on the Colony. Keep an eye on Willa.

After a while, he headed out for a stroll and a swim. There was a spot at the far northern tip of the island, about a forty-minute walk, where the dunes disappeared and the waves crashed right up into the jungle, a tangle of coral rock and storm-felled trees and arching mangrove. He would linger there for hours, swimming and smoking and clambering over the rocks and tree trunks, like a little boy playing at his *Treasure Island* adventure. When he got back, a little after noon, drained by the heat, he had a cool shower and something to eat. Willa was in the studio: he could make her out through the bank of closed windows, standing at the easel and then backing off and pacing. No predicting what her mood might be at the end of the day. It was too late to catch the morning ferry, too damned hot outside, the dry cool house and the soft leather sofa too seductive. He poured a bourbon, swallowed a Dolophine—Bobby had branched out; anything but heroin, it seemed—smoked half a stick, and lay back on the sofa, listening to a Charles Mingus record, his eyes closed. Floating, levitating.

He didn't hear her come in. She was standing by the sofa, glaring at him, at the bourbon and the dope cigarette in the ashtray, her face rigid, a veneer of sweat on her forehead, her hair and clothes saturated with the stink of Gauloises and oils. He raised his head, startled at the sound of her voice. "For Christ's sake, Philip. Shut off that goddamn noise. It's driving me up the wall."

He knew that she couldn't hear the record player in the studio, not with the air-conditioner running. He got up and lifted the needle.

She said nothing, climbing the stairs, slamming the bedroom door. Whatever it was, it was worse now. The call that morning had set it off. He sat in the silence, the hum, for half an hour, reading the papers, until he couldn't fight it any longer. She was waiting for him. To get it out of her. He went upstairs and tried the door. It was open. The bedroom was dark, the blinds closed behind the drawn curtain. She was still in her work clothes, on top of the bedspread, balled up like a fetus. He sat on the bed and laid his hand on her thigh. Though the bedroom was rather warm she was shivering, ever so slightly. "Willa. Come down and have something to eat. A glass of wine."

"Leave me alone. There's nothing you can do. Please. Just go away."

"Who was on the phone this morning?"

She uncoiled sufficiently to face him. "So sorry you couldn't listen in, Philip. Don't think I can't see it. The way you're always sniffing around. Trying to pick up the scent. It was nothing. I wasn't even talking on the phone. I hung up."

She was taunting him. Lying. "Grow up, goddamn it. So, you had a lousy day in the studio. Big deal. It's just goddamn pictures, Willa. You made them before. You'll make them again."

"Pictures? That's what you think of me? Polaroids make *pictures*. John Wayne makes *pictures*." She turned away, balled herself up again. "I can't stand it," she muttered, her face pressed into the bedspread. "I don't want it anymore. I can't face it."

He tried to pull her forward, to compel her to look at him. "Let me help you. Whatever it is, let me help you."

That made her whip around. "Don't be such an arrogant ass. You, help me?" She laughed. "I picked you up on the beach, remember? I took you in, gave you comfort in the storm."

"That's not how I remember it. I remember a frightened little girl, afraid to wade across the creek."

She had perhaps only been trying to push him away—thrusting her hands upward just as he was leaning closer and catching him square in the throat, with her forearm. He jerked back, gasping, trying to clear his windpipe. If she wanted him to strike back, slap her around, she was out of luck. He wasn't about to debase himself, hitting a woman. After a moment, his breathing calmed, he spoke to her, to her balled-up form on the bed. "I'll be downstairs." The blow had left a rasp in his voice. He got up and for some reason he reached behind the curtain and opened the blinds, filling the room with a blue-tinted light.

After a while, from the sofa, he heard her moving about overhead, climbing off the bed and starting the shower. The running water would cover the sound of her making a call, if that's what she was up to. Ten minutes later she came down in her short kimono, her hair wet, her eyes a bit glazed. "Philip," she said, coming to a rest on the second step, "would you be so kind as to open a bottle of wine."

He put down the newspaper. She had managed to regain her equilibrium. With the help of the cocaine, he assumed. A few moths ago, after one of her frequent trips to New York, he had found a vial in her purse. Her secret vice. He never told her that he had found it—that would have meant admitting that he went through her things—and she never mentioned it, never sniffed it in front of him or offered any. Not that he wanted it: cocaine, heroin, injections, nothing that rocketed you upward and then exploded under your feet, leaving you in free fall. Ever since Havana he had disciplined himself, adjusting his daily intake of amphetamines, narcotics, marijuana, alcohol, balancing one against another. Keeping fit—swimming, running on the beach, push-ups and sit-ups and barbells—fending off the lethargy, the gut. The cocaine would throw it all into confusion.

It was medicine for her, he supposed. Like his Dolophine. Only she couldn't control it. Nobody could, not that kind of dope.

He went into the kitchen. Her reserve of Sauvignon Blanc took up half the refrigerator. He carried an uncorked bottle and two glasses. She was sitting in the low slung chair, smoking, her legs crossed, looking rather serene now, untouched. He poured out two glasses, handed one to her, and sat on the sofa.

"Thank you, Philip."

"Feeling better?"

"I'm exhausted. That's all it is, really. And the heat. I had to shut off the air-conditioner in the studio. I can't abide that noise when I'm trying to work. I hate shutting out the sound of the ocean. Anyway, it's intolerable in there. I can't work here anymore. Not in this weather." She paused, smoking. "How about you?"

She wasn't going to apologize, apparently, for jabbing him in the throat. "I'm all right. Went for a swim earlier, before it got too unbearable."

There was something she wanted to say, but she couldn't get it out. She was staring at the glass-topped table. "The two preoccupations of modern man," she said, finally, extending her foot to indicate the stack of magazines he'd been reading, "fornication, and reading the newspaper."

He laughed. "Well, I suppose I could always take up fishing."

"God forbid! But, well, what exactly do you get out of all that? Combing through all that noise, that chatter? You're not just passing the time, are you? You're looking for something in particular." She put down the wine glass and picked up the copy of *Newsweek*, folded open to the international pages. "Leaving behind an atmosphere of tension and rising disorder in his native Congo, newly-appointed Premiere Patrice Lumumba arrived in Washington on Friday for talks with State Department officials. Reports of increasing shipments of food and other aid to the Congo from the Soviet Union have raised serious concerns ..." She let the magazine drop on the table. "You've put a mark by it, as if you were cramming for an exam."

He smiled. She wasn't mocking him anymore. She was desperate to get beyond herself, crawl out of the darkness. "Lumumba. Interesting character. A few years ago, when the Belgians were Lord and Master, he was a nothing. A beer salesman, I believe. Now he's a hero to half his people, marching through the streets of Kinshasa chanting *we are the masters now*. The other half, they want his head on a spear. He's got something of a cult behind him, some tribal magic nonsense, so I understand. A hashish addict, rumor has it, with a taste for white women. Blondes. That might be a point of common interest between Lumumba and our dashing new president."

"You're a voyeur. It's power that fascinates you, the pretense of it all."

"I like to keep my eye on world events. I got run over once. As you well know. Caught unawares. I'd like to keep out of the way, the next time they start ringing the alarms."

"Philip. In all the time I've known you—and I say this with all due respect—I've never seen you do a day's work. Never seen you write a check, or pick up the phone to make a business call. I've never even met anyone who knows you, aside from your Negro friends, in Miami. And, well, I'd hardly call people like that your associates. I've never seen where you live, the house you've told me about. Or the land you say you own."

"You told me none of that mattered. That you liked not knowing. Pretending I was a stranger. Someone you picked up on the beach. The famous Willa Branton, showing herself, giving her body to a stranger. A nobody."

"Yes. Well, everything has a limit. I never know how to react, when I reach a limit. I don't know how to live with it, that sense of stasis. Paralysis."

She was mocking him and inciting him at the same time. She was going to betray him, use him up. And there was nothing he could do about it. "What it is you want from me, Willa? What do you need?"

"I don't know. But. It's beginning to frighten me. Having a stranger in my house. Do you understand?"

"Maybe we should call it quits. Is that your point?"

"My god. You say it so cavalierly. Could you really give me up, just like that?"

"No. You know I couldn't."

She thought about it for a moment. "I suppose this is where one of us is supposed to say, perhaps we should consider marriage. Children. A family. Frankly," she said, stubbing out the cigarette, "I'd rather hang myself. A mercy killing. To save you, and the children."

"Well, don't start tying the noose. I don't want that, either."

"Then what? We can't be friends. Because of the sex. If it weren't for the isolation here, the protection of the island, it would have already ended. Don't you agree?"

"How the hell should I know?"

"You must have had other lovers, while I was away. You can tell me. I won't be angry."

"Sorry to disappoint you, but there's nothing to tell. What about you? There must be any number of men in New York who'd line up to take you to bed."

She lit another cigarette. "Darling. Half the men I know in New York are homosexuals. The other half are pompous assholes. Or sloppy drunks. Or married. Even some of the homosexuals are married. When I'm not here, not with you, I prefer to go without. I think about you, instead. About how it is with you, the things we do. I fantasize. Let it build up. So that when I come back, it's something like a fantasy becoming real. Only that's the problem, isn't it? If it's real, it's no longer a fantasy. It fails to sustain. And I'm here now, with you, and you're still a stranger, only you can't be a stranger anymore."

"You want to see my house? See how I live? I'll take you."

"But, Philip, I really can't …"

"Go upstairs and get dressed. Pack a bag. I'm sick of this place, anyway."

"Now? But. I can't leave the studio."

"We'll have to go in my truck. You get ready while I walk over to the lighthouse. It'll take me half an hour."

"Why not take the Guilieta?"

"The Guilieta can't make it, not where we're going."

"What do you mean?"

"The road's not paved. You car would bottom out. Come to think of it, pack up some wine, too. And whatever else you can't live without, for the next few days." He got up and looked for his rucksack. "We still have time to make the afternoon ferry. You coming? Or do you prefer to stay here? Alone."

7

THE SUN LASERED ITS WAY through the gaps in the blinds. Moaning, shielding his eyes, he struggled out of bed and yanked the cord, restoring the room to darkness. Feeling sick, his skin clammy and his throat raw, his breathing shallow, he stood under the tepid shower, trying to wake himself up, shake it off. Willa was asleep, sprawled face-down on top of the sheets. Toweling dry, he let his eye run over her, her hair and shoulders and neck, the sleek dimpled curve of her lower back and the frizz of her wheat-colored tuft poking out from behind. Her leg, just below her ass, was marred by a nasty bruise—yellowed, blotched with black and swollen beneath the skin. As if someone had struck her with a bat or truncheon. But there was no blood or scab, the skin unbroken. No other marks of violence that he could see. She had fallen, that was all. Though where or how, if she had tripped or been pushed, he couldn't remember.

Out cold, her cheek crushed against the pillow and her mouth slack, her arms limp at her side, the rise and fall of her breathing almost imperceptible. It wouldn't take much, holding the pillow over her head for a couple of minutes, pressing down with the strength of his swimmer's arms. He doubted she would even stir, perhaps only a frantic involuntary spasm of her hips, her ass thrusting upward in a jolt of resistance, a final offering of sex before shuffling off the mortal coil.

It made him queasy, looking at her like that. He went into the other room. Warm in here, too. He raised his palm and held it by the vent. Once a veritable arctic gale the air-conditioning at the Calvado now produced little more than a musty luke-warm seepage. The final stage in the hotel's long decline, Sid Black squeezing out every last penny before the collapse into insolvency and foreclosure.

His watch was on the table. It was eleven already. He was meeting Black at one. There was time for a swim, maybe, if he felt up for it.

He stepped out on the terrace, squinting into the glare. A storm was blowing in, towering masses of blue-black thunder-heads clotting the horizon. The swells were rough, the water a turbid milky green. The Calvado no longer offered cabanas. At high tide the beach behind the hotel virtually disappeared. During the big storms the water sloshed right up against the concrete seawall, leaving the narrow strip of coarse sand lit-tered with heaps of seaweed rotting in the sun, swarming with flies.

He would have to stand up to Black, maybe even threaten him. Narby had done everything Black had asked, the charade with the mortgages and the foreclosures. In fact, he had rather enjoyed it, buying land for the Jew behind the backs of the Lacoosa County Commissioners. Only now Black was taking too much, threatening to destroy what little Narby had left, ruining Narby's friendship with Sam Waters. Only how the hell was he going to stand up to Sid Black when he could barely summon the will to roll a cigarette? His hands were trembling.

He stepped inside and called room service. The Calvado had closed its kitchen months ago, but you could still get some-thing resembling breakfast—a pot of warmed-over coffee and a plate of ham and eggs that they brought in from the greasy spoon down the block. Willa's purse was on the floor. He picked it up and dumped the contents on the coffee table, looking for the vials, finding nothing of interest except a blue circular pill dispenser, half full of little pink pills. What the hell was Enovid? Maybe he ought to try one. But then he realized what they were. She'd gone off the diaphragm a year ago. Always going up to New York to see her gynecologist and her shrink and Sidney Janis. And who else?

If one of those black sons-of-a-bitch had laid a hand on her. The bass player, a tall lanky rather good-looking Negro. Narby had seen it in the man's eyes, that look of immense self-regard as he flirted with her, sharing the joint with her, the end of it slavered with his spit. Her mouth running like a sewer: fuck this, fuck that, fuck fuck fuck. Talking like that all night long, in front of them, like a drunken slut. Bobby had taunted him, warned him. *Some of these cats got a theory, man. White pussy the true path to Black Man's equality. Hit on white chicks every chance they get, man. Real hard. Especially them cats that been up to New York. You better keep your chick on a tight leash, man. She got that come hither look, you dig? That freak scene jag, you dig?*

He got on his hands and knees and searched under the love seat and then ran his hand under the cabinet, his face pressed against the worn-down carpet that stank of mildew and spilled booze. Crawling around in the filth, groveling like a dog. Because of her.

After a moment he got up off his knees and dressed. He needed his medicine, that was all. He shook out the dosage from the little brown bottle and washed it down with water and smoked a cigarette on the terrace. Room service came—the eternal white-haired Negro in gold buttons—and he ate, forcing himself for his own good, splashing a bit of Jim Beam into the coffee to render it palatable. He'd been stupid, weak. She was using him up, and instead of resisting he was urging her on, inciting her. Because he liked it, because he couldn't help himself. The only thing worse than the fear of losing her was the fear that it would go on like this, spiraling down until he was nothing, had nothing. And then she would leave him anyway. It had to stop.

They had left Sanmora three days ago, the same day she had forearmed him in the throat. Sitting close in the truck, sidled next to him, drinking wine from the bottle—like teenagers out on a necking spree. She had been desperate to get away from the studio, he realized, had wanted him to force her to let it go, at least for a few days. Maybe her talent, her inspiration, had finally dried up, abandoned her. Eight, ten hours a day, batting her head against the wall, staring down an empty canvas. But then, he could hardly think of it as talent, that intangible trait that had made her famous. It was nerve. Daring. Maybe that was what Endicott Ward and Sydney Janis valued in her, in conjunction with her corn-fed middle-American girl-next-door sex appeal—the outrageous unmitigated nerve, her intransigent acerbic disdain for *pictures*, for even the most minimal appeasement towards the normal entertainments of the eye. Her mockery of faces and landscapes and flowers in vases. Even Jackson Pollock had been a traitor to Willa's cause, because he reveled in the cunning excess of his splatters and swirls. *Jack the dripper.* By making chaos pleasing, making disorder so obvious a spectacle, he, too, had sinned against the artist's sacred calling.

I don't care how other men live, he told her, driving from the ferry landing at Punta Rasca, through the monotonous miles of palmetto brush, the cattle enclosures and gladiola farms and trailer parks, everything seared by the paralytic heat, the blinding glare. I run my business my way. When I want. How I want. Matter of fact, I just sold about two thousand acres. I'll show you. I never got anything from my father, not a cent. After Korea, I couldn't go back. Mommy. Daddy. Little Sis. It's a weakness, a liability, all that sentimental attachment. They're better off without me.

She stroked his hair adoringly as he drove. Let me be your sister, she said. There's no one closer than a brother and a sister. No one who understands better than a sister. No one else who can give you everything and shut out the rest. Make you forget what happened in Korea. Make you whole again.

He had never felt more love for her than at that moment, in the truck. The feeling would fall away, decay, he knew that very well. But for an hour or two, even a day, he might know what a woman could be: a lover, a mother, a sister. To have them all at once, in the same woman's body. Martha, Janet, Becca, the mother, the sister, the whore. Only never a friend. There were no friends, not in his world. Only enemies of enemies.

He stopped when they reached the fork. Her head on his shoulder, clinging to his arm, she had closed her eyes. "Willa. It's going to be a rough ride now. You need to brace yourself, so you don't hit your head."

She looked up, her face matted with sweat. "Where are we, Philip?"

"My land."

She held on to him as they bounced over the ruts. The jungle had nearly reclaimed the lane. It was more like a tunnel now, worming through the high brush, broadening out when they reached the stand of Australian Pines where he parked the truck in the shade. Sam's flatbed was gone. That was a relief. The old Colored man would disapprove, seeing Willa here, knowing they were sharing a bed. He led her by the hand up the stone steps and onto the porch, under the wide eaves. The pretty Caribbean colors, the yellows and greens, had succumbed to the fungal omnipotence of the tropical climate, the house hemmed in now by the prodigious growth of the jungle and the gardens, not a single plank free of vines or mold or the webbing of insect life—a mottled, vegetal, human cocoon. The heavy slab-like door had never swung open easily. He shoved it with his shoulder. He escorted her down the hall into the back room, the floor planks groaning. It was something of a shambles, filthy really, a welter of books and papers amidst the moldering junk-store furnishings, the brocade and rattan and water-stained silk lampshades, the threadbare Persian rugs gray with pulverized dust. The room was always dim now, the harsh sunlight filtering in through the tall thick bamboo and the branches of the grove that pressed against the screens, throwing a dense green shade.

"Sorry about the mess. I'm not much of a housekeeper. I'll turn on the generator and get the fans going. I warned you it was rustic."

She sat in the one of the wicker thrones and lit a Gauloises, crossing her legs and holding herself a bit tight, adjusting to the murky atmosphere, the dust, like someone inching into frigid water. When he came back, the ceiling fan chugging, she was sitting at the table. He had left out his papers, the notebooks and diaries and folders of clippings. "I don't mean to pry," she said.

"Feel free. Carte blanche. You want to know who I am? Do me a favor. When you discover the secret, let me know, would you? The contest ends at midnight."

She opened one of the black leather-bound diaries, flipping through the entries on Campos, the mundane lists of serial numbers, like bookkeeping. She picked up another and opened it at random, reading aloud: "*Where the Department of National Defense rather than the State Department has governed our policy, as in Germany, we have pursued a dangerous political course, snubbing the Socialists and trade unionists and restoring to power the great cartel-masters—the men whose political imbecility and cowardice when they were last in power brought about the rise of Hitler.* Oh dear. I was hoping to find something salacious about me in here."

She turned the page. "*In Europe Communism robs people of cherished freedom. But Asia and Africa have little freedom to lose. The Mongolian or Iranian who has never read a newspaper and cannot tell a habeas corpus from an eggbeater is not likely to regard the absence of a bill of rights as a major issue.* Well, that's nicely put, especially the eggbeater." She ran her eyes down the page. "*The same Nehru who worked with the Communists in the days of British domination today throws them in prison.* That's hardly fair. But I do admire Nehru's sense of fashion, those smart collarless jackets. You'd look fetching in one of those, darling. Let's see. *Democracy, by its nature, dissipates rather than concentrates its moral force…. The advocate of free society defines himself by telling what he is against.* I certainly agree with that. *When philosophies of blood and violence arise to take up the slack between democracy's thin optimism and the bitter agonies of experience, democracy by comparison seems pale and feeble.* Yes. The death drive. Blood and violence. Wherever Eros wanders, Thanatos lurks in the shadows, waiting for the denouement, the sad uncoupling."

She closed the notebook and looked up at him.

"Those aren't my words. I like to jot things down when I read, anything that strikes me. Sorry to disappoint you. It's all business and politics. I keep my personal life out of it."

"You're hiding out here, aren't you? It's your way of saying what you're against. This room. It's like an animal's burrow. A solitary animal that's run off with bits and scraps of human civilization, hoarding them."

"Yeah, well, like I said. I'm not much of a housekeeper."

"That's not what I mean, darling." She stood and put her arms around him and for the first time since the night before she kissed him on the mouth, tenderly. Almost chaste. "Show me around. I want to see everything."

He took her by the hand and led her through the groves of mango and avocado and citrus and the gardens with the low roughly-hewn coral-rock walls and around the pond, choked with lilies and floating hearts—showed her Sam's two-room cottage and the shed and the generator and the stand of oaks and took her down one of the footpaths into the forest of stunted blackened pines, the trunks still stained by the slather of crusted yellow sap where the buckets had been nailed to collect the resin. When she could no longer bear the heat and mosquitoes he took her back inside and together they stood under the cool shower. She was naked now in a way that he had never understood, like a girl bathing in a river, her sex natural and innocent and unattached to their lust, their fucking. Her caresses and kisses filled him with longing, as if everything might start over and he was a little boy again and his mother was bathing him and cuddling and teasing.

Waters didn't return that night. Probably visiting his son in Tampa. They were alone. No one around for miles and miles. Against the heat Willa had rejected her own clothing, putting on one of his old T-shirts that hung to her mid-thighs. There was plenty of white wine in the cooler she had packed, plenty of Jim Beam, heaps of marijuana, the screened-in room enclosing them like soil around roots, the fan stirring the warm moist air just enough to keep them from wilting, in a state of immanent lethargic stimulation.

The afternoon storm arrived on schedule, a brief torrential pounding followed by the monotony of drizzle and drip. She had never heard it like that before, the room sheltering them more like a great tree than a house of wood and stone. For a while nothing existed but the rain and the sodden heat and she nestled into him on the sunken couch. The darkness, the night, came slowly, the gloom of the storm merging into dusk. He put on music, the jazz from his record player spooling out with a muted distant quality, as if overheard through an open window—a second-hand machine, its vintage fidelity quite unlike the warm crisp state-of-the-art stereo that Richard Lansdale had bequeathed his former fiancée.

When they sent me to Korea, he told her, they destroyed my ambitions, my career. Maybe you're right, that I'm hiding out here. I don't know. I don't care. There's no difference between hiding and living, anyway. However I choose to live, I'd always be hiding from something. Always looking over my shoulder. It's preparation, the notebooks and my reading. My voyeurism, as you call it. My vindication. He spoke like that for hours, holding her close, the jazz seeping through the thrumming of the insects, drinking and smoking his half-dope cigarettes. At first, buying the land had been a way of investing the money, he tried to explain. He didn't like banks, didn't want anything to do with stock brokers. It was a violent ugly piece of earth, Sawfish Point. Unfit for decent chamber-of-commerce humans. A good place for him to wait it out, to become something more than whatever it was he had been, before Korea. As an artist, maybe she could understand what he was trying to say. Oh, he had plenty of money. He didn't have to live like this. Only he liked it, the heat and the jungle dirt and the damp odors. Like a prison camp, an internment of his own devising. And when at last those who had promised to help him finally arrived, perhaps he would refuse them. Tell them to go to hell. Was there help without betrayal? Friends who were more than enemies of enemies?

To all this she had listened silently, nestled against his chest, her eyes closed—fortunately, because the rain had driven in the silverfish and earwigs and palmetto bugs, enormous winged roaches that scurried across the floor in mad waddling sprints. She was nearly in a trance. He had pried her away from the paralysis of the studio; for a night or two she wanted to stop being Willa Branton. And so, during those first hours of darkness, a space had opened for them: Narby wanting her to know, to understand, bringing her here, and Willa wanting to void herself of fame and reputation and the horror of what awaited her when the renown—her spectacular audacity, her talent—crumbled away.

When he got up to put on another record, around ten or so, she excused herself to use the bathroom, taking her purse. None of the doors in the house closed tightly, the wood in a constant state of warp and swell, the hinges sagging in the pith. It would be better for her, for both of them, after all, if she didn't hide it. So, after a moment he followed her and swung open the bathroom door with a push of his foot. She was sitting on the closed lid of the toilet dipping a tiny implement, a spoon, into the glass vial. Ignoring the intrusion she raised the spoon to her nostril and snorted and leaned back, her head raised slightly. Only then, after the drug connected, did she deign to acknowledge his presence. "Where are your manners, Philip? Didn't your mother teach you to knock?"

He held out his hand and reluctantly she took it and he led her back into the room and he watched as she fed the other nostril. "I'm sorry Philip," she said, screwing the vial closed and putting it safely in her purse. "Forgive me."

"For what?"

"For being such a bloody fucking bore." Her eyes had hardened and yet she looked at him softly, with tenderness. "I'm in something of a spiral these days. Thank you. For bringing me here. For not leaving me alone." She tried to explain, make excuses. She only used it when things got difficult with her work. It was a release, that was all. Freud himself had used cocaine, had recognized its therapeutic value when taken judiciously. Had she ever raised an eyebrow at all the marijuana he smoked, all the pills he took? And they both drank like fish, didn't they? She laughed. God, they were pathetic, both of them, weren't they? Pathetic and glorious. She began to kiss him, running her hand over his bare chest. The sister swooning into the lover, the mother revealing her admiration for the strong magnificent man her little boy had become. Would he like a little sample? She would have offered sooner, only she never had much. She got it from a painter she knew who lived on St. Mark's in the East Village. She was selfish by nature, she knew that about herself, didn't pretend otherwise. Her selfishness, her filthy moods, the cocaine, her sexual compulsions—anything to feed the hunger of her art, her painting. It was like an inferno, her need to paint, burning up everything else in her life.

She reached into her purse and handed him the vial. He was the only person in the world, the only man she would ever want to share with. The only person who knew—well, except of course for Hendrik, the painter on St. Mark's. An addict and a homosexual. He didn't count.

He took a tiny spoonful in each nostril. His system seemed to welcome the drug like an old lost friend, come home at last from years of aimless wandering. The wandering was over, and the feast might begin.

Willa had stretched out on the sofa, her head resting on his lap. He ran his hand over her body, under the flimsy T-shirt. She looked up at him, a vacant stare in her colorless dilated eyes, her thick pale lips parted, showing the tip of her tongue. Their lovemaking took a long time, as if the ecstatic climax had come first and their laborious mechanical movements were merely an effort to catch up to it. Afterwards, trying to get some sleep, she had murmured, "Your friends at Sir Jack's. They could get some for us, couldn't they? You wouldn't mind asking them, would you, darling? You'd do that for me. For us. Why don't we go into Miami, tomorrow or the next day, whenever you like. You'll ask them, won't you, my love?"

He woke before her. It was late morning. Waters still hadn't returned. The generator would be running low on gas. He went out to refill it—Waters usually kept the gas cans full—and then made coffee and rolled a few cigarettes. There was an empty vial on the table; the other was in her purse. He felt a sharp senseless anger. She was using him. What difference did it make, as long as he got what he wanted?

He hung a cigarette on his lip and lighted it and went out to the grove and picked the morning's fruit: mango, and oranges for juice. He had cheese and a dozen eggs in the icebox, not yet spoiled, enough coffee for a pot or two, but little else. He would ask Waters to pick up supplies. Only where the hell was he? Why hadn't he told Narby he was leaving for a few days? Waters was far more to him than a caretaker, a groundskeeper. Narby had offered to put something in writing, to insure that whatever else happened, Waters would always have a place here, a right to live on the property. But Waters had demurred. "Ain't no paper gwine to change things," he had said. "If we ain't getting along, ain't no paper gwine to make things stick. If you ain't around, ain't no paper gwine to stop the white folk from taking what they want."

Waters had never disappeared like this, without leaving word.

After an hour or so he cajoled Willa out of bed. She didn't seem so amenable now to the shabby surroundings. It was a long way from the island, the sterile comforts of the steel and glass house and the humming air-conditioner. Without her car, hardly knowing where she was, she was rather at his mercy. As if he were keeping her against her will. She was wrapped up in his T-shirt, hugging herself on the decrepit sofa despite the sweltering heat. He fed her what little food he had and they sat under the fan looking out into the shade of the grove, smoking cigarettes, sipping the gritty coffee and the orange juice he had squeezed, a bit sour, spiked with the white wine. Despite her jagged mood he understood that she was grateful not to have to face the studio again that morning, to have been bodily removed from that burden. Grateful, too, that he would help her, once the vial in her purse was empty.

He told her to get dressed. He wanted to show her the other side of his jungle kingdom. The rape and pillage undertaken by his business partner, Sid Black. On the way back they'd stop at the Piggly Wiggly in Myerton and pick up a few things for dinner, a romantic repast in his jungle bower, entertained by Coltrane and Davis. One more night chez Narby. In the morning they'd take the truck across the Everglades, have one hell of a weekend in America's year-round fun-in-the-sun playground. Splurge, go for broke. People like them couldn't drop their cares so easily. A day at the racetrack, a ball game, would hardly suffice.

She went into the bedroom and came out in a bright floral-print backless halter-style sundress. "Could you cinch me, darling? It's my summery wife-dress."

He put on a pair of khaki trousers and a freshly laundered sport shirt and the jaunty narrow-brim straw fedora. "Not yet," he said, staying her hand when she snapped opened the purse. Bring it along, for later."

"All right, Philip. Whatever you say."

He had hoped to spot Waters' flatbed truck somewhere along the way, but there was no sign of him anywhere.

From the highway he turned onto Burnt Ranch Road—smooth now, the fresh coat of asphalt paid for by the Sun American Land Corporation. After Narby's loans had gone into default, his acreage foreclosed by Wilson's bank and then sold to Sun American—twenty-thousand acres of pine and palmetto waste and mangrove muck, with all right-of-ways and easements and variances appertaining thereto—Sid Black personally had won over the Commissioners, or at least enough of them. Bob Sunderland was a veritable Zionist these days. Besides, Black had assured them.—no Miami Beach for Lacoosa County. They were selling *home-sites*, not hotel rooms with kosher smorgasbord. Building schools and hospitals and churches. Using local builders, whoever the County Commissioners recommended, while keeping out the east coast labor unions. Everything wholesome and American, through and through. Black had showed Sunderland the list of the first hundred home-site buyers: Swanson, Beckridge, Marshall. Russo. Fenton. Not a single Hebraic name among them. Folks from Michigan, Indiana, Illinois. The Jews from up north preferred the Gold Coast, they flocked with their own—the Goldberg Coast, Sid joked. Coco Reef was something different, the kind of place where the average American could stake his claim in the sun.

Two miles down the road they came to the intersection with Coco Reef Boulevard. A highway-style billboard loomed up from the trampled brush: *Welcome to COCO REEF, Waterway Wonder City of the future. More miles of canals than Venice Italy! Home-site sales office five miles ahead.*

Narby pulled over to let Willa have a good look. She stared in disbelief. "Venice, Italy?" All around nothing but the low ugly scrub, colorless under the glaring blanched sky. She laughed.

"Shall we have a café espresso while we wait for the next vaporetto, darling?"

In the distance he could make out the smudges of black smoke rising from the enormous pyres of bulldozed vegetation, staining the haze. Once the road had been finished—sturdy and wide enough to bring in the draglines—Black had started at the southern tip of Sawfish Point, working inland and up the mangrove coast toward Vetch's store. Bulldozing, scraping the land clean, and gouging out the canals.

Willa passed him the vial.

"Maybe just a taste," he said. In the halter sundress, her complexion clear and lightly tanned, her legs and arms bare, her eyes hidden seductively behind the dark glasses, her mouth in a little pout as she sniffed, she was like the neighbor's wife in the Ten Commandants, the one you'd risk everything for—job, family, reputation, the gamble on eternal life—to covet. "Only take it easy, OK?"

"Whatever you say, my love."

They drove down Coco Reef Parkway, a four-lane macadam road only a year old yet already cracking and buckling from the heat and the punishing weight of the heavy equipment. Along the shoulder a series of black creosote-oozing power poles receded into the distance, a pair of wires sagging from one pole to the next. The road was deserted but for a single car speeding in the opposite direction—a black sedan with dark tinted windows. Last winter, the high season, they'd been bringing them down by the busload, on junkets with tickets to Weeki Wachee and the glass bottom boat rides and the free fried-chicken dinners. Now, with the wretched heat, it was just the stragglers, suckers who'd been drawn in by the television commercials or came out of curiosity, wondering what the hell kind of wonderland went for ten dollars down and ten a month.

They reached the cut line, where the jungle ended. He drove a little further and pulled over into the weeds.

"What's this, Philip? It looks like a desert. What happened?"

"Sid Black. That's what happened. Let me show you."

They got out. Every living thing had been scraped away as if with a titanic razor. Mile after mile of blank naked land, covered in a whitish scaly residue that had dried hard and cracked in the sun. Like the dead spot behind Narby's pond. He took Willa by the hand, the white ground reflecting the heat upward, as if they were walking across the top of a furnace. Ahead was what looked like a wide gouge. There were only weeds, a grasslike stalk topped with sharp burrs, the only life form capable of pushing up through the baked cracked surface. "Watch out for those motherfuckers. Here we are. The fabulous waterways of Coco Reef."

It was the butt-end of a canal. The banks were steep and barren and straight, showing the tooth marks of the dragline buckets. The water sat some twelve feet below, dark and still, like run-off pooled in an industrial ditch. There was a faint smell of riverbank, brackish tannin mud. He pointed out where the canal intersected with another just like it, and another after that. The space in between, though you couldn't see it, was already divided up into narrow lots and nests of streets that went nowhere, a circuitry within a circuitry with a little bridge here and there over a canal to connect it up to the other circuitries. Eventually, miles away, the wider canals reached the mangrove at the mouth of the Lacoosa River where it mixed with the incoming tides of the Gulf. Or rather, where the mangrove used to be. It was all gone now, plowed under, burnt, buried under tons of crushed rock.

"Just like Venice Italy, after a couple of hydrogen bombs."

"It's utterly surreal, Philip." They were walking back to the truck, flying on the cocaine. "What next? The Plaza San Marcos?"

"The tour isn't complete without a stop at the sales office." He offered her the flask and lit a cigarette. "You game for that?"

"Sales office? What is there to sell? There's nothing here."

"Very good. You're catching on."

They sat for a moment in the truck, kissing and groping, Willa rather moist under the sundress, her thighs slick with sweat, and then they drove off. After another mile or so a few houses appeared, scattered against the vast sterile blank, concrete-block and stucco with screened-in patios facing the canal in the backyard, each house set within its own isolate square of sod. A desperate attempt at landscaping festooned the median strip running down the center of the so-called boulevard—young coconut palms, jaundiced and nut-less, propped up with two-by-fours nailed into the curving trunks, and pale hibiscus bushes struggling to flower. Black had poisoned the soil by filling and elevating the scraped-away jungle with the muck and marl from the bottom of the canals. Only Black didn't see it as poisoning, but rather sterilization. He knew exactly what he was doing. He was letting in the light, the water. Obliterating the dirt and darkness and chaos. Everything clean and bright and simple and transparent. And it was damned cost-effective, too. Economies of scale. Creating miles and miles of waterfront and ready-to-build-on land in one fell swoop. Nothing like it anywhere in America, anywhere in the world. Even the redneck County Commissioners had to admit: Sid Black—decorated Korean War veteran, the kind of Jewish fellow you could do business with—was a genius.

Narby pulled into the gravel lot and parked next to a gold-tinted two-toned Cadillac El Dorado. Narby didn't recognize it. Another new salesman, probably. There were a few other cars in the lot—the powerfully air-conditioned Oldsmobiles and Lincolns that the Company used to show people around, and a new white Ford pickup, splattered with mud. Sid kept his Corvette in a shed at the Coco Reef airstrip for his personal use, whenever he deigned to fly in from Coral Gables in the Company Cessna. No more Lincolns for Sid, no more thug drivers like Lou. Sid was in the advertising and marketing business now. Keeping up with the trends.

"Let's have a little fun, shall we? Most of these people here won't recognize me, but they might know my name. Who should we be?"

Inspired by another snort they decided on Mr. and Mrs. Bland. Jack and Jill. Newlyweds, from Normal, Illinois. Narby would do the talking; Willa would play the obedient wife. The sales office was a low, long, concrete building coated in gay yellow stucco, roaring air-conditioners dripping rust- brown water jutting out from every other window. Inside was a small reception room, the wood-paneled walls decorated with charcoal-line drawings and watercolor renderings of lushly gardened modern homes and lavishly landscaped open-air shopping plazas, pools and tennis courts and golf courses and motor boats docked in backyards. Willa paused to examine the illustrators' artistry. "It's god damned freezing in here," she whispered. "My nipples are hard as rocks, darling." After a moment the salesman came out and greeted them. The blather came fast and furious: "Welcome to Coco Reef, waterway city of the future… Irv Segal, like the bird… how are you, glad to meet you, where you folks down from?… something to drink, a nice cold Coca Cola or a cup of coffee?… Jack, Jill, you're in for a real treat today, I can promise you that."

Sid Black's script. Segal was in the prescribed Sun American haberdash: blue blazer over a white short-sleeve shirt, striped tie, hair combed back stiff as a helmet and stinking of Vitalis, the morning's razor nicks dotting his loose-skinned bristling cheeks, face and neck daubed in styptic. "And not only the waterfront Florida dream house you never thought you could afford, but the return on your investment guaranteed, better than the stock market, and you can quote me on that… how did you hear about Coco Reef? Television? Magazine ad? Or have some of your friends already bought their home-sites? I wouldn't be surprised… moved down from Baltimore myself and let me tell you, I don't miss that snow and sleet and slush… the Puerto Ricans, the crime, the juvenile delinquency, the dirty streets? Well, you can forget about all that. None of those worries down here.... Let me get the keys to the Cadillac and I'll show you around. You can pick out your home-site today."

Segal had addressed his remarks to the husband, of course, but Narby saw the man's reptilian eyes drifting toward Willa—her frozen-stiff nipples poking against the floral print and her lovely legs crossed, exposing the creamy flesh stippled with goose bumps. Segal stood, ready to escort them, a pair of sunglasses in his hand—enormous jutting nose, thick protruding ears, bulging deeply underscored eyes set below an overhung brow, a complexion like the skin of a wilting red grape, his features exaggerated by the dark glasses, his entire aspect like some totemic figure chiseled in stone, a Semite incarnation of an Easter Island statue, an Olmec head. Christ, compared to Irv Segal you'd think Sid Black had just stepped off the Mayflower.

"Beautiful day, huh? Another one. Look at all that sunshine."

Black would have worked out the off-season sales routine with cunning precision, the blathering salesman detaining the prospects in the frigid office air-conditioning just long enough so that, stepping back into the Coco Reef swelter, the heat came as a relief, a soothing warm embrace. Segal swung open the passenger door to the El Dorado, but Mr. Bland insisted that his wife take the front seat, next to Irv. "No you, darling." "No you." "He treats me like a princess," she explained to Segal, smiling. "He's a wonderful husband, really, in every possible way. So attentive. So strong."

Segal nodded. He was wondering, perhaps, where their car was. They couldn't have come from Illinois in that broken down pickup truck with the Florida plates. He started the engine and turned on the air-conditioning and pulled out into the desert void, the glare ameliorated through the tinted windows. Blathering: "No kids yet? By the time they're old enough, Coco Reef will have the best schools in the State... the fishing is fabulous around here, best in the world... dock your boat right in your own backyard. Now how incredible is that?... more miles of canals than Venice, Italy... absolute best investment on the market... build right away or purchase on surprisingly easy terms .... low as ten dollars down twenty a month I kid you not... unfortunately, many of the best homesites have already sold... only a few premium sites left until we develop the next section... selling like hotcakes... shopping plazas, hospitals, parks, PGA approved golf courses, all at your fingertips."

They came to a spit of land, the only acreage in Sawfish Point tangent to the open waters of the Lacoosa River as it widened into the mangrove islets and sandbar ridges and mixed with the Gulf. Not far, in fact, from where Narby and Campos had been left to die, on the sandbar. Only now, instead of jungle and mangrove swamp there was dry white hard cracked land, like a staging-area or landing strip, raised several feet above the sluggish brown water. More houses were scattered about, little blotches of colored stucco and yellowish-green sod dotting the blank. At the end of the boulevard they reached a large active construction site, the skeleton of a warehouse-sized A-frame building already in place. The blather came thicker now: "Million-Dollar-Yacht-and-Racquet-Club, championship tennis courts, a five-hundred boat marina, a thousand-foot fishing pier, two Olympic-size swimming pools, a fantastic fully air-conditioned club house... absolutely free lifetime membership when you purchase a home-site... a limited offer... we can sign the contract today... no banks, no mortgages, no credit requirements, no realtor fees, none of that bother. The paperwork is ready to go."

"Mind if I get out and take a look around?"

"You can see better from the car, Jack. Jill. Now hold on, folks. All right. Let's get out and take a short stroll."

Obviously, Segal loathed the withering heat. Grunting, he peeled off the blazer and tossed it in the backseat. Narby took Willa by the hand, walking past the trucks and skirting the construction debris until they came to the river. The last time he'd been down here, with Sid, they had just started the work.

Now the rock-hard ground went right up to the water's edge, where the trucks had dumped enormous chunks of limestone and rock and heaps of broken concrete blocks. Of the billowing miles of mangrove—the dark green thickets laden with pelican nests, the warm brackish lapping waters filtering through the towering maze of arching roots—nothing was left. It might be the very spot where he and Campos had come ashore.

Segal caught up to them, panting, his face purple and streaming sweat.

"You in Korea?" Narby blurted out.

"Sorry? What was that?"

"Darling. Please. Don't be like that." Willa looked at Segal. Maybe she even winked. She took Narby's arm. He could see now how much Willa was enjoying their little cocaine-inspired charade. "My husband is a war hero, Mr. Segal. He fought in the Korean conflict. But, well, the adjustment to civilian life hasn't always been easy."

"It's an honor to meet him," Segal blathered. He cajoled them back to the El Dorado, the engine left idling and the air-conditioner roaring. The blather picked up: "one of the best neighborhoods close to the river the widest canals the Million-Dollar-Yacht-and-Racquet-Club only a few home-sites today tomorrow we'll be sold out PGA-approved eighteen holes the best construction money can buy all-electric appliances no dangerous gas no open flames wall-to-wall carpeting you don't want wood construction in Florida you want quality top-grade concrete-block virtually maintenance free in a fantastic climate like this what's to maintain?" Segal steered them into a net-work of circling streets and cul-de-sacs, the connecting canal spanned by a short squat concrete bridge. At the end of the block stood a cluster of four houses, their sod yards contiguous, creating the illusion of life and human habitation. He pulled into a driveway. "This is the Verona, our most popular model for the young family." Inside the house was cool, but Segal dialed up the air-conditioner higher, blotting the sweat from his face with a tissue. He opened the refrigerator. "How about a nice cold soda, Jack? Jill? Look at that view, would you?" Through the sliding glass door was a screened-in swimming pool and behind that ten more yards of sod and then the canal with a concrete seawall and a concrete dock with a four-seat outboard motor boat roped to the davits. Narby stepped outside, leaving Willa to play with Irv. He lit a cigarette and stood on the dock, looking at the canal, the steep bare dirt banks and the dark pooled semi-stagnant water, and then across the canal, out toward the barren plane of white hard ground, scantily fuzzed with sandburs, not an upright thing in sight but for the black creosote-oozing power poles. He started to laugh. Sid Black was out of his mind.

Irv Segal watched him from behind the glass doors while at his side Mrs. Bland went on coquettishly, "How marvelous, how convenient, how clever, how nice." Back in the El Dorado, a Pall Mall pinioned between Irv's lips, Jack Bland sitting in the front now where he belonged, Irv blathered: "opportunity of a lifetime you're not one-hundred percent satisfied you get your deposit back ninety-day refund never had a taker yet."

"I don't know, Irv. I'm not sure it's for us."

"What's not for you, Jack? The best investment you'll ever make in your life? That's not for you? Owning a piece of fabulous Florida waterfront property for pennies? That's not for you? Knowing that one day you and your lovely wife and family can leave the ice and slush and crime and delinquency and god-knows-what-else and have a piece of paradise waiting for you? With your own boat right in the backyard, minutes from the river, the Gulf of Mexico, the best fishing in the world. A free lifetime membership in the brand new Million Dollar Yacht and Racquet Club? That's not for you? Well, excuse me. But I took you for a pretty sharp fellow, Jack. Remember, Jack, Jill. Those home-sites I showed are selling faster that we can keep up. In a week, maybe two, we'll be sold out. So, when you come back, after you've thought it over and changed your mind, well, I'm afraid I can't guarantee the same premium quality home-sites, the same ridiculously low terms. Jack, look, it's nothing to me. I just hate to see you and Jill miss out on a once-in-a-lifetime opportunity. That's all. Tell you what. We have a lovely room at the office where you and Jill can sit in private and discuss." He looked at her in the rearview. "I saw that twinkle in Jill's eyes when she stepped into that all-electric kitchen. Isn't that right Jill?"

"Come on now, Jack. Let's talk it over, like Mr. Segal says. I'm twinkling all over, darling."

"I guess there's no harm in talking it over. Only I don't like to be pushed, Irv. Understand? I didn't like being pushed around in Korea and I don't like it here, either."

"Whose pushing? I'm only telling you the honest-to-god truth, Jack. I'd hate to see you and Jill miss out. That's all. Believe me, I'm up to my neck in commissions. I got paperwork on my desk piled up to here. The last thing I need is more paper, another contract to do the work on. It's not about me, it's about you and Jill." He took a drag from Pall Mall to slow himself down, let the pressure off. "So, Jack, what line you in, up in Normal?"

"I'm a butcher, Jack. In the meat business."

"That right? Good for you. Everyone's got to eat. Ha ha."

At the sales office Irv left them in the conference room, the door closed, the window-unit air-conditioner blowing. They sat at the table where Irv had set down a Sun American contract-for-deed and the brochures and the passes for Weeki Wachee and the complimentary coffee and donuts. Narby lit one of his cigarettes and Willa a Gauloises. "Darling, Ph…"

He shushed her, pressing his hand gently against her lips and gesturing for her to look under the table. There was a metal device screwed to the underside with a wire that ran down the table leg and under the carpet. A microphone. He pointed to his ear and then the wall. Irv Segal would be sitting in the adjacent room with a headset on, listening to all their private concerns, their intimate marital squabbles—whatever actionable intelligence the salesman could gather to pressure them or shame them into signing. Sun American was a pioneer in the burgeoning field of innovative sales techniques. Sid had even managed to place three Sun American executives on the Florida State Board of Land Sales, just in case there were complaints.

"I don't know," Narby began. "I don't like that man Segal. Don't trust him. Yeah, it would be nice to have a little place down here. But these guys are shysters."

"Oh, darling. Don't be like that. I think he's very nice." Willa paused, her eyes gleaming as she snapped open the purse, unscrewed the vial. "Dear, it's rather chilly in here. It's giving me a sniffle."

"Let me look at this contract thing. Too good to be true, a waterfront lot for ten bucks down. It's a gimmick. There's got to be a catch. They're probably selling to a lot of spics and jungle bunnies. You know how these Jewish people are. All they care about is money."

"Don't be dreadful, darling. We're not at war anymore, darling. You're not in Korea now. Come here. Let Jill calm you down."

Narby lit a cigarette. Sitting back, smiling, he began to moan, just loud enough to be picked up by the microphone. "Oh, baby. That feels good." Under the table, so that it could be clearly heard, he zipped and unzipped his trousers a few times. "Oh, yeah."

Willa chimed in. "Oh, darling. No no, don't touch me like that." She gave a little squeal. "Darling, please, you'll drive me crazy. I won't be able to control myself. Oh yes, right there. Like that. Oh, it's getting so hot now. What if someone walks in?"

"That Segal clown was making eyes at you. I saw it. And you liked it, didn't you?"

"No. Of course not. I was only—oh oh oh—thinking about you, darling."

"He looks at you like that again, I'll break his neck."

"Darling. Calm down. Please. Oh, yeah, baby. Jackie poo? Won't you buy Jillie-poo a nice waterfront all-electric house?"

"I got to admit. You'd look damn good sitting by that pool in your bikini. Or without your bikini. Bend over a minute would you?"

Her eyes widened. She lit a Gauloises. "Like this?"

"Yeah." Narby slapped his hands together. "You like that, don't you?" He clapped again.

She was gritting her teeth, trying to choke down the laughter. "You know I do, Jackie-poo."

"All right. That's enough. Pull down your dress, for god's sake."

She paused, considering her next line. "Well? Are we going to buy or not? Be a man, Jack. Make up your mind. This is a wonderful opportunity for us. After all, do you really want to spend the rest of your life chopping meat in boring old Normal? This could be a new start for us, my love."

"All right. Let me look at this contract. Blah blah blah. Who can read this kind of crap? It's a gimmick, I'm telling you."

There was a knock at the door. Segal came in, careful to keep his eyes off Willa. He blathered for a moment, explaining the contract, the down payment and monthly installments, how the deed to the property would be transferred once the final payment had been deposited. "I can see you're a man who knows his own mind, Jack. It was tough for you men in Korea. As an American, I appreciate that. I served in the Second World War myself. But you younger men. Well, it's a new world now and it belongs to you. I don't need to sell you on anything. You're the best judge of your own destiny. A man who takes charge. It's clear as day. But—if I may, let me explain this particular clause, *Caucasians only*. It's just a precaution. We're only marketing our unique city to the best kind of people. I guarantee it. And if someone decided to transfer his investment, he couldn't just transfer to anybody. You understand?"

"You mean no niggers or spics allowed?"

Irv smiled, his face stretching like rubber. "Caucasians only. That's correct."

"What about Chinks? Gooks? After what happened to me in Korea, I wouldn't want any gooks moving next door. Drooling over my wife in her bikini when's she sunning herself by the pool. Got that?"

Irv stepped back. "No Orientals. I assure you."

"Not even the women?"

"Sorry. The what?"

"Well, naturally, having served in both Japan and Korea, I developed a fondness for the pan-pan type." He picked up the pen. "Maybe this clause should read, Caucasian *males* only. See what I'm saying. That way, we could liven the place up. May I?"

"Now wait a minute. You can't change that."

"Well, in that case, forget it." Narby stood. "Come on, my dear. We're not welcome around here. Christ, you'd think we were communists or something."

Segal's face had gone purple. "What do you mean, forget it? What the hell you trying to pull?" He followed them out, blathering: "What kind of people are you? You're walking away from the chance of a lifetime. Look, come back in here, have a nice cold soda… your tickets to Weeki Wachee… what the hell's wrong with you, goddamn perverts. Caucasian only! What the hell more do you want?"

They sped away in the truck, letting out the laughter, taking another little snort, touched for the moment with the madness of love.

That was two days ago. The plateau of the spree. But by the second night, Willa's patience had run out. "You'll ask your friend? Bobby, isn't it? Just enough to see me through this bad patch, and then I'm finished with it. I've got to be in New York in September, anyway. When I come back, things will be better. I won't need it."

Sam Waters had returned late that night. Narby had heard the truck around midnight. Waters had gone straight to his cabin. In the morning, early, Willa sleeping, Narby knocked on his door. "Where the hell have you been, Sam? I've been worried about you."

Waters looked away. Something like contempt in the man's clouded eyes, Narby thought. "You broke your word," he said at last. "You told me them men could stay. Told me the camp was on your land. That you protecting em. Only they ain't no more camp. They done tore it down. Just like Cap'm Vetch said they'd do. Flatten it to nothing."

Goddamn Sid Black. He had promised Narby he would keep away from the camp for at least another year. Sun American had already cleared thousands of acres. There was no need, no reason. "I'm sorry. It couldn't be helped." But it was no good explaining, pleading his case. It would only make Narby look weak. "I'm going to find them work, better work. We'll build houses for them and their families. You know as well as I that they couldn't have lived like that forever. Living out there like animals. Hell, Sam. Things are different now for you people. They can't treat you like they used to."

"I done took em over to the cane fields. Took em with they belongings in the flatbed. That's where I was. Over to Belle Glade and 'Mokalee. They plenty work now in the cane. In the winter they got the vegetables to pick, too. If that work run out they can travel up north and spray them o'nge trees and such."

Narby knew those places—the squalid crowded migrant hovels, the long days of backbreaking labor in the burning sun. With the embargo on Cuban sugar and prices in flux there was a frenzy to harvest and mill as quickly and cheaply as possible. The bosses would grind them into the dust.

"Look, I'll explain it to my business partner ..." But Waters had turned away. It was trouble between Whites. Water wouldn't want to hear, to know. "Sam."

"We need more wire, Boss. Need maybe two more men."

"Fine. Get whoever you want, Sam."

Five hundred acres, that was all Narby had left. He was girding it with a barbed-wire fence. If Black tried to take an inch more, he would kill him. Kill Black with his own revolver. The five bullets still awaiting their destiny. Sid Black, his lawyer, his accountant, that son-of-a-bitch Irving Segal—he'd kill them all.

Later, after Waters had gone to purchase the fence materials, he and Willa left for Miami Beach. The Calvado, their decaying little honeymoon nest, ripe for fouling. By the time they caught a taxi for Sir Jack's they were pretty-damned soused. The cocaine doubled one's capacity. He had to bargain with the cracker cabbie to take them to niggertown that late at night. Willa's last vial empty, vacuumed clean, and Willa growing apprehensive with each passing hour, clinging to Narby, wearing the flouncy little dress with the scoop front that showed her nipples when she leaned forward. The ice-blue neon arrow, haloed in the thick humid air, glowing in the middle of the dark narrow street. After the more renowned Overtown venues closed for the night—the Lyric, the Harlem Square, the Hotel Flamingo—there was a crowd, come to drink and score dope in the comfort of air-conditioning, feeble as it was. Narby still caused a stir when he came in, nodding to Red or whoever sat at the door. The White Money Man who had helped Red and Bobby get the place off the ground, made Sir Jack's the only joint in Dixie where you could catch the latest sounds, the newest angles from the Big Apple, out-of-this-world shit, in orbit. Negro-owned, Negro-operated, damned historic, if anyone had bothered to set down a chronicle. Not that anyone came for the music, really. Wasn't soul, wasn't R and B. Wasn't Ray Charles or Sam Cooke or Etta James. They crowded instead into the front room, the bar, an uproar of voices and laughing. What was so damn funny, what they were all so damn eager to yammer about, Narby never could figure out. He and Willa had to squeeze through, his arm tight around her waist. Bobby's table was next to the stage. The band was in full sound. They were good, only not that good. Music easy to imitate but hard to play right. A fraction of a tone off, a muffed sixteenth-note run, and the best tightest shit wobbled into cliché and crap. Narby was too far gone to discern, to care. They never had been able to get the heavy cats down from New York, only the locals who traveled back and forth every couple months until they made it and stayed up North for good or failed and came back to wallow and burn-out and die.

"Bobby, my man, you remember Willa." Talking loudly over the music, Bobby with the crescent-moon face, wearing that tablecloth caftan or whatever the hell it was. They pulled up a couple of chairs and crowded his table, all the cats giving Willa the eye, a drunken White chick in that flouncy dress, Narby's woman, White Man's property no trespassing step to the back of the bus.

"I don't deal that shit, man, you know that. No junk, no poo-dray." Bobby was wound up tighter than usual. "Man, where you been? I got to talk to you, Phil. We getting notices about some eminent domain shit, like the whole block getting summoned, like what's the hell's going down, Phil? You got to talk to that Jew Goldfarb, he'll straighten it out, cat owns half of Overtown, the half worth owning anyway."

He wasn't going to break his promise to Willa. "Come on, Bobby. You know where to get it, man. Just this one time. I'll make it worth your while. You know that, right? See, it's a special night, man. Willa and me getting married, yeah, it's a wedding present." Bobby didn't like the pressure, that tease with the money, but in the end he got up and came back about half an hour later and handed it to Narby under the table and Willa, barely able to stand on her own two feet, excused herself to use the powder room and when she came out her eyes were bright and everyone saw and everyone knew and she started swaying to the jagged swinging music and flirting and every other word *fuck fuck fuck* out of her mouth.

At the break Bobby took Narby into the office behind the bar to show him the notices, five of them now, about the City Council meetings and the eminent domain. Only Narby was too far gone. "I'll get Goldfarb to take care of it, man. What's wrong with you Bobby, where's that red porkpie hat you used to wear? Come on, man, let's go outside, get straight with the fellows." That's when he saw Willa, in the alley with the lanky good looking arrogant son-of-a-bitch bass player and a few of the others, passing the joint and her dress all messed up and the black-as-coal hand on her arm. Both of them laughing. Laughing at him, the White Man who couldn't keep his pussy on a leash. Blathering the jazz talk: "White Man can play it but he can't create it. It's Black music Black emotion Black passion Black intellect, a straight line right from Satchmo and Duke to Mingus and the Trane. Ain't a single shade of White, ain't a single White branch in the family tree. African roots baby, thick and strong and hot."

He dragged Willa out of there, into the street. She had what she wanted. That was enough. On NW Second there was trouble with the Negro cab driver, reluctant to venture across the General Douglas B MacArthur Causeway, afraid he'd get stopped by the Miami Beach police. Narby had to pay him triple. And then, goddamn, he couldn't quite remember, maybe that's when Willa had tripped, getting into the cab and bruising her leg and ass, only he remembered, oh yes, how in the back of the cab somehow he had pulled up her dress and she was naked and on her back, legs bent at the knees and Narby, sitting upright, had his finger inside her, his eyes glued to the rearview mirror, watching the driver's eyes, knowing that he knew, that he could see the tops of Willa's knees, pretended that he didn't, a gleam of terror and perhaps also fascination in his eyes, and Willa moaning and naked and convulsing. "You like it," he said. "You like me rubbing your cunt with that colored man in the front seat, watching, listening? That's what you want, isn't it?" But she was too far gone to speak, moaning and clasping his hand, begging him to stop or don't stop or leave her alone or keep going. He couldn't tell which. He didn't care.

8

HE LEFT HER SLEEPING, dead to the world ten stories above the milky-green sea, and walked down Collins to the Wolfies on Twenty-First. On the opposite corner stood the Place Pigalle, shabbier with every passing season. Narby paused to finish his cigarette, admiring the poster:

> *Dixie Evans, the Marilyn Monroe of Burlesque!*
> *The sensation of the nation, hotter than the hydrogen*
> *bomb*
> *Florida's biggest most sexciting girlie revue*
> *25 long-stemmed lovelies!!!*

All of lower Collins stumbling toward decay, with the Calvado leading the descent into squalor. Dade Boulevard too, the classy nightclubs and piano bars choked into bankruptcy by the gargantuan new hotels up the Beach, the Fontainebleau, the Americana, the Eden Roc. What had Sid called it? The American Plan.

It was a vast delicatessen-type restaurant, always crowded. Narby waded through the sea of tables, the air tangy with sauerkraut and pickles and pastrami and cigar smoke. Black was sitting against the mirrored wall, in a red booth. The short, barrel-chested, rodent-faced Master Supply Sergeant had certainly come a long way since his Tokyo days dealing in pilfered scrap metal and stolen Army materiel and contraband luxury goods. McCoy and his ilk might have felt the need to wash their hands after doing business with Black. But nevertheless, they had done business with him. Narby had to admire Black. Because Black had turned their snobbish bigotry, their disgust, to his own benefit. Somehow Black had managed to stay out of the way of the Military Police and the biggest Jew-haters of all—MacArthur and Willoughby and the entire S.C.A.P. HQ. Narby's hatred of Black, his admiration, his outrage, was rather complicated. Enemies of enemies of enemies. Without Black's money, Black's pushing, he never would have run, never deserted. He would have found Bill Knowles instead, somehow, when his head had cleared and he was out of the hospital. Only he wouldn't have made it that far. Because in the hospital they would have strapped him to the gurney, juiced him with electro-shock. Burned his brain. "Who sent you that filthy slanderous infamy about General Willoughby? What were you doing at the Kansas City that night? Who else was there besides McCoy? What else do you know? Appeaser, communist, homosexual, pervert. It's because of scum like you that we lost China. You're going to pay for that. You're going to pay and pay and pay, for the rest of your life."

"The pastrami is good, but I prefer the brisket." Black waived his hand at a passing waitress. "Doll. Take this man's order, would you."

"Just a beer."

"Hair of the dog, eh? Christ, you look terrible. You ought to take it easy, friend."

"You're making things difficult for me, Sid. You're not keeping your end of the bargain, Sid. Goddamn it."

"Calm down. What are you talking about? I took care of that redneck Vetch for you, didn't I? You've got enough socked away for your old age, right? I fixed everything with Wilson at the bank, did I not? Fraud, extortion, illegal transfer of funds, conspiracy—you were wading in deep shit, my friend. And now? Now you're not in trouble anymore. Because I vouched for you. All things considered, I don't think it's fair for you to be complaining. Capiche?"

"Those Colored men living on my land. I told you to keep away from them."

"Oh. Right. That." He shrugged, tapping his cigar ash. "Couldn't be helped. It's all about accounting, the books. It's out my hands. I've got shareholders, Phil. I've got bankers and lawyers breathing down my neck. I got the salesmen, out in the field, furious with me, because they got clydes eating out of their hands, hook line and sinker, and then, bam, they run into some of your rustic Colored friends. You can imagine how well that goes over. They got to go, Phil. I waited as long as possible. Besides. I already have four out of every six home-sites in that section under contract. There's only so far I can overextend before it starts to attract undue attention. Murray can only finagle the books so far. If there's anything more important than knowing when to get out, it's never paying for something you intend to re-sell until you've already sold it. The whole contract-for-deed system hinges on this neck-and-neck race between over-capitalization and sales. In plain English, that means I got to keep selling, even when I haven't yet acquired. Every quarter we got to leap through the same hoops. I went to a hell of a lot of effort to develop the appropriate instruments and investment climate for Coco Reef. You think it's cheap to build a city, a Venice, Italy? You think it's cheap to advertise on Jack Parr?"

"I want that land back, Sid. That was part of the thousand acres we agreed on. I want you to find jobs for those men. They'll work a hell of a lot harder than those Southern-fried scabs you hire."

"What are you, on dope or something? Those scabs belong to Sunderland. How do you think we keep pushing through the new variances on the elevations? Eight feet and I'm dead. Six feet and I'm still not breaking even. Three feet I can live with, as long we get the lakes for drainage. Capiche? I got to keep Sunderland greased along with everyone else. He's depending on those Tampa kickbacks. I can't disappoint him. Not yet, anyway."

"My thousand acres, Sid. We agreed."

"Wrong. *A* thousand acres. I never stipulated *which* thousand. Believe me, I know what I agree to and what I don't. That five hundred is sitting smack in the middle of where we have to put in the cross canal. It's engineering, my friend, pure and simple. Can't be helped."

"I'm putting up a fence. Anyone crosses it, I'll shoot them. I'll kill them."

"Calm down, would you? What's with you goyim and violence? Always with the shooting and the fistfights. No one's going to touch your homestead. All right? Just keep your Colored men out of sight. That's all I'm asking. The salesmen get nervous whenever they see your truck. You ever think about getting something a little classier to drive? I can get you a good price on a Corvette. You ought to clean up your act, Phil. Get with the times."

"What if I turn myself in, Sid? Go to the Army, go to the State Department. Tell them about Tokyo, about the radio batteries, or our discussions at the hospital in Kobe and the money I deposited at the Banco del República?"

"Be my guest. You're a deserter, Phil. You abandoned your post, during wartime. That's a death sentence, my friend. Look. I can still make it happen, if you want. Just like we talked about. A passport, a place in the Bahamas. Give me three months and you can stop being Philip Narby. Forever. No one will bother you there. No one will even know you exist."

Narby drained off the beer. "No thanks, Sid. You've already done me enough favors. I don't think I could withstand any more of your kindness. But, thanks for the drink."

When he returned to the suite he saw his rucksack on the love seat, gaping open. The bedroom door was locked. He looked in the sack. The gun was gone. "Willa?" he said, trying the door again, shaking it. "Willa? Are you all right? Open the door. Willa?"

After a moment the door opened. Willa was wearing his T-shirt. The gun in her hand, her arm dangling at her side. He stepped toward her and she backed away, limping a little. "Where were you?" Her voice rasped. She raised the gun, her wrist limp, the gun level with her chin and the barrel, trembling, pointing loosely at her mouth, her head, her finger curled feebly about the trigger.

"I was at a meeting. With Sid Black. Willa. Give me that, would you?" He extended his arm.

"Stay back," she said, slurring. "Finder's keepers."

"Willa. It's loaded. It's dangerous. Please."

"A thing of beauty," she said. "Do you like Keats? A thing of beauty. Is a joy forever. The point is, Keats died at twenty-six. That's the point, I suppose. To die before 'forever' runs out."

She backed away, her legs bumping against the mattress and her knees buckling as she tipped backwards. He snapped forward and grabbed the gun and dropped it to the floor, falling with her, on top of her, and held her on the bed, pinning her, stroking her hair and letting her sob and quiver until, at last, she quieted. Then he got up and looked in her purse and finding nothing crawled around the floor and under the bed until he found the vial. There was enough left, he hoped, to get her back to New York.

9

WILLA SPENT THE SUMMER and early fall in New York. Endicott Ward had arranged studio space for her, an atelier a short walk from her Greenwich Village apartment. Narby had the Colony to himself. He would spend a few days of the week working with Sam

Waters—Sid Black's bulldozers roaring at the eastern boundary of his remaining five hundred acres, scraping away the jungle, with the draglines not far behind. The rest of the week he lived in Sanmora, swimming in the bath-warm Gulf and wandering the deserted shoreline and luxuriating in the gently humming air-conditioning and the high-fidelity stereo phonograph.

Willa telephoned every Sunday and Thursday evening. With the help of her analyst and her physician and Ward, she had recovered her equanimity, was painting again. Their conversations were brief and reassuring and rather chaste. She loved him, missed him. When she returned in October they would start over again, talk about the future. She didn't invite him to come visit her in the city, nor did he offer to do so. In the chilly balanced tones of her voice he detected a certain dullness, a resignation. She was off the cocaine, and probably the wine, too. The doctor would have prescribed tranquilizers to quell the agitation, the craving. If she had taken a lover, she was doing a good job of hiding it. But he figured that she was on the wagon with the sex, too. Her handlers in New York had got her back on track—producing fresh Brantons for the international trade in American Contemporary.

In her absence he had taken the Guilieta to Miami, maybe half a dozen trips. Things were changing, and not just on the Beach. The racial disturbances in Alabama and Mississippi had led to a backlash, even though the Negroes of Dade County had no taste for confrontation. There had been police shootings of young Negro men, beatings and KKK intimidation. An unidentified Negro male had been strung up by the heels, naked, and left for dead under one of the bridges crossing Biscayne Bay. Miami was among the most segregated cities in the South, and the local crackers meant to keep it that way. The atmosphere at Sir Jack's, the fantasy of a mixed-race clientele, was poisoned. Narby kept his visits short, getting what he needed from Bobby—or if Bobby wasn't around, from a couple of other enterprising young Negroes who weren't about to let racial politics spoil their business—catching the first set and then getting the hell out of Overtown before midnight. Bobby wasn't so eager to pal around now with his white benefactor, resented Narby for pressuring him about the cocaine. The crescent-moon faced hipster hardly spoke to him anymore. No more jive and jazz talk. It was all business now.

"You find out anything more about that eviction notice, man, that eminent domain shit?"

"Just forward the notices to the address I gave you, Bobby. I'll take care of it."

"Says they going to be meetings with the City Council. About that interstate highway they want to put in. Sure as hell ain't no Negro going to speak at that meeting."

"I'll talk to Goldfarb. He still holds the deed to the property. He'll know how to handle it. Don't worry."

Out of curiosity, Narby had stayed one weekend at the fabulous Fontainebleau. The hookers who frequented the Bleu Bar and the poolside lounge were reputed to be among the best looking and most talented in town. Sitting by himself with a cocktail and a cigarette, wearing his Lincoln Road silk and linen, he had no trouble attracting their attention. But after the initial goose of eye contact, the little game of glances, he turned away, giving no sign of recognition or desire to do business. If he were going to debase himself, risk disease, he decided, it wouldn't be with one of these missile-breasted rhinestone-studded mannequins reeking of Chanel. His compulsion in that regard could only find accommodation at the lower depths where there was no pretense, no make-believe. Girls like Becca, like La China or the has-been strippers who trolled the dives along Alton Road. For now, though, he willed himself to do without.

The Willa Branton who returned to Sanmora that November—a few weeks later than promised—was not quite the same person. Something, or someone, had taken her down a few pegs. About her contemporaries she was as arrogant as ever. But her drinking was much diminished, her dirty sex-talk restrained, her moods evened-out. They took up something of their old rhythm, Narby staying for three or four days and then absenting himself for the same, their love-making confined now to more conventional hours and positions, late at night, in the bedroom, the blinds closed and the curtains drawn. Afterwards, Willa would entwine him in her arms and fall asleep, never asking for more, and more, as she used to. She was taking Equinal and Miltown, as her doctor recommended. But so was half the population of Manhattan, it seemed. The important thing was her work. She was in the studio eight hours a day. Crates of older paintings arrived—she was entering a new phase and wanted to have her older attempts in front of her, as if better to chart a new course. The studio was off-limits to everyone. Remarkably, though, she had hung a few of her older works, still unsold, in the house—the first adornment she had allowed to the soaring silken-concrete walls.

Seeing it like that, everyday—the ostentatious smears and washed out streaks, in various lights and moods— Narby began to accept her genius as a given. It reminded him, oddly, of photos he had seen in a magazine of Edward Teller's blackboard, every square inch covered in a chaos of incomprehensible and random symbols, the scribbling of a madman. Yet to another of Teller's ilk, an Oppenheimer, there was beauty and logic and awe—even fear, considering the consequences when the welter of abstractions and symbols became manifest in the pragmatic world, became instrument and policy in the hands of lesser men.

Only how long would it last? By January, it seemed, she was on edge again, spending more and more hours in the studio, sometimes staying after dark, working by floodlight. Still, she was off the cocaine and holding steady at half a bottle of Sauvignon Blanc a day. She was quiet, affectionate, passionate enough, always willing to give him pleasure even if she were exhausted. The promised talk about their future had yet to materialize, and they drifted through the idyllic island winter in a haze of mild satisfactions.

Twice now, Campos had written from Havana. He described the precipitous exodus of the colonial-class, the unbridled support for the Revolution of the masses, worker and peasant alike—with each letter an invitation, as well, for Narby to join him and his comrades in the creation of an egalitarian social order, the flowering of the true Cuban culture.

Not yet, he wrote back. It was too soon. He would remain where he was, watching and waiting. The forces of reaction were gathering from East and West, like a distant storm. Better to gauge the weather from outside, yes? His business, the business for which he had been sent here, was unfinished. True, he might still be of service to the Revolution—but only out of affection for their friendship. He trusted nothing else, no one else. Beware of the false dawn, he admonished, of poets with machine guns becoming finance ministers. Beware the young handsome president with the wavy hair. There might be a fresh coat of paint on the white house, but the mortgage is held by the same old bank.

The end-of-season party at the Pembakers in March was especially festive that year—a celebration, rather than the usual farewell to winter's tropical splendor. Tara had finally got her bird sanctuary.

The entire Colony, and a number of their well-heeled well-connected guests—maybe sixty in all, including a scatter of children—milled about the flagstone patio, the walkways and gardens and swimming pool illuminated by dozens of blazing Polynesian torches. Three uniformed Negro domestics circulated the crowd, bearing trays of sweated iced cocktails, flutes of champagne, and platters of canapés. Dalton had even borrowed some of Narby's jazz records for the occasion, to set a more sophisticated mood. As he and Willa came through the gate, he could hear the trumpet and double-bass and cymbals drifting out from the French doors.

There was a guest of honor, too. Endicott Ward had flown down from New York, just for the occasion. Ward had been one of the original founders of the Colony, along with Pembaker and Atlee. Tara liked to say that it was Endicott who had "discovered" Willa. His presence—he hadn't been back to the island since selling the "machine-in-the-jungle" to Willa almost a decade ago—made the celebration complete. No sooner had Narby and Willa walked through the gate than Willa abandoned her lover to the throng on the patio and went inside to seek out Ward.

Narby plucked a drink from a passing tray. The Negro help sure as hell weren't from Lacoosa County—South American or Caribbean, probably, where Pembaker had his newspapers. Most of the Colony knew Narby now, by sight and repute— Willa's *fiancé*, connected with all that development going on over on the mainland, dabbled in real estate and investing. Several people nodded. He smiled, lighting a cigarette, scanning the crowd. Looking for Atlee.

Tara was holding forth about her triumph, Dalton listening and nodding in approval or interjecting a correction or amplification. Narby moved closer, to listen. Getting the County on board hadn't been easy, she was explaining. Sanctified defenders of private property, weekend sportsmen for whom the creatures of air and water were little more than moving targets for buckshot and hook, the Lacoosa County Commissioners had shown no sympathy for birdwatchers and butterfly collectors. But Tara and her supporters had connections to Washington, reaching back to the days of Teddy Roosevelt. Her tireless entreaties—to the County, the State of Florida, the Department of the Interior—had been not only eloquent and impassioned but soundly pragmatic. Farsighted stewardship of South Florida's natural patrimony would ensure a diversified tourist-and-development economy. It was a good tack and she had stuck to it, with Dalton's help, of course. Miami Beach and the high-rise bonanza of the Gold Coast were at one end of the spectrum, Sanmora Island and the unspoiled beauty of the Gulf islands at the other. She had won over Sanmora Village, too. The island's thin layer of arable topsoil was depleted. Every few years a tropical storm blew across, spoiling the grapefruit and key-lime harvest, wrecking half the fishing boats. Backed into a corner, the Village had at last bargained away its rights to the estuary. The Village school, the Island fire department, the water and roads and electric service, would all benefit. Besides, the Villagers had little affection for the swamp, as they called it, so beloved of Tara and her committee: six hundred acres of wooded wetlands, winter grounds for heron and egret and ibis, gallinule and coot, osprey and wood stork and fat lipped roseate spoonbill. Not to mention alligators, raccoons, snakes—a reptilian horde that would now feast on a diet of government-protected eggs and feathered flesh. *The Tara Pembaker National Wildlife Preserve.*

After a round of applause, Dalton took over. With Peterman's Beach State Park, and the land trust held by the Colony, and now the Preserve, it was guaranteed that Sanmora would be spared the rampant Coney-Islandism spreading up and down the Florida coast. Of course, with the inevitable construction of the causeway to the mainland, Sanmora was bound to undergo a new round of development. But there would now be a maximum of control and rational planning. In fact, he announced, the new resort at the northern tip of the island—in which, Narby knew, Isadora Trust was heavily invested—was slated to open next winter. Fifteen cozy luxury bungalows, built right into the jungle. A small marina, tennis courts, and a first-rate restaurant. The entire resort accessible only by private boat or seaplane. Tara herself had come up with the resort's name, redolent of pirate adventure and Gauguin-esque charm: *South Seas Plantation.*

There was another round of applause. The crowd began to break up. Narby wandered through the French doors, took a sandwich from the buffet, looked around for his next drink. Willa had someone cornered in the book-lined alcove off the living room, her back to the rest of the party. Lost in conversation, it appeared. It was Endicott Ward, he assumed: the graying goatee, the ascot, his yellowed teeth clamped down on an ivory cigarette holder. Narby took his drink across the room. As he passed the alcove, Endicott looked up over Willa's shoulder and caught his eye. Ward would perhaps have recognized Narby from Willa's descriptions. But obviously, it was not the moment for introductions. Willa seemed to be haranguing him. The critic and collector gave Narby a wan smile, as if to say, *it's one of Willa's moods. You must know them quite well by now.* Whatever they were talking about, it didn't look as though Ward was having much fun.

His gaze settled on one of the Colored girls, the most exotic of the three. Brazilian, he guessed, an African-Indian, her skin like coffee and cream, with high cheekbones, her smooth jet-black hair pulled back tight under the maid's headpiece. He followed her and smiling plucked a cocktail off her tray.

"Philip."

He felt Dalton's hand on his shoulder.

"It's been a while. How have you been?"

They shook hands. "Good to see you, Dalt. Busy. Over in Sawfish Point most days."

"Willa's here, isn't she?"

"Yes. All wrapped up with Endicott Ward at the moment."

"Talking shop."

"Suppose so."

"You like those?" He nodded doubtfully at the cocktail in Narby's hand.

"The gin and tonic? Well, it was just passing by ..."

"Come on. I brought something home from the Isle of Skye last year. All smoke and peat."

He followed Pembaker down the hallway to his office, the inner sanctum. Atlee was waiting for them, sitting in one of the leather club chairs, in a black polo shirt and suntan trousers, his legs crossed. He was paging through a large atlas spread open on his lap, absently rattling the ice in his tumbler. At their entrance he raised his head.

"Well, well. Our fledgling land magnate."

"Hello, Dan. That's all right, don't get up." Narby leaned and shook Atlee's heavy gripping hand.

Altee closed the atlas and laid it on the desk and tilted the last of the drink into his mouth.

But for a few words in passing along the dunes Narby hadn't spoken to Dan Atlee since the day on the Miranda. For all his pride in his Colony credentials, Atlee didn't actually spend much time on the island. His shipping company, the oil tankers, kept him traveling. The big wood-shingled Cape Cod house on Sanmora was a place to deposit Sheila and the kids, keep them amused during the winter season while he attended to business—or whatever the hell he did while he was away. When he deigned to join his family, Atlee in fact spent most of his island-time on the Miranda, fishing, chasing sailfish and tarpon and blue marlin.

"A single cube," Pembaker was saying, dipping a pair of tongs into the ice bucket. "It's better than drinking it neat, in my opinion. Brings out the depth." He poured from the decanter and handed the heavy tumbler to Narby and then took the empty tumbler from Atlee. Atlee had been sitting here all evening, Narby guessed, siphoning off Pembaker's precious booze, and browsing through Pembaker's atlases—there were two others at arm's reach, piled on the desk.

"Thank God this bird thing is over." Pembaker lowered himself into the third club chair. "Tara's been bouncing around like a damn rubber ball. Still, it's a good thing for Sanmora. Even with the causeway we'll have a firm grip on the entire island.

And it's kept Tara out of my hair," he said, smiling, as if it were a clever remark.

"Sheila, too," Atlee put in. "The wives' cabal."

"They've been at it since Caracas, haven't they? Always plotting against the rapacious forces of progress."

"The American Women's Service Organization. Wasn't that it?"

"A.W.S.O. Remember, Dan, when you pointed out to our fair wives that the first way they had it, the Service Organization of American Woman, spelled out S.O.A.W. Sow. Saved them a good deal of embarrassment."

Atlee laughed. "I should've kept my mouth shut."

"So, Philip," Pembaker said after a moment, "this Coco Reef development is getting a lot of attention. I've been keeping an eye on Sun American stock ever since they went public. How about an insider tip? Good time for Dan and I to buy some shares?"

"I wish I could tell you, Dalt. It was just luck that I bought up all that land right before Sun American came looking. Well. Not entirely luck." Atlee was watching him, his face dull, expectant, waiting for the right moment to butt in, challenge him. "My timing was good. The lumber company had already pulled out. No one back then would have thought that all that pine-and-palmetto scrub was worth developing. It was like buying up old furniture at a fire sale. I figured, it's so damned cheap, might as well gather it up and sit on it, wait for things to change. And along came Sid Black." He sipped his scotch. "Thing is, I've got nothing to do with Sun American anymore. Sold them everything, except for the five hundred acres around my house. Your guess is as good as mine, whether the whole thing will fly or crash."

"That's not they way I hear it, Phil," Atlee said. "I heard that you're the silent partner. Every time I take out the Miranda I like to swing around that maze of mangrove to see how much more riverfront they've cleared off. Finally got curious enough to drive over there one day, talk to some of the salesmen. Your name came up. More than once."

Narby lit a cigarette, deciding. "Well. I helped Sid Black deal with the County. That's all. Got him in with Bob Sunderland. Folks around the County aren't used to dealing with people like Sid Black. More of a liaison really, than what you'd call a silent partner." He turned toward Pembaker. "You know Bob Sunderland, don't you, Dalt?"

"I do. A reasonable enough fellow. One of those scratch-my-back types, I'd say."

"In any case, as far as I'm concerned, my dealings with Sid Black are finished."

"But you plan to stay out there, in your house, for the time being?"

"When he's not here, you mean, nesting with Willa." Atlee interjected. "Any intimation of wedding bells? It's not fair, Phil. That you're still single, still free. I mean, isn't there some time limit on being the fiancé?"

Narby shrugged. "Willa and I like things the way they are. Why risk spoiling it?"

"Why, indeed? Nice work, if you can get it." He was fairly drunk, but he held it well. The talk turned to Cuba, as it had on the Miranda. "Used to be a hell of a fun place. Yeah, Dalt? So, when exactly were you in Havana, Phil?"

"I went a few times, after Korea. Winter of fifty-four, fifty-five. You're right. It was a damned good time. As long you belonged to the right crowd." He paused. Dan was flaming up a cigar—one from the box on the desk, not from the drawer. "A hell of a lot of misery, too. Under Batista."

"Where the hell in the world isn't there misery? A little-known fact, Phil. Cuba had the highest standard of living of any of those Latin countries. Now it's going to go down the toilet. Batista was harsh, maybe too harsh. But now, with Castro wanting to go it alone, without our business expertise, our efficiency, our capital, well—they don't know how to drive, been in the back seat too long."

"They can learn, can't they?" Narby said.

"Can they?" Pembaker said. "The revolution has opened a can of worms, a real power vacuum. No one really knows how loyal the Army is to the new government, or to Castro himself. My sense is that they could turn, just like that. Bring in a new strongman. Someone even worse than Batista. It's certainly happened before."

"Disclosure," Atlee said suddenly. "I had friends in that crowd around Batista. At least he had a grip, and you knew who to go to. You wanted to build a new hotel, you went through Batista. You wanted to renew a nickel or magnesium concession, you went through Batista. Met him once. Can't say I was much impressed. At the Lake, at Dayton Hedges' funeral. You remember, Dalt. Let me tell you, Phil." He lurched a bit in his chair. "There wasn't a thing wrong with that country that couldn't have been fixed with a little American know-how, a little pressure applied in the right places. Even Batista. Easily fixed. Too late for that now. They've thrown the baby out with the bathwater. What did you say your business was over there, Phil?"

"I don't think I did say."

"Well then, what *was* your connection? Apparently you have a lot of feeling for our Cuban neighbors."

Pembaker was watching Narby now. He wanted a good answer, something to take Dan off balance.

Narby breathed, leaned back. "I can't name any names, I'm afraid."

"Why not?" Atlee's face had gone a bit rigid. "Ashamed of your *nationalista* friends?"

"Because. Well. She was married."

Pembaker smiled. "Oh?"

He had hit the right note. "A miserable marriage, she assured me. An American gal, stranded in Havana. Her business-man husband was always out in the countryside, inspecting his company's mills, or something like that. And playing around with the local fauna, so she claimed. I was single, just out of the service." He looked at Atlee. "Very pretty, very… eager. She had a fair number of Cuban friends, too. So, I got to know the country a little. As far as I could tell, for the kind of things she and I were doing, well, we didn't need to go through Batista. "

Atlee drew on his cigar. "You dog," he said, frowning and then laughing. "Unfortunately, I married young, when I was still in the Marines. But once we had the kids, Sheila usually stayed stateside when I travelled on business. When in Havana, eh?"

"God," said Pembaker. "I shudder to imagine. All those lovely Cuban girls, the pall cast over them if they fall into the Soviet Bloc. Have you seen the women in Hungary, in Poland? With legs like tree trunks."

"Won't happen," Atlee said, enjoying himself, letting the tension go. "Castro's a damn prude, a scold in fatigues. But the Cuban people thrive on that cha-cha-cha theory of life. Christ, with all those damn five-hour speeches he'll suck the vavoom right out of them." His face went absent for a moment. "There was that little house, just off the Prado… "

"Dan," Pembaker interrupted.

"I didn't. Wouldn't. Touch married women. Not that I didn't have plenty of opportunity. Hell, that's why they flocked down there, to have their flings. What was it called? La Casa Miel. The Honey House."

Atlee fell into silence, looking down into his drink. Pembaker leaned forward. "Well, we all seem to be up-to-speed on our Cuban affairs. Dan? Shall we make our proposal?"

"All right."

"A little adventure, Phil. While we still have the opportunity. We've had reports of blue marlin running between the Straits and the Old Bahama Channel, off the Camaguey coastline. A big run. The Miranda can handle that distance, no problem. But we'd have to stop somewhere along the Cuban coast to fuel up. And we'd need to have safe harbor in the vicinity, if the weather turned."

Atlee picked up the nautical atlas from the desk. "Here. Take a look. We'd shoot through the Keys under the Marathon bridge. Remember the time we got hung up on that shoal, Dalt? Had to spend the night on a damn forty-five degree tilt waiting for the tide. And we weren't even drinking!"

"We'd be gone three, maybe four days. Hook a few marlin, if the gods are willing. Maybe take a little tour of that stretch of coast. Put in for the night here, at Cariboca."

"Before Castro closes the country down." Altee said. "Or before we close it down for him."

"We'd like to have you on board. What do you say?"

Narby looked at the atlas. "They're not exactly welcoming Americans these days, are they?"

"There aren't any restrictions. Border's relatively open. Castro wants to boost tourism. At least that was his line a few months ago. Remember all that publicity about Joe Louis in Havana? There won't be a problem. If there is, well, there's always Guantánamo. It's a bit far, but we'll be within radio contact. As I said, it'll be an adventure."

"You haven't gone fishing until you've landed a blue. You haven't *lived* until you've landed a blue. Might be our last chance for a while ..."

Someone tapped at the door. It swung open. It was Tara. "Sorry to disturb you, Dalton."

"Quite all right."

"Phillip. It's Willa. Something's happened. She ran out of the living room very upset. Just a moment ago. I think, oh dear, I think she was crying. Everyone noticed. I went out to the patio and I heard the gate slam. She's probably on her way home. Maybe you'd better see what's wrong."

10

AFTER AN HOUR—WALKING ALONG the dunes back to the house, then out again, all the way to the creek and backtracking to the Pembakers'—he gave up the search. At least he was certain she wouldn't try to drown herself. Of all her fears, real and imagined, her terror of the water took first place. He looked in the rucksack. The pistol was there. She was hiding somewhere, in the jungle or further up the beach. He wasn't about to wander aimlessly in the dark, calling out her name. She'd show herself when she was ready. Only what the hell had happened? Endicott Ward was her champion, her biggest booster. What the hell could he have said that would put her in such a panic?

He telephoned the Pembakers. Tara answered. He could hear the sounds of the party in the background, the Miles Davis record. "Don't worry, Tara. She's always been a bit unpredictable. Did you speak to Endicott?"

"Yes, of course. He said that they had chatted for a while, the usual art world gossip, New York, the Venice Biennial—nothing that they hadn't talked about dozens of times. He said he can't imagine what set her off like that."

"That's odd. Looked to me like they were having a rather intense conversation."

"I don't know what to say, Philip. I don't mean to pry. Everything all right between you two?"

"Far as I know." There was a silence. "She's probably walking it off, whatever it is. I wouldn't worry." He promised to telephone in the morning, to reassure her that Willa was safe and sound.

He took the flask and pouch and sat on the cantilevered terrace, waiting. Even without moonlight the dunes showed white against the darkness, the waves rolling in rimmed with phosphorescent foam. Thinking about what had transpired in

Pembaker's office: as soon as he knew when, had a firm date, he'd wire Campos. They'd be waiting at the harbor in Cariboca, confiscate the Miranda, arrest Atlee and Pembaker and charge them with colluding with Batista, spying for the reactionaries in Miami, preparing a counterstrike against the new government. That ought to satisfy the Fidelistas as to whose side Philip Narby was on. Then he would track down Bill Knowles, the way Knowles had tracked him, trapped him. This was the chance Narby had been waiting for. Whatever Atlee had in store for him, he'd turn the tables.

Or not. Depending on what happened between now and then, the news coming out of Cuba and Miami and Washington, or if things changed while they were out at sea. Instead of betraying Atlee and Pembaker he would warn them, steer them away just in time. Play both hands at once. The only real man now was the man with no sides. He wasn't the congressman's boy anymore.

Around midnight he got up. The flask was empty. Goddamn it, he felt like a swim. Who was going to stop him? Willa hated it, when he wanted to swim at night. It terrified her and she would plead with him not to go. Only she liked it. She liked it that he scared her like that, purging her fear. And now she was trying to scare him. Only it wasn't working. He didn't give a damn where she was, or why.

He changed into his swimsuit and slung a towel over his shoulder, finding that he had to steady himself with the hand-rail as he thumped down the floating-step staircase. At the bottom he stopped and gazed up at the Willa Branton hanging on the wall above him, dominating the room. What a joke! She and that aging fairy Endicott Ward had cast a pall over the eyes of the art-gapers, the Arab sheik collectors and gallery touts, convincing them to see what wasn't there, conjuring wonders where there were only smears and stains. He lurched forward. He needed another drink, that was all. That would get him out to the waves.

Take it easy, he told himself. He made it out to the garden and satisfied at his progress sprawled in one of the poolside chaises. He remembered reading something once, about blue marlin. A three-hour struggle to reel it in. Hands cramping and burning from holding the rod. When they finally pulled it along-side the boat the thing was nothing but a ragged-head corpse, gnawed by the sharks to a bloody stump. The skipper got out his shotgun and started blasting away, but to no avail. A sad story, a moral disaster. Waste and futility and shame. But the blunderers had acted like men, struggling, refusing to give up, leaving a river of blood in their wake, like a signature.

Only where the hell was Willa? Maybe it had something to do with these new paintings Willa was so wrapped up with? Christ, maybe she'd decided to actually paint a picture, some-thing you could see for yourself that didn't have to be explained, justified. He pushed out of the chaise and crossed the garden. She usually kept the studio locked. He tried the knob and to his surprise it turned and he opened the door and switched on the light.

She was sitting on the stool, her party dress hiked up over her knees, the floor beneath her littered with butts. A large can-vas was propped against the ladder, directly in front of her.

"There you are. I knew you were all right. You had them all damn worried."

She looked up. Didn't seem upset at all. "I couldn't see it. In the light. Isn't that funny, Philip?" Her voice rasped, ravaged from the Gauloises. "Because I had to see it in the dark. Had to look through the darkness. All this blather, these theories about light. It's apt to throw you off, if you don't have a mind of your own."

"Huh? See what?" He stood beside her and looked. The can-vas was blank. Only there was a sheen, pale yellow. Like some-one had smeared it with piss. "What is it you can't see in the light?" He didn't care for her riddles anymore. "I give up."

She got off the stool and kissed him very lightly, very sweetly, on his mouth, and took his hand. "Let's go. Yes?"

"Sure." He thought she meant upstairs. To fuck.

"I'll pack a bag. Let's go to the jazz club, darling. Go see your friends. I have to get away from these pathetic middlebrow bourgeois. These spiritual eunuchs. All right?"

"Too late. We missed the last ferry. Hours ago."

"Dalton paid them to run all night. Because some of their party guests have to get back to the mainland. Dalton and Tara run this island. They get everything they want."

"For the birds," he said. "Tara's birds."

She laughed. "You've had more than usual, haven't you?"

"Maybe. Yeah. You better drive."

It was near dawn when they mounted the causeway over Biscayne Bay. Willa insisted they stay at the Calvado. She wanted nothing to do with the middle-class glamour-whoring at the Fontainebleau or the Eden Roc, the faux-European kitsch. She preferred a rat hole, something suitably down yet not-quite out. They'd sleep late and he could have his afternoon swim and then they'd make a night of it, hear some music, something real, at Sir Jack's. Thank god you don't buy into the mass mediocrity, she told him. Flattering him, softening him up. Because she was thinking he might not be so willing this time. To get the cocaine for her. Debase himself again in front of his Negro pals.

He felt pretty good the next day, considering. The weather was ideal, the sea calm and cool, the air crisp and ethereal blue. Must have swum three miles, paralleling the shore far enough out to clear the rock jetties, while Willa took a nice long stroll. They had dinner on Espanola Way—snapper ala putanesca and a bottle of a dry, acidic Italian white wine. She was trying to be playful, at ease. When he asked again about the party last night she shrugged it off. It was nothing, darling. Just a passing mood.

It was around nine when they left the restaurant. "Shall we get a cab, darling? Or take the car?"

"We can't go to the club tonight. There's been some trouble. It's not a good idea."

"What do you mean? It's such a fascinating place. It's the other side of the world from the people I have to deal with. I can't endure all those prigs anymore, those patrician know-nothings. I need some fresh air."

She was flailing a bit. He felt sorry for her. "I can't take you to Overtown. Believe me, Willa. You wouldn't find it amusing. Not tonight."

"Oh, come on, Philip. Don't be such a milquetoast."

"You really want to go? Well, there's nothing stopping you. Go on, hail a cab. I'll wait for you back at the hotel. Have fun."

That shut her up. She clung to his arm. Helpless. They walked east and turned on Alton Road. He hadn't come this way in years: the dull brick facades, the neon flashing through grimy window-grills, the gray metal doors. They passed Roberto's, where the queers congregated. The Tiki. The Roost. The Bradford, where he had met his first American girlfriend, a shellacked blonde smeared with lipstick and rouge. At the corner of Fourteenth he saw the place he was looking for. The Ship Ahoy. He led her inside. A dark dank box, the moldering lifesaver rings nailed up on the wall, the big ship's wheel behind the bar, some nautical rope and a cobwebbed fisherman's net hanging from the ceiling. Billie Holiday was coming from the jukebox. He sat her in a booth along the wall and went to the bar and brought back two gin rickeys and slid in next to her. "Here," he said, taking them from his shirt pocket. "Take these."

"What is it?"

"Medicine."

"Philip. Darling. Couldn't you possibly—"

"Not tonight. Go ahead, take them. It'll make you feel better, I promise."

A flash of anger came over her face. Then she shrugged and swallowed them with her cocktail and leaned back against the cushion, lighting a cigarette, closing her eyes for a moment and then letting herself look around. "Come here often?" she said, not quite sarcastically.

"Only on special occasions."

"They mix a lousy drink."

"Good jukebox, though."

Her face had gone blank. She was slipping, spiraling down. But the dope would catch her in a few minutes, lift her. Not like the cocaine, of course. More like dropping from a height into a safety net, catching her and holding her aloft and then, in a couple of hours, with the drinks, easing her down.

He waited a few minutes, smoking, holding her hand under the table. "Willa. What happened last night? What did Endicott say to you?"

"Please, Philip. Don't. Just leave it alone."

"Maybe I can help you. If you would just tell me what it's all about."

"You want to help me, Philip? Then leave it alone. And get me another drink, would you? They go down like water."

It was pointless. He went to the bar and brought back their drinks. "Dalton and Dan Atlee are planning a fishing expedition," he said, trying another tack. "They were talking to me about it last night. Asked me to come along."

"Oh? To the Keys?"

"Further. Off the coast of Cuba. In fact, they plan to stop somewhere along the Cuban coast."

"You're becoming quite the chum with those two." She thought for a moment. "That's something that interests you, isn't it? Not fishing, darling. Cuba. I saw it in your notebooks. All those clippings about Castro."

"Yes. It interests me very much."

"Dan Atlee, too. The scourge of the communists. It was his idea, I take it?" The dope, the second gin rickey, was loosening her tongue. "Don't let him bully you, darling."

Narby laughed, tensing a bit. "Bully me? I don't think so. You don't like Dan Atlee much, do you?"

"Oh, he's all right I suppose. A lot of bluff, that's all. With all that asinine he-man fisherman's philosophy." She paused, to drink. Then she looked at him. "I had to slap him once. Rather hard, right across the face."

"Slap him? What the hell for?"

"I never told anyone. Least of all Sheila. It was years ago. Before I met you, darling. Ancient history."

" Why? What did he do?"

The Billie Holiday had switched off. A bossa nova was playing, a woman singing in a low urgent whisper. "But, darling. You might not want to go fishing with Dan if I told you. I don't want to spoil it."

"Oh, come off it. He made a pass at you, is that it?" he said, carelessly. "Big deal."

She laughed. "A pass? More like a stab, actually. Partially my own fault. I must admit."

"Come on." He tried to sound light. "Spill it."

"If you insist." She was in the net, her fall broken, her voice neutral, weightless. "It was the first season I spent on the island. Richard had to go back to New York, but I stayed on. It was all so new, so exotic and enchanting. The dunes and the jungle and the sound of the waves. And I had the studio and the work was satisfying, new ideas coming to me every week, it seemed. Anyway, I already knew Dalton and Tara through Endicott and that winter I met Dan and Sheila for the first time. The Colony was just getting off the ground then and Dan, the founding father, the solider-adventurer, liked to play up his superior status. It seemed to suit him. We were all a bit in awe of him, I suppose.

"From the very first, I had noticed something in Dan. He didn't try to hide it, really. That hungry searching look that husbands of a certain age seem to acquire, as if the family they had seeded and nurtured was now choking them to death with their affection. A predatory look. There was something else about Dan, too. I didn't find it unattractive. What should I call it? The aura of command, no doubt a by-product of his military days. Or the way Dan would go on so sincerely about the nightmare of communism, the danger of subversion, the fragility of our democratic freedoms. But not like a vulgar politician, grubbing for votes. He took it much more personally, as if it were a challenge to his masculinity. And while I found that aspect of him rather foolish, it was also forceful. He had that strength of character that affects you, regardless of whether you like the person or agree with him. He repulsed me, but repulsion is a force, like attraction, and so a force existed.

"Anyway, well, you know how I like to sun by the pool. Richard and I would spend hours out there, the gate closed, behind the hedge, feeling perfectly private, perfectly safe. After Richard went back to the City and I was on my own, well, I suppose I was a bit careless. But Endicott had given me the house for the year and I cherished that freedom, that chance to experience the tropical weather, the sun, against my body. And I would take the sun naked, as I like to do. Didn't give it a second thought. And because Dan is what he is, I suppose, my lack of modesty must have given him the idea that he could approach me. That I was an open target. I suppose he had glimpsed Richard and me once or twice, or had seen me alone. He was always patrolling that winter, walking the beach like a sentry. And it didn't take much to peek over the hedge, if you really wanted to see. For Dan, I imagine it was like being intoxicated, knowing I was alone and without a stitch, with only the dunes and a fence separating me from his hunger, his right to break the rules.

"It was maybe a week after Richard had left. I was by the pool, reading, and I got up to go inside for a moment. He must have been watching. Waiting for the right moment. As I was coming back, still without anything on, I saw him through the

French doors. He was shirtless, in his bathing trunks, a towel draped over his shoulder, as if just coming from the beach. He was quite good-looking back then, taut and compact and muscular. I put something on and went out to see what he wanted. He smiled. With perfectly guileless innocence—oh, he had done this kind of thing before, no doubt about it—he told me that his pool was out of commission and asked if I wouldn't mind him taking a dip. I couldn't very well refuse, not without sounding rude, or even worse, sounding afraid. On the face of it, it was an entirely innocent request.

"Of course not, I told him, jump in, make yourself at home. He asked if I wouldn't join him, smiling, dropping the towel, standing rather close to me, and looking at me in that way of his. I told him no, that I was busy inside, and he shrugged and dove in. Rather gracefully, I noticed. Like you, darling, he was a swimmer. I decided to go into the studio until he went away. I remember watching Dan for a moment, gliding under the water, and at the same time feeling Richard's absence rather strongly, missing him in a way that hadn't quite yet registered until that moment. Well, I went into the studio, ready to work. Must have sat there for a good fifteen minutes. Doing nothing. Because that man was still out there, in my garden, exerting his force, ruining my solitude, my concentration. Well, I wanted him gone—only I wasn't sure how to manage it—wanted to send him back to wife, his children, his suffocation. So, rather stupidly I suppose, I decided to beat him at his game. Meet him face to face and say, there, I swam with you, the two of us alone, and I want nothing more to do with you, so go home. I went back to the house and put on my most modest swimsuit. But when I stepped out to the pool, there was no one there. Very odd. Only he had left his towel on the grass. I called out, 'Dan?' And all of a sudden, from behind me, I felt two arms snake around my waist, embracing me and pulling me back, and I twisted and turned around, rather startled. And here's the point of it, really. He was naked, pressing himself against me. 'Come on Willa,' he said, 'let's take a dip, au naturel.' His cock was already stiff. He was smiling, perfectly at ease. It was repulsive and rather comic, too. I don't know what I was feeling at that moment: fear, or humiliation, or disgust. But mixed in with all that was something else. That force between us. I felt it, like an electric shock. And I pulled away and slapped him in the face. Quite hard. I remember rather vividly the bright red swatch it raised on his cheek.

"He let go. He was calm. Receiving a slap was apparently not so unprecedented for him. 'You didn't have to do that,' he said. 'I know you like to lie out here. Au naturel. A simple yes or no would have done the trick.' He could stick his cock against my backside unwanted, uninvited, and yet he couldn't bring himself to say *naked* or *nude*. He had to use that prudish old-ladyish phrase. *Au naturel.*

"It was quite a performance. He began to droop, I couldn't help noticing. And yet, he continued to stand there, not exactly smiling but not visibly upset. I had to turn away, physically turn around to get him out of my sight. And after all that he nevertheless had the audacity to say, 'So, no swim I take it? Too bad, Willa, I'm a damn good swimmer. I've got a damn good stroke.'

"What could I do? I simply went inside, ignoring him, slamming the door behind me and turning the lock. I went into the kitchen from where I could see him, without him seeing me. He had put his suit on, slung the towel over his shoulder, and he was making his way toward the gate. The kitchen window was open and I could hear him. It's a rather telling detail, I think. He was whistling. Some marching tune, not the Battle Hymn but something equally martial. Bucking himself up in the face of what I am sure he considered a minor retreat, a skirmish of little strategic importance."

"The fact was that I knew of course I would have to see him again, in front of his wife and his children and Dalton and Tara and the rest. He had done that to me, made it so that I would have to carry that around. I knew that I would say nothing and he knew I would say nothing. So there was an unspoken pact between us: I'll say nothing and he'll leave me alone because if he ever did anything like that again I'd call for help, I'd shout rape. And on his part he must have thought, well, if she does, no one will believe her, because she sprawls around naked and screws her boyfriend outdoors by the pool, in the bright light of day, like a slut. There's no raping a woman like Willa.

"In any case, Philip, he's left me alone ever since. Hardly has the nerve to look me in the eye. Especially when you're in the vicinity. Oh, dear. I've spoiled it, haven't I? You won't want to go on his little boy-scout trip to Cuba. But do go. For Dalton's sake. Dalton likes you so, darling. He and Tara. Very much."

11

THREE DAYS AFTER HER CONFESSION—or whatever the hell it was— Willa flew back to New York, earlier than planned, leaving the studio cluttered with unfinished paintings and the wooden crates packed with her earlier, unsold works. To consult her Park Avenue shrink and her gynecologist, find solace with Sidney Janis and the third-rate homosexual painter who trafficked in cocaine. And who else?

Even had he been willing, Narby wouldn't have been able to get what she craved that night. Bobby had found some other roost and no one at Sir Jack's wanted to tell Narby where to find him. Soon, it would start all over again: cutting back on the pills and the grass, drinking too much, sweating it out until he found another Bobbie, another Sylvio. Grubbing around in the squalor, debasing himself. He couldn't go back to that.

He'd give it a week or two and try Sir Jack's again. He wasn't particularly welcome there anymore. So what? They couldn't keep him out. He went home and spent a few days working alongside Sam Waters. The fence now girded half the perimeter of Narby's five-hundred. Thickly twined barbed wire, KEEP OUT, NO TRESPASSING, PRIVATE PROPERY, signs hung every twenty yards. Filthy killing work in the miasmic heat and the mosquito swarms, but at night, after all the exertion, at least he might sleep, induce oblivion, blanking her from his mind.

Then he returned to Sanmora. He understood now what Atlee really was—a peeping tom, a bully who preyed on lone women, a half-hearted rapist. The type of swaggering sycophant MacArthur liked to surround himself with.

On his way through Myerton Narby stopped at the Smoker's Den. Campos might have written again. There was always the remote chance of something from Knowles. But it was only magazines and a couple of record catalogues. Hank always showed him the latest photos of little William, a stocky dusky-skinned child with his father's dark Levantine eyes and thick black hair. "Already he is five. Next year he will start his schooling. I am enrolling him in the Jackson Elementary, Mr. Norby. He will become a true American. I teach him the pledge of allegiance, in preparation. Maybe he can even become the President. Eh? A fantastic idea, I admit. But anything is possible in America."

He got to the ferry landing a little early for the afternoon run. Waiting in the truck, flipping through the *New Yorker*, something in the *Talk of the Town* section caught his eye. *Last Monday the Museum of Modern Art in New York announced with characteristically austere fanfare the roster for its much anticipated fall exhibition, 'Sixteen Americans.' The show will no doubt materialize as an historic occasion for the Modern, the first time that the august institution, with its blue-chip Picassos and Cezannes, its sterling De Koonings and Rothkos, has lavished such attention on the freshest, youngest, most daring domestic artists, some of whom, like the twenty-three year old Frank Stella, are virtual unknowns north of Fourteenth Street.*

He recognized the names—Johns, Rauschenberg, Kelly, Stella—artists whose work, Narby seemed to recall, had traveled on exhibition along with Willa's, through the capitals of the free world, from Venice to Sao Paulo. Emblems, like Minuteman Missiles and self-cleaning ovens, of American supremacy. The only woman on the list, Louise Nevelson, a sculptor, was older than Willa, a rival perhaps. What had Willa caller her? "The grand dame of the junkyard aesthetes."

One of the museum's exhibition organizers, critic and curator Endicott Ward, has assured us that the show would not merely break new ground but "reconfigure the necessity of painting itself, its most profound compulsions and deepest anxieties."

So that was it—Willa hadn't made the cut. The night of the party she would have pressed Ward to assure her she was one of the anointed. No wonder Ward had looked so helpless and cornered. Willa was thirty-five, her income generated by a single Manhattan gallery. The traveling exhibitions had come to an end—that would account for the crates sitting in her studio. Despite Willa's disdain for corporations and committees, she was desperate for the imprimatur of the lofty unassailable Modern. The rejection had crushed her. Lifted the veil from her audacious performance. Her objectless fears and anxieties, her moods of isolation and doom, had finally banged up against the wall of something very concrete, very consequential.

In New York she would find sympathy, perhaps. And cocaine. And what else? He could give her nothing. Everything they had experienced together seemed to hinge on that high-wire act of her fame, from the very moment when he had carried the young newly-ascendant Willa Branton across the creek. Now that the wire was sagging, her feet dragging the ground, she might not find Philip Narby so irresistible.

The studio was locked. Willa had hidden the key. He searched around the house for her medicine, the tranquilizers and mood-lifters prescribed by her Park Avenue doctor. She had cleaned the place out. Only two bottles remained, chilling in the fridge, of her beloved Sauvignon Blanc.

The next day, after a swim, he walked over to the Pembakers. They were usually the last to leave at the end of the season. As he came through the gate a tiny Yorkshire terrier came scurrying across the flagstones, trembling, yipping in frenzy. The French doors opened. Tara came out, looking to see what the commotion was. The dog ran to her and she scooped it up and smiled.

"Phillip. What a pleasant surprise." She cuddled the quivering lozenge until it calmed and set it down again on the flagstones. "Poor little Zulu. She's nothing but nerves these days. The little thing's been everywhere with us, from Caracas to San Juan." She laughed, watching the dog retreat on its matchstick legs. "She's got some old-age dog disease, endemic to the smaller breeds. As if her clock had been over-wound and now her little springs are going haywire."

Their eyes met for a second. "Come inside. It's gotten awful muggy of a sudden, hasn't it?" She wore beige Capri pants and a sleeveless top that showed her tanned arms and shoulders. For a woman her age, with grown children, she was quite attractive, her warm brown eyes bright and alive, and she knew how to dress, so that her petite figure showed to advantage. "I'm afraid you missed Dalton. He left yesterday. Some urgent business in Washington."

"Oh. Well, in that case, don't let me bother you."

"Nonsense. I'm delighted you stopped by. Whenever you're here you're always sneaking off with Dalton and Dan. I've got you to myself, for once. Please, sit down, Philip. Would you like a drink? Gin and tonic suit you?"

"If you're having one. Sure. Thanks."

"I'll have Sarah fix them." She walked into the next room and came back a moment later, sitting across from him, her legs crossed, leaning forward, smiling, offered him a cigarette from a silver box and then taking one herself, flicking the lighter. "Was there something you needed to talk to Dalton about? Perhaps I could help. Or is it, well"—she laughed easily—"just between men?"

"Nothing important. We'd been knocking around an idea for a fishing trip. Taking out the Miranda. Thought I'd check in with Dalton about it."

Tara spoke for a moment about her husband. How busy he was, the stress of his work, the constant travel, the byzantine politics of doing business abroad, and how much being on the island, fishing and boating and walking the beach, had relaxed him, despite the fact that the poor man had hardly been there at all this season. Sarah brought their cocktails on a tray, two tall glasses shimmering with condensation—one of the Colored help that Narby had noticed at the party. All the while Tara let her gaze meet his, her eyes darting away and then flitting back. He got the picture. Dalton was gone a lot, for weeks at a stretch. Now that they were alone, he found her more attractive than he had realized. Well, not quite alone. There was Sarah.

"Philip," she said after a few moments. "I can't help wondering. Is Willa all right? After what happened, at the party. Well, I'm concerned."

"She's fine. No need to worry. Matter of fact, she's in New York. Left last week. Rather suddenly." He leaned back, drink in hand, one arm thrown over the top of the sofa. "She didn't say when she was coming back."

"Oh. That's a shame. We might miss her. Dalton and I plan to close up the house in a couple of weeks. And what about you, Philip? Are you going to stay on for a while?"

He shrugged. "It depends." He tossed back the rest of the drink. "Very refreshing. Just what I needed."

"Well, then. Let's have another." This time, rather then get up, she called out to Sarah. She'd hardly touched her drink, but now she seemed eager to catch up to him.

He thought for a moment. Then, he said, "You know, that night of the party, when Willa ran out. It was because Endicott had told her that she wasn't going to be included in that big show they're putting up at the Modern this fall. At least, that's what I think happened. Pretty sure."

"Oh, dear. I can well imagine how upsetting that must have been."

"It's childish. The way she reacted. Willa's one of the most remarkable people I've ever met. She rarely gives a damn what anyone else thinks. But sometimes, she acts like a spoiled little girl. Throwing a tantrum when she doesn't get what she wants."

Tara took this in, leaning forward to tap her cigarette, meeting his eyes more directly. "She's certainly a bold young woman. Still, it must be a precarious existence, earning your bread as an artist. And especially as a woman. I admire her very much for what she's tried to do. So does Dalton. That's why he offered to help her when Endicott first invited her down here, years ago. Despite her, what shall I call it, her proud independence, well, Willa certainly never refused Dalton's help. Why should she? The artistic personality …"

She paused while Sarah brought their drinks and took the empty glasses away. "Thank you, Sarah. Sarah? Would you mind taking a run to Turner's? There's a list on the kitchen table. No hurry. Take your time."

When Sarah had left the room, Tara continued. "The artistic personality always has a childlike side, don't you think? A sort of innocence about the nuts and bolts of practical life. A need to be taken care of, nurtured. The European exhibitions were just the thing Willa needed to find her audience."

"Dalton helped her? Funny, she never mentioned it. If you don't mind my asking, how did he do that?"

"Dalton has known all those fellows at the Congress for Cultural Freedom for years. He and Mike Josselson were rather great friends in Berlin and Paris. They served together in Strategic Services. It was Mike and the CCF that arranged all those tours, made it all happen. It's a wonderful organization. They hold conferences and exhibitions and such, very influential all over Europe. We attended some of their art gatherings in Paris. Though Dalton never really had anything substantive to do with it." She laughed. "Dalton's many fine qualities, his impressive grasp of the issues, don't quite extend to T.S. Eliot or abstract expressionism. In his office you'll find all the latest cloak and dagger dime novels, but not a single issue of *Encounter*. I believe Ross MacDonald is his current passion. Or is it John McDonald? In any case, yes, that was how Willa got her big start, from Endicott pushing for her inclusion in the American Painting tour, which was one of the Congress's projects. So naturally, when Endicott introduced us to Willa and raved about her work, her originality and freshness, the indelibly American quality of her vision—what did he call it, her limitless frontier sensibility—well, Dalton was more than happy to make a few calls on her behalf."

The Congress for Cultural Freedom? He'd heard that name before, only where? Some kind of propaganda outfit, a front run by some obscure office in the State Department. "So, Dalton gave Willa a leg up. Put her in circulation, more or less." Tara liked that, smiling, as if they were both on the same track. She had sent Sarah away so they could be alone. "It's pretty out-there stuff, Willa's art. Not so easy to like at first."

"Well, it is rather telling. That it requires a connoisseur to tell you what to look for in that severely abstract type of work, to explain why you should like it. Endicott's very persuasive. He knows just about everything about painting. One minute he's talking about Cezanne and the next he's describing the caves at Lascaux. It's hard not to give in to that kind of authority."

She was testing him perhaps, his loyalty. He wouldn't mind kissing her, a test of both their loyalties. She wouldn't mind it, either, he was pretty sure.

"Of course, I'm talking in general. Not just about Willa. Take Jackson Pollock, for instance. There's physical energy, there's a sensuous appeal in all that chaos, there's bravado. But. Are we really required to take it so seriously?" She sipped at her drink, shifting her legs. "Well, I suppose if someone is willing to pay tens of thousands of dollars for it, then we don't really have a choice but to take it seriously. Or if they put it in the Museum of Modern Art."

"And if they don't put it in the Museum?"

She turned away for a moment, realizing perhaps the insensitivity of her remarks. "But, of course, even without that, Willa will do fine. She's got a strong reputation. Some Arab oil sheik has been collecting her. And she's always painting, always creating. That's the important thing. She's following her passion. How many of us can say that about ourselves?"

"You can, Tara. Congratulations on the wildlife preserve." He raised his glass for a toast. Their eyes met, held. Her hand trembled a bit as she clinked. She looked away. She was nervous, now. Because he was letting her know. All she had to do was touch him, graze his hand, make the decisive gesture. He had the advantage.

"Thank you, Philip. You know, it might be old-fashioned, but I still believe that all our ideas of beauty ultimately derive from nature. Even the most au courant abstract art would wither without some connection to biological forms, to waves and mountaintops and the stars blazing at night. We have to be on guard not to squander that sense of natural wonder. They ought to pass a law in Congress, stipulating that with every atomic weapon we build we establish another national park." She laughed. "How do you like that?"

"I couldn't agree more. Only, don't say it too loudly, or someone's bound to accuse you of being soft on communism."

She laughed again. "Thank god, Philip, that you're not another one of these warrior political types. Believe me, between Dalton and Dan Atlee I'd go soft or hard on anything not to hear another word on the subject. Thank goodness for President Kennedy. After eight years of Ike's golf and mumbling and saber rattling, how gratifying to have someone in the White House with an appreciation for art and culture." She leaned back, lighting another cigarette. "Doesn't hurt that he's so damn good-looking, either."

Tara asked him about the house he had built, his land, the species of trees on his property. Having worked for years on the preserve and the expansion of the Everglades Park, a personal friend of Marjorie Douglas, Tara was conversant with all the native flora. He told her about the stands of live oak, the mango and avocado groves, the lone gumbo-limbo tree that Sam Waters had shown him when they were working on the fence. She got up and pulled a few books from the shelves, Florida nature guides, and sat next to him, flipping through photos of Spanish bayonet and Indian almond and locust Berry. She wore a subtle perfume. He could sense her excitement, her distraction, feel the brush of her hand as she turned the pages.

"You must come on the tour of the preserve," she said, setting the books aside. "We're just now building the road, creating a series of small bridges and sluices so as not to disturb the tidal ebb and flow. Have you seen much of the Everglades, Philip? There's a beautiful book, *River of Grass*, that captures it perfectly. Water flow is everything. Disturb the flow and you've started a domino effect of extinction. The last expansion of the park was back in fifty-nine. We have our eyes on a new parcel, just south of Lake Okeechobee. If the sugar people don't get it first. But, well, don't mention anything to Dalton. Not yet. He's still recovering from my last crusade."

After a few moments the conversation drifted back to Sanmora, the Colony. Tara asked if he and Willa would be spending part of the summer on the island, as they had done last year.

"Not sure. Frankly, I don't know much when it comes to Willa anymore. I—sorry, don't want to bore with you my personal woes."

She leapt at that. "Please, Philip. I'm a good listener." She moved her hand, as if to place it on his, hesitated, turning away and fidgeting with a cigarette. "Maybe I can help."

"Willa's changed. Half the time now it's as if she's drifted into some other world and there's no reaching her. Sometimes she tells me the most outrageous things as though she were reciting trifles or giving her order to a waiter. I don't know what to make of it."

"Obviously, Willa is not a conventional person. But neither are you. For that matter, neither am I." She cocked her head, her mouth in a little pout, sitting close to him. Somewhere along the way the top button of her blouse had come undone.

"What was her other boyfriend like, if you don't mind my asking. Her fiancé. Did you know him?"

"Richard? Yes. We knew him quite well, actually. He and Willa met in New York, at a party Endicott threw, as a matter of fact. Richard comes from a very established New York family, related on his mother's side to the Roosevelts. I never thought Richard was right for Willa. He's so buttoned-up and Willa's such a free spirit, such an iconoclast. It was before Willa had her first show at the Janis. A classic case of being swept off one's feet, it seems to me, what with Richard's family and the trips to Europe and his doting on her. But once they were engaged, well, Willa came to her senses. It broke up rather quickly after that. Richard—I shouldn't be telling you this, Phillip, but Richard told us that Willa had cheated on him. She'd been seeing another man the whole time, it seems. Secretly. Part of me was disgusted. And part of me thought, good for you, Willa. You've found an escape route." She leaned back, her gaze sweeping over him, looking for a reaction. "After it was all over, I remember Willa saying that she couldn't have married Richard anyway, that it would have been bigamy, because Richard was already married. To his bond broker."

Was Willa doing the same to him, in New York? The Dan Altee story had been some twisted way of warning him, trying to throw him off track. "Any idea who the other fellow was? Mr. Secret?"

"No." Her face went a little red under the suntan. "It was a strained situation. Richard and Willa should never have been together in the first place. She adores you, Philip. Anyone can see that."

He leaned over to put out his cigarette and stood. "Perhaps I should go. Any idea when Dalton will be back?"

"Philip. I didn't in any way mean to imply—"

"Of course not."

"Please. Don't go." She stood, her face pointed up at his. "How about another drink?"

"But you've hardly started the one you have."

She took the glass from the table and drank it down like cold lemonade. "There. Now you can't refuse."

He laughed. "All right. One more."

"Sarah?" She turned to look toward the other room. "She must have gone already. I'll fix them." He went with her to the bar by the dining room and she asked him about the fishing trip.

"They want to go all the way to Cuba. A couple days there and back."

"Cuba? But …" She stopped, and then, as if taking up the thread in a different way, handing him his drink, said, "But why in the world do you have to go all the way to Cuba just to catch fish? Don't they reel them in by the dozen all around here?"

"Not blue marlin. At least, not according to Dan. It's his holy grail, landing a marlin in Cuba waters."

"They're all besotted by Hemingway, these fishing fanatics. That's my diagnosis. Cheers."

She was coming undone, drinking so early in the afternoon. He could reach over and unbutton her blouse and she would swoon. But it was only the idea of it that excited him. The idea that Dalton's wife wanted him, was practically throwing herself at him. Touch her, kiss her, and suddenly he would lose the advantage.

"Cheers."

She was practically leaning on him. He moved away slightly and they went back into the living room. The furniture was Polynesian-style, hard shiny black bamboo covered in colorful batik fabrics. She lit a cigarette, trying to fight it off, he suspected. Trying to keep her self-respect. "Oh Philip. I just remembered. We still have your jazz records, the ones we borrowed for the party." She went to the cabinet on the far wall. Underneath the record player was a shelf of record albums. Rather nimbly, she squatted down to look. "Are any of these yours?"

He squatted beside her. She laid her hand on his shoulder, as if to balance herself, their faces almost touching. Her breathing was a bit labored, almost a shallow pant. "Nope. Not these." He straightened and gave her his hand to help her up. She held it for a few seconds longer than necessary and he gently pulled it away.

"Dalton probably put them in his office. Let's have a look." They carried their drinks down the hall. The door was closed and Tara opened it. "I'm sure they're in here somewhere. Let me see." She reached behind and rather nonchalantly closed the door behind them. With the club chairs and the large desk, the antique globe on the stand and the shelves crammed with books, there wasn't much room to maneuver. "There they are, behind the chair." He was about to lean over when Tara, from behind, wrapped her arms around his waist, and he felt her face, her cheek, pressed flat against his back. An embrace more desperate for touch, for contact, than explicitly carnal. He twisted about to face her and releasing him she took half a step back, leaning against the desk. She had undone another button, showing her cleavage at the top of her brassiere. Small well-formed breasts, as far as he could tell, though her skin, just above the creamy white, was crinkled and mottled from the sun, showing her age. "Hello," she said, her eyes tearing slightly. She was giddy. "So nice to finally get to you know, Philip."

"Tara. I don't think ..."

"That's right. Don't think ..."

From another room in the house a phone started ringing. She glanced at her watch. "Excuse me. I have to get that. Wait here." She opened the door. "You won't leave, will you?"

"No."

She went out. He heard her footsteps climbing the stairs. The phone stopped ringing. The atlas of the Caribbean they had been looking at the night of the party was on the desk, in a pile with a few others. There were slips of paper inserted into the atlas, marking specific pages. He opened it. The marked pages were small-scale maps of a section of the Cuban coast. Someone, Dalton or Atlee, had marked several locations in light pencil— Trinidad, Cochinos Bay, Cienfuegos—with faintly drawn arrows running toward the interior. Then he found the photographs, tucked between the pages, black-and-white aerial views of a jungle coastline. He pulled them out, turned them over—there was nothing written, no place names—and then carefully tucked them back, exactly as he had found them.

He listened. Tara was still on the phone. He opened the desk drawers and found a stack of folders. Newspaper and magazine clippings. Like the ones Narby himself clipped and saved. Only Dalton's had more range: *Los Angeles Mirror, St. Louis Dispatch, Hispanic American Report, Nation, Miami Herald.* Most of the clippings were from the last few months. All about Cuba: the agrarian reforms, the nationalization of the banks and utilities, the flow of exiles into the U.S. and Spain from Guantanamo, the mass trials for political crimes, the bombings and sporadic attacks all across the island, Castro's campaign against illiteracy, the outlawing of gambling and prostitution, the Cuban exile militias training in Guatemala.

He heard Tara coming down the stairs. He bent down and picked up the stack of record albums. Maybe he ought to take the atlas, but it was too large to conceal between the record covers.

"Ah," she said. "You found them."

"Yes. Thanks."

This time she left the door open. "That was Dalton on the phone. Calling from Washington. It seems he has to go on directly to Mexico City. He'll be gone another two weeks and—oh shoot, I forget to mention your fishing trip to him. I'm sorry."

"That's all right. I don't suppose the fish are going anywhere."

Talking to Dalton had given her a little jolt, it seems. Something had drained out of her. She looked tired. The afternoon drinks were dragging her down.

"Maybe I better go, Tara."

She stood in the doorway, hesitating. "Yes. I suppose you should."

"Thanks for the drinks. It was good to talk."

She walked him to the patio, the albums under his arm. Zulu came bolting out from somewhere, yipping and quivering, and she scooped him up in her arms. She was safe now.

"Philip. I don't know what came over me. In the office. I ..."

"Forget it. Never happened."

She smiled, but it dropped away. "Please give my best to Willa. In case I don't see her before we pack up. She'll be all right. She's a winner."

"I'll do that."

With the ridiculous bundle of fur in her arms, he could risk it. He leaned over and without otherwise touching or embracing kissed her on the mouth, letting his mouth open just a little, letting his lips linger a few seconds. She was rather dry. As he pulled back he saw that she was grateful, for both the kiss and the restraint. He could come back now, anytime he wished. To get a better look at Dalton's papers.

The next day he posted the letter to Campos. It had been a while since he last heard from the revolutionary psychologist. He hoped the Havana address was still good. "Look out for that storm. Blowing off the coast of southern Florida in the next few weeks. Turbulence centered near Cienfuegos or Trinidad. Will issue further weather reports as conditions develop."

12

HE WAITED ACROSS THE STREET in the Guilieta, reading the newspaper, watching the parking lot. With the pills running low he was losing his balance, the levitation act: it was up and down now, in jagged spikes, with intervening spans of dull insufferable aching neutrality. The gun was in the rucksack. Four bullets remained. After the close call with Dan Atlee on the Miranda he had fired a test shot in the jungle, into the gut of a scrub pine at close range, the black-rimmed hole oozing pale yellow sap. One for Goldfarb, then Atlee, then Vetch, and the last for Sid Black. He could, of course, purchase more of the same gauge bullets at any gun shop along the Dixie Highway or the Tamiami Trail. Only then, there would be no end to it. He preferred restraint, honoring Robinson Crusoe's eminently rational Providence: the gun and the bullets had come to Narby for a reason, and it was his moral duty to use them to his advantage. Once the bullets were discharged, regardless of whose flesh they extinguished, Narby's work was finished, and he would be rescued.

Around six o'clock Goldfarb exited the office building. A tall semi-corpulent man with a shining bald head and the golden sun-kissed complexion of the Miami Beach Oriental Jew. Despite the heat he wore a shiny blue suit, though without the constriction of a tie, his shirt open at the neck. The door from the lobby led to the shaded parking area under the portico. Goldfarb got into his car, a white sedan of foreign make, and after lighting a cigar he backed out of the lot. Narby started his engine and followed: left on Ninth Street, north on Washington, right on Dade Boulevard and continuing on to Pine Tree Drive. A neighborhood of expensive sprawling homes—ranch, Spanish colonial, Moroccan, boxy modernist—with wide-open front lawns, the courtyard patios and swimming pools and tennis courts hidden behind exotically planted hedges and gardens. After a few turns

Goldfarb pulled into a driveway on Forty-third Street, near the corner of Sheridan Avenue. Not bothering to garage the car, he got out, trailing cigar smoke, unlocked the front door, and went in. A plain looking single-story house, one of the more modest on the block. Narby parked on the street, waited a few minutes, and then with the gun tucked into his waistband walked up the driveway and rang the bell. He could hear the chime echoing through the house. He was about to ring again when Goldfarb opened the door. He was in his shirtsleeves now, a drink in his hand.

He took the cigar out of his mouth. "Can I help you?"

"Don't you recognize me? You took my money, you wrote out the contract-for-deed even though you already knew that the property was doomed. You timed it just right, so that I would lose everything. The entire block, that whole section of Overtown." He stopped to take a breath, reciting the words he had practiced a dozen times. "You knew what was happening. That's why you sold the Harlem Square, found some sucker to take everything off your hands. You and the Dade County Chamber of Commerce and the City of Miami Planning department. All along they pretended the highway was going to be built along the old railway corridor. That it wouldn't barrel right through the Negro community. But that was all lies, a diversion, so you and the businessmen you eat lunch with, the great liberal Jews and the rapacious Crackers and the Country Club bigots, all of you together in shameless rapacious collusion. You knew. "

Goldfarb blinked, stepping back as if to check whether there was anyone else with Narby. His face had drained of color, but he hadn't flinched, the drink in one hand, the cigar in the other "It's progress," he said. "Urban renewal. It's good for everybody. The Negro people most of all. They're going to put up decent housing. Better than Liberty City. Most of it is slum, anyway. You're Philip Narby. Now I recognize you. If you'd been paying attention you'd have understood this two, three years ago. You had plenty of time to get out. It's not my concern. I'm not a charity, my friend. I'm not a public information agency. How dare you come to my home and insult me like this. In front of my wife and children. Not get the hell off my property."

The door slammed and he heard Goldfarb slide the bolt. The gun was eating into his waist and gut, draining his strength like a parasite. He wedged it out, his hand trembling, his finger curled against the trigger, aware now from the test shot of the effort it took to squeeze it, his arm bent with his elbow pinned against his side to maintain stability, the barrel pointed straight at the door at the height of Goldfarb's belly. His head was hot and the sweat rolled down his face. He heard something from above and looked up. It was only the breeze shaking the fronds of the tall Royal Palms growing in front of Goldfarb's house. For a moment it mesmerized him, the sudden cool against his damp face and the pom-pom like quivering of the plume of huge green fronds high above his head. He lowered his head and rang the bell again and he listened to the musical chime and then the shallow echo.

Wife and children. The words caught up to him now. The door remained closed, locked. He looked up again at the quivering fronds, maybe thirty feet above his head, shifting and unfurling, unreal against the hazy pale blue ether.

Wife and children. That was war, killing women and children and whoever else blundered into your line of fire. He wasn't a goddamn soldier. Would he have to spend the rest of his existence proving that he was not a soldier, that he hadn't deserted? Who would he have to kill, to prove he wasn't a soldier?

He lowered the gun and walked away, letting it hang at its side, and sat in the car, drinking from the flask and looking up through the windshield at the dancing frolicking fronds. Sooner or later, someone had to pay, had to bear the brunt of all the treason, all their lies.

13

TWO WEEKS AFTER HIS COZY CHAT with Tara Pembaker the news broke. He was staying in a suite at the Calvado—Willa would return at the end of the week and he had arranged to pick her up in the Guilieta at Miami International. The Pembakers and the Atlees and the rest of them had packed up for the season, the Colony deserted, a row of secluded villas and mansions—unoccupied but well-maintained, the gardens trimmed, the pools and tennis courts covered against the storms, the windows and the shutters locked, the air-conditioners humming to protect the furnishings—hidden behind the dunes on a small otherwise undeveloped barrier island on the Gulf of Mexico a hundred-and-ten miles from Havana. He had seen neither Dalton nor Dan Atlee since the night of the party, when Willa's outburst, her sobbing flight, had interrupted their discussion of the trip to Cuba, the hunt for the blue marlin.

Anyone who had been reading the newspapers carefully, the articles about the Cuban exiles in Guatemala, would have known something was in the works, but not so soon; not in that unpropitious stretch of swampy coastline so far from Havana; not so closely managed and so thoroughly bungled by their American handlers. But Narby had known, had pinpointed the where and when. The note he had written Campos after seeing the marked pages in the atlas on Pembaker's desk had perhaps turned the tide in favor of Castro. Still, he could hardly believe it was happening. Couldn't believe that he had come so close. Only whose side was he supposed to be on? What role had he played? It drove him half mad, burning with envy: he had been at the center of things and yet they ignored him, as if he didn't exist. It was Willa's fault. Her inane painting, her hysterical outburst at the party that had cut him out at the decisive moment.

Hadn't he warned them, goddamn it! On the Miranda that day, when he had wanted to kill Atlee, and in Pembaker's office—had told them point blank that Castro could not be defeated like this, that it would only push him deeper into the embrace of the Soviets. He had written words to the same effect to Knowles, years ago. And they ignored him. Because he was on the outside, because he wasn't one of them.

What a farce, a comedy with corpses. How could they have been so inept? The fishing trip—a reconnaissance, with the innocent stop along the coast to refuel—must have been canceled at the last minute. That's why Pembaker had been called away. Otherwise, the invaders would have known to steer clear of the offshore reefs around the Bahía de Cochinos, avoid the morass of coastal swamps that had fouled the landing.

What cravenness, what mental disorganization and magical thinking that America could do no wrong, might explain the higher farce of Kennedy lecturing the world that the United States would never intervene in Cuban affairs? And Adlai Stevenson at the U.N. the day after the first wave of bombings, disavowing all American involvement. Nobody, from Moscow to Miami Beach, was suckered by Kennedy's charming well-bred spew. He was a liar, a disgrace. A coward.

Minute by minute, day after day, anyone who cared to sniff around would smell the exalted bullshit. Two bullet-riddled B26's, hastily painted in the colors of the Cuban Air Force, landing in Miami and Key West. Their Cuban pilots claiming to be defectors who had lead the raid from inside Castro's Cuba. It wasn't an invasion, they sputtered, it was a spontaneous uprising of the Cuban people against the communist dictator Castro. But Cuban B26s have plexiglass noses; American B26s have opaque noses, just like these. The patterns of bullet holes suggested air-to-air combat typical of an attack from offshore. The so-called defector pilot whose picture appeared on the front page of the *Miami Herald* bore a striking resemblance to a former Cuban Air Force Captain well known to have been living in

Florida, a long-standing ally of Batista. Even the propaganda, the lies, were shamelessly bungled.

In Miami the exiles were seething. At the eleventh hour Kennedy had lost his nerve, withheld the air support he had promised and left their comrades to be slaughtered like dogs, floundering in the swamps of Playa Giron. Kennedy, they had been told, was a real man; Kennedy, they all said, had cajones. It was all lies. Mentiras! Mierda! With every new revelation that the botched invasion was an American-directed disaster, with every echo of bombast from the exiles fuming in the cafes along Calle Ocho, with every hypocritical scolding from the East Coast magazine intellectuals, in every phony denial issued by the administration, every call for Castro's blood from the floor of the House, in the cackling of Khrushchev and the relentless drone of Castro himself as his prophecy of historical absolution was made true—La Historia Me Absolverá—Narby discerned the nightmare pattern of his life. What did it matter if it were MacArthur and Willoughby or Kennedy and Dulles and Stevenson? There were only two sides, now and forevermore: them, the jackals with generals' stars and the Harvard-suckled backstabbers and assassins, and us, the men who didn't matter, fodder left to rot in the swamps and the jungles and the shit-water ditches.

He picked her up at the airport around noon. She wasn't hungry, didn't care to stop for a drink. She wanted to go home, to the island and the dunes and her studio. Speeding across the Everglades at ninety, the Highway Patrol not so vigilant during the months of miasmic off-season heat, running his hand up and down her thigh, over the metallic-green satiny trousers. She seemed more to endure his touch than relish it. "I'm tired, Philip." She leaned her head back, her eyes hidden behind the dark glasses. Shutting him out.

They had used her, too. Given her paintings and her reputation a free lift around the world, from Athens to Caracas, because they needed her audacity, an original spirit so much more striking in a woman like Willa, with her tawny hair and clear complexion, her girl-next-door American sex appeal. Only now the ride was over. That meant, perhaps, it was over with him, too. She could no longer afford to be so blasé about what other people thought or with whom she sought intimate association. Maybe if he found cocaine for her, he could stretch it out a little longer, trading the dope for sex. For love.

Without the dollies, rationing the splash, he had to make do with the pot and the booze. Torpor drugs. With nothing to cut his gathering lust, he was afraid of what might happen if she refused him, of what he might do.

They stopped for a bite before getting on the ferry, a new roadside diner about ten miles south of Myerton. All along the highway now buildings were going up: low, narrow, concrete-block, with five or six store-fronts, fronted by asphalt parking lots. Liquor stores, gun shops, car repair, drive-in burger joints, carpet and flooring, discount shoes. She perked up a bit, holding his hand as they walked from the lot into the air-conditioned space. But once they had settled in the booth, away from the glare and heat of the windows, she began to recoil. It was one of those malignant void-like places, reeking of vinyl and ammonia, that sterilized placelessness of all things leached of human warmth or personality. And yet it wasn't a cave or a hole in the ground. Someone, a sentient creature, had made it so.

Innocently, or so he thought, he asked about New York, the gallery, her plans for the summer.

"I don't want to think about that right now, Philip. My head is killing me. I just want to see the ocean. Clear out all the noise and garbage."

It was the same toneless voice in which she had recited the ballad of Dan Atlee's stiff cock, her admission of the "force" between them, the attraction of repulsion. He poured a dollop of bourbon into the coffee and lit a cigarette, trying to stay quiet. But he couldn't. "I saw the piece in the *New Yorker*. The one that mentioned Endicott and that show at the Modern. What's it called? Sixteen Americans."

"Did you? Good for you."

"You ought to eat something, Willa. You've been traveling all day."

"I would, if this mess was edible." She pushed away the plate of eggs and took out a pack of cigarettes, clawing at the cellophane.

"Is that what you and Endicott were talking about?"

She snapped her lighter a few times, blew the smoke in his face from across the table. "Among other things. What's your point?"

"You told me you didn't care about that kind of thing. That those splashy museum exhibits are all about pandering to the public, attracting the big donors."

"That's what I said. So why the hell don't you believe it?"

"Because of the way you've been acting ever since you ran out of Tara's party. You were counting on that exhibit. The Congress for Cultural Freedom had stopped sponsoring the tours, haven't they? Someone in Washington managed to cut off the funding. So I heard."

"I have no idea what the hell you're talking about. I don't *count* on anyone to validate my worth. Christ, Philip. After all this time, you don't know me better than that?" Her eyes had welled a bit. He didn't care. It was a crack in her coldness through which he still might crawl, to get inside her, touch her.

They caught the six o'clock ferry. The island and the dunes and the beautiful desolation of the Colony seemed to soften her. They sat on the terrace watching the sun go down. In May the heat and the haze bleached the drama out of the subtropical skies, and the sun sank without benefit of its rosy palette, leaving only a dullish burnt-orange afterglow. After half a bottle of white wine she went inside and lay down on the bed, still in her clothes, and fell asleep. He took the opportunity to go through her things. She was back on the Equinal. Her found her appointment book. She had met with a Dr. K. at least half a dozen times. There were other doctors' names, scribbled hastily. And a number of evening assignations, if he were reading it right, with "R." He watched her sleeping, sprawled on top of the spread. She had lost weight. The pills she was on were making her haggard. He couldn't bear looking at her like that and not having her, whether she wanted it or not. The thought of pulling off her clothes, turning her over like a mannequin, made him dizzy. He closed the bedroom door behind him and descended the stairs, stopping for a moment halfway down to regard the painting she had hung last year, on the wall opposite the picture window. Now that no one wanted it, no one worshipped it, he decided he rather liked it. It was like a bit of his own sickness, a bit of hers, spewed up and splattered as if in a panic. Not even sickness, but the intimation of it. The tremor coiling inside before it spreads and doubles you over.

The house was humming from the air-conditioning, the windows shut tight. Standing on the stairs he looked down at the clustered island of furniture in the midst of the spacious room, the black leather and chrome and glass, the low-slung chairs, the dark rug with the blood-red streak. Remembering how it had been, those first months. Then he put on a jazz record and lay on the sofa, drinking and smoking dope until he nodded off. He woke up very early, before dawn, and without bothering with his bathing suit went out the garden gate, naked, and swam, back and forth paralleling the dunes, until the pale seepage of light spread across the top of the jungle. There was no one to see and he didn't give a goddamn if there was. Too bad Tara wasn't around. He needed someone and she would have gladly taken him to bed. Well, perhaps not gladly—excited, fearful, risking everything. He would have had to force it a little, he supposed, to push past the whine of betrayal. And that would have satisfied him, though she was too old and her skin somewhat leathered from the sun.

Coming in through the French doors he heard Willa in the kitchen. He dried off in the downstairs bathroom and wrapped the towel around his waist. Willa was in her short kimono, her hair wet from the shower, making coffee. He came up from behind and put his arms around her, pulling her close, and she let her head drop back and rest against his shoulder while he kissed her on the neck and the ear, pressing against her and then spinning her around and kissing her on the mouth. She let him. But as he ran his hands up her legs, under the kimono, she pushed him away, gently.

"I can't right now, Philip. I'm sorry. I've been to the doctor in New York. He took me off the Enovid, because of an infection of some sort. I'm not—I don't know what it is. I just can't. I'm sorry."

He looked at her, unbelieving. She was lying, making excuses.

Out of pity, perhaps, she said, "I'll suck you off, if you want."

He supposed that she expected him to refuse, gallantly. Instead, he said, "Yeah. All right." He let the towel drop and took her by the hand to one of the low chairs and he sat with his legs apart and she kneeled in front of him until he was finished. Then she got up and went into the bathroom and he heard water running in the sink. Spitting him out, down the drain. What would be next? Treating him as she had treated Atlee, an intruder, a pervert lurking in the garden?

He offered to go to the Village and pick up groceries at Turner's. His truck was parked in her garage and he backed the Guilieta out of the driveway and pulled the truck out and garaged the Guilieta in its place. When he got back Willa was dressed for the studio in loose fitting shorts and a splattered T-shirt. They had breakfast together. She tried to make a little talk. She would have to return to New York in June. She was looking for a new gallery. The Janis was starting to feel rather staid. "Richard Bellamy and Bob Scull are looking around. They have a new space on 57th, the Green Gallery. I've got some things from the place on Jane Street I'd like to show them."

"When do you plan to come back?"

"It depends. You can stay here, of course. As long as you like."

"Play caretaker? Is that what you mean?"

"Of course not. Look. I'm sorry everything's not as you wish it to be. I can't help what's happening and I'm not apologizing for anything. Past or present."

"Why should you? What's there to apologize for?"

She reached over and caressed his hand. "Philip. I love you. I'm sorry I'm so—on guard. You know how it goes for me. You've known it all along. You were right, about Endicott. It wasn't that I wanted to be in that show so very badly. It was more, I don't know, the shock of it. Because I had been told, promised, I was included. I had been misled. Maliciously misled."

He thought for a moment. "I'll fly up with you. I haven't been to New York in ages. Haven't been much of anywhere, since Korea. I feel like traveling again."

"That's a nice thought, Philip. But I'm going to be very busy. And I can't—well, I can't take you around with me. That's just not the way I do things. Another time, perhaps."

"Forget it."

She clenched her jaw. "You never wanted to come before. You never even mentioned it. So now, all of a sudden, you think you can tell me how to live? That I need to have a man attached to my arm, wherever I go."

"I said forget it."

She closed her eyes and took a few deep breaths, sitting very still. Then she opened them. "I would love for you to come to New York with me, Philip. Only it's frustrating that you bring it up, after all this time, on the one occasion when I'm under a certain amount of pressure. When I really need to be alone, without any other obligations or personal concerns. Do you understand?"

"Sure. We'll do it another time. Or maybe we'll go to Paris or Rome."

She tried to smile. "I'd like that, Philip. Very much." She stood. "I'll be in the studio for most of the day. Why don't we reconvene around six? I'll make dinner. And then, we can talk."

"Fine with me."

On her way out she kissed him, letting him caress her for a moment. As if, perhaps, she was suddenly afraid he might not be around when she was finished in the studio.

He hung about a while, not sure what to do, and then got in the truck and drove to the northern tip of the island, about three miles past the Village and another mile past the *Tara Pembaker Wildlife Preserve*. At the dead-end of the road stood a high chain-link fence and behind that nothing but the low coastal scrub. He knew from walking the dunes that a half-mile or so beyond the fence the long narrow barrier island broke up at its northern tip, where the jungle ran into the sea in a welter of tiny mangrove islets. That end of the island belonged to South Seas Plantation Company—probably some kind of dummy entity, a tax dodge perhaps, for the Isadora Land Trust, the group led by Pembaker that owned the Colony. They were putting up luxury bungalows and a restaurant and tennis courts and a small marina. A discrete hideaway for the elite, coming and going by yacht and seaplane. That would have been part of the thinking behind the nature preserve, he now understood— to buffer that end of the island, insuring absolute privacy and security. No wonder Tara had gotten help from Dalton's pals at the Department of the Interior.

He drove back to the Village. They had fixed up the local tavern, the Mucky Duck. A harbinger of the change coming once the causeway was finished. He went in. It was cool and dark, with windows on one side facing north, looking out over the quaint marina. The Miranda was either at sea or in dry dock.

Or perhaps sunk on a reef off the Bahía de Chochinos. He had a beer and a cup of grouper chowder—rather good, he thought—and then drove back down the spine of the Island, the road shaded by the tall Australian Pines planted along the shoulder, and parked in the dirt lot by the lighthouse and got out and started walking up the beach, toward the creek, smoking and sipping from the flask. The tide was out, so when he reached the inlet he had only to roll up his trousers and wade across. At the foot of the walkway he hesitated. It infuriated him that she was forcing him to behave like this, like a pervert. Like a Dan Atlee. Quietly, he came through the gate into the garden and went around the gardenias and the bamboo so he could see into the studio. Willa wasn't there. He walked around again and without caring anymore came through the French doors. He could hear her. She was on the phone in the bedroom upstairs, her voice muffled because even though she thought she was alone she had nevertheless closed the bedroom door.

He sprawled on the sofa and waited. The door upstairs clicked open. Halfway down the stairs she saw him and stopped, frozen, and then came down.

"I heard the truck earlier. I thought you'd gone into Myerton."

"Nope."

"Oh. Well, I got so tired all of a sudden, thought I'd take a little cat nap."

"You were on the phone. I heard you."

"Spying on me again? Christ, Philip. What the hell is it with you?"

"It's Richard, isn't it? Your old flame. Your Wall Street fiancé? Yeah?"

"Yes."

"You saw him in New York, didn't you?"

"I see a lot of people in New York. That's what New York is. A lot of people, very many people. That's what you do there. You see them."

"You saw him, didn't you? Had dinner, drinks. Got cozy."

"What if I did?"

"And you slept with him? Fucked him. Didn't you?"

The obscenity, an element of their bedroom repertoire since the beginning, seemed to pain her now. She was standing at the foot of the stairs, keeping her distance. He stood and positioned himself in front of her, as if to block her from reaching the kitchen or the French doors. She had one hand on the cable banister. "You never wanted to come to New York with me. Never showed any real interest in my work, or the gallery. I don't owe you an explanation."

"I take that as a yes. An affirmative. So why not just say it?"

"All right. I fucked him. I fucked Richard."

"Once? Twice? What about your infection?"

"Oh, for Christ's sake." She bolted forward, as if to make a run for the garden, but he caught her by the wrist. "That was in New York, Philip. Now I'm here. With you. Isn't that enough? That I choose to be with you."

"But you're going back. Very soon."

"Philip. The summer is unbearable here. You know that." A slight whine wobbled her voice. "I've tried to get through it for two years now, but not again. I've got to see about getting a new gallery. I told you all that. Are you asking me to stay? Is that what you want? To have me at your beck and call?"

Feeling her yank away he let go of her wrist. "It's either me or him. I can't bear it any other way. Understand?"

"You're jumping to conclusions. It's not what you think. I have no idea if I'll ever see him again. It just… happened."

"Then what's with the phone calls? Waiting till I'm not here, closing the door so you can talk to him in private."

"You're imagining things. I told you, I came in for a catnap and the phone rang. I couldn't very well hang up on him."

"You're lying. I can see it in your face."

"Please, Philip. Drop it. It's not worth it. You're blowing it out of proportion."

"I don't think so. Look at you. Like a lovesick schoolgirl, caught making out on the couch by Daddy, with your panties down."

"Go to hell, Philip. You don't have a clue. All right. Maybe it was a mistake to sleep with Richard. But not because you tell me I can't. Richard means nothing to me. If it hadn't been Richard it would have been someone else. You have your private world, don't you? Don't tell me you haven't strayed a bit, dear Philip, while I was away. With the women you meet at those dives you like to frequent. You and your Negro friends."

"You can't have us both, Willa. I don't give a damn if it's Richard or the fucking mailman."

"Oh for God's sake, Philip, drop the clichés. I don't *have* anybody, nobody *has* anyone else."

"You're such a goddamn phony, Willa. You think you're a mile above the rest of us, that you don't have to speak the same language everyone speaks. Or like with your painting. Like it's an insult if someone asks you what it is, or what it means."

"I won't abuse words simply because others abuse them. I won't conform to their false thinking, their *group-speak*."

"Maybe you just need to accept the fact that you're not so unique after all. That you're just like me. That maybe it eats you up that you're not on top anymore, that they locked you out of the Modern Art museum. Is that how you deal with setbacks, Willa? By fucking whoever you happen to bump into? But, well, Richard. He's not just anybody, is he? Richard's got connections. Tara filled me in. On Richard Lansdale and his sterling family—"

"Please. Shut up. I can't stand it." She closed her eyes. Pleading. "Just leave. For a few days. Just let me think. Let me breathe."

"Willa. Look at me."

But she wouldn't open her eyes.

"Do you love me? Tell me that you love me. That you're through with him. And then I'll leave."

"Yes, Philip. I love you. Now go."

He was halfway out the door when she called after him. "You'll come back? In a few days. Promise me."

She was afraid. At least there was that, for him to grasp on to. "I promise."

14

SHE WAS GONE, July and August and September. In October they would meet again, start over or finish, once and for all.

Every time he passed the pharmacy on the way to the Smoker's Den he felt the allure of the gun in his rucksack. Come in at the dead hour, two in the afternoon, pull the stocking over his face, the old man behind the counter trembling in fear as Narby ordered him to fill the sack—dexies, cartwheels, dollies, codeine, all the amphetamines and narcotics in stock—while the fat slow somnolent deputy sheriff slumped in his bubble-gum-machine cruiser, glutted on pecan pie, his eyes lowered in reveries of beating niggers, spraying them with fire hoses, burning down their churches.

With Goldfarb spared there was a discretionary bullet. For Janet's delightful spouse Sergeant Frank Swanson, perhaps, if circumstances were propitious. What pleasure to rid her forever of that meat-faced malignancy, corroding her soul, blighting her sex like a cancer. He would kill Frank and take her far away, nurture her like a sick pale flower until she showed color and opened, purged of the poison. Bring into the light all he had sensed in her that day at the library when she had looked at him with a sea of longing brimming in her eyes, drowning her in darkness and regret.

He went down the five steps and pulled at the glass door. It was locked. On the other side the little brass bells gave a choked tinkle. Odd. Once in a while, ever since Hank had become a father five years ago, he might run home during business hours to attend to some domestic contingency. But he would always hang the "back soon" sign, the cardboard-clock hands set to the hour of his return. Today, there was only the locked door. The Egyptian's mercantile zeal was not so easily diverted. Something was wrong.

Narby bent to peer inside, cupping his eyes against the glare. The beaded curtain that separated the sales counter from the backroom was swaying, as if just parted. He needed tobacco. Was hoping for something from Campos. The Bay of Pigs debacle had shifted the ground. There were new enemies, new enemies of enemies. Peering in, he rapped on the glass with his knuckles, showing his face. The beaded curtain shook. When Hank saw who it was he came from behind the counter and opened the door and then, pushing past Narby in the cluttered space, locked it behind him.

"Hello, Hank. Everything all right?"

"No." The man's voice had lost its usual playful lilt. "Thank God you have come, Mr. Norby. You must help me."

"What is it? What's happened?"

"Come away from the door, please." The shopkeeper lifted the hinged section of the counter and led Narby behind the curtain into the chilled cave-like store-room, the walls stacked with cartons and bags, smelling of damp cardboard and pipe tobacco. There was a card table for a desk, two folding chairs, a telephone, a hot plate and kettle, a tea glass in a silver holder, piles of invoices, and an ashtray over-spilling with the husks of the nuts and seeds on which the Egyptian habitually chewed.

"Mr. Norby. You are a citizen of America. As am I. But I know nothing. What they are trying to do to me, it cannot be. You must help me. They tell me I must put Will'am in the nigger school. I beg you, sir ..."

"Whoa. Wait a minute Hank, slow down."

"Please. I am sorry. Please, sit down. These are my troubles, not your own. But I am lost. Please. May I offer you a glass of tea?"

"No, thanks." But seeing the panic in the man's eyes, the pleading, he corrected himself. "All right. Sure. Thanks."

"It is fine black pekoe, imported from Ceylon." The Egyptian filled the kettle and turned on the hotplate, brought out another tea glass in its silver filigree holder, his hand trembling as he spooned the leaves from the tin. Despite the refrigerated air his white shirt was spotted with sweat. He reached in his trouser pocket for the box of Turkish Ovals and offered one to Narby and then cleared a spot on the table and poured the hot water and finally sat down, his elbows on the table, his head lowered, thumb and forefinger massaging his furrowed nut-brown brow.

"I am ashamed," he said. "It is a disgrace. I will close the shop and move from here."

"What's going on, Hank? Maybe I can help."

"I register Will'em for school. He is five years old and already he knows his letters in English and Arabic. Very smart boy. When I get the paper from the county I think, this is not the school in the district. We are in district one, you understand, but then I see the paper says Woodford Elementary. So I find the school, I go to look at it. Across Henderson Avenue. Is it an abomination, a school for dirty niggers, half the children without shoes, dressed in rags. I think to myself, this murst be a mistake. Clerical error. I telephone. I visit the office of the School Board. I take Will'em with me, holding him by the hand. I say to the woman, look, is he a nigger? Look at his nose, his fine lips. Look how he dresses, how clean he is! No! He is an American citizen, born in Chicago. What is wrong with you! Don't you understand? The Arab people had nigger slaves before the English, before the American! We are not black African, we are high civilization."

"I'm sure that went over well. Let me see the paper, Hank. So, what did they say?"

He handed Narby a single sheet, many times folded. One sentence, no explanation, with a typographical error.

"They laugh at me, Mr. Norby. They tell me, oh no, my son is not a nigger. That he is Colored. Mr. Norby. I will not send my son to a school like this. Let me tell you something, sir. I do not care if you are a nigger or an English or a bloody wog like myself. We are all the same color beneath the skin, are we not? But the nigger here is a degraded man. Shoeshine boy, janitor, yardman, cleaning other people's dirt but neglectful of his own cleanliness, his own dignity. I cannot help the nigger. Do you understand, Mr. Norby? How can I send my son to be among them? I ask you, sir? Would you do that to your own son? Would you?"

"You say they switched school districts on you? It's against the law now, Hank. If they switched schools on you because they say you're son is Colored …"

"Excuse me, Mr. Norby," he broke in, shrieking a bit. "They tell me I live in district so and so, that the districts have changed. But I have gone to the County office. I have seen the map. They lie to me. Laugh behind my back. Like the British. Sand nigger— that was the slur from my own youth. I can still hear it, burning my ears."

"Settle down, Hank. Let me think." He sipped the tea. Two men who had drifted halfway across the world, stuck in a place they didn't belong. All these years Hank had kept his mouth shut about Narby's mail. And Narby had spent plenty in the shop. Hank's best customer—a more solid foundation for loyalty, perhaps, than race or creed. "Maybe I can find a lawyer, someone who could determine which school your boy should go to."

"Yes? You think so, Mr Norby?"

Only who? There was an A.C.L.U. office in Miami. But would they really help a man who kept shouting *I'm not a nigger*? "It's worth a try."

"Yes," the tobacconist said, cheering up. "A lawyer! This is a country of laws, is it not? We will make a test, yes?"

"A test?"

"Of the American system. I passed the examination to become an American citizen. Now the examination is the other way round. The citizen tests America."

"America's one thing, Hank. Lacoosa County is something else."

"I cannot tell you what it means to me, sir. To have a friend like you, Mr. Norby. So kind, so intelligent. How can I repay you?"

"Just keep the shop open. You're like an outpost of civilization around here. All right?"

"Yes, of course. Today I was too angry. I locked the door out of shame. What if one of them came in here, to taunt me? Now I have equanimity. I shall resume regular shop hours."

Narby laughed. "Equanimity. Good for you."

Narby stocked up on Danish shag. There was no mail. It might be impossible for Campos to get a letter out. Castro had the whole island under martial law, rounding up counter-revolutionaries by the busload. The tobacconist saw his advocate to the door. "Mr. Norby," he said, lowering his voice, his hand on the bolt. "I suspect it is a Jew behind all this trouble. A Zionist who wishes to keep my son out of the regular school."

"A Jew on the Lacoosa County School Board? Come on, Hank. Not a chance."

The Egyptian shrugged. "Why not? The Jews are everywhere."

"Hank. The Jews are not your problem. I assure you."

He shook his head sadly, pushing the glass door open. "Suez, Mr. Norby. The Sinai. Every day in the newspaper I expect to read that the Jews have again attacked my country, my people."

"Your country? I thought you were an American citizen, Hank."

"So I am. But some things cannot be altered by a document, a piece of paper."

Narby found out what he could. Anticipating future court decisions, apparently, the county school board had declared the county's schools as segregated "de facto," but not "de jure." So far, no one had brought a challenge. The district maps, drawn up before the boom of the 1920s when Myerton's population had doubled, were obsolete. "Talk to your neighbors," Narby advised Hank a few days later. "Ask them which school their children attend. Let's start with that."

The tobacconist's house was on a street near the train tracks, in a neighborhood that since the First World War had housed a handful of Greek and Italian immigrants. The only neighbors Hank felt comfortable approaching were Catholics, but they told him that they sent their children to St. Pius, the only private school in the county. He advised Hank to write letters to the school board, the County Commissioners and the Myerton News Press. Don't mention Negroes or Arabic civilization, Narby instructed, just a respectful request to send his son to Jackson Elementary, "where he would be among his peers, his equals. It is the fair and legal course of action." Hank even brought little William into the shop one day, against his wife's wishes, so that he might show Narby how bright the boy was, how deserving. Shy, unused to strangers, the sullen confused kid cowered behind the glass cases, his father impatiently prodding him to come out and recite his alphabet. Narby's heart sank as the boy stood before him—thick set, nut-brown, with jet black hair and big ears, just like his old man—warbling his ABC's in a tiny terrified voice.

Hank's case was hopeless. He wasn't a Negro and he wasn't White and wasn't a Christian and he despised the Jews. No one would help him, not the N.A.A.C.P., not the S.C.L.C., not the A.C.L.U. Still, by the end of summer things seemed back to normal at the shop. The Egyptian must somehow have reconciled himself to the inevitable. One afternoon in August Narby swung open the glass doors, setting off the little brass bells. Hank came out from behind the curtain, the sour pall of his face melting when he saw it was Narby, his friend and confidante.

"Mr. Norby! So good to see you. Where have you been, my friend? I have for you two special order magazines, and a package of your musical record albums."

The tobacconist set the pile on the counter. Narby rifled through, hoping to find a letter from Campos or Willa." Good to see you, Hank. Everything all right? Business good?"

"Very good, sir. A rising tide, my friend, a rising tide."

They busied themselves for a moment in commerce. After Hank had tendered his change, Narby summoned the nerve. "How's the family, Hank? Your wife and William and the new baby?"

"Ah, they are on expedition. I have sent them to Chicago on the train. So the boy can know his uncles and cousins."

"That's great." That settles it, Narby thought. He'll have the boy go to school up north. "You must miss them, yeah?"

"Frankly, I am enjoying the peace and quiet. As a confirmed bachelor you have no idea of the disruption of young children. On Sunday, however, they return." Hank's smile faded a bit. He leaned over the counter. "You remember the subject we have been discussing?"

"Yes, of course."

"I have found the solution."

"Good, Hank, I knew you would."

"I am planning to send the boy to Jackson Elementary, the school that by right and law he should attend. When they see how smart he is, how well-prepared, how well-mannered and neatly dressed and shoes shined, there will be no problem." He paused, nervously popping a sunflower seed into his mouth, chewing. "Do you agree this is the correct course of action? My letters have fallen on deaf ears, I'm afraid. I can think of nothing else."

"Hank. Have you considered letting William stay with your brother in Chicago? They've got better schools up there. You know that, don't you?"

"Yes. I have considered this and I reject it. He belongs with his mother and father and baby sister. They will accept him. I have faith. You will see."

"Good luck, Hank. I hope it works out."

"Thank you, Mr. Norby. If only more people here were like you, we would have no trouble like this. A little kindness, a little understanding, and the world would cease to hate."

School started that Monday. Narby, unaware that disaster was so close at hand, dropped by the shop on Friday, only to find it closed, dark inside. There were web-like cracks in the plate glass window—as if someone had thrown a rock or brick—dressed with masking tape. He went by the library to look at the week's Myerton News Press. *A scuffle broke out yesterday at Jackson Elementary… local merchant Hassim "Hank" Duballa arrested for disorderly conduct, inciting a riot… his six-year old son William temporarily barred from the public school system.* He drove by Hank's house: there was a moving truck, furniture out on the lawn, a man loading boxes. He pulled over and went through the open door. The house was empty. The owners had already left town, one of the movers told him.

There was nothing he could have done. He'd been stupid not to have arranged a back-up address. It made him sick to think about it. The one decent human being he could count on, chased out of town like a rabid dog.

15

HE RENTED A POST-OFFICE BOX in Myerton and left a message for Willa at the Janis Gallery. Then, he waited. With his bourbon and his dwindling supply of marijuana, his jazz records and notebooks and newspapers and magazines that he had to buy now in Miami or Coral Gables, working with Sam Waters and a couple of hired hands every morning, girding his property with barbed wire while Sid Black's bulldozers and draglines closed in from every direction. The machines were herding the snakes and possums and woodrats into Narby's five hundred, the last of the Sawfish Point jungle, a slithering plague, Sam shooting at the snakes all day long, a shotgun by his side as they worked in the killing heat. Waiting with his guns, the five-chambered snub nose and his new Winchester rifle and the strongbox buried under the floorboards. Checking the post office every other day. Hanging around, getting sick again, and for what?

The first week of October he received her note. *Dear Philip, I'm back on Sanmora. After New York I needed a week of solitary peace, just me and the dunes. I hope you understand why I didn't write sooner. Well, now you know where to find me. Willa.*

He waited a few days. He wasn't a pet, leaping into her lap at the sound of her fingers snapping, at the smell of her treat. *Now you know where to find me.* It sounded more like a trap than an invitation. A dare. It was about six in the evening when he parked the truck at the lighthouse. The creek was high and he had to take off his clothes and swim across, keeping the rucksack above his head. He took his time drying off, getting dressed. By the time he came through the garden gate it was dark. The pool lights threw a blue aqueous shimmer against the side of the house. He tried the French doors. They were locked. She was there, though. He caught a glimpse of her going up the stairs. He went around to the side door that opened from the kitchen and found it open. She would have just come in from the studio, perhaps. He slipped inside and put the rucksack down. A bottle of white wine sat uncorked on the counter. The air was cool, the house humming quietly. He stepped into the living room. From upstairs he heard the shower. He went up. Her handbag was on the dresser, next to an empty wine glass. He took a quick look and then went through the drawers, finding the Enovid dispenser. She was taking them again, if in fact she had ever stopped. And a bottle of something called Librium. Equilibrium pills. *Caution: do not take with alcohol.* Good luck with that, he thought, almost laughing.

The shower went off and he heard her get out, drying herself, just on the other side of the wall. They hadn't seen each other, hadn't touched, for months. He didn't care now if she had been with half a dozen men. Afterwards, then he would care. If it were half a dozen men, then he would forgive her, perhaps even enjoy it, because it was her nature. But if it was only one, Lansdale. Then he wasn't sure what he would do.

Standing there, he might give her a damn good fright as she stepped out of the bathroom. Scare her half to death. But that was Atlee's way, the pervert's way. Instead he went quietly down the stairs again and let himself out the kitchen door and around to the pool, waiting until she'd had a chance to put something on, and then he rapped on the glass. She would know it was him, of course. The rest of the Colony wouldn't return until mid-November. He rapped again. She came down in the short kimono, her tawny hair wet from the shower, her breasts shifting under the silken fabric. "Oh, Philip. I'm so glad you're here." He put his arms around her and kissed her. As if in a dance he guided her floatingly toward the sofa, feeling her yield, her mouth open and her head back, sliding his hands under the kimono, her flesh taut and prickled with goose bumps. Not giving her a chance to say no or yes or wait or stop or don't stop. Knowing the places that gave her the most pleasure, that pushed her beyond words and reason. And she let him. But that was all. Allowed it to happen, but with a certain detachment, as if to say, do you what you want, but don't expect me to help you, to induce you. Well, he didn't need any inducing.

After he was through she slipped away for a minute, to the bathroom, and he dressed, feeling like a fool, a pervert, after all.

She came out wrapped in the kimono, smoking a cigarette, and went to the kitchen for another glass of wine. He followed her and fixed a bourbon. Stroking her hair, smiling at her. Apparently, the equilibrium pills had a dampening effect on her usual running commentary, the steady drip of sarcasm. "That was nice," she said, rather blandly, after a moment. "It was good to be here by myself. Now it's good to have company."

"It's that what I am? Company?"

She just looked at him. "We need to talk. Things are changing."

"Things are always changing."

She smiled again, looking away. "That's odd, Philip. There's your rucksack."

He'd made a mistake, apparently. "Yeah?"

"But. I just let you in." She put down her glass. "You came in before. While I was in the studio. Or in the shower. Didn't you?" Her voice flat, calm but rising. "To spy on me. Eavesdrop. Again. What is it with you?"

He took his drink into the living room, leaving her at the kitchen counter. After a moment she followed. The wine was knocking her out. "Philip. Would you mind if I went upstairs? All of a sudden I'm… I'm going to crawl into bed and read until I fall asleep. We can talk in the morning. I'll feel better in the morning." She paused. "I *am* glad to see you, Philip. You believe me, don't you?"

"Why not? Go ahead. I'll stay down here."

"Thank you, Philip. Good night."

He slept in the downstairs bedroom. She was already up and fixing breakfast when he woke, dressed for the studio. After eating they went for a walk along the dunes. Hand in hand. The morning was blissfully cool, the breeze up and the sky streaked with dark moving clouds, the swells rougher than usual and the water turbid. She told him that the Green Gallery had not yet decided when to mount her next show. Her life was in flux. She might go to Europe for a year. She loved living on the island, but she couldn't control the course of her life anymore than she could control the course of her heart. "It's the same for you, Philip. I know it is. One day, something will happen, and you'll be gone. Nothing roots you here. You're looking for something else, something you've been waiting for, hoping for. Isn't that right?"

"Maybe it's you. What I've been waiting for."

She didn't answer. She was playing with him, setting him up. Instead of answering, she said, "I've never seen it like this. Look at how fast the clouds are moving across the sky. The air feels strange, and the water, the way it's churning."

"There's a hurricane. They've been issuing reports on the radio. It hit the Virgin Islands pretty hard. Last I heard it was north of Haiti, coming up towards Cuba. Hurricane Cora. They're calling it *the storm of the century*. Makes good newspaper copy. It'll blow over, like all the others."

"I've always wanted to see what that's like. To be in a storm like that."

"Yeah? There's a chance it might come this way. You never know. I've been here for every storm season since 1953. So far, it's just been a lot of rain and a few big gusts. Nothing much."

"Look at it. There's something very angry out there. It's beautiful. The air feels so alive, as if it's carrying some message from afar." She took his arm. They headed back, walking in silence. When they reached the walkway she said, "There's something I need help with. In the studio. Would you mind giving me a hand?"

She'd never wanted anyone to help her with anything in the studio. "Yeah. Sure."

She unlocked the sacred space. He saw now what she'd been doing all week—packing up. The big swinging racks were empty and there were three more tall wooden crates standing next to the one that had been delivered last spring. About ten large canvases—finished or unfinished, rejects or masterworks—were stacked against the far wall. She pointed at them. "I want to take these out to the beach."

"The beach?"

"Yes. I'm going to have a bonfire."

"What's going on Willa?"

"Inventory," she said. "It's time to make a reckoning. Then, I can start over."

"You're kidding? They must be worth a hell of lot. I mean, they're Willa Brantons."

She laughed. "Well, it's a bit like gold, isn't it? The more that circulates, the less valuable per ounce. Let's just pretend we're driving up prices."

"Still, you don't have to destroy them. Why not just put them away somewhere?"

She looked at him, a bit surprised, he thought.

"Philip. I know you have no feeling for my work, one way or the other. I don't mind. In a way, I think that's what's allowed us to spend time together. To enjoy each other. I remember what you said, the first time I brought you in here, showed you what I was working on. You said, 'I believe it.' That was rather beautiful, I thought. Because at least you didn't lie, you didn't pretend. You found a way for us to proceed, to go forward, without all the misplaced adoration, the ego stroking. Well, now, maybe you still believe it. But I don't. It's not about putting them away somewhere. It's about their ceasing to exist. Un-painting them."

He carried them out to the dunes just beyond the walkway, two at a time, and tossed them unceremoniously in a heap. When he got to the last one, he stood for a moment, looking at it. It was no different from the others, he supposed. Bland and washed out and formless. There had to be some reason she was destroying them. As if she didn't want any evidence left behind. "Willa. Can I have this one? For my house. You've seen my house, the way I live. It's as good as burning it, if you're worried about anyone else laying eyes on it."

"I'd rather not, Philip."

"Afraid I'll try to sell it? Is that it?"

"It's not that."

"Then why not?" He titled it forward and looked on the back. "It's not even signed. What's the harm? It would mean a lot to me."

She turned away. "I've got some kerosene in the garage. I'll be right back."

He lifted the canvas and placed it out of sight, behind one of the crates. Then he met her on the beach. Either she hadn't noticed or didn't care to resist him any further. They watched the fire, the smoke oily and acrid. It began to drizzle, the blaze flaring and then fighting to keep its heat. When it started to rain in earnest they went inside. An hour later they come out again. The downpour had left a sodden stinking mess of charred wooden frames, globs of congealed paint and molten canvas. Too wet to re-ignite, and there was more rain on the way. She couldn't bear to leave it there, fouling the beach so close to her house. So he helped her cart the remains into the thick jungle growth that in accordance with the Colony master plan had been left wild to provide privacy and natural beauty between the villas and mansions.

That afternoon he took the Guilieta to Turner's store. The store was crowded with Villagers swapping information and rumors. The radio was on, with news about Cora. The winds were estimated at an unprecedented 170 miles per hour, leaving hundreds dead, thousands more homeless, across Puerto Rico and Cuba. The Keys were being evacuating. The storm path was unpredictable—after the Keys it might veer out into the Gulf and up toward the Panhandle or Texas, or move westward into the Yucatan, or swing out into Florida Bay and then, like a big-game fish taking the hook and running with it, head inland again toward Cape Romano. Or it might ride the Gulf Coast, ripping straight up Lacoosa County like a circular saw chewing through soft pine.

Regardless, no one in Sanmora Village was leaving. They'd seen it before. Some of them had been around in '26—nameless storms back then, you hardly knew they were coming until it was too late to do anything but tough it out—when it came right across the Glades, wrecking everything from Miami Beach to Pensacola, or Labor Day '35, the giant storm that wiped out the Bonus March Veterans on Metecumbe Key, or October '41 that felt more like a bloated summer thunderstorm than a true hurricane, and '47 wasn't so bad either. The Villagers knew what to do: filling bathtubs and barrels, hauling up the fishing boats, boarding up windows, trusting in providence.

The next morning there was a knock on Willa's door, a Lacoosa County deputy sheriff in a cowboy hat. They were advising everyone to leave the island while there was still a chance. The ferry would be running continually until the water got too rough. "There's a gigantic storm surge, that's what we're hearing from the reports. The Keys are getting it right now, m'am. The water just might come right up over them dunes."

The morning sky was remarkably clear and blue, a strong salt-sweet breeze rustling the jungle.

"Do you really think it's that bad?"

"Could be. I wouldn't recommend you remaining here, m'am, 'specially if y'all alone."

"No. No, I'm not alone."

"Good chance you'll lose your 'lectricity and phone and water and such. You don't want to get stranded out here, now do you? You best catch that ferry, soon as you can."

"Thank you, officer." She closed the door. Narby was standing behind her. The deputy hadn't seen him. "What do you think, Philip?"

Since she'd returned there had been only stalemate. She had said nothing yet about Lansdale, or her true motive for clearing out the studio. Twice, she had let him make love to her, but her passivity had spoiled it—as if she were giving herself out of pity, knowing that she would soon be free of him. Or maybe the pills, the equilibrium dope, sapped her sex drive. But evidently the storm, the idea of it, stimulated her. Perhaps it would change something. Besides, how bad could it be? Chances are it wouldn't be much more than a glancing hit. The Gulf would never rise high enough to breach the dunes. The sleek modern concrete and steel house was safe.

"Let's ride it out. Might be interesting. Unless you're scared."

She gave a moment's thought, lighting a cigarette. "All right, Philip. I'm game if you are."

"Just in case, let's do some provisioning."

They filled empty wine and beer bottles with water, and the tub downstairs, and found candles and matches and the flashlight, stowed the patio furniture and flower pots and trash cans in the garage. After their chores they fixed sandwiches and cocktails and sat up on the terrace in the wet heavy wind, the clouds now dominating the sky after the bright clear morning, shifting and layering in constant turmoil, the air plangent with the rustling of the jungle and the rising pound of the waves, the entire island vibrating in sibilant anticipation.

Around dusk, she said, "Philip, should we turn on the radio?"

"It's too late to leave. The ferry can't run in wind like this. What difference does it make?"

"You're right. It's better like this. Not knowing."

"Come on," he said, standing, "let's go down to the water, while there's still a little light."

She took his hand and he led her downstairs and through the gate. The blowing sand stung their faces. From the terrace it didn't look so bad, but as soon as they crossed between the dunes they stopped. The water was higher than Narby had ever seen it, the waves thundering and boiling forward then heaving back, leaving the sand dark with the coarse detritus dredged from the deep.

"It's horribly beautiful, isn't it?" She had to shout. "Philip! Don't get any closer. It won't get much higher, will it, Philip? Philip! Are you out of your mind!"

Wanting to test the force against his body, he waded up to his waist and a wave had knocked him over and he came running back, soaked. He was laughing. He grabbed her and kissed her and she clung to him, backing away, a look of hatred and envy and panic on her face. "You're freezing, goddamn it," she shouted. "Come inside. Please! Stop it!"

Now they waited. The electricity went out. They huddled downstairs in candlelight, every window in the house rattling and the gusts pounding as if a giant were smashing his fists on the roof, determined to chase them out and crush them. Hour after hour, the wind calming for a moment, teasing, only to gust again in redoubled force, pounding in relentless fury.

The rain began to seep in through the window frames and under the doors. Willa spread out towels to soak it up. Despite her efforts a thin layer of water was spreading across the floor, pooling in the corners of the living room. He took her upstairs, holding the flashlight. They lay on the bed, in the dark, Willa holding on to him, breathing deeply, saying nothing. Behind the curtain and the blinds the glass doors that opened to the terrace were rattling madly, as if on the verge of shattering.

Willa began to rant. "God, Philip, how long will it last? I can't take it anymore. We're safe up here, aren't we, Philip? The water can't rise this high, can it, Philip? Oh God, it's going to wash away the whole house, it's going to come pouring in and drown us. I can't stand it anymore. It has to stop. God, please make it stop."

"Calm down. It's not the ocean. It's the creek. The creek's flooding, that's what's happening. And the pool most likely. Calm down. It's going to pass."

She stared at him. "I'm suffocating. I can't breath. You made me stay here. Goddamn you, Philip. I'm drowning ..."

Then came a moment of genuine terror, as if summoned forth to validate her panic. A prosaic piece of lumber, swept up in the maelstrom—a length of two-by-four, probably from the resort bungalows under construction down the dunes—shot through the glass doors like a missile, exploding three feet from where they lay, showering them with shards, the rain slashing in as they both dived instinctively to the floor, Willa screaming, Narby covering his head and at the same time throwing himself over her, protecting her, the bedroom, the sterile inviolability of the house, instantly transformed into a ruin, filthy and soaked as the wind blasted in the sand and debris.

For the next hour they cowered in the windowless upstairs bathroom, Willa silent in his arms.

"Listen," he said, "it's stopping."

He opened the door. Morning light was streaming in from the terrace. The two-by-four had come to rest atop the filthy rain-soaked bedspread, surrounded in a halo of shards. He stepped over the broken glass onto the terrace. The surge had bitten well into the dunes, but they had not been breached. The garden was torn to pieces, the surface of the pool clotted with debris and the bottom lined with mud. Sections of the jungle were flattened, as if trampled by a giant.

"Willa. Come out here. Look. We're in the eye." All around the island arose a towering circular wall of dark cloud, the light from above pouring through a ragged hole of brilliant blue.

"Should we try to leave?"

"No. It won't last very long, and then the wind will come from the opposite direction."

"We can't stay up here, Philip. What should we do?"

They went downstairs. The flooding had receded, leaving a patina of slime and grit on the floor. A jagged brown water stain ran along the walls, just over the top of the baseboards. "The back of the storm might be just as bad." They circled the house, looking for damage. So far, except for the glass doors upstairs and the seepage, it was holding its own. The Guilieta was safe in the garage but a toppled pine blocked the driveway, the lane that threaded though the Colony littered with felled trees and branches. The jungle had gone silent: no birds, no insect thrum, the breeze so gentle it barely rustled the coastal scrub.

They checked the studio. It was dry, untouched. The rows of louvered windows, the smaller thicker panes, could withstand more wind than the plate glass. They decided to wait it out there, in the empty high bare cube, among the wooden crates. They gathered up what food they had, the bottles of water, the wine and bourbon and cigarettes. Then, just as the wind was starting to pick up, they went out the gate—blown open; unhinged—to assess the dunes. The plank walkway was buried, but the native dune plants—the sea grape and the bunched grasses—seemed to have hardly been disturbed. The surge had carved a steep three-foot ledge into the face of the dunes, and the roiling seawater, lower now, was a clouded bluish-gray, the foam dirty with pulverized black particles. The beach was littered with chunks of wood and branches and a spew of nautical junk, shreds of rope and fiberglass, rubber and plastic. In the water, just beyond where the waves broke, thousands of blackish-green mangrove seedpods bobbed on the surface, like an invading flotilla.

They closed themselves in the studio. Willa had been up all night and now, worn out by fear, swallowing her pills with half a bottle of wine, she fell asleep on a blanket spread over the paint-spattered floor. Narby sat beside her, smoking, listening to the howling passage of the storm, half its fury spent. The crates, he now saw, had shipping labels. Addressed to the Lundson Gallery, Southampton, New York. Lansdale territory.

Ever since she had returned it was clear as day, and yet he had refused to see. And now for five hours he had to stare at it, swallow it down, breath it in with the residual stink of the oil paints, Willa next to him unconscious on the floor, the world outside blown to bits.

★

The Village Fire Department didn't bother with the Colony lane. It was a private road. The wealthy snowbirds were never around at this time of year, anyway. There was more important work in the Village, clearing the main road to the ferry and the lighthouse.

With no electricity, no air-conditioning, the sun bearing down on the sodden jungle, the air a malefic steam swarming with horseflies and mosquitoes, Willa lost all patience. She couldn't bear to deal with the house—the ruined floors, the dead garden and garbage-filled swimming pool, half the windows cracked or broken, the leather-and-chrome furniture and the bed upstairs beginning to molder. "We have to get out of here. I can't stand another night of this. Tara and Dalton will know what to do, they'll hire people to clean up. Not that it matters anymore. I should have told you sooner, Philip. I've decided to let go of the house. I've worked everything out with Endicott."

"You're going back to Lansdale, aren't you?"

"You're obsessed with him, aren't you? I'm not going *back*. I'm going forward. We had our time together, Philip. Surely, you didn't think it could go on forever?"

"They threw you over, didn't they? The Congress for Cultural Freedom, Pembaker and his OSS pals, the people who were using you, showing you off like a high-class call girl?" He laughed. "A fucking self-cleaning oven."

"I have no idea what the hell you're talking about. And I don't care. I can't bear another night here. I'll lose my mind. Please, Philip. Help me."

"Why? What's in it for me?"

She stared at him, her eyes brimming, the words catching in her throat. "If you don't want to help me, then leave me the hell alone! I don't need you. I'll find a way."

The lane and driveway were blocked. No phone, no lights. And no one else from the Colony around. Without his help she might be stuck for weeks. "Calm down. I'll do what I can. The truck is parked by the lighthouse. I'm going to walk down the beach, see if it's still in one piece. I should be back in an hour or two. Depending on what I find."

"I'm coming with you. I can't stay here alone."

He took his rucksack and they walked down the dunes, Willa wearing her wide-brim straw hat against the sun. It all looked so strange. The creek inlet was almost unrecognizable, a skein of trickles oozing out from under a mass of tangled brush. The storm had diverted the creek channel, the drifts of sand choking off the flow. It was a different sea, a different island.

The truck had escaped damage. He opened the tailgate and let the water drain. There was room to maneuver around the debris, but it was stop-and-go on the island road. Unlike the native scrub oaks and hardwoods, the shallow-rooted Australian pines planted along the shoulder—with their fine shaggy needles, their deep sheltering shade—had gone down in the storm. Cars and trucks were backed up wherever men were working, sawing the felled trunks into manageable pieces and hauling them onto the shoulder and then stepping aside to let a few vehicles pass, first in one direction and then the other. Twice, coming to a standstill, Narby got out to help. He asked about the ferry. It was running now, continually, on an emergency schedule.

The Colony lane, passing mostly through low coastal scrub, was passable where it met the main road. Narby managed to get the truck close to the house, about thirty yards from the driveway. Willa got out, went ahead, saying nothing. He followed her inside. She ran upstairs, flinging things into her suitcase. He followed her, packed his few belongings, and went downstairs, looking through the jazz records, taking the ones on the second shelf that hadn't been ruined and putting them in the cab of the truck. The rucksack, the revolver, was on the seat.

In a few hours it would be over. He would never see her again, never touch her. It occurred to him, at that moment, that with no phone service Willa hadn't been able to contact anyone since the storm. Not even Lansdale. Just now, driving back from the lighthouse, she had stayed in the truck while he had helped clear the road; no one had paid Willa any mind. The sheriff who had come to the door, who had asked if she were alone, hadn't seen Narby. With the jungle flooded and stewing in the heat, a pervasive rot had risen over the entire island, growing stronger with each passing hour. Wherever you looked there were vultures circling. A decaying body, buried in the scrub, might go unnoticed for months and months. He felt his pulse pound. There must be at least twenty large canvases in the crates. Vintage Brantons. He could load them in the bed of the truck, pull a tarp over them. There would be a lot of ferry traffic for the next several days, pick-up trucks just like his hauling in supplies, hauling out all kinds of junk. No one would give him a second look. It was rather perfect. All he need do was go inside, right now. If he didn't have the nerve to use the gun he could do it some other, quieter way. With the pills. Get her to take more, somehow; get a bottle of wine down her throat. Once she passed out he would use the pillow. Two, three minutes of exertion: he could withstand that.

After dark he would take the body to where the creek used to be, drag it far back in the brush. By the time they found her, with the rot and worms and carrion-eating animals, it would be impossible to determine the cause of death. Foolish of her not to evacuate. Everyone who knew Willa knew how stubborn she was. How she loved the ocean, how she romanticized, how impractical and irrational she sometimes behaved. The drama of the storm had mesmerized her. Foolishly, despite all warnings, she had gone for a walk along the crashing surf. Another victim of Cora, the killer storm of the century.

He slung the sack over his shoulder and went into the house. She was upstairs. Gathering what she could from the ruin. He took a drink from the flask and lit a cigarette and waited at the foot of the staircase with the cable banister and the floating steps, feeling the grit and slime under his shoe. Without her, without the island, he was nothing. He wasn't about to simply let her go like this, without getting something in return. He was sick of it. Ever since Korea, sick of them all.

She was coming down, carrying a valise, her handbag hanging over her shoulder. "Philip, I'm dying in this heat. I'm going rinse off in the tub, before we—." He was blocking the way. "Philip?" She reared back a step. He felt nothing. It was necessary to feel nothing. Only the effort was choking him. "Don't hate me," she said. "Please please don't hate me. Just let me go. I can't help it, Philip. Please help me."

"What about the crates? Your paintings? All those years of hard work. You're not going to abandon all that? And the Guilieta?"

"Dalton will take care of it. Or Endicott. I'll lock the studio and arrange to have everything shipped. Philip? Please, don't look at me like that. Here." She set the valise down and went through her bag. "Take one of these. It will relax you." She held out the bottle, as if offering him the poison of a suicide pact.

"No thanks. Wouldn't want to deprive you. Maybe you ought to take a few more. Yeah. You relax, and I'll put your things in the truck. You can sleep on the ride. I'll take you to Miami International. They hardly felt a breeze over on the Atlantic side. Once we're a few miles inland it will be smooth sailing."

"I don't want to take any more, Philip. I don't want to sleep. I just want to get the hell out of here. But... if there are planes coming in and out of Myerton, there's no point in driving all the way to Miami. Just drop me ..."

"Can't stand to be next to me for that long? Is that it?"

She began to weep, the bottle of pills in her hand, the tears streaming down her drawn defeated face, her mouth drooping open. Tears, but no heaving or sobbing, a cry void of pain or pity.

"Take the pills," he demanded. Blocking her way, he offered her the flask. "Go to sleep."

"No." She gripped the valise and came toward him, the tears unabated. "Get out of my way. Let me go."

He felt himself unclenching, his body slacking a bit, his knees buckling, and he made a little bow, almost involuntarily but then, aware of his posture, exaggerating it, with a little flourish of his hand as he let her pass. Like a perfect gentleman. He heard her in the bathroom, splashing her face in the tub and then probably changing into clean clothes. Or cowering, locking the door, terrified.

That was enough. He was sick of it. He went out and put the rucksack and his valise in the truck. Then he walked around the side of the garage to the studio. There was a roll of waxed paper in one of the cabinet shelves. He tucked it under his arm and lifted the painting that he had rescued from the bonfire and brought it to the truck, hastily wrapping it and then sliding it into the gap behind the seat. He backed the truck down the lane until there was space to turn around. Waiting in line for the ferry, he waved over one of the sheriff's deputies. "There's a woman, over at the Colony. Number twelve. By herself. She's not hurt, but she's pretty damn shaken up. Can't get her car out, apparently. Just thought I'd let you know."

He nodded, a big jowly face blotched and boiling with sweat under the cowboy hat. "Lot of folks needing help. We'll see to her," he said, "by and by."

16

THE BLOCK WAS DESERTED—NO MORE cool-blue neon to guide him down the row of sagging wooden houses and empty storefronts. Of the sign that had hung above the door only a protruding tangle of wires remained. He peered through the window but it was too dark to see much—overturned chairs, a chaos of empty bottles and boxes and trash. Ransacked.

He walked toward the Avenue. The marquee above the Harlem Square Club was blank. El Castillo was closed down, gutted. It was as if someone had reached into Overtown and pulled out its heart, still beating, and crushed it. He didn't like the way people were looking at him. No cops around tonight, either. He stuck out like a ghost. White as a sheet. He walked faster until he found a side street where there were flashing lights in a window. He turned, pulled down the brim of his hat, and flexed his shoulders. Just go in, get a measure of the place.

He sat at the end of the bar and ordered a bourbon. There was a Ray Charles record playing. Then Chubby Checker. A few couples got up to dance in the cramped space between the tables and the jukebox. The noise of the electric fans muddied the sound of the music, the air muddied with dank and smoke. He was breaking into a sweat—needles pricking him under his clothes and then a chilling clinging damp.

Two girls were sitting at the other end. He thought he recognized one of them from Sir Jack's. He finished off the bourbon and had another. Without the pills, alcohol and marijuana enflamed him and then burned him out. He felt the pyre catching again, one more time. He kept looking over until he caught her eye, the skinny one. He got up and moved to the stool next to her. She pretended not to notice, talking to her friend. He would have to convince her first that he wasn't a cop.

"Can I buy you a drink?"

She shrugged. "I won't say no, sugar."

"What you having?"

"Gin rickey."

"You recognize me, don't you? From Sir Jack's. I'm a friend of Bobby's. You remember."

She turned, shrugging, shaking her head. "Maybe. All you White folk look the same to me." She mugged at her friend and they had a little laugh at his expense. That was all right. Keep laughing. After a moment, he said, "I'd like to know you better. You're a very beautiful girl. How about we go out?" Petite with short frizzy hair and small conical breasts, pushed upward by the bra visible under her thin blouse. Her face flat, the cheekbones sunken, the eyes yellowed and pink. A small round red mouth. Like Becca.

"Depends, sugar. I only go out with the finest gentlemen. Ain't that right?" she asked her friend.

"I know how to treat a girl," he said, his face very close now to her ear, almost nuzzling her hair, smelling the sweet musky perfume and hairspray and powder shielding her from the indignities of the heat and the night. "I'm very generous, very attentive to a girl's needs. Especially a fine looking high-class girl like yourself. Come on. I've got a beautiful hotel room, a suite overlooking the beach. We can have a couple of cocktails, watch the moonlight rippling in the water, that big beautiful Miami moon." Under the bar he had found her hand and pressed a ten into her warm moist palm. "That's just for talking to me. Just for letting me sit here, next to you."

She was interested. It wasn't cop talk; she would have smelled the dope smoke clinging to his hair and clothes. She let him caress her leg under the table, her thigh under the dress, the smooth dark flesh and the concavity of the inner muscle as it twisted toward her sex. "What beach you talking about, sugar?"

"Miami Beach, beautiful."

"You crazy, sugar. I ain't going over the water."

"There's nothing to worry about, gorgeous. I'll take you over and I'll bring you back." He was talking softly, very close to her. "No one's going to bother you as long as you're with me."

She laughed. "Who you? The mayor?"

"The mayor of Miami Beach happens to be a very good friend of mine. Jewish fellow. Very liberal, very progressive. Just like me."

"That right? You Joosh too, baby?"

"Hell no. Come on." He hooked his arm around her tiny waist. "It's getting late."

"I know a place right round the corner, sugar. Real close by. Got everything we need."

"Forget that. I've got a fabulous oceanfront room. You can hear the waves crashing, right from the bed. Feel that cool ocean breeze. Come on. No one's going to bother you, no one's going to say a word. You have rights, beautiful. Beautiful civil rights. Come on. We're going to exercise those civil rights. In my oceanfront suite."

"You ain't going to start preaching me about my freedom now, are you, sugar?"

"That wasn't my intention."

"Why ask for trouble, baby? I can do whatever you like right round the corner."

He put another bill in her hand. Nuzzling her, kissing her neck and then pulling away. "That one's just for the ride. I got a hot little Corvette parked right down the street. We can ride with the top down. Just like two movie stars, you and me and the moon above and the water sparkling down below. I've got plenty of booze, I've got some fine reefer. I'll treat you like you deserve." His arm around her waist he led her out the door. He had found her at last. He didn't need to ask her name. Whoever she was, she was Becca.

The truck had broken down on the Tamiami, crossing the Everglades. It wasn't worth fixing and he had abandoned it at the garage where they had towed it, taking his things—the valise, the rucksack, the Willa Branton wrapped in waxed paper—in a cab. The Corvette he had rented from the Hertz in Coral Gables. Candy red, like Sid's. It was late and the streets were deserted. They had ripped out the heart of Overtown, pulled the plug. When she saw the Corvette, new and shiny, he felt her relax. It would be worth her while after all. They rode with the top down, the warm damp night air streaming over them and his hand on her thigh under her dress gently caressing and massaging. Across the tracks and past the tall office buildings downtown. As they approached the causeway he put up the roof, to shield her from the bullnecked cracker cops. He parked on Twenty-first near Collins under the looming Wolfies sign, its swirling yellow neon switched off for the night, the gaudy light-bulb fes-tooned facade of the Pigalle on the opposite corner still flash-ing. He held her close, like an ardent honeymooner. Fortunately, the Calvado had dispensed with doormen. No more gold but-tons, no more epaulettes. From the porte-cochère they slipping through the glass doors into the glaring sterility of the lobby, its once glamorous appurtenances long since sold off or simply left to crumble in neglect.

There was only the night clerk. At the front desk, across from the elevators. At the sound of their footsteps clicking against the terrazzo floor he lowered his newspaper. Narby had the key in his hand. He put himself between the girl and the clerk, shielding her, and passed her the room key. "Tenth floor. You go on. I'll be up in a minute. Just go. Now." The elevator was waiting and she stepped in. The door dinged and slid closed. The clerk, his paper down, rose to his full height. "Hey," he said. "Hey you."

Narby stepped toward the desk. "Philip Narby. Room 1014." He nodded. "Good night."

"Hey. Hold on a minute."

"It's very late, my friend, and as you can no doubt discern I've had a bit to drink. So, if you'll excuse me."

"Who was that with you? That woman. She can't stay here."

"I have a suite. Double occupancy. Paid in full."

The clerk was as tall as Narby but broader, heavier, his white shirt pulling tight against his paunch as he leaned forward, the brow of his broad mottled oily face creased in distress. "Sorry, pal. That don't matter. She's got to find somewhere else to park it for the night."

"She's an old friend. I wouldn't dream of sending her out in the streets at this hour."

"Don't be a wise guy. We don't allow no Negroes here. You know that."

Narby lurched forward, planting his elbows on the counter. He saw that the night clerk was unclean, his shirt yellowed under the armpits, the plump sausage-like body exuding a rancid odor. A pint bottle of Four Aces, half consumed, sat at his elbow, and the ashtray held the plastic butts of half a dozen Tiparillos. A big-city cracker, a big-city cousin of Carl Vetch.

"Listen to me. Pal." He could feel himself tightening, the fever coiling his spine. "I'm a veteran of the Korean War, a citizen of the United States, a customer paid in full. You know what it was like, in Korea? The filthy lies, the pointless slaughter, the shit-water ditches. Well, there you have it." He swayed backward, as if preparing to strike. "If I want my lady friend to spend the evening with me in my hotel suite, then there's nothing more to be said. Case closed."

"Look, pal. I got a job to do. It's nothing personal. It's the law." A strain of pleading threaded through the bullying tone. "Either you go upstairs and bring her down, or I have to call the cops."

"You're wrong. If you'd been in Korea, you'd understand my position."

"Yeah, well I wasn't in Korea. Screw Korea. That's go nothing to do with anything. Look, buddy, I don't want trouble. I don't want to call the cops. Just get her out. Look," he said, leaning forward, the fabric of his soiled shirt stretching, releasing the rancid odor from the folds, his breath ashen and sour.

"Go up there and do your business with her and then get her the hell out. I'll give you an hour. How's that? Get her out of here in an hour and I'll look the other way."

"I'm afraid I don't understand. Do my business? What are you implying?"

"Oh, Christ. Come off it. She's a hooker." He tilted back. A man of the world, apparently. Willing to negotiate. A pragmatist with a preference for containment, rather than direct confrontation. "I ain't got no argument with that. Only why the hell did you have bring in a nigger, for Jesus sake? One hour. OK? She ain't out of here by then, I got no choice. I call the cops."

"Why a *Negro*?" Narby laughed. "Obviously, you've never had the pleasure. Have you?"

The clerk turned his head, perhaps eyeing the door to the lobby. It was three a.m. The hotel was empty. A dead sweltering month between summer's end and the beginning of the winter season, in a doomed hotel. "The pleasure of what?"

Narby leaned forward again. "She's very good. Very talented. And you know what? She loves big White men. Craves 'em. You're definitely her type. She's something else, man. Believe me. That little twitching ass. That hot little mouth. Those sweet little jiggling titties."

"Can't say I got a very good look at her. She's um ..." He cleared his throat. He was yellowing his shirt as they spoke, the sweat eating through the fabric. "She's young."

"Like fruit off the vine. Young and hot. And very eager. I mean. Seeing how you're willing to look the other way. Why not come upstairs? She's got enough spunk for both of us. I am not exaggerating. I assure you. It's in the Negro blood. I'm serious. Come upstairs. On the house. You can go first, take as long as you'd like."

" Christ. I don't know. I mean."

"Come up, have a drink. She'll love it. I'll throw her another twenty. That will stoke her up. Besides. When are you ever going to get another chance like this? Right here, in the hotel. For free. My treat."

"Oh my god." His face was flushed, his chest heaving. He kept looking at his watch and then at the door to the lobby, back and forth, back and forth.

"Hey. I don't want to keep the young lady waiting. She's probably out of the shower by now, waiting in her birthday suit. Hot and wet and waiting. Come on." He laughed. "Get it while it's hot, brother."

After the clerk locked the lobby doors they went up together in the elevator, the man's nervous stink filling the space. "Just a minute. Wait here while I explain to her. I don't want her to think there's something wrong. Hold on." He knocked, his face to the peephole. The door opened and he went in. "Where you been?" she said. "Quiet. Come here." He counted out a hundred dollars from the roll in his pocket. She was staring at him, unbelieving. "I want you to do something. Just go into the bathroom and close the door. All right?" He leaned over and kissed her. "I love you. Shh. Just go into the bathroom and close the door and don't come out until I say so."

"What you gonna ..."

"Shh. Go on."

Once she was in the bathroom with the door closed he gathered the few items of his clothing strewn about and put them in his valise, and then closed the door to the bedroom and turned on the radio to the all-night station. At that hour they played swing and big band: Goodman, Basie, Bunny Berigan, Artie Shaw. Then he took the revolver from the rucksack and tucked it in his waistband under his shirt and opened the door. "Come on in. She's in the bedroom, getting ready. How about a drink?"

The clerk looked at the bedroom door. She had left her shoes by the love seat. He saw the shoes and said, "all right."

Narby poured two bourbons and handed one to the clerk. "Cheers. To one hell of a night." The clerk, pale with nerves, joylessly clinked his glass. "Fabulous view from up here." Narby stepped over to the sliding glass doors and opened them. "Come out for a minute, cool off. I want to show you something."

"What?" "Just come out here and I'll show you."

The clerk was standing in front of the bedroom door, his mouth hanging open, panting a bit.

"Christ, relax, would you. You'll spoil it for yourself," Narby said. "Step out here and cool off."

The curtains billowed gently, an invitation to delight in the ocean breeze. The clerk stepped out onto the terrace, the drink in his hand. Narby moved back and as the clerk went to the rail Narby turned toward him. Blanking his mind, the tension in his spine uncoiling in a single spasm, he thrust out his arms as if pushing away an enormous disgusting burden, the vile putrid presence he could no longer tolerate after so many years. He could feel the clerk toppling as his palms were suddenly set free of the pressure, the clerk buckling at the knees, grappling piti-fully in the empty air, his arms whirling for something to grab on to but oddly unable to let go of the glass of bourbon as if it were glued to his hand, the liquid shooting upward over his shoulder and the railing hardly creaking as it gave way. He thought per-haps he heard a whoosh or sucking sound, or was it only the waves? But then, distinctly, there was a crash and a heavy muf-fled thud. He took a breath, finished his drink, stepped inside and opened the bedroom door and let her out of the bathroom.

"What's wrong, sugar?"

"It's my old Korean war wound. Acting up again. Puts me right out of the mood, I'm afraid. Here's a little more for your trouble." He handed her another hundred, five crisp twenties. "I love you." He leaned and kissed her dry pale lips. They barely yielded, a mere twitch. It was enough.

"But what you want, sugar?"

"I don't want anything. I just wanted to tell you that I love you."

She was staring at him, stuffing the money in her purse. "You going to take me home, ain't you? You ain't going to leave me here. Cause ..."

"Of course I'm going to take you home. Right now. Put on your shoes, my love."

He took his valise and slung the sack over his shoulder and taking the canvas from the closet he gripped it by the frame, crinkling the waxed paper. In the lobby he told her to wait. He went behind the front desk, found the hotel register and put it in the rucksack, hesitating, for a moment fighting the urge to cross the lobby and take a look outside, at the poolside patio. A ten-story fall. He would have landed on his back or his head, hitting the stone-hard terrazzo deck. Verification seemed an unnecessary risk. He came out from behind the desk and unbolted the front doors. They passed a couple of drunks staggering out of the Pigalle. No one else. Unfortunately, in order to accommodate the painting in the two-seat Corvette he had to lower the roof, asking Becca to cradle it on her knees. Collins to Fifth and then over Biscayne Bay—a Negro prostitute, a White man in sporty linen and silk reeking of marijuana and Jim Beam, and an abstract expressionist painting, riding over the General Douglas MacArthur Causeway in a candy-red Corvette convertible at four o'clock in the morning, an outrage of conspicuousness of which he was hardly aware—and through downtown and over the tracks. The demolition for the Interstate highway had eaten like a plague into the heart of Overtown. She asked nothing, said nothing. Because whatever it was it had nothing to do with her. Some kind of trouble between Whites.

17

HE GOT A ROOM at a roadside motel on the Tamiami about a mile beyond the city limits and slept until noon. Then he returned the rented Corvette and bought a '57 Chevy pick-up at a used car lot, not too banged up, the new cobalt-blue paint job hiding the subtropical rust and corrosion. Four hours across the Everglades, the hot wind in his face, drinking steadily from the flask. Passing through Myerton he saw the Smoker's Den had re-opened. Only now it was Al's Smoke and News. He parked and went down the five steps. The tinkling brass bells had been removed.

"Don't carry that," the new man said. "We got Top. We got Bugler. Which you want?"

Narby explained that he had been picking up his mail at the shop for years, special-order magazines, an occasional package or letter. "The previous owner and I had an arrangement. I live pretty far out in the county. It was a convenience."

Al shrugged. "I don't do no special orders. I'm running a business, not a post office. I got *Time, Newsweek, Life, Playboy*. Everything out on the rack, 'cept for what the kids ain't supposed to see. For that stuff, just ask. So, what can I get for you?"

"Have you run across any mail addressed to Philip Narby? Or just PN?"

"I t'rew out a lot of old piles of junk. The Arab left a real mess, let me tell you. Hey, pull the door closed, would you? Jesus frickin' hot down here. The humidity must be a hundred, heh? Thank god for air-conditioning, heh? Thank god they got the juice going again. Jesus, what a storm! Florida, it's a dream, right? Been down here long, have you? Like to roll your own, heh? Old school. Like my old man. Myself, I couldn't be bothered. The guy who used to own this place, the Arab. I hear he got mixed up with the law. Just curious. Heard he was something of a troublemaker. I don't get it, all these agitators. I mean, we're on top of the world, why the hell stir the pot? You looking for something special, are you? I've got some very racy stuff, the best available. If that's what interests you."

Although the risk on the island had been great—had the surge been a foot or two higher the dunes might have washed away—the chaos around Myerton was far worse. Thousands without water or power or sewage or shelter, their stucco gimcrack bungalows and cottages stripped of roofing and siding, their trailer-homes toppled and gashed. There were rumors of typhoid and rabies. It was as if some malignant feral force had boiled forth out of the cypress swamps and pine wastes. An infestation of raccoon and possum and skunk gorging on the wreckage of supermarkets and diners and barbecue joints, the kitchens and cupboards and refrigerators spilt open to the poisonous heat, the wild dogs roaming the aisles of the Piggly Wiggly, the plague of rats and field mice flushed out by the floods burrowing through the broken cases of festering meat.

But not so Coco Reef. As if in preparation, the land had been scraped clear of life, bare, sterile, the circuitry of asphalt roads clear of debris, the power poles along Coco Reef Parkway the first in the County to be righted by the emergency crews, their trucks meeting no obstacles. No trees to fall, the low featureless concrete-block houses and isolate shopping-plazas offering little resistance to the gales, the sheets of rain running off the hard white sterile land and draining into the steep-banked canals, the snakes and alligators and possums and rats long ago annihilated, chased by bulldozer and dragline and fire into the ever-receding line of scrub.

Already the charter flights and busses were rolling in again, folks down from Indiana and Michigan and Ohio. No sign of destruction remained, no hint that the *killer hurricane of the century* had struck Coco Reef in full force. Cora, a mere tantrum-prone child of nature, was no match for Sid Black.

His land was exposed—a five-hundred-acre square of pine and palmetto waste surrounded on every side by the manufactured desert-like void. The gate to his lane like a portal between two geographic zones. The barbed wire fence like a border between hostile realms.

The native jungle scrub had been ruffled, a few old pines toppled, but nothing worse. The island-style house, raised two feet off the ground on limestone pillars, had held. Waters had battened the shutters, boarded up the screens, secured tools and lumber and anything that could fly, done everything he could think of to protect Narby's property and his own two-room cottage. One of the sheds had collapsed. The pond had spilled over into the groves. About a dozen Australian Pines had toppled. As Narby came down the lane he heard the noise. Sam was standing in the roadway, bare-chested in his overalls, a roaring chainsaw dangling at the end of his arm as easily as if it were a toy.

As Narby came from the truck, he turned it off.

"I been wondering if that storm done blew you away."

"I'm all right."

"You don't look all right. You sick, boss?"

"Just tired, that's all."

"You sure look sick. They sickness go round, after a storm like that. Fever and such. Come on, now. Just leave your things. You go on indoors. Go on and rest. Sam take care of everything."